RICH MAN, POOR MAN

IRWIN SHAW

Rich Man, Poor Man

DELACORTE PRESS / NEW YORK

TO MY SON

PART
ONE

PART

ONE

Chapter 1

I

Mr. Donnelly, the track coach, ended the day's practice early because Henry Fuller's father came down to the high-school field to tell Henry that they had just got a telegram from Washington announcing that Henry's brother had been killed in action in Germany. Henry was the team's best shot-putter. Mr. Donnelly gave Henry a chance to go in and change his clothes alone and go home with his father, then whistled to gather the whole squad in a group and said they could all go home, as a gesture of respect.

The baseball team was practicing on the diamond, but nobody on the baseball team had lost a brother that afternoon, so they kept on practicing.

Rudolph Jordache (two-twenty low hurdles) went into the locker room and took a shower, although he hadn't run enough to work up a sweat. There never was enough hot water at home and when he could he showered at the gym. The high school had been built in 1927, when everybody had money, and the showers were roomy and with plenty of hot water. There was even a swimming pool. Usually, Rudolph took a swim too, after practice, but he didn't today, out of respect.

The boys in the locker room spoke in low tones and there was none of the usual horsing around. Smiley, the captain of the team, got up on a bench and said he thought that if there was a funeral service for Henry's brother, they all ought to chip in and buy a wreath. Fifty cents a man would do it, he thought. You could tell by the looks on the boys' faces who could spare the fifty cents and who couldn't. Rudolph couldn't spare it, but he made a conscious effort to look as though he could. The boys who agreed most readily were the ones whose parents took them down to New York City before the school term to buy the year's clothes for them. Rudolph bought his clothes in town, in Port Philip, at Bernstein's Department Store.

He was dressed neatly, though, with a collar and tie and a sweater under a leather windbreaker, and brown pants, from an old suit whose jacket had gone through at the elbows. Henry Fuller was one of the boys who got his clothes in New York, but Rudolph was sure Henry wasn't getting any pleasure from the fact this afternoon.

Rudolph got out of the locker room quickly because he didn't want to walk home with any of the other fellows and talk about Henry Fuller's brother. He wasn't particularly friendly with Henry, who was rather stupid, as the weight men were likely to be, and he preferred not to pretend to any excessive sympathy.

The school was in a residential part of the town, to the north and east of the business center, and was surrounded by semi-detached one-family houses that had been built at about the same time as the school, when the town was expanding. They were all the same originally, but through the years their owners had painted the trim and doors in different colors and here and there had added a bay window or a balcony in forlorn attempts at variety.

Carrying his books, Rudolph strode along the cracked sidewalks of the neighborhood. It was a windy early spring day, although not very cold, and he had a sense of well-being and holiday because of the light workout and the short practice. Most of the trees had already put out their leaves and there were buds everywhere.

The school was built on a hill and he could see the Hudson River below him, still looking cold and wintry, and the spires of the churches of the town, and in the distance to the south, the chimney of the Boylan Brick and Tile Works, where his sister Gretchen worked, and the tracks of the New York Central, along the river. Port Philip was not a pretty town, although once it had been, with big white Colonial houses mingled with solid Victorian stone. But the boom in the 1920's had brought a lot of new people into town, working people whose homes were narrow and dark, spreading out into all neighborhoods. Then the Depression had thrown almost everybody out of work and the jerry-built houses had been neglected, and as Rudolph's mother complained, the entire town had become a single slum. This wasn't absolutely true. The northern part of the town still had many fine big houses and wide streets and the houses had been kept up through everything. And even in the neighborhoods that were run down there were big houses that families had refused to leave and were still presentable behind generous lawns and old trees.

The war had brought prosperity once again to Port Philip and the Brick and Tile Works and the cement plant were going full blast and even the tannery and the Byefield Shoe Factory had started up again with Army orders. But with the war on, people had other things to do than worry about keeping up appearances and, if possible, the city looked more dilapidated than ever.

With the town spread before him like that, planless and jumbled in the windy afternoon sun, Rudolph wondered if anybody would give his life to defend it or to take it, as Henry Fuller's brother had given his life to take some nameless town in Germany.

Secretly, he hoped that the war would last another two years, although it didn't look now as though it would. He was going to be seventeen years old soon and another year after that he could enlist. He saw himself with a lieutenant's silver bars, taking an enlisted man's salute, waving a platoon to follow him under machine-gun fire. It was the sort of experience a man ought to have. He was sorry there was no more cavalry. That must have been something—waving a saber, at a full gallop, charging the despicable foe.

He didn't dare mention anything like this around the house. His mother became hysterical when anybody as much as suggested that perhaps the war would last and her Rudolph would be taken. He knew that some boys lied about their age to enlist—there were stories about fifteen-year-old boys, even fourteen-year-olds, who were in the Marines and who had won medals—but he couldn't do anything like that to his mother.

As usual, he made a detour to pass the house where Miss Lenaut lived. Miss Lenaut was his French teacher. She was nowhere in sight.

Then he walked down to Broadway, the main street of the town, which ran parallel to the river and which was also the through highway from New York to Albany. He dreamed of having a car, like the ones he saw speeding through town. Once he had a car he would go down to New York every weekend. He wasn't quite sure what he would do in New York, but he would go there.

Broadway was a nondescript thoroughfare, with shops of all kinds mixed together, butcher shops and markets next to quite large stores that sold women's clothes and cheap jewelry and sporting goods. He stopped, as he often did, before the window of the Army and Navy Store, which had fishing equipment displayed along with work shoes and chino pants and shirts and flashlights and penknives. He stared at the fishing rods, thin and elegant, with their expensive reels. He fished in the river and, when the season was on, in the trout streams that were open to the public, but his equipment was primitive.

He went down another short street and turned to his left on Vanderhoff Street, where he lived. Vanderhoff Street ran parallel to Broadway and seemed to be trying to emulate it, but doing it badly, like a poor man in a baggy suit and scuffed shoes pretending he had arrived in a Cadillac. The shops were small and the wares in their windows were dusty, as though the owners knew there really was no use. Quite a few of the shop fronts were still boarded up, having closed down in 1930 or 1931. When new sewer lines were laid down before the war the WPA had felled all the trees which had shaded the sidewalks and nobody had bothered to plant new ones. Vanderhoff was a long street and as he approached his own house the street became shabbier and shabbier, as though just the mere act of going south was somehow spiritually a decline.

His mother was in the bakery, behind the counter, with a shawl around her shoulders, because she was always cold. The building was on a corner, so there were two big windows and his mother kept complaining that with all that glass there was no way of keeping the shop warm. She was putting a dozen hard rolls in a brown paper bag for a little girl. There were cakes and tarts displayed in the front window, but they were no longer baked in the cellar. At the start of the war, his father, who did the baking, had decided that it was more trouble than it was worth and now a truck from a big commercial bakery stopped every morning to deliver the cakes and pastries and Axel confined himself to baking the bread and rolls. When pastries had remained in the window three days, his father would bring them upstairs for the family to eat.

Rudolph went in and kissed his mother and she patted his cheek. She always looked tired and was always squinting a little, because she was a chain smoker and the smoke got into her eyes.

"Why so early?" she asked.

"Short practice today," he said. He didn't say why. "I'll take over here. You can go upstairs now."

"Thank you," she said. "My Rudy." She kissed him again. She was very affectionate with him. He wished she would kiss his brother or his sister once in a while, but she never did. He had never seen his mother kiss his father.

"I'll go up and make dinner," she said. She was the only one in the family who called supper dinner. Rudolph's father did the shopping, because he said his wife was extravagant and didn't know good food from bad, but most of the time she did the cooking.

She went out the front door. There was no door that opened directly from the bakery to the hallway and the staircase that led up to the two floors above, where they lived, and he saw his mother pass the show window, framed in pastry and shivering as the wind hit her. It was hard for him to remember that she was only a little over forty years old. Her hair was graying and she shuffled like an old lady.

He got out a book and read. It would be slow in the shop for another hour. The book he was reading was Burke's speech *On Conciliation With the Colonies*, for his English class. It was so convincing that you wondered how all those supposedly smart men in Parliament hadn't agreed with him. What would America have been like if they had listened to Burke? Would there have been earls and dukes and castles? He would have liked that. Sir Rudolph Jordache, Colonel in the Port Philip Household Guards.

An Italian laborer came in and asked for a loaf of white bread. Rudolph put down Burke and served him.

The family ate in the kitchen. The evening meal was the only one they all ate together because of the father's hours of work. They had lamb stew tonight. Despite rationing, they always had plenty of meat because Rudolph's father was friendly with the butcher, Mr. Haas, who didn't ask for ration tickets because he was German, too. Rudolph felt uneasy about eating black market lamb on the same day that Henry Fuller had found out his brother had been killed, but all he did about it was ask for a small portion, mostly potatoes and carrots, because he couldn't talk to his father about fine points like that.

His brother, Thomas, the only blond in the family, besides the mother, who really couldn't be called blonde anymore, certainly didn't seem to be worried about anything as he wolfed down his food. Thomas was just a year younger than Rudolph, but was already as tall and much stockier than his brother. Gretchen, Rudolph's older sister, never ate much, because she worried about her weight. His mother just picked at her food. His father, a massive man in shirt-sleeves, ate enormously, wiping his thick, black moustache with the back of his hand from time to time.

Gretchen didn't wait for the three-day-old cherry pie that they had for dessert, because she was due at the Army hospital just outside town where she worked as a volunteer nurse's aide five nights a week. When she stood up, the father made his usual joke. "Be careful," he said. "Don't let those soldiers grab you. We don't have enough rooms in this house to set up a nursery."

"Pa," Gretchen said reproachfully.

"I know soldiers," Axel Jordache said. "Just be careful."

Gretchen was a neat, proper, beautiful girl, Rudolph thought, and it pained him that his father talked like that to her. After all, she was the only one in the family who was contributing to the war effort.

When the meal was over, Thomas went out, too, as he did every night. He never did any homework and he got terrible marks in school. He was still a freshman in the high school, although he was nearly sixteen. He never listened to anybody.

Axel Jordache went into the living room up front to read the evening newspaper before going down to the cellar for the night's work. Rudolph stayed in the kitchen to dry the dishes after his mother had washed them. If I ever get married, Rudolph thought, my wife will not have to wash dishes.

When the dishes were done, the mother got out the ironing board and Rudolph went upstairs to the room he shared with his brother, to do his homework. He knew that if ever he was going to escape from eating in a kitchen and listening to his father and wiping dishes it was going to be through books, so he was always the best prepared student in the class for all examinations.

II

Maybe, Axel Jordache thought, at work in the cellar, I ought to put poison in one of them. For laughs. For anything. Serve them right. Just once, just one night. See who gets it.

He drank the blend straight out of the bottle. By the end of the night the bottle would be almost gone. There was flour all the way up to his elbows and flour on his face, where he had wiped away the sweat. I'm a goddamn clown, he thought, without a circus.

The window was open to the March night and the weedy Rhenish smell of the river soaked into the room, but the oven was cooking the air in the basement. I am in hell, he thought, I stoke the fires of hell to earn my bread, to make my bread. I am in hell making Parker House rolls.

He went to the window and took a deep breath, the big chest muscles, age-ridged, tightening against his sweaty skivvy shirt. The river a few hundred yards away, freed now of ice, carried the presence of North with it like the rumor of passing troops, a last cold marching threat of winter, spreading on each side of its banks. The Rhine was four thousand miles away. Tanks and cannon were crossing it on improvised bridges. A lieutenant had run across it when a bridge had failed to blow up. Another lieutenant on the other side had been court-martialed and shot because he had failed to blow the bridge as ordered. Armies. Die Wacht am Rhein. Churchill had pissed in it recently. Fabled river. Jordache's native water. Vineyards and sirens. Schloss Whatever. The cathedral in Cologne was still standing. Nothing much else. Jordache had seen the photographs in the newspapers. Home sweet home in old Cologne. Bulldozed ruins with the ever-remembered stink of the dead buried under collapsed walls. It couldn't have happened to a nicer city. Jordache thought dimly of his youth and spat up and out of the window in the direction of the other river. The invincible German Army. How many dead? Jordache spat again and licked his black moustache that drooped down at the corners of his mouth. God bless America. He had killed to get there. He took one last breath of the river's presence and limped back to work.

His name was on view on the window of the shop above the basement. BAKERY, A. Jordache, Pro. Twenty years ago, when the sign had been put up, it had read A. Jordache, Prop., but one winter the *p* had fallen off and he hadn't bothered to have it put back on. He sold just as many Parker House rolls without the *p*.

The cat lay close to the oven, staring at him. They had never bothered to give the cat a name. The cat was there to keep the mice and rats out of the flour. When Jordache had to address it, he said, "Cat." The cat probably thought its name was Cat. The cat watched him steadily all night, every night. She lived on one bowl of milk a day and all the mice and rats she could catch. The way the cat looked at him, Jordache was sure the cat wished she was ten times bigger than she was, as big as a tiger, so she could spring on him one night and have one real meal.

The oven was hot enough now and he limped over and put in the first tray of the night. He grimaced when he opened the oven door and the heat hit him.

III

Upstairs, in the narrow room he shared with his brother, Rudolph was looking up a word in an English-French dictionary. He had finished his homework. The word he was looking for was longing. He had already looked up hints and visions. He was writing a love letter in French to his French teacher, Miss Lenaut. He had read *The Magic Mountain,* and while most of the book had bored him, with the exception of the chapter about the seance, he had been impressed by the fact that the love scenes were in French and had painfully translated them for himself. To make love in French seemed to him to be distinguished. One sure thing, there was no other sixteen-year-old boy writing a love letter in French that night anywhere in the whole Hudson Valley.

"*Enfin*"—he wrote, in a carefully fashioned, almost printed script that he had developed over the last two years—"*enfin, je dois vous dire, chère Madame, quand je vous vois par hasard dans les couloirs de l'école ou se promenant dans votre manteau bleu-clair dans les rues, j'ai l'envie*"—that was the closest he could get to longing—"*très profond de voyager dans le monde d'où vous êtes sortie et des visions délicieuses de flâner avec vous à mes côtés sur les boulevards de Paris, qui vient d'être libéré par les braves soldats de votre pays et le mien. Votre cavalier servant,* Rudolph Jordache (French 32b)."

He reread the letter, then read it in the English in which he had first written it. He had tried to make the English as much like French as possible. "Finally, I must tell you, Dear Madame, that when I see you by accident in the hallways of the school or walking along in your light-blue coat on the street, I have a deep longing to travel in the world you came from and wonderful visions of strolling arm in arm with you along the boulevards of Paris, which has just been liberated by the brave soldiers of your country and mine."

He read the French version again with satisfaction. There was no doubt about it. If you wanted to be elegant, French was the language for it. He liked the way Miss Lenaut pronounced his name, correctly, Jordahsh, making it soft and musical, not Jawdake, as some people said it, or Jordash.

Then, regretfully, he tore both letters into small pieces. He knew he was never going to send Miss Lenaut any letters. He had already written her six letters and torn them up because she would think he was crazy and would probably tell the principal. And he certainly didn't want his father or mother or Gretchen or Tom to find any love letters in any language in his room.

Still, the satisfaction was there. Sitting in the bare little room above the bakery, with the Hudson flowing a few hundred yards away, writing the letters was like a promise to himself. One day he would make long voyages, one day he would sail the river and write in new languages to beautiful women of high character, and the letters would actually be mailed.

He got up and looked at himself in the wavy little mirror above the battered oak dresser. He looked at himself often, searching his face for the man he wanted to be. He was very careful with his looks. His straight, black hair was always perfectly brushed; occasionally he plucked two or three bits of dark fuzz from the space between his eyebrows; he avoided candy so that he would have a minimum of pimples; he remembered to smile, not laugh aloud, and even that not frequently. He was very conservative with the colors he chose to wear and had worked on the way he walked, so that he never seemed hurried or exuberant, but walked in an easy gliding motion with his shoulders squared. He kept his nails filed and his sister gave him a manicure once a month and he kept out of fights because he didn't want to have his face marred by a broken nose or his long, thin hands twisted by swollen knuckles. To keep in shape, there was the track team. For the pleasures of nature and solitude he fished, using a dry fly when somebody was watching, worms at other times.

"*Votre cavalier servant,*" he said into the mirror. He wanted his face to look French when he spoke the language, the way Miss Lenaut's face suddenly looked French when she addressed the class.

He sat down at the little yellow oak table he used for a desk and pulled a piece of paper toward him. He tried to remember exactly what Miss Lenaut looked like. She was quite tall, with flat hips and full breasts always prominently propped up, and thin, straight legs. She wore high heels and ribbons and a great deal of lipstick. First he drew her with her clothes on, not achieving much of a likeness but getting the two curls in front of her ears and making the mouth convincingly prominent and dark. Then he tried to imagine what she might look like without any clothes. He drew her naked, sitting on a stool looking at herself in a hand-mirror. He stared at his handiwork.

O, *God, if ever!* He tore up the naked drawing. He was ashamed of himself. He deserved to live over a bakery. If they ever found out downstairs what he thought and did upstairs . . .

He began to undress for bed. He was in his socks, because he didn't want his mother, who slept in the room below, to know that he was still awake. He had to get up at five o'clock every morning to deliver the bread in the cart attached to a bicycle and his mother kept after him for not getting enough sleep.

Later on, when he was rich and successful, he would say, I got up at five o'clock in the morning, rain or shine, to deliver rolls to the Depot Hotel and the Ace Diner and Sinowski's Bar and Grill. He wished his name wasn't Rudolph.

IV

At the Casino Theater Errol Flynn was killing a lot of Japs. Thomas Jordache was sitting in the dark at the rear of the theater eating caramels from a package that he had taken from the slot machine in the lobby with a lead slug. He was expert at making lead slugs.

"Slip me one, Buddy," Claude said, making it sound tough, like a movie gangster asking for another clip of 45 cartridges for his rod. Claude Tinker had an uncle who was a priest and to overcome the damaging implications of the relationship he tried to sound tough at all times. Tom flipped a caramel in the air and Claude caught it and started chewing on it loudly. The boys were sitting low on their spines, their feet draped over the empty seats in front of them. They had sneaked in as usual, through a grating that they had pried loose last year. The grating protected a window in the men's room in the cellar. Every once in a while, one or the other of them would come up into the auditorium with his fly open, to make it look for real.

Tom was bored with the picture. He watched Errol Flynn dispose of a platoon of Japs with various weapons. "Phonus bolonus," he said.

"What language you speaking, Professor?" Claude said, playing their game.

"That's Latin," Tom said, "for bullshit."

"What a command of tongues," Claude said.

"Look," Tom said, "down there to the right. That GI with his girl."

A few rows in front of them a soldier and a girl were sitting, entwined. The theater was half-empty and there was nobody in the row they were in or in the rows behind them. Claude frowned. "He looks awful big," Claude said. "Look at that neck on him."

"General," Tom said, "we attack at dawn."

"You'll wind up in the hospital," Claude said.

"Wanna bet?" Tom swung his legs back from the chair in front of him and stood up and started toward the aisle. He moved silently, his sneakered feet light on the worn carpet of the Casino floor. He always wore sneakers. You had to be sure-footed and ready to make the fast break at all times. He hunched his shoulders, bulky and easy under his sweater, and tucked in his gut, enjoying the hard, flat feeling under the tight belt. Ready for anything. He smiled in the darkness, the excitement beginning to get him, as it always did at these preliminary choosing moments.

Claude followed him, uneasily. Claude was a lanky, thin-armed boy, with a long-nosed squirrely wedge of a face and loose, wet lips. He was nearsighted and wore glasses and that didn't make him look any better. He was a manipulator and behind-the-scenes man and slid out of trouble like a corporation lawyer and conned teachers into giving him good marks although he almost never opened a school book. He wore dark suits and neckties and had a kind of literary stoop and shambled apologetically when he walked and looked insignificant, humble, and placating. He was imaginative, his imagination concentrating on outrages against society. His father ran the bookkeeping department of the Boylan Brick and Tile Works and his mother, who had a degree from St. Anne's College for Women, was the president of the draft board, and what with all that and the priest-uncle besides, and his harmless and slightly repulsive appearance, Claude maneuvered with impunity through his plot-filled world.

The two boys moved down the empty row and sat directly behind the GI and his girl. The GI had his hand in the girl's blouse and was methodically squeezing her breast. The GI hadn't removed his overseas cap and it peaked down steeply over his forehead. The girl had her hand somewhere down in the shadows between the soldier's legs. Both the GI and the girl were watching the picture intently. Neither of them paid any attention to the arrival of the boys.

Tom sat behind the girl, who smelled good. She was liberally doused with a flowery perfume which mingled with the buttery, cowlike aroma from a bag of popcorn they had been eating. Claude sat behind the soldier. The soldier had a small head, but he was tall, with broad shoulders, and his cap obscured most of the screen from Claude, who had to squirm from side to side to glimpse the film.

"Listen," Claude whispered, "I tell you he's too big. I bet he weighs one seventy, at least."

"Don't worry," Tom whispered back. "Start in." He spoke confidently, but he could feel little shivers of doubt in his fingertips and under his armpits. That hint of doubt, of fear, was familiar to him and it added to his expectation and the beauty of the final violence. "Go ahead," he whispered harshly to Claude. "We ain't got all night."

"You're the boss," Claude said. Then he leaned forward and tapped the soldier on the shoulder. "Pardon me, Sergeant," he said. "I wonder if you'd be so kind as to remove your cap. It's difficult for me to see the screen."

"I ain't no sergeant," the soldier said, without turning. He kept his cap on and continued watching the picture, squeezing the girl's breast.

The two boys sat quietly for more than a minute. They had practiced the tactic of provocation so often together that there was no need for signals. Then Tom leaned forward and tapped the soldier heavily on the shoulder. "My friend made a polite request," he said. "You are interfering with his enjoyment of the picture. We will have to call the management if you don't take your cap off."

The soldier swiveled a little in his seat, annoyedly. "There's two hundred empty seats," he said. "If your friend wants to see the picture let him sit someplace else." He turned back to his two preoccupations, sex and art.

"He's on the way," Tom whispered to Claude. "Keep him going."

Claude tapped the soldier on the shoulder again. "I suffer from a rare eye disease," Claude said. "I can only see from this seat. Everywhere else it's a blur. I can't tell whether it's Errol Flynn or Loretta Young up there."

"Go to an eye doctor," the soldier said. The girl laughed at his wit. She sounded as though she had drunk some water the wrong way when she laughed. The soldier laughed, too, to show that he appreciated himself.

"I don't think it's nice to laugh at people's disabilities," Tom said.

"Especially with a war on," Claude said, "with all those crippled heroes."

"What sort of an American are you?" Tom asked, his voice rising patriotically. "That's the question I would like to ask, what sort of an American are you?"

The girl turned. "Get lost, kids," she said.

"I want to remind you, sir," Tom said, "that I hold you personally responsible for anything your lady friend says."

"Don't pay them no mind, Angela," the soldier said. He had a high, tenor voice.

The boys sat in silence again for a moment.

"Marine, tonight you die," Tom said in a high falsetto, in his Japanese imitation. "Yankee dog, tonight I cut off your balls."

"Watch your goddamn language," the soldier said, turning his head.

"I bet he's braver than Errol Flynn," Tom said. "I bet he's got a drawer full of medals back home but he's too modest to wear them."

The soldier was getting angry now. "Why don't you kids shut up? We came here to see a movie."

"We came to make love," Tom said. He caressed Claude's cheek elaborately. "Didn't we, hotpants?"

"Squeeze me harder, darrrling," Claude said. "My nipples're palpitating."

"I am in ecstasy," Tom said. "Your skin is like a baby's ass."

"Put your tongue in my ear, honey," Claude said. "Ooooh—I'm coming."

"That's enough," the soldier said. Finally he had taken his hand out of the girl's blouse. "Get the hell out of here."

He had spoken loudly and angrily and a few people were turning around up front and making shushing noises.

"We paid good money for these seats," Tom said, "and we're not moving."

"We'll see about that." The soldier stood up. He was about six feet tall. "I'm going to get the usher."

"Don't let the little bastards get your goat, Sidney," the girl said. "Sit down."

"Sidney, remember I told you I hold you personally responsible for your lady friend's language," Tom said. "This is a last warning."

"Usher!" the soldier called across the auditorium, to where the lone attendant, dressed in frayed gold braid, was sitting in the last row, dozing under an exit light.

"Sssh, sssh!" came from spots all over the theater.

"He's a real soldier," Claude said. "He's calling for reinforcements."

"Sit down, Sidney." The girl tugged at the soldier's sleeve. "They're just snotty kids."

"Button your shirt, Angela," Tom said. "Your titty's showing." He stood up, in case the soldier swung.

"Sit down, please," Claude said politely, as the usher came down the aisle toward them, "this is the best part of the picture and I don't want to miss it."

"What's going on here?" the usher asked. He was a big weary-looking man of about forty who worked in a furniture factory during the day.

"Get these kids out of here," the soldier said. "They're using dirty language in front of this lady."

"All I said was, please take your hat off," Claude said. "Am I right, Tom?"

"That's what he said, sir," Tom said, sitting down again. "A simple polite request. He has a rare eye disease."

"What?" the usher asked, puzzled.

"If you don't throw them out," the soldier said, "there's going to be trouble."

"Why don't you boys sit someplace else?" the usher said.

"He explained," Claude said. "I have a rare eye disease."

"This is a free country," Tom said. "You pay your money and you sit where you want to sit. Who does he think he is—Adolf Hitler? Big shot. Just because he's wearing a soldier suit. I bet he never got any nearer to the Japs than Kansas City, Missouri. Coming here, giving a bad example to the youth of the country, screwing girls in public. In uniform."

"If you don't throw them out, I'm going to clout them," the soldier said thickly. He was clenching and unclenching his fists.

"You used bad language," the usher said to Tom. "I heard it with my own ears. Not in this theater. Out you go."

By now most of the audience was booing. The usher leaned over and grabbed Tom by his sweater. By the feel of the big hand on him Tom knew there was no chance with the man. He stood up. "Come on, Claude," he said. "All right, Mister," he said to the usher. "We don't want to cause any disturbance. Just give us our money back and we'll leave."

"Fat chance," the usher said.

Tom sat down again. "I know my rights," he said. Then very loudly, so that his voice rang through the entire auditorium over the sound of the gunfire from the screen, "Go ahead and hit me, you big brute."

The usher sighed. "Okay, okay," he said. "I'll give you your money back. Just get the hell out of here."

The boys stood up. Tom smiled up at the soldier. "I warned you," he said. "I'll be waiting for you outside."

"Go get your ma to change your diapers," the soldier said. He sat down heavily.

In the lobby, the usher gave them each thirty-five cents out of his own pocket, making them sign receipts to show to the owner of the theater. Tom signed the name of his algebra teacher and Claude signed the name of the president of his father's bank. "And I don't want to see you ever trying to get in here again," the usher said.

"It's a public place," Claude said. "You try anything like that and my father'll hear about it."

"Who's your father?" the usher said, disturbed.

"You'll find out," Claude said menacingly. "In due time."

The boys stalked deliberately out of the lobby. On the street they clapped each other on the back and roared with laughter. It was early and the picture wouldn't end for another half hour, so they went into the diner across the street and had a piece of pie and some coffee with the usher's money. The radio was on behind the counter and a newscaster was talking about the gains the American Army had made that day in Germany and about the possibility of the German high command falling back into a redoubt in the Bavarian Alps for a last stand.

Tom listened with a grimace twisting his round baby face. The war bored him. He didn't mind the fighting, it was the crap about sacrifice and ideals and our brave boys all the time that made him sick. It was a cinch they'd never get *him* in any army.

"Hey, lady," he said to the waitress, who was buffing her nails behind the counter, "can't we have some music?" He got enough patriotism at home, from his sister and brother.

The waitress looked up languidly. "Ain't you boys interested in who's winning the war?"

"We're Four F," Tom said. "We have a rare eye disease."

"Oh, my rare eye disease," Claude said, over his coffee. They burst into laughter again.

They were standing in front of the Casino when the doors opened and the audience began to stream out. Tom had given Claude his wristwatch to hold so that it wouldn't get broken. He stood absolutely still, purposely controlling himself, his hands hanging loosely at his sides, hoping that the soldier hadn't left before the end of the picture. Claude was pacing up and down nervously, his face sweating and pale from excitement. "You're sure now?" he kept saying.

"You're absolutely sure? He's an awful big sonofabitch. I want you to be *sure*."

"Don't you worry about me," Tom said. "Just keep the crowd back so I have room to move. I don't want him grappling me." His eyes narrowed. "Here he comes."

The soldier and his girl came out onto the sidewalk. The soldier looked about twenty-two or twenty-three. He was a little pudgy, with a heavy, sullen face. His tunic bulged over a premature paunch, but he looked strong. He had no hash marks on his sleeve and no ribbons. He had his hand possessively on the girl's arm, steering her through the stream of people. "I'm thirsty," he was saying. "Let's go get ourselves a coupla beers." Tom went over to him and stood in front of him, barring his way.

"You here again?" the soldier said, annoyed. He stopped for a moment. Then he started moving again, pushing Tom with his chest.

"You better stop pushing," Tom said. He grabbed the soldier's sleeve. "You're not going anywhere."

The soldier stopped in surprise. He looked down at Tom, who was at least three inches shorter than he, blond and cherubic looking in his old blue sweater and basketball sneakers. "You sure are perky for a kid your size," the soldier said. "Now get out of my way." He pushed Tom to one side with his forearm.

"Who do you think you're pushing, Sidney?" Tom said and jabbed sharply at the soldier's chest with the heel of his hand. By now people were stopping around them and looking on curiously. The soldier's face reddened in slow anger. "Keep your hands to yourself, kid, or you'll get hurt."

"What's the matter with you, boy?" the girl said. She had redone her mouth before coming out of the theater but there were still lipstick smears on her chin and she was uncomfortable at all the attention they were getting. "If this is some kind of joke, it's not funny."

"It's not a joke, Angela," Tom said.

"Stop that Angela crap," the soldier said.

"I want an apology," Tom said.

"That's the least," Claude said.

"Apology? Apology for what?" The soldier appealed to the small crowd that by now had collected around them. "These kids must be nuts."

"Either you apologize for the language your lady friend used to us in there," Tom said, "or you take the consequences."

"Come on, Angela," the soldier said, "let's go get that beer." He started to take a step, but Tom grabbed his sleeve and pulled. There was a tearing noise and a seam broke open at the shoulder.

The soldier twisted around to view the damage. "Hey, you little sonofabitch, you tore my coat."

"I told you you weren't going nowhere," Tom said. He backed away a little, his arms crooked, his fingers outspread.

"Nobody gets away with tearing my coat," the soldier said. "I don't care who he is." He swung with his open hand. Tom moved in and let the blow fall on his left shoulder. "Ow!" he screamed, putting his right hand to his shoulder and bending over as though he were in terrible pain.

"Did you see that?" Claude demanded of the spectators. "Did you see that man hit my friend?"

"Listen, soldier," a gray-haired man in a raincoat said, "you can't beat up on a little kid like that."

"I just gave him a little slap," the soldier turned to the man apologetically. "He's been dogging me all . . ."

Suddenly Tom straightened up and hitting upward, with his closed fist, struck the soldier, not too hard, so as not to discourage him, along the side of the jaw.

There was no holding the soldier back now. "Okay, kid, you asked for it." He began to move in on Tom.

Tom retreated and the crowd pushed back behind him.

"Give them room," Claude called professionally. "Give the men room."

"Sidney," the girl called shrilly, "you'll kill him."

"Nah," the soldier said, "I'll just slap him around a little. Teach him a lesson."

Tom snaked in and hit the soldier with a short left hook to the head and went in deep to the belly with his right. The soldier let the air out of his lungs with a large, dry sound, as Tom danced back.

"It's disgusting," a woman said. "A big oaf like that. Somebody ought to stop it."

"It's all right," her husband said. "He said he'd only slap him a couple of times."

The soldier swung a slow, heavy right hand at Tom. Tom ducked under it and dug both his fists into the soldier's soft middle. The soldier bent almost double in pain and Tom hooked both hands to the face. The soldier began to spurt blood and he waved his hands feebly in front of him and tried to clinch. Contemptuously, Tom let the soldier grapple him, but kept his right hand free and clubbed at the soldier's kidneys. The soldier slowly went down to one knee. He looked up blearily at Tom through the blood that was flowing from his cut forehead. Angela was crying. The crowd was silent. Tom stepped back. He wasn't even breathing hard. There was a little glow under the light, blond fuzz on his cheeks.

"My God," said the lady who had said that somebody ought to stop it, "he looks just like a baby."

"You getting up?" Tom asked the soldier. The soldier just looked at him and swung his head wearily to get the blood out of his eyes. Angela knelt beside him and started using her handkerchief on the cuts. The whole thing hadn't taken more than thirty seconds.

"That's all for tonight, folks," Claude said. He was wiping sweat off his face.

Tom strode out of the little circle of watching men and women. They were very quiet, as though they had seen something unnatural and dangerous that night, something they would like to be able to forget.

Claude caught up to Tom as they turned the corner. "Boy, oh boy," Claude said, "you worked fast tonight. The combinations, boy, oh boy, the combinations."

Tom was chuckling. "Sidney, you'll kill him," he said, trying to imitate the girl's voice. He felt wonderful. He half-closed his eyes and remembered the shock of his fists against skin and bone and against the brass buttons of the uniform. "It was okay," he said. "Only it didn't last long enough. I should have carried him a while. He was just a pile of shit. Next time let's pick somebody can *fight*."

"Boy," Claude said, "I really enjoyed that. I sure would like to see that fella's face tomorrow. When you going to do it again?"

Tom shrugged. "When I'm in the mood. Good night." He didn't want Claude hanging around him anymore. He wanted to be alone and remember every move of the fight. Claude was used to these sudden rejections and treated them respectfully. Talent had its prerogatives. "Good night," he said. "See you tomorrow."

Tom waved and turned off down the avenue for the long walk toward his house. They had to be careful to go to other parts of town when Tom wanted to fight. He was too well known in his own neighborhood. Everybody avoided him when they sensed one of his moods coming on.

He walked swiftly toward home down the dark street toward the smell of the river, dancing a little around a lamppost here and there. He'd shown them, he'd shown them. And he was going to show them a lot more. *Them.*

As he turned the last corner, he saw his sister Gretchen approaching the house from the other end of the street. She was hurrying and she had her head down and she didn't see him. He slipped into a doorway across the street and waited. He didn't want to have to talk to his sister. She hadn't said anything that he wanted to hear since he was eight years old. He watched her almost run up to the door next to the bakery window and get her key out of her bag. Maybe once he would follow her and really find out what she did with her nights.

Gretchen opened the door and went in. Tom waited until he was sure that she was safely upstairs and in her room, then crossed the street and stood in front of the weathered gray frame building. Home. He had been born in that house. He had come unexpectedly, early, and there had been no time to get his mother to the hospital. How many times he had heard *that* story. Big deal, being born at home. The Queen did not leave the Palace. The Prince first saw the light of day in the royal bedchamber. The house looked desolate, ready to be torn down. Tom spat again. He stared at the building, all exhilaration gone. There was the usual light from the basement window, where his father was working. The boy's face hardened. A whole life in a cellar. What do they know? he thought. Nothing.

He let himself in quietly with the key and climbed to the room he shared with Rudolph on the third floor. He was careful on the creaky stairs. Moving soundlessly was a point of honor with him. His exits and entrances were his own business. Especially on a night like this. There was some blood on the sleeve of his sweater and he didn't want anybody coming in and howling about it.

He could hear Rudolph breathing steadily, asleep, as he closed the door quietly behind him. Nice, proper Rudolph, the perfect gentleman, smelling of toothpaste, right at the head of his class, everybody's pet, never coming home with blood on him, getting a good night's sleep, so he wouldn't miss a good morning, Ma'am, or a trigonometry problem the next day. Tom undressed in the dark, throwing his clothes carelessly over a chair. He didn't want to answer any questions from Rudolph, either. Rudolph was no ally. He was on the other side. Let him be on the other side. Who cared?

But when he got into the double bed, Rudolph awoke. "Where you been?" Rudolph asked sleepily.

"Just to the show."

"How was it?"

"Lousy."

The two brothers lay still in the darkness. Rudolph moved a bit toward the other side of the bed. He thought it was degrading to have to sleep in the same bed with his brother. It was cold in the room, with the window open and the wind coming off the river. Rudolph always opened the window wide at night. If there was a rule, you could bet Rudolph would obey it. He slept in pajamas. Tom just stripped to his shorts for sleeping. They had arguments about that twice a week.

Rudolph sniffed. "For Christ's sake," he said, "you smell like a wild animal. What've you been doing?"

"Nothing," Tom said. "I can't help the way I smell." If he wasn't my brother, he thought, I'd beat the shit out of him.

He wished he'd had the money to go to Alice's behind the railroad station. He'd lost his virginity there for five dollars and he'd gone back several times after that. That was in the summer. He had had a job on a dredge in the river and he told his father he made ten dollars a week less than he actually did. That big dark woman, that Florence girl, up from Virginia, who had let him come twice for the same five dollars because he was only fourteen and he was cherry, that would have really finished the night off. He hadn't told Rudolph about Alice's either. Rudolph was still a virgin, that was for sure. He was above sex or he was waiting for a movie star or he was a fairy or something. One day, he, Tom, was going to tell Rudolph everything and then watch the expression on his face. Wild animal. Well, if that's what they thought of him, that's what he was going to be—a wild animal.

He closed his eyes and tried to remember what the soldier looked like, down on one knee on the pavement with the blood leaking all over his face. The image was clear, but there was no pleasure in it any more.

He started to tremble. The room was cold, but that wasn't why he was trembling.

V

Gretchen sat in front of the little mirror which was propped up on the dressing table against the wall of her room. It was an old kitchen table she had bought at a junk sale for two dollars and painted pink. There were some cosmetic jars on it and a silver-backed brush she had gotten as a present on her eighteenth birthday and three small bottles of perfume and a manicure set all neatly laid out on a clean towel. She had on an old bathrobe. The worn flannel was warm against her skin and gave her some of the same feeling of coziness she used to have when she came in out of the cold and put it on before bedtime as a young girl. She needed what comfort she could find tonight.

She scrubbed the cold cream off her face with a piece of Kleenex. Her skin was very white, a heritage from her mother, like her blue, shading-to-violet eyes. Her straight, black hair was like her father's. Gretchen was beautiful, her mother said, just as she had been when she was Gretchen's age. Her mother was constantly imploring her not to allow herself to decay, as she had done. Decay was the word her mother used. With marriage, her mother intimated, decay set in immediately. Corruption lay in the touch of a man. Her mother did not lecture her about men; she was sure of what she called Gretchen's virtue (that was another word she used freely), but she used her influence to get Gretchen to wear loose clothes that did not show off her figure. "There's no sense in seeking out trouble," her mother said. "It comes finding you out soon enough. You have an old-fashioned figure, but your troubles will be strictly up-to-date."

Her mother had once confided to Gretchen that she had wanted to be a nun. There was a bluntness of sensibility there that disturbed Gretchen when she thought about it. Nuns had no daughters. She existed, aged nineteen, seated in front of a mirror on a March night in the middle of the century because her mother had failed to live up to her destiny.

After what had happened to her tonight, Gretchen thought bitterly, she herself would be tempted to enter a nunnery. If only she believed in God.

She had gone to the hospital as usual after work. The hospital was a military one on the outskirts of town, full of soldiers convalescing from wounds received in Europe. Gretchen was a volunteer worker five nights a week, distributing books and magazines and doughnuts, reading letters to soldiers with eye wounds and writing letters for soldiers with hand and arm injuries. She wasn't paid anything, but she felt it was the least she could do. Actually, she enjoyed the work. The soldiers were grateful and docile, made almost childlike by their wounds, and there was none of the tense sexual parading and reconnoitering that she had to endure in the office all day. Of course, many of the nurses and some of the other volunteers slipped off with the doctors and the more active officer-wounded, but Gretchen had quickly shown that she wasn't having any of that. So many girls were available and willing, that very few of the men persisted. To make it all easier, she had arranged to be assigned to the crowded enlisted men's wards, where it was almost impossible for a soldier to be alone with her for more than a few seconds at a time. She was friendly and easy with men conversationally, but she couldn't bear the thought of any man touching her. She had been kissed by boys from time to time, of course, at parties and in cars after dances, but their clumsy gropings had seemed meaningless to her, unsanitary and vaguely comic.

She never was interested in any of the boys who surrounded her in school and she scorned the girls who had crushes on football heroes or boys with cars. It all seemed so *pointless*. The only man she had ever speculated about in that way was Mr. Pollack, the English teacher, who was an old man, maybe fifty, with tousled gray hair, and who spoke in a low, gentlemanly voice and read Shakespeare aloud in class. " 'To-morrow, and to-morrow, and to-morrow, creeps in this petty pace from day to day . . .' " She could imagine herself in his arms, and his poetic and mournful caresses, but he was married and had daughters her age and never remembered anyone's name. As for her dreams . . . She forgot her dreams.

Something enormous was going to happen to her, she was sure, but it wasn't going to be this year or in this town.

As she went on her rounds in the loose, gray smock provided by the hospital, Gretchen felt motherly and useful, making up in a small way for what these courteous, uncomplaining young men had suffered for their country.

The lights were low in the wards and all the men were supposed to be in bed. Gretchen had made her usual special visit to the bedside of a soldier named Talbot Hughes, who had been wounded in the throat and couldn't speak. He was the youngest soldier in the ward and the most pitiful and Gretchen liked to believe that the touch of her hand and her good-night smile made the long hours before dawn more bearable for the boy. She was tidying the common room, where the men read and wrote letters, played cards and checkers and listened to the phonograph. She stacked the magazines neatly on the center table, cleared off a chessboard and put the pieces in their box, dropped two empty Coca-Cola bottles into a wastebasket.

She liked the little housewifely end of the night, conscious of the hundreds of young men sleeping around this central, warm core of the hospital block, young men saved from death, acquitted of war, young men healing and forgetting fear and agony, young men one day nearer to peace and home.

She had lived in small, cramped quarters all her life and the spaciousness of the common room, with its pleasant light-green walls and deep upholstered chairs, made her feel almost like a hostess in her own elegant home, after a successful party. She was humming as she finished her work and was just about to turn out the light and start for the locker room to change her clothes when a tall young Negro in pajamas and the Medical Corps maroon bathrobe limped in.

"Evening, Miss Jordache," the Negro said. His name was Arnold. He had been in the hospital a long time and she knew him fairly well. There were only two Negroes in the block and this was the first time Gretchen had seen one without the other. She always made a particular point of being agreeable to them. Arnold had had his leg smashed when a shell hit the truck he was driving in France. He came from St. Louis, he had told her, and had eleven brothers and sisters, and had finished high school.

He spent many hours reading and wore glasses while doing so. Although he seemed to read at random, comic books, magazines, the plays of Shakespeare, anything that happened to be lying around, Gretchen had decided that he was ripe for literature. He did look bookish, like a brilliant, lonely student from an African country, with his Army-issue glasses. From time to time Gretchen brought him books, either her own or her brother Rudolph's, or sometimes from the public library in town. Arnold read them promptly and returned them conscientiously, in good condition, without ever offering any comment on them. Gretchen felt that he was silent out of embarrassment, not wanting to pretend to be an intellectual in front of the other men. She read a great deal herself, but omnivorously, her taste guided in the last two years by Mr. Pollack's catholic enthusiasms. So she had through the months offered Arnold such disparate works as *Tess of the D'Urbervilles*, the poems of Edna St. Vincent Millay and Rupert Brooke, and *This Side of Paradise*, by F. Scott Fitzgerald.

She smiled as the boy came into the room. "Good evening, Arnold," she said. "Looking for something?"

"Naw. Just wanderin'. Couldn't get to sleep, somehow. Then I saw the light in here and I say to myself, 'I'll go in and visit with that pretty li'l Miss Jordache, pass the time of day.'" He smiled at her, his teeth white and perfect. Unlike the other men, who called her Gretchen, he always used her last name. His speech was somehow countrified, as though his family had carried the burden of their Alabama farm with them when they had migrated north. He was quite black, gaunt in the loose bathrobe. It had taken two or three operations to save his leg, Gretchen knew, and she was sure she could see the lines of suffering around his mouth.

"I was just going to put the light out," Gretchen said. The next bus passed the hospital in about fifteen minutes and she didn't want to miss it.

Pushing off his good leg, Arnold bounced up onto the table. He sat there swinging his legs. "You don't know the pleasure a man can get," Arnold said, "just looking down and seeing his own two feet. You just go on home, Miss Jordache, I imagine you got some fine young man waiting outside for you and I wouldn't like him to be upset your not coming on time."

"Nobody's waiting for me," Gretchen said. Now she felt guilty that she had wanted to hustle the boy out of the room just to catch a bus. There'd be another bus along. "I'm in no hurry."

He took a package of cigarettes out of his pocket and offered her one. She shook her head. "No, thank you. I don't smoke."

He lit his cigarette, his hand very steady, his eyes narrowed against the smoke. His movements were all deliberate and slow. He had been a football player in high school in St. Louis before he was drafted, he had told her, and the athlete remained in the wounded soldier. He patted the table next to him. "Why don't you set awhile, Miss Jordache?" he said. "You must be weary, on your feet all night, running around the way you do for us."

"I don't mind," Gretchen said. "I sit most of the day in the office." But she hoisted herself up to the table beside him, to show that she was not anxious to leave. They sat side by side, their legs hanging over the side of the table.

"You got pretty feet," Arnold said.

Gretchen looked down at her sensible, low-heeled, brown shoes. "I suppose they're all right," she said. She thought she had pretty feet, too, narrow and not too long, and slender ankles.

"I became an expert on feet in this man's army," Arnold said. He said it without self-pity, as another man might have said, "I learned how to fix radios in the Army," or, "The Army taught me how to read maps." His absence of compassion for himself made her feel a rush of pity for the soft-spoken, slow-moving boy. "You'll be all right," she said. "The nurses tell me the doctors've done wonders for your leg."

"Yeah." Arnold chuckled. "Just don't bet on old Arnold gaining a lot of ground from here on in."

"How old are you, Arnold?"

"Twenty-two. You?"

"Nineteen."

He grinned. "Good ages, huh?"

"I suppose so. If we didn't have a war."

"Oh, I'm not complaining," Arnold said, pulling at his cigarette. "It got me out of St. Louis. Made a man of me." There was the tone of mockery in his voice. "Ain't a dumb kid no more. I know what the score is now and who adds up the numbers. Saw some interesting places, met some interesting folk. You ever been in Cornwall, Miss Jordache? That's in England."

"No."

"Jordache," Arnold said. "That a name from around these parts?"

"No," Gretchen said. "It's German. My father came over from Germany. He was wounded in the leg too. In the First War. He was in the German army."

Arnold chuckled. "They get a man coming and going, don't they?" he said. "He do much running, your pa?"

"He limps a little," Gretchen spoke carefully. "It doesn't seem to interfere too much."

"Yeah, Cornwall." Arnold rocked back and forth a little on the table. He seemed to have had enough of talk about wars and wounds. "They got palm trees, little old towns, make St. Louis look like it was built the day before yesterday. Big, wide beaches. Yeah. Yeah, England. Folk're real nice. Hospitable. Invite you to their homes for Sunday dinner. They surprised me. Always felt the English were uppity. Anyway, that was the general impression about 'em in the circles in which I moved in St. Louis as a young man."

Gretchen felt he was making fun of her, gently, with the ironic formal pronouncement. "People have to learn about each other," she said stiffly, unhappy about how pompous she was sounding, but somehow put off, disturbed, forced on the defensive by the soft, lazy, country voice.

"They sure do," he agreed. "They sure enough do." He leaned on his hands and turned his face toward her. "What have I got to learn about you, Miss Jordache?"

"Me?" A forced little laugh was surprised out of her. "Nothing. I'm a small-town secretary who's never been anyplace and who'll never go anyplace."

"I wouldn't agree to that, Miss Jordache," Arnold said seriously. "I wouldn't agree to that at all. If ever I saw a girl that was due to rise, it's you. You got a neat, promising style of handling yourself. Why, I bet half the boys in this building'd ask you to marry them on the spot, you gave them any encouragement."

"I'm not marrying anyone yet," Gretchen said.

"Of course not." Arnold nodded soberly. "No sense in rushing, lock yourself in, a girl like you. With a wide choice." He stubbed his cigarette out in an ash tray on the table, then reached automatically into the package in the pocket of the bathrobe for a fresh one, which he neglected to light. "I had a girl in Cornwall for three months," he said. "The prettiest, most joyous, loving little girl a man could ever hope to see. She was married, but that made never no mind. Her husband was out in Africa somewhere since 1939 and I do believe she forgot what he looked like. We went to pubs together and she made me Sunday dinner when I got a pass and we made love like we was Adam and Eve in the Garden."

He looked thoughtfully up at the white ceiling of the big empty room. "I became a human being in Cornwall," he said. "Oh, yeah, the Army made a man out of little Arnold Simms from St. Louis. It was a sorrowful day in that town when the orders came to move to fight the foe." He was silent, remembering the old town near the sea, the palm trees, the joyous, loving little girl with the forgotten husband in Africa.

Gretchen sat very still. She was embarrassed when anybody talked of making love. She wasn't embarrassed by being a virgin, because that was a conscious choice on her part, but she was embarrassed by her shyness, her inability to take sex lightly and matter-of-factly, at least in conversation, like so many of the girls she had gone to high school with. When she was honest with herself, she recognized that a good deal of her feeling was because of her mother and father, their bedroom separated from hers by only a narrow hallway. Her father came clumping up at five in the morning, his slow footsteps heavy on the stairs, and then there would be the low sound of his voice, hoarsened by the whiskey of the long night, and her mother's complaining twitterings and then the sounds of the assault and her mother's tight, martyred expression in the morning.

And tonight, in the sleeping building, in the first really intimate conversation she had had alone with any of the men, she was being made a kind of witness, against her will, of an act, or the ghost and essence of an act, that she tried to reject from her consciousness. Adam and Eve in the Garden. The two bodies, one white, one black. She tried not to think about it in those terms, but she couldn't help herself. And there was something meaningful and planned in the boy's revelations—it was not the nostalgic, late-at-night reminiscences of a soldier home from the wars—there was a direction in the musical, flowing whispers, a target. Somehow, she knew the target was herself and she wanted to hide.

"I wrote her a letter after I was hit," Arnold was saying, "but I never got no answer. Maybe her husband come home. And from that day to this I never touched a woman. I got hit early on and I been in the hospital ever since. The first time I got out was last Saturday. We had an afternoon pass, Billy and me." Billy was the other Negro in the ward. "Nothin' much for two colored boys to do in this valley. It ain't Cornwall, I'll tell you that." He laughed. "Not even any colored folk around. Imagine that, being sent to maybe the one hospital in the United States that's in a town without any colored folk. We drank a couple of beers that we got in the market and we took the bus upriver a bit, because we heard there was a colored family up at the Landing. Turned out it was just an old man from South Carolina, living all by himself in an old house on the river, with all his family gone and forgotten. We gave him some beer and told him some lies about how brave we were in the war, and said we'd come back fishin' on our next pass. Fishin'!"

"I'm sure," Gretchen said, looking at her watch, "that when you get out of the hospital for good and go back home you'll find a beautiful girl and be very happy again." Her voice sounded prissy and false and nervous all at the same time and she was ashamed of herself, but she knew she had to get out of that room. "It's awfully late, Arnold," she said. "I've enjoyed our little talk, but now I'm afraid I . . ." She started to get off the table, but he held her arm in his hand, not hard, but firmly.

"It ain't all that late, Miss Jordache," Arnold said. "To tell you the truth, I been waiting for just such an occasion, all alone like this."

"I have to catch a bus, Arnold. I . . ."

"Wilson and me, we've been discussing you." Arnold didn't let go of her arm. "And we decided on our next pass, that's this Saturday, we would like to invite you to spend the day with us."

"That's very kind of you and Wilson," Gretchen said. She had difficulty trying to keep her voice normal. "But I'm terribly busy on Saturdays."

"We figured it wouldn't do to be seen in the company of two black boys," Arnold went on, his voice flat, neither menacing nor inviting, "being as how this is your town and they're not used to seeing things like that around here, and we're only enlisted men . . ."

"That really has nothing to do with . . ."

"You take the bus up to the Landing at twelve-thirty," Arnold continued, as though there had been no interruption. "We'll go earlier and give that old man five bucks to buy himself a bottle of whiskey and go to the show and we'll fix up a nice meal for the three of us in his house. You turn left directly at the bus stop and walk on about a quarter of a mile down to the river and it's the only house there, sitting real pretty on the bank, with nobody around to snoop or make a fuss, just the three of us, all folksy and friendly."

"I'm going home now, Arnold," Gretchen said loudly. She knew she would be ashamed to call out, but she tried to make him think she was ready to shout for help.

"A good meal, a couple of nice long drinks," Arnold said, whispering, smiling, holding her. "We been away a long time, Miss Jordache."

"I'm going to yell," Gretchen said, finding it hard to speak. How could he do it—be so polite and friendly in one breath and then . . . She despised herself for her ignorance of the human race.

"We have a high opinion of you, Miss Jordache, Wilson and me. Ever since I first laid eyes on you I can't think about anybody else. And Wilson says it's the same with him . . ."

"You're both crazy. If I tell the Colonel . . ." Gretchen wanted to pull her arm away, but if anybody happened to come in and saw them struggling, the explanations would be painful.

"As I said, our opinion is high," Arnold said, "and we're willing to pay for it. We got a lot of back pay accumulated, Wilson and me, and I been particularly lucky in the crap game in the ward. Listen careful, Miss Jordache. We got eight hundred dollars between us and you're welcome to it. Just for one little afternoon on the river . . ." He took his hand off her arm and, unexpectedly, jumped down from the table, landing lightly on his good foot. He started limping out, his big body made clumsy by the floating maroon bathrobe. He turned at the door. "No need to say yes or no this minute, Miss Jordache," he said politely. "Think on it. Saturday's two days away. We'll be there at the Landing, from eleven A.M. on. You just come anytime you get your chores done, Miss Jordache. We'll be waiting on you." And he limped out of the room, standing very straight and not holding onto the walls for support.

For a moment, Gretchen sat still. The only sound she heard was the hum of a machine somewhere in the basement, a sound she didn't remember ever having heard before. She touched her bare arm, where Arnold's hand had held it, just below the elbow. She got off the table and turned off the lights, so that if anybody came in, they wouldn't see what her face must look like. She leaned against the wall, her hands against her mouth, hiding it. Then she hurried to the locker room and changed into her street clothes and almost ran out of the hospital to the bus stop.

She sat at the dressing table wiping off the last of the cold cream from the delicately veined pale skin under her swollen eyes. On the table before her stood the jars and vials with the Woolworth names of beauty—Hazel Bishop, Coty. *We made love like Adam and Eve in the Garden.*

She mustn't think about it, she mustn't think about it. She would call the Colonel tomorrow and ask to be transferred to another block. She couldn't go back *there* again.

She stood up and took off her bathrobe and for a moment she was naked in the soft light of the lamp over the dressing table. Reflected in the mirror, her high, full breasts were very white and the nipples stood disobediently erect. Below was the sinister, dark triangle, dangerously outlined against the pale swell of her thighs. *What can I do about it, what can I do about it?*

She put on her nightgown and put out the light and climbed into the cold bed. She hoped that this was not going to be one of the nights that her father picked to claim her mother. There was just so much that she could bear in one night.

The bus left every half hour on the way upriver toward Albany. On Saturday it would be full of soldiers on weekend passes. All the battalions of young men. She saw herself buying the ticket at the bus terminal, she saw herself seated at the window looking out at the distant, gray river, she saw herself getting off at the stop for the Landing, standing there alone, in front of the gas station; under her high-heeled shoes she felt the uneven surface of the gravel road, she smelled the perfume she couldn't help but wear, she saw the dilapidated, unpainted frame house on the bank of the river, and the two dark men, glasses in their hands, waiting silently, knowing executioners, figures of fate, not rising, confident, her shameful pay in their pockets, waiting, knowing she was coming, watching her come to deliver herself in curiosity and lust, knowing what they were going to do together.

She took the pillow from beneath her head and put it between her legs and clamped it hard.

VI

The mother stands at the lace-curtained window of the bedroom staring out at the cindery back yard behind the bakery. There are two spindly trees there, with a board nailed between them, from which swings a scuffed, heavy, leather cylinder, stuffed with sand like the heavy bags prize fighters use to train on. In the dark enclosure, the bag looks like a hanged man. In other days in the back gardens on the same street, there were flowers and hammocks strung between the trees. Every afternoon, her husband puts on a pair of wool-lined gloves and goes out into the back yard and flails at the bag for twenty minutes. He goes at the bag with a wild, concentrated violence, as though he is fighting for his life. Sometimes, when she happens to see him at it, when Rudy takes over the store for her for awhile to let her rest, she has the feeling that it isn't a dead bag of leather and sand her husband is punishing, but herself.

She stands at the window in a green sateen bathrobe, soiled at the collar and cuffs. She is smoking a cigarette and the ash drifts down unnoticed onto the robe. She used to be the neatest and most meticulous of girls, clean as a blossom in a glass vase. She was brought up in an orphanage and the Sisters knew how to inculcate strict habits of cleanliness. But she is a slattern now, loose-bodied and careless about her hair and skin and her clothes. The Sisters taught her a love of religion and affection for the ceremonies of the Church, but she has not been to Mass for almost twenty years. When her first child, her daughter, Gretchen, was born, she arranged with the Father for the christening, but her husband refused to appear at the font and forbade her then or ever again to give as much as a penny in contribution to the Church. And he a born Catholic.

Three unbaptized and unbelieving children and a blaspheming, Church-hating husband. Her burden to bear.

She had never known her father or mother. The orphanage in Buffalo had been her mother and father. She was assigned a name. Pease. It might have been her mother's name. When she thought of herself it was always as Mary Pease, not Mary Jordache, or Mrs. Axel Jordache. The Mother Superior had told her when she left the orphanage that it might well have been that her mother was Irish, but nobody knew for sure. The Mother Superior had warned her to beware of her fallen mother's blood in her body and to abstain from temptation. She was sixteen at the time, a rosy, frail girl with bright golden hair. When her daughter had been born she had wanted to name the baby Colleen, to memorialize her Irish descendance. But her husband didn't like the Irish and said the girl's name would be Gretchen. He had known a whore in Hamburg by that name, he said. It was only a year after the wedding, but he already hated her.

She had met him in the restaurant on the Buffalo lake front where she worked as a waitress. The orphanage had placed her there. The restaurant was run by an aging German-American couple named Mueller and the people at the orphanage had chosen them as employers because they were kindly and went to Mass and allowed Mary to stay with them in a spare room above their apartment. The Muellers were good to her and protected her and none of the customers dared to speak improperly to her in the restaurant. The Muellers let her off three times a week to continue her education at night school. She was not going to be a waitress in a restaurant all her life.

Axel Jordache was a huge, silent young man with a limp, who had emigrated from Germany in the early 1920's and who worked as a deckhand on the Lake steamers. In the winter, when the Lakes were frozen over, he sometimes helped Mr. Mueller in the kitchen as a cook and baker. He hardly spoke English then and he frequented the Muellers' restaurant so that he could have someone to talk to in his native tongue. When he had been wounded in the German army and couldn't fight any more they had made him into a cook at the hospital in Frankfurt.

Because, during another war, a young man had come out of a hospital alienated and looking for exile, she was standing tonight in a shabby room, over a shop in a slum, where every day, twelve hours a day, she had given up her youth, her beauty, her hopes. And no end in sight.

He had been most polite. He never as much as tried to hold her hand and when he was in Buffalo between voyages he would walk her to night school and wait to accompany her home. He had asked her to correct his English. Her English was a source of pride to her. People told her they thought she came from Boston when they heard her talk and she took it as a great compliment. Sister Catherine, whom she admired above all the teachers in the orphanage, came from Boston, and spoke crisply and with great precision and had the vocabulary of an educated woman. "To speak slovenly English," Sister Catherine had said, "is to live the life of a cripple. There are no aspirations denied a girl who speaks like a lady." She had modeled herself on Sister Catherine and Sister Catherine had given her a book, a history of Irish heroes, when she had left the orphanage. "To Mary Pease, my most hopeful student," was written in a bold, upright hand on the flyleaf. Mary had modeled her handwriting on Sister Catherine's, too. Somehow, Sister Catherine's teaching had made her believe that her father, whoever he was, must have been a gentleman.

With Mary Pease coaching him in the silvery Back Bay accents of Sister Catherine, Axel Jordache had learned how to speak proper English very quickly. Even before they were married, he spoke so well that people were surprised when he told them that he had been born in Germany. There was no denying it, he was an intelligent man. But he used his intelligence to torment her, torment himself, torment everyone around him.

He hadn't even kissed her before he proposed to her. She was nineteen at the time, her daughter Gretchen's age, and a virgin. He was unfailingly attentive, always cleanly bathed and shaved and he always brought her small gifts of candy and flowers when he returned from his trips.

He had known her for two years before he proposed. He hadn't dared to speak earlier, he said, because he was afraid she would reject him because he was a foreigner and because he limped. How he must have laughed to himself as he saw the tears come to her eyes at his modesty and his lack of confidence in himself. He was a diabolical man, weaving lifetime plots.

She said yes, conditionally. Perhaps she thought she loved him. He was a good-looking man, with that Indian head of black hair and a sober, industrious, thin face and clear, brown eyes that seemed soft and considerate when they looked at her. When he touched her it was with the utmost deceptive gentleness, as though she were made of china. When she told him she had been born out of wedlock (her phrase) he said he already knew it, from the Muellers, and that it didn't make any difference, in fact, it was a good thing, there wouldn't be any in-laws to disapprove of him. He himself was cut off from what remained of his family. His father had been killed on the Russian front in 1915 and his mother had remarried a year later and moved to Berlin from Cologne. There was a younger brother he had never liked, who had married a rich German-American girl who had come to Berlin after the war to visit relatives. The brother now lived in Ohio, but Axel never saw him. His loneliness was apparent and it matched her own.

Her conditions were stringent. He was to give up his job on the Lakes. She didn't want a husband who was away most of the time and who had a job that was no better than a common laborer's. And they were not to live in Buffalo, where everyone knew about her birth and the orphanage and where at every turn she would meet people who had seen her working as a waitress. And they were to be married in church.

He had agreed to everything. Oh, diabolical, diabolical. He had some money saved up and through Mr. Mueller he got in touch with a man who had a bakery in Port Philip whose lease was for sale. She made him buy a straw hat for the trip to Port Philip to conclude the deal. He was not to go wearing his usual cloth cap, that hangover from Europe. He was to look like a respectable American businessman.

Two weeks before the wedding, he took her to see the shop in which she was going to spend her life and the apartment above it in which she was going to conceive three children. It was a sunny day in May and the shop was freshly painted, with a large, green awning to protect the plate-glass window, with its array of cakes and cookies, from the sun. The street was a clean, bright one, with other little shops, a hardware store, a dry-goods store, a pharmacy on the corner. There was even a milliner's shop, with hats wreathed in artificial flowers on stands in the window. It was the shopping street for a quiet residential section that lay between it and the river. Large, comfortable houses behind green lawns. There were sails on the river and a white excursion boat, up from New York, passed as they sat on a bench under a tree looking across the broad stretch of summer-blue water. They could hear the band on board playing waltzes. Of course, with his limp, they never danced.

Oh, the plans she had that sunny May waltzing rivery day. Once they were established, she would put in tables, redecorate the shop, put up curtains, set out candles, serve chocolate and tea, then, later, buy the shop next door (it was empty that first day she saw it) and start a little restaurant, not one like the Muellers', for working men, but for traveling salesmen and the better class of people of the town. She saw her husband in a dark suit and bow tie showing diners to their table, saw waitresses in crisp muslin aprons hurrying with loaded platters out of the kitchen, saw herself seated behind the cash register, smiling as she rang up the checks, saying, "I hope you enjoyed your dinner," sitting down with friends over coffee and cake when the day's work was over.

How was she to know that the neighborhood was going to deteriorate, that the people she would have liked to befriend would consider her beneath them, that the people who would have liked to befriend her she would consider beneath her, that the building next door was to be torn down and a large, clanging garage put up beside the bakery, that the millinery shop was to vanish, that the houses facing the river would be turned into squalid apartments or demolished to make place for junkyards and metal-working shops?

There were never any little tables for chocolate and cakes, never any candles and curtains, never any waitresses, just herself, standing on her feet twelve hours a day summer and winter, selling coarse loaves of bread to grease-stained mechanics and slatternly housewives and filthy children whose parents fought drunkenly with each other in the street on Saturday nights.

Her torment began on her wedding night. In the second-class hotel in Niagara Falls (convenient to Buffalo). All the fragile hopes of the timid, rosy, frail young girl who had been photographed smiling in bridal white beside her unsmiling, handsome groom just eight hours before disappeared in the blood-stained, creaking Niagara bed. Speared helplessly under the huge, scarred, demonically tireless, dark, male body, she knew that she had entered upon her sentence of life imprisonment.

At the end of her week of honeymoon she wrote a suicide note. Then she tore it up. It was an act she was to repeat again and again through the years.

During the day, they were like other honeymooning couples. He was unfailingly considerate, he held her elbow when they crossed the street, he bought her trinkets and took her to the theater (the last week in which he ever showed any generosity to her. Very soon she discovered she had married a fanatical miser). He took her into ice cream parlors and ordered huge whipped cream sundaes (she had a child's sweet tooth) and smiled indulgently at her like a favorite uncle as she spooned down the heaped confections. He took her for a ride on the river under the Falls and held her hand lovingly when they walked in the sunlight of the northern summer. They never discussed the nights. When he closed the door behind them after dinner it was as though two different and unconnected souls swooped down to inhabit their bodies. They had no vocabulary with which to discuss the grotesque combat in which they were engaged. The severe upbringing of the Sisters had left her inhibited and full of impossible illusions of gentility. Whores had educated him and perhaps he believed all women who were worthy of marriage lay still and terrified in the marriage bed. Or perhaps he thought all American women.

In the end, of course, after months had passed, he recognized that fatalistic, lifeless rejection for what it was, and it enraged him. It spurred him on, made his attacks wilder. He never went with other women. He never looked at another woman. His obsession slept in his bed. It was her misfortune that the one body he craved was hers and was at his disposal. For twenty years he besieged her, hopelessly, hating her, like the commander of a great army incredibly being held at bay before the walls of a flimsy little suburban cottage.

She wept when she discovered that she was pregnant.

When they fought it was not about this. They fought about money. She learned that she had a sharp and hurtful tongue. She became a shrew for small change. To get ten dollars for a new pair of shoes and, later on, for a decent dress for Gretchen to wear to school, took months of bitter campaigning. He begrudged her the bread she ate. She was never to know how much money he had in the bank. He saved like a lunatic squirrel for a new ice age. He had been in Germany when a whole population had been ruined and he knew it could happen in America, too. He had been shaped by defeat and understood that no continent was immune.

The paint was flaking off the walls of the shop for years before he bought five cans of whitewash and repainted. When his prosperous, garage-owning brother came from Ohio to visit him and offered him a share in a new automobile agency he was acquiring, for a few thousand dollars which he could borrow from his brother's bank, Axel threw his brother out of the house as a thief and schemer. The brother was chubby and cheerful. He took a two-week holiday in Saratoga every summer and went to the theater in New York several times a year with his fat, garrulous wife. He was dressed in a good wool suit and smelled nicely of bay rum. If Axel had been willing to borrow money like his brother, they would have lived in comfort all their lives, could have been freed from the slavery of the bakery, escaped from the slum into which the neighborhood was sinking. But her husband would not draw a penny from the bank or put his name on a note. The paupers of his native country, with their tons of worthless money, watched with gaunt eyes over every dollar that passed through his hands.

When Gretchen graduated from high school, although, like her brother Rudolph, she was always at the head of her class, there was no question of her going to college. She had to go to work immediately and hand half her salary over to her father every Friday. College ruined women, turned them into whores. The Father has spoken. Gretchen would marry young, the mother knew, would marry the first man who asked her, to escape her father. Another life destroyed, in the endless chain.

Only with Rudolph was her husband generous. Rudolph was the hope of the family. He was handsome, well-mannered, well-spoken, admired by his teachers, affectionate. He was the only member of the family who kissed her when he left in the morning and returned in the evening. Both she and her husband saw the redemption of their separate failures in their older son. Rudolph had a talent for music and played the trumpet in the school band. At the end of the last school year Axel had bought a trumpet for him, a gleaming, golden instrument. It was the one gift to any of them that Axel had ever made. Everything else he had given to them had come as a result of ferocious bargaining. It was strange to hear the soaring, triumphant horn notes resounding through the gray, undusted apartment when Rudolph was practicing. Rudolph played club dates at dances and Axel had advanced him the money for a tuxedo, thirty-five dollars, an unheard-of outpouring. And he permitted Rudolph to hold onto the money he earned. "Save it," he said. "You'll be able to use it when you get to college." It was understood from the beginning that Rudolph was going to go to college. Somehow.

She feels guilty about Rudolph. All her love is for him. She is too exhausted to love anybody but her chosen son. She touches him when she can, she goes into his room when he is sleeping and kisses his forehead, she washes and irons his clothes when she is dizzy from fatigue so that his splendor will be clear to all eyes at every moment. She cuts out items from the school newspaper when he wins a race and pastes his report cards neatly in a scrapbook that she keeps on her dresser next to her copy of *Gone With the Wind*.

Her younger son, Thomas, and her daughter are inhabitants of her house. Rudolph is her blood. When she looks at him she sees the image of her ghostly father.

She has no hopes for Thomas. With his blond, sly, derisive face. He is a ruffian, always brawling, always in trouble at school, insolent, mocking, going his own way, without standards, sliding in and out of the house on his own secret schedule, impervious to punishment. On some calendar, somewhere, disgrace is printed in blood red, like a dreadful holiday, for her son Thomas. There is nothing to be done about it. She does not love him and she cannot hold out a hand to him.

So, the mother, standing on swollen legs at the window, surrounded by her family in the sleeping house. Insomniac, unfastidious, over-worked, ailing, shapeless, avoiding mirrors, a writer of suicide notes, graying at the age of forty-two, her bathrobe dusted with ash from her cigarette.

A train hoots far away, troops piled into the rattling coaches, on their way to distant ports, on their way to the sound of the guns. Thank God Rudolph is not yet seventeen. She would die if they took him for a soldier.

She lights a last cigarette, takes off her robe, the cigarette hanging carelessly from her lower lip, and gets into bed. She lies there smoking. She will sleep a few hours. But she knows she will wake when she hears her husband coming heavily up the steps, rank with the sweat of his night's work and the whiskey he has drunk.

Chapter 2

The office clock stood at five to twelve. Gretchen kept typing. Since it was Saturday, the other girls had already stopped working and were making up, ready to depart. Two of them, Luella Devlin and Pat Hauser, had invited her to go out and have a pizza with them, but she was in no mood for their brainless gabble this afternoon. When she was in high school she had had three good friends, Bertha Sorel, Sue Jackson, Felicity Turner. They were the brightest girls in the school and they had made a small, superior, isolated clique. She wished all three of them or any one of them were in town today. But they all came from well-off families and had gone to college and she had found no one else to take their place in her life.

Gretchen wished that there were enough work to give her an excuse to remain at her desk the whole afternoon, but she was typing out the final items of the last bill of lading Mr. Hutchens had put on her desk and there was no way of dragging it out.

She hadn't gone to the hospital the last two nights. She had phoned in and said she was sick and had gone home directly after work and stayed there. She had been too restless to read and had fussed over her entire wardrobe, washing blouses that were already spotlessly clean, pressing dresses that didn't have a crease in them, washing her hair and setting it, manicuring her nails, insisting on giving Rudy a manicure, although she had given him one just the week before.

Late on Friday night, unable to sleep, she had gone down into the cellar where her father was working. He looked up at her in surprise as she came down the steps, but didn't say anything, even when she sat down on a chair and said, "Here, pussy, pussy," to the cat. The cat backed away. The human race, the cat knew, was the enemy.

"Pa," she said, "I've been wanting to talk to you."

Jordache didn't say anything.

"I'm not getting anywhere in this job I have," Gretchen said. "There's no chance of more money and no place to go. And once the war is over, they'll be cutting down and I'll be lucky if I can hang on."

"The war's not over yet," Jordache said. "There's still a lot of idiots waiting that have to be killed."

"I thought I ought to go down to New York and look for a real job there. I'm a good secretary now and I see ads for all sorts of jobs with twice the pay I'm getting now."

"You talk to your mother about this?" Jordache began to shape the dough into rolls, with quick little flips of his hand, like a magician.

"No," Gretchen said. "She's not feeling so well and I didn't want to disturb her."

"Everyone's so damn thoughtful in this family," Jordache said. "Warms the cockles."

"Pa," Gretchen said, "be serious."

"No," he said.

"Why not?"

"Because I said so. Be careful, you're going to get flour all over that fancy gown."

"Pa, I'll be able to send back a lot more money . . ."

"No," Jordache said. "When you're twenty-one, you can fly off anyplace you want. But you're not twenty-one. You're nineteen. You have to bear up under the hospitality of the ancestral home for two years. Grin and bear it." He took the cork out of the bottle and took a long swig of whiskey. With deliberate coarseness, he wiped his mouth with the back of his hand, leaving a smudge of flour across his face.

"I've got to get out of this town," Gretchen said.

"There are worse towns," Jordache said. "I'll see you in two years."

Five minutes past twelve, the clock read. She put the neatly typed papers in the drawer of her desk. All the other clerks were gone. She put the cover on her typewriter and went into the washroom and stared at herself in the mirror. She looked feverish. She dabbed some cold water on her forehead, then took out a vial of perfume from her bag and put a little on under each ear.

She went out of the building and through the main gate, under the big sign, "Boylan's Brick and Tile Works." The plant and the sign, with its ornate lettering that looked as though it advertised something splendid and amusing, had been there since 1890.

She looked around to see if Rudy was by any chance waiting for her. Sometimes he came by the Works and walked her home. He was the only one in the family she could talk to. If Rudy had been there, they could have had lunch in a restaurant and then perhaps splurged on a movie. But then she remembered that Rudy had gone with the high-school track team to a neighboring town for a meet.

She found herself walking toward the bus terminal. She walked slowly, stopping often to look into shop windows. Of course, she told herself, she was not going to take the bus. It was daytime now and the fantasies of night were safely behind her. Although it would be refreshing to drive along the river and get out somewhere and breathe a little country air. The weather had changed and spring was announcing itself. The air was warm and there were little white clouds high in the blue sky.

Before leaving the house in the morning, she had told her mother she was going to work in the hospital that afternoon to make up for the time she had lost. She didn't know why she had suddenly invented the story. She rarely lied to her parents. There was no need. But by saying she had to be on duty at the hospital, she avoided being asked to come and work in the store to help her mother handle the Saturday afternoon rush. It had been a sunny morning and the idea of long hours in the stuffy store had been distasteful to her.

A block from the terminal she saw her brother Thomas. He was pitching pennies in front of a drugstore with a gang of rowdyish-looking boys. A girl who worked in the office had been at the Casino Wednesday night and had seen the fight and told Gretchen about it. "Your brother," the girl said. "*He's scary*. A little kid like that. He's like a snake. I sure wouldn't like to have a kid like that in *my* family."

Gretchen told Tom that she knew about the fight. She had heard similar stories before. "You're a hideous boy," she said to Tom. He had just grinned, enjoying himself.

If Tom had seen her she would have turned back. She wouldn't have dared to go into the bus terminal with him watching. But he didn't see her. He was too busy pitching a penny at a crack in the sidewalk.

She drifted into the terminal. She looked at the clock. Twelve thirty-five. The bus upriver must have left five minutes ago and of course she wouldn't hang around there for twenty-five more minutes waiting for the next one. But the bus was late and was still standing there. She went up to the ticket window. "One for King's Landing," she said.

She got into the bus and sat up front near the driver. There were a lot of soldiers on the bus, but it was still early in the day and they hadn't had time to get drunk yet and they didn't whistle at her.

The bus pulled out. The motion of the bus lulled her and she drowsed with her eyes open. Trees flashed by, newly budded; houses, stretches of river; there were glimpses of faces in a town. Everything seemed washed and beautiful and unreal. Behind her the soldiers sang, young men's voices blending together, in "Body and Soul." There was a Virginia voice among the others, a slow Southern tone, sweetening the song's lament. Nothing could happen to her. Nobody knew where she was. She was between event and event, choiceless, unchoosing, floating among soldiers' yearning voices.

The bus drew to a halt. "King's Landing, miss," the driver said.

"Thank you," she said and stepped down neatly onto the side of the road. The bus pulled away. Soldiers blew kisses at her through the windows. She kissed her fingers to the young men in return, smiling. She would never see them again. They knew her not, nor she them, and they could not guess her errand. Singing, their voices waning, they disappeared north.

She stood on the side of the empty road in the hushed Saturday afternoon sunlight. There was a gas station and a general store. She went into the store and bought herself a Coke from a white-haired old man in a clean, faded, blue shirt. The color pleased her eye. She would buy herself a dress that color, fine, clean, pale cotton, to wear on a summer evening.

She went out of the store and sat down on a bench in front of it to drink her Coke. The Coke was icy and sweet and stung the back of her mouth in little tart explosions. She drank slowly. She was in no hurry. She saw the graveled road leading away from the highway to the river. The shadow of a little cloud raced down it, like an animal running. It was silent from one coast to the other. The wood of the bench under her was warm. No cars passed. She finished her Coke and put the bottle down under the bench. She heard the ticking of the watch on her wrist. She leaned back, to catch the weight of the sun on her forehead.

Of course she wasn't going to go to the house on the river. Let the food go cold, let the wine go unpoured, let the suitors languish by the side of the river. Unknown to them, their lady is near, playing her single, teasing game. She wanted to laugh, but would not break the wilderness silence.

It would be delicious to push the game further. To go halfway down the gravel road between the stands of second-growth birch, white pencils in the woodshade. Go halfway and then return, in inner mirth. Or better still, weave through the forest, in and out of the shadows, Iroquois maiden, silent on her stockinged feet over last year's leaves, down to the river, and there, from the protection of the trees, spy out, Intelligence agent in the service of all virgins, and watch the two men, their lusty plans prepared, sitting waiting on the porch. And then steal back, her crisp dress flecked with bark and sticky buds, safe, safe, after the edge of danger, but feeling her power.

She stood up and crossed the highway toward the leafy entrance of the gravel-top road. She heard a car coming fast, from the south. She turned and stood there, as though she were waiting for a bus to take her in the direction of Port Philip. It wouldn't do to be seen plunging into the woods. Secrecy was all.

The car swept toward her, on the far side of the road. It slowed, came to a halt opposite her. She did not look at it, but kept searching for the bus she knew wouldn't appear for another hour.

"Hello, Miss Jordache." She had been named, in a man's voice. She could feel the blush rising furiously to her cheeks as she turned her head. She knew it was silly to blush. She had every right to be on the road. No one knew of the two black soldiers waiting with their food and liquor and their eight hundred dollars. For a moment she didn't recognize the man who had spoken, sitting alone at the wheel of a 1939 Buick convertible, with the top down. He was smiling at her, one hand, in a driving glove, hanging over the door of the car on her side. Then she saw who it was. Mr. Boylan. She had only seen him once or twice in her life, around the plant which bore his family's name. He was rarely there, a slender, blond, tanned, cleanly shaven man, with bristly blond eyebrows and highly polished shoes.

"Good afternoon, Mr. Boylan," she said, not moving. She didn't want to get close enough for him to be able to notice her blush.

"What in the world are you doing all the way up here?" Privilege his voice suggested. He sounded as though this unexpected discovery, the pretty girl alone in her high heels at the edge of the woods, amused him.

"It was such a lovely day." She almost stammered. "I often go on little expeditions when I have an afternoon off."

"All alone?" He sounded incredulous.

"I'm a nature lover," she said lamely. What a clod he must think I am, she thought. She caught him smiling as he looked down at her high-heeled shoes. "I just took the bus on the spur of the moment," she said, inventing without hope. "I'm waiting for the bus back to town." She heard a rustle behind her and turned, panic-stricken, sure that it must be the two soldiers, growing impatient and come to see if she had arrived. But it was only a squirrel, racing across the gravel of the side road.

"What's the matter?" Boylan asked, puzzled by her spasmodic movement.

"I thought I heard a snake." Oh, good-bye, she thought.

"You're pretty jittery," Boylan said gravely, "for a nature lover."

"Only snakes," she said. It was the stupidest conversation she had ever had in her life.

Boylan looked at his watch. "You know, the bus won't be along for quite some time," he said.

"That's all right," she said, smiling widely, as though waiting for buses in the middle of nowhere was her favorite Saturday afternoon occupation. "It's so nice and peaceful here."

"Let me ask you a serious question," he said.

Here it comes, she thought. He's going to want to know whom I'm waiting for. She fumbled for a serviceable short list. Her brother, a girl friend, a nurse from the hospital. She was so busy thinking, she didn't hear what he said, although she knew he had said something.

"I'm sorry," she said. "I missed that."

"I said, have you had your lunch yet, Miss Jordache?"

"I'm not hungry, really. I . . ."

"Come." He gestured to her with his gloved hand. "I'll buy you lunch. I despise lunching alone."

Obediently, feeling small and childish, under adult orders, she crossed the road behind the Buick and stepped into the car, as he leaned over from his side to open the door for her. The only other person she had ever heard use the word "despise" in normal conversation was her mother. Shades of Sister Catherine, Old Teacher. "It's very kind of you, Mr. Boylan," she said.

"I'm lucky on Saturdays," he said as he started the car. She had no notion of what he meant by that. If he hadn't been her boss, in a manner of speaking, and old besides, forty, forty-five at least, she would have somehow managed to refuse. She regretted the secret excursion through the woods that now would never take place, the obscene, tantalizing possibility that perhaps the two soldiers would have glimpsed her, pursued her . . . Limping braves on tribal hunting grounds. Eight hundred dollars worth of war paint.

"Do you know a place called The Farmer's Inn?" Boylan asked as he started the car.

"I've heard of it," she said. It was a small hotel on a bluff above the river about fifteen miles farther on and supposed to be very expensive.

"It's not a bad little joint," Boylan said. "You can get a decent bottle of wine."

There was no more conversation because he drove very fast and the wind roared across the open car, making her squint against the pressure on her eyes and swirling her hair. The wartime speed limit was supposed to be only thirty-five miles an hour, to conserve gasoline, but of course a man like Mr. Boylan didn't have to worry about things like gasoline.

From time to time, Boylan looked over at her and smiled a little. The smile was ironical, she felt, and had to do with the fact that she was sure he knew she had been lying about her reasons for being alone so far from town, waiting senselessly for a bus that wouldn't arrive for another hour. He leaned over and opened the glove case and brought out a pair of dark Air Force glasses and handed it to her. "For your pretty blue eyes," he shouted, over the wind. She put the glasses on and felt very dashing, like an actress in the movies.

The Farmer's Inn had been a relay house in the post-colonial days when travel between New York and upstate had been by stagecoach. It was painted red with white trim and there was a large wagon wheel propped up on the lawn. It proclaimed the owner's belief that Americans liked to dine in their past. It could have been a hundred miles or a hundred years away from Port Philip.

Gretchen combed her hair into some sort of order, using the rear-view mirror. She was uncomfortable and conscious of Boylan watching her. "One of the nicest things a man can see in this life," he said, "is a pretty girl with her arms up, combing her hair. I suppose that's why so many painters have painted it."

She was not used to talk like that from any of the boys who had gone through high school with her or who hung around her desk at the office and she didn't know whether she liked it or not. It seemed to invade her privacy, talk like that. She hoped she wasn't going to blush any more that afternoon. She started to put on some lipstick, but he reached out and stopped her. "Don't do that," he said authoritatively. "You've got enough on. More than enough. Come." He leaped out of the car, with surprising agility, she thought, for a man that age, and came around and opened the door for her.

Manners, she noted automatically. She followed him from the parking lot, where there were five or six other cars ranged under the trees, toward the entrance to the hotel. His brown shoes, well they weren't really shoes (jodhpur boots, she was later to discover they were called), were highly shined, as usual. He was wearing a houndstooth tweed jacket, and gray flannel slacks, and a scarf at the throat of his soft wool shirt, instead of a tie. He's not real, she thought, he's out of a magazine. What am I doing with him?

Beside him, she felt dowdy and clumsy in the short-sleeved navy-blue dress that she had taken so much care to choose that morning. She was sure he was already sorry he had stopped for her. But he held the door open for her and touched her elbow helpfully as she passed in front of him into the bar.

There were two other couples in the bar, which was decorated like an eighteenth-century tap room, all dark oak and pewter mugs and plates. The two women were youngish and wore suede skirts with tight, flat jerseys and spoke in piercing, confident voices. Looking at them, Gretchen was conscious of the gaudiness of her own bosom and hunched over to minimize it. The couples were seated at a low table at the other end of the room and Boylan guided Gretchen to the bar and helped her sit on one of the heavy, high, wooden stools. "This end," he said in a low voice. "Get away from those ladies. They make a music I can do without."

A Negro in a starched white jacket came to take their order. "Afternoon, Mr. Boylan," the Negro said soberly. "What is your pleasure, sir?"

"Ah, Bernard," Boylan said, "you ask the question that has stumped philosophers since the beginning of time."

Phoney, Gretchen thought. She was a little shocked that she could think it about a man like Mr. Boylan.

The Negro smiled dutifully. He was as neat and spotless as if he were ready to conduct an operation. Gretchen looked at him sideways. I know two friends of yours not far from here, she thought, who aren't giving anybody any pleasure this afternoon.

"My dear," Boylan turned to her, "what do you drink?"

"Anything. Whatever you say." The traps were multiplying. How did she know what she drank? She never drank anything stronger than Coke. She dreaded the arrival of the menu. Almost certainly in French. She had taken Spanish and Latin in school. Latin!

"By the way," Boylan said, "you *are* over eighteen."

"Oh, yes," she said. She blushed. What a silly time to blush. Luckily it was dark in the bar.

"I wouldn't want to be dragged into court for leading minors into corruption," he said, smiling. He had nice, well-cared-for dentist's teeth. It was hard to understand why a man who looked like that, with teeth like that and such elegant clothes, and all that money, would ever have to have lunch alone.

"Bernard, let's try something sweet. For the young lady. A nice Daiquiri, in your inimitable manner."

"Thank you, sir," Bernard said.

Inimitable, she thought. Who uses words like that? Her sense of being the wrong age, wrongly dressed, wrongly made-up, made her hostile.

Gretchen watched Bernard squeeze the limes and toss in the ice and shake the drink, with expert, manicured black-and-pink hands. *Adam and Eve in the Garden.* If Mr. Boylan had had an inkling . . . There wouldn't be any of that condescending talk about corruption.

The frothy drink was delicious and she drank it like lemonade. Boylan watched her, one eye raised, a little theatrically, as the drink disappeared.

"Once again, please, Bernard," he said.

The two couples went into the dining room and they had the bar to themselves, as Bernard prepared the second round. She felt more at ease now. The afternoon was opening up. She didn't know why those were the words that occurred to her, but that's the way it seemed—*opening up*. She was going to sit at many dark bars and many kindly older men in peculiar clothes were going to buy her delicious drinks.

Bernard put the drink in front of her.

"May I make a suggestion, pet?" Boylan said. "I'd drink this one more slowly, if I were you. There *is* rum in them, after all."

"Of course," she said, with dignity. "I guess I was thirsty, standing out there in the hot sun."

"Of course, pet," he said.

Pet. Nobody had ever called her anything like that. She liked the word, especially the way he said it, in that cool, unpushy voice. She took little ladylike sips of the cold drink. It was as good as the first one. Maybe even better. She was beginning to feel that she wasn't going to blush anymore that afternoon.

Boylan called for the menu. They would order in the bar while they were finishing their drinks. The headwaiter came in with two large, stiff cards, and said, bowing a little, "Glad to see you again, Mr. Boylan."

Everybody was glad to see Mr. Boylan, in his shiny shoes.

"Should I order?" Boylan asked her.

Gretchen knew, from the movies, that gentlemen often ordered for ladies in restaurants, but it was one thing to see it on the screen and another thing to have it happen right in front of you. "Please do," she said. Right out of the book, she thought triumphantly. My, the drink was good.

There was a brief but serious discussion about the menu and the wine between Mr. Boylan and the headwaiter. The headwaiter disappeared, promising to call them when their table was ready. Mr. Boylan took out a gold cigarette case and offered her a cigarette. She shook her head.

"You don't smoke?"

"No." She felt that she was not living up to the level of the place and the rules of the situation by not smoking, but she had tried two or three times and it had made her cough and go red eyed and she had given up the experiment. Also, her mother smoked, day and night, and anything her mother did Gretchen didn't want to do.

"Good," Boylan said, lighting his cigarette with a gold lighter he took from his pocket and put down on the bar beside the monogrammed case. "I don't like girls to smoke. It takes away the fragrance of youth."

Fancy talk, she thought. But it didn't offend her now. He was putting himself out to please her. She was suddenly conscious of the odor of the perfume that she had dabbed on herself in the washroom at the office. She worried that it might seem cheap to him. "I must say," she said, "I was surprised you knew my name."

"Why?"

"Well, I don't think I've seen you more than once or twice at the Works. And you never come through the office."

"I've seen you," he said. "I wondered what a girl who looked like you was doing in a dreary place like Boylan's Brick and Tile Works."

"It isn't as awful as all that," she said defensively.

"No? I'm glad to hear that. I was under the impression that all my employees found it intolerable. I make it a point not to visit it more than fifteen minutes a month. I find it depresses me."

The headwaiter appeared. "Ready now, sir."

"Leave your drink, pet," Boylan said, helping her off her stool. "Bernard'll bring it in."

They followed the headwaiter into the dining room. Eight or ten of the tables were occupied. A full colonel and a party of young officers. Other tweedy couples. There were flowers on the polished fake-colonial tables and rows of shining glasses. There is nobody here who makes less than ten thousand dollars a year, she thought.

The conversation in the room dropped as they followed the headwaiter to a small table at the window, overlooking the river far below. She felt the young officers regarding her. She touched her hair. She knew what was going on in their minds. She was sorry Mr. Boylan wasn't younger.

The headwaiter held the chair for her and she sat down and put the large, creamy napkin demurely over her lap. Bernard came in with their unfinished Daiquiris on a tray and put them down on the table.

"Thank you, sir," he said as he backed off.

The headwaiter appeared with a bottle of red wine from France and the table waiter came up with their first course. There was no manpower shortage at The Old Farmer's Inn.

The headwaiter ceremoniously poured a little of the wine into a huge, deep glass. Boylan sniffed it, tasted it, looked up, squinting, at the ceiling, as he kept it for a moment in his mouth before swallowing. He nodded at the headwaiter. "Very good, Lawrence," he said.

"Thank you, sir," the headwaiter said. With all those thank you's, Gretchen thought, the bill was going to be horrendous.

The headwaiter poured the wine into her glass, then into Boylan's. Boylan raised his glass to her and they both sipped the wine. It had a strange dusty taste and was warm. Eventually, she was sure, she was going to learn to like that taste.

"I hope you like hearts of palm," Boylan said. "I developed the taste in Jamaica. That was before the war, of course."

"It's delicious." It tasted like a flat nothing to her, but she liked the idea that a whole noble palm tree had been cut down just to serve her one small, delicate dish.

"When the war is over," he said, picking at his plate, "I'm going to go down there and settle. Jamaica. Just lie on the white sand in the sun from year's end to year's end. When the boys come marching home this country's going to be impossible. A world fit for heroes to live in," he said mockingly, "is hardly fit for Theodore Boylan to live in. You must come and visit me."

"Sure," she said. "I'll rhumba on down on my salary from the Boylan Brick and Tile Works."

He laughed. "It is the proud boast of my family," he said, "that we have underpaid our help since 1887."

"Family?" she said. As far as she knew, he was the only Boylan extant. It was common knowledge that he lived alone in the mansion behind the stone walls of the great estate outside town. With servants, of course.

"Imperial," he said. "We are spread in our glory from coast to coast, from pine-clad Maine to orange-scented California. Aside from the Boylan Cement plant and the Boylan Brick and Tile Works in Port Philip, there are Boylan shipyards, Boylan oil companies, Boylan heavy-duty machinery plants throughout the length and breadth of this great land, each with a Boylan brother or uncle or cousin at its head, supplying the sinews of war at cost-plus to our beloved country. There is even a Major General Boylan who strikes shrewd blows in his nation's cause in the Service of Supply in Washington. Family? Let there be the sniff of a dollar in the air and there you will find a Boylan, first on the line."

She was not used to people running down their own families; her loyalties were simple. Her face must have showed her disappointment.

"You're shocked," Boylan said. Again that crooked look of amusement.

"Not really," she said. She thought of her own family. "Only people inside a family know how much love they deserve."

"Oh, I'm not all bad," Boylan said. "There's one virtue which my family has in abundance and I admire it without reservation."

"What's that?"

"They're rich. They're verrry, verrry rich." He laughed.

"Still," she said, hoping that he wasn't as bad as he sounded, that it was just a show-off lunchtime act that he was performing to impress an empty-headed girl, "still, you work. The Boylans've done a lot for this town . . ."

"They certainly have," he said. "They have bled it white. Naturally, they feel a sentimental interest in it. Port Philip is the most insignificant of the imperial possessions, not worth the time of a true, one hundred percent, up-and-at-em male Boylan, but they do not abandon it. The last and the least of the line, your humble servant, is delegated to the lowly home province to lend the magic of the name and the authority of the living family presence at least once or twice a month to the relic. I perform my ritual duties with all due respect and look forward to Jamaica when the guns have fallen silent."

He not only hates the family, she thought, he hates himself.

His quick, pale eyes noted the minute change in her expression. "You don't like me," he said.

"That isn't true," she said. "It's just that you're different from anyone I know."

"Different better or different worse?"

"I don't know," she said.

He nodded gravely. "I abide the question," he said. "Drink up. Here comes another bottle of wine."

Somehow, they had gone through the whole bottle of wine and they hadn't reached the main course yet. The headwaiter gave them fresh glasses and there was the ceremony of tasting once more. The wine had flushed her face and throat. The conversation in the rest of the restaurant seemed to have receded and came to her ears now in a regular, reassuring rhythm, like the sound of distant surf. She suddenly felt at home in the polished old room and she laughed aloud.

"Why are you laughing?" Boylan asked suspiciously.

"Because I'm here," she said, "and I could be so many other places instead."

"You must drink more often," he said. "Wine becomes you." He reached over and patted her hand. His hand was dry and firm on her skin. "You're beautiful, pet, beautiful, beautiful."

"I think so, too," she said.

It was his turn to laugh.

"Today," she said.

By the time the waiter brought their coffee she was drunk. She had never been drunk before in her life so she didn't know that she was drunk. All she knew was that all colors were clearer, that the river

below her was cobalt, that the sun lowering in the sky over the faraway western bluffs was of a heartbreaking gold. All the tastes in her
mouth were like summertime and the man opposite her was not a
stranger and her employer, but her best and most intimate friend, his
fine, tanned face kindly and marvelously attentive, the occasional
touch of his hand on hers of a welcome calm dryness, his laugh an
accolade to her wit. She could tell him anything, her secrets were his.

She told him anecdotes about the hospital—about the soldier who
had been hit over the eye by a bottle of wine that an enthusiastic
French woman had thrown to welcome him to Paris and who had
been awarded the Purple Heart because he suffered from double vision incurred in the line of duty. And the nurse and the young officer
who made love every night in a parked ambulance and who, one
night, when the ambulance had been called out, had been driven all
the way to Poughkeepsie stark naked.

As she spoke, it became clear to her that she was a unique and interesting person who led an incident-crammed, full life. She described the problems she had when she had played Rosalind in *As
You Like It* in the school play in her senior year. Mr. Pollack, the director, who had seen a dozen Rosalinds, on Broadway and elsewhere,
had said that it would be a crime if she wasted her talent. She had
also played Portia the year before and wondered briefly if she
wouldn't make a brilliant lawyer. She thought women ought to go in
for things like that these days, not settle for marriage and babies.

She was going to tell Teddy (he was Teddy by dessert) something
that she hadn't confided to a soul, that when the war was over she
was going to go down to New York to be an actress. She recited a
speech from *As You Like It,* her tongue lively and tripping from the
Daiquiris, the wine, the two glasses of Benedictine.

"*Come, woo me, woo me,*" she said, "*for now I am in a holiday
humor, and like enough to consent. What would you say to me now,
an I were your very, very Rosalind?*"

Teddy kissed her hand as she finished and she accepted the tribute
graciously, delighted with the flirtatious aptness of the quotation.

Warmed by the man's unflagging attention, she felt electric, sparkling, and irresistible. She opened the top two buttons of her dress.
Let her glories be displayed. Besides, it was warm in the restaurant.
She could speak of unmentionable things, she could use words that
until now she had only seen scrawled on walls by naughty boys. She
had achieved candor, that aristocratic privilege.

"I never pay any attention to them." She was responding to a
question from Boylan about the men in the office. "Squirming

around like puppies. Small-town Don Juans. Taking you to the movies and an ice-cream soda and then necking in the back seat of a car, grabbing at you as though you're the brass ring on a merry-go-round. Making a noise like a dying elk and trying to put their tongues in your mouth. Not for me. I've got other things on my mind. They try it once and after that they know better. I'm in no hurry!" She stood up suddenly. "Thank you for a delicious lunch," she said. "I have to go to the bathroom." She had never before said to any of her dates that she had to go to the bathroom. Her bladder had nearly burst from time to time in movie houses and at parties.

Teddy stood up. "The first door in the hall to the left," he said. He was a knowing man, Teddy, informed on all subjects.

She sauntered through the room, surprised that it was empty. She walked slowly, knowing that Teddy was following her every step with his pale, intelligent eyes. Her back was straight. She knew that. Her neck was long and white under the black hair. She knew that. Her waist was slender, her hips curved, her legs long and rounded and firm. She knew all that and walked slowly to let Teddy know it once and for all.

In the ladies' room, she looked at herself in the mirror and wiped off the last of the lipstick from her mouth. I have a wide, striking mouth, she told her reflection. What a fool I was to paint it just like any old mouth.

She went out into the hall from the ladies' room. Teddy was waiting for her at the entrance to the bar. He had paid the bill and he was drawing on his left glove. He stared at her somberly as she approached him.

"I am going to buy you a red dress," he said. "A blazing red dress to set off that miraculous complexion and that wild, black hair. When you walk into a room, the men will drop to their knees."

She laughed, red her color. That was the way a man should talk.

She took his arm and they went out to the car.

He put the top up because it was getting cold and they drove slowly south, his bare right hand, thoughtfully ungloved, on hers on the seat between them. It was cosy in the car, with all the windows up. There was the flowery fragrance of the alcohol they had drunk, mixed with the smell of leather.

"Now," he said, "tell me. What were you *really* doing at the bus stop at King's Landing?"

She chuckled.

"That was a dirty chuckle," he said.

"I was there for a dirty reason," she said.

He drove without speaking for awhile. The road was deserted, and they drove through stripes of long shadows and pale sunshine down the tree-lined highway.

"I'm waiting," Teddy said.

Why not? she thought. All things could be said on this blessed afternoon. Nothing was unspeakable between them. They were above the trivia of prudery. She began to speak, first hesitantly, then more easily, as she got into it, of what had happened at the hospital.

She described what the two Negroes were like, lonely and crippled, the only two colored men in the ward, and how Arnold had always been so reserved and gentlemanly and had never called her by her first name, like the other soldiers, and how he read the books she loaned him and seemed so intelligent and sad, with his wound and the girl in Cornwall who had never written to him again. Then she told about the night he found her alone when all the other men were asleep and the conversation they had and how it led up to the proposition, the two men, the eight hundred dollars. "If they'd been white, I'd have reported them to the Colonel," she said, "but this way . . ."

Teddy nodded understandingly at the wheel, but said nothing, just drove a little faster down the highway.

"I haven't been back to the hospital since," she said. "I just couldn't. I begged my father to let me go to New York. I couldn't bear staying in the same town with that man, with his knowing what he said to me. But my father . . . There's no arguing with my father. And naturally, I couldn't tell him why. He'd have gone out to the hospital and killed those two men with his bare hands. And then, this morning—it was such a lovely day—I didn't *go* to the bus, I *drifted* into it. I knew I didn't want to go to that house, but I guess I wanted to know if they really were there, if there were men who actually acted like that. Even so, even after I got out of the bus, I just waited on the road. I had a Coke, I took a sunbath . . . I . . . Maybe I would have gone a bit down the road. Maybe all the way. Just to see. I knew I was safe. I could run away from them easily, even if they saw me. They can hardly move, with their legs . . ."

The car was slowing down. She had been looking down at her shoes, under the dashboard of the car, as she spoke. Now she glanced up and saw where they were. The gas station. The general store. Nobody in sight.

The car came to a halt at the entrance to the gravel road that led down to the river.

"It was a game," she said, "a silly, cruel, girl's game."

"You're a liar," Boylan said.

"What?" She was stunned. It was terribly hot and airless in the car.

"You heard me, pet," Boylan said. "You're a liar. It wasn't any game. You were going to go down there and get laid."

"Teddy," she said, gasping, "please . . . please open the window. I can't breathe."

Boylan leaned across her and opened the door on her side. "Go ahead," he said. "Walk on down, pet. They're still there. Enjoy yourself. I'm sure it'll be an experience you'll cherish all your life."

"Please, Teddy . . ." She was beginning to feel very dizzy and his voice faded in her ears and then came up again, harshly.

"Don't worry about transportation home," Boylan said. "I'll wait here for you. I have nothing better to do. It's Saturday afternoon and all my friends are out of town. Go ahead. You can tell me about it when you come back. I'll be most interested."

"I've got to get out of here," she said. Her head was expanding and contracting and she felt as though she were choking. She stumbled out of the car and threw up by the side of the road in great racking heaves.

Boylan sat immobile at the wheel, staring straight ahead of him. When she was finished and the throat-tearing convulsions had ceased, he said, curtly, "All right, come back in here."

Depleted and fragile, she crept back into the car, cold sweat on her forehead, holding her hand up to her mouth against the smell.

"Here, pet," Boylan said kindly. He gave her the large colored silk handkerchief from his breast pocket. "Use this."

She dabbed at her mouth, wiped the sweat from her face. "Thank you," she whispered.

"What do you *really* want to do, pet?" he asked.

"I want to go home," she whimpered.

"You can't go home in that condition," he said.

He started the car.

"Where're you taking me?"

"My house," he said.

She was too exhausted to argue and she lay with her head against the back of the seat, her eyes closed, as they drove swiftly south along the highway.

He made love to her early that evening, after she had rinsed her mouth a long time with a cinnamon-flavored mouthwash in his bathroom and had slept soddenly on his bed for two hours. Afterward, silently, he drove her home.

Monday morning, when she came into the office at nine o'clock, there was a long, white, plain envelope on her desk, with her name printed on it and "Personal" scribbled in one corner. She opened the envelope. There were eight one-hundred-dollar bills there.

He must have gotten up at dawn to drive all the way into town and get into the locked factory before anyone appeared for work.

Chapter 3

The classroom was silent, except for the busy scratching of pens on paper. Miss Lenaut was seated at her desk reading, occasionally raising her head to scan the room. She had set a half-hour composition for her pupils to write, subject, "Franco-American Friendship." As Rudolph bent to his task at his desk toward the rear of the room, he had to admit to himself that Miss Lenaut might be beautiful, and undoubtedly French, but that her imagination left something to be desired.

Half a point would be taken off for a mistake in spelling or a misplaced accent, and a full point for any errors in grammar. The composition had to be at least three pages long.

Rudolph filled the required three pages quickly. He was the only student in the class who consistently got marks of over 90 on compositions and dictation, and in the last three tests he had scored 100. He was so good in the language that Miss Lenaut had grown suspicious and had asked him if his parents spoke French. "Jordache," she said. "It is not an American name." The imputation hurt him. He wanted to be different from the people around him in many respects, but not in his American-ness. His father was German, Rudolph told Miss Lenaut, but aside from an occasional word in that language, all Rudolph ever heard at home was English.

"Are you sure your father wasn't born in the Alsace?" Miss Lenaut persisted.

"Cologne," Rudolph said and added that his grandfather had come from Alsace-Lorraine.

"Alors," Miss Lenaut said. "It is as I suspected."

It pained Rudolph that Miss Lenaut, that incarnation of feminine beauty and worldly charm and the object of his feverish devotion, might believe, even for a moment, that he would lie to her or take secret advantage of her. He longed to confess his emotion and had fantasies of returning to the high school some years hence, when he was a suave college man, and waiting outside the school for her and addressing her in French, which would by that time be fluent and perfectly accented, and telling her, with an amused chuckle for the shy child he had been, of his schoolboy passion for her in his junior year. Who knew what then might happen? Literature was full of older women and brilliant young boys, of teachers and precocious pupils . . .

He reread his work for errors, scowling at the banality which the subject had imposed upon him. He changed a word or two, put in an accent he had missed, then looked at his watch. Fifteen minutes to go.

"Hey!" There was a tortured whisper on his right. "What's the past participle of venir?"

Rudolph turned his head slightly toward his neighbor, Sammy Kessler, a straight D student. Sammy Kessler was hunched in a position of agony over his paper, his eyes flicking desperately over at Rudolph. Rudolph glanced toward the front of the room. Miss Lenaut was engrossed in her book. He didn't like to break the rules in her class, but he couldn't be known by his contemporaries as a coward or a teacher's pet.

"Venu," he whispered.

"With two o's?" Kessler whispered.

"A u, idiot," Rudolph said.

Sammy Kessler wrote laboriously, sweating, doomed to his D.

Rudolph stared at Miss Lenaut. She was particularly attractive today, he thought. She was wearing long earrings and a brown, shiny dress that wrinkled skin-tight across her girdled hips and showed a generous amount of her stiffly armored bosom. Her mouth was a bright-red gash of lipstick. She put lipstick on before every class. Her family ran a small French restaurant in the theatrical district of New York and there was more of Broadway in Miss Lenaut than the Faubourg St. Honoré, but Rudolph was happily unaware of this distinction.

Idly, Rudolph began to sketch on a piece of paper. Miss Lenaut's face took shape under his pen, the easily identifiable two curls that she wore high on her cheeks in front of her ears, the waved, thick hair, with the part in the middle. Rudolph continued drawing. The earrings, the rather thick, beefy throat. For a moment, Rudolph hesitated. The territory he was now entering was dangerous. He glanced once more at Miss Lenaut. She was still reading. There were no problems of discipline in Miss Lenaut's class. She gave out punishments for the slightest infractions with merciless liberality. The full conjugation of the reflexive irregular verb *se taire*, repeated ten times, was the lightest of her sentences. She could sit and read with only an occasional lifting of her eyes to reassure herself that all was well, that there was no whispering, no passing of papers between desk and desk.

Rudolph gave himself to the delights of erotic art. He continued the line down from Miss Lenaut's neck to her right breast, naked. Then he put in her left breast. He was satisfied with the proportions. He drew her standing, three-quarter view, one arm extended, with a piece of chalk in her hand, at the blackboard. Rudolph worked with relish. He was getting better with each opus. The hips were easy. The mons veneris he drew from memory of art books in the library, so it was a bit hazy. The legs, he felt, were satisfactory. He would have liked to draw Miss Lenaut barefooted, but he was bad on feet, so he gave her the high-heeled shoes, with straps above the ankle, that she habitually wore. Since he had her writing on the blackboard, he decided to put some words on the blackboard. "*Je suis folle d'amour,*" he printed in an accurate representation of Miss Lenaut's blackboard script. He started to shade Miss Lenaut's breasts artistically. He decided that the entire work would be more striking if he drew it as though there were a strong light coming from the left. He shaded the inside of Miss Lenaut's thigh. He wished there were someone he knew in school he could show the drawing to who would appreciate it. But he couldn't trust the boys on the track team, who were his best friends, to treat the picture with appropriate sobriety.

He was shading in the straps on the ankles when he became conscious of someone standing beside his desk. He looked up slowly. Miss Lenaut was glaring down at the drawing on his desk. She must have moved down the aisle like a cat, high heels and all.

Rudolph sat motionless. No gesture seemed worthwhile at the moment. There was fury in Miss Lenaut's dark, mascaraed eyes and she was biting the lipstick off her lips. She reached out her hand, silently. Rudolph picked up the piece of paper and gave it to her. Miss

Lenaut turned on her heel and walked back to her desk, rolling the paper in her hands so that no one could see what was on it.

Just before the bell rang to end the class, she called out, "Jordache."

"Yes, ma'am," Rudolph said. He was proud of the ordinary tone he managed to use.

"May I see you for a moment after class?"

"Yes, ma'am," he said.

The bell rang. The usual chatter broke out. The students hurried out of the room to rush for their next classes. Rudolph, with great deliberation, put his books into his briefcase. When all the other students had quit the room, he walked up to Miss Lenaut's desk.

She was seated like a judge. Her tone was icy. "*Monsieur l'artiste*," she said. "You have neglected an important feature of your *chef d'oeuvre*." She opened the drawer of her desk and took out the sheet of paper with the drawing on it and smoothed it with a rasping noise on the blotter of the desk top. "It is lacking a signature. Works of art are notoriously more valuable when they are signed authentically by the artist. It would be deplorable if there were any doubts as to the origin of a work of such richness." She pushed the drawing across the desk toward Rudolph. "I will be much indebted to you, Monsieur," she said, "if you would have the kindness to affix your name. Legibly."

Rudolph took out his pen and signed his name on the lower right hand corner of the drawing. He did it slowly and deliberately and he made sure that Miss Lenaut saw that he was studying the drawing at the same time. He was not going to act like a frightened kid in front of her. Love has its own requirements. Man enough to draw her naked, he was man enough to stand up to her wrath. He underlined his signature with a little flourish.

Miss Lenaut reached over and snatched the drawing to her side of the desk. She was breathing hard now. "Monsieur," she said shrilly, "you will go get one of your parents immediately after school is over today and you will bring it back for a conversation with me speedily." When she was excited, there were little, queer mistakes in Miss Lenaut's English. "I have some important things to reveal to them about the son they have reared in their house. I will be waiting here. If you are not here with a representative of your family by four o'clock the consequences will be of the gravest. Is it understood?"

"Yes, ma'am. Good afternoon, Miss Lenaut." The "good afternoon" took courage. He went out of the room, neither more quickly nor more slowly than he usually did. He remembered his gliding motion. Miss Lenaut sounded as though she had just run up two flights of stairs.

When he reached home after school was over, he avoided going into the store where his mother was serving some customers and went up to the apartment, hoping to find his father. Whatever happened, he didn't want his mother to see that drawing. His father might whack him, but that was to be preferred to the expression that he was sure would be in his mother's eyes for the rest of her life if she saw that picture.

His father was not in the house. Gretchen was at work and Tom never came home until five minutes before supper. Rudolph washed his hands and face and combed his hair. He was going to meet his fate like a gentleman.

He went downstairs and into the shop. His mother was putting a dozen rolls into a bag for an old woman who smelled like a wet dog. He waited until the old woman had left, then went and kissed his mother.

"How were things at school today?" she asked, touching his hair.

"Okay," he said. "The usual. Pa around anywhere?"

"He's probably down at the river. Why?" The "Why?" was suspicious. It was unusual for anyone in the family to seek out her husband unnecessarily.

"No reason," Rudolph said carelessly.

"Isn't there track practice today?" she probed.

"No." Two customers came into the shop, the little bell over the door tingling, and he didn't have to lie any more. He waved and went out as his mother was greeting the customers.

When he was out of sight of the shop he began to walk quickly down toward the river. His father kept his shell in the corner of a ramshackle warehouse on the waterfront and usually spent one or two afternoons a week working on the boat there. Rudolph prayed that this was one of those afternoons.

When he reached the warehouse he saw his father out in front of it, sandpapering the hull of the one-man shell, which was propped, upside down, on two sawhorses. His father had his sleeves rolled up and was working with great care on the smooth wood. As Rudolph approached, he could see the ropy muscles of his father's forearms hardening and relaxing with his rhythmic movements. It was a warm day, and even with the wind that came off the river his father was sweating.

"Hi, Pa," Rudolph said.

His father looked up and grunted, then went back to his work. He had bought the shell in a half-ruined condition for practically nothing from a boys' school nearby that had gone bankrupt. Some river memory of youth and health from his boyhood on the Rhine was behind the purchase and he had reconstructed the shell and varnished it over and over again. It was spotless and the mechanism of the sliding seat gleamed with its coating of oil. After he had gotten out of the hospital in Germany, with one leg almost useless and his big frame gaunt and weak, Jordache had exercised fanatically to recover his strength. His work on the Lake boats had given him the strength of a giant and the grueling miles he imposed on himself sweeping methodically up and down the river had kept him forbiddingly powerful. With his bad leg he couldn't catch anybody, but he gave the impression of being able to crush a grown man in those hairy arms.

"Pa . . ." Rudolph began, trying to conquer his nervousness. His father had never hit him, but Rudolph had seen him knock Thomas unconscious with one blow of his fist just last year.

"What's the matter?" Jordache tested the smoothness of the wood, with broad, spatulate fingers. The back of his hands and his fingers were bristling with black hairs.

"It's about school," Rudolph said.

"You in trouble? *You?*" Jordache looked over at his son with genuine surprise.

"Trouble might be too strong a word," Rudolph said. "A situation has come up."

"What kind of situation?"

"Well," Rudolph said, "there's this French woman who teaches French. I'm in her class. She says she wants to see you this afternoon. Now."

"Me?"

"Well," Rudolph admitted, "she said one of my parents."

"What about your mother?" Jordache asked. "You tell her about this?"

"It's something I think it's better she doesn't know about," Rudolph said.

Jordache looked across the hull of the shell at him speculatively. "French," he said. "I thought that was one of your good subjects."

"It is," Rudolph said. "Pa, there's no sense in talking about it, you've got to see her."

Jordache flicked a spot off the wood. Then he wiped his forehead with the back of his hand and began rolling down his sleeves. He swung his windjacket over his shoulder, like a workingman, and picked up his cloth cap and put it on his head, and started walking. Rudolph followed him, not daring to suggest that perhaps it would be a good idea if his father went home and put on a suit before the conversation with Miss Lenaut.

Miss Lenaut was seated at her desk correcting papers when Rudolph led his father into the room. The school building was empty, but there were shouts from the athletic field below the classroom windows. Miss Lenaut had put lipstick on at least three more times since Rudolph's class. For the first time, he realized that she had thin lips and plumped them out artificially. She looked up when they came into the room and her mouth set. Jordache had put his windjacket on before entering the school and had taken off his cap, but he still looked like a workman.

Miss Lenaut stood up as they approached the desk.

"This is my father, Miss Lenaut," Rudolph said.

"How do you do, sir?" she said, without warmth.

Jordache said nothing. He stood there, in front of the desk, chewing at his moustache, his cap in his hands, proletarian and subdued.

"Has your son told you why I asked you to come this afternoon, Mr. Jordache?"

"No," Jordache said, "I don't remember that he did." That peculiar, uncharacteristic mildness was in his voice, too. Rudolph wondered if his father was afraid of the woman.

"It embarrasses me even to talk about it." Miss Lenaut immediately became shrill again. "In all my years of teaching . . . The indignity . . . From a student who has always seemed ambitious and diligent. He did not say what he had done?"

"No," Jordache said. He stood there patiently, as though he had all day and all night to sort out the matter, whatever it turned out to be.

"*Eh, bien,*" Miss Lenaut said, "the burden devolves upon my shoulders." She bent down and opened the desk drawer and took out the drawing. She did not look at it, but held it down and away from her as she spoke. "In the middle of my classroom, when he was supposed to be writing a composition, do you know what he was doing?"

"No," said Jordache.

"*This!*" She poked the drawing dramatically in front of Jordache's nose. He took the paper from her and held it up to the light from the windows to get a better look at it. Rudolph peered anxiously at his father's face, searching for signs. He half expected his father to turn and hit him on the spot and wondered if he would have the courage to just stand there and take it without flinching or crying out. Jordache's face told him nothing. He seemed quite interested, but a little puzzled.

Finally, he spoke. "I'm afraid I can't read French," he said.

"That is not the point," Miss Lenaut said excitedly.

"There's something written here in French." Jordache pointed with his big index finger to the phrase, "*Je suis folle d'amour*," that Rudolph had printed on the drawing of the blackboard in front of which the naked figure was standing.

"I am crazy with love, I am crazy with love." Miss Lenaut was now striding up and down in short trips behind her desk.

"What's that?" Jordache wrinkled his forehead, as though he was trying his best to understand but was out in waters too deep for him.

"That's what's written there." Miss Lenaut pointed a mad finger at the sheet of paper. "It's a translation of what your talented son has written there. 'I am crazy with love, I am crazy with love.'" She was shrieking now.

"Oh, I see," Jordache said, as though a great light had dawned on him. "Is that dirty in French?"

Miss Lenaut gained control of herself with a visible effort, although she was biting her lipstick again. "Mr. Jordache," she said, "have you ever been to school?"

"In another country," Jordache said.

"In whatever country you went to school, Mr. Jordache, would it be considered proper for a young boy to draw a picture of his teacher nude, in the classroom?"

"Oh!" Jordache sounded surprised. "Is this you?"

"Yes, it is," Miss Lenaut said. She glared bitterly at Rudolph.

Jordache studied the drawing more closely. "By God," he said, "I see the resemblance. Do teachers pose nude in high school these days?"

"I will not have you mock of me, Mr. Jordache," Miss Lenaut said with cold dignity. "I see there is no further point to this conversation. If you will be so good as to return the drawing to me . . ." She stretched out her hand. "I will say good day to you and take the matter up elsewhere, where the gravity of the situation will be appreciated. The office of the principal. I had wanted to spare your son the embarrassment of putting his obscenity on the principal's desk, but I see no other course is open to me. Now, if I may have the drawing please, I won't detain you further . . ."

Jordache took a step back, holding onto the drawing. "You say my son did this drawing?"

"I most certainly do," Miss Lenaut said. "His signature is on it."

Jordache glanced at the drawing to confirm this. "You're right," he said. "It's Rudy's signature. It's his drawing, all right. You don't need a lawyer to prove that."

"You may expect a communication from the principal," Miss Lenaut said. "Now, please return the drawing. I'm busy and I've wasted enough time on this disgusting affair."

"I think I'll keep it. You yourself said it's Rudy's," Jordache said placidly. "And it shows a lot of talent. A very good likeness." He shook his head in admiration. "I never guessed Rudy had it in him. I think I'll have it framed and hang it up back home. You'd have to pay a lot of money to get a nude picture as good as this one on the open market."

Miss Lenaut was biting her lips so hard she couldn't get a word out for the moment. Rudolph stared at his father, dumbfounded. He hadn't had any clear idea of how his father was going to react, but this falsely innocent, sly, country-bumpkin performance was beyond any concept that Rudolph might ever have had of how his father would behave.

Miss Lenaut gave tongue. She spoke in a harsh whisper, leaning malevolently over her desk and spitting out the words at Jordache. "Get out of here, you low, dirty, common foreigner, and take your filthy son with you."

"I wouldn't talk like that, Miss," Jordache said, his voice still calm. "This is a taxpayer's school and I'm a taxpayer and I'll get out when I'm good and ready. And if you didn't strut around with your tail wiggling in a tight skirt and half your titties showing like a two dollar whore on a street corner, maybe young boys wouldn't be tempted to draw pictures of you stark-assed naked. And if you ask me, if a man took you out of all your brassieres and girdles, it'd turn out that Rudy was downright complimentary in his art work."

Miss Lenaut's face was congested and her mouth writhed in hatred. "I know about you," she said. "*Sale Boche.*"

Jordache reached across the desk and slapped her. The slap resounded like a small firecracker. The voices from the playing field had died down and the room was sickeningly silent. Miss Lenaut remained bent over, leaning on her hands on the desk, for another moment. Then she burst into tears and crumpled onto her chair, holding her hands to her face.

"I don't go for talk like that, you French cunt," Jordache said. "I didn't come all the way here from Europe to listen to talk like that. And if I was French these days, what with running like rabbits the first shot the dirty Boche fired at them, I'd think twice about insulting anybody. If it'll make you feel any better, I'll tell you I killed a Frenchman in 1916 with a bare bayonet and it won't surprise you that I stuck it in his back while he was trying to run home to his Mama."

As his father talked, calmly, as though he were discussing the weather or an order for flour, Rudolph began to shiver. The malice in the words was made intolerable by the conversational, almost friendly, tone in which they were delivered.

Jordache was going on, inexorably. "And if you think you're going to take it out on my boy here, you better think twice about that, too, because I don't live far from here and I don't mind walking. He's been an A student in French for two years and I'll be here to ask some questions if he comes back at the end of the term with anything less. Come on, Rudy."

They went out of the room, leaving Miss Lenaut sobbing at her desk.

They walked away from the school without speaking. When they came to a trash basket on a corner, Jordache stopped. He tore the drawing into small pieces, almost absently, and let the pieces float down into the basket. He looked over at Rudolph. "You are a silly bastard, aren't you?" he said.

Rudolph nodded.

They resumed walking in the direction of home.

"You ever been laid?" Jordache said.

"No."

"That the truth?"

"I'd tell you."

"I suppose you would," Jordache said. He walked silently for awhile, with his rolling limp. "What're you waiting for?"

"I'm in no hurry," Rudolph said defensively. Neither his father nor his mother had ever mentioned anything about sex to him and this afternoon was certainly the wrong day to start. He was haunted by the sight of Miss Lenaut, dissolved and ugly, weeping on her desk, and he was ashamed that he had ever thought a silly, shrill woman like that worthy of his passion.

"When you start," Jordache said, "don't get hung up on one. Take 'em by the dozen. Don't ever get to feel that there's only one woman for you and that you got to have her. You can ruin your life."

"Okay," Rudolph said, knowing that his father was wrong, dead wrong.

Another silence as they turned a corner.

"You sorry I hit her?" Jordache said.

"Yes."

"You've lived all your life in this country," Jordache said. "You don't know what real hating is."

"Did you really kill a Frenchman with a bayonet?" He had to know.

"Yeah," Jordache said. "One of ten million. What difference does it make?"

They were nearly home. Rudolph felt depressed and miserable. He should have thanked his father for sticking up for him that way, it was something that very few parents would have done, and he realized that, but he couldn't get the words out.

"It wasn't the only man I killed," Jordache said, as they stopped in front of the bakery. "I killed a man when there was no war on. In Hamburg, Germany, with a knife. In 1921. I just thought you ought to know. It's about time you learned something about your father. See you at supper. I got to go put the shell under cover." He limped off, down the shabby street, his cloth cap squarely on top of his head.

When the final marks were posted for the term, Rudolph had an A in French.

Chapter 4

I

The gymnasium of the elementary school near the Jordache house was kept open until ten o'clock five nights a week. Tom Jordache went there two or three times a week, sometimes to play basketball, sometimes merely to shoot the breeze with the boys and young men who gathered there or to play in the mild game of craps that occasionally was held in the boys' toilet, out of sight of the gym teacher refereeing the permanent game on the basketball court.

Tom was the only boy his age allowed in the crap game. He had gained entrance with his fists. He had found a place between two of the players in the ring and had kneeled on the floor one night and thrown a dollar into the pot and said, "You're faded," to Sonny Jackson, a boy of nineteen waiting to be drafted, and the guiding spirit of the group that congregated around the school. Sonny was a strong, stocky boy, pugnacious and quick to take offense. Tom had chosen Sonny purposely for his debut. Sonny had looked at Tom, annoyed, and pushed Tom's dollar bill back along the floor toward him. "Go way, punk," he said. "This game is for men."

Without hesitation, Tom had leaned across the open space and backhanded Sonny, without moving from his knees. In the fight that followed, Tom made his reputation. He had cut Sonny's eyes and lips and had finished by dragging Sonny into the showers and turning the cold water on him and keeping him there for five minutes before he turned the water off. Since then, whenever Tom joined the group in the gymnasium, they made room for him.

Tonight, there was no game in progress. A gangling twenty-year-old by the name of Pyle, who had enlisted early in the war, was displaying a samurai sword he said he had captured himself at Guadalcanal. He had been discharged from the Army after having malaria three times and nearly died. He was still alarmingly yellow.

Tom listened skeptically as Pyle described how he had thrown a hand grenade into a cave just for luck. Pyle said he heard a yell inside and had crawled in with his lieutenant's pistol in his hand to find a dead Jap captain, with the sword at his side. It sounded to Tom more like Errol Flynn in Hollywood than anybody from Port Philip in the South Pacific. But he didn't say anything, because he was in a peaceful mood and you couldn't beat up on a guy who looked that sick and yellow, anyway.

"Two weeks later," Pyle said, "I cut off a Jap's head with this sword."

Tom felt a tug at his sleeve. It was Claude, dressed in a suit and tie, as usual, and bubbling a little at the lips. "Listen," Claude whispered, "I got something to tell you. Let's get out of here."

"Wait a minute," Tom said. "I want to hear this."

"The island was secured," Pyle was saying, "but there were still Japs hiding out, coming out at night, and shooting up the area and knocking off guys. The C.O. got pissed off and he sent out patrols three times a day. He told us to clean every last one of the bastards out of the area.

"Well, I'm on one of those patrols and we see one of 'em trying to wade across a creek so we let him have it. He was hit but not bad and he's sitting up, holding his hands over his head, saying something in Jap. There wasn't no officers on the patrol, just a corporal and six other guys, and I says, 'Hey, listen, you guys, just hold him here and I'll go back to get my samurai sword and we'll have a regular execution.' The corporal was a little chicken about it, the orders were to bring in prisoners, but like I said, there were no officers present and after all, that's what the bastards did all the time to our guys, cut off their heads, and we took a vote and they tied the fucker up and I went back and got my samurai sword. We made him kneel down in the regular way and he did it just like he was used to it. It was my sword so I got to do the job. I picked it up way over my head and clunk! there was his head rolling on the ground like a coconut, with his eyes wide open. The blood spurted out, it must have been close to ten feet. I tell you," Pyle said, touching the edge of the weapon lovingly, "these swords are something."

"Horseshit," Claude said loudly.

"What's that?" Pyle asked, blinking. "What'd you say?"

"I said horseshit," Claude repeated. "You never cut off no Jap's head. I bet you bought that sword in a souvenir shop in Honolulu. My brother Al knows you and he told me you haven't got the guts to kill a rabbit."

"Listen, kid," Pyle said, "sick as I am, I'll give you the beating of your life, if you don't shut up and get out of here. Nobody says horseshit to me."

"I'm waiting," Claude said. He took off his glasses and put them in the breast pocket of his suit. He looked pathetically defenseless.

Tom sighed. He stepped in front of Claude. "Anybody wants to pick on my friend," he said, "he has to go through me first."

"I don't mind," Pyle began, handing the sword to one of the other boys. "You're young, but you're fresh."

"Knock it off, Pyle," said the boy who now was holding the sword. "He'll murder you."

Pyle looked uncertainly at the circling faces. There was something sobering that he saw there. "I didn't come back from fighting in the Pacific," he said loudly, "to get into arguments with little kids in my home town. Give me my sword, I'm due back at the house."

He beat a retreat. The others drifted off without a word, leaving Tom and Claude in possession of the boys' toilet.

"What'd you want to do that for?" Tom asked, irritated. "He didn't mean no harm. And you know they wouldn't let him take me on."

"I just wanted to see the expression on their faces," Claude said, sweating and grinning. "That's all. Power. Raw power."

"You're going to get me killed one day with your raw power," Tom said. "Now what the hell did you have to tell me?"

"I saw your sister," Claude said.

"Hooray for you, you saw my sister. I see her every day. Sometimes twice a day."

"I saw her in front of Bernstein's Department Store. I was riding around on the bike and I went around the block again to make sure and she was getting into a big convertible Buick and a guy was holding the door open for her. She was waiting for him in front of Bernstein's, that's for sure."

"So, big deal," Tom said. "She got a ride in a Buick."

"You want to know who was driving the Buick?" Behind his glasses, Claude's eyes were joyous with information. "You'll drop dead."

"I won't drop dead. Who?"

"Mr. Theodore Boylan, Esquire," Claude said. "That's who. How do you like that for moving up in class?"

"What time you see them?"

"An hour ago. I've been looking for you all over."

"He probably drove her to the hospital. She works in the hospital on week nights."

"She isn't in any hospital tonight, Buddy," Claude said. "I followed them part of the way on the bike. They took the road up the hill. Toward his place. You want to find your sister tonight, I advise you to look in on the Boylan estate."

Tom hesitated. It would have been different if Gretchen was with one of the fellows around her own age, off in a car to the lover's lane down near the river for a little simple necking. Tease her a little later on. *Hideous boy.* Get a little of his own back. But with an old man like Boylan, a big shot in the town . . . He would rather not have to get mixed up in it. You never knew where something like that could lead you.

"I'll tell you something," Claude said, "if it was my sister, I'd look into it. That Boylan has quite a reputation around town. You don't know some of the things I hear around the house when my father and uncle are talking and they don't know I'm listening. Your sister may be asking for a big load of trouble . . ."

"You got the bike outside?"

"Yeah. But we need some gas." The motorcycle belonged to Claude's brother Al, who had just been drafted two weeks before. Al had promised to break every bone in Claude's body if he came back and found that Claude had used the machine, but whenever his parents went out at night, Claude pushed it out of the garage, after siphoning off a little gas from the family's second car, and raced around town for an hour or so, avoiding the police, because he was too young to have a license.

"Okay," Tom said. "Let's see what's happening up the hill."

Claude had a length of rubber tubing slung on the motorcycle and they went behind the school, where it was dark, and opened the gas tank of a Chevy that was parked there and Claude put the tube in and sucked hard, then, as the gasoline came up, filled the tank of the motorcycle.

Tom got on behind and with Claude driving they spurted through back streets toward the outskirts of town and began to climb the long winding road that went up the hill to the Boylan estate.

When they got to the main gate, made of huge wrought-iron wings standing open and set into a stone wall that seemed to run for miles on each side, they parked the motorcycle behind some bushes. The rest of the way they'd have to go on foot, so as not to be heard. There was a gatekeeper's cottage, but since the war nobody had lived in it. The boys knew the estate well. For years, they had been jumping over the wall and hunting for birds and rabbits with BB guns. The estate had been neglected for years and it was more like a jungle than the meadowed park it had been originally.

They walked through the woods toward the main house. When they got near it, they saw the Buick parked in front. There were no lights on outside, but there was a gleam from a big French window downstairs.

They moved cautiously toward the flower bed in front of the window. The window came down almost to the ground. One side of it was ajar. The curtains had been drawn carelessly and with Claude kneeling in the loam and Tom standing astride him, they both could look inside at the same time.

As far as they could see, the room was empty. It was big and square, with a grand piano, a long couch, and big easy chairs and tables with magazines on them. A fire was going in the fireplace. There were a lot of books on the shelves along the walls. A few lamps did for the lighting. The double doors facing the window were open and Tom could see a hallway and the lower steps of a staircase.

"That's the way to live," Claude whispered. "If I had a joint like this, I'd have every broad in town."

"Shut up," Tom said. "Well, there's nothing doing here. Let's move."

"Come on, Tom," Claude protested. "Take it easy. We just got here."

"This isn't my idea of a big night," Tom said. "Just standing out in the cold looking at a room with nobody in it."

"Give it a chance to develop, for Christ's sake," Claude said. "They're probably upstairs. They can't stay there all night."

Tom knew that he didn't want to see anybody come into that room. Anybody. He wanted to get away from that house. And stay away. But he didn't want to look as though he was chickening out. "All right," he said, "I'll give it a couple of minutes." He turned away from the window, leaving Claude on his knees peering in. "Call me if anything happens," he said.

The night was very still. The mist rising from the wet ground was getting heavier and there were no stars. In the distance, below them, there was the faint glow of the lights of Port Philip. The Boylan grounds swept away from the house in all directions, a myriad of great old trees, the outline of the fence of a tennis court, some low buildings about fifty yards away that had once been used as stables. One man living in all that. Tom thought of the bed he shared with his brother. Well, Boylan was sharing a bed tonight, too. Tom spat.

"Hey!" Claude beckoned to him excitedly. "Come here, come here."

Slowly, Tom went back to the window.

"He just came in, down the stairs," Claude whispered. "Look at that. Just look at that, will you."

Tom looked in. Boylan had his back to the window, on the far side of the room. He was at a table with bottles, glasses and a silver ice container on it. He was pouring whiskey into two glasses. He was naked.

"What a way to walk around a house," Claude said.

"Shut up," Tom said. He watched as Boylan carelessly dropped some ice into the glasses and splashed soda from a siphon into the glasses. Boylan didn't pick up the glasses right away. He went over to the fireplace and threw another log on the fire, then went to a table near the window and opened a lacquered box and took out a cigarette. He lit it with a foot-long silver cigarette lighter. He was smiling a little.

Standing there, so close to the window, he was clearly outlined in the light of a lamp. Mussed, bright blond hair, skinny neck, pigeony chest, flabby arms, knobby knees, and slightly bowed legs. His dick hung down from the bush of hair, long, thick, reddened. A dumb rage, a sense of being violated, of being a witness to an unspeakable obscenity, seized Tom. If he had had a gun he would have killed the man. That puny stick, that strutting, smiling, satisfied weakling, that feeble, pale, hairy slug of a body so confidently displayed, that long, fat, rosy instrument. It was worse, infinitely worse, than if he and Claude had seen his sister come in naked.

Boylan walked across the thick carpet, the smoke from his cigarette trailing over his shoulder, out into the hall. He called up the stairs. "Gretchen, do you want your drink up there or do you want to come down for it?" He listened. Tom couldn't hear the answer. Boylan nodded and came back into the room and picked up the two glasses. Then, carrying the whiskey, he went out of the room and up the stairs.

"Jesus, what a sight," Claude said. "He's built like a chicken. I guess if you're rich you can be built like the Hunchback of Notre Dame and the broads still come running."

"Let's get out of here," Tom said thickly.

"What the hell for?" Claude looked up at him in surprise, the light that came through the parted curtains reflecting damply on his eyeglasses. "The action is just beginning."

Tom reached down and grabbed Claude by the hair and jerked him savagely to his feet.

"Hey, for Christ's sake, watch what you're doing," Claude said.

"I said let's get out of here." Tom held Claude roughly by his necktie. "And you keep quiet about what you saw tonight."

"I didn't see anything," Claude whined. "What the hell did I see! A skinny crock with a dick on him like an old rubber hose. What's there to keep quiet about?"

"Just keep quiet, that's all," Tom said, his face close to Claude's. "If I ever hear a word from anyone, you'll get a beating you'll never forget. Got it?"

"Jesus, Tom," Claude said reproachfully, rubbing his sore scalp, "I'm your friend."

"Got it?" Tom said fiercely.

"Sure, sure. Anything you say. I don't know what there's to get so excited about."

Tom let him go and wheeled and strode across the lawn away from the house. Claude followed him, grumbling. "Guys tell me you're crazy," he said, as he caught up to Tom, "and I always tell them they're nuts, but now I'm beginning to see what they mean, I swear to God I do. Boy, are you temperamental."

Tom didn't answer. He was almost running as they neared the gate house. Claude wheeled out the bike and Tom swung on behind him. They drove into town without talking to each other.

II

Replete and drowsy, Gretchen lay in the wide soft bed, her hands behind her head, staring up at the ceiling. The ceiling reflected the fire that Boylan had lit before he had undressed her. The arrangements for seduction were planned meticulously and smoothly practiced up here on the hill. The house was hushed and luxurious, the servants were never in evidence, the telephone never rang, there was never any fumbling or hurrying. Nothing clumsy or unforeseen was allowed to intrude on their evening ritual.

Downstairs, a clock chimed softly. Ten o'clock. It was the hour the common room in the hospital emptied and the wounded men made their way, on crutches and in wheelchairs, back to the wards. These days Gretchen only went to the hospital two or three times a week. Her life was centered, with a single urgency, on the bed in which she lay. The days were passed in expectation of it, the nights away from it in its memory. She would make restitution to the wounded some other time.

Even when she had opened the envelope and seen the eight one-hundred-dollar bills, she had known she would return to this bed. If it was one of Boylan's peculiarities that he had to humiliate her, she accepted it. She would make the man pay for it later.

Neither Boylan nor she had ever spoken of the envelope on her desk. On Tuesday, as she was coming out of the office after work, the Buick was there, with Boylan at the wheel. He had opened the car door without a word and she had gotten in and he had driven to his house. They had made love and after that gone to The Farmer's Inn for dinner and after that had driven home and made love again. When he took her into town, toward midnight, he had dropped her off two blocks from her home and she had walked the rest of the way.

Teddy did everything perfectly. He was discreet—secrecy was to his taste; it was a necessity for her. Nobody knew anything about them. Knowledgeable, he had taken her to a doctor in New York to be fitted for a diaphragm, so that she didn't have to worry about *that*. He had bought her the red dress, as promised, on the same trip to New York. The red dress hung in Teddy's wardrobe. There would come a time when she would wear it.

Teddy did everything perfectly, but she had little affection for him and certainly didn't love him. His body was flimsy and unprepossessing; only when he was dressed in his elegant clothes could he be considered in any way attractive. He was a man without enthusiasms, self-indulgent and cynical, a confessed failure, friendless and shunted off by a mighty family to a crumbling shipwreck of a Victorian castle in which most of the rooms were permanently closed off. An empty man in a half-empty house. It was easy to understand why the beautiful woman whose photograph still stood on the piano downstairs had divorced him and run away with another man.

He was not a lovable or admirable man, but he had other uses. Having renounced the ordinary activities of the men of his class, work, war, games, friendship, he dedicated himself to one thing: he copulated with all his hoarded force and cunning. He demanded nothing of her except to be there, the material of his craft. His triumph was in his own performance. The battles he had declined elsewhere, he won in the face below his on the pillow. The fanfares of victory were her sighs of pleasure. For her part, Gretchen was not concerned with Boylan's profits and losses. She lay passively under him, not even putting her arms around the unimportant body, accepting, accepting. He was anonymous, nobody, the male principle, an abstract, unconnected priapus, for which she had been waiting, unknowing, all her life. He was a servant to her pleasures, holding a door open to a palace of marvels.

She was not even grateful.

The eight hundred dollars lay folded into the leaves of her copy of the works of Shakespeare, between Acts II and III of *As You Like It*.

A clock chimed somewhere and his voice floated into the room from downstairs. "Gretchen, do you want your drink up there or do you want to come down for it?"

"Up here," she called. Her voice was lower, huskier. She was conscious of new, subtler tonalities in it; if her mother's ear for such things had not been deafened by her own disaster, she would have known with one sentence that her daughter was sunnily sailing that dangerous sea in which she herself had foundered and drowned.

Boylan came into the room, naked in the firelight, bearing the two glasses. Gretchen propped herself up and took the glass from his hand. He sat on the edge of the bed, flicking ashes from his cigarette into the ash tray on the bed table.

They drank. She was developing a liking for Scotch. He leaned over and kissed her breast. "I want to see how it tastes with whiskey on it," he said. He kissed the other breast. She took another sip from her glass.

"I don't have you," he said. "I don't have you. There's only one time when I can make myself believe I have you—when I'm in you and you're coming. All the rest of the time, even when you're lying right beside me naked and I have my hand on you, you've escaped. Do I have you?"

"No," she said.

"Christ," he said. "Nineteen years old. What are you going to be like at thirty?"

She smiled. He would be forgotten by that year. Perhaps before. Much before.

"What were you thinking about up here while I was down getting the drinks?" he asked.

"Fornication," she said.

"Do you have you to talk like that?" His own language was strangely prissy, some hangover fear of a domineering nanny quick with the kitchen soap to wash out the mouths of little boys who used naughty words.

"I never talked like that until I met you." She took a satisfying gulp of whiskey.

"I don't talk like that," he said.

"You're a hypocrite," she said. "What I can do, I can name."

"You don't do so damn much," he said, stung.

"I'm a poor little, inexperienced, small-town girl," she said. "If the nice man in the Buick hadn't come along that day and got me drunk and taken advantage, I probably would have lived and died a withered, dried-up old maid."

"I bet," he said. "You'd have been down there with those two niggers."

She smiled ambiguously. "We'll never know, now, will we?"

He looked at her thoughtfully. "You could stand some education," he said. Then he stubbed out his cigarette, as though he had come to a decision. "Excuse me." He stood up. "I have to make a telephone call." He put on a robe this time and went downstairs.

Gretchen sat, propped against the pillows, slowly finishing her drink. She had paid him off. For the moment earlier in the evening when she had delivered herself so absolutely to him. She would pay him off every time.

He came back into the room. "Get dressed," he said. She was surprised. Usually they stayed until midnight. But she said nothing. She got out of bed and put on her clothes. "Are we going somewhere?" she asked. "How should I look?"

"Look anyway you want," he said. Dressed, he was important and privileged again, a man to whom other men deferred. She felt diminished in her clothes. He criticized the things she wore, not harshly, but knowingly, sure of himself. If she weren't afraid of her mother's questions, she would have taken the eight hundred dollars out from between Acts II and III of *As You Like It* and bought herself a new wardrobe.

They went through the silent house and into the car and drove off. She asked no more questions. They drove through Port Philip and sped on down south. They didn't speak. She wouldn't give him the satisfaction of asking where they were going. There was a scorecard in her head in which she kept track of the points they gained against each other.

They went all the way to New York. Even if they turned back promptly, she wouldn't get home much before dawn. There probably would be hysterics from her mother. But she didn't remonstrate. She refused to show him that she allowed herself to be worried by things like that.

They stopped in front of a darkened four-story house on a street lined with similar houses on both sides of it. Gretchen had only come down to New York a few times in her life, twice with Boylan in the last three weeks, and she had no idea of what neighborhood they were in. Boylan came over to her side of the car, as usual, and opened the door for her. They went down three steps into a little cement courtyard behind an iron fence and Boylan rang a doorbell. There was a long wait. She had the feeling that they were being inspected. The door opened. A big woman in a white evening gown stood there, her dyed red hair piled heavily on her head. "Good evening, honey," she said. Her voice was hoarse. She closed the door behind them. The lights in the entrance hall were low and the house was hushed, as though it was heavily carpeted throughout and its walls hung with muffling cloth. There was a sense of people moving about it softly and carefully.

"Good evening, Nellie," Boylan said.

"I haven't seen you in a dog's age," the woman said, as she led them up a flight of steps and into a small pinkly lit living room on the first floor.

"I've been busy," Boylan said.

"So I see," the woman said, looking at Gretchen, appraising, then admiring. "How old are you, darling?"

"A hundred and eight," Boylan said.

He and the woman laughed. Gretchen stood soberly in the small, draped room hung with oil paintings of nudes. She was determined to show nothing, respond to nothing. She was frightened, but tried not to feel it or show it. In numbness there was safety. She noticed that all the lamps in the room were tasseled. The woman's white dress had fringes at the bosom and at the hem of the skirt. Was there a connection there? Gretchen made herself speculate on these matters to keep from turning and fleeing from the hushed house with its malevolent sense of a hidden population moving stealthily between rooms on the floors above her head. She had no notion of what would be expected of her, what she might see, what would be done with her. Boylan looked debonair, at ease.

"Everything is just about ready, I think, honey," the woman said. "Just a few more minutes. Would you like something to drink, while waiting?"

"Pet?" Boylan turned toward Gretchen.

"Whatever you say." She spoke with difficulty.

"I think a glass of champagne might be in order," Boylan said.

"I'll send a bottle up to you," the woman said. "It's cold. I have it on ice. Just follow me." She led the way out into the hall and Gretchen and Boylan climbed the carpeted stairs behind her up to a dim hallway on the second floor. The stiff rustling of the woman's dress sounded alarmingly loud as she walked. Boylan was carrying his coat. Gretchen hadn't taken off her coat.

The woman opened a door off the hallway and switched on a small lamp. They went into the room. There was a large bed with a silk canopy over it, an oversized maroon velvet easy chair, and three small gilt chairs. A large bouquet of tulips made a brilliant splash of yellow on a table in the center of the room. The curtains were drawn and the sound of a car passing on the street below was muffled. A wide mirror covered one wall. It was like a room in a slightly old-fashioned, once-luxurious hotel, now just a little bit déclassé.

"The maid will bring you your wine in a minute," the woman said. She rustled out, closing the door softly but firmly behind her.

"Good old Nellie," Boylan said, throwing his coat down on an up-holstered bench near the door. "Always dependable. She's famous." He didn't say what she was famous for. "Don't you want to take your coat off, pet?"

"Am I supposed to?"

Boylan shrugged. "You're not supposed to do anything."

Gretchen kept her coat on, although it was warm in the room. She went over and sat on the edge of the bed and waited. Boylan lit a cigarette and sat comfortably in the easy chair, crossing his legs. He looked over at her, smiling slightly, amused. "This is a brothel," he said matter-of-factly. "In case you haven't guessed. Have you ever been in one before, pet?"

She knew he was teasing her. She didn't answer. She didn't trust herself to speak.

"No, I suppose not," he said. "Every lady should visit one. At least once. See what the competition is doing."

There was a low knock on the door. Boylan went over to it and opened it. A frail middle-aged maid in a white apron over a short, black dress came in carrying a silver tray. On the tray there was a bucket of ice with a champagne bottle sticking out of it. There were two champagne glasses on the tray. The maid set the tray down on the table next to the tulips without speaking. There was no expression on her face. Her function was to appear not to be present. She began to pry open the cork. She was wearing felt slippers, Gretchen noticed.

She struggled with the cork, her face becoming flushed with the effort, and a strand of graying hair fell over her eyes. It made her look like the aging, slow-moving women with varicose veins, to be seen at early Mass, before the working day begins.

"Here," Boylan said, "I'll do that." He took the bottle from her hands.

"I'm sorry, sir," the maid said. She had betrayed her function. She was there, made noticeable by her failure.

Boylan couldn't get the bottle open, either. He pulled, he pushed at the cork with his thumbs, holding the bottle between his legs. He, too, began to get red in the face, as the maid watched him apolo-getically. Boylan's hands were slender and soft, useful only for gentler work.

Gretchen stood up and took the bottle. "I'll do it," she said.

"Do you open many bottles of champagne at the brick works?" Boylan asked.

Gretchen paid no attention to him. She grasped the cork firmly.

Her hands were quick and strong. She twisted the cork. It popped and flew out of her hands and hit the ceiling. The champagne bubbled out and soaked her hands. She handed the bottle to Boylan. One more mark on the scorecard. He laughed. "The working classes have their uses," he said. He poured the champagne as the maid gave Gretchen a towel to dry her hands. The maid left in her felt slippers. Soft, mouselike traffic in the hallways.

Boylan gave Gretchen the glass of champagne. "The shipments are now steady from France, although they tell me the Germans made important inroads," he said. "Last year, I understand, was a mediocre one for the vintage." He was plainly angered by his fiasco with the bottle and Gretchen's success.

They sipped the champagne. There was a diagonal red line on the label. Boylan made an approving face. "One can always be assured of the best in Nellie's place," he said. "She would be hurt if she knew that I called her establishment a brothel. I think she thinks of it as a kind of salon where she can exercise her limitless sense of hospitality for the benefit of her many gentlemen friends. Don't think all whore houses are like this, pet. You'll only be in for a disappointment." He was still smarting from the tussle over the bottle and he was getting his own back. "Nellie's is one of the last hangovers from a more gracious era, before the Century of the Common Man and Common Sex engulfed us all. If you develop a taste for bordellos ask me for the proper addresses, pet. You might find yourself in terribly sordid places otherwise, and we wouldn't want that, would we? Do you like the champagne?"

"It's all right," Gretchen said. She seated herself once more on the bed, holding herself together rigidly.

Without warning, the mirror lit up. Somebody had turned on a switch in the next room. The mirror was revealed as a one-way window through which Boylan and Gretchen could see what was going on next door to them. The light in the next room came from a lamp hanging from the ceiling, its brightness subdued by a thick silk shade.

Boylan glanced at the mirror. "Ah," he said, "the orchestra is tuning up." He took the bottle of champagne from the bucket and came over and sat down on the bed beside Gretchen. He set the bottle on the floor next to him.

Through the mirror, they could see a tall young woman with long blonde hair. Her face was pretty enough, with the pouting, greedy, starlet expression of a spoiled child. But when she threw off the pink, frilly negligee she was wearing, she revealed a magnificent body with long, superb legs. She never even glanced toward the mirror, although the routine must have been familiar to her, and she knew she was being watched. She threw back the covers on the bed and let herself fall back on it, all her movements harmonious and unaffected. She lay there, waiting, content to let hours go past, days, lazily allowing herself to be admired. Everything passed in utter silence. No sound came through the mirror.

"Some more champagne, pet?" Boylan asked. He lifted the bottle.

"No, thank you." Gretchen found it difficult to speak.

The door opened and a young Negro came into the other room.

Oh, the bastard, Gretchen thought, oh the sick, revengeful bastard. But she didn't move.

The young Negro said something to the girl on the bed. She waved a little in greeting and smiled a baby-beauty-contest-winner's smile. Everything happened on the other side of the mirror in pantomime and gave an air of remoteness, of unreality, to the two figures in the other room. It was falsely reassuring, as though nothing serious could happen there.

The Negro was dressed in a navy-blue suit and white shirt and a dotted red bow-tie. He had on sharply pointed light-brown shoes. He had a nice, young, smiling "Yes, suh" kind of face.

"Nellie has a lot of connections in night clubs up in Harlem," Boylan said as the Negro began to undress, hanging his jacket neatly on the back of a chair. "He's probably a trumpet player or something in one of the bands, not unwilling to make an extra buck of an evening, entertaining the white folk. A buck for a buck." He chuckled briefly at his own *mot*. "You sure you don't want some more to drink?"

Gretchen didn't answer. The Negro started to unbutton his pants. She closed her eyes.

When she opened her eyes the man was naked. His body was the color of bronze, with gleaming skin, wide, sloping muscular shoulders, a tapering waist, like an athlete at the height of training. The comparison with the man beside her made her rage.

The Negro moved across the room. The girl opened her arms to receive him. Lightly as a cat, he dropped down onto the long white body. They kissed, and her hands clutched at his back. Then he rolled over and she began to kiss him, first on the throat, then his nipples, slowly and expertly, while her hand caressed his mounting penis. The blonde hair tangled over the coffee-colored gleaming skin, went down lower as the girl licked the tight skin over the flat muscles of the man's belly and he tautened convulsively.

Gretchen watched, fascinated. She found it beautiful and fitting, a promise to herself that she could not formulate in words. But she could not watch it with Boylan at her side. It was too unjust, filthily unjust, that these two magnificent bodies could be bought by the hour, like animals in a stable, for the pleasure or perversity or vengeance of a man like Boylan.

She stood up, her back to the mirror. "I'll wait for you in the car," she said.

"It's just beginning, pet," Boylan said mildly. "Look what she's doing now. After all, this is really for your instruction. You'll be very popular with the . . ."

"I'll see you in the car," she said, and ran out of the room and down the stairs.

The woman in the white dress was standing near the hall doorway. She said nothing, although she smiled sardonically as she opened the door for Gretchen.

Gretchen went and sat in the car. Boylan came out fifteen minutes later, walking unhurriedly. He got into the car and started the motor. "It's a pity you didn't stay," he said. "They earned their hundred dollars."

They drove all the way back without a word. It was nearly light when he stopped the car in front of the bakery. "Well," he said after the hours of silence, "did you learn anything tonight?"

"Yes," she said. "I must find a younger man. Good night."

She heard the car turn around as she unlocked the door. As she climbed the stairs, she saw the light streaming from the open door of her parents' bedroom, across from hers. Her mother was sitting upright on a wooden chair, staring out at the hallway. Gretchen stopped and looked at her mother. Her mother's eyes were those of a madwoman. It could not be helped. Mother and daughter stared at each other.

"Go to bed," the mother said. "I'll call the Works at nine o'clock to say you're sick, you won't be in today."

She went into her room and closed the door. She didn't lock it because there were no locks on any of the doors in the house. She took down her copy of Shakespeare. The eight one-hundred-dollar bills were no longer between Acts II and III of *As You Like It*. Still neatly folded in the envelope, they were in the middle of Act V of *Macbeth*.

Chapter 5

There were no lights on in the Boylan house. Everybody was downtown celebrating. Thomas and Claude could see the rockets and roman candles that arched into the night sky over the river and could hear the booming of the little cannon that was used at the high-school football games when the home team scored a touchdown. It was a clear, warm night and from the vantage point on the hill, Port Philip shimmered brightly, with every light in town turned on.

The Germans had surrendered that morning.

Thomas and Claude had wandered around town with the crowds, watching girls kissing soldiers and sailors in the streets and people bringing out bottles of whiskey. Throughout the day Thomas grew more and more disgusted. Men who had dodged the draft for four years, clerks in uniform who had never been more than a hundred miles away from home, merchants who had made fortunes off the black market, all kissing and yelling and getting drunk as though they, personally, had killed Hitler.

"Slobs," he had said to Claude, as he watched the celebrants. "I'd like to show 'em."

"Yeah," Claude said. "We ought to have a little celebration of our own. Our own private fireworks." He had been thoughtful after that, not saying anything, as he watched his elders cavorting. He took off his glasses and chewed on an earpiece, a habit of his when he was preparing a coup. Thomas recognized the signs, but braced himself against anything rash. This was no time for picking on soldiers and any kind of fight, even with a civilian, would be a wrong move today.

Finally, Claude had come up with his VE Day plan and Thomas conceded that it was worthy of the occasion.

So there they were on the Boylan hill, with Thomas carrying the can of gasoline and Claude the bag of nails and the hammer and the bundle of rags, making their way cautiously through the underbrush toward a dilapidated greenhouse standing on a bare knoll about five hundred yards from the main house. They had not come the usual way, but had approached the estate on a small dirt road that was on the inland side, away from Port Philip, and led to the rear of the house. They had broken in through a gardener's gate and left the bike hidden near an abandoned gravel pit outside the estate walls.

They reached the greenhouse on the knoll. Its glass panes were dusty and broken and a musty odor of rotten vegetation came from it. There were some long, dry planks along one side of the sagging structure, and a rusty shovel that they had noticed on other occasions when they had prowled the grounds. When Thomas began to dig, Claude selected two big planks and began to hammer them into a cross. They had perfected their plans during the day and there was no need for words.

When the cross was finished, Claude soaked the boards with gasoline. Then they both lifted it and jammed it into the hole that Thomas had dug. He put dirt around the base of the cross, and stamped it down hard with his feet and the back of the shovel, to keep everything firm. Claude soaked the rags he had been carrying with the rest of the gasoline. Everything was ready. The boom of the cannon floated up the hill from the high-school lawn and rockets glared briefly far off in the night sky.

Thomas was calm and deliberate in his movements. As far as he was concerned it wasn't anything very important that they were doing. Once more, in his own way, he was thumbing his nose at all those grown-up phoneys down there. With the extra pleasure of doing it on that naked prick Boylan's property. Give them all something to think about, between kisses and the "Star-Spangled Banner." But Claude was all worked up. He was gasping, as though he couldn't get any air in his lungs, and he was bubbling, almost drooling at the mouth, and he had to keep wiping his glasses off with his handkerchief because they kept clouding up. It was an act of huge significance for Claude, with an uncle who was a priest, and a father who made him go to Mass every Sunday and who lectured him daily on Mortal Sin, keeping away from loose Protestant women, and remaining pure in the eyes of Jesus.

"Okay," Thomas said softly, stepping back.

Claude's hands trembled as he struck a match and bent over and touched it to the gasoline-soaked rags at the base of the cross. Then he screamed and began to run, as the rags flared up. His arm was on fire and he ran blindly across the clearing, screaming. Thomas ran after him, yelling to him to stop, but Claude just kept running, crazily. Thomas caught up with him and tackled him, then rolled on Claude's arm, using his chest, which was protected by his sweater, to smother the flames.

It was over in a moment. Claude lay on his back, moaning, holding his burnt arm, and whimpering, unable to say anything.

Thomas stood up and looked down at his friend. Every drop of sweat on Claude's face could be clearly made out, in the light of the flaming cross. They had to get out of there fast. People were bound to arrive at any minute. "Get up," Thomas said. But Claude didn't move. He rolled a little from side to side, with his eyes staring, but that was all.

"Get up, you stupid son of a bitch." Thomas shook Claude's shoulder. Claude looked up at him, his face rigid with fear, dumb. Thomas bent over and picked Claude up and threw him over his shoulder and began to run down off the crown of the hill in the direction of the gardener's gate, crashing through underbrush, trying not to listen to Claude saying, "Oh, Jesus, oh, Jesus, oh, sweet Mother Mary."

There was a smell Thomas recognized, as he stumbled down the hill under the weight of his friend. It was the smell of broiling meat.

The cannon was still booming down in the town.

II

Axel Jordache rowed slowly out toward the center of the river, feeling the pull of the current. He wasn't rowing for exercise tonight. He was out on the river to get away from the human race. He had decided to take the night off, the first weekday night he had not worked since 1924. Let his customers eat factory bread tomorrow. After all, the German army only lost once every twenty-seven years.

It was cool on the river, but he was warm enough, in his heavy blue turtle-neck sweater, from his deckhand days on the Lakes. And he had a bottle with him to take the nip out of the air and to drink to the health of the idiots who had once more led Germany to ruin. Jordache was a patriot of no country, but he reserved his hatred for the land in which he was born. It had given him a life-long limp, had cut short his education, had exiled him, and had armed him with an utter contempt for all policies and all politicians, all generals, priests, ministers, presidents, kings, dictators, all conquests and all defeats, all candidates and all parties. He was pleased that Germany had lost the war, but he was not happy that America had won it. He hoped he'd be around twenty-seven years from now, when Germany would lose another war.

He thought of his father, a little, God-fearing, tyrannical man, a clerk in a factory office, who had gone marching off, singing, with a posy of flowers in his rifle barrel, a happy, militant sheep, to be killed at Tannenburg, proud to leave two sons who soon would be fighting for the *Vaterland*, too, and a wife who had remained a widow less than a year. Then at least she had had the wisdom to marry a lawyer who spent the war managing tenements behind the Alexander Platz in Berlin.

"*Deutschland, Deutschland, über alles*," Jordache sang mockingly, resting on his oars, letting the waters of the Hudson carry him south, as he lifted the bottle of bourbon to his lips. He toasted the youthful loathing with which he had regarded Germany when he had been demobilized, a cripple among cripples, and which had driven him across the ocean. America was a joke, too, but at least he was alive tonight as were his sons, and the house in which he lived was still standing.

The noise of the little cannon carried across the water and the reflections from the rockets twinkled in the river. Fools, Jordache thought, what're they celebrating about? They never had it so good in their whole lives. They'd all be selling apples on street corners in five years, they'd be tearing each other to pieces on the lines outside factories waiting for jobs. If they had the brains they were born with they'd all be in the churches tonight praying that the Japanese would hold out for ten years.

Then he saw the fire flare up suddenly on the hill outside the town, a small, clear spurt of flame which quickly defined itself as a cross, burning on the rim of the horizon. He laughed. *Business as usual and screw victory. Down with the Catholics, the Niggers, and the Jews, and don't forget it. Dance tonight and burn tomorrow. America is America. We're here and we're telling you what the score really is.*

Jordache took another drink, enjoying the spectacle of the flaming cross dominating the town, savoring in advance the mealy-mouthed lamentations that would appear tomorrow in the town's two newspapers on the subject of the affront to the memory of the brave men of all races and creeds who had died defending the ideals on which America was founded. And the sermons on Sunday! It would almost be worthwhile to go to a church or two to listen to what the holy bastards would say.

If I ever find out who put up that cross, Jordache thought, I'm going to shake their hands.

As he watched, he saw the fire spread. There must have been a building right near the cross, down wind from it. It must have been good and dry, because in no time at all the whole sky was lit up.

In a little while, he heard the bells of the fire engines racing through the streets of the town and up the hill.

Not a bad night, Jordache thought, all things considered.

He took a last drink and then started to row leisurely toward the river bank.

III

Rudolph stood on the steps of the high school and waited for the boys at the cannon to shoot it off. There were hundreds of boys and girls milling around on the lawn, shouting, singing, kissing. Except for the kissing, it was very much like the Saturday nights after the team had won a big football game.

The cannon went off. A huge cheer went up.

Then Rudolph put his trumpet to his lips and began to play, "America." First the crowd fell silent and the slow music rang out all alone, note by solemn note over their heads. Then they began to sing and in a moment all the voices joined in: "*America, America, God shed His grace on thee, And crown thy good with brotherhood, From sea to shining sea . . .*"

There was a big cheer after the song was over and he began to play the "Stars and Stripes Forever." He couldn't stand still while playing the "Stars and Stripes Forever," so he began to march around the lawn. People fell in behind him and soon he was leading a parade of boys and girls, first around the lawn and then into the street, marching to the rhythm of his horn. The boys serving the cannon trundled it along at the head of the procession just behind him and at every intersection they stopped and fired it and the boys and girls cheered and grownups along the route applauded and waved flags at them.

Striding at the head of his army, Rudolph played "When the Caissons Go Rolling Along," and "Columbia the Gem of the Ocean," and the high-school hymn, and "Onward Christian Soldiers," as the parade wound its jubilant way through the streets of the town. He led them down toward Vanderhoff Street and stopped in front of the bakery and played, "When Irish Eyes Are Smiling," for his mother's sake. His mother opened the window upstairs and waved to him and he could see her dabbing at her eyes with a hand-kerchief. He ordered the boys at the cannon to give a salute to his mother and they fired the piece and the hundreds of boys and girls roared and his mother wept openly. He wished his mother had combed her hair before opening the window and it was too bad she never took the cigarette out of her mouth. There was no light from the cellar tonight, so he knew his father wasn't there. He wouldn't have known what to play for him. It would have been hard to choose the proper selection for a veteran of the German army on this partic-ular night.

He would have liked to go out to the hospital and serenade his sister and her soldiers, but the hospital was too far away. With a last flourish for his mother, he led the parade toward the center of town, playing "Boola-Boola." Perhaps he would go to Yale when he finished school next year. Nothing was impossible tonight.

He didn't really decide to do it, but he found himself on the street on which Miss Lenaut lived. He had stood outside the house often enough, hidden in the shadow of a tree across the street, looking up at the lighted window on the second floor which he knew was hers. The light was on now.

He stopped boldly in the middle of the street in front of the house, looking up at the window. The narrow street with its modest two-family dwellings and tiny lawns was packed with his followers. He felt sorry for Miss Lenaut, alone, so far from home, thinking of her friends and relatives joyously flooding the streets of Paris at this moment. He wanted to make amends to the poor woman, show that he forgave her, demonstrate that there were depths to him she had never guessed, that he was more than a dirty little boy with a foul-mouthed German father, who specialized in pornographic drawings. He put the trumpet to his lips and began to play the "Marseillaise." The complicated, triumphant music, with its memories of flags and battles, of desperation and heroism, rang in the shabby little street, and the boys and girls chanted along with it, without words, because they didn't know the words. By God, Rudolph thought, no high-school teacher in Port Philip ever had anything like this happen to her before. He played it through straight once, but Miss Lenaut didn't appear at the window. A girl with a blonde pigtail down her back came out of the house next door and stood near Rudolph, watching him play. Rudolph started all over again, but this time as a tricky solo, playing with the rhythm, improvising, now soft and slow, now brassy and loud. Finally, the window opened. Miss Lenaut stood there, in a dressing gown. She looked down. He couldn't see the expression on her face. He took a step so that the light of a street-lamp illuminated him clearly and pointed his trumpet directly up at Miss Lenaut and played loud and clear. She had to recognize him. For another moment she listened, without moving. Then she slammed the window down and pulled the blind.

French cunt, he thought, and finished the *"Marseillaise"* with a mocking sour note. He took the trumpet from his lips. The girl who had come out of the house next door was standing next to him. She put her arm around his neck and kissed him. The boys and girls around him cheered and the cannon went off. He grinned. The kiss was delicious. He knew the girl's address, too, now. He put the trumpet to his lips and began playing "Tiger Rag," as he marched, swinging, down the street. The boys and girls danced behind him in a gigantic swirling mass as they headed toward Main Street.

Victory was everywhere.

IV

She lit another cigarette. Alone in an empty house, she thought. She had closed all the windows, to mute the sounds from the town, the cheering and the noise of the fireworks and the blares of music. What did she have to celebrate? It was a night on which husbands turned to wives, children to parents, friends to friends, when even strangers embraced on street corners. Nobody had turned to her, she had been taken in no embrace.

She went into her daughter's room and turned on the light. The room was spotlessly clean, with the bedspread freshly ironed, a polished brass reading lamp, a brightly painted dressing table with jars and instruments of beauty. The tricks of the trade, Mary Jordache thought bitterly.

She went over to the small mahogany bookcase. The books were all neatly in place, carefully arranged. She took out the thick book of the works of Shakespeare. She opened it to where the envelope parted the pages of *Macbeth*. She peered into the envelope. The money was still there. Her daughter didn't even have the grace to try to hide it somewhere else, even knowing now that her mother knew. She took the envelope out of the Shakespeare and stuffed the book carelessly on the shelf. She took out another book at random, an anthology of English poetry Gretchen had used in her last year of high school. The fine food of her fine daughter's mind. She opened the book and put the envelope between the pages. Let her daughter worry about her money. If her father ever discovered there was eight hundred dollars in the house, she wouldn't find it just by going through her bookshelves.

She read a few lines.

> Break, break, break,
> On thy cold gray stones, O Sea!
> And I would that my tongue could utter
> The thoughts that arise in me.

Oh, fine, fine . . .

She put the book back in its place on the shelf. She didn't bother to turn out the light when she went out of the room.

She went into the kitchen. The pots and dishes that she had used for the dinner she had eaten alone that night lay unwashed in the sink. She doused her cigarette in a frying pan, half-filled with greasy water. She had had a pork chop for her dinner. Coarse food. She looked at the stove, turned on the gas in the oven. She dragged a chair over to the oven and opened the oven door and sat down and put her head in. The smell was unpleasant. She sat like that for a little while. Sounds of cheering in the town filtered in through the closed kitchen window. She had read somewhere that there were more suicides on holidays than at any other time, Christmas, New Year's. What better holiday would she ever find?

The smell of the gas grew stronger. She began to feel giddy. She took her head out of the oven and turned the gas off. There was no rush.

She went into the living room, mistress of the house. There was a faint smell of gas in the small room, with the four wooden chairs arranged geometrically around the square oak table in the center of the worn, reddish carpet. She sat down at the table, took a pencil out of her pocket and looked around for some paper, but there was only the student's exercise book in which she kept her daily accounts in the bakery. She never wrote letters and never received any. She tore several sheets of paper out of the back of the book and began to write on the ruled paper.

"Dear Gretchen," she wrote. "I have decided to kill myself. It is a mortal sin and I know it, but I can't go on any more. I am writing from one sinner to another. There is no need for me to say more. You know what I mean.

"There is a curse on this family. On me, on you, on your father and your brother Tom. Only your brother Rudolph may have escaped it and perhaps in the end he too will feel it. I am happy that I will not live to see that day. It is the curse of sex. I will tell you now something I have hidden from you all your life. I was an illegitimate child. I never knew my father or my mother. I cannot bear to think what sort of life my mother must have led and the degradation she must have wallowed in. That you should be following in her footsteps and have gone to the gutter should not surprise me. Your father is an animal. You sleep in the room next to ours, so you must know what I mean. He has crucified me on his lust for twenty years. He is a raging beast and there have been times when I was sure he was going to kill me. I have seen him nearly beat a man to death with his fists over an eight-dollar bakery bill. Your brother Thomas inherits from his father and it would not surprise me if he winds up in jail or worse. I am living in a cage of tigers.

"I am guilty, I suppose. I have been weak and I have permitted your father to drive me from the Church and to make heathens of my children. I was too worn out and beaten down to love you and protect you from your father and his influence. And you always seemed so neat and clean and well-behaved that my fears were put to sleep. With the results that you know better than I do."

She stopped writing and read what she had written with satisfaction. Finding her mother dead and this address from the grave on her pillow would poison the whore's guilty pleasures. Each time she allowed a man to put a hand on her, Gretchen would remember her mother's last words to her.

"Your blood is tainted," she wrote, "and it is now plain to me that your character is tainted too. Your room is clean and dainty but your soul is a stable. Your father should have married someone like you. You would have been fitting partners for each other. My last wish is for you to leave the house and go far away so that your influence cannot corrupt your brother Rudolph. If only one decent human being comes out of this terrible family, perhaps it will make a balance in God's eyes."

There was a confused sound of music and cheering growing stronger outside. Then she heard the trumpet, and recognized it. Rudolph was playing beneath the window. She got up from the table and opened the window and looked out. There he was, at the head of what looked like a thousand boys and girls, playing "When Irish Eyes Are Smiling," up to her.

She waved down at him, feeling the tears start. Rudolph ordered the boys with the cannon to fire a salute for her and the boom echoed along the street. She was crying frankly now and had to take

out her handkerchief. With a last wave, Rudolph led his army down
the street, his trumpet playing them on.

She went in and sat down at the table, sobbing. He has saved my
life, she thought, my beautiful son has saved my life.

She tore up the letter and went into the kitchen and burned the
scripts in the soup pot.

v

A good many of the soldiers were drunk. Everybody who could walk
and get into a uniform had fled the hospital without waiting for
passes as soon as the news had come over the radio, but some of
them had come back with bottles and the common room smelled
like a saloon as men in wheel chairs and on crutches reeled around
the room, shouting and singing. The celebration had degenerated
into destruction after supper and men were breaking windows with
canes, tearing posters down from the walls, ripping books and magazines into handfuls of confetti, with which they conducted Mardi-
gras battles amid drunken whoops of laughter.

"I am General George S. Patton," shouted a boy to no one in particular. He had a steel contraption around his shoulders that kept his
shattered arm sticking out above his head. "Where's your necktie,
soldier? Thirty years KP." Then he seized Gretchen with his good
arm and insisted on dancing with her in the middle of the room to
the tune of "Praise the Lord and Pass the Ammunition," which the
other soldiers obligingly sang for him. Gretchen had to hold the boy
tight to keep him from falling. "I'm the greatest, highest-class, one-
armed, 105-millimeter ballroom dancer in the world and I'm going to
Hollywood tomorrow to waltz with Ginger Rogers. Marry me, baby,
we'll live like kings on my total disability pension. We won the war,
baby. We made the world safe for total disability." Then he had to
sit down, because his knees wouldn't support him anymore. He sat
on the floor and put his head between his knees and sang a verse of
"Lili Marlene."

There was nothing Gretchen could do for any of them tonight.
She kept a fixed smile on her face, trying to intervene when the confetti battles became too rough and looked as though they would become real fights. A nurse came to the door of the room and
beckoned to Gretchen. Gretchen went over to her. "I think you'd
better get out of here," the nurse said in a low, worried voice. "It's
going to be wild in a little while."

"I don't really blame them," Gretchen said. "Do you?"

"I don't blame them," the nurse said, "but I'm staying out of their way."

There was a crash of glass from the room. A soldier had thrown an empty whiskey bottle through a window. "Fire for effect," the soldier said. He picked up a metal waste basket and hurled it through another window. "Put the mortars on the bastards, Lieutenant. Take the high ground."

"It's a lucky thing they took their guns away from them before they came here," said the nurse. "This is worse than Normandy."

"Bring on the Japs," someone shouted. "I'll beat 'em to death with my first-aid kit. Banzai!"

The nurse tugged at Gretchen's sleeve. "Go on home," she said. "This is no place for a girl tonight. Come early tomorrow and help pick up the pieces."

Gretchen nodded and started toward the locker room to change, as the nurse disappeared. Then she stopped and turned back and went down the corridor from which the wards angled off. She went into the ward where the bad head and chest wounds were cared for. It was dimly lit here, and quiet. Most of the beds were empty, but here and there she could see a figure lying still under blankets. She went to the last bed in the corner, where Talbot Hughes lay, with the glucose dripping into his arm from the bottle rigged on its stand next to the bed. He was lying there with his eyes open, enormous and feverishly clear in the emaciated head. He recognized her and smiled. The shouting and singing from the distant common room sounded like the confused roar from a football stadium. She smiled down at him and sat on the edge of his bed. Although she had seen him only the night before, he seemed to have grown ominously thinner in the last twenty-four hours. The bandages around his throat were the only solid thing about him. The doctor in the ward had told her Talbot was going to die within the week. There really was no reason for him to die, the wound was healing, the doctor said, although he would never be able to speak again, of course. But by this time, by any normal calculation, he should have been taking nourishment and even walking around a little. Instead, he was fading quietly away day by day, politely and irresistibly insisting upon dying, making no fuss, a trouble to no one.

"Would you like me to read to you tonight?" Gretchen asked.

He shook his head on the pillow. Then he put out his hand toward hers. He grasped her hand. She could feel all the fragile birdlike bones. He smiled again and closed his eyes. She sat there, motionless, holding his hand. She sat like that for more than fifteen minutes, not saying anything. Then she saw that he was sleeping. She disengaged her hand gently, stood up, and walked softly out of the room. Tomorrow she would ask the doctor to tell her when he thought Talbot Hughes, victorious, was about to go. She would come and hold his hand, representative of his country's sorrow, so that he would not be alone when he died, twenty years old, everything unspoken.

She changed into her street clothes quickly and hurried out of the building.

As she went out the front door, she saw Arnold Simms leaning against the wall next to the door, smoking. This was the first time she had seen him since the night in the common room. She hesitated for a moment, then started toward the bus stop.

"Evenin', Miss Jordache." The remembered voice, polite, countrified.

Gretchen made herself stop. "Good evening, Arnold," she said. His face was bland, memoryless.

"The boys finally got themselves something to yell about, didn't they?" Arnold gestured with a little movement of his head toward the wing which contained the common room.

"They certainly did," she said. She wanted to get away, but didn't want to appear as if she were afraid of him.

"These little old Yoonited States went and did it," Arnold said. " 'Twas a mighty fine effort, wouldn't you say?"

Now he was making fun of her. "We all should be very happy," she said. He had the trick of making her pompous.

"I'm very happy," he said. "Yes, indeed. Mighty happy. I got good news today, too. Special good news. That's why I waited on you out here. I wanted to tell you."

"What is it, Arnold?"

"I'm being discharged tomorrow," he said.

"That *is* good news," she said. "Congratulations."

"Yup," he said. "Officially, according to the Yoonited States Medical Corps, I can walk. Transportation orders to installation nearest point of induction and immediate processing of discharge from the service. This time next week I'll be back in St. Louis. Arnold Simms, the immediate civilian."

"I hope you'll be . . ." She stopped. She had nearly said happy, but that would have been foolish. "Lucky," she said. Even worse.

"Oh, I'm a lucky fella," he said. "No one has to worry about l'il ole Arnold. Got some more good news this week. It was a big week for me, a giant of a week. I got a letter from Cornwall."

"Oh, isn't that nice." Prissy. "That girl you told me about wrote you." Palm trees. Adam and Eve in the Garden.

"Yep." He flicked away his cigarette. "She just found out her husband got killed in Italy and she thought I'd like to know."

There was nothing to say to this, so she kept quiet.

"Well, I won't be seeing you any more, Miss Jordache," he said, "unless you happen to be passin' through St. Louis. You can find me in the telephone book. I'll be in an exclusive residential district. I won't keep you no longer. I'm sure you got a victory ball or a country club dance to go to. I just wanted to thank you for everything you done for the troops, Miss Jordache."

"Good luck, Arnold," she said coldly.

"Too bad you didn't find the time to come on down to the Landing that Saturday," he said, drawling it out flatly. "We got ourselves two fine chickens and roasted them and had ourselves quite a picnic. We missed you."

"I'd hoped you weren't going to talk about that, Arnold," she said. Hypocrite, hypocrite.

"Oh, God," he said, "you so beautiful I just want to sit down and cry."

He turned and opened the door to the hospital and limped in.

She walked slowly toward the bus stop, feeling battered. Victory solved nothing.

She stood under the light, looking at her watch, wondering if the bus drivers were also celebrating tonight. There was a car parked down the street in the shadow of a tree. The motor started up and it drove slowly toward her. It was Boylan's Buick. For a moment she thought of running back into the hospital.

Boylan stopped the car in front of her and opened the door. "Can I give you a lift, ma'am?"

"Thank you very much, no." She hadn't seen him for more than a month, not since the night they had driven to New York.

"I thought we might get together to offer fitting thanks to God for blessing our arms with victory," he said.

"I'll wait for the bus, thank you," she said.

"You got my letters, didn't you?" he asked.

"Yes." There had been two letters, on her desk at the office, asking her to meet him in front of Bernstein's Department Store. She hadn't met him and she hadn't answered the letters.

"Your reply must have been lost in the mail," he said. "The service these days is very hit and miss, isn't it?"

She walked away from the car. He got out and came up to her and held her arm.

"Come up to the house with me," he said harshly. "This minute."

His touch unnerved her. She hated him but she knew she wanted to be in his bed. "Let go of me," she said, and pulled her arm savagely out of his grasp. She walked back to the bus stop, with him following her.

"All right," he said. "I'll say what I came to say. I want to marry you."

She laughed. She didn't know why she laughed. Surprise.

"I said I want to marry you," he repeated.

"I'll tell you what," she said, "you go on down to Jamaica, as you planned, and I'll write you there. Leave your address with my secretary. Excuse me, here's my bus."

The bus rolled to a stop and she jumped up through the door as soon as it opened. She gave the driver her ticket and went and sat in the back by herself. She was trembling. If the bus hadn't come along, she would have said yes, she would marry him.

When the bus neared Port Philip she heard the fire engines and looked up the hill. There was a fire on the hill. She hoped it was the main building, burning to the ground.

VI

Claude hung on to him with his good arm, as Tom drove the bike down the narrow back road behind the Boylan estate. He hadn't had much practice and he had to go slowly and Claude moaned in his ear every time they skidded or hit a bump. Tom didn't know how bad the arm was, but he knew something had to be done about it. But if he took Claude to the hospital, they'd ask how he happened to get burned and it wouldn't take Sherlock Holmes to figure out the connection between the boy with the burned arm and the cross flaming on the Boylan hill. And Claude sure as hell wouldn't take the blame alone. Claude was no hero. He'd never die under torture with his secret forever clamped between his lips, that was for sure.

"Listen," Tom said, slowing the bike down so that they were hardly moving, "you got a family doctor?"

"Yeah," Claude said. "My uncle."

That was the kind of a family to have. Priests, doctors, there probably was a lawyer uncle, too, who would come in handy later on, after they were arrested.

"What's the address?" Tom asked.

Claude mumbled the address. He was so frightened he found it almost impossible to speak. Tom speeded up and keeping on back roads, found his way to the big house on the outskirts of the town, with a sign on the lawn that said, "Dr. Robert Tinker, M.D."

Tom stopped the bike and helped Claude off. "Listen," he said, "you're going in there alone, you understand, and no matter what you tell your uncle, you don't mention my name. And you better get your father to send you out of town tonight. There's going to be an awful mess in this town tomorrow and if anybody sees you walking around with a burned hand it'll take them just about ten seconds to come down on you like a load of bricks."

For answer, Claude moaned, and hung onto Tom's shoulder. Tom pushed him away. "Stand on your own two feet, man," Tom said. "Now get in there and make sure you see your uncle and nobody else. And if I ever find out that you gave me away I'll kill you."

"Tom," Claude whimpered.

"You heard me," Tom said. "I'll kill you. And you know I mean it." He pushed him toward the door of the house.

Claude staggered toward the door. He reached up his good hand and rang the bell. Tom didn't wait to see him go in. He hurried off down the street. Above the town the fire was still blazing, lighting up the sky.

He went down to the river near the warehouse in which his father kept his shell. It was dark along the bank and there was the acid odor of rusting metal. He took off his sweater. It had the sick smell of burnt wool, like vomit. He found a stone and tied it into the sweater and heaved the bundle out into the river. There was a dull splash and he could see the little fountain of white water against the black of the current, as the sweater sank. He hated to lose the sweater. It was his lucky sweater. He had won a lot of fights while wearing it. But there were times when you had to get rid of things and this was one of them.

He walked away from the river toward home, feeling the chill of the night through his shirt. He wondered if he really was going to have to kill Claude Tinker.

Chapter 6

I

With his German food, Mary Jordache thought, as Jordache came in from the kitchen, carrying the roast goose on a platter with red cabbage and dumplings. Immigrant.

She didn't remember when she had seen her husband in such a high mood. The surrender of the Third Reich that week had made him jovial and expansive. He had devoured the newspapers, chuckling over the photographs of the German generals signing the papers at Rheims. Now, on Sunday, it was Rudolph's seventeenth birthday, and Jordache had decreed a holiday. No other birthday in the family was celebrated by more than a grunt. He had bought Rudolph a fancy fishing rod, God knew how much it cost, and had told Gretchen that she could keep half her salary from now on instead of the usual quarter. He had even given Thomas the money for a new sweater to replace the one he said he lost. If the German army could be brought to surrender every week, life might be tolerable in the home of Axel Jordache.

"From now on," Jordache had said, "we eat Sunday dinner together." The bloody defeat of his race, it seemed, had given him a sentimental interest in the ties of blood.

So they were all seated at the table, Rudolph self-consciously the focus of the occasion, wearing a collar and tie, and sitting very erect, like a cadet at table at West Point; Gretchen in a lacy, white shirtwaist looking as though butter wouldn't melt in her mouth, the whore; and Thomas, with his gambler's dodgy smile, all neatly washed and combed. Thomas had changed unaccountably since VE day, too, coming right home from school, studying all evening in his room, and even helping out in the shop for the first time in his life. The mother permitted herself the first glimmerings of timid hope. Perhaps by some unknown magic, the falling silent of the guns in Europe would make them a normal family.

Mary Jordache's idea of a normal American family was largely formed by the lectures of the nuns in the orphanage and later on by glances at the advertisements in popular magazines. Normal American families were always well-washed and fragrant and smiled at each other constantly. They showered each other with gifts for Christmas, birthdays, weddings, anniversaries, and Mother's Day. They had hale old parents who lived on farms in the country and at least one automobile. The sons called the father sir and the daughters played the piano and told their mothers about their dates and everybody used Listerine. They had breakfast, dinner, and Sunday lunch together and attended the church of their choice, and took holidays at the seashore en masse. The father commuted to business every day in a dark suit and had a great deal of life insurance. None of this was completely formulated in her mind, but it was the misty standard of reference against which she compared her own circumstances. Both too shy and too snobbish to mix with her own neighbors, the reality of the life of the other families who lived in the town was unknown to her. The rich were out of her reach and the poor were beneath her contempt. By her reckoning, hazy and unsystematic as it was, she, her husband, Thomas, and Gretchen, were not a family in any way that she could accept or that might give her pleasure. Rather they were an abrasive group collected almost at random for a voyage which none of them had chosen and during which the best that could be hoped for was that hostilities could be kept to a minimum.

Rudolph, of course, was excepted.

II

Axel Jordache put the goose down on the table with satisfaction. He had spent all morning preparing the meal, keeping his wife out of the kitchen, but without the usual insults about her cooking. He carved the bird roughly, but competently, and set out huge portions for all, serving the mother first, to her surprise. He had bought two bottles of California Riesling and he filled all their glasses ceremoniously. He raised his glass in a toast. "To my son Rudolph, on his birthday," he said huskily. "May he justify our hopes and rise to the top and not forget us when he gets there."

They all drank seriously, although the mother saw Thomas make a little grimace. Perhaps he thought the wine was sour.

Jordache did not specify just which top he expected his son to rise to. Specifications were unnecessary. The top existed, a place with boundaries, densities, privileges. When you got there you recognized it and your arrival was greeted with hosannahs and Cadillacs by earlier arrivals.

III

Rudolph ate the goose delicately. It was a little fatty to his taste and he knew that fat caused pimples. And he ate sparingly of the cabbage. He had a date later in the afternoon with the girl with the blonde pigtail who had kissed him outside Miss Lenaut's house and he didn't want to be smelling of cabbage when he met her. He only sipped at his wine. He had decided that he was never going to get drunk in his whole life. He was always going to be in full control of his mind and his body. He had also decided, because of the example of his mother and father, that he was never going to get married.

He had gone back to the house next to Miss Lenaut's the following day and loitered obviously across the street from it. Sure enough, after about ten minutes the girl had come out wearing blue jeans and a sweater and waved to him. She was just about his age, with bright-blue eyes and the open and friendly smile of someone who has never had anything bad happen to her. They had walked down the street together and in half an hour Rudolph felt that he had known her for years. She'd just moved into the neighborhood from Connecticut. Her name was Julie and her father had something to do with the Power Company. She had an older brother who was in the Army in France and that was the reason she'd kissed him that night, to celebrate her brother's being alive in France with the war over for him. Whatever the reason, Rudolph was glad that she had kissed him, although the memory of that first brush of the lips between strangers made him diffident and awkward for awhile.

Julie was crazy about music and liked to sing and thought he played a marvelous trumpet and he had half promised her that he would get his band to take her along with them to sing with them on their next club date.

She liked serious boys, Julie said, and there was no doubt about it, Rudolph was serious. He had already told Gretchen about Julie. He liked to keep saying her name. "Julie, Julie . . ." Gretchen had merely smiled, being a little bit too patronizingly grown-up for his taste. She had given him a blue-flannel blazer for his birthday.

He knew his mother would be disappointed that he wasn't going to take her for a walk this afternoon, but the way his father was be-

having all of a sudden, the miracle might happen and his father
might actually take her for a walk himself.

He wished he was as confident about getting to the top as his father and mother were. He was intelligent, but intelligent enough to
know that intelligence by itself carried no guarantees along with it.
For the kind of success his mother and father expected of him you
had to have something special—luck, birth, a gift. He did not know
yet if he was lucky. He certainly could not count upon his birth to
launch him on a career and he was doubtful of his gifts. He was a
connoisseur of others' gifts and an explorer of his own. Ralph
Stevens, a boy in his class, could hardly make a *B* average overall, but
he was a genius in mathematics and was doing problems in calculus
and physics for fun while his classmates were laboring with elementary algebra. Ralph Stevens had a gift which directed his life like a
magnet. He knew where he was going because it was the only way he
could go.

Rudolph had many small talents and no definite direction. He
wasn't bad on the horn, but he didn't fool himself that he was any
Benny Goodman or Louis Armstrong. Of the four other boys who
played in the band with him, two were better than he and the other
two were just about as good. He listened to the music he made with
a cool appreciation of what it was worth and he knew it wasn't
worth much. And wouldn't be worth much more, no matter how
hard he worked on it. As an athlete, he was top man in one event,
the two-twenty hurdles, but in a big city high school, he doubted if
he could even make the team, as compared with Stan O'Brien, who
played fullback for the football team, and had to depend upon the
tolerance of his teachers to get marks just good enough to keep him
eligible to play. But on a football field O'Brien was one of the
smartest players anybody had ever seen in the state. He could feint
and find split-second holes and make the right move every time, with
that special sense of a great athlete that no mere intelligence could
ever compete with. Stan O'Brien had offers of scholarships from colleges as far away as California and if he didn't get hurt would probably make All-American and be set for life. In class, Rudolph did better on the English Literature tests than little Sandy Hopewood, who
edited the school paper and who flunked all his science courses
regularly, but all you had to do was read one article of his and you
knew that nothing was going to stop Sandy from being a writer.

Rudolph had the gift of being liked. He knew that and knew that
was why he had been elected president of his class three times in a
row. But he felt it wasn't a real gift. He had to *plan* to be liked, to

be agreeable to people, and seem interested in them, and cheerfully take on thankless jobs like running school dances and heading the advertising board of the magazine and working hard at them to get people to appreciate him. His gift of being liked wasn't a true gift, he thought, because he had no close friends and he didn't really like people himself very much. Even his habit of kissing his mother morning and evening and taking her for walks on Sundays was planned for her gratitude, to maintain the notion he knew she had of him as a thoughtful and loving son. The Sunday walks bored him and he really couldn't stand her pawing him when he kissed her, though, of course, he never showed it.

He felt that he was built in two layers, one that only he knew about and the other which was displayed to the world. He wanted to be what he seemed but he was doubtful that he could ever manage it. Although he knew that his mother and his sister and even some of his teachers thought he was handsome, he was uncertain about his looks. He felt he was too dark, that his nose was too long, his jaws too flat and hard, his pale eyes too light and too small for his olive skin, and his hair too lower-class dull black. He studied the photographs in the newspapers and the magazines to see how boys at good schools like Exeter and St. Paul's dressed and what college men at places like Harvard and Princeton were wearing, and tried to copy their styles in his own clothes and on his own budget.

He had scuffed white-buckskin shoes with rubber soles and now he had a blazer but he had the uneasy feeling that if he were ever invited to a party with a group of preppies he would stand out immediately for what he was, a small-town hick, pretending to be something he wasn't.

He was shy with girls and had never been in love, unless you could call that stupid thing for Miss Lenaut love. He made himself seem uninterested in girls, too busy with more important matters to bother with kid stuff like dating and flirting and necking. But in reality he avoided the company of girls because he was afraid that if he ever got really close to one, she would find out that behind his lofty manner he was inexperienced and clownish.

In a way he envied his brother. Thomas wasn't living up to anyone's estimate of him. His gift was ferocity. He was feared and even hated and certainly no one truly liked him, but he didn't agonize over which tie to wear or what to say in an English class. He was all of one piece and when he did something he didn't have to make a painful and hesitant selection of attitudes within himself before he did it.

As for his sister, she was beautiful, a lot more beautiful than most of the movie stars he saw on the screen, and that gift was enough for anybody.

"This goose is great, Pop," Rudolph said, because he knew his father expected him to comment on the meal. "It really is something." He had already eaten more than he wanted, but he held out his plate for a second portion. He tried not to wince when he saw the size of the piece that his father put on the plate.

IV

Gretchen ate quietly. When am I going to tell them, what's the best moment? On Friday she had been given two weeks notice at the Works. Mr. Hutchens had called her into his office and after a little distracted preliminary speech about how efficient she was and conscientious and how her work was always excellent and how agreeable it was to have her in the office, he had come out with it. He had received orders that morning to give her notice, along with another girl in the office. He had gone to the manager to remonstrate, Mr. Hutchens said, his dry voice clicking with real distress, but the manager had said he was sorry, there was nothing he could do about it. With the end of the war in Europe there were going to be cutbacks on government contracts. A falling-off in business was expected and they had to economize on staff. Gretchen and the other girl were the last two clerks to be hired in Mr. Hutchens' department and so they had to be the first to go. Mr. Hutchens had been so disturbed that he had taken out his handkerchief several times while talking to her and blown his nose aridly, to prove to her that it was none of his doing. Three decades of working with paper had left Mr. Hutchens rather papery himself, like a paid bill that has been tucked away for many years and is brittle and yellowed and flaking at the edges, when it is brought out to be examined. The emotion in his voice as he spoke to her was incongruous, like tears from a filing cabinet.

Gretchen had to console Mr. Hutchens. She had no intention of spending the rest of her life working for the Boylan Brick and Tile Works, she told him, and she understood why the last to be hired had to be the first to go. She did not tell Mr. Hutchens the real reason why she was being fired and she felt guilty about the other girl, who was being sacrificed as camouflage to Teddy Boylan's act of vengeance.

She had not yet figured out what she was going to do and she hoped to be able to wait until her plans were set before telling her father about her dismissal. There was bound to be an ugly scene and she wanted to have her defenses ready. Today, though, her father was behaving like a human being for once, and perhaps at the end of the meal, ripened by wine and basking in his pleasure in the one child, he might prove to be lenient with another. With the dessert, she decided.

V

Jordache had baked a birthday cake and he came in from the kitchen carrying it, eighteen candles alight on the icing, seventeen and one to grow on, and they all actually were singing "Happy birthday to you, dear Rudolph," when the doorbell rang. The sound stopped the song in mid-verse. The doorbell almost never rang in the Jordache house. No one ever came to visit them and the mailman dropped the letters through a slot.

"Who the hell is that?" Jordache asked. He reacted pugnaciously to all surprises, as though anything new could only be an attack of one kind or another.

"I'll go," Gretchen said. She had the instantaneous certainty that it must be Boylan downstairs at the door, with the Buick parked in front of the shop. It was just the sort of demented thing he was liable to do. She was running down the stairs as Rudolph blew out the candles. She was glad that she was all dressed up and had done her hair that morning for Rudolph's party. Let Teddy Boylan mourn over what he was never going to get anymore.

When she opened the door, there were two men standing there. She knew them both, Mr. Tinker and his brother, the priest. She knew Mr. Tinker from the Works and everybody knew Father Tinker, a burly, red-faced man, who looked like a longshoreman who had made a mistake in his profession.

"Good afternoon, Miss Jordache," Mr. Tinker said, taking off his hat. His voice was sober, and his long, flabby face looked as though he had just discovered a terrible error in the books.

"Hello, Mr. Tinker. Father," Gretchen said.

"I hope we're not interrupting anything," Mr. Tinker said, his voice more ceremoniously churchly than that of his ordained brother. "But we have to speak to your father. Is he in?"

"Yes," Gretchen said. "If you'll come up . . . We're just at dinner, but . . ."

"I wonder if you'd be good enough to ask him to come down, child," said the priest. He had the round, assured voice of a man who inspired confidence in women. "We have a most important matter to discuss with him in private."

"I'll go get him," Gretchen said. The men came into the dark little hallway and shut the door behind them, as though unwilling to be observed from the street. Gretchen put the light on. She felt peculiar about leaving the two men standing crowded together in the dark. She hurried up the steps, knowing that the Tinker brothers were looking at her legs as she mounted.

Rudolph was cutting the cake as she went into the living room. Everybody looked at her inquiringly.

"What the hell was that about?" Jordache asked.

"Mr. Tinker's down there," Gretchen said. "With his brother, the priest. They want to speak to you, Pa."

"Well, why didn't you ask them to come up?" Jordache accepted a slice of cake on a plate from Rudolph and took a huge bite.

"They didn't want to. They said they had a most important matter to discuss with you in private."

Thomas made a little sucking sound, pulling his tongue over his teeth, as though he had a morsel of food caught between one tooth and another.

Jordache pushed back his chair. "Christ," he said, "a priest. You'd think the bastards would at least leave a man in peace on a Sunday afternoon." But he stood up and went out of the room. They could hear his heavy limping tread as he descended the staircase.

Jordache didn't greet the two men standing in the feeble light of the forty-watt bulb in the hallway. "Well, gentlemen," he said, "what the hell is so important that you've got to take a working man away from his Sunday dinner to talk about?"

"Mr. Jordache," Tinker said, "could we talk to you in private?"

"What's wrong with right here?" Jordache asked, standing above them on the last step, still chewing on his cake. The hallway smelled of the goose.

Tinker looked up the stairway. "I wouldn't like to be overheard," he said.

"As far as I can tell," Jordache said, "we got nothing to say to each other that the whole goddamn town can't hear. I don't owe you any money and you don't owe me none." Still, he took the step down into the hallway and opened the door to the street and unlocked the front door of the bakery with the key he always carried in his pocket.

The three men went into the bakery, its big window covered from within by a canvas blind for Sunday.

VI

Upstairs, Mary Jordache was waiting for the coffee to boil. Rudolph kept looking at his watch, worried that he'd be late for his date with Julie. Thomas sat slumped in his chair, humming tunelessly and tapping an annoying rhythm on his glass with his fork.

"Stop that, please," the mother said. "You're giving me a headache."

"Sorry," Thomas said. "I'll take up the trumpet for my next concert."

Never a courteous moment, Mary Jordache thought. "What's keeping them down there?" she asked querulously. "The one day we're having a normal family meal." She turned accusingly on Gretchen. "You work with Mr. Tinker," she said. "Have you done something disgraceful downtown?"

"Maybe they discovered I stole a brick," Gretchen said.

"Even one day," her mother said, "is too much for this family to be polite." She went into the kitchen to get the coffee, her back a drama of martyrdom.

There was the sound of Jordache coming up the staircase. He came into the living room, his face expressionless. "Tom," he said flatly, "come on downstairs."

"I got nothing to say to the Tinker family," Thomas said.

"They got something to say to you." Jordache turned and went out of the room and down the stairs again. Thomas shrugged. He pulled at his fingers, tugging with one hand against the other, the way he did before a fight, and followed his father.

Gretchen frowned. "Do you know what it's all about?" she asked Rudolph.

"Trouble," Rudolph said gloomily. He knew he was going to be late for Julie.

VII

In the bakery the two Tinkers, one in a navy-blue suit and the other in his shiny, black, priest's suit, looked like two ravens against the bare shelves and the gray marble counter. Thomas came in and Jordache closed the door behind him.

I'm going to have to kill him, Thomas thought. "Good afternoon, Mr. Tinker," he said, smiling boyishly. "Good afternoon, Father."

"My son," the priest said portentously.

"Tell him what you told me," Jordache said.

"We know all about it, son," the priest said. "Claude confessed everything to his uncle, as was only right and natural. From confession flows repentance and from repentance forgiveness."

"Save that crap for Sunday school," Jordache said. He was leaning with his back against the door, as though to make sure nobody was going to escape.

Thomas didn't say anything. He was wearing his little prefight smile.

"The shameful burning of the cross," the priest said. "On a day consecrated to the memory of the brave young men who have fallen in the struggle. On a day when I celebrated a holy mass for the repose of their souls at the altar of my own church. And with all the trials and intolerance we Catholics have undergone in this country and our bitter efforts to be accepted by our bigoted countrymen. And to have the deed perpetrated by two Catholic boys." He shook his head sorrowfully.

"He's no Catholic," Jordache said.

"His mother and father were born in the Church," the priest said. "I have made inquiries."

"Did you do it or didn't you do it?" Jordache asked.

"I did it," Thomas said. That yellow, gutless son of a bitch Claude.

"Can you imagine, my son," the priest went on, "what would happen to your family and Claude's family if it ever became known who raised that flaming cross?"

"We'd be driven out of town," Mr. Tinker said excitedly. "That's what would happen. Your father wouldn't be able to *give* away a loaf of bread in this town. The people of this town remember you're foreigners, Germans, even if you'd like to forget it."

"Oh, Christ, now," Jordache said. "The red, white, and blue."

"Facts are facts," Mr. Tinker said. "You might as well face it. I'll give you another fact. If Boylan ever finds out who it was that set fire to his greenhouse he'll sue us for our lives. He'll get a smart lawyer that'll make that old greenhouse seem like the most valuable property between here and New York." He shook his fist at Thomas. "Your father won't have two pennies to rub against each other in his pocket. You're minors. *We're* responsible, your father and me. The savings of a lifetime . . ."

Thomas could see his father's hands working, as though he would like to put them around Thomas's neck and strangle him.

"Keep calm, John," the priest said to Tinker. "There's no sense in getting the boy too upset. We have to depend upon his good sense to save us all." He turned to Thomas. "I will not ask you what devilish impulse moved you to incite our Claude to do this awful deed . . ."

"He said it was my idea?" Thomas asked.

"A boy like Claude," the priest said, "growing up in a Christian home, going to Mass every Sunday, would never dream up a desperate scheme like that on his own."

"Okay," Thomas said. He sure as hell was going to be out looking for Claude.

"Luckily," the priest went on, in measured Gregorian tones, "when Claude visited his uncle, Dr. Robert Tinker, that awful night, with his cruelly wounded arm, Dr. Tinker was alone. He treated the boy and extracted the story from him and took him home in his own car. By the grace of God, he was not observed. But the burns are severe and Claude will be in bandages for at least three more weeks. It was not possible to keep him hidden at home safely until he was fully recovered. A maid might become suspicious, a delivery boy might get a glimpse of him, a school friend might pay a visit out of pity . . ."

"Oh, Christ, Anthony," Mr. Tinker said, "get out of the pulpit!" His face pale and working convulsively, his eyes bloodshot, he strode over to Thomas. "We drove the little bastard down to New York last night and we put him on a plane to California this morning. He's got an aunt in San Francisco and he'll be stashed away until he can get the bandages off and then he's going to military school and I don't care if he doesn't come back to this town before he's ninety. And if he knows what's good for him your father'd damn well better get you out of town, too. As far away as possible, where nobody knows you and nobody'll ask any questions."

"Don't worry, Tinker," Jordache said. "He'll be out of town by nightfall."

"He'd better be," Tinker said threateningly.

"All right now." Jordache opened the door. "I've had enough of the both of you. Get out."

"I think we ought to go now, John," the priest said. "I'm certain Mr. Jordache will do the proper thing."

Tinker had to get in the last word. "You're being let off easy," he said. "All of you." He marched out of the store.

"God forgive you, my son," the priest said, and followed his brother.

Jordache locked the door and faced Thomas. "You've hung a sword over my head, you little shit," he said. "You've got something coming to you." He limped toward Thomas and swung his fist. It landed high on Thomas's head. Thomas staggered and then, instinctively, hit back, going off the floor and catching his father flush on the temple with the hardest right hand he had ever thrown. Jordache didn't fall, but swayed a little, his hands out in front of him. He stared disbelieving at his son, at the blue eyes icy with hatred. Then he saw Thomas smile and drop his hands to his side.

"Go ahead and get it over with," Thomas said contemptuously. "Sonny boy won't hit his brave daddy any more."

Jordache swung once more. The left side of Thomas's face began to swell immediately and became an angry wine red, but he merely stood there, smiling.

Jordache dropped his hands. The one blow had been a symbol, nothing more. Meaningless, he thought dazedly. Sons.

"Okay," he said. "That's over. Your brother's going to take you on the bus to Grafton. From there you'll take the first train to Albany. In Albany you'll change for Ohio. Alone. My brother'll have to take care of you. I'll call him today and he'll be expecting you. Don't bother packing. I don't want anybody to see you leaving town with a valise." He unlocked the bakery door. Thomas went out, blinking in the Sunday afternoon sunlight.

"You wait here," Jordache said. "I'll send your brother down. I don't fancy any farewell scenes with your mother." He locked the bakery door and limped into the house.

Only after his father was gone did Thomas touch the tender, swollen side of his jaw.

VIII

Ten minutes later, Jordache and Rudolph came down. Thomas was leaning against the bakery window, staring calmly across the street. Rudolph was carrying the jacket of Thomas's one suit, striped and greenish. It had been bought two years before and was too small for him. He couldn't move his shoulders freely when he put it on and his hands dangled far out of the tight sleeves.

Rudolph looked dazed and his eyes widened when he saw the welt on Thomas's cheek. Jordache had the appearance of a sick man. Under the naturally dark tint of his skin, there was a wash of pallid green and his eyes were puffy. One punch, Thomas thought, and look what happens to him.

"Rudolph knows what he has to do," Jordache said. "I gave him some money. He'll buy you your ticket to Cleveland. Here's your uncle's address." He handed Thomas a slip of paper.

I'm moving up in class, Thomas thought, I have uncles for emergencies, too. Call me Tinker.

"Now get moving," Jordache said. "And keep your trap shut."

The boys started down the street. Jordache watched, feeling the vein throb in his temple where Thomas had hit him and not seeing anything very clearly. His sons moved off in a blur down the sunny empty slum street, the one tallish and slender and well dressed in the gray-flannel slacks and a blue blazer, the other almost as tall but wider and looking childish in the jacket that was too small for him. When the boys had disappeared around a corner, Jordache turned and walked in the opposite direction, toward the river. This was one afternoon he had to be alone. He would call his brother later. His brother and his wife were just slobs enough to take in the son of a man who had kicked them out of his house and hadn't even said thank you for the yearly Christmas card that was the only evidence that two men who had been born long ago in the same house in Cologne and who were living in different parts of America were, in fact, brothers. He could just hear his brother saying to his fat wife, in that ineradicable German accent, "After all, vat can ve do? Blut is thicker than vater."

"What in hell happened?" Rudolph asked as soon as they were out of their father's sight.

"Nothing," Thomas said.

"He hit you," Rudolph said. "Your jaw's a sight."

"It was a terrible blow," Thomas said mockingly. "He's next in line for a shot at the title."

"He came upstairs looking sick," Rudolph said.

"I clipped him one." Thomas grinned, remembering.

"You *hit* him?"

"Why not?" Thomas said. "What's a father for?"

"Christ! And you're still alive?"

"I'm alive," said Thomas.

"No wonder he's getting rid of you." Rudolph shook his head. He couldn't help being angry at Thomas. Because of Thomas he was missing his date with Julie. He would have liked to pass her house, it was only a few blocks out of the way to the bus station, but his father had said he wanted Thomas out of town immediately and with nobody knowing about it. "What the hell is the matter with you, anyway?"

"I'm a high-spirited, red-blooded, normal American boy," Thomas said.

"It must be real trouble," Rudolph said. "He gave me fifty bucks for the train fare. Anytime he shells out fifty bucks, it must be something enormous."

"I was discovered spying for the Japs," Thomas said placidly.

"Oh, boy, you're smart," Rudolph said, and they walked the rest of the way to the bus station in silence.

They got off the bus at Grafton near the railroad station and Thomas sat under a tree in a little park across the square from the station while Rudolph went in to see about Thomas's ticket. The next train to Albany was in fifteen minutes and Rudolph bought the ticket from the wizened man with a green eyeshade behind the wicket. He didn't buy the ticket for the connection to Cleveland. His father had told him he didn't want anybody to know Thomas's final destination, so Thomas was going to have to buy the ticket himself at the station in Albany.

As he took the change, Rudolph had an impulse to buy another ticket for himself. In the opposite direction. To New York. Why should Thomas be the first one to escape? But of course, he didn't buy any ticket to New York. He went out of the station and past the dozing drivers waiting in their 1939 taxis for the arrival of the next train. Thomas was sitting on a bench under a tree, his legs sprawled out in a V, his heels dug into the scrubby lawn. He looked unhurried and peaceful, as though nothing was happening to him.

Rudolph glanced around to make sure nobody was watching them. "Here's your ticket," he said, handing it to Thomas, who looked at it lazily. "Put it away, put it away," Rudolph said. "And here's the change for the fifty dollars. Forty-two fifty. For your ticket from Albany. You'll have a lot left over, the way I figure it."

Thomas pocketed the money without counting it. "The old man must have shit blood," Thomas said, "when he took it out from wherever he hides his dough. Did you see where he keeps it?"

"No."

"Too bad. I could come back some dark night and lift it. Although I don't suppose you'd tell me, even if you knew. Not my brother Rudolph."

They watched a roadster drive up with a girl at the wheel and a lieutenant in the Air Force beside her. They got out of the car and went into the shade of the tiled overhang of the depot. Then they stopped and kissed. The girl was wearing a pale-blue dress and the summery wind twirled it around her legs. The lieutenant was tall and very tan, as though he had been in the desert. He had medals and wings on his green Eisenhower jacket and he was carrying a stuffed flight bag. Rudolph heard the roar of a thousand engines in foreign skies as he watched the couple. Again, he felt the pang because he had been born too late and missed the war.

"Kiss me, darling," Thomas said, "I bombed Tokyo."

"What the hell are you proving?" Rudolph said.

"You ever get laid?" Thomas asked.

The echo of his father's question the day Jordache hit Miss Lenaut disturbed Rudolph. "What's it to you?"

Thomas shrugged, watching the two people go through the open door of the station. "Nothing. I just thought I'm going to be away a long time, maybe we ought to have a heart-to-heart talk."

"Well, if you must know, I haven't," Rudolph said stiffly.

"I was sure of it," Thomas said. "There's a place called Alice's in town on McKinley, you can get a good piece of tail for five bucks. Tell them your brother sent you."

"I'll take care of myself my own way," Rudolph said. Although he was a year older than Thomas, Thomas was making him feel like a kid.

"Our loving sister is getting hers regularly," Thomas said. "Did you know that?"

"That's her business." But Rudolph was shocked. Gretchen was so *clean* and neat and politely spoken. He couldn't imagine her in the sweaty tangle of sex.

"Do you want to know who with?"

"No."

"Theodore Boylan," Thomas said. "How do you like that for class?"

"How do you know?" Rudolph was sure that Thomas was lying.

"I went up and watched through the window," Thomas said. "He came down into the living room bare-assed, with his thing hanging down to his knees, he's a regular horse, and made two whiskies and called up the stairs, 'Gretchen, do you want your drink up there or do you want to come down for it?'" Thomas simpered as he imitated Boylan.

"Did she come down?" Rudolph didn't want to hear the rest of the story.

"No. I guess she was having too good a time where she was."

"So you didn't see whoever it was." Rudolph fell back on logic to preserve his sister. "It might have been anybody up there."

"How many Gretchens you know in Port Philip?" Thomas said. "Anyway, Claude Tinker saw them drive up the hill together in Boylan's car. She meets him in front of Bernstein's when she's supposed to be at the hospital. Maybe Boylan got wounded in a war, too. The Spanish-American War."

"Jesus," Rudolph said. "With an ugly old man like Boylan." If it had been with someone like the young lieutenant who had just gone into the station, she would still have remained his sister.

"She must be getting something out of it," Thomas said carelessly. "Ask her."

"You ever tell her you knew?"

"Nah. Let her screw in peace. It's not my cock. I just went up there for laughs," Thomas said. "She don't mean anything to me. La-di-da, la-di-da, where do babies come from, Mummy?"

Rudolph wondered how his brother could have perfected his hatred so young.

"If we were Italians or something," Thomas said, "or Southern gentlemen, we'd go up that hill and avenge the honor of the family. Cut off his balls or shoot him or something. I'm busy this year, but if you want to do it, I give you permission."

"Maybe you'll be surprised," Rudolph said. "Maybe I will do something."

"I bet," Thomas said. "Anyway, just for your information, I've already done something."

"What?"

Thomas looked consideringly at Rudolph. "Ask your father," he said, "he knows." He stood up. "Well, I better be getting along. The train's due."

They went out onto the platform. The lieutenant and the girl were kissing again. He might never come back, this might be the last kiss, Rudolph thought; after all, they were still fighting out in the Pacific, there were still the Japanese. The girl was weeping as she kissed the lieutenant and he was patting her back with one hand to comfort her. Rudolph wondered if there ever would be a girl who would cry on a station platform because he had to leave her.

The train came in with a whoosh of country dust. Thomas swung up onto the steps.

"Look," Rudolph said, "if there's anything you want from the house, write me. I'll get it to you somehow."

"There's nothing I want from that house," Thomas said. His rebellion was pure and complete. The undeveloped, childish face seemed merry, as if he were going to a circus.

"Well," Rudolph said lamely. "Good luck." After all, he was his brother and God knew when they would ever see each other again.

"Congratulations," Thomas said. "Now you got the whole bed to yourself. You don't have to worry about my smelling like a wild animal. Don't forget to wear your pajamas."

Giving nothing, right up to the last moment, he went into the vestibule and into the car without looking back. The train started and Rudolph could see the lieutenant standing at an open window waving to the girl, who was running along the platform.

The train gathered speed and the girl stopped running. She became conscious of Rudolph looking at her and her face closed down, erasing public sorrow, public love. She wheeled and hurried off, the wind whipping her dress about her body. Warrior's woman.

Rudolph went back to the park and sat on the bench again and waited for the bus back to Port Philip.

What a goddamn birthday.

IX

Gretchen was packing a bag. It was a big, frayed, yellow-stippled, cardboardish rectangle, studded with brass knobs, that had held her mother's bridal trousseau when she arrived in Port Philip. Gretchen had never spent a night away from home in her whole life so she had never had a valise of her own. When she had made her decision, after her father had come up from the conference with Thomas and the Tinkers, to announce that Thomas was going away for a long time, Gretchen had climbed to the narrow little attic where the few things that the Jordaches had collected and had no further use for were stored. She had found the bag and brought it down to her own room. Her mother had seen her with the bag and must have guessed what it meant, but had said nothing. Her mother hadn't talked to her in weeks, ever since the night she had come in at dawn after the trip to New York with Boylan. It was as though she felt that conversation between them brought with it the contagion of Gretchen's rank corruption.

The air of crisis, of hidden conflicts, the strange look in her father's eyes when he had come back into the living room and told Rudolph to come with him, had finally pushed Gretchen to action. There would never be a better day to leave than this Sunday afternoon.

She packed carefully. The bag wasn't big enough to take everything she might need and she had to choose deliberately, putting things in, then taking them out in favor of other things that might be more useful. She hoped that she could get out of the house before her father came back, but she was prepared to face him and tell him that she had lost her job and was going down to New York to look for another. There had been something in his face as he started downstairs with Rudolph that was passive and stunned and she guessed that today might be the one day she could walk past him without a struggle.

She had to turn almost every book upside down before she found the envelope with the money in it. That crazy game her mother played. There was a fifty-fifty chance that her mother would wind up in an asylum. Eventually, she hoped, she would be able to learn to pity her.

She was sorry that she was going without a chance to say good-bye to Rudolph but it was growing dark already and she didn't want to reach New York after midnight. She had no notion of where she was going to go in New York. There must be a Y.W.C.A. somewhere. Girls had spent their first nights in New York in worse places.

She looked around her stripped room without emotion. Her good-bye to her room was flippant. She took the envelope, now empty of money, and laid it squarely in the middle of her narrow bed.

She lugged the suitcase out into the hallway. She could see her mother sitting at the table, smoking. The remains of the dinner, the goose carcass, the cold cabbage, the dumplings jellied in slime, the stained napkins, had remained untouched all these hours on the table, as her mother had sat there, wordless, staring at the wall. Gretchen went into the room. "Ma," she said, "this is going-away day, I guess. I'm packed and I'm leaving."

Her mother turned her head slowly and blearily toward her. "Go to your fancy man," she said thickly. Her vocabulary of abuse dated from earlier in the century. She had finished all the wine and she was drunk. It was the first time Gretchen had seen her mother drunk and it made her want to laugh.

"I'm not going to anybody," she said. "I lost my job and I'm going to New York to look for another one. When I'm settled, I'll write you and let you know."

"Harlot," the mother said.

Gretchen grimaced. Who said harlot in 1945? It made her going unimportant, comic. But she forced herself to kiss her mother's cheek. The skin was rough and seamed with broken capillaries.

"False kisses," the mother said, staring. "The dagger in the rose."

What books she must have read as a young girl!

The mother pushed back a wisp of hair from her forehead with the back of her hand, in the gesture that had been weary since she was twenty-one years old. It occurred to Gretchen that her mother had been born worn out and that much should be forgiven her because of it. For a moment she hesitated, searching for some vestige of affection within her for the drunken woman sitting wreathed in smoke at the cluttered table.

"Goose," her mother said disdainfully. "Who eats goose?"

Gretchen shook her head hopelessly and went out into the hallway and picked up the bag and struggled down the staircase with it. She unlocked the door below and pushed the suitcase out over the sill into the street. The sun was just setting and the shadows on the street were violet and indigo. As she picked up the bag, the streetlamps went on, lemony and pale, doing premature and useless service.

Then she saw Rudolph hurrying down the street toward the house. He was alone. She put down her bag and waited for him. As he approached she thought how well the blazer fit him, how neat he looked, and was glad she had spent the money.

When Rudolph saw her, he broke into a run. "Where're *you* going?" he said as he came up to her.

"New York," she said lightly. "Come along?"

"I wish I could," he said.

"Help a lady to a taxi?"

"I want to talk to you," he said.

"Not here," she said, glancing at the bakery window. "I want to get away from here."

"Yeah," Rudolph said, picking up her bag. "This is for sure no place to talk."

They started down the street together to look for a taxi. Good-bye, good-bye, Gretchen sang to herself, as she passed the familiar names, good-bye Clancy's Garage, Body Work, good-bye Soriano's Hand

Laundry, good-bye Fenelli's, Prime Beef, good-bye the A and P, good-bye Bolton's Drug Store, good-bye Wharton's Paints and Hardware, good-bye Bruno's Barber Shop, good-bye Jardino's Fruits and Vegetables. The song inside her head was lilting as she walked briskly beside her brother, but there was a minor undertone in it. You leave no place after nineteen years without regrets.

They found a taxi two blocks farther on and drove to the station. While Gretchen went over to the window to buy her ticket, Rudolph sat on the old-fashioned valise, thinking, I am spending my eighteenth year saying good-bye in every station of the New York Central railroad.

Rudolph couldn't help but feel a little bruised by the rippling lightness in his sister's movements and the pinpoints of joy in her eyes. After all, she was not only leaving home, she was leaving *him*. He felt strange with her now, since he knew she had made love with a man. *Let her screw in peace.* He must find a more melodious vocabulary.

She touched him on the sleeve. "The train won't be along for more than a half hour," she said. "I feel like a drink. Celebrate. Put the valise in the baggage room and we'll go across the street to the Port Philip House."

Rudolph picked up the valise. "I'll carry it," he said. "It costs ten cents in the baggage room."

"Let's be big for once." Gretchen laughed. "Squander our inheritance. Let the dimes flow."

As he took a check for the valise, he wondered if she had been drinking all afternoon.

The bar of the Port Philip House was empty except for two soldiers who were moodily staring at glasses of wartime beer near the entrance. The bar was dark and cool and they could look out through the windows at the station, its lights now on in the dusk. They sat at a table near the back and when the bartender came over to them, wiping his hands on his apron, Gretchen said, firmly, "Two Black and White and soda, please."

The barman didn't ask whether or not they were over eighteen. Gretchen had ordered as if she had been drinking whiskey in bars all her life.

Actually, Rudolph would have preferred a Coke. The afternoon had been too full of occasions.

Gretchen poked at his cheek with two fingers. "Don't look so glum," she said. "It's your birthday."

"Yeah," he said.

"Why did Pa send Tommy away?"

"I don't know. Neither of them would tell me. Something happened with the Tinkers. Tommy hit Pa. I know *that*."

"Wooh . . ." Gretchen said softly. "Quite a day, isn't it?"

"It sure is," Rudolph said. It was a bigger day than she realized, he thought, remembering what Tom had told him earlier about her. The barman came over with their drinks and a siphon bottle. "Not too much soda, please," Gretchen said.

The barman splashed some soda in Gretchen's glass. "How about you?" He held the siphon over Rudolph's glass.

"The same," Rudolph said, acting eighteen.

Gretchen raised her glass. "To that well-known ornament to Port Philip society," she said, "the Jordache family."

They drank. Rudolph had not yet developed a taste for Scotch. Gretchen drank thirstily, as though she wanted to finish the first one fast, so that there would be time for another one before the train came in.

"What a family." She shook her head. "The famous Jordache collection of authentic mummies. Why don't you get on the train with me and come live in New York?"

"You know I can't do that," he said.

"I thought I couldn't do it, too," she said. "And I'm doing it."

"Why?"

"Why what?"

"Why're you going? What happened?"

"A lot of things," she said vaguely. She took a long swig of her whiskey. "A man mostly." She looked at him defiantly. "A man wants to marry me."

"Who? Boylan?"

Her eyes dilated, grew darker in the dim saloon. "How do you know?"

"Tommy told me."

"How does he know?"

Well, why not, he thought. She asked for it. Jealousy and shame for her made him want to hurt her. "He went up to the hill and looked in through a window."

"What did he see?" she asked coldly.

"Boylan. Naked."

"He didn't get much of a show, poor Tommy." She laughed. The laugh was metallic. "He's not much to look at, Teddy Boylan. Did he have the good luck to see me naked, too?"

"No."

"Too bad," she said. "It would have made his trip worthwhile." There was something hard and self-wounding in his sister that Rudolph had never seen in her before. "How did he know I was there?"

"Boylan called upstairs to ask you if you wanted to have your drink there."

"Oh," she said. "That night. That was a big night. Some time I'll tell you about it." She studied his face. "Don't look so stormy. Sisters have a habit of growing up and going out with fellas."

"But Boylan," he said bitterly. "That puny old man."

"He's not that old," she said. "And not that puny."

"You liked him," he said accusingly.

"I liked *it*," she said. Her face became very sober. "I liked it better than anything that ever happened to me."

"Then why're you running away?"

"Because if I stay here long enough, I'll wind up marrying him. And Teddy Boylan's not fit for your pure, beautiful little sister to marry. It's complicated, isn't it? Is your life complicated, too? Is there some dark, sinful passion you're nursing in your bosom, too? An older woman you visit while her husband's at the office, a . . . ?"

"Don't make fun of me," he said.

"Sorry." She touched his hand, then gestured toward the bartender. When he came over, she said, "One more, please." As the bartender went back to fill the order, she said, "Ma was drunk when I left. She finished all your birthday wine. The blood of the lamb. That's all that family needs—" She spoke as though they were discussing the idiosyncracies of strangers. "A drunken crazy old lady. She called me a harlot." Gretchen chuckled. "A last loving farewell to the girl going to the big city. Get out," she said harshly, "get out before they finish crippling you. Get out of that house where nobody has a friend, where the doorbell never rings."

"I'm not crippled," he said.

"You're frozen in an act, Brother." The hostility was out in the open now. "You don't fool me. Everybody's darling, and you don't give a good goddamn if the whole world lives or dies. If that's not being crippled, put me in a wheel chair any day."

The bartender came over and put her drink down in front of her and half filled the glass with soda.

"What the hell," Rudolph said, standing up, "if that's what you think of me, there's no sense in my hanging around any more. You don't need me."

"No, I don't," she said.

"Here's the ticket for your bag." He handed her the slip of paper.

"Thanks," she said woodenly. "You've done your good deed for the day. And I've done mine."

He left her sitting there in the bar, drinking her second whiskey, her lovely, oval face flushed at the cheek bones, her eyes shining, her wide mouth avid, beautiful, hungry, bitter, already a thousand miles removed from the dingy apartment above the bakery, removed from her father and mother, her brothers, her lover, on her way to a city that engulfed a million girls a year.

He walked slowly toward home, tears for himself in his eyes. They were right, they were right about him, his brother, his sister; their judgments on him were just. He had to change. How do you change, what do you change? Your genes, your chromosomes, your sign of the zodiac?

As he neared Vanderhoff Street, he stopped. He couldn't bear the thought of going home yet. He didn't want to see his mother drunk, he didn't want to see that stunned, hating look, like a disease, in his father's eyes. He walked on down toward the river. There was a faint afterglow from the sunset and the river slid by like wet steel, with a smell like a deep, cool cellar in chalky ground. He sat on the rotting wharf near the warehouse in which his father kept his shell and looked out toward the opposite shore.

Far out, he could see something moving. It was his father's shell, the oars going in a fierce, even rhythm, biting the water, going upstream.

He remembered that his father had killed two men, one with a knife, one with a bayonet.

He felt empty and beaten. The whiskey he had drunk burned in his chest and there was a sour taste in his mouth.

I'll remember this birthday, he thought.

X

Mary Pease Jordache sat in the living room, in darkness and in the fumes of smoke from the roast goose. She was oblivious to them and to the vinegary aroma of the cabbage that lay cold on the disordered platter. Two of them gone, she thought, the thug and the harlot. I have Rudolph alone now, she exulted drunkenly. If only a storm came up and swamped the shell, far, far out on the cold river, what a day it would be.

Chapter 7

I

A horn blew outside the garage and Tom climbed out from under the Ford on which he was working in the grease pit, and wiping his hands on a rag, went out to where the Oldsmobile was standing next to one of the pumps.

"Fill'er up," Mr. Herbert said. He was a steady customer, a real estate man who had taken options on outlying properties near the garage at low, wartime prices, lying in wait for the post-war boom. Now that the Japanese had surrendered, his car passed the garage frequently. He bought all his gas at the Jordache station, using the black-market ration stamps Harold Jordache sold him.

Thomas unscrewed the tank cap and ran the gasoline in, holding onto the trigger of the hose nozzle. It was a hot afternoon and the fumes from the flowing gasoline rose in visible waves from the tank. Thomas turned his head, trying to avoid breathing in the vapor. He had a headache every night from this job. The Germans are using chemical warfare on me, he thought, now that the war is over. He thought of his uncle as German in a way that he didn't think of his father as German. There was the accent, of course, and the two pale-blonde daughters who were dressed in vaguely Bavarian fashion on holidays, and the heavy meals of sausage, smoked pork, and kraut, and the constant sound of people singing Wagner and Schubert *lieder* on the phonograph in the house, because Mrs. Jordache loved music. Tante Elsa, she asked Thomas to call her.

Thomas was alone in the garage. Coyne, the mechanic, was sick this week, and the second man was out on a call. It was two o'clock in the afternoon and Harold Jordache was still home at lunch.

Sauerbraten mit spetzli and three bottles of Miller High Life and a nice snooze on the big bed upstairs with his fat wife to make sure they didn't overwork and have premature heart attacks. Thomas was just as glad that the maid gave him two sandwiches and some fruit in a bag for his lunch to eat at the garage. The less he saw of his uncle and his family, the better he liked it. It was enough he had to live in the house, in the minuscule room in the attic, where he lay sweating all night in the heat that had collected there under the roof in the summer sun during the day. Fifteen dollars a week. His Uncle Harold had made a good thing out of that burning cross in Port Philip.

The tank overflowed a little and Thomas hung up the hose and put on the cap and wiped away the splash of gasoline on the rear fender. He washed the windshield down and collected four dollars and thirty cents from Mr. Herbert, who gave him a dime tip.

"Thanks," Thomas said, with a good facsimile of gratitude, and watched the Oldsmobile drive off into town. The Jordache garage was on the outskirts of town, so they got a lot of transient traffic, too. Thomas went into the office and charged up the sale on the register and put the money into the till. He had finished the grease job on the Ford and for the moment he had nothing to do, although if his uncle were there, he would have no trouble finding work for him. Probably cleaning out the toilets or polishing the chrome of the shining hulks in the Used Car Lot. Thomas thought idly of cleaning out the cash register instead, and taking off somewhere. He rang the No Sale key and looked in. With Mr. Herbert's four dollars and thirty cents, there was exactly ten dollars and thirty cents in the drawer. Uncle Harold had lifted the morning's receipts when he went home for lunch, just leaving five one-dollar bills and a dollar in silver in case somebody had to have change. Uncle Harold hadn't become the owner of a garage and a Used Car Lot and a filling station and an automobile agency in town by being careless with his money.

Thomas hadn't eaten yet, so he picked up his lunch bag and went out of the office and sat tilted on the cracked wooden chair against the wall of the garage, in the shade, watching the traffic go by. The view was not unpleasant. There was something nautical about the cars in diagonal lines in the lot, with gaily colored banners overhead announcing bargains. Beyond the lumberyard diagonally across the road, there were the ochre and green of patches of the farmland all around. If you sat still, the heat wasn't too bad and just the absence of Uncle Harold gave Thomas a sense of well-being.

Actually, he wasn't unhappy in the town. Elysium, Ohio, was smaller than Port Philip, but much more prosperous, with no slums and none of the sense of decay that Thomas had taken as a natural part of his environment back home. There was a small lake nearby, with two hotels that were open for the summer, and holiday cottages owned by people who came there from Cleveland, so the town itself had some of the spruced-up air of a resort, with good shops, restaurants, and entertainments like horse shows and regattas for small sailboats on the lake. Everybody seemed to have money in Elysium and that was a real change from Port Philip.

Thomas dug into the bag and pulled out a sandwich. It was wrapped neatly in waxed paper. It was a bacon, lettuce, and tomato sandwich, with a lot of mayonnaise, on fresh, thinly cut rye bread. Recently, Clothilde, the Jordaches' maid, had begun to give him fancy sandwiches, different ones every day, instead of the unrelieved diet of bologna on thick hunks of bread that he had had to make do with the first few weeks. Tom was a little ashamed, seeing his grease-stained hands with the black nails on the elaborate tea-shoppe sandwich. It was just as well that Clothilde couldn't see him as he ate her offerings. She was nice, Clothilde, a quiet French-Canadian woman of about twenty-five who worked from seven in the morning until nine at night, with every other Sunday afternoon off. She had sad, dark eyes and black hair. Her uniform somberness of coloring set her off as being ineluctably lower in the social scale than the aggressively blonde Jordaches, as though she had been born and marked specifically to be their servant.

She had taken to leaving a piece of pie out on the kitchen table for him, too, at night, when he left the house after dinner, to wander around the town. Uncle Harold and Tante Elsa couldn't keep him in the house at night any more than his own parents could. He had to wander. Nighttime made him restless. He didn't do much—sometimes he'd play in a pickup softball game under the lights in the town park or he'd go to a movie and have a soda afterward, and he'd found some girls. He had made no friends who might ask embarrassing questions about Port Philip and he'd been careful to be civil to everyone and he hadn't had a fight since he'd come to town. He'd had enough trouble for the time being. He wasn't unhappy. Being out from under his mother and father was a blessing and not living in the same house and sharing the same bed with his brother, Rudolph, was soothing to the nerves. And not having to go to school was a big improvement. He didn't mind the work at the garage, although Uncle Harold was a nuisance, always fussing and worrying. Tante Elsa clucked over him and kept giving him glasses of orange juice under the impression that his lean fitness was a sign of malnutrition. They meant well enough, even if they were slobs. The two little girls stayed out of his way.

Neither of the senior Jordaches knew why he had been sent away from home. Uncle Harold had pried, but Thomas had been vague and had merely said that he was doing badly at school, which was true enough, and that his father had thought it would be good for his character to get away from home and earn some money on his own. Uncle Harold was not one to underestimate the moral beauties of sending a boy out to earn money on his own. He was surprised, though, that Thomas never got any mail from his family and that after that first Sunday afternoon telephone call from Axel telling him that Thomas was on his way, there had been no further communication from Port Philip. Harold Jordache was a family man, himself, extravagantly affectionate with his two daughters and lavish with gifts for his wife, whose money it had been in the first place that had enabled him to take his comfortable place in Elysium. In talking about Axel Jordache to Tom, Uncle Harold had sighed over the differences in temperament between the brothers. "I think, Tom," Uncle Harold had said, "it was because of the wound. He took it very hard, your father. It brought out the dark side in him. As though nobody ever was wounded before."

He shared one conception with Axel Jordache. The German people, he believed, had a streak of childishness in them, which drove them into waging war. "Play a band and they march. What's so attractive about it?" he said. "Clumping around in the rain with a sergeant yelling at you, sleeping in the mud instead of a nice, warm bed with your wife, being shot at by people you don't know, and then, if you're lucky, winding up in an old uniform without a pot to piss in. It's all right for a big industrialist, the Krupps, making cannons and battleships, but for the small man—" He shrugged. "Stalingrad. Who needs it?" With all his German-ness, he had kept clear of all German-American movements. He liked where he was and what he was and he was not to be lured into any associations that might compromise him. "I got nothing against anybody," was one of the foundations of his policy. "Not against the Poles, or the French, or the English, or the Jews or anybody. Not even the Russians. Anybody who wants can come in and buy a car or ten gallons of gas from me and if he pays in good American money, he's my friend."

Thomas lived placidly enough in Uncle Harold's house, observing the rules, going his own way, occasionally annoyed at his uncle's reluctance to see him sitting down for a few minutes during the working day, but by and large more grateful than not for the sanctuary that was being offered him. It was only temporary. Sooner or later, he knew he was going to break away. But there was no hurry.

He was just about to dig into the bag for the second sandwich, when he saw the twins' 1938 Chevy approaching. It curved in toward the filling station and Tom saw that there was only one of the twins in it. He didn't know which one it was, Ethel or Edna. He had laid them both, as had most of the boys in town, but he couldn't tell them apart.

The Chevy stopped, gurgling and creaking. The twins' parents were loaded with money, but they said the old Chevy was good enough for two sixteen-year-old girls who had never earned a cent in their lives.

"Hi, twin," Tom said, to be on the safe side.

"Hi, Tom." The twins were nice-looking girls, well tanned, with straight, brown hair and plump little, tight asses. They had skin that always looked as if they had just come out of a mountain spring. If you didn't know that they had laid every boy in town, you'd be pleased to be seen with them anywhere.

"Tell me my name," the twin said.

"Aw, come on," Tom said.

"If you don't tell me my name," the twin said, "I'll buy my gas somewhere else."

"Go ahead," Tom said. "It's my uncle's money."

"I was going to invite you to a party," the twin said. "We're cooking some hot dogs down at the lake tonight and we have three cases of beer. I won't invite you if you don't tell me my name."

Tom grinned at her, stalling for time. He looked into the open Chevy. The twin was going swimming. She had a white bathing suit on the seat beside her. "I was only kidding you, Ethel," he said. Ethel had a white bathing suit and Edna had a blue one. "I knew it was you all the time."

"Give me three gallons," Ethel said. "For guessing right."

"I wasn't guessing," he said, taking down the hose. "You're printed on my memory."

"I bet," Ethel said. She looked around at the garage and wrinkled her nose. "This is a dumb old place to work. I bet a fellow like you could get something a lot better if he looked around. At least in an office."

He had told her he was nineteen years old and graduated from high school when he had first met her. She had come over to talk to him after he had spent fifteen minutes one Saturday afternoon down at the lake, showing off on the diving board. "I like it here," he said. "I'm an outdoor man."

"Don't I know," she said, chuckling. They had screwed out in the woods on a blanket that she kept in the rumble seat of the car. He had screwed her sister Edna in the same place on the same blanket, although on different nights. The twins had an easygoing family spirit of share and share alike. The twins did a lot toward making Tom willing to stay in Elysium and work in his uncle's garage. He didn't know what he was going to do in the winter, though, when the woods were covered in snow.

He put the cap back on the tank and racked up the hose. Ethel gave him a dollar bill, but no ration coupons. "Hey," he said, "where's the tickets?"

"Surprise, surprise," she said, smiling. "I'm all out."

"You got to have 'em."

She pouted. "After everything you and I are to each other. Do you think Antony asked Cleopatra for ration tickets?"

"She didn't have to buy gas from him," Tom said.

"What's the difference?" Ethel asked. "My old man buys the coupons from your uncle. In one pocket and out the other. There's a war on."

"It's over."

"Only just."

"Okay," Tom said. "Just because you're beautiful."

"Do you think I'm prettier than Edna?" she asked.

"One hundred per cent."

"I'll tell her you said that."

"What for?" Tom said. "There's no sense in making people unhappy." He didn't relish the idea of cutting his harem down by half by an unnecessary exchange of information.

Ethel peered into the empty garage. "Do you think people ever do it in a garage?"

"Save it for tonight, Cleopatra," Tom said.

She giggled. "It's nice to try everything once. Do you have the key?"

"I'll get it sometime." Now he knew what to do in the winter.

"Why don't you just leave this dump and come on down to the lake with me? I know a place we can go skinny bathing." She wriggled desirably on the cracked leather of the front seat. It was funny how two girls in the same family could be such hot numbers. Tom wondered what their father and mother thought when they started out to church with their daughters on Sunday morning.

"I'm a working man," Tom said. "I'm essential to industry. That's why I'm not in the Army."

"I wish you were a captain," Ethel said. "I'd love to undress a captain. One brass button after another. I'd unbuckle your sword."

"Get out of here," Tom said, "before my uncle comes back and asks me if I collected your ration tickets."

"Where should I meet you tonight?" she asked, starting the motor.

"In front of the Library. Eight-thirty okay?"

"Eight-thirty, Lover Boy," she said. "I'll lay out in the sun and think about you all afternoon and pant." She waved and went off.

Tom sat down in the shade on the broken chair. He wondered if his sister, Gretchen, talked like that to Theodore Boylan.

He reached into the lunch bag and took out the second sandwich and unwrapped it. There was a piece of paper, folded in two, on the sandwich. He opened up the paper. There was writing on it in pencil. "I love you," in careful, schoolgirlish script. Tom squinted at the message. He recognized the handwriting. Clothilde wrote out the list of things she had to phone for in the market every day and the list was always in the same place on a shelf in the kitchen.

Tom whistled softly. He read aloud. "I love you." He had just passed his sixteenth birthday but his voice was still adolescently high. A twenty-five-year-old woman to whom he'd hardly ever spoken more than two words. He folded the paper carefully and put it in his pocket and stared out at the traffic sweeping along the road toward Cleveland for a long time before he began eating the bacon, lettuce, and tomato sandwich, soaked in mayonnaise.

He knew he wasn't going out to the lake tonight, for any old weeny roast.

II

The River Five played a chorus of "Your Time Is My Time," and Rudolph took a solo on the trumpet, putting everything he had into it, because Julie was in the room tonight, sitting alone at a table, watching and listening to him. The River Five was the name of

Rudolph's band, himself on the trumpet, Kessler on the bass, Westerman on the saxophone, Dailey on the percussion, and Flannery on the clarinet. The River Five was Rudolph's name for the band, because they all lived in Port Philip, on the Hudson, and because Rudolph thought it had an artistic and professional sound to it.

They had a three-week engagement, six nights a week, at a roadhouse outside Port Philip. The place, called Jack and Jill's, was a huge clapboard shack that shook to the beat of the dancers' feet. There was a long bar and a lot of small tables and most of the people just drank beer. The Saturday night standard of dress was relaxed. Boys wore T-shirts and many of the girls came in slacks. Groups of girls came unescorted and waited to be asked to dance or the girls danced with each other. It wasn't like playing the Plaza or 52nd Street in New York, but the money wasn't bad.

As he played, Rudolph was pleased to see Julie shake her head in refusal when a boy in a jacket and tie, obviously a preppie, came over and asked her to dance.

Julie's parents allowed her to stay out late with him on Saturday nights because they trusted Rudolph. He was a born parent-pleaser. With good reason. But if she fell into the clutches of a hard-drinking preppie, smooching around the floor, with his superior Deerfield or Choate line of talk, there was no telling what sort of trouble she might get into. The shake of the head was a promise, a bond between them as solid as an engagement ring.

Rudolph played the three trick bars of the band's signature for the fifteen-minute break, put his horn down, and signaled to Julie to come out with him for a breath of air. All the windows were open in the shack, but it was hot and wet inside, like the bottom of the Congo.

Julie held his hand as they walked out under the trees where the cars were parked. Her hand was dry and warm and soft and dear in his. It was hard to believe that you could have so many complicated sensations all through your body just holding a girl's hand.

"When you played that solo," Julie said, "I just sat there shivering. I curled up inside—like an oyster when you squirt lemon on it."

He chuckled at the comparison. Julie laughed too. She had a whole list of oddball phrases to describe her various states of mind. "I feel like a PT boat," when she raced him in the town swimming pool. "I feel like the dark side of the moon," when she had to stay in and do the dishes at home and missed a date with him.

They went all the way to the end of the parking lot, as far away as possible from the porch outside the shack, where the dancers were coming out for air. There was a car parked there and he opened the door for her to slide in. He got in after her and closed the door behind them. In the darkness, they locked in a kiss. They kissed interminably, clutching each other. Her mouth was a peony, a kitten, a peppermint, the skin of her throat under his hand was a butterfly's wing. They kissed all the time, whenever they could, but never did anything more.

Drowned, he was gliding and diving, through fountains, through smoke, through clouds. He was a trumpet, playing his own song. He was all of one piece, loving, loving . . . He took his mouth away from hers softly and kissed her throat as she put her head back against the seat. "I love you," he said. He was shaken by the joy he had in saying the words for the first time. She pulled his head fiercely against her throat, her swimmer's smooth summer arms wonderfully strong, and smelling of apricots.

Without warning the door opened and a man's voice said, "What the hell are you two doing in here?"

Rudolph sat up, an arm tightening protectively around Julie's shoulder. "We're discussing the atom bomb," he said coolly. "What do you think we're doing?" He would die rather than let Julie see that he was embarrassed.

The man was on his side of the car. It was too dark for him to see who it was. Then, unexpectedly, the man laughed. "Ask a foolish question," he said, "and get a foolish answer." He moved a little and a pale beam from one of the lights strung under the trees hit him. Rudolph recognized him. The yellow tightly combed hair, the thick, double bushes of blond eyebrows.

"Excuse me, Jordache," Boylan said. His voice was amused.

He knows me, Rudolph thought. How does he know me?

"This happens to be my car, but please make yourself at home," Boylan said. "I do not want to interrupt the artist at his moments of leisure. I've always heard that ladies show a preference for trumpet players." Rudolph would have preferred to hear this in other circumstances and from another source. "I didn't want to leave anyway," Boylan said. "I really need another drink. When you've finished, I'd be honored if you and the lady would join me for a nightcap at the bar." He made a little bow and softly closed the door and strolled off through the parking lot.

Julie was sitting at the other side of the car, straight up, ashamed. "He knows us," she said in a small voice.

"Me," Rudolph said.

"Who is he?"

"A man called Boylan," Rudolph said. "From the Holy Family."

"Oh," Julie said.

"That's it," said Rudolph. "Oh. Do you want to leave now? There's a bus in a few minutes." He wanted to protect her to the end, although he didn't know exactly from what.

"No," Julie said. Her tone was defiant. "I've got nothing to hide. Have you?"

"Never."

"One more kiss." She slid toward him and put out her arms.

But the kiss was wary. There was no more gliding through clouds.

They got out of the car and went back into the shack. As they passed through the door, they saw Boylan at the end of the bar, his back to it, leaning on it with his elbows behind him, watching them. He gave a little salute of recognition, touching the tips of his fingers to his forehead.

Rudolph took Julie to her table and ordered another ginger ale for her and then went back on the bandstand and began arranging the music sheets for the next set.

When the band played "Good Night Ladies" at two o'clock and the musicians began packing their instruments as the last dancers drifted off the floor, Boylan was still at the bar. A medium-sized, confident man, in gray-flannel slacks and a crisp linen jacket. Negligently out of place among the T-shirts and enlisted men's suntans and the young workingmen's Saturday night blue suits, he strolled leisurely away from the bar as Rudolph and Julie left the bandstand.

"Do you two children have transportation home?" he asked as they met.

"Well," Rudolph said, not liking the *children*, "one of the fellows has a car. We usually all pile into that." Buddy Westerman's father loaned him the family car when they had a club date and they lashed the bass and the drums onto the top. If any of them had girls along, they dropped the girls off first and all went to the Ace All Night Diner for hamburgers, to wind down.

"You'll be more comfortable with me," Boylan said. He took Julie's arm and guided her through the doorway. Buddy Westerman raised his eyebrows questioningly as he saw them leaving. "We've got a hitch into town," Rudolph said to Buddy. "Your bus is over-crowded." The fraction of betrayal.

Julie sat between them on the front seat of the Buick as Boylan swung out of the parking lot and onto the road toward Port Philip. Rudolph knew that Boylan's leg was pressing against Julie's. That same flesh had been pressed against his sister's naked body. He felt peculiar about the whole thing, all of them clamped together in the same front seat on which he and Julie had kissed just a couple of hours before, but he was determined to be sophisticated.

He was relieved when Boylan asked for Julie's address and said he'd drop her off first. He wasn't going to have to make a scene about leaving her alone with Boylan. Julie seemed subdued, not like herself, as she sat between the two of them, watching the road rush at them in the Buick's headlights.

Boylan drove fast and well, passing cars in racing-driver spurts, his hands calm on the wheel. Rudolph was disturbed because he had to admire the way the man drove. There was a disloyalty there some-where.

"That's a nice little combination you boys have there," Boylan said.

"Thanks," Rudolph said. "We could do with some more practice and some new arrangements."

"You manage a smooth beat," Boylan said. *Amateur.* "It made me regret that my dancing days are over."

Rudolph couldn't help but approve of this. He thought people over thirty dancing were ludicrous, obscene. Again he felt guilty about approving of anything about Theodore Boylan. But he was glad that at least Boylan hadn't danced with Gretchen and made fools in public of both of them. Older men dancing with young girls were the worst.

"And you, Miss . . . ?" Boylan waited for one or the other of them to supply the name.

"Julie," she said.

"Julie what?"

"Julie Hornberg," she said defensively. She was sensitive about her name.

"Hornberg?" Boylan said. "Do I know your father?"

"We just moved into town," Julie said.

"Does he work for me?"

"No," Julie said.

Moment of triumph. It would have been degrading if Mr. Horn-berg was another vassal. The name was Boylan, but there were some things beyond his reach.

"Are you musical, too, Julie?" Boylan asked.

"No," she said, surprisingly. She was making it as hard as she could for Boylan. He didn't seem to notice it. "You're a lovely girl, Julie," he said. "You make me happy that my kissing days, unlike my dancing days, are not yet over."

Dirty old lecher, Rudolph thought. He fingered his black trumpet case nervously and thought of asking Boylan to stop the car so that he and Julie could get out. But walking back to town, he wouldn't get Julie to her door before four o'clock. He marked a sorrowful point against his character. He was practical at moments that demanded honor.

"Rudolph . . . It is Rudolph, isn't it?"

"Yes." His sister must have run off at the mouth like a faucet.

"Rudolph, do you intend to make a profession of the trumpet?" Kindly old vocational counselor, now.

"No. I'm not good enough," Rudolph said.

"That's wise," Boylan said. "It's a dog's life. And you have to mix with scum."

"I don't know about that," Rudolph said. He couldn't let Boylan get away with *everything*. "I don't think people like Benny Good-man and Paul Whiteman and Louis Armstrong are scum."

"Who knows?" Boylan said.

"They're artists," Julie said tightly.

"One thing does not preclude the other, child." Boylan laughed gently. "Rudolph," he said, dismissing her, "what *do* you plan to do?"

"When? Tonight?" Rudolph knew that Boylan meant as a career, but he didn't intend to let Boylan know too much about himself. He had a vague idea that all intelligence might one day be used against him.

"Tonight I hope you're going to go home and get a good night's sleep, which you eminently deserve after your hard evening's work," Boylan said. Rudolph bridled a little at Boylan's elaborate language. The vocabulary of deceit. Trapped English. "No, I mean, later on, as a career," Boylan said.

"I don't know yet," Rudolph said. "I have to go to college first."

"Oh, you're going to college?" The surprise in Boylan's voice was clear, a pinprick of condescension.

"Why shouldn't he go to college?" Julie said. "He's a straight A student. He just made Arista."

"Did he?" Boylan said. "Forgive my ignorance, but just what is Arista?"

"It's a scholastic honor society," Rudolph said, trying to extricate Julie. He didn't want to be defended in the terms of adolescence. "It's nothing much," he said. "If you can just read and write, practically . . ."

"You know it's a lot more than that," Julie said, her mouth bunched in disappointment at his self-deprecation. "The smartest students in the whole school. If *I* was in the Arista, I wouldn't poor-mouth it."

Poor-mouth, Rudolph thought, she must have gone out with a Southern boy in Connecticut. The worm of doubt.

"I'm sure it's a great distinction, Julie," Boylan said soothingly.

"Well it is." She was stubborn.

"Rudolph's just being modest," Boylan said. "It's a commonplace male pretense."

The atmosphere in the car was uncomfortable now, with Julie in the middle angry at both Boylan and Rudolph. Boylan reached over and turned on the radio. It warmed up and a radio announcer's voice swam out of the rushing night, with the news. There had been an earthquake somewhere. They had tuned in too late to hear where. There were hundreds killed, thousands homeless, in the new whistling, 186,000-miles-per-second darkness which was the world of radio land.

"You'd think with the war just over," Julie said, "God would lay off for awhile."

Boylan looked at her in surprise and turned off the radio. "God never lays off," he said.

Old faker, Rudolph thought. Talking about God. After what he's done.

"What college do you intend to go to, Rudolph," Boylan talked across Julie's plump, pointy, little chest.

"I haven't made up my mind yet."

"It's a very grave decision," Boylan said. "The people you meet there are likely to change your whole life. If you need any help, perhaps I can put in a good word at my Alma Mater. With all the heroes coming back, boys of your age are going to have difficulties."

"Thank you." The last thing in the world. "I don't have to apply for months yet. What college did you go to?"

"Virginia," Boylan said.

Virginia, Rudolph thought disdainfully. Anybody can go to Virginia. Why does he talk as though it's Harvard or Princeton, or at least Amherst?

They drew up in front of Julie's house. Automatically, Rudolph looked up at Miss Lenaut's window, in the next building. It was dark.

"Well, here we are, child," Boylan said, as Rudolph opened the door on his side and got out. "It's been delightful talking to you."

"Thank you for the ride," Julie said. She got out and bounced past Rudolph toward her front door. Rudolph went after her. He could kiss her good night, at least, in the shadow of the porch. As she felt in her bag for her key, her head down, her pony tail swinging down over her face, he tried to pick up her chin so he could kiss her, but she pulled away fiercely. "Kowtower," she said. She mimicked him savagely. "It's nothing much. If you can just read and write, practically . . ."

"Julie . . ."

"Suck up to the rich." He had never seen her face looking like that, pale and closed down. "Scaly old man. He bleaches his hair. *And* his eyebrows. Boy, some people'll do anything for a ride in a car, won't they?"

"Julie, you're being unreasonable." If she knew the whole truth about Boylan, he might understand her anger. But just because he was ordinarily polite . . .

"Take your hands off me." She had the key out and was fumbling at the door, still smelling of apricot.

"I'll come by tomorrow about four . . ."

"That's what you think," she said. "Wait until I have a Buick and then come around. That's more your speed." She had the door open now and was through it, a rustle of girl, a fragrant, snapping shadow, and was gone as the door slammed shut.

Rudolph went back to the car slowly. If this was love, the hell with it. He got into the car and closed the door. "That was a quick good night," Boylan said as he started the car. "In my day, we used to linger."

"Her folks like her to get in early."

Boylan drove through the town in the direction of Vanderhoff Street. Of course he knows where I live, Rudolph thought. He doesn't even bother to hide it.

"A charming girl, little Julie," Boylan said.

"Yeah."

"You do anything more than kiss her?"

"That's my business, sir," Rudolph said. Even in his anger at the man, he admired the way the words came out, clipped and cold. Nobody could treat Rudolph Jordache as though Rudolph Jordache was a cad.

"Of course it is," Boylan said. He sighed. "The temptation must be great. When I was your age . . ." He left it unfinished, a suggestion of a procession of virgins, virginal no more.

"By the way," he said in a flat conversational tone, "do you hear from your sister?"

"Sometimes," Rudolph said guardedly. She wrote to him care of Buddy Westerman. She didn't want her mother reading her letters. She was living in a Y.W.C.A. downtown in New York. She had been making the rounds of theatrical offices, looking for a job as an actress but producers weren't falling all over themselves to hire girls who had played Rosalind in high school. She hadn't found any work yet, but she loved New York. In her first letter she had apologized for being so mean to Rudolph the day she left, at the Port Philip House. She had been all churned up and not really responsible for what she was saying. But she still thought it was bad for him to stay on at home. The Jordache family was quicksand, she wrote. Nothing was going to change her opinion about that.

"Is she well?" Boylan asked.

"Okay."

"You know I know her," Boylan said, without emphasis.

"Yes."

"She spoke to you about me?"

"Not that I remember," Rudolph said.

"Ah-hah." It was difficult to know what Boylan meant to convey by this. "Do you have her address? I sometimes go down to New York and I might find the time to buy the child a good dinner."

"No, I don't have her address," Rudolph said. "She's moving."

"I see." Boylan saw through him, of course, but didn't press. "Well, if you do hear from her, let me know. I have something of hers she might like to have."

"Yeah."

Boylan turned into Vanderhoff and stopped in front of the bakery.

"Well, here we are," he said. "The home of honest toil." The sneer was plain. "I bid you good night, young man. It's been a most agreeable evening."

"Good night," Rudolph said. He got out of the car. "Thanks."

"Your sister told me you liked to fish," Boylan said. "We have quite a good stream on the property. It's stocked every year. I don't know why. Nobody goes near it anymore. If you'd like to give it a try, just come any time."

"Thank you," Rudolph said. Bribery. And he knew he would be bribed. The slippery innocence of trout. "I'll be along."

"Good," Boylan said. "I'll have my cook do up the fish for us and we can have dinner together. You're an interesting boy and I enjoy talking to you. Maybe when you come up, you'll have heard from your sister, with her new address."

"Maybe. Thanks again."

Boylan waved and drove off.

Rudolph went in and up to his room through the dark house. He could hear his father snoring. It was Saturday night and his father didn't work on Saturday night. Rudolph walked past his parents' door and up the steps to his room carefully. He didn't want to wake his mother and have to talk to her.

III

"I'm going to sell my body, I do declare," Mary Jane Hackett was saying. She came from Kentucky. "They don't want talent anymore, just bare, fruity flesh. The next call anybody puts out for showgirls I'm going to say, Farewell Stanislavsky, and wiggle my little old Dixie behind for pay."

Gretchen and Mary Jane Hackett were sitting in the cramped, poster-lined anteroom of the Nichols office on West 46th Street, waiting with a collection of other girls and young men to see Bayard Nichols. There were only three chairs behind the railing which divided the aspirants from the desk of Nichols's secretary, who was typing with spiky malice, her fingers stabbing at the keys, as though the English language were her personal enemy, to be dispatched as swiftly as possible.

The third chair in the anteroom was occupied by a character actress who wore a fur stole, even though it was eighty-five degrees in the shade outside.

Without losing a syllable on her machine, the secretary said, "Hello, dear," each time the door opened for another actor or actress. The word was that Nichols was casting a new play, six characters, four men, two women.

Mary Jane Hackett was a tall, slender, bosomless girl, who made her real money modeling. Gretchen was too curvy to model. Mary Jane Hackett had been in two flops on Broadway and had played a half-season of summer stock and already spoke like a veteran. She looked around her at the actors standing along the walls, lounging gracefully against the posters of Bayard Nichols's past productions. "You'd think, with all those hits," Mary Jane Hackett said, "going all the way back to the dark ages, 1935, for God's sake, Nichols could afford something grander than this foul little rat trap. At least air conditioning, for heaven's sake. He must have the first nickel he ever made. I don't know what I'm doing here. He dies if he has to pay more than minimum and even then, he gives you a long lecture about how Franklin D. Roosevelt has ruined this country."

Gretchen looked uneasily over at the secretary. The office was so small, there was no possibility that she hadn't heard Mary Jane. But the secretary typed on, stolidly disloyal, defeating English.

"Look at the size of them." Mary Jane gestured with a toss of her head at the young men. "They don't come up to my shoulder. If they wrote women's parts playing all three acts on their knees, I'd stand a chance of getting a job. The American theater, for God's sake! The men're midgets and if they're over five feet tall they're fairies."

"Naughty, naughty, Mary Jane," a tall boy said.

"When was the last time you kissed a girl?" Mary Jane demanded.

"Nineteen-twenty-eight," the boy said. "To celebrate the election of Herbert Hoover."

Everybody in the office laughed good-naturedly. Except the secretary. She kept on typing.

Even though she still had to get her first job, Gretchen enjoyed this new world into which she had been thrown. Everybody talked to everybody else, everybody called everybody by his first name; Alfred Lunt was Alfred to anyone who had ever been in a play with him, even if it was only for two lines at the beginning of the first act; everybody helped everybody else. If a girl heard of a part that was up for casting, she told all her friends and might even lend a particular dress for the interview. It was like being a member of a generous club, whose entrance requirements were not birth or money, but youth and ambition and belief in one another's talent.

In the basement of Walgreen's drugstore, where they all congregated over endless cups of coffee, to compare notes, to denigrate success, to mimic matinee idols and lament the death of the Group

Theatre, Gretchen was now accepted, and talked as freely as anyone about how idiotic critics were, about how Trigorin should be played in *The Sea Gull*, about how nobody acted like Laurette Taylor any more, about how certain producers tried to lay every girl who came into their offices. In two months, in the flood of youthful voices, speaking with the accents of Georgia, Maine, Texas, and Oklahoma, the mean streets of Port Philip had almost disappeared, a dot on the curve of memory's horizon.

She slept till ten in the morning, without feeling guilty. She went to young men's apartments and stayed there till all hours, rehearsing scenes, without worrying what people would think. A Lesbian at the Y.W.C.A., where she was staying until she found a job, had made a pass at her, but they were still good friends and sometimes had dinner and went to the movies together. She worked out in a ballet class three hours a week, to learn how to move gracefully on a stage, and she had changed the way she walked completely, keeping her head so still that she could have balanced a glass of water on it, even when going up and down stairs . . . Primitive serenity, the ex-ballerina who taught the class, called it.

She felt that when people looked at her they were sure she had been born in the city. She believed that she was no longer shy. She went out to dinners with some of the young actors and would-be directors whom she met at Walgreen's and in producers' offices and rehearsal classes and she paid for her own meals. She didn't mind cigarette smoke any more. She had no lovers. She had decided she would wait for that until she had a job. One problem at a time.

She had almost made up her mind to write Teddy Boylan and ask him to send down the red dress he had bought for her. There was no telling when she would be invited to that kind of party.

The door to the inner office opened and Bayard Nichols came out with a short, thin man in the suntan uniform of a captain in the Air Force. ". . . if anything comes up, Willie," Nichols was saying, "I'll let you know." He had a sad, resigned voice. He remembered only his failures. His eyes made a sweep of the people who were waiting to see him, like the beam of a lighthouse, sightless, casting shadows.

"I'll come by next week sometime and mooch a meal off you," the Captain said. He had a voice in the low tenor range, unexpected in a man who couldn't have weighed more than a hundred and thirty pounds and wasn't more than five feet, six inches, tall. He held himself very erect, as though he were still in Air Cadets' school. But his face was unmilitary, and his hair was chestnut, unruly, long for a sol-

dier, making you disbelieve the uniform. His forehead was high, a little bulgy, an unsettling hint of Beethoven, massive and brooding,
and his eyes were Wedgwood blue.

"You're still being paid by Uncle," Nichols was saying to the Captain. "My taxes. I'll mooch the meal off you." He sounded like a
man who would not cost much to feed. The theater was an
Elizabethan tragedy being played nightly in his digestive tract.
Murders stalked the duodenum. Ulcers lurked. He was always going
on the wagon next Monday. A psychiatrist or a new wife might help.

"Mr. Nichols . . ." The tall young man who had had the exchange with Mary Jane took a step away from the wall.

"Next week, Bernie," Mr. Nichols said. One more sweep of the
beam. "Miss Saunders," he said to the secretary, "can you come inside for a moment, please?" A languid, dyspeptic wave of the hand
and he disappeared into his office. The secretary sprayed a last mortal burst out of the typewriter, enfilading the Dramatists' Guild,
then stood up and followed him, carrying a shorthand pad. The door
closed behind her.

"Ladies and gentlemen," the Captain said to the room at large,
"we are all in the wrong business. I suggest Army surplus. The
demand for used bazookas will be overwhelming. Hello, Tiny." This
was for Mary Jane, who stood up, towering over him, and leaning
over, kissed his cheek.

"I'm glad to see you got home alive from that party, Willie,"
Mary Jane said.

"I confess, it was a little drunk out," the Captain said. "We were
washing the somber memories of combat from our souls."

"Drowning, I'd say," Mary Jane said.

"Don't begrudge us our poor little entertainments," the Captain
said. "Remember, you were modeling girdles while we were walking
on flak in the terrible skies over Berlin."

"Were you ever over Berlin, Willie?" Mary Jane asked.

"Of course not." He grinned at Gretchen, disclaiming valor. "I am
standing here patiently, Tiny," he said.

"Oh," she said. "Gretchen Jordache, Willie Abbott."

"I am happy I walked down 46th Street this morning," Abbott
said.

"Hello," said Gretchen. She nearly stood up. After all, he *was* a
captain.

"I suppose you're an actress," he said.

"Trying."

"Dreadful trade," Abbott said. "To quote Shakespeare on samphire?"

"Don't show off, Willie," Mary Jane said.

"You will make some man a fine wife and mother, Miss Jordache," Abbott said. "Mark my words. Why haven't I seen you before?"

"She just came to town," Mary Jane said, before Gretchen could answer. It was a warning, a go slow sign. Jealousy?

"Oh, the girls who have just come to town," Abbott said. "May I sit in your lap?"

"Willie!" Mary Jane said.

Gretchen laughed and Abbott laughed with her. He had very white, even, small teeth. "I was not mothered sufficiently as a child."

The door to the inner office opened and Miss Saunders came out. "Miss Jordache," she said, "Mr. Nichols can see you now."

Gretchen stood up, surprised that Miss Saunders remembered her name. This was only the third time she had been in the Nichols office. She hadn't talked to Nichols at all, ever. She brushed out the wrinkles in her dress nervously, as Miss Saunders held open the little swinging gate in the partition.

"Ask for a thousand dollars a week and ten per cent of the gross," Abbott said.

Gretchen went through the gate and toward Nichols's door. "Everybody else can go home," Miss Saunders said. "Mr. Nichols has an appointment for lunch in fifteen minutes."

"Beast," said the character woman with the stole.

"I just work here," Miss Saunders said.

Confusion of feelings. Pleasure and fright at the prospect of being tested for a job. Guilt because the others had been dismissed and she chosen. Loss, because now Mary Jane would leave with Willie Abbott. Flak above Berlin.

"See you later," Mary Jane said. She didn't say where. Abbott didn't say anything.

Nichols's office was a little larger than the anteroom. The walls were bare and his desk was piled with playscripts in leatherette covers. There were three yellowish wooden armchairs and the windows were coated with dust. It looked like the office of a man whose business was somehow shady and who had trouble meeting the rent on the first of the month.

Nichols stood up as she came into the office and said, "It was good of you to wait, Miss Jordache." He waved to a chair on one side of his desk and waited for her to sit down before he seated himself. He stared at her for a long time, without a word, studying her with the slightly sour expression of a man who is being offered a painting with a doubtful signature. She was so nervous that she was afraid her knees were shaking. "I suppose," she said, "you want to know about my experience. I don't have much to . . ."

"No," he said. "For the moment we can dispense with experience. Miss Jordache, the part I'm considering you for is frankly absurd." He shook his head sorrowfully, pitying himself for the grotesque deeds his profession forced him to perform. "Tell me, do you have any objections to playing in a bathing suit? In three bathing suits to be exact."

"Well . . ." She laughed uncertainly. "I guess it all depends." Idiot. Depends upon what? The size of the bathing suit? The size of the part? The size of her bosom? She thought of her mother. Her mother never went to the theater. Lucky.

"I'm afraid it isn't a speaking role," Nichols said. "The girl just walks across the stage three times, once in each act, in a different suit each time. The whole play takes place at a beach club."

"I see," Gretchen said. She was annoyed with Nichols. Because of him, she had let Mary Jane walk off with Willie Abbott, out into the city. *Captain, Captain* . . . Six million people. Get into an elevator and you are lost forever. For a walk-on. Practically naked.

"The girl is a symbol. Or so the playwright tells me," Nichols said, long hours of struggle with the casuistry of artists tolling like a ship-wreck's bell under the phrase. "Youth. Sensual beauty. The Mystery of Woman. The heartbreaking ephemeralness of the flesh. I am quoting the author. Every man in the audience must feel as she walks across the stage, 'My God, why am I married?' I am still quoting. Do you have a bathing suit?"

"I . . . I think so." She shook her head, annoyed with herself now. "Of course."

"Could you come to the Belasco at five with your bathing suit? The author and the director will be there."

"At five." She nodded. Farewell, Stanislavsky. She could feel the blush starting. Prig. A job was a job.

"That's most kind of you, Miss Jordache." Nichols stood, mourn-fully. She stood with him. He escorted her to the door and opened it for her. The anteroom was empty, except for Miss Saunders, blazing away.

"Forgive me," Nichols murmured obscurely. He went back into his office.

"So long," Gretchen said as she passed Miss Saunders.

"Goodbye, dear," Miss Saunders said, without looking up. She smelled of sweat. Ephemeral flesh. I am quoting.

Gretchen went out into the corridor. She didn't ring for the elevator until the blush had subsided.

When the elevator finally came, there was a young man in it carrying a Confederate officer's uniform and a cavalry saber in a scabbard. He was wearing the hat that went with the uniform, a dashing wide-brimmed felt, plumed. Under it his beaked, hard-boiled 1945 New York face looked like a misprint. "Will the wars never end?" he said amiably to Gretchen as she got into the elevator.

It was steamy in the little grilled car and she felt the sweat break out on her forehead. She dabbed at her forehead with a piece of Kleenex.

She went out into the street, geometric blocks of hot, glassy light and concrete shadow. Abbott and Mary Jane were standing in front of the building, waiting for her. She smiled. Six million people in the city. Let there be six million people. They had waited for her.

"What I thought," Willie was saying, "was lunch."

"I'm starving," Gretchen said.

They walked off toward lunch on the shady side of the street, the two tall girls, with the slender, small soldier between them, jaunty, remembering that other warriors had also been short men, Napoleon, Trotsky, Caesar, probably Tamerlane.

Naked, she regarded herself in the dressing-room mirror. She had gone out to Jones Beach with Mary Jane and two boys the Sunday before and the skin of her shoulders and arms and legs was a faint rosy tan. She didn't wear a girdle any more and in the summer heat she dispensed with stockings, so there were no prosaic ridges from clinging elastic on the smooth arch of her hips. She stared at her breasts. *I want to see how it tastes with whiskey on it.* She had had two Bloody Marys at lunch, with Mary Jane and Willie, and they had shared a bottle of white wine. Willie liked to drink. She put on her one-piece, black bathing suit. There were grains of sand in the crotch, from Jones Beach. She walked away from the mirror, then toward it, studying herself critically. The Mystery of Woman. Her walk was too modest. Remember Primitive Serenity. Willie and Mary Jane were waiting for her at the bar of the Algonquin, to find out how it all came out. She walked less modestly. There was a knock on the door. "Miss Jordache," the stage manager said, "we're ready when you are."

She began to blush as she opened the door. Luckily, in the harsh work light of the stage, nobody could tell.

She followed the stage manager. "Just walk across and back a couple of times," he said. There were shadowy figures sitting toward the tenth row of the darkened auditorium. The stage floor was unswept and the bare bricks of the back wall looked like the ruins of Rome. She was sure her blush could be seen all the way out to the street. "Miss Gretchen Jordache," the stage manager called out into the cavernous darkness. A message in a bottle over the night waves of seats. *I am adrift*. She wanted to run away.

She walked across the stage. She felt as though she were stumbling up a mountain. A zombie in a bathing suit.

There was no sound from the auditorium. She walked back. Still no sound. She walked back and forth twice more, worried about splinters in her bare feet.

"Thank you very much, Miss Jordache." Nichols's dejected voice, thin in the empty theater. "That's fine. If you'll stop in the office tomorrow we'll arrange about the contract."

It was as simple as that. Abruptly, she stopped blushing.

Willie was sitting alone at the small bar in the Algonquin, erect on a stool, nursing a whiskey in the greenish, submarine dusk that was the constant atmosphere of the room. He swiveled around to greet her as she came in carrying the little rubberized beach bag with her bathing suit in it. "The beautiful girl looks like a beautiful girl who has just landed herself a job as the Mystery of Woman at the Belasco Theatre," he said. "I am quoting." Over lunch, they had all laughed at Gretchen's account of her interview with Nichols.

She sat down on the stool next to his. "You're right," she said. "Sarah Bernhardt is on her way."

"She never could have handled it," Willie said. "She had a wooden leg. Do we drink champagne?"

"Where's Mary Jane?"

"Gone. She had a date."

"We drink champagne." They both laughed.

When the barman set their glasses in front of them, they drank to Mary Jane. Delicious absence. It was the second time in her life Gretchen had drunk champagne. The hushed, gaudy room in the four-story house on a side street, the one-way mirror, the magnificent whore with the baby face, stretched triumphantly on the wide bed.

"We have many choices," Willie said. "We can stay here and drink wine all night. We can have dinner. We can make love. We can go to a party on Fifty-sixth Street. Are you a party girl?"

"I would like to be," Gretchen said. She ignored the "make love." Obviously it was a joke. Everything was a joke with Willie. She had the feeling that even in the war, at the worst times, he had made fun of the bursting shells, the planes diving in, the flaming wings. Images from newsreels, war movies. *"Old Johnny bought it today, chaps. This is my round."* Was it like that? She would ask him later, when she knew him better.

"The party it is," he said. "There's no hurry. It'll go on all night. Now, before we fling ourselves into the mad whirl of pleasure, are there things I should know about you?" Willie poured himself another glass of champagne. His hand was not quite steady and the bottle made a little clinking music against the rim of the glass.

"What kind of things?"

"Begin at the beginning," he said. "Place of residence?"

"The Y.W.C.A. downtown," she said.

"Oh, God." He groaned. "If I dress in drag could I pass as a young Christian woman and rent a room next to yours? I'm petite and I have a light beard. I could borrow a wig. My father always wanted daughters."

"I'm afraid not," Gretchen said. "The old lady at the desk can tell a boy from a girl at a hundred yards."

"Other facts. Fellas?"

"Not at the moment," she said after a slight hesitation. "And you?"

"The Geneva Convention stipulates that when captured, a prisoner of war must only reveal his name, rank, and serial number." He grinned at her and laid his hand on hers. "No," he said. "I'll tell you everything. I shall bare my soul. I shall tell you, in many installments, how I wished to murder my father when I was a babe in a crib and how I was not weaned from my mother's breast until I was three and what us boys used to do behind the barn with the neighbor's daughter in the good old summertime." His face became serious, the forehead prominent, as he brushed back his hair with his hand. "You might as well know now as later," he said. "I'm married."

The champagne burned in her throat. "I liked you better when you were joking," she said.

"Me, too," he said soberly. "Still, there's a brighter side to it. I'm working on a divorce. The lady found other divertissements while daddy was away playing soldier."

"Where is she? Your wife?" The words came out leadenly. Absurd, she thought. I've only known him for a few hours.

"California," he said. "Hollywood. I guess I have a thing for actresses."

A continent away. Burning deserts, impassable peaks, the fruited plain. Beautiful, wide America. "How long have you been married?"

"Five years."

"How old are you anyway?" she asked.

"Will you promise not to discard me if I tell you the truth?"

"Don't be silly. How old?"

"Twenty fucking nine," he said. "Ah, God."

"I'd have said twenty-three at the outside," Gretchen shook her head wonderingly. "What's the secret?"

"Drink and riotous living," Willie said. "My face is my misfortune. I look like an ad for the boys' clothing department of Saks. Women of twenty-two are ashamed to be seen with me in public places. When I made captain the Group Commander said, 'Willie, here's your gold star for being a good boy in school this month.' Maybe I ought to grow a moustache."

"Wee Willie Abbott," Gretchen said. His false youthfulness was reassuring to her. She thought of the gross, dominating maturity of Teddy Boylan. "What did you do before the war?" she asked. She wanted to know everything about him. "How do you know Bayard Nichols?"

"I worked for him on a couple of shows. I'm a flak. I'm in the worst business in the world. I'm a publicity man. Do you want your picture in the paper, little girl?" The disgust was not put on. If he wanted to look older, there was no need to grow a moustache. All he had to do was talk about his profession. "When I went into the Army, I thought I'd finally get away from it. So they looked up my card and put me in public relations. I ought to be arrested for impersonating an officer. Have some more champagne." He poured for them again, the bottle clinking an icy code of distress against the glasses, the nicotined fingers trembling minutely.

"But you were overseas. You did fly," she said. During lunch, he had talked about England.

"A few missions. Just enough to get an Air Medal, so I wouldn't feel naked in London. I was a passenger. I admired other men's wars."

"Still, you could've been killed." His bitterness disturbed her and she would have liked to move him out of it.

"I'm too young to die, Colonel." He grinned. "Finish your bubbly. They're waiting for us all over town."

"When do you get out of the Air Force?"

"I'm on terminal leave now," he said. "I wear the uniform because I can get into shows free with it. I also have to go over to the hospital on Staten Island a couple of times a week for therapy for my back and nobody'd believe I was a Captain if I didn't wear the suit."

"Therapy? Were you wounded?"

"Not really. We made an aggressive landing and bounced. I had a little operation on my spine. Twenty years from now I'll say the scar came from shrapnel. All drunk up, like a good little girl?"

"Yes," Gretchen said. The wounded were everywhere. Arnold Simms, in the maroon bathrobe, sitting on the table and looking down at the foot that no longer was any good for running. Talbot Hughes, with everything torn out of his throat, dying silently in his corner. Her own father, limping from another war.

Willie paid for the drinks and they left the bar. Gretchen wondered how he could walk so erectly with a bad back.

Twilight made a lavender puzzle out of New York as they came out of the bar onto the street. The stone heat of the day had gentled down to a meadowed balminess and they walked against a soft breeze, hand in hand. The air was like a drift of pollen. A three-quarter moon, pale as china in the fading sky, sailed over the towered office buildings.

"You know what I like about you?" Willie said.

"What?"

"You didn't say you wanted to go home and change your dress when I said we were going to a party."

She didn't feel she had to tell him she was wearing her best dress and had nothing to change to. It was cornflower-blue linen, buttoned all the way down the front, with short sleeves and a tight red cloth belt. She had changed into it when she had gone down to the Y.W.C.A. after lunch to get her bathing suit. Six ninety-five at Ohrbach's. The only piece of clothing she had bought since she came to New York. "Will I shame you in front of your fine friends?" she said.

"A dozen of my fine friends will come up to you tonight and ask for your telephone number," he said.

"Shall I give it to them?"

"Upon pain of death," Willie said.

They went slowly up Fifth Avenue, looking in all the windows. Finchley's was displaying tweed sports jackets. "I fancy myself in one of those," Willie said. "Give me bulk. Abbott, the tweedy Squire."

"You're not tweedy," Gretchen said. "I fancy you smooth."

"Smooth I shall be," Willie said.

They stopped a long time in front of Brentano's and looked at the books. There was an arrangement of recent plays in the window. Odets, Hellman, Sherwood, Kaufman and Hart. "The literary life," Willie said. "I have a confession to make. I'm writing a play. Like every other flak."

"It will be in the window," she said.

"Please God, it will be in the window," he said. "Can you act?"

"I'm a one-part actress. The Mystery of Woman."

"I am quoting," he said. They laughed. They knew the laughter was foolish, but it was dear because it was for their own private joke.

When they reached Fifty-fifth Street, they turned off Fifth Avenue. Under the St. Regis canopy, a wedding party was disembarking from taxis. The bride was very young, very slender, a white tulip. The groom was a young infantry lieutenant, no hashmarks, no campaign ribbons, razor-nicked, peach-cheeked, untouched.

"Bless you, my children," Willie said as they passed.

The bride smiled, a whitecap of joy, blew a kiss to them. "Thank you, sir," said the lieutenant, restraining himself from throwing a salute, by the book.

"It's a good night for a wedding," Willie said as they walked on. "Temperature in the low eighties, visibility unlimited, no war on at the moment."

The party was between Park and Lexington. As they crossed Park, at Fifty-fifth Street, a taxi swung around the corner and down toward Lexington. Mary Jane was sitting alone in the taxi. The taxi stopped midway down the street and Mary Jane got out and ran into a five-story building.

"Mary Jane," Willie said. "See her?"

"Uhuh." They were walking more slowly now.

Willie looked across at Gretchen, studying her face. "I have an idea," he said. "Let's have our own party."

"I was hoping you'd say that," Gretchen said.

"Company, about face," he barked out. He made a smart military turn, clicking his heels. They started walking back toward Fifth Avenue. "I don't cotton to the idea of all those guys asking for your telephone number," he said.

She squeezed his hand. She was almost sure now that Willie had slept with Mary Jane, but she squeezed his hand just the same.

They went to the Oak Room Bar of the Plaza and had mint juleps in frosted pewter mugs. "For Kentucky's sake," Willie explained. He didn't mind mixing his drinks. Scotch, champagne, bourbon. "I am an exploder of myths," he said.

After the mint juleps they left the Plaza and got onto a Fifth Avenue bus heading downtown. They sat on the top deck, in the open air. Willie took off his overseas cap with the two silver bars and the officer's braid. The wind of the bus's passage tumbled his hair, making him look younger than ever. Gretchen wanted to take his head and put it down on her breast and kiss the top of his head, but there were people all around them so she took his cap and ran her fingers along the braid and the two bars instead.

They got off the bus at Eighth Street and found a table on the sidewalk at the Brevoort and Willie ordered a Martini. "To improve my appetite," he said. "Give notice to the gastric juices. Red Alert."

The Algonquin, the Plaza, the Brevoort, a job, a captain. All in one day. It was a cornucopia of firsts.

They had melon and a small roast chicken for dinner and a bottle of California red wine from the Napa Valley. "Patriotism," Willie said. "And because we won the war." He drank most of the bottle himself. Nothing of what he had drunk seemed to affect him. His eyes were clear, his speech the same.

They weren't talking much any more, just looking at each other across the table. If she couldn't kiss him soon, Gretchen thought, they would carry her off to Bellevue.

Willie ordered brandy for both of them after the coffee. What with paying for lunch and all the eating and drinking of the evening, Gretchen figured that it must have cost Willie at least fifty dollars since noon. "Are you a rich man?" she asked, as he was paying the bill.

"Rich in spirit only," Willie said. He turned his wallet upside down and six bills floated down onto the table. Two were for a hundred apiece, the rest were fives. "The complete Abbott fortune," he said. "Shall I mention you in my will?"

Two hundred and twenty dollars. She was shocked at how little it was. She still had more than that in the bank herself, from Boylan's eight hundred, and she never paid more than ninety-five cents for a meal. Her father's blood? The thought made her uneasy.

She watched Willie gather up the bills and stuff them carelessly into his pocket. "The war taught me the value of money," he said.

"Did you grow up rich?" she asked.

"My father was a customs inspector, on the Canadian border," he said. "And honest. And there were six children. We lived like kings. Meat three times a week."

"I worry about money," she confessed. "I saw what not having any did to my mother."

"Drink hearty," Willie said. "You will not be your mother's daughter. I will turn to my golden typewriter in the very near future."

They finished their brandies. Gretchen was beginning to feel a little lightheaded, but not drunk. Definitely not drunk.

"Is it the opinion of this meeting," Willie said, as they stood up from the table and passed through the boxed hedges of the terrace onto the avenue, "that a drink is in order?"

"I'm not drinking any more tonight," she said.

"Look to women for wisdom," Willie said. "Earth mother. Priestesses of the oracle. Delphic pronouncements, truth cunningly hidden in enigmas. No more drink shall be drunk tonight. Taxi!" he called.

"We can walk to the Y.W.C.A. from here," she said. "It's only about fifteen minutes . . ."

The taxi braked to a halt and Willie opened the door and she got in.

"The Hotel Stanley," Willie said to the driver as he got into the cab. "On Seventh Avenue."

They kissed. Oasis of lips. Champagne, Scotch, Kentucky mint, red wine of Napa Valley in Spanish California, brandy, gift of France. She pushed his head down onto her breast and nuzzled into the thick silkiness of his hair. The hard bone of skull under it. "I've been wanting to do this all day," she said. She held him against her, child soldier. He opened the top two buttons of her dress, his fingers swift, and kissed the cleft between her breasts. Over his cradled head, she could see the driver, his back toward her, busy with red lights, green lights, rash pedestrians, what the passengers do is the passengers' business. His photograph stared at her from the lighted tag. A man of about forty with glaring, defiant eyes and kidney trouble, a man who had seen everything, who knew the whole city. Eli Lefkowitz, his name, prominently displayed by police order. She would remember his name forever. Eli Lefkowitz, unwatching charioteer of love.

There was little traffic at this hour and the cab swept uptown. Airman in the quick sky.

One last kiss for Eli Lefkowitz and she buttoned her dress, proper for the bridal suite.

The facade of the Hotel Stanley was imposing. The architect had been to Italy, or had seen a photograph. The Doges' Palace, plus Walgreen's. The Adriatic coast of Seventh Avenue.

She stood to one side of the lobby while Willie went to the desk for the key. Potted palms, Italianate dark wood chairs, glaring light. Traffic of women with the faces of police matrons and hair the frizzed blonde of cheap dolls. Horse-players in corners, G.I.'s on travel orders, two show girls, high-assed, long-lashed, an old lady in men's work shoes, reading *Seventeen*, somebody's mother, traveling salesmen after a bad day, detectives, alert for Vice.

She drifted toward the elevator shaft, as though she were alone, and did not look at Willie when he came up to her with the key. Deception easily learned. They didn't speak in the elevator.

"Seventh floor," Willie said to the operator.

There was no hint of Italy on the seventh floor. The architect's inspiration had run out on the way up. Narrow corridors, peeling dark-brown metal doors, uncarpeted tile floors that must have once been white. *Sorry, folks, we can't kid you anymore, you might as well know the facts, you're in America.*

They walked down a narrow corridor, her heels making a noise like a pony trotting. Their shadows wavered on the dim walls, uncertain poltergeists left over from the 1925 boom. They stopped at a door like all the other doors. 777. On Seventh Avenue, on the seventh floor. The magic orderliness of numbers.

Willie worked the key and they went into Room 777 of the Stanley Hotel on Seventh Avenue. "You'll be happier if I don't put on a light," Willie said. "It's a hole. But it's the only thing I could get. And even so, they'll only let me stay five days. The town's full up."

But enough light filtered in from electric New York outside the chipped tin blinds, so that she could see what the room was like. A small cell, a slab of a single bed, one upright wooden chair, a basin, no bathroom, a shadowy pile of officer's shirts on the bureau.

Deliberately, he began to undress her. The red cloth belt first, then the top button of her dress and then, going all the way, one button after another. She counted with his movements as he kneeled before her. ". . . seven, eight, nine, ten, eleven . . ." What conferences, what soul searching in the workrooms farther down on Seventh Avenue to come to that supreme decision—not ten buttons, not twelve buttons, ELEVEN!

"It's a full day's work," Willie said. He took the dress from her shoulders and put it neatly over the back of the chair. Officer and gentleman. She turned around so that he could undo her brassiere. Boylan's training. The light coming in through the blinds cut her into a tiger's stripes. Willie fumbled at the hooks on her back. "They must finally invent something better," he said.

She laughed and helped him. The brassiere fell away. She turned to him again and he gently pulled her innocent white cotton panties down to her ankles. She kicked off her shoes. She went over to the bed and with a single movement ripped off the cover and the blanket and top sheet. The linen wasn't fresh. Had Mary Jane slept there? No matter.

She stretched out on the bed, her legs straight, her ankles touching, her hands at her sides. He stood over her. He put his hand between her thighs. Clever fingers. "The Vale of Delight," he said.

"Get undressed," she said.

She watched him rip off his tie and unbutton his shirt. When he took his shirt off, she saw that he was wearing a medical corset with hooks and laces. The corset went almost up to his shoulders and down past the web belt of his trousers. That's why he stands so erectly, the young Captain. *We made an aggressive landing and bounced.* The punished flesh of soldiers.

"Did you ever make love to a man with a corset before?" Willie asked, as he started pulling at the laces.

"Not that I remember," she said.

"It's only temporary," he said. He was embarrassed by it. "A couple of months more. Or so they tell me at the hospital." He was struggling with the laces.

"Should I turn the light on?" she asked.

"I couldn't bear it."

The telephone rang.

They looked at each other. Neither of them moved. If they didn't move, perhaps it wouldn't ring again.

The telephone rang again.

"I guess I'd better answer it," he said.

"I guess."

He picked up the phone from the bedtable next to her head. "Yes?"

"Captain Abbott?" Willie held the phone loosely and she could hear clearly. It was a man's voice, aggrieved.

"Yes," Willie said.

"We believe there is a young lady in your room." The royal We, from the Mediterranean throne room.

"I believe there is," Willie said. "What of it?"

"You have a single room," the voice said, "for the occupancy of one individual."

"All right," Willie said. "Give me a double room. What's the number?"

"I'm sorry, every room is occupied," the voice said. "We're all booked until November."

"Let's you and I pretend this is a double room, Jack," said Willie. "Put it on my bill."

"I'm afraid I can't do that," the voice said. "Room number 777 is definitely a single room for a single occupancy. I'm afraid the young lady will have to leave."

"The young lady isn't *living* here, Jack," Willie said. "She isn't occupying anything. She's visiting me. Anyway, she's my wife."

"Do you have your marriage certificate, Captain?"

"Dear," Willie said loudly, holding the phone out over Gretchen's head, "have you got our marriage certificate?"

"It's home," Gretchen said, close to the receiver.

"Didn't I tell you never to travel without it?" Marital annoyance.

"I'm sorry, dear," Gretchen said meekly.

"She left it home," Willie said into the phone. "We'll show it to you tomorrow. I'll have it sent down by special delivery."

"Captain, young ladies are against the rules of the establishment," the voice said.

"Since when?" Willie was getting angry now. "This dive is famous from here to Bangkok as a haunt of pimps and bookies and hustlers and dope peddlers and receivers of stolen goods. One honest policeman could fill the Tombs from your guest list."

"We are under new management," the voice said. "A well-known chain of respectable hotels. We are creating a different image. If the young lady is not out of there in five minutes, Captain, I'm coming up."

Gretchen was out of bed now and pulling on her panties.

"No," Willie said beseechingly.

She smiled gently at him.

"Fuck you, Jack," Willie said into the phone and slammed it down. He started to do up his corset, pulling fiercely at the laces.

"Go fight a war for the bastards," he said. "And you can't find another room at this hour in the goddamn town for love or money."

Gretchen laughed. Willie glared at her for a moment, then he burst into laughter too. "Next time," he said, "remember for Christ's sake to bring your marriage license."

They walked grandly through the lobby, blatantly arm in arm, pretending they were not defeated. Half the people in the lobby looked like house detectives, so there was no way of knowing which one was the voice on the telephone.

They didn't want to leave each other, so they went over to Broadway and had orangeades at a Nedick stand, faint taste of tropics in a Northern latitude, then continued on to 42nd Street and went into an all-night movie and sat among derelicts and insomniacs and perverts and soldiers waiting for a bus and watched Humphrey Bogart playing Duke Mantee in *The Petrified Forest.*

When the picture ended, they still didn't want to leave each other, so they saw *The Petrified Forest* over again.

When they got out of the movie house, they still didn't want to leave each other, so he walked her all the way down to the Y.W.C.A., among silent, empty buildings which looked like fortresses that had fallen, no quarter shown.

Dawn was breaking as they kissed in front of the Y.W.C.A. Willie looked with loathing at the dark bulk of the building, one lamp on at the entrance, lighting proper young ladies out on the town to their proper beds. "Do you think that in the entire, glorious history of this structure," he said, "that anybody got laid here?"

"I doubt it," she said.

"It sends shivers down your spine, doesn't it?" he said gloomily. He shook his head. "Don Juan," he said. "The corseted lover. Call me schmuck."

"Don't take it so hard," she said. "There're other nights."

"Like when?"

"Like tonight," she said.

"Like tonight," he repeated soberly. "I can live through the day. I suppose. I'll spend the hours in good works. Like looking for a hotel room. It may be in Coney Island or Babylon or Pelham Bay, but I'll find a room. For Captain and Mrs. Abbott. Bring along a valise, for Queen Victoria. Fill it with old copies of *Time*, in case we get bored and want something to read."

A last kiss and he strode off, small and defeated in the fresh dawn

light. It was a lucky thing he would still be in uniform tonight. In civilian clothes, she doubted that any desk clerk would believe he was
old enough to be married.

When he had disappeared, she climbed the steps and went
demurely into the Y.W.C.A. The old lady at the desk leered at her
knowingly, but Gretchen took her key and said, "Good night," as
though the dawn coming in through the windows was merely a
clever optical illusion.

Chapter 8

I

As Clothilde washed his hair, he sat in Uncle Harold's and Tante
Elsa's big bathtub, steaming in the hot water, his eyes closed, drows-
ing, like an animal sunning himself on a rock. Uncle Harold, Tante
Elsa, and the two girls were at Saratoga for their annual two-week
holiday and Tom and Clothilde had the house to themselves. It was
Sunday and the garage was closed. In the distance a church bell was
ringing.

The deft fingers massaged his scalp, caressed the back of his neck
through foaming, perfumed suds. Clothilde had bought a special
soap for him in the drugstore with her own money. Sandalwood.
When Uncle Harold came back, he'd have to go back to good old
Ivory, five cents a cake. Uncle Harold would suspect something was
up if he smelled the sandalwood.

"Now, rinse, Tommy," Clothilde said.

Tom lay back in the water and stayed under as her fingers worked
vigorously through his hair, rinsing out the suds. He came up
blowing.

"Now your nails," Clothilde said. She kneeled beside the tub and
scrubbed with the nail brush at the black grease ground into the skin
of his hands and under his nails. Clothilde was naked and her dark
hair was down, falling in a cascade over her low, full breasts. Even
kneeling humbly, she didn't look like anybody's servant.

His hands were pink, his nails rosy, as Clothilde scrubbed away, her wedding ring glistening in foam. Clothilde put the brush on the rim of the tub, after a last meticulous examination. "Now the rest," she said.

He stood up in the bath. She rose from her knees and began to soap him down. She had wide, firm hips and strong legs. Her skin was dark and with her flattish nose, wide cheek bones, and long straight hair she looked like pictures he had seen in history books of Indian girls greeting the first white settlers in the forest. There was a scar on her right arm, a jagged crescent of white. Her husband had hit her with a piece of kindling. Long ago, she said. In Canada. She didn't want to talk about her husband. When he looked at her something funny happened in his throat and he didn't know whether he wanted to laugh or cry.

Motherly hands touched him lightly, lovingly, doing unmotherly things. Between his buttocks, slipperiness of scented soap, between his thighs, promises. An orchestra in his balls. Woodwinds and flutes. Hearing Tante Elsa's phonograph blaring all the time, he had come to love Wagner. "We are finally civilizing the little fox," Tante Elsa had said, proud of her unexpected cultural influence.

"Now the feet," Clothilde said.

He obediently put a foot up on the rim of the tub, like a horse being shod. Bending, careless of her hair, she soaped between his toes and used a washcloth devotedly, as though she were burnishing church silver. He learned that even his toes could give him pleasure.

She finished with his other foot and he stood there, glistening in the steam. She looked at him, studying him. "A boy's body," she said. "You look like Saint Sebastian. Without the arrows." She wasn't joking. She never joked. It was the first intimation of his life that his body might have a value beyond its functions. He knew that he was strong and quick and that his body was good for games and fighting, but it had never occurred to him that it would delight anybody just to look at it. He was a little ashamed that he had no hair yet on his chest and that it was so sparse down below.

With a quick motion of her hands, she did her hair up in a knot on top of her head. Then she stepped into the bathtub, too. She took the bar of soap and the suds began to glisten on her skin. She soaped herself all over methodically, without coquetry. Then they slid down into the tub together and lay quietly with their arms around each other.

If Uncle Harold and Tante Elsa and the two girls fell sick and died in Saratoga, he would stay in this house in Elysium forever.

When the water began to cool they got out of the tub and Clothilde took one of the big special towels of Tante Elsa and dried him off. While she was scrubbing out the tub, he went into the Jordaches' bedroom and lay down on the freshly made crisp bed.

Bees buzzed outside the screened windows, green shades against the sun made a grotto of the bedroom, the bureau against the wall was a ship on a green sea. He would burn a thousand crosses for one such afternoon.

She came padding in, her hair down now, for another occasion. On her face the soft, distant, darkly concentrated expression he had come to look for, yearn for.

She lay down beside him. Wave of sandalwood. Her hand reached out for him, carefully. The touch of love, cherishing him, an act apart from all other acts, profoundly apart from the giggly high-school lust of the twins and the professional excitement of the woman on McKinley Street back in Port Philip. It was incredible to him that anyone could want to touch him like that.

Sweetly, gently, he took her while the bees foraged in the window boxes. He waited for her, adept now, taught, well and quickly taught, by that wide Indian body, and when it was over, they lay back side by side and he knew that he would do anything for her, anything, any time she asked.

"Stay here." A last kiss under the throat. "I will call you when I am ready."

She slipped out of the bed and he heard her in the bathroom, dressing, then going softly down the stairs toward the kitchen. He lay there, staring up at the ceiling, all gratitude, and all bitterness. He hated being sixteen years old. He could do nothing for her. He could accept her rich offering of herself, he could sneak into her room at night, but he couldn't even take her for a walk in the park or give her a scarf as a gift, because a tongue might wag, or Tante Elsa's sharp eye might search out the new color in the warped bureau drawer in the room behind the kitchen. He couldn't take her away from this grinding house in which she slaved. If only he were twenty . . .

Saint Sebastian.

She came silently into the room. "Come eat," she said.

He spoke from the bed. "When I'm twenty," he said, "I'm coming here and taking you away."

She smiled. "My man," she said. She fingered her wedding ring absently. "Don't take long. The food is hot."

He went into the bathroom and dressed and went on down to the kitchen.

There were flowers on the kitchen table, between the two places laid out there. Phlox. Deep blue. She did the gardening, too. She had a knowing hand with flowers. "She's a pearl, my Clothilde," he had heard Tante Elsa say. "The roses're twice as big this year."

"You should have your own garden," Tom said as he sat before his place. What he could not give her in reality he offered in intention. He was barefooted and the linoleum felt cool and smooth against his soles. His hair, still damp, was neatly combed, the blond, tight curls glistening darkly. She liked everything neat and shining clean, pots and pans, mahogany, front halls, boys. It was the least he could do for her.

She put a bowl of fish chowder in front of him.

"I said you should have your own garden," he repeated.

"Drink your soup," she said, and sat down at her own place across from him.

A leg of lamb, small, tender and rare, came next, served with parsleyed new potatoes, roasted in the same pan with the lamb. There was a heaped bowl of buttered young string beans and a salad of crisp romaine and tomatoes. A plate of fresh, hot biscuits stood to one side, and a big slab of sweet butter, next to a frosted pitcher of milk.

Gravely, she watched him eat, smiled when he offered his plate again. During the family's holiday, she got on the bus every morning to go to the next town to do her shopping, using her own money. The shopkeepers of Elysium would have been sure to report back to Mrs. Jordache about the fine meats and carefully chosen first fruits for the feasts prepared in her kitchen in her absence.

For dessert there was vanilla ice cream that Clothilde had made that morning, and hot chocolate sauce. She knew her lover's appetites. She had announced her love with two bacon and tomato sandwiches. Its consummation demanded richer fare.

"Clothilde," Tom said, "why do you work here?"

"Where should I work?" She was surprised. She spoke in a low voice, always without inflection. There was a hint of French Canada in her speech. She almost said *v* for *w*.

"Anyplace. In a store. In a factory. Not as a servant."

"I like being in a house. Cooking meals," she said. "It is not so bad. Your aunt is proper with me. She appreciates me. It was kind of her to take me in. I came here, two years ago, I didn't know a soul, I didn't have a penny. I like the little girls very much. They are always so clean. What could I do in a store or a factory? I am very slow at adding and subtracting and I'm frightened of machines. I like being in a house."

"Somebody else's house," Tom said. It was intolerable that those two fat slobs could order Clothilde around.

"This week," she said, touching his hand on the table, "it is our house."

"We can never go out with each other."

"So?" She shrugged. "What are we missing?"

"We have to sneak around," he cried. He was growing angry with her.

"So?" She shrugged again. "There are many things worth sneaking around for. Not everything good is out in the open. Maybe I like secrets." Her face gleamed with one of her rare soft smiles.

"This afternoon . . ." he said stubbornly, trying to plant the seed of revolt, arouse that placid peasant docility. "After a . . . a *banquet* like this . . ." He waved his hand over the table. "It's not right. We should go out, do something, not just sit around."

"What is there to do?" she asked seriously.

"There's a band concert in the park," he said. "A baseball game."

"I get enough music from Tante Elsa's phonograph," she said. "You go to the baseball game for me and tell me who won. I will be very happy here, cleaning up and waiting for you to come home. As long as you come home, I do not want anything else, Tommy."

"I'm not going anywhere without you today," he said, giving up. He stood up. "I'll wipe the dishes."

"There's no need," she said.

"I'll wipe the dishes," he said, with great authority.

"My man," she said. She smiled again, beyond ambition, confident in her simplicities.

The next evening after work, on his way home from the garage on his wobbly Iver Johnson he was passing the town library. On a sudden impulse, he stopped, leaned the bike against a railing, and went in. He hardly read anything at all, not even the sports pages of the newspapers, and he was not a frequenter of libraries. Perhaps in reaction to his brother and his sister, always with their noses in books, and full of fancy sneering ideas.

The hush of the library and the unwelcoming examination of his grease-stained clothes by the lady librarian made him ill at ease, and he wandered around among the shelves, not knowing which book of all these thousands held the information he was looking for. Finally, he had to go to the desk and ask the lady.

"Excuse me," he said. She was stamping cards, making out prison sentences for books with a little mean snapping motion of her wrist.

"Yes?" She looked up, unfriendly. She could tell a non-book-lover at a glance.

"I want to find out something about Saint Sebastian, ma'am," he said.

"What do you want to find out about him?"

"Just anything," he said, sorry he had come in now.

"Try the Encyclopaedia Britannica," the lady said. "In the Reference Room. SARS to SORC." She knew her library, the lady.

"Thank you very much, ma'am." He decided that from now on he would change his clothes at the garage and use Coyne's sandsoap to get out the top layer of grease from his skin, at least. Clothilde would like that better, too. No use being treated like a dog when you could avoid it.

It took him ten minutes to find the Encyclopaedia Britannica. He pulled out SARS to SORC and took it over to a table and sat down with the book. SEA-URCHIN–SEA-WOLF, SEA-WRACK–SEBASTIANO DEL PIOMBO. The things that some people fooled with!

There it was, "SEBASTIAN, ST., a Christian martyr whose festival is celebrated on Jan. 20." Just one paragraph. He couldn't have been so damned important.

"After the archers had left him for dead," Tom read, "a devout woman, Irene, came by night to take his body away for burial, but finding him still alive, carried him to her house, where his wounds were dressed. No sooner had he wholly recovered than he hastened to confront the emperor, who ordered him to be instantly carried off and beaten to death with rods."

Twice, for Christ's sake, Tom thought. Catholics were nuts. But he still didn't know why Clothilde had said Saint Sebastian when she had looked at him naked in the bathtub.

He read on. "St. Sebastian is specially invoked against the plague. As a young and beautiful soldier, he is a favorite subject of sacred art, being most generally represented undraped, and severely though not mortally wounded with arrows."

Tom closed the book thoughtfully. "A young and beautiful soldier, being most generally represented undraped . . ." Now he knew. Clothilde. Wonderful Clothilde. Loving him without words, but saying it with her religion, with her food, her body, everything.

Until today he had thought he was kind of funny looking, a snotty kid with a flat face and a sassy expression. Saint Sebastian. The next time he saw those two beauties, Rudolph and Gretchen, he could look them straight in the eye. I have been compared by an older, experienced woman to Saint Sebastian, a young and beautiful soldier. For the first time since he had left home he was sorry he wasn't going to see his brother and sister that night.

He got up and put the book away. He was about to leave the reference room when it occurred to him that Clothilde was a Saint's name, too. He searched through the volumes and took out CASTIR to COLE.

Practiced now, he found what he was looking for quickly, although it wasn't Clothilde, but "CLOTILDA, ST. (d. 544) daughter of the Burgundian king Chilperic, and wife of Clovis, king of the Franks."

Tom thought of Clothilde sweating over the stove in the Jordache kitchen and washing Uncle Harold's underwear and was saddened. Daughter of the Burgundian king Chilperic, and wife of Clovis, king of the Franks. People didn't think of the future when they named babies.

He read the rest of the paragraph, but Clotilda didn't seem to have done all that much, converting her husband and building churches and stuff like that, and getting into trouble with her family. The book didn't say what entrance requirements she had met to be made a saint.

Tom put the book away, eager to get home to Clothilde. But he stopped at the desk to say, "Thank you, ma'am," to the lady. He was conscious of a sweet smell. There was a bowl of narcissus on the desk, spears of green, with white flowers, set in a bed of multicolored pebbles. Then, speaking without thinking, he said, "Can I take out a card, please?"

The lady looked at him, surprised. "Have you ever had a card anywhere before?" she asked.

"No, ma'am. I never had the time to read before."

The lady gave him a queer look, but pulled out a blank card and asked him his name, age, and address. She printed the information in a funny backward way on the card, stamped the date, and handed the card to him.

"Can I take out a book right away?" he asked.

"If you want," she said.

He went back to the Encyclopaedia Britannica and took out SARS to SORC. He wanted to have a good look at that paragraph and try to memorize it. But when he stood at the desk to have it stamped, the lady shook her head impatiently. "Put that right back," she said. "That's not supposed to leave the Reference Room."

He returned to the Reference Room and put the volume back. They keep yapping at you to read, he thought resentfully, and then when you finally say okay, I'll read, they throw a rule in your face.

Still, walking out of the library, he patted his back pocket several times, to feel the nice stiffness of the card in there.

There was fried chicken, mashed potatoes, and apple sauce for dinner and blueberry pie for dessert. He and Clothilde ate in the kitchen, not saying much.

When they had finished and Clothilde was clearing off the dishes, he went over to her and held her in his arms and said, "Clotilda, daughter of the Burgundian king Chilperic, and wife of Clovis, king of the Franks."

She looked at him, wide-eyed. "What's that?"

"I wanted to find out where your name came from," he said. "I went to the library. You're a king's daughter and a king's wife."

She looked at him a long time, her arms around his waist. Then she kissed him on the forehead, gratefully, as if he had brought home a present for her.

II

There were two fish in the straw creel already, speckled on the bed of wet fern. The stream was well stocked, as Boylan had said. There was a dam at one edge of the property where the stream entered the estate. From there the stream wound around the property to another dam with a wire fence to keep the fish in, at the other edge of the property. From there it fell in a series of cascades down toward the Hudson.

Rudolph wore old corduroys and a pair of fireman's rubber boots, bought secondhand and too big for him, to make his way along the banks, with the thorns and the interlaced branches tearing at him. It was a long walk up the hill from the last stop on the local bus line, but it was worth it. His own private trout stream. He hadn't seen Boylan or anybody else on the property any of the times he had come up there. The stream was never closer at any point to the main house than five hundred yards.

It had rained the night before and there was rain in the gray, late-afternoon air. The brook was a bit muddy and the trout were shy. But just slowly moving upstream, getting the fly lightly, lightly, where he wanted it, with nobody around, and the only sound the water tumbling over the rocks, was happiness enough. School began again in a week and he was making the most of the last days of the holiday.

He was near one of the stream's two ornamental bridges, working the water, when he heard footsteps on gravel. A little path, overgrown with weeds, led to the bridge. He reeled in and waited. Boylan, hatless, dressed in a suede jacket, a paisley scarf, and jodhpur boots, came down the path and stopped on the bridge. "Hello, Mr. Boylan," Rudolph said. He was a little uneasy, seeing the man, worried that perhaps Boylan hadn't remembered inviting him to fish the stream, or had merely said it for politeness' sake, not really meaning it.

"Any luck?" Boylan asked.

"There're two in the basket."

"Not bad for a day like this," Boylan said, examining the muddied water. "With flies."

"Do you fish?" Rudolph moved nearer the bridge, so that they wouldn't have to talk so loud.

"I used to," Boylan said. "Don't let me interfere. I'm just taking a walk. I'll be back this way. If you're still here, perhaps you'll do me the pleasure of joining me in a drink up at the house."

"Thank you," Rudolph said. He didn't say whether he'd wait or not.

With a wave, Boylan continued his walk.

Rudolph changed the fly, taking the new one from where it was stuck in the band of the battered old brown felt hat he used when it rained or when he went fishing. He made the knots precisely, losing no time. Perhaps one day he would be a surgeon, suturing incisions. "I think the patient will live, nurse." How many years? Three in premed, four in medical school, two more as an intern. Who had that much money? Forget it.

On his third cast, the fly was taken. There was a thrash of water, dirty white against the brown current. It felt like a big one. He played it carefully, trying to keep the fish away from rocks and brushwood anchored in the stream. He didn't know how long it took him. Twice the fish was nearly his and twice it streaked away, taking line with it. The third time, he felt it tiring. He waded out with his net. The water rushed in over the top of his fireman's boots, icy cold.

It was only when he had the trout in the net that he was conscious that Boylan had come back and was on the bridge watching him.

"Bravo," Boylan said, as Rudolph stepped back on shore, water squelching up from the top of his boots. "Very well done."

Rudolph killed the trout and Boylan came around and watched him as he laid the fish with the two others in the creel. "I could never do that," Boylan said. "Kill anything with my hands." He was wearing gloves. "They look like miniature sharks," he said, "don't they?"

They looked like trout to Rudolph. "I've never seen a shark," he said. He plucked some more fern and stuffed it in the creel, around the fish. His father would have trout for breakfast. His father liked trout. A return on his investment in the birthday rod and reel.

"Do you ever fish in the Hudson?" Boylan asked.

"Once in awhile. Sometimes, in season, a shad gets up this far."

"When my father was a boy, he caught salmon in the Hudson," Boylan said. "Can you imagine what the Hudson must have been like when the Indians were here? Before the Roosevelts. With bear and lynx on the shores and deer coming down to the banks."

"I see a deer once in awhile," Rudolph said. It had never occurred to him to wonder what the Hudson must have looked like with Iroquois canoes furrowing it.

"Bad for the crops, deer, bad for the crops," Boylan said.

Rudolph would have liked to sit down and take his boots off and get the water out, but he knew his socks were darned, and he didn't cherish the idea of displaying the thick patches of his mother's handiwork to Boylan.

As though reading his mind, Boylan said, "I do believe you ought to empty the water out of those boots. That water must be cold."

"It is." Rudolph pulled off one boot, then another. Boylan didn't seem to notice. He was looking around him at the overgrown woods that had been in his family's possession since just after the Civil War. "You used to be able to see the house from here. There was no underbrush. Ten gardeners used to work this land, winter and summer. Now the only ones who come are the state fisheries people once a year. You can't get anybody anymore. No sense to it, really, anyway." He studied the massed foliage of the shrub oak and blossomless dogwood and alder. "Trash trees," he said. "The forest primeval. Where only Man is vile. Who said that?"

"Longfellow," Rudolph said. His socks were soaking wet, as he put his boots back on.

"You read a lot?" Boylan said.

"We had to learn it in school." Rudolph refused to boast.

"I'm happy to see that our educational system does not neglect our native birds and their native wood-notes wild," Boylan said.

Fancy talk again, Rudolph thought. Who's he impressing? Rudolph didn't much like Longfellow, himself, but who did Boylan think he was to be so superior? What poems have you written, brother?

"By the way, I believe there's an old pair of hip-length waders up at the house. God knows when I bought them. If they fit you, you can have them. Why don't you come up and try them on?"

Rudolph had planned to go right on home. It was a long walk to the bus and he had been invited for dinner at Julie's house. After dinner they were to go to a movie. But waders . . . They cost over twenty dollars new. "Thank you, sir," he said.

"Don't call me sir," Boylan said. "I feel old enough as it is."

They started toward the house, on the overgrown path. "Let me carry the creel," Boylan said.

"It's not heavy," Rudolph said.

"Please," said Boylan. "It will make me feel as though I've done something useful today."

He's sad, Rudolph thought with surprise. Why, he's as sad as my mother. He handed the creel to Boylan, who slung it over his shoulder.

The house sat on the hill, huge, a useless fortress in Gothic stone, with ivy running wild all over it, defensive against knights in armor and dips in the Market.

"Ridiculous, isn't it?" Boylan murmured.

"Yes," Rudolph said.

"You have a nice turn of phrase, my boy." Boylan laughed. "Come on in." He opened the massive oak front doors.

My sister has passed through here, Rudolph thought. I should turn back.

But he didn't.

They went into a large, dark, marble-floored hall, with a big staircase winding up from it. An old man in a gray alpaca jacket and bow tie appeared immediately, as though merely by entering the house Boylan set up waves of pressure that drove servants into his presence.

"Good evening, Perkins," Boylan said. "This is Mr. Jordache, a young friend of the family."

Perkins nodded, the ghost of a bow. He looked English. He had a for King and Country face. He took Rudolph's battered hat and laid it on a table along the wall, a wreath on a royal tomb.

"I wonder if you could be kind enough, Perkins, to go into the Armory," Boylan said, "and hunt around a bit for my old pair of waders. Mr. Jordache is a fisherman." He opened the creel. "As you can see."

Perkins regarded the fish. "Very good size, sir." Caterer to the Crown.

"Aren't they?" The two men played an elaborate game with each other, the rules of which were unknown to Rudolph. "Take them in to Cook," Boylan said to Perkins. "Ask her if she can't do something with them for dinner. You are staying to dinner, aren't you, Rudolph?"

Rudolph hesitated. He'd miss his date with Julie. But he *was* fishing Boylan's stream, and he *was* getting a pair of waders. "If I could make a telephone call," he said.

"Of course," Boylan said. Then to Perkins. "Tell Cook we'll be two." Axel Jordache would not eat trout for breakfast. "And while you're at it," Boylan said, "bring down a pair of nice, warm socks and a towel for Mr. Jordache. His feet are soaked. He doesn't feel it now, being young, but as he creaks to the fireside forty years from now, he will feel the rheumatism in his joints, even as you and I, and will remember this afternoon."

"Yes, sir," Perkins said and went off to the kitchen or to the Armory, whatever that was.

"I think you'll be more comfortable if you take your boots off here," Boylan said. It was a polite way of hinting to Rudolph that he didn't want him to leave a trail of wet footprints all over the house. Rudolph pulled off the boots. Silent reproach of darned socks.

"We'll go in here." Boylan pushed open two high carved wooden doors leading off the hallway. "I think Perkins has had the goodness to start a fire. This house is chilly on the best of days. At the very best it is always November in here. And on a day like this, when there's rain in the air, one can ice-skate on one's bones."

One. One, Rudolph thought, as, bootless, he went through the door which Boylan held open for him. One can take a flying hump for oneself.

The room was the largest private room Rudolph had ever been in. It didn't seem like November at all. Dark-red velvet curtains were drawn over the high windows, books were ranged on shelves on the walls, there were many paintings, portraits of highly colored ladies in nineteenth-century dresses and solid, oldish men with beards, and big cracked oils. Rudolph recognized the latter as views of the neighboring valley of the Hudson that must have been painted when it was all still farmland and forest. There was a grand piano with a lot of bound music albums strewn on it, and a table against a wall with bottles. There was a huge upholstered couch, some deep leather armchairs, and a library table heaped with magazines. An immense pale Persian carpet that looked hundreds of years old, was shabby and worn to Rudolph's unknowing eye. Perkins had, indeed, started a fire in the wide fireplace. Three logs crackled on heavy andirons and six or seven lamps around the room gave forth a tempered evening light. Instantly, Rudolph decided that one day he would live in a room like this.

"It's a wonderful room," he said sincerely.

"Too big for a single man," Boylan said. "One rattles around in it. I'm making us a whiskey."

"Thank you," Rudolph said. His sister ordering whiskey in the bar in the Port Philip House. She was in New York now, because of this man. Good or bad? She had a job, she had written. Acting. She would let him know when the play opened. She had a new address. She had moved from the Y.W.C.A. Don't tell Ma or Pa. She was being paid sixty dollars a week.

"You wanted to phone," Boylan said, pouring whiskey. "On the table near the window."

Rudolph picked up the phone and waited for the operator. A beautiful blonde woman with an out-of-style hair-do smiled at him from a silver frame on the piano. "Number, please," the operator said.

Rudolph gave her Julie's number. He hoped that Julie wasn't home, so that he could leave a message. Cowardice. Another mark against him in the Book of Himself.

But it was Julie's voice that answered, after two rings.

"Julie . . ." he began.

"Rudy!" Her pleasure at hearing his voice was a rebuke. He wished Boylan were not in the room. "Julie," he said, "about tonight. Something's come up . . ."

"What's come up?" Her voice was stony. It was amazing how a pretty young girl like that, who could sing like a lark, could also make her voice sound like a gate clanging, between one sentence and the next.

"I can't explain at the moment, but . . ."

"Why can't you explain at the moment?"

He looked across at Boylan's back. "I just can't," he said. "Anyway, why can't we make it for tomorrow night? The same picture's playing and . . ."

"Go to hell." She hung up.

He waited for a moment, shaken. How could a girl be so . . . so *decisive?* "That's fine, Julie," he said into the dead phone. "See you tomorrow. 'Bye." It was not a bad performance. He hung up.

"Here's your drink," Boylan called to him across the room. He made no comment on the telephone call.

Rudolph went over to him and took the glass. "Cheers," Boylan said as he drank.

Rudolph couldn't bring himself to say Cheers, but the drink warmed him and even the taste wasn't too bad.

"First one of the day," Boylan said, rattling the ice in his glass. "Thank you for joining me. I'm not a solitary drinker and I needed it. I had a boring afternoon. Please do sit down." He indicated one of the big armchairs near the fire. Rudolph sat in it and Boylan stood to one side of the hearth, leaning against the mantelpiece. There was a Chinese clay horse on the mantelpiece, stocky and warlike-looking. "I had insurance people here all afternoon," Boylan went on. "About that silly fire I had here on VE Day. Night, rather. Did you see the cross burn?"

"I heard about it," Rudolph said.

"Curious that they should have picked my place," Boylan said. "I'm not Catholic and I'm certainly not black or Jewish. The Ku Klux Klan up in these parts must be singularly misinformed. The insurance people keep asking me if I have any particular enemies. Perhaps you've heard something in town?"

"No," Rudolph said carefully.

"I'm sure I have. Enemies, I mean. But they don't advertise," Boylan said. "Too bad the cross wasn't nearer the house. It would be a blessing if this mausoleum burnt down. You're not drinking your drink."

"I'm a slow drinker," Rudolph said.

"My grandfather built for eternity," Boylan said, "and I'm living through it." He laughed. "Forgive me if I talk too much. There're so few opportunities of talking to anybody who has the faintest notion of what you're saying around here."

"Why do you live here, then?" Rudolph asked, youthfully logical.

"I am doomed," said Boylan, with mock melodrama. "I am tied to the rock and the bird is eating my liver. Do you know that, too?"

"Prometheus."

"Imagine. Is that school, too?"

"Yes." I know a lot of things, mister, Rudolph wanted to say.

"Beware families," Boylan said. He had finished his drink fast and he left the mantelpiece to pour another for himself. "You pay for their hopes. Are you family-ridden, Rudolph? Are there ancestors you must not disappoint?"

"I have no ancestors," Rudolph said.

"A true American," said Boylan. "Ah, the waders."

Perkins was in the room, carrying a hip-length pair of rubber boots and a towel, and a pair of light-blue wool socks. "Just put everything down, please, Perkins," Boylan said.

"Very good, sir." Perkins put the waders within Rudolph's reach and draped the towel over the edge of the armchair. He put the socks on the end table next to the chair.

Rudolph stripped off his socks. Perkins took them from him, although Rudolph had intended to put them in his pocket. He had no idea what Perkins could do with a pair of soggy patched cotton socks in that house. He dried his feet with the towel. The towel smelled of lavender. Then he drew on the socks. They were of soft wool. He stood up and pulled on the waders. There was a triangular tear at the knee of one of them. Rudolph didn't think it was polite to mention it. "They fit fine," he said. Fifty dollars. At least fifty dollars, he thought. He felt like D'Artagnan in them.

"I think I bought them before the war," Boylan said. "When my wife left me, I thought I'd take up fishing."

Rudolph looked over quickly to see if Boylan was joking, but there was no glint of humor in the man's eyes. "I tried a dog for company. A huge Irish wolfhound. Brutus. A lovely animal. I had him for five years. We were inordinately attached to each other. Then someone poisoned him. My surrogate." Boylan laughed briefly. "Do you know what surrogate means, Rudolph?"

The school-teacherly questions were annoying. "Yes," he said.

"Of course," said Boylan. He didn't ask Rudolph to define it. "Yes, I must have enemies. Or perhaps he was just chasing somebody's chickens."

Rudolph took off the boots and held them uncertainly. "Just leave them anywhere," Boylan said. "Perkins will put them in the car when I take you home. Oh, dear." He had seen the rip in the boot. "I'm afraid they're torn."

"It's nothing. I'll have it vulcanized," Rudolph said.

"No. I'll have Perkins attend to it. He loves mending things." Boylan made it sound as though Rudolph would be depriving Perkins of one of his dearest pleasures if he insisted upon mending the boot himself. Boylan was back at the bar table. The drink wasn't strong enough for him and he added whiskey to his glass. "Would you like to see the house, Rudolph?" He kept using the name.

"Yes," Rudolph said. He was curious to find out what an armory was. The only armory he had ever seen was the one in Brooklyn where he had gone for a track meet.

"Good," Boylan said. "It may help you when you become an ancestor yourself. You will have an idea of what to inflict upon your descendants. Take your drink along with you."

In the hall there was a large bronze statue of a tigress clawing the back of a water buffalo. "Art," Boylan said. "If I had been a patriot I would have had it melted down for cannon." He opened two enormous doors, carved with cupids and garlands. "The ballroom," he said. He pushed at a switch on the wall.

The room was almost as big as the high school gymnasium. A huge crystal chandelier, draped in sheets, hung from the two-story-high ceiling. Only a few of the bulbs in the chandelier were working and the light through the muffling sheets was dusty and feeble. There were dozens of sheet-draped chairs around the painted wooden walls. "My father said his mother once had seven hundred people here. The orchestra played waltzes. Twenty-five pieces. Quite a club date, eh, Rudolph? You still play at the Jack and Jill?"

"No," Rudolph said, "our three weeks are finished."

"Charming girl, that little . . . what's her name?"

"Julie."

"Oh, yes, Julie. She doesn't like me, does she?"

"She didn't say."

"Tell her I think she's charming, will you? For what it's worth."

"I'll tell her."

"Seven hundred people," Boylan said. He put his arms up as though he were holding a partner and made a surprising little swooping waltz step. The whiskey sloshed over from his glass onto his hand. "I was in great demand at debutantes' parties." He took a handkerchief out of his pocket and dabbed at his hand. "Perhaps I'll give a ball myself. On the eve of Waterloo. You know about that, too?"

"Yes," Rudolph said. "Wellington's officers. I saw Becky Sharp." He had read Byron, too, but he refused to show off for Boylan.

"Have you read *The Charterhouse of Parma*?"

"No."

"Try it, when you're a little older," Boylan said, with a last look around the dim ballroom. "Poor Stendhal, rotting in Civitavecchia, then dying unsung, with his mortgage on posterity."

All right, Rudolph thought, so you've read a book. But he was flattered at the same time. It was a literary conversation.

"Port Philip is my Civitavecchia," Boylan said. They were in the hall again and Boylan switched off the chandelier. He peered into the sheeted darkness. "The haunt of owls," he said. He left the doors open and walked toward the rear of the house. "That's the library," he said. He opened a door briefly. It was an enormous room, lined with books. There was a smell of leather and dust; Boylan closed the door. "Bound sets. All of Voltaire. That sort of thing. Kipling."

He opened another door. "The armory," Boylan said, switching on the lights. "Everybody else would call it a gun room, but my grandfather was a large man."

The room was in polished mahogany, with racks of shotguns and hunting rifles locked in behind glass. Trophies lined the walls, antlers, stuffed pheasants with long brilliant tails. The guns shone with oil. Everything was meticulously dusted. Mahogany cabinets with polished brass knobs made it look like a cabin on a ship.

"Do you shoot, Rudolph?" Boylan asked, sitting astride a leather chair, shaped like a saddle.

"No." Rudolph's hands itched to touch those beautiful guns.

"I'll teach you, if you want," Boylan said. "There's an old skeet trap somewhere on the property. There's nothing much left here, a rabbit or so, and once in a while a deer. During the season I hear the guns popping around the house. Poachers, but there's nothing much to be done about it." He gazed around the room. "Convenient for suicide," he said. "Yes, this was game country. Quail, partridge, doves, deer. I haven't fired a gun in years. Perhaps teaching you will reawaken my interest. A virile sport. Man, the hunter." His tone showed what he thought of this description of himself. "When you're making your way in the world it may help you one day to be known as a good gun. A boy I knew in college married into one of the biggest fortunes in North Carolina because of his keenness of eye and steadiness of hand. Cotton mills. The money, I mean. Reeves, his name was. A poor boy, but he had beautiful manners, and that helped. Would you like to be rich, Rudolph?"

"Yes."

"What do you plan to do after college?"

"I don't know," Rudolph said. "It depends upon what comes along."

"Let me suggest law," Boylan said. "This is a lawyer's country. And it's becoming more so each year. Didn't your sister tell me that you were the captain of the debating team at school?"

"I'm on the debating team." The mention of his sister made him wary.

"Perhaps you and I will drive down to New York some afternoon and visit her," Boylan said.

As they left the gun room, Boylan said, "I'll have Perkins set up the skeet trap this week, and order some pigeons. I'll give you a ring when it's ready."

"We don't have a phone."

"Oh, yes," Boylan said. "I believe I once tried looking it up in the directory. I'll drop you a line. I think I remember the address." He looked vaguely up the marble staircase. "Nothing much up there to interest you," he said. "Bedrooms. Mostly closed off. My mother's upstairs sitting room. Nobody sits there anymore. If you'll excuse me a moment, I'll go up and change for dinner. Make yourself at home. Give yourself another drink." He looked frail going up the sweeping staircase to the other floors, which would be of no interest to his young guest, except, of course, if his young guest were interested in seeing the bed upon which his sister had lost her virginity.

III

Rudolph went back into the living room and watched Perkins laying a table for dinner in front of the fire. Priestly hands on chalices and goblets. Westminster Abbey. Graves of the poets. A bottle of wine poked out of a silver ice bucket. A bottle of red wine, uncorked, was on a sideboard.

"I have made a telephone call, sir," Perkins said. "The boots will be ready by Wednesday next."

"Thank you, Mr. Perkins," Rudolph said.

"Happy to be of service, sir."

Two sirs in twenty seconds. Perkins returned to his sacraments.

Rudolph would have liked to pee, but he couldn't mention anything like that to a man of Perkins' stature. Perkins whispered out of the room, a Rolls-Royce of a man. Rudolph went to the window and parted the curtains a little and looked out. A fog swirled up from the valley in the darkness. He thought of his brother, Tom, at the window, peering in at a naked man with two glasses in his hands.

Rudolph sipped at his drink. Scotch got a grip on you. Maybe one day he would come back and buy this place, Perkins and all. This was America.

Boylan came back into the room. He had merely changed from

the suede jacket to a corduroy one. He still was wearing the checked wool shirt and paisley scarf. "I didn't take the time for a bath," Boylan said. "I hope you don't mind." He went over to the bar. He had put some sort of cologne on himself. It gave a tang to the air around him.

"The dining room is chilling," Boylan said, glancing at the table in front of the fire. He poured himself a fresh drink. "President Taft once ate there. A dinner for sixty notables." Boylan walked over to the piano and sat down on the bench, putting his glass beside him. He played some random chords. "Do you play the violin, by any chance, Rudolph?"

"No."

"Any other instrument besides the trumpet?"

"Not really. I can fake a tune on the piano."

"Pity. We could have tried some duets. I don't think I know of any duets for piano and trumpet." Boylan began to play. Rudolph had to admit he played well. "Sometimes one gets tired of canned music," he said. "Do you recognize this, Rudolph?" He continued playing.

"No."

"Chopin, Nocturne in D-flat. Do you know how Schumann described Chopin's music?"

"No." Rudolph wished Boylan would just play and stop talking. He enjoyed the music.

"A cannon smothered in flowers," Boylan said. "Something like that. I think it was Schumann. If you have to describe music, I suppose that's as good a way as any."

Perkins came in and said, "Dinner is served, sir."

Boylan stopped playing and stood up. "Rudolph, do you want to pee or wash your hands or something?"

Finally. "Thank you, yes."

"Perkins," Boylan said, "show Mr. Jordache where it is."

"This way, sir," Perkins said.

As Perkins led him out of the room, Boylan sat down at the piano again and started playing from where he left off.

The bathroom near the front entrance was a large room with a stained-glass window, which gave the place a religious air. The toilet was like a throne. The faucets on the basin looked like gold. The strains of Chopin drifted in as Rudolph peed. He was sorry he had agreed to stay for dinner. He had the feeling that Boylan was trapping him. He was a complicated man, with his piano-playing, his waders and whiskey, his poetry and guns and his burning cross and poisoned dog. Rudolph didn't feel equipped to handle him. He could understand now why Gretchen had felt she had to get away from him.

When he went out into the hall again, he had to fight down the impulse to sneak out through the front door. If he could have gotten his boots without anyone's seeing him, he might have done it. But he couldn't see himself walking down to the bus stop and getting on it in stockinged feet. Boylan's socks.

He went back into the living room, enjoying Chopin. Boylan stopped playing and stood up and touched Rudolph's elbow formally as he led him to the table, where Perkins was pouring the white wine. The trout lay in a deep copper dish, in a kind of broth. Rudolph was disappointed. He liked trout fried.

They sat down facing each other. There were three glasses in front of each place, and a lot of cutlery. Perkins transferred the trout to a silver platter, with small boiled potatoes on it. Perkins stood over Rudolph and Rudolph served himself cautiously, uneasy with all the implements and determined to seem at ease.

"*Truit au bleu*," Boylan said. Rudolph was pleased to note that he had a bad accent, or at least different from Miss Lenaut's. "Cook does it quite well."

"Blue trout," Rudolph said. "That's the way they cook it in France." He couldn't help showing off on this one subject, after Boylan's phoney accent.

"How do you know?" Boylan looked at him questioningly. "Have you ever been in France?"

"No. In school. We get a little French newspaper for students every week and there was an article about cooking."

Boylan helped himself generously. He had a good appetite. "*Tu parle français?*"

Rudolph made a note of the *tu*. In an old French grammar he had once looked through, the student was instructed that the second-person singular was to be used for servants, children, noncommissioned soldiers, and social inferiors.

"*Un petit peu.*"

"*Moi, j'étais en France quand j'étais jeune,*" Boylan said, the accent rasping. "*Avec mes parents. J'ai veçu mon premier amour à Paris. Quand c'était? Mille neuf cent vingt-huit, vingt-neuf. Comment s'appelait-elle? Anne? Annette? Elle était délicieuse.*"

She might have been delicious, Boylan's first love, Rudolph thought, tasting the profound joys of snobbery, but she sure didn't work on his accent.

"*Tu as l'envie d'y aller? En France?*" Boylan asked, testing him. He had said he could speak a little French and Boylan wasn't going to let him get away with it unchallenged.

"*J'irai, je suis sûr,*" Rudolph said, remembering just how Miss Lenaut would have said it. He was a good mimic. "*Peut-être après l'Universite. Quand le pays sera rétabli.*"

"Good God," Boylan said, "you speak like a Frenchman."

"I had a good teacher." Last bouquet for poor Miss Lenaut, French cunt.

"Maybe you ought to try for the Foreign Service," Boylan said. "We could use some bright young men. But be careful to marry a rich wife first. The pay is dreadful." He sipped at the wine. "I thought I wanted to live there. In Paris. My family thought differently. Is my accent rusty?"

"Awful," Rudolph said.

Boylan laughed. "The honesty of youth." He grew more serious. "Or maybe it's a family characteristic. Your sister matches you."

They ate in silence for awhile, Rudolph carefully watching how Boylan used his knife and fork. A good gun, with beautiful manners.

Perkins took away the fish dishes and served some chops and baked potatoes and green peas. Rudolph wished he could send his mother up for some lessons in the kitchen here. Perkins presided over the red wine, rather than poured it. Rudolph wondered what Perkins knew about Gretchen. Everything, probably. Who made the bed in the room upstairs?

"Has she found a job yet?" Boylan asked, as though there had been no interruption in the conversation. "She told me she intended to be an actress."

"I don't know," Rudolph said, keeping all information to himself. "I haven't heard from her recently."

"Do you think she'll be successful?" Boylan asked. "Have you ever seen her act?"

"Once. Only in a school play." Shakespeare battered and reeling, in homemade costumes. The seven ages of man. The boy who played Jacques nervously pushing at his beard, to make sure it was still pasted on. Gretchen looking strange and beautiful and not at all like a young man in her tights, but saying the words clearly.

"Does she have talent?" Boylan asked.

"I think so. She has *something.* Whenever she came onto the stage everybody stopped coughing."

Boylan laughed. Rudolph realized that he had sounded like a kid. "What I mean . . ." He tried to regain lost ground. "Is, well, you could feel the audience focusing on her, being for her, in a way that they weren't for any of the other actors. I guess that's talent."

"It certainly is." Boylan nodded. "She's an extraordinarily beautiful girl. I don't suppose a brother would notice that."

"Oh, I noticed it," Rudolph said.

"Did you?" Boylan said absently. He no longer seemed interested. He waved for Perkins to take the dishes away and got up and went over to a big phonograph and put on the Brahms Second Piano Concerto, very loud, so that they didn't talk for the rest of the meal. Five kinds of cheese on a wooden platter. Salad. A plum tart. No wonder Boylan had a paunch.

Rudolph looked surreptitiously at his watch. If he could get out of there early enough maybe he could catch Julie. It would be too late for the movies, but maybe he could make up to her, anyway, for standing her up.

After dinner, Boylan had a brandy with the demitasse, and put on a symphony. Rudolph was tired from the long afternoon's fishing. The two glasses of wine he had drunk made him feel blurred and sleepy. The loud music was crushing him. Boylan was polite, but distant. Rudolph had the feeling the man was disappointed in him because he hadn't opened up about Gretchen.

Boylan sat sunk in a deep chair, his eyes almost closed, concentrating on the music, occasionally taking a sip of the brandy. He might just as well have been alone, Rudolph thought resentfully, or with his Irish wolfhound. They probably had some lively evenings here together, before the neighbors put out the poison. Maybe he's getting ready to offer me a position as his dog.

There was a scratch on the record now and Boylan made an irritated gesture as the clicking recurred. He stood up and turned off the machine. "I'm sorry about that," he said to Rudolph. "The revenge of the machine age on Schumann. Shall I take you on down to town now?"

"Thank you." Rudolph stood up, gratefully.

Boylan looked down at Rudolph's feet. "Oh," he said. "You can't go like that, can you?"

"If you'll give me my boots . . ."

"I'm sure they're still soaking wet inside," Boylan said. "Wait here a minute. I'll find something for you." He went out of the room and up the stairway.

Rudolph took a long look around the room. How good it was to be rich. He wondered if he ever was going to see the room again. Thomas had seen it once, although he had not been invited in. *He came down into the living-room bare-assed, with his thing hanging down to his knees, he's a regular horse, and made two whiskies and called up the stairs, "Gretchen, do you want your drink up there or do you want to come down for it?"*

Now that he had had a chance to listen to Boylan, Rudolph recognized that Tom's caricature of the man's voice had been an accurate one. He had caught the educated flattening out on the "there," and the curious way he had of making questions not sound like questions.

Rudolph shook his head. What could Gretchen have been thinking of? *"I liked it."* He heard her voice again in the Port Philip House bar. *"I liked it better than anything that had ever happened to me."*

He walked restlessly around the room. He looked at the album of the symphony that Boylan had cut off. Schumann's Third, the Rhenish Symphony. Well, at least he had learned something today. He would recognize it when he heard it again. He picked up a silver cigarette lighter a foot long and examined it. There was a monogram on it. T.B. Purposely expensive gadgets for doing things that cost nothing to the poor. He flicked it open. It spouted flame. The burning cross. Enemies. He heard Boylan's footsteps on the marble floor in the hall and hurriedly doused the flame and put the lighter down.

Boylan came into the room. He was carrying a little overnight bag and a pair of mahogany-colored moccasins. "Try these on, Rudolph," he said.

The moccasins were old but beautifully polished, with thick soles and leather tassels. They fit Rudolph perfectly. "Ah," Boylan said, "you have narrow feet, too." One aristocrat to another.

"I'll bring them back in a day or two," Rudolph said, as they started out.

"Don't bother," Boylan said. "They're old as the hills. I never wear them."

Rudolph's rod, neatly folded, and the creel and net were on the back seat of the Buick. The fireman's boots, still damp inside, were on the floor behind the front seat. Boylan swung the overnight bag onto the back seat and they got into the car. Rudolph had retrieved the old felt hat from the table in the hallway, but didn't have the courage to put it on with Perkins watching him. Boylan turned on the radio in the car, jazz from New York, so they didn't talk all the way to Vanderhoff Street. When Boylan stopped the Buick in front of the bakery, he turned the radio off.

"Here we are," he said.

"Thank you very much," Rudolph said. "For everything."

"Thank *you*, Rudolph," Boylan said. "It's been a refreshing day." As Rudolph put his hand on the handle of the car door, Boylan reached out and held his arm lightly.

"Ah, I wonder if you'd do me a favor."

"Of course."

"In that bag back there . . ." Boylan twisted a little, holding onto the wheel, to indicate the presence of the leather overnight bag behind him. ". . . there's something I'd particularly like your sister to have. Do you think you could get it to her?"

"Well," Rudolph said, "I don't know when I'll be seeing her."

"There's no hurry," Boylan said. "It's something I know she wants, but it's not pressing."

"Okay," Rudolph said. It wasn't like giving away Gretchen's address, or anything like that. "Sure. When I happen to see her."

"That's very good of you, Rudolph." He looked at his watch. "It's not very late. Would you like to come and have a drink with me someplace? I don't fancy going back to that dreary house alone for the moment."

"I have to get up awfully early in the morning," Rudolph said. He wanted to be by himself now, to sort out his impressions of Boylan, to assess the dangers and the possible advantages in knowing the man. He didn't want to be loaded with any new impressions, Boylan drunk, Boylan with strangers at a bar, Boylan perhaps flirting with a woman, or making a pass at a sailor. The idea was sudden. Boylan, the fairy? Making a pass at *him*. The delicate hands on the piano, the gifts, the clothes that were like costumes, the unobtrusive touching.

"What's early?" Boylan asked.

"Five," Rudolph said.

"Good God!" Boylan said. "What in the world does anyone do up at five o'clock in the morning?"

"I deliver rolls on a bicycle for my father," Rudolph said.

"I see," Boylan said. "I suppose *somebody* has to deliver rolls." He laughed. "You just don't *seem* like a roll-deliverer."

"It's not my main function in life," Rudolph said.

"What is your main function in life, Rudolph?" Absently, Boylan switched off the headlights. It was dark in the car because they were directly under a lamppost. There was no light from the cellar. His father hadn't begun his night's work. If his father were asked, would he say that his main function in life was baking rolls?

"I don't know yet," Rudolph said. Then aggressively, "What's yours?"

"I don't know," Boylan said. "Yet. Have you any idea?"

"No." The man was split into a million different parts. Rudolph felt that if he were older he might be able to assemble Boylan into one coherent pattern.

"A pity," Boylan said. "I thought perhaps the clear eyes of youth would see things in me I am incapable of seeing in myself."

"How old are you, anyway?" Rudolph asked. Boylan spoke so much of the past that he seemed to stretch far, far back, to the Indians, to President Taft, to a greener geography. It occurred to Rudolph that Boylan was not old so much as old-fashioned.

"What would you guess, Rudolph?" Boylan asked, his tone light.

"I don't know." Rudolph hesitated. Everybody over thirty-five seemed almost the same age to Rudolph, except for real tottering graybeards, hunching along on canes. He was never surprised when he read in the papers that somebody thirty-five had died. "Fifty?"

Boylan laughed. "Your sister was kinder," he said. "Much kinder." Everything comes back to Gretchen, Rudolph thought. He just can't stop talking about her. "Well," Rudolph said, "how old *are* you?"

"Forty," Boylan said. "Just turned forty. With all my life still ahead of me, alas," he said ironically.

You have to be damn sure of yourself, Rudolph thought, to use a word like "alas."

"What do you think you'll be like when you're forty, Rudolph?" Boylan asked lightly. "Like me?"

"No," Rudolph said.

"Wise young man. You wouldn't want to be like me, I take it?"

"No." He'd asked for it and he was going to get it.

"Why not? Do you disapprove of me?"

"A little," Rudolph said. "But that's not why."

"What's the reason you don't want to be like me?"

"I'd like to have a room like yours," Rudolph said. "I'd like to have money like you and books like you and a car like you. I'd like to be able to talk like you—some of the time, anyway—and know as much as you and go to Europe like you . . ."

"But . . ."

"You're lonesome," Rudolph said. "You're sad."

"And when you're forty you do not intend to be lonesome and sad?"

"No."

"You will have a loving, beautiful wife," Boylan said, sounding like someone reciting a fairy story for children, "waiting at the station each evening to drive you home after your day's work in the city, and handsome, bright children who will love you and whom you will see off to the next war, and . . ."

"I don't expect to marry," Rudolph said.

"Ah," Boylan said. "You have studied the institution. I was different. I expected to marry. And I married. I expected to fill that echoing castle on the hill with the laughter of little children. As you may have noticed, I am not married and there is very little laughter of any kind in that house. Still, it isn't too late . . ." He took out a cigarette from his gold case and used his lighter. In its light his hair looked gray, his face deeply lined with shadows. "Did your sister tell you I asked her to marry me?"

"Yes."

"Did she tell you why she wouldn't?"

"No."

"Did she tell you she was my mistress?"

The word seemed dirty to Rudolph. If Boylan had said, "Did she tell you that I fucked her?" it would have made him resent Boylan less. It would have made her seem less like another of Theodore Boylan's possessions. "Yes," he said. "She told me."

"Do you disapprove?" Boylan's tone was harsh.

"Yes."

"Why?"

"You're too old for her."

"That's my loss," Boylan said. "Not hers. When you see her, will you tell her the offer still holds?"

"No."

Boylan seemed not to have noticed the no. "Tell her," he said, "that I cannot bear to lie in my bed without her. I'll tell you a secret, Rudolph. I wasn't at Jack and Jill's that night by accident. I never go to places like that, as you can well imagine. I made it a point to find out where you were playing. I followed you out to my car. I was looking for Gretchen. Maybe I had some foolish notion I could find something of the sister in the brother."

"I'd better go to sleep," Rudolph said cruelly. He opened the car door and got out. He reached into the back for his rod and creel and net and the fireman's boots. He put on the ridiculous felt hat. Boylan sat smoking, squinting through the smoke at the straight line of lights of Vanderhoff Street, like a lesson in drawing class in perspective. Parallel to infinity, where lines meet or do not meet, as the case may be.

"Don't forget the bag, please," Boylan said.

Rudolph took the bag. It was very light, as though there were nothing in it. Some new scientific infernal machine.

"Thank you for your delightful visit," Boylan said. "I'm afraid I got all the best of it. Just for the price of an old pair of torn waders that I was never going to use anymore anyway. I'll let you know when the skeet trap is up. Roll on, young unmarried roll-deliverer. I'll think of you at five A.M." He started the motor of the car and drove off abruptly.

Rudolph watched the red tail lights speeding off toward infinity, twin signals saying Stop! then unlocked the door next to the bakery and lugged all the stuff into the hall. He turned on the light and looked at the bag. The lock was open. The key, on a leather thong, hung from the handle. He opened the bag, hoping that his mother hadn't heard him come in.

There was a bright-red dress lying in a careless heap in the bag. Rudolph picked it up and studied it. It was lacy and cut low in front, he could tell that. He tried to imagine his sister wearing it, showing practically everything.

"Rudolph?" It was his mother's voice, from above, querulous.

"Yes, Ma." He turned the light out hurriedly. "I'll be right back. I forgot to get the evening papers." He picked up the bag and got out of the hallway before his mother could come down. He didn't know whom he was protecting, himself or Gretchen or his mother.

He hurried over to Buddy Westerman's, on the next block. Luckily, there were still lights on. The Westerman house was big and old. Buddy's mother let the River Five practice in the basement. Rudolph whistled. Buddy's mother was a jolly, easy-going woman who liked boys and served them all milk and cake after the practice sessions, but he didn't want to have to talk to her tonight. He took the key of the bag off the handle and locked the bag and put the key in his pocket.

After awhile, Buddy came out. "Hey," he said, "what's up? This time of night?"

"Listen, Buddy," Rudolph said, "will you hold onto this for me for a couple of days?" He thrust the bag at Buddy. "It's a present for Julie and I don't want my old lady to see it." Inspired lie. Everybody knew what misers the Jordaches were. Buddy also knew that Mrs. Jordache didn't like the idea of Rudolph going around with girls.

"Okay," Buddy said carelessly. He took the bag.

"I'll do as much for you some day," Rudolph said.

"Just don't play flat on 'Stardust.'" Buddy was the best musician in the band and that gave him the right to say things like that. "Any other little thing?"

"No."

"By the way," Buddy said, "I saw Julie tonight. I was passing the movie. She was going in. With a guy I didn't know. An old guy. Twenty-two, at least. I asked her where you were and she said she didn't know and didn't care."

"Pal," Rudolph said.

"No use living your life in total ignorance," Buddy said. "See you tomorrow." He went in, carrying the bag.

Rudolph went down to the Ace Diner to buy the evening paper. He sat at the counter reading the sports page while drinking a glass of milk and eating two doughnuts. The Giants had won that afternoon. Other than that, Rudolph couldn't decide whether it had been a good day or a bad day.

IV

Thomas kissed Clothilde good night. She was lying under the covers, with her hair spread on the pillow. She had turned on the lamp so that he could find his way out without bumping into anything. There was the soft glow of a smile as she touched his cheek. He opened the door without a sound and closed it behind him. The crack of light under the door disappeared as Clothilde switched off the lamp.

He went through the kitchen and out into the hallway and mounted the dark steps carefully, carrying his sweater. There was no sound from Uncle Harold's and Tante Elsa's bedroom. Usually, there was snoring that shook the house. Uncle Harold must be sleeping on his side tonight. Nobody had died in Saratoga. Uncle Harold had lost three pounds, drinking the waters.

Thomas climbed the narrow steps to the attic and opened the door to his room and put on the light. Uncle Harold was sitting there in striped pajamas, on the bed.

Uncle Harold smiled at him peculiarly, blinking in the light. Four of his front upper teeth were missing. He had a bridge that he took out at night.

"Good evening, Tommy," Uncle Harold said. His speech was gappy, without the bridge.

"Hi, Uncle Harold," Thomas said. He was conscious that his hair was mussed and that he smelled of Clothilde. He didn't know what Uncle Harold was doing there. It was the first time he had come to the room. Thomas knew he had to be careful about what he said and how he said it.

"It is quite late, isn't it, Tommy?" Uncle Harold said. He was keeping his voice down.

"Is it?" Thomas said. "I haven't looked at a clock." He stood near the door, away from Uncle Harold. The room was bare. He had few possessions. A book from the library lay on the dresser. *Riders of the Purple Sage.* The lady at the library had said he would like it. Uncle Harold filled the little room in his striped pajamas, making the bed sag in the middle, where he sat on it.

"It is nearly one o'clock," Uncle Harold said. He sprayed because of the missing teeth. "For a growing boy who has to get up early and do a day's work. A growing boy needs his sleep, Tommy."

"I didn't realize how late it was," Thomas said.

"What amusements have you found to keep a young boy out till one o'clock in the morning, Tommy?"

"I was just wandering around town."

"The bright lights," Uncle Harold said. "The bright lights of Elysium, Ohio."

Thomas faked a yawn and stretched. He threw his sweater over the one chair of the room. "I'm sleepy now," he said. "I better get to bed fast."

"Tommy," Uncle Harold said, in that wet whisper, "you have a good home here, hey?"

"Sure."

"You eat good here, just like the family, hey?"

"I eat all right."

"You have a good home, a good roof over your head." The "roof" came out "woof," through the gap.

"I'm not complaining." Thomas kept his voice low. No sense in waking Tante Elsa and getting her in on the conference.

"You live in a nice clean house," Uncle Harold persisted. "Everybody treats you like a member of the family. You have your own personal bicycle."

"I'm not complaining."

"You have a good job. You are paid a man's wages. You are learning a trade. There will be unemployment now, millions of men coming home, but for the mechanic, there is always a job. Am I mistaken?"

"I can take care of myself," Thomas said.

"You can take care of yourself," Uncle Harold said. "I hope so. You are my flesh and blood. I took you in without a question, didn't I, when your father called? You were in trouble, Tommy, in Port Philip, weren't you, and Uncle Harold asked no questions, he and Tante Elsa took you in."

"There was a little fuss back home," Thomas said. "Nothing serious."

"I ask no questions." Magnanimously, Uncle Harold waved away all thought of interrogation. His pajamas opened. There was a view of plump, pink rolls of beer-and-sausage belly over the drawstrings of the pajama pants. "In return for this, what do I ask? Impossibilities? Gratitude? No. A little thing. That a young boy should behave himself properly, that he should be in bed at a reasonable hour. His own bed, Tommy."

Oh, that's it, Thomas thought. The sonofabitch knows. He didn't say anything.

"This is a clean house, Tommy," Uncle Harold said. "The family is respected. Your aunt is received in the best homes. You would be surprised if I told you what my credit is at the bank. I have been approached to run for the State Legislature in Columbus on the Republican ticket, even though I have not been born in this country. My two daughters have clothes . . . I challenge any two young ladies to dress better. They are model students. Ask me one day to show you their report cards, what their teachers say about them. They go to Sunday school every Sunday. I drive them myself. Pure young souls, sleeping like angels, right under this very room, Tommy."

"I get the picture," Thomas said. Let the old idiot get it over with.

"You were not wandering around town tonight till one o'clock, Tommy," Uncle Harold said sorrowfully. "I know where you were. I was thirsty. I wanted a bottle of beer from the Frigidaire. I heard noises. Tommy, I am ashamed even to mention it. A boy your age, in the same house with my two daughters."

"So what?" Thomas said sullenly. The idea of Uncle Harold outside Clothilde's door nauseated him.

"So what? Is that all you have to say, Tommy? So what?"

"What do you want me to say?" He would have liked to be able to say that he loved Clothilde, that it was the best thing that had ever happened to him in his whole rotten life, that she loved him, that if he were older he would take her away from Uncle Harold's clean, goddamn house, from his respected family, from his model, pale-blonde daughters. But, of course, he couldn't say it. He couldn't say anything. His tongue strangled him.

"I want you to say that you are sorry for the filthy thing that ignorant, scheming peasant has done to you," Uncle Harold whispered. "I want you to promise you will never touch her again. In this house or anywhere else."

"I'm not promising anything," Thomas said.

"I'm being kind," Uncle Harold said. "I am being delicate. I am speaking quietly, like a reasonable and forgiving man, Tommy. I do not want to make a scandal. I don't want your Aunt Elsa to know her house has been dirtied, that her children have been exposed to . . . *Ach*, I can't find the words, Tommy."

"I'm not promising anything," Thomas said.

"Okay. You are not promising anything," Uncle Harold said. "You don't have to promise anything. When I leave this room, I am going down to the room behind the kitchen. She will promise plenty, I assure you."

"That's what you think." Even to his own ears, it sounded hollow, childish.

"That's what I know, Tommy," Uncle Harold whispered. "She will promise anything. She's in trouble. If I fire her, where will she go? Back to her drunken husband in Canada who's been looking for her for two years so he can beat her to death?"

"There're plenty of jobs. She doesn't have to go to Canada."

"You think so. The authority on International Law," Uncle Harold said. "You think it's as easy as that. You think I won't go to the police."

"What've the police got to do with it?"

"You are a child, Tommy," Uncle Harold said. "You put it up in between a married woman's legs like a grown man, but you have the mind of a child. She has corrupted the morals of a minor, Tommy. You are the minor. Sixteen years old. That is a crime, Tommy. A serious crime. This is a civilized country. Children are protected in this country. Even if they didn't put her in jail, they would deport her, an undesirable alien who corrupts the morals of minors. She is not a citizen. Back to Canada she would go. It would be in the papers. Her husband would be waiting for her. Oh, yes," Uncle Harold said. "She will promise." He stood up. "I am sorry for you, Tommy. It is not your fault. It is in your blood. Your father was a whoremaster. I was ashamed to say hello to him in the street. And your mother, for your information, was a bastard. She was raised by the nuns. Ask her some day who her father was. Or even her mother. Get some sleep, Tommy." He patted him comfortingly on the shoulder. "I like you. I would like to see you grow up into a good man. A credit to the family. I am doing what is best for you. Go—get some sleep."

Uncle Harold padded out of the room, barefooted, beery mastodon in the shapeless striped pajamas, all weapons on his side.

Thomas put out the light. He lay face down on the bed. He punched the pillow, once, with all his strength.

The next morning, he went down early, to try to talk to Clothilde before breakfast. But Uncle Harold was there, at the dining-room table, reading the newspaper.

"Good morning, Tommy," he said, looking up briefly. His teeth were back in. He sipped noisily at his coffee.

Clothilde came in with Thomas's orange juice. She didn't look at him. Her face was dark and closed. Uncle Harold didn't look at Clothilde. "It is terrible what is happening in Germany," he said. "They are raping women in Berlin. The Russians. They have been waiting for this for a hundred years. People are living in cellars. If I hadn't met your Tante Elsa and come to this country when I was a young man, God knows where I would be now."

Clothilde came in with Thomas's bacon and eggs. He searched her face for a sign. There was no sign.

When he finished breakfast, Thomas stood up. He would have to get back later in the day, when the house was empty. Uncle Harold looked up from his paper. "Tell Coyne, I'll be in at nine-thirty," Uncle Harold said. "I have to go to the bank. And tell him I promised Mr. Duncan's car by noon, washed."

Thomas nodded and went out of the room as the two daughters came down, fat and pale. "My angels," he heard Uncle Harold say as they went into the dining room and kissed him good morning.

He had his chance at four o'clock that afternoon. It was the daughters' dentist day for their braces and Tante Elsa always took them, in the second car. Uncle Harold, he knew, was down at the showroom. Clothilde should be alone.

"I'll be back in a half-hour," he told Coyne. "I got to see somebody."

Coyne wasn't pleased, but screw him.

Clothilde was watering the lawn when he pedaled up. It was a sunny day and rainbows shimmered in the spray from the hose. The lawn wasn't a big one and was shadowed by a linden tree. Clothilde was in a white uniform. Tante Elsa liked her maids to look like nurses. It was an advertisement of cleanliness. You could eat off the floor in my house.

Clothilde looked at Thomas once as he got off his bicycle, then continued watering the lawn.

"Clothilde," Thomas said, "come inside. I have to talk to you."

"I'm watering the lawn." She turned the nozzle and the spray concentrated down to a stream, with which she soaked a bed of petunias along the front of the house.

"Look at me," he said.

"Aren't you supposed to be at work?" She kept turned away from him.

"Did he come down to your room last night?" Thomas said. "My uncle?"

"So?"

"Did you let him in?"

"It's his house," Clothilde said. Her voice was sullen.

"Did you promise him anything?" He knew he sounded shrill, but he couldn't help himself.

"What difference does it make? Go back to work. People will see us."

"Did you promise him anything?"

"I said I wouldn't see you alone anymore," she said flatly.

"You didn't mean it, though," Thomas pleaded.

"I meant it." She fiddled with the nozzle again. The wedding ring on her finger gleamed. "We are over."

"No, we're not!" He wanted to grab her and shake her. "Get the hell out of this house. Get another job. I'll move away and . . ."

"Don't talk nonsense," she said sharply. "He told you about my crime." She mocked the word. "He will have me deported. We are not Romeo and Juliet. We are a schoolboy and a cook. Go back to work."

"Couldn't you say anything to him?" Thomas was desperate. He was afraid he was going to break down and cry, right there on the lawn, right in front of Clothilde.

"There is nothing to say. He is a wild man," Clothilde said. "He is jealous. When a man is jealous you might as well talk to a wall, a tree."

"Jealous?" Thomas said. "What do you mean?"

"He has been trying to get into my bed for two years," Clothilde said calmly. "He comes down at night when his wife is asleep and scratches on the door like a kitten."

"That fat bastard," Thomas said. "I'll be there waiting for him the next time."

"No you won't," Clothilde said. "He is going to come in the next time. You might as well know."

"You're going to let him?"

"I'm a servant," she said. "I lead the life of a servant. I do not want to lose my job or go to jail or go back to Canada. Forget it," she said. "*Alles kaput*. It was nice for two weeks. You're a nice boy. I'm sorry I got you into trouble."

"All right, all right," he shouted. "I'm never going to touch another woman again as long as—"

He was too choked to say anything more and ran over to his bicycle and rode blindly away, leaving Clothilde watering the roses. He didn't turn around. So he didn't see the tears on the dark, despairing face.

St. Sebastian, well supplied with arrows, he headed for the garage. The rods would come later.

Chapter 9

I

When she came out of the Eighth Street subway station she stopped for six bottles of beer and then went into the cleaner's for Willie's suit. It was dusk, the early dusk of November, and the air was nippy. People were wearing coats and moving quickly. A girl in slacks and a trench coat slouched in front of her, her hair covered by a scarf. The girl looked as though she had just gotten out of bed, although it was after five o'clock in the afternoon. In Greenwich Village, people might get out of bed at any time of the day or night. It was one of the charms of the neighborhood, like the fact that most of the population was young. Sometimes, when she walked through the neighborhood, among the young, she thought, "I am in my native country."

The girl in the trench coat went into Corcoran's Bar and Grill.

Gretchen knew it well. She was known in a dozen bars of the neighborhood. A good deal of her life was spent in bars now.

She hurried toward Eleventh Street, the beer bottles heavy in the big brown-paper sack and Willie's suit carefully folded over her arm. She hoped Willie was home. You never could know when he'd be there. She had just come from an understudy rehearsal uptown and she had to go back for the eight o'clock call. Nichols and the director had her read for the understudy's job and had told her that she had talent. The play was a moderate success. It would almost certainly last till June. She walked across the stage in a bathing suit three times a night. The audience laughed each time, but the laughter was nervous. The author had been furious the first time he had heard the laughter, at a preview, and had wanted to cut her out of the play, but Nichols and the director had persuaded him that the laughter was good for the play. She received some peculiar letters backstage and telegrams asking her if she wanted to go out to supper and twice there were roses. She never answered anybody. Willie was always there in her dressing room after the show to watch her wash off the body make-up and get into her street clothes. When he wanted to tease her, he said, "Oh, God, why did I ever get married? I am quoting."

His divorce was dragging along, he said.

She went into the hallway of the walkup and looked to see if there was any mail in the box. Abbott–Jordache. She had printed the little card herself.

She opened the downstairs door with her key and ran up the three flights of stairs. She was always in a hurry, once she got into the house. She opened the door of the apartment, a little breathless from the stairs. The door opened directly on the living room. "Willie . . ." she was calling. There were only two small rooms, so there was no real reason to call out. She found excuses to say his name.

Rudolph was sitting on the tattered couch, a glass of beer in his hand.

"Oh," Gretchen said.

Rudolph stood up. "Hello, Gretchen," he said. He put down his glass and kissed her cheek, over the bag full of beer bottles and Willie's suit.

"Rudy," she said, getting rid of the bag and dropping the suit over the back of a chair, "what're you doing here?"

"I rang the bell," Rudolph said, "and your friend let me in."

"Your friend is getting dressed," Willie called from the next room. He often sat around in his bathrobe all day. The apartment was so small that you heard everything that was said in either of the rooms. A little kitchenette was concealed by a screen from the living room. "I'll be right out," Willie said from the bedroom. "I blow you a kiss."

"I'm so glad to see you." Gretchen took off her coat and hugged Rudolph hard. She stepped back to look at him. When she had been seeing him every day she hadn't realized how handsome he was, dark, straight, a button-down blue shirt and the blazer she had given him for his birthday. Those sad, clear, greenish eyes.

"Is it possible you've grown? In just a couple of months?"

"Almost six months," he said. Was there an accusation there?

"Come on," she said. "Sit down." She pulled him down on the couch next to her. There was a little leather overnight bag near the door. It didn't belong to Willie or her, but she had a feeling that she had seen it someplace before.

"Tell me about everything," she said. "What's happening at home? Oh, God, it's good to see you, Rudy." Still, her voice didn't sound completely natural to her. If she had known he was coming she'd have warned him about Willie. After all, he was only seventeen, Rudolph, and just to come barging in innocently and discover that his sister was living with a man . . . Abbott–Jordache.

"Nothing much is happening at home," Rudolph said. If he was embarrassed, he didn't show it. She could take lessons in control from Rudy. He sipped at his beer. "I am bearing the brunt of everybody's love, now that I'm the only one left."

Gretchen laughed. It was silly to worry. She hadn't realized how grown-up he was.

"How's Mom?" Gretchen asked.

"Still reading *Gone With the Wind*," Rudolph said. "She's been sick. She says the doctor says it's phlebitis."

Messages of cheer and comfort from the family hearth, Gretchen thought. "Who takes care of the store?" she asked.

"A Mrs. Cudahy," Rudolph said. "A widow. She costs thirty dollars a week."

"Pa must love that," Gretchen said.

"He isn't too happy."

"How is he?"

"To tell the truth," Rudolph said, "I wouldn't be surprised if he's actually sicker than Ma. He hasn't been out in the yard to hit the bag in months and I don't think he's been out on the river since you left."

"What is it?" Gretchen was surprised to find out that she was really concerned.

"I don't know," Rudolph said. "He just moves that way. You know Pa. He never says anything."

"Do they talk about me?" Gretchen asked carefully.

"Not a word."

"And Thomas?"

"Gone and forgotten," Rudolph said. "I never did find out what happened. He never writes, of course."

"Our family," Gretchen said. They sat in silence, honoring the clan Jordache for a moment. "Well . . ." Gretchen shook herself. "How do you like our place?" She gestured to indicate the apartment, which she and Willie had rented furnished. The furniture looked as though it had come out of somebody's attic, but Gretchen had bought some plants and tacked some prints and travel posters on the walls. An Indian in a sombrero in front of a pueblo. Visit New Mexico.

"It's very nice," Rudolph said gravely.

"It's awfully tacky," Gretchen said. "But it has one supreme advantage. It's not Port Philip."

"I understand what you mean," Rudolph said. She wished he didn't look so serious. She wondered what had brought him down to see her.

"How's that pretty girl," she asked. Her voice was falsely bright. "Julie?"

"Julie," Rudolph said. "We have our ups and downs."

Willie came into the room combing his hair. He wasn't wearing a jacket. She had seen him only some five hours earlier, but if they had been alone she would have enfolded him as if they were meeting again after an absence of years. Willie kissed Gretchen quickly, leaning over the couch. Rudolph stood up politely. "Sit down, sit down, Rudy," Willie said. "I'm not your superior officer."

Briefly, Gretchen regretted Willie was so short.

"Ah," Willie said, seeing the beer and the pressed suit, "I told her the day I saw her for the first time that she would make some man a good wife and mother. Is it cold?"

"Uhuh."

Willie busied himself opening a bottle. "Rudy?"

"This will do me for awhile," Rudolph said, sitting down again.

Willie poured the beer in a glass that had been used and still had a rim of foam around it. He drank a lot of beer, Willie. "We can speak frankly," Willie said, grinning. "I have explained everything to

Rudy. I have told him that we are only technically living in sin. I've told him I have asked for your hand in marriage and that you've rejected me, although not for long."

This was true. He *had* asked her to marry him again and again. Quite often she was sure that he meant it.

"Did you tell him you were married?" she asked. She was anxious to have Rudy leave with no questions unanswered.

"I did," Willie said. "I hide nothing from brothers of women I love. My marriage was a whim of youth, a passing cloud, no bigger than a man's hand. Rudy is an intelligent young man. He understands. He will go far. He will dance at our wedding. He will support us in our old age."

For once, Willie's jokes made her uneasy. Although she had told him about Rudolph and Thomas and her parents, this was the first time he had had to cope with the actual presence of her family and she was worried that it was setting his nerves on edge.

Rudolph said nothing.

"What're you doing in New York, Rudy?" she said, to cover up for Willie.

"I got a ride down," Rudolph said. Plainly, he had something to say to her and he didn't feel like saying it in front of Willie. "It's a half-holiday at school."

"How's it going at school?" After she had said it she was afraid it sounded condescending, the sort of thing you say to other people's children because you don't know what else to talk about.

"Okay." Rudolph dismissed school.

"Rudy," Willie said, "what would you think of me as a brother-in-law?"

Rudolph looked at him soberly. Considering green eyes. "I don't know you," he said.

"That's it, Rudy, don't give anything away. That's my big trouble. I'm too open. I wear my heart on my tongue." Willie poured himself some more beer. He couldn't stay in one place. By contrast Rudy seemed settled, sure of himself, judging. "I told Rudy I'd take him to see your show tonight," Willie said. "The toast of New York."

"It's a silly show," Gretchen said. She didn't like the idea of her brother watching her practically nude in front of a thousand people. "Wait till I play Saint Joan."

"I'm busy anyway," Rudolph said.

"I invited him to supper after the show, too," Willie said. "He pleads a prior engagement. See what you can do with him. I like him. I am tied to him by profound bonds."

"Some other night, thank you," Rudolph said. "Gretchen, there's something for you in that bag." He indicated the little overnight bag. "I was asked to deliver it to you."

"What is it?" Gretchen asked. "Who's it from?"

"Somebody called Boylan," Rudolph said.

"Oh." Gretchen touched Willie's arm. "I think I'd like a beer, too, Willie." She got up and went over to the bag. "A present. Isn't that nice?" She picked the bag up and put it on a table and opened it. When she saw what was in the bag, she knew that she had known all along. She held the dress up against her. "I didn't remember that it was so *red*," she said calmly.

"Holy man," Willie said.

Rudolph was watching them closely, first one, then the other.

"A memento of my depraved youth," Gretchen said. She patted Rudolph's arm. "That's all right, Rudy," she said. "Willie knows about Mr. Boylan. Everything."

"I will shoot him down like a dog," Willie said. "On sight. I'm sorry I turned in my B-17."

"Should I keep it, Willie?" Gretchen asked doubtfully.

"Of course. Unless it fits Boylan better than it fits you."

Gretchen put the dress down. "How come he got you to deliver it?" she asked Rudolph.

"I happened to meet him," Rudolph said. "I see him from time to time. I didn't give him your address, so he asked me . . ."

"Tell him I'm most grateful," Gretchen said. "Tell him I'll think of him when I wear it."

"You can tell him yourself, if you want," Rudolph said. "He drove me down. He's in a bar on Eighth Street, waiting for me now."

"Why don't we all go and have a drink with the bugger?" Willie said.

"I don't want to have a drink with him," Gretchen said.

"Should I tell him that?" Rudolph asked.

"Yes."

Rudolph stood up. "I'd better go," he said. "I told him I'd be right back."

Gretchen stood, too. "Don't forget the bag," she said.

"He said for you to keep it."

"I don't want it." Gretchen handed the smart little leather bag to her brother. He seemed reluctant to take it. "Rudy," she said curiously, "do you see much of Boylan?"

"A couple of times a week."

"You like him?"

"I'm not sure," Rudy said. "He's teaching me a lot."

"Be careful," she said.

"Don't worry." Rudolph put out his hand to Willie. "Good-bye," he said. "Thanks for the beer."

Willie shook his hand warmly. "Now you know where we are," he said, "come and see us. I mean it."

"I will," Rudolph said.

Gretchen kissed him. "I hate to see you run off like this."

"I'll come down to New York soon," Rudolph said. "I promise."

Gretchen opened the door for him. He seemed to want to say something more, but finally he just waved, a small troubled movement of his hand, and went down the stairs, carrying the bag. Gretchen closed the door slowly.

"He's nice, your brother," Willie said. "I wish I looked like that."

"You look good enough," Gretchen said. She kissed him. "I haven't kissed you for ages."

"Six long hours," Willie said. They kissed again.

"Six long hours," she said, smiling. "Please be home every time I come home."

"I'll make a point of it," Willie said. He picked up the red dress and examined it critically. "Your brother's awfully grown-up for a kid that age."

"Too, maybe."

"Why do you say that?"

"I don't know." She took a sip of beer. "He figures things out too carefully." She thought of her father's unlikely generosity toward Rudolph, of her mother's standing at night over an ironing board doing Rudolph's shirts. "He collects on his intelligence."

"Good for him," Willie said. "I wish I could collect on mine."

"What did you two talk about before I came?" she asked.

"We praised you."

"Okay, okay, aside from that?"

"He asked me about my work. I guess he wondered what his sister's feller was doing home in the middle of the afternoon while his sister was out earning her daily bread. I hope I put his fears to rest."

Willie had a job on a new magazine that a friend of his had just started. It was a magazine devoted to radio and a lot of Willie's work consisted of listening to daytime programs and he preferred listening to them at home rather than in the little cramped office of the magazine. He was making ninety dollars a week and with her sixty they got along well enough, although they usually found themselves broke by the end of the week, because Willie liked to eat out in restaurants and stay up late in bars.

"Did you tell him you were a playwright, too?" Gretchen said.

"No. I'll leave him to find that out for himself. Some day."

Willie hadn't shown her his play yet. He only had an act and a half done and he was going to rewrite that completely.

Willie draped the dress against his front and walked like a model, with an exaggerated swing of the hips. "Sometimes I wonder what sort of a girl I would have made. What do you think?"

"No," she said.

"Try it on. Let's see what it looks like." He gave her the dress. She took it and went into the bedroom because there was a full-length mirror there on the back of a closet door. She had made the bed neatly before leaving the house, but the bedcover was mussed. Willie had taken a nap after lunch. They had been living together only a little over two months but she had amassed a private treasury of Willie's habits. His clothes were strewn all over the room. His corset was lying on the floor near the window. Gretchen smiled as she took off her sweater and skirt. She found Willie's childish disorder endearing. She liked picking up after him.

She zipped up the dress with difficulty. She had only put it on twice before, once in the shop and once in Boylan's bedroom, to model it for Boylan. She had never really worn it. She looked at herself critically in the mirror. She had the feeling that the lacy top exposed too much of her bosom. Her reflection in the red dress was that of an older woman, New Yorkish, certain of her attractions, a woman ready to enter any room, disdainful of all competition. She let her hair down so that it flowed darkly over her shoulders. It had been piled up in a practical knot on top of her head for the day's work.

After a last look at herself she went back into the living room. Willie was opening another bottle of beer. He whistled when he saw her. "You scare me," he said.

She pirouetted, making the skirt flare out. "Do you think I dare wear it?" she said. "Isn't it a little naked?"

"Dee-vine," Willie drawled. "It is the perfectly designed dress. It is designed to make every man want to take you out of it immediately." He came over to her. "Suiting action to the thought," he said, "the gentleman unzips the lady." He pulled at the zipper and lifted the dress over her head. His hands were cold from the beer bottle and she shivered momentarily. "What are we doing in this room?" he said.

They went into the bedroom and undressed quickly. The one time she had put on the dress for Boylan they had done the same thing. There was no avoiding echoes.

Willie made love to her sweetly and gently, almost as though she were frail and breakable. Once, in the middle of love-making the word *respectfully* had crossed her consciousness and she chuckled. She didn't tell Willie what had caused the chuckle. She was very different with Willie than with Boylan. Boylan had overcome her, obliterated her. It had been an intense and ferocious ceremony of destruction, a tournament, with winners and losers. After Boylan, she had come back into herself like someone returning from a long voyage, resentful of the rape of personality that had taken place. With Willie the act was tender and dear and sinless. It was a part of the flow of their lives together, everyday and natural. There was none of that sense of dislocation, abandonment, that Boylan had inflicted upon her and that she had hungered for so fiercely. Quite often she did not come with Willie, but it made no difference.

"Precious," she murmured and they lay still.

After awhile Willie rolled carefully on his back and they lay side by side, not touching, only their hands entwined, childishly, between them.

"I'm so glad you were home," she said.

"I will always be home," he said.

She squeezed his hand.

He reached out with his other hand for the package of cigarettes on the bedside table and she disentangled her fingers, so that he could light up. He lay flat, his head on the thin pillow, smoking. The room was dark except for the light that was coming in through the open door from the living room. He looked like a small boy who would be punished if he were caught smoking. "Now," he said, "that you have finally had your will of me, perhaps we can talk a bit. What sort of day did you have?"

Gretchen hesitated. Later, she thought. "The usual," she said. "Gaspard made a pass at me again." Gaspard was the leading man of the show and during a break in the rehearsal he had asked her to come into his dressing room to run over some lines and had practically thrown her on the couch.

"He knows a good thing when he sees one, old Gaspard," Willie said comfortably.

"Don't you think you ought to talk to him and tell him he'd better leave your girl alone?" Gretchen said. "Or maybe hit him in the nose?"

"He'd kill me," Willie said, without shame. "He's twice my size."

"I'm in love with a coward," Gretchen said, kissing his ear.

"That's what happens to simple young girls in from the country." He puffed contentedly on his cigarette. "Anyway, in this department a girl's on her own. If you're old enough to go out at night in the Big City you're old enough to defend yourself."

"I'd beat up anybody who made a pass at *you*," Gretchen said.

Willie laughed. "I bet you would, too."

"Nichols was at the theater today. After the rehearsal he said he might have a part for me in a new play next year. A big part, he said."

"You will be a star. Your name will be in lights," Willie said. "You will discard me like an old shoe."

Just as well now as any other time, she thought. "I may not be able to take a job next season," she said.

"Why not?" He raised on one elbow and looked at her curiously.

"I went to the doctor this morning," she said. "I'm pregnant."

He looked at her hard, studying her face. He sat up and stubbed out his cigarette. "I'm thirsty," he said. He got out of bed stiffly. She saw the shadow of the long scar low on his spine. He put on an old cotton robe and went into the living room. She heard him pouring his beer. She lay back in the darkness, feeling deserted. I shouldn't have told him, she thought. Everything is ruined. She remembered the night it must have happened. They had been out late, nearly four o'clock, there had been a long loud argument in somebody's house. About Emperor Hirohito, of all things. Everybody had had a lot to drink. She had been fuzzy and hadn't taken any precautions. Usually, they were too tired when they came home to make love. That one goddamn night, they hadn't been too tired. One for the Emperor of Japan. If he says anything, she thought, I'm going to tell him I'll have an abortion. She knew she could never have an abortion, but she'd tell him.

Willie came back into the bedroom. She turned on the bedside lamp. This conversation was going to be adequately lit. What Willie's face told her was going to be more important than what he said. She pulled the sheet over herself. Willie's old cotton robe flapped around his frail figure. It was faded with many washings.

"Listen," Willie said, seating himself on the edge of the bed. "Listen carefully. I am going to get a divorce or I am going to kill the bitch. Then we are going to get married and I am going to take a course in the care and feeding of infants. Do you read me, Miss Jordache?"

She studied his face. It was all right. Better than all right.

"I read you," she said softly.

He leaned over her and kissed her cheek. She clutched the sleeve of his robe. For Christmas, she would buy him a new robe. Silk.

II

Boylan was standing at the bar in his tweed topcoat, staring at his glass, when Rudolph came down the little flight of steps from Eighth Street, carrying the overnight bag. There were only men standing at the bar and most of them were probably fairies.

"I see you have the bag," Boylan said.

"She didn't want it."

"And the dress?"

"She took the dress."

"What are you drinking?"

"A beer, please."

"One beer, please," Boylan said to the bartender. "And I'll continue with whiskey."

Boylan looked at himself in the mirror behind the bar. His eyebrows were blonder than they had been last week. His face was very tan, as though he had been lying on a southern beach for months. Two or three of the fairies at the bar were equally brown. Rudolph knew about the sun lamp by now. "I make it a point to look as healthy and attractive as I can at all times," Boylan had explained to Rudolph. "Even if I don't see anybody for weeks on end. It's a form of self-respect."

Rudolph was so dark, anyway, that he felt he could respect himself without a sun lamp.

The bartender put the drinks down in front of them. Boylan's fingers trembled a little as he picked up his glass. Rudolph wondered how many whiskies he had had.

"Did you tell her I was here?" Boylan asked.

"Yes."

"Is she coming?"

"No. The man she was with wanted to come and meet you, but she didn't." There was no point in not being honest.

"Ah," Boylan said. "The man she was with."

"She's living with somebody."

"I see," Boylan said flatly. "It didn't take long, did it?"

Rudolph drank his beer.

"Your sister is an extravagantly sensual woman," Boylan said. "I fear for where it may lead her."

Rudolph kept drinking his beer.

"They're not married, by any chance?"

"No. He's still married to somebody else."

Boylan looked at himself in the mirror again for a while. A burly young man in a black turtle-neck sweater down the bar caught his eye in the glass and smiled. Boylan turned away slightly, toward Rudolph. "What sort of fellow is he? Did you like him?"

"Young," Rudolph said. "He seemed nice enough. Full of jokes."

"Full of jokes," Boylan repeated. "Why shouldn't he be full of jokes? What sort of place do they have?"

"Two furnished rooms in a walkup."

"Your sister has a romantic disregard of the advantages of money," Boylan said. "She will regret it later. Among the other things she will regret."

"She seemed happy." Rudolph found Boylan's prophecies distasteful. He didn't want Gretchen to regret anything.

"What does her young man do for a living? Did you find out?"

"He writes for some kind of radio magazine."

"Oh," Boylan said. "One of those."

"Teddy," Rudolph said, "if you want my advice I think you ought to forget her."

"Out of the depths of your rich experience," Boylan said, "you think I ought to forget her."

"Okay," Rudolph said, "I haven't had any experience. But I *saw* her. I saw how she looked at the man."

"Did you tell her I still was willing to marry her?"

"No. That's something you'd better tell her yourself," Rudolph said. "Anyway, you didn't expect me to say it in front of her fellow, did you?"

"Why not?"

"Teddy, you're drinking too much."

"Am I?" Boylan said. "Probably. You wouldn't want to walk back there with me and go up and pay your sister a visit, would you?"

"You know I can't do that," Rudolph said.

"No you can't," Boylan said. "You're like the rest of your family. You can't do a fucking thing."

"Listen," Rudolph said, "I can get on the train and go home. Right now."

"Sorry, Rudolph." Boylan put out his hand and touched Rudolph's arm. "I was standing here, telling myself she was going to walk through that door with you and she didn't walk through. Disappointment makes for bad manners. It's a good reason never to put yourself in a position in which you can be disappointed. Forgive me. Of course, you're not going home. We're going to take advantage of our freedom to have a night on the town. There's quite a good restaurant a few blocks from here and we'll start with that. Barman, may I have the check, please?"

He put some bills on the bar. The young man in the turtle-neck sweater came up to them. "May I invite you gentlemen for a drink?" He kept his eyes on Rudolph, smiling.

"You're a fool," Boylan said, without heat.

"Oh, come off it, dearie," the man said.

Without warning, Boylan punched him, hard, on the nose. The man fell back against the bar, the blood beginning to seep from his nose.

"Let's go, Rudolph," Boylan said calmly.

They were out of the place before the barman or anyone else could make a move.

"I haven't been there since before the war," Boylan said, as they headed toward Sixth Avenue. "The clientele has changed."

If Gretchen had walked through the door, Rudolph thought, there would have been one less nosebleed in New York City that night.

After dinner at a restaurant where the bill, Rudolph noted, was over twelve dollars, they went to a night club in a basement that was called Cafe Society. "You might get some ideas for the River Five," Boylan said. "They have one of the best bands in the city. And there's usually a new colored girl who can sing."

The place was crowded, mostly with young people, many of whom were black, but Boylan got them a little table next to the small dance floor with an accurate tip. The music was deafening and wonderful. If the River Five was to learn anything from the band at Cafe Society it would be to throw their instruments into the river.

Rudolph leaned forward intently, gloriously battered by the music, his eyes glued on the Negro trumpeter. Boylan sat back smoking and drinking whiskies, in a small, private zone of silence. Rudolph had ordered a whiskey, too, because he had to order something, but it stood untouched on the table. With all the drinking Boylan had done that afternoon and evening, he would probably be in no condition to drive and Rudolph knew that he had to remain sober to take the wheel. Boylan had taught him to drive on the back roads around Port Philip.

"Teddy!" A woman in a short evening dress, with bare arms and shoulders, was standing in front of the table. "Teddy Boylan, I thought you were dead."

Boylan stood up. "Hello, Cissy," he said. "I'm not dead."

The woman flung her arms around him and kissed him, on the mouth. Boylan looked annoyed and turned his head. Rudolph stood up uncertainly.

"Where on earth have you been *hiding* yourself?" The woman stepped back a little, but held onto Boylan's sleeve. She was wearing a lot of jewelry that glittered in the reflection of the spotlight on the trumpet. Rudolph couldn't tell whether the jewelry was real or not. She was startlingly made up, with colored eyeshadow and a brilliantly rouged mouth. She kept looking at Rudolph, smiling. Boylan didn't make any move to introduce him and Rudolph didn't know whether he ought to sit down or not. "It's been *centuries*," she went on, not waiting for any answers, continuing to look boldly at Rudolph. "There've been the *wildest* rumors. It's just *sinful*, the way your nearest and dearest drop out of sight these days. Come on over to the table. The whole gang's there. Susie, Jack, Karen . . . They're just *longing* to see you. You're looking absolutely marvelous, darling. Ageless. Imagine finding you in a place like this. Why, it's an absolute *resurrection*." She still kept smiling widely at Rudolph. "Do come over to the table. Bring your beautiful young friend with you. I don't think I caught the name, darling."

"May I present Mr. Rudolph Jordache," Boylan said stiffly. "Mrs. Alfred Sykes."

"Cissy to my friends," the woman said. "He *is* ravishing. I don't blame you for switching, darling."

"Don't be more idiotic than God originally made you, Cissy," Boylan said.

The woman laughed. "I see you're just as much of a shit as ever, Teddy," she said. "Do come over to the table and say hello to the group." With a fluttery wave of the hand, she turned and made her way through the jungle of tables toward the back of the room.

Boylan sat down and motioned to Rudolph to sit down, too. Rudolph could feel himself blushing. Luckily, it was too dark for anyone to tell.

Boylan drained his whiskey. "Silly woman," he said. "I had an affair with her before the war. She wears badly." Boylan didn't look at Rudolph. "Let's get out of here," he said. "It's too damned noisy. And there are too many of our colored brethren on the premises. It's like a slave ship after a successful mutiny."

He waved to a waiter and got the check and paid it and they redeemed their coats from the hatcheck girl and went out. Mrs. Sykes, Cissy to her friends, was the first person Boylan had ever introduced Rudolph to, not counting Perkins, of course. If that's what Boylan's friends were like, you could understand why Boylan stayed up on his hill, alone. Rudolph was sorry the woman had come over to the table. The blush reminded him painfully that he was young and unworldly. Also, he would have liked to stay in there and listen to that trumpeter all night.

They walked east on Fourth Street, toward where the car was parked, past darkened shop fronts and bars which were little bursts of light and music and loud conversation on their way.

"New York is hysterical," Boylan said. "Like an unsatisfied, neurotic woman. It's an aging nymphomaniac of a city. God, the time I've wasted here." The woman's appearance had plainly disturbed him. "I'm sorry about that bitch," he said.

"I didn't mind," Rudolph said. He did mind, but he didn't want Boylan to think it bothered him.

"People're filthy," Boylan said. "The leer is the standard expression on the American face. Next time we come to town, bring your girl along. You're too sensitive a boy to be exposed to rot like that."

"I'll ask her," Rudolph said. He was almost sure Julie wouldn't come. She didn't like his being friendly with Boylan. Beast of prey, she called him, and the Peroxide Man.

"Maybe we'll ask Gretchen and her young man and I'll go through my old address books and see if any of the girls I used to know are still alive and we'll make it a party."

"It ought to be fun," Rudolph said. "Like the sinking of the *Titanic*."

Boylan laughed. "The clear vision of youth," he said. "You're a rewarding boy." His tone was affectionate. "With any luck, you'll be a rewarding man."

They were at the car now. There was a parking ticket under the windshield wiper. Boylan tore it up without looking at it.

"I'll drive, if you like," Rudolph said.

"I'm not drunk," Boylan said curtly and got behind the wheel.

III

Thomas sat in the cracked chair, tilted back against the garage wall, a grass-stalk between his teeth, looking across at the lumberyard. It was a sunny day and the light reflected metallically off the last blaze of autumn leaves on the trees along the highway. There was a car that was supposed to be greased before two o'clock, but Thomas was in no hurry. He had had a fight the night before at a high-school dance and he was sore all over and his hands were puffed. He had kept cutting in on a boy who played tackle for the high-school team because the tackle's girl was giving him the eye all night. The tackle had warned him to lay off, but he'd kept cutting in just the same. He knew it was going to wind up in a fight and he'd felt the old mixture of sensations, pleasure, fear, power, cold excitement, as he saw the tackle's heavy face getting darker and darker while Thomas danced with his girl. Finally the two of them, he and the tackle, had gone outside the gym where the dance was taking place. The tackle was a monster, with big, heavy fists, and fast. That sonofabitch Claude would have pissed in his pants with joy if he had been there. Thomas had put the tackle down in the end, but his ribs felt as though they were caving in. It was his fourth fight in Elysium since the summer.

He had a date with the tackle's girl for tonight.

Uncle Harold came out of the little office behind the filling station. Thomas knew that people had complained to Uncle Harold about his fights, but Uncle Harold hadn't said anything about them. Uncle Harold also knew that there was a car to be greased before two o'clock, but he didn't say anything about that either, although Thomas could tell from the expression on Uncle Harold's face that it pained him to see Thomas lounging like that against the wall, chewing lazily on a stalk of grass. Uncle Harold didn't say anything about anything anymore. Uncle Harold looked bad these days—his plump pink face was now yellowish and sagging and he had the expression on his face of a man waiting for a bomb to go off. The bomb was Thomas. All he had to do was hint to Tante Elsa about what was going on between Uncle Harold and Clothilde and they wouldn't be singing Tristan and Isolde for a long time to come in the Jordache household. Thomas had no intention of telling Tante Elsa, but he didn't let Uncle Harold in on the news. Let him stew.

Thomas had stopped bringing his lunch from home. For three days running he had left the paper bag of sandwiches and fruit that Clothilde prepared for him lying on the kitchen table when he had gone off to work. Clothilde hadn't said anything. After three days she had caught on, and there were no more sandwiches waiting for him. He ate at the diner down the highway. He could afford it. Uncle Harold had raised him ten dollars a week. Slob.

"If anybody wants me," Uncle Harold said, "I'm down at the showroom."

Thomas kept staring out across the highway, chewing on the stalk of grass. Uncle Harold sighed and got into his car and drove off.

From inside the garage there came the sound of Coyne working a lathe. Coyne had seen him in one of his fights on a Sunday down at the lake and now was very polite with him and if Thomas neglected a job, Coyne more often than not would do it himself. Thomas played with the idea of letting Coyne do the two o'clock grease job.

Mrs. Dornfeld drove up in her 1940 Ford, and stopped at a pump. Thomas got up and walked over to the car slowly, not rushing anything.

"Hello, Tommy," Mrs. Dornfeld said.

"Hi."

"Fill her up, please, Tommy," Mrs. Dornfeld said. She was a plump blonde of about thirty with disappointed, childish, blue eyes. Her husband worked as a teller in the bank, which was convenient, as Mrs. Dornfeld always knew where he was during business hours.

Thomas hung up the hose and screwed the cap back on and started washing the windshield.

"It would be nice if you paid me a visit today, Tommy," Mrs. Dornfeld said. That was always what she called it—a visit. She had a prissy way of talking, with little flutterings of her eyelids and lips and hands.

"Maybe I can break loose at two o'clock," Thomas said. Mr. Dornfeld was settled behind the bars of his teller's cage from one-thirty on.

"We can have a nice long visit," Mrs. Dornfeld said.

"If I can break loose." Thomas didn't know how he would feel after lunch.

She gave him a five-dollar bill and clutched at his hand when he gave her change. Every once in a while after one of his visits she slipped him a ten-dollar bill. Mr. Dornfeld must be giving her nothing, but nothing.

There was always lipstick on his collar when he came from visiting

Mrs. Dornfeld and he left it on purposely so that when Clothilde collected his clothes for washing she'd be sure to see it. Clothilde never mentioned the lipstick. The shirt would be neatly washed and ironed and left on his bed the next day.

None of it really worked. Not Mrs. Dornfeld, nor Mrs. Berryman, nor the twins, nor any of the others. Pigs, all of them. None of them really helped him get over Clothilde. He was sure Clothilde knew— you couldn't hide anything in this stinking little town—and he hoped it made her feel bad. At least as bad as he felt. But if she did feel bad, she didn't show it.

"Two o'clock is happy time," Mrs. Dornfeld said.

It was enough to make a man throw up.

Mrs. Dornfeld started the motor and fluttered off. He went back and sat down on the chair tilted against the wall. Coyne came out of the garage, wiping his hands. "When I was your age," Coyne said, looking after the Ford disappearing down the highway, "I was sure it would fall off if I did it with a married woman."

"It doesn't fall off," Thomas said.

"So I see," Coyne said. He wasn't a bad guy, Coyne. When Thomas had celebrated his seventeenth birthday Coyne had broken out a pint of bourbon and they'd finished it off together in one afternoon.

Thomas was wiping the gravy of the hamburger off his plate with a piece of bread when Joe Kuntz, the cop, came into the diner. It was ten to two and the diner was almost empty, just a couple of the hands from the lumberyard finishing up their lunch, and Elias, the counterman, swabbing off the grill. Thomas hadn't decided yet whether or not he was going to visit Bertha Dornfeld.

Kuntz came up to where Thomas was sitting at the counter and said, "Thomas Jordache?"

"Hi, Joe," Thomas said. Kuntz stopped in at the garage a couple of times a week to shoot the breeze. He was always threatening to leave the force because the pay was so bad.

"You acknowledge that you are Thomas Jordache?" Kuntz said in his cop voice.

"What's going on, Joe?" Thomas asked.

"I asked you a question, son," Kuntz said, bulging out of his uniform.

"You know my name," Thomas said. "What's the joke?"

"You better come with me, son," Kuntz said. "I have a warrant for your arrest." He grabbed Thomas's arm above the elbow. Elias stopped scrubbing the grill and the guys from the lumberyard stopped eating and it was absolutely quiet in the diner.

"I ordered a piece of pie and a cup of coffee," Thomas said. "Take your meathooks off me, Joe."

"What's he owe you, Elias?" Kuntz asked, his fingers tight on Thomas's arm.

"With the coffee and pie or without the coffee and pie?" Elias said.

"Without."

"Seventy-five cents," Elias said.

"Pay up, son, and come along quiet," Kuntz said. He didn't make more than twenty arrests a year and he was getting mileage out of this one.

"Okay, okay," Thomas said. He put down eighty-five cents. "Christ, Joe," he said, "you're breaking my arm."

Kuntz walked him quickly out of the diner. Pete Spinelli, Joe's partner, was sitting at the wheel of the prowl car, with the motor running.

"Pete," Thomas said, "will you tell Joe to let go of me."

"Shut up, kid," Spinelli said.

Kuntz shoved him into the back seat and got in beside him and the prowl car started toward town.

"The charge is statutory rape," Sergeant Horvath said. "There is a sworn complaint. I'll notify your uncle and he can get a lawyer for you. Take him away, boys."

Thomas was standing between Kuntz and Spinelli. They each had an arm now. They hustled him off and put him in the lockup. Thomas looked at his watch. It was twenty past two. Bertha Dornfeld would have to go without her visit today.

There was one other prisoner in the single cell of the jail, a ragged, skinny man of about fifty, with a week's growth of beard on his face. He was in for poaching deer. This was the twenty-third time he had been booked for poaching deer, he told Thomas.

IV

Harold Jordache paced nervously up and down the platform. Just tonight the train had to be late. He had heartburn and he pushed anxiously at his stomach with his hand. When there was trouble, the trouble went right to his stomach. And ever since two-thirty yesterday afternoon; when Horvath had called him from the jail, it had been nothing but trouble. He hadn't slept a wink, because Elsa had cried all night, in between bouts of telling him that they were disgraced for life, that she could never show her face in town again, and what a fool he had been to take a wild animal like that into the house. She was right, he had to admit it, he had been an idiot, his heart was too big. Family or no family, that afternoon when Axel called him from Port Philip, he should have said no.

He thought of Thomas down in the jail, talking his head off like a lunatic, admitting everything, not showing any shame or remorse, naming names. Who could tell what he would say, once he started talking like that? He knew the little monster hated him. What was to stop him from telling about the black-market ration tickets, the faked-up secondhand cars with gear boxes that wouldn't last for more than a hundred miles, the under-the-counter mark-ups on new cars to get around the Price Control, the valve and piston jobs on cars that had nothing more wrong with them than a clogged fuel line? Even about Clothilde? You let a boy like that into your house and you became his prisoner. The heartburn stabbed at Uncle Harold like a knife. He began to sweat, even though it was cold on the station, with the wind blowing.

He hoped Axel was bringing plenty of money along with him. And the birth certificate. He had sent Axel a telegram asking Axel to call him because Axel didn't have a telephone. In this day and age! He had made the telegram sound as ominous as he could, to make sure Axel would call, but even so he was half-surprised when the phone rang in his house and he heard his brother's voice on the wire.

He heard the train coming around the curve toward the station and stepped back nervously from the edge of the platform. In his state he wouldn't be surprised if he had a heart attack and fell down right where he stood.

The train slowed to a halt and a few people got off and hurried away in the wind. He had a moment of panic. He didn't see Axel. It would be just like Axel to leave him alone with the problem. Axel was an unnatural father; he hadn't written once to either Thomas or himself, all the time that Thomas had been in Elysium. Neither had the mother, that skinny hoity-toity whore's daughter. Or the other two kids. What could you expect from a family like that?

Then he saw a big man in a workman's cap and a mackinaw limping slowly toward him on the platform. What a way to dress. Harold was glad it was dark and there were so few people around. He must have been crazy that time in Port Philip when he'd invited Axel to come in with him.

"All right, I'm here," Axel said. He didn't shake hands.

"Hello, Axel," Harold said. "I was beginning to worry you wouldn't come. How much money you bring with you?"

"Five thousand dollars," Axel said.

"I hope it's enough," Harold said.

"It better be enough," Axel said flatly. "There isn't any more." He looked old, Harold thought, and sick. His limp was worse than Harold remembered.

They walked together through the station toward Harold's car.

"If you want to see Tommy," Harold said, "you'll have to wait till tomorrow. They don't let anybody in after six o'clock."

"I don't want to see the sonofabitch," Axel said.

Harold couldn't help feeling that it was wrong to call your own child a sonofabitch, even under the circumstances, but he didn't say anything.

"You have your dinner, Axel?" he asked. "Elsa can find something in the icebox."

"Let's not waste time," Axel said. "Who do I have to pay off?"

"The father, Abraham Chase. He's one of the biggest men in town. Your son had to pick somebody like that," Harold said aggrievedly. "A girl in a factory wasn't good enough for him."

"Is he Jewish?" Axel asked, as they got into the car.

"What?" Harold asked, irritatedly. That would be great, that would help a lot, if Axel turned out to be a Nazi, along with everything else.

"Why should he be Jewish?"

"Abraham," Axel said.

"No. It's one of the oldest families in town. They own practically everything. You'll be lucky if he takes your money."

"Yeah," Axel said. "Lucky."

Harold backed out of the parking lot and started toward the Chase house. It was in the good section of town, near the Jordache house. "I talked to him on the phone," Harold said. "I told him you were coming. He sounded out of his mind. I don't blame him. It's bad enough to come home and find one daughter pregnant. But *both* of them! And they're twins, besides."

"They can get a wholesale rate on baby clothes." Axel laughed.

The laughter sounded like a tin pitcher rattling against a sink. "Twins. He had a busy season, didn't he, Thomas?"

"You don't know the half of it," Harold said. "He's beat up a dozen people since he came here, besides." The stories that had reached Harold's ears had been exaggerated as they passed along the town's chain of gossip. "It's a wonder he hasn't been in jail before this. Everybody's scared of him. It's the most natural thing in the world that something like this comes up, they pin it on him. But who suffers? Me. And Elsa."

Axel ignored his brother's suffering and the suffering of his brother's wife. "How do they know it was my kid?"

"The twins told their father." Harold slowed the car down. He was in no hurry to confront Abraham Chase. "They've done it with every boy in town, the twins, and plenty of the men too, everybody knows that, but when it comes to naming names, naturally the first name anybody'd pick would be your Tommy. They're not going to say it was the nice boy next door or Joe Kuntz, the policeman, or the boy from Harvard whose parents play bridge with the Chases twice a week. They pick the black sheep. Those two little bitches're smart. And your son had to tell them he was nineteen years old. Big shot. Under eighteen, my lawyer says, you can't be held for statutory rape."

"So what's the fuss?" Axel said. "I have his birth certificate."

"Don't think it's going to be that easy," Harold said. "Mr. Chase swears he can have him locked up until he's twenty-one as a juvenile delinquent. And he can. That's four years. And don't think Tommy is making it any easier for himself telling the cops he knows twenty fellows personally who've been in there with those girls and giving a list of names. It just makes everybody sorer, that's all. It gives the whole town a bad name and they'll make him pay for it. And me and Elsa. That's my shop," he said automatically. They were passing the showroom. "I'll be lucky if they don't put a brick through the window."

"You friendly with Abraham?"

"I do some business with Mr. Chase," Harold said. "I sold him a Lincoln. I can't say we move in the same circles. He's on the waiting list for a new Mercury. I could sell a hundred cars tomorrow if I could get delivery. The goddamn war. You don't know what I've been going through for four years, just to keep my head above water. And now, just when I begin to see a little daylight, this has to come along."

"You don't seem to be doing so bad," Axel said.

"You have to keep up appearances." One thing was sure. If Axel thought for a minute that he was going to borrow any money, he was barking up the wrong tree.

"How do I know Abraham won't take my money and the kid'll go to jail just the same?"

"Mr. Chase is a man of his word," Harold said. He had a sudden horrible fear that Axel was going to call Mr. Chase Abraham in his own house. "He's got this town in his pocket. The cops, the judge, the mayor, the party organization. If he tells you the case'll be dropped, it'll be dropped."

"It better be," Axel said. There was a threat in his voice and Harold remembered what a rough boy his brother had been when they had both been young back home in Germany. Axel had gone off to war and had killed people. He was not a civilized man, with that harsh, sick face and that hatred of everybody and everything, including his own flesh and blood. Harold wondered if maybe he hadn't made a mistake calling his brother and telling him to come to Elysium. Maybe it would have been better if he had just tried to handle it himself. But he had known it was going to cost money and he'd panicked. The heartburn gripped him again as they drove up to the white house, with big pillars, where the Chase family lived.

The two men went up the walk to the front door and Harold rang the bell. He took off his hat and held it across his chest, almost as if he were saluting the flag. Axel kept his cap on.

The door opened and a maid stood there. Mr. Chase was expecting them, she said.

v

"They take millions of clean-limbed young boys." The poacher was chewing on a wad of tobacco and spitting into a tin can on the floor beside him, as he talked. "Clean-limbed boys, and send them off to kill and maim each other with inhuman instruments of destruction and they congratulate themselves and hang their chests with medals and parade down the main thoroughfares of the city and they put me in jail and mark me as an enemy of society because every once in awhile I drift out into the woodlands of America and shoot myself a choice buck with an old 1910 Winchester 22." The poacher originally had come from the Ozarks and he spoke like a country preacher.

There were four bunks in the cell, two on one side and two on the other. The poacher, whose name was Dave, was lying in his bunk and Thomas was lying in the lower bunk on the other side of the cell. Dave smelled rather ripe and Thomas preferred to keep some space between them. It was two days now that they had been in the cell together and Thomas knew quite a bit about Dave, who lived alone in a shack near the lake and appreciated a permanent audience. Dave had come down from the Ozarks to work in the automobile industry in Detroit and after fifteen years of it had had enough. "I was in there in the paint department," Dave said, "in the stink of chemicals and the heat of a furnace, devoting my numbered days on this earth to spraying paint on cars for people who didn't mean a fart in hell to me to ride around in and the spring came and the leaves burgeoned and the summer came and the crops were taken in and the autumn came and city folk in funny caps with hunting licenses and fancy guns were out in the woods shooting the deer and I might just as well have been down in the blackest pit, chained to a post, for all the difference the seasons meant to me. I'm a mountain man and I pined away and one day I saw where my path laid straight before me and I took to the woods. A man has to be careful with his numbered days on this earth, son. There is a conspiracy to chain every living child of man to an iron post in a black pit, and you mustn't be fooled because they paint it all the bright colors of the rainbow and pull all sorts of devilish tricks to make you think that it isn't a pit, it isn't an iron post, it isn't a chain. The president of General Motors, up high in his glorious office, was just as much chained, just as deep down in the pit as me coughing up violet in the paint shop."

Dave spat tobacco juice into the tin can on the floor next to his bunk. The gob of juice made a musical sound against the side of the can.

"I don't ask for much," Dave said, "just an occasional buck and the smell of woodsy air in my nostrils. I don't blame nobody for putting me in jail from time to time, that's their profession just like hunting is my profession, and I don't begrudge 'em the coupla months here and there I spend behind bars. Somehow, they always seem to catch me just as the winter months're drawing on, so it's really no hardship. But nothing they say can make me feel like a criminal, no sir. I'm an American out in the American forest livin' off American deer. They want to make all sorts of rules and regulations for those city folk in the gun clubs, that's all right by me. They don't apply, they just don't apply."

He spat again. "There's just one thing that makes me a mite forlorn—and that's the hypocrisy. Why, once the very judge that condemned me had eaten venison I shot just the week before and ate it right at the dining-room table in his own house and it was bought with his own money by his own cook. The hypocrisy is the canker in the soul of the American people. Why, just look at your case, son. What did you do? You did what everybody knows he'd do if he got the chance—you were offered a nice bit of juicy tail and you took it. At your age, son, the loins're raging, and all the rules in the book don't make a never-no-mind. I bet that the very judge who is going to put you away for years of your young life, if he got the offer from those two little plump-assed young girls you told me about, if that same judge got the offer and he was certain sure nobody was around to see him, he'd go cavorting with those plump-assed young girls like a crazy goat. Like the judge who ate my venison. Statutory rape." Dave spat in disgust. "Old man's rules. What does a little twitching young tail know about statutory? It's the hypocrisy, son, the hypocrisy, son, the hypocrisy everywhere."

Joe Kuntz appeared at the cell door and opened it. "Come on out, Jordache," Kuntz said. Ever since Thomas had told the lawyer Uncle Harold had got for him that Joe Kuntz had been in there with the twins, too, and Kuntz had heard the news, the policeman had not been markedly friendly. He was married, with three kids.

Axel Jordache was waiting in Horvath's office with Uncle Harold and the lawyer. The lawyer was a worried-looking young man with a bad complexion and thick glasses. Thomas had never seen his father looking so bad, not even the day he hit him.

He waited for his father to say hello, but Axel kept quiet, so he kept quiet, too.

"Thomas," the lawyer said, "I am happy to say that everything has been arranged to everybody's satisfaction."

"Yeah," Horvath said behind the desk. He didn't sound terribly satisfied.

"You're a free man, Thomas," the lawyer said.

Thomas looked doubtfully at the five men in the room. There were no signs of celebration on any of the faces. "You mean I can just walk out of this joint?" Thomas asked.

"Exactly," the lawyer said.

"Let's go," Axel Jordache said. "I wasted enough time in this goddamn town as it is." He turned abruptly and limped out.

Thomas had to make himself walk slowly after his father. He wanted to cut and run for it, before anybody changed his mind.

Outside it was sunny late afternoon. There were no windows in
the cell and you couldn't tell what the weather was from in there.
Uncle Harold walked on one side of Thomas and his father on the
other. It was another kind of arrest.

They got into Uncle Harold's car. Axel sat up in front and
Thomas had the back seat all to himself. He didn't ask any questions.

"I bought your way out, in case you're curious," his father said.
His father didn't turn in the seat, but talked straight ahead, at the
windshield. "Five thousand dollars to that Shylock for his pound of
flesh. I guess you got the highest-priced lay in history. I hope it was
worth it."

Thomas wanted to say he was sorry, that somehow, some day, he'd
make it up to his father. But the words wouldn't come out.

"Don't think I did it for you," his father said, "or for Harold
here . . ."

"Now, Axel," Harold began.

"You could both die tonight and it wouldn't spoil my appetite,"
his father said. "I did it for the only member of the family that's
worth a damn—your brother Rudolph. I'm not going to have him
start out in life with a convict brother hanging around his neck. But
this is the last time I ever want to see you or hear from you. I'm taking the train home now and that's the end of you and me. Do you
get that?"

"I get it," Thomas said flatly.

"*You're* getting out of town, too," Uncle Harold said to Thomas.
His voice was quivering. "That's the condition Mr. Chase made and
I couldn't agree with him more. I'll take you home and you pack
your things and you don't sleep another night in my house. Do you
get that too?"

"Yeah, yeah," Thomas said. They could have the town. Who
needed it?

There was no more talking. When Uncle Harold stopped the car
at the station, his father got out without a word and limped away,
leaving the door of the car open. Uncle Harold had to reach over
and slam it shut.

In the bare room under the roof, there was a small, battered valise
on his bed. Thomas recognized it. It belonged to Clothilde. The bed
was stripped down and the mattress was rolled up, as though Tante

Elsa were afraid that he might sneak in a few minutes' sleep on it. Tante Elsa and the girls were not in the house. To avoid contamination, Tante Elsa had taken the girls to the movies for the afternoon.

Thomas threw his things into the bag quickly. There wasn't much. A few shirts and underwear and socks, an extra pair of shoes and a sweater. He took off the garage uniform that he had been arrested in and put on the new gray suit Tante Elsa had bought for him on his birthday.

He looked around the room. The book from the library, the *Riders of the Purple Sage*, was lying on a table. They kept sending postcards saying he was overdue and they were charging him two cents a day. He must owe them a good ten bucks by now. He threw the book into the valise. Remember Elysium, Ohio.

He closed the valise and went downstairs and into the kitchen. He wanted to thank Clothilde for the valise. But she wasn't in the kitchen.

He went out through the hallway. Uncle Harold was eating a big piece of apple pie in the dining room, standing up. His hands were trembling as he picked up the pie. Uncle Harold always ate when he was nervous. "If you're looking for Clothilde," Uncle Harold said, "save your energy. I sent her to the movies with Tante Elsa and the girls."

Well, Thomas thought, at least she got a movie out of me. One good thing.

"You got any money?" Uncle Harold asked. "I don't want you to be picked up for vagrancy and go through the whole thing again." He wolfed at his apple pie.

"I have money," Thomas said. He had twenty-one dollars and change.

"Good. Give me your key."

Thomas took the key out of his pocket and put it on the table. He had an impulse to push the rest of the pie in Uncle Harold's face, but what good would that do?

They stared at each other. A piece of pie dribbled down Uncle Harold's chin.

"Kiss Clothilde for me," Thomas said, and went out the door, carrying Clothilde's valise.

He walked to the station and bought twenty dollars' worth of transportation away from Elysium, Ohio.

Chapter 10

The cat stared at him from its corner, malevolent and unblinking. Its enemies were interchangeable. Whoever came down in the cellar each night, to work in the hammering heat, was regarded by the cat with the same hatred, the same topaz lust for death in his yellow eyes. The cat's night-long cold stare disconcerted Rudolph as he put the rolls in the oven. It made him uneasy when he was not liked, even by an animal. He had tried to win the cat over with an extra bowl of milk, with caresses, with a "Nice, kitty," here and there, but the cat knew it wasn't a nice kitty and lay there, it's tail twisting, contemplating murder.

Axel had been gone for three days now. There had been no word from Elysium and there was no telling how many more nights Rudolph would have to come down into the cellar and face the heat, the flour dust, the arm-numbing lifting and shoving and hauling. He didn't know how his father could stand it. Year in and year out. After only three nights, Rudolph was almost completely worn out, with purplish bruises of fatigue under his eyes and his face haggard. And he still had to take the bicycle and deliver the rolls in the morning. And school after that. There was an important exam in math the next day and he hadn't been able to prepare for it and he never was all that good in math anyway.

Sweating, fighting the greasy, huge trays, the flour smearing chalkily over his bare arms and face, after three nights he was his father's ghost, staggering under the punishment his father had endured six thousand nights. Good son, faithful son. Shit on that. Bitterly, he regretted the fact that he had come down to help his father on holidays, when there was a rush on, and had learned, approximately, his father's profession. Thomas had been wiser. Let the family go to hell. Whatever trouble Thomas was in now (Axel had not told Rudolph what it was when he got the telegram from Elysium), Thomas just had to be better off than the dutiful son in the blazing cellar.

As for Gretchen, just walking across a stage three times a night for sixty dollars a week . . .

In the last three nights Rudolph had figured out approximately how much the Jordache Bakery earned. About sixty dollars a week, on the average, after rent and expenses, and the thirty dollars for salary for the widow who took care of the shop now that his mother was sick.

He remembered the bill for more than twelve dollars that Boylan had paid in the restaurant in New York, and all the money for drinks that one night.

Boylan had gone down to Hobe Sound, in Florida, for two months. Now that the war was over, life was returning to normal.

He put another tray of rolls into the oven.

He was awakened by the sound of voices. He groaned. Five o'clock so soon? He got out of bed mechanically. He noticed that he was dressed. He shook his head stupidly. How could he be dressed? He looked blearily at his watch. A quarter to six. Then he remembered. It wasn't morning. He had come home from school and thrown himself on the bed to get some rest before the night's work. He heard his father's voice. His father must have come home while he was asleep. His first thought was selfish. I don't have to work tonight.

He lay down again.

The two voices, the one high and excited, the other low and explaining, came up from downstairs. His father and mother were fighting. He was too tired to care. But he couldn't go to sleep, with all that noise downstairs, so he listened.

Mary Pease Jordache was moving out. She wasn't moving far. Just to Gretchen's room across the hall. She stumbled back and forth, her legs hurting from the phlebitis, carrying dresses, underwear, sweaters, shoes, combs, photographs of the children when they were young, Rudolph's scrapbook, a sewing kit, *Gone With the Wind*, a rumpled package of Camels, old handbags. Everything she owned, getting it out of the room she had hated for twenty years and piling everything on Gretchen's unmade bed, raising a small cloud of dust every time she came in with a new load in her arms.

She kept up a surging monologue as she went back and forth. "I'm through with this room. Twenty years too late, but I'm finally through. No one shows any consideration for me, I'm going to go my own way from now on. I am not going to be at the disposal of a fool. A man who travels halfway across the country to give away five thousand dollars to a perfect stranger. The savings of a lifetime. *My* life-time. I slaved, day in and day out, I denied myself everything, I be-came an old woman, to save that money. My son was going to go to college, my son was going to be a gentleman. But now he's not going anywhere, he's not going to be anything, my brilliant husband had to show what a great man he was—handing out thousand dollar bills to millionaires in Ohio, so that his precious brother and his fat wife wouldn't be embarrassed when they went to the opera in their Lin-coln Continental."

"It wasn't for my brother or his fat wife," Axel Jordache said. He was sitting on the bed, his hands dangling between his knees. "I ex-plained to you. It was for Rudy. What good would it do going to college if one day all of a sudden people found out he had a brother in jail?"

"He belongs in jail," Mary Pease Jordache said. "Thomas. It's the natural place for him. If you're going to hand out five thousand dol-lars each time they want to put him in jail, you'd better get out of the bakery right away and go into the oil business or become a banker. I bet you felt *good* giving that man the money. You felt *proud*. Your son. A chip off the old block. Full of sex. Potent. Right on the target. It isn't enough for him to get one girl pregnant at a time. Oh, no, not Axel Jordache's son. Two at a time, that's the kind of family *he* comes from. Well, if Axel Jordache wants to show what a great big he-man he is in bed from now on he'd better start looking for a couple of twins on his own. It's all finished here. My Calvary is over."

"Oh, Christ," Jordache said. "Calvary."

"Filth, filth!" Mary Jordache screamed. "From one generation to another. Your daughter's a whore, too, I saw the money she took from men for her services, right in this house, eight hundred dollars, I saw it with my own eyes, she hid it in a book. *Eight hundred dol-lars*. Your children command a good price. Well, I'm going to have a price, too. You want anything from me, you want me to go down into that store, you want to come to my bed, you pay. We give that woman downstairs thirty dollars a week, and she only does half the job, she goes home at night. Thirty dollars a week is my price. I'm giving you a bargain rate. Only I want my back pay first. Thirty dol-lars a week for twenty years. I figured it out. Thirty thousand dol-lars. You put thirty thousand dollars on the table and I'll talk to you. Not before."

She had the last bundle of clothes in her arms now and she rushed out of the room. The door to Gretchen's room slammed behind her.

Jordache shook his head, then got up and limped up the stairs to Rudolph's room.

Rudolph was lying on the bed, his eyes open.

"You heard, I suppose," Jordache said.

"Yeah," Rudolph said.

"I'm sorry," Jordache said.

"Yeah," said Rudolph.

"Well, I'm going down to the shop, see how things are." Jordache turned away.

"I'll come down and give you a hand tonight," Rudolph said.

"You sleep," Jordache said. "I don't want to see you down there."

He went out of the room.

Chapter 11

1946

I

The lights were down low in the Westerman basement. They had it fixed up as a sort of den and they gave parties there. There was a party on tonight, about twenty boys and girls, some of them dancing, some of them necking a little in the dark corners of the room, some of them just listening to Benny Goodman playing "Paper Doll" on a record.

The River Five didn't practice much anymore there because some guys back from the Army had started a band, too, and were getting most of the dates. Rudolph didn't blame people for hiring the other band. The guys were older and they played a lot better than the River Five.

Alex Dailey was dancing closely with Lila Belkamp in the middle of the room. They told everybody they were going to get married when they got out of school in June. Alex was nineteen and a little slow in school. Lila was all right, a little gushy and silly, but all right. Rudolph wondered if his mother had looked anything like Lila when she was nineteen. Rudolph wished he had a recording of his mother's speech the night his father came home from Elysium, to play to Alex. It should be required listening for all prospective bridegrooms. Maybe there wouldn't be such a rush to the church.

Julie was sitting on Rudolph's lap in a broken-down old easy chair in a corner of the den. There were other girls sitting on boys' laps around the room, but Rudolph wished she wouldn't do it. He didn't like the idea of people seeing him like that and guessing how he was feeling. There were some things that ought to be kept private. He couldn't imagine Teddy Boylan letting any girl sit in his lap in public, at any age. But if he even hinted about it to Julie, she'd blow up.

Julie nuzzled her head around and kissed him. He kissed her back, of course, and enjoyed it, but wished she'd quit.

She had applied to Barnard for the fall and was pretty sure of getting in. She was smart in school. She wanted Rudolph to try to get into Columbia, so they would be right next to each other in New York. Rudolph pretended he was considering Harvard or Yale. He never could get himself to tell Julie that he wasn't going to college.

Julie snuggled closer, her head under his chin. She made a purring sound that at other times made him chuckle. He looked over her head at the other people at the party. He was probably the only virgin among the boys in the room. He was sure about Buddy Westerman and Dailey and Kessler and most of the others, although maybe there were one or two who probably lied when the question came up. That wasn't the only way he was different from the others. He wondered if they'd have invited him if they knew that his father had killed two men, that his brother had been in jail for rape, that his sister was pregnant (she had written him to tell him, so that it wouldn't come as a horrid surprise, she said) and living with a married man, that his mother had demanded thirty thousand dollars from his father if he wanted to go to bed with her.

The Jordaches were special, there was no doubt about that.

Buddy Westerman came over and said, "Listen, kids, there's punch upstairs and sandwiches and cake."

"Thanks, Buddy," Rudolph said. He wished Julie would get the hell off his lap.

Buddy went around passing the word along to the other couples. There was nothing wrong with Buddy. He was going to Cornell, and then to law school, because his father had a solid law practice in town. Buddy had been approached by the new group to play bass for them, but out of loyalty to the River Five had said no. Rudolph gave Buddy's loyalty just about three weeks to wear out. Buddy was a born musician and as he said, "Those guys really make music," and you couldn't expect Buddy to hold out forever, especially as they didn't get more than one date a month any more.

As he looked at the boys in the room, Rudolph realized that almost every one of them knew where he was going. Kessler's father had a pharmacy and Kessler was going to go to pharmaceutical school after college and take over the old man's business. Starrett's father dealt in real estate and Starrett was going to Harvard and to the school of business there, to make sure he could tell his father how to use his money. Lawson's family had an engineering concern and Lawson was going to study engineering. Even Dailey, who probably was too slow to get into college, was going into his father's plumbing supply business.

There was a great opening for Rudolph in the ancestral oven. "I am going into grains." Or perhaps, "I intend to join the German army. My father is an alumnus."

Rudolph felt a sick surge of envy for all his friends. Benny Goodman was playing the clarinet like silver lace on the phonograph and Rudolph envied *him*. Maybe most of all.

On a night like this you could understand why people robbed banks.

He wasn't going to come to any more parties. He didn't belong there, even if he was the only one who knew it.

He wanted to go home. He was tired. He was always tired these days, somehow. Aside from the bicycle route in the morning, he had to tend the store every day from four to seven, after school closed. The widow had decided she couldn't work the whole day, she had children at home to take care of. It had meant giving up the track and the debating teams and his marks were slipping, too, as he never seemed to find the energy to study. He'd been sick, too, with a cold that started after Christmas and seemed to be hanging on all winter.

"Julie," he said, "let's go home."

She sat up straight on his lap, surprised.

"It's early," she said, "it's a nice party."

"I know, I know," he said, sounding more impatient than he intended. "I just want to get out of here."

"We can't do anything in my house," she said. "My folks have people over for bridge. It's Friday."

"I just want to go home," he said.

"You go." She got off his lap and stood over him angrily. "I'll find somebody else to take me home."

He was tempted to spill out everything he had been thinking. Maybe she'd understand then.

"Boy, oh boy," Julie said. There were tears in her eyes. "This is the first party we've been to in months and you want to go home practically before we get here."

"I just feel lousy," he said. He stood up.

"It's peculiar," she said. "Just the nights you're with me you feel lousy. I bet you feel just fine the nights you go out with Teddy Boylan."

"Oh, lay off Boylan, will you, Julie?" Rudolph said, "I haven't seen him for weeks."

"What's the matter—he run out of peroxide?"

"Joke," Rudolph said wearily.

She turned on her heel, her pony tail swinging, and went over to the group around the phonograph. She was the prettiest girl in the room, snub-nosed, scrubbed, smart, slender, dear, and Rudolph wished she would go away someplace for six months, a year, and then come back, after he had gotten over being tired, and had a chance to figure everything out in peace and they could start all over again.

He went upstairs and put on his coat and left the house without saying good night to anyone. Judy Garland was on the phonograph now, singing "The Trolley Song."

It was raining outside, a cold, drifting, February misty river rain, blowing at him in the wind. He coughed inside his coat, with the wet trickling down inside his turned-up collar. He walked slowly toward home, feeling like crying. He hated these spats with Julie, and they were becoming more and more frequent. If they made love to each other, really made love, not that frustrating, foolish necking that made them both ashamed after it, he was sure they wouldn't be scratching at each other all the time. But he couldn't bring himself to do it. It would have to be hidden, they'd have to lie, they'd have to sneak off somewhere like criminals. He had long ago made up his mind. It was going to be perfect or it wasn't going to happen.

The hotel manager threw open the door of the suite. There was a balcony overlooking the Mediterranean. There was a smell of jasmine and thyme in the air. The two bronzed young people looked around the room coolly, glanced at the Mediterranean. Uniformed bellboys brought in many pieces of leather luggage and distributed them around the rooms.

"*Ça vous plaît, Monsieur?*" *the manager asked.*

"*Ça va,*" *the bronzed young man said.*

"*Merci, Monsieur.*" *The hotel manager backed out of the room.*

The two bronzed young people went out onto the balcony and looked at the sea. They kissed against the blueness. The smell of jasmine and thyme became stronger.

Or . . .

It was only a small log cabin, with the snow piled high against its sides. The mountains reared behind it. The two bronzed young people came in shaking the snow from their clothes, laughing. There was a fire roaring in the fireplace. The snow was so high it covered the windows. They were all alone in the high world. The two bronzed young people sank down to the floor in front of the fire.

Or . . .

The two bronzed young people walked along the red carpet on the platform. The Twentieth Century to Chicago stood on the tracks, gleaming. The two young people went past the porter in his white coat, into the car. The stateroom was full of flowers. There was the smell of roses. The two bronzed young people smiled at each other and strolled through the train to the club car for a drink.

Or . . .

Rudolph coughed miserably in the rain as he turned into Vanderhoff Street. I've seen too goddamn many movies, he thought.

The light from the cellar was coming up through the grating in front of the bakery. The Eternal Flame. Axel Jordache, the Unknown Soldier. If his father died, Rudolph thought, would anyone remember to put out the light?

Rudolph hesitated, the keys to the house in his hand. Ever since the night his mother had made that crazy speech about thirty thousand dollars, he had felt sorry for his father. His father walked around the house slowly and quietly, like a man who has just come out of a hospital after a major operation, a man who had felt the warning tap of death on his shoulder. Axel Jordache had always seemed strong, terrifyingly strong, to Rudolph. His voice had been loud, his movements abrupt and careless. Now his long silences, his hesitant gestures, his slow, apologetic way of spreading a newspaper or fixing himself a pot of coffee, careful not to make any unnecessary noise, was somehow frightening. Suddenly, it seemed to Rudolph that his father was preparing himself for his grave. Standing in the dark hallway with his hand on the banister, for the first time since he was a little boy he asked himself whether he loved his father or not.

He went over to the door leading to the bakery, unlocked it and passed through it to the back room and descended into the cellar.

His father wasn't doing anything, just sitting on his bench, staring ahead of him at the oven, the bottle of whiskey on the floor beside him. The cat lay crouched in the corner.

"Hello, Pa," Rudolph said.

His father turned his head slowly toward him and nodded.

"I just came down to see if there was something I could do."

"No," his father said. He reached down and picked up the bottle and took a small swig. He offered the bottle to Rudolph. "Want some?"

"Thanks." Rudolph didn't want any whiskey, but he felt his father would like it if he took some. The bottle was slippery from his father's sweat. He took a swig. It burned his mouth and throat.

"You're soaking wet," his father said.

"It's raining out."

"Take off your coat. You don't want to sit there in a wet coat."

Rudolph took off his coat and hung it on a hook on the wall. "How're things, Pa?" he asked. It was a question he had never asked his father before.

His father chuckled quietly, but didn't answer. He took another swig of the whiskey.

"What'd you do tonight?" Axel asked.

"I went to a party."

"A party." Axel nodded. "Did you play your horn?"

"No."

"What do people do at a party these days?"

"I don't know. Dance. Listen to music. Kid around."

"Did I ever tell you I went to dancing school when I was a boy?" Axel said. "In Cologne. In white gloves. They taught me how to bow. Cologne was nice in the summertime. Maybe I ought to go back there. They'll be starting everything up from scratch there now, maybe that's the place for me. A ruin for the ruins."

"Come on, Pa," Rudolph said. "Don't talk like that."

Axel took another drink. "I had a visitor today," he said. "Mr. Harrison."

Mr. Harrison was the owner of the building. He came on the third of each month for the rent. He was at least eighty years old, but he never missed collecting. In person. It wasn't the third of the month, so Rudolph knew that the visit must have been an important one. "What'd he want?" Rudolph said.

"They're tearing down the building," Axel said. "They're going to put up a whole block of apartments with stores on the ground floor. Port Philip is expanding, Mr. Harrison says, progress is progress. He's eighty years old, but he's progressing. He's investing a lot of money. In Cologne they knock the building down with bombs. In America they do it with money."

"When do we have to get out?"

"Not till October. Mr. Harrison says he's telling me early, so I'll have a chance to find something else. He's a considerate old man, Mr. Harrison."

Rudolph looked around him at the familiar cracked walls, the iron doors of the ovens, the window open to the grating on the sidewalk. It was queer to think of all this, the house he had known all his life, no longer there, vanished. He had always thought he would leave the house. It had never occurred to him that the house would leave him.

"What're you going to do?" he asked his father.

Axel shrugged. "Maybe they need a baker in Cologne. If I happen to find a drunken Englishman some rainy night along the river maybe I could buy passage back to Germany."

"What're you talking about, Pa?" Rudolph asked sharply.

"That's how I came to America," Axel said mildly. "I followed a drunken Englishman who'd been waving his money around in a bar in the Sankt Pauli district of Hamburg and I drew a knife on him. He put up a fight. The English don't give up anything without a fight. I put the knife in him and took his wallet and I dropped him into the canal. I told you I killed a man with a knife that day with your French teacher, didn't I?"

"Yes," Rudolph said.

"I've always meant to tell you the story," Axel said. "Anytime any of your friends says his ancestors came over on the Mayflower, you can say *your* ancestors came over on a wallet full of five-pound notes. It was a foggy night. He must've been crazy, that Englishman, going around a district like Sankt Pauli with all that money. Maybe he thought he was going to screw every whore in the district and he didn't want to be caught short of cash. So that's what I say, maybe if I can find an Englishman down by the river, maybe I'll make the return trip."

Christ, Rudolph thought bitterly, come on down and have a nice cosy little chat with old Dad in his office . . .

"If you ever happened to kill an Englishman," his father went on, "you'd want to tell your son about it, now, wouldn't you?"

"I don't think you ought to go around talking about it," Rudolph said.

"Oh," Axel said, "you planning to turn me over to the police? I forgot you were so high principled."

"Pa, you ought to forget about it. It's no good thinking about it after all these years. What good does it do?"

Axel didn't answer. He drank reflectively from the bottle.

"Oh, I remember a lot of things," he said. "I get a lot of remembering-time down here at night. I remember shitting my pants along the Meuse. I remember the way my leg smelled the second week in the hospital. I remember carrying two-hundred-pound sacks of cocoa on the docks in Hamburg, with my leg opening up and bleeding every day. I remember what the Englishman said before I pushed him into the canal. 'I say there,' he said, 'you can't do that.' I remember the day of my marriage. I could tell you about that, but I think you'd be more interested in your mother's report. I remember the look on the face of a man called Abraham Chase in Ohio when I laid five thousand dollars on the table in front of him to make him feel better for getting his daughters laid." He drank again. "I worked twenty years of my life," he went on, "to pay to keep your brother out of jail. Your mother has let it be known that she thinks I was wrong. Do you think I was wrong?"

"No," Rudolph said.

"You're going to have a rough time from now on, Rudy," Axel said. "I'm sorry. I tried to do my best."

"I'll get by," Rudolph said. He wasn't at all sure he would.

"Go for the money," Axel said. "Don't let anybody fool you. Don't go for anything else. Don't listen to all that crap they write in the papers about Other Values. That's what the rich preach to the poor so that they can keep raking it in, without getting their throats cut. Be Abraham Chase with that look on his face, picking up the bills. How much money you got in the bank?"

"A hundred and sixty dollars," Rudolph said.

"Don't part with it," Axel said. "Not with a penny of it. Not even if I come dragging up to your door starving to death and ask you for the price of a meal. Don't give me a dime."

"Pa, you're getting yourself all worked up. Why don't you go upstairs and go to bed. I'll put in the hours here."

"You stay out of here. Or just come and talk to me, if you want. But stay away from the work. You got better things to do. Learn your lessons. All of them. Step careful. The sins of the fathers. Unto how many generations. My father used to read the Bible after dinner in the living room. I may not be leaving you much, but I sure as hell am leaving you well visited with sins. Two men killed. All my whores. And what I did to your mother. And letting Thomas grow up like wild grass. And who knows what Gretchen is doing. Your mother seems to have some information. You ever see her?"

"Yeah," Rudolph said.

"What's she up to?"

"You'd rather not hear," Rudolph said.

"That figures," his father said. "God watches. I don't go to church, but I know God watches. Keeping the books on Axel Jordache and his generations."

"Don't talk like that," Rudolph said. "God doesn't watch anything." His atheism was firm. "You've had some bad luck. That's all. Everything can change tomorrow."

"Pay up, God says." Rudolph had the feeling his father wasn't talking to him anymore, that he would be saying the same things, in the same dreamlike dead voice if he were alone in the cellar. "Pay up, Sinner, I will afflict you and your sons for your deeds." He took a long drink, shook himself, as though a shiver had run coldly through his body. "Go to bed," he said. "I got work to do."

"Good night, Pa." Rudolph took his coat off the hook on the wall. His father didn't answer, just sat there, staring, holding the bottle.

Rudolph went upstairs. Christ, he thought, and I thought it was Ma who was the crazy one.

II

Axel took another drink from the bottle, then went back to work. He worked steadily all night. He found himself humming as he moved around the cellar. He didn't recognize the tune for a while. It bothered him, not recognizing it. Then he remembered. It was a song his mother used to sing when she was in the kitchen.

He sang the words, low,

> *Schlaf', Kindlein, schlaf'*
> *Dein Vater hüt' die Schlaf'*
> *Die Mutter hüt die Ziegen,*
> *Wir wollen das Kindlein wiegen?*

His native tongue. He had traveled too far. Or not far enough.

He had the last pan of rolls ready to go into the oven. He left it standing on the table and went over to a shelf and took down a can. There was a warning skull-and-bones on the label. He dug into the can and measured out a small spoonful of the powder. He carried it over to the table and picked up one of the raw rolls at random. He kneaded the poison into the roll thoroughly, then reshaped the roll and put it back into the pan. My message to the world, he thought.

The cat watched him. He put the pan of rolls into the oven and went over to the sink and stripped off his shirt and washed his hands and face and arms and torso. He dried himself on flour sacking and redressed. He sat down, facing the oven, and put the bottle, now nearly empty, to his lips.

He hummed the tune his mother had sung in her kitchen when he was a small boy.

When the rolls were baked, he pulled out the pan and left them to cool. All the rolls looked the same.

Then he turned off the gas in the ovens and put on his mackinaw and cap. He went up the steps into the bakery and went out. He let the cat follow him. It was dark and still raining. The wind had freshened. He kicked the cat and the cat ran off.

He limped toward the river.

He opened the rusty padlock of the warehouse and turned on a light. He picked up the shell and carried it to the rickety wharf. The river was rough, with whitecaps, and made a sucking, rushing sound as it swept past. The wharf was protected by a curling jetty and the water there was calm. He put the shell down on the wharf and went back and got the oars and turned out the light and snapped the padlock shut. He carried the oars back to the wharf and lay them down along the edge, then put the shell in the water. He stepped in lightly and put the oars into the outriggers.

He pushed off and guided the shell out toward open water. The current caught him and he began to row steadily out toward the river's center. He went downstream, the waves washing over the sides of the shell, the rain beating in his face. In a little while the shell was low in the water. He continued to row steadily, as the river ran swiftly down toward New York, the bays, the open ocean.

The shell was almost completely awash as he reached the heart of the river.

The shell was found, overturned, the next day, near Bear Mountain. They didn't ever find Axel Jordache.

PART
TWO

Chapter 1

1949

Dominic Joseph Agostino sat at the little desk in his office behind the gym with the newspaper spread out in front of him to the sports page, reading about himself. He had his Ben Franklin reading glasses on and they gave a mild, studious look to his round, ex-pug's face, with the broken nose and the small, dark eyes under the heavy scar tissue. It was three o'clock, the mid-afternoon lull, and the gym was empty, the best time of day. There wouldn't be anything much doing until five o'clock when he gave a calisthenics class to a group of club members, middle-aged businessmen most of them, fighting their waistlines. After that he might spar a few rounds with some of the more ambitious members, being careful not to damage anybody.

The article about him had come out the night before, in a box on the sports page. It was a slow day. The Red Sox were out of town and weren't going anyplace, anyway, and they had to fill the sports page with something.

Dominic had been born in Boston, and had been introduced in his fighting days as Joe Agos, the Boston Beauty, because he lacked a punch and had to do a lot of dancing around to keep from getting killed. He had fought some good lightweights in the late twenties and thirties and the sportswriter, who was too young ever to have seen him fight, had written stirring accounts of his matches with people like Canzoneri and McLarnin, when Canzoneri and McLarnin were on the way up. The sportswriter had written that he was still in good shape, which wasn't all that true. The sportswriter quoted Dominic as saying jokingly that some of the younger members of the exclusive Revere Club were beginning to get to him in the sparring sessions in the gym and that he was thinking of getting an assistant or putting on a catcher's mask to protect his beauty in the near future. He hadn't said it all that jokingly. The article was friendly, and made Dominic sound like a wise old veteran of the golden days of the sport who had learned to accept life philosophically in his years in the ring. He had lost every cent he'd ever made, so there wasn't much else left but philosophy. He hadn't said anything about that to the writer and it wasn't in the article.

The phone on his desk rang. It was the doorman. There was a kid downstairs who wanted to see him. Dominic told the doorman to send the kid up.

The kid was about nineteen or twenty, wearing a faded blue sweater and sneakers. He was blond and blue-eyed and baby-faced. He reminded Dominic of Jimmy McLarnin, who had nearly torn him apart the time they had fought in New York. The kid had grease-stained hands, even though Dominic could see that he had tried to wash it all out. It was a cinch none of the members of the Revere Club had invited the kid up for a workout or a game of squash.

"What is it?" Dominic asked, looking up over his Ben Franklin glasses.

"I read the paper last night," the kid said.

"Yeah?" Dominic was always affable and smiling with the members and he made up for it with non-members.

"About how it's getting a little tough for you, Mr. Agostino, at your age, with the younger members of the club and so on," the kid said.

"Yeah?"

"I was thinking maybe you could take on an assistant, kind of," the kid said.

"You a fighter?"

"Not exactly," the kid said. "Maybe I want to be. I seem to fight an awful lot of the time . . ." He grinned. "I figure I might as well get paid for it."

"Come on." Dominic stood up and took off his glasses. He went out of the office and through the gym to the locker room. The kid followed him. The locker room was empty except for Charley, the attendant, who was dozing, sitting up at the door, his head on a pile of towels.

"You got any things with you?" Dominic asked the kid.

"No."

Dominic gave him an old sweat suit and a pair of shoes. He watched as the kid stripped. Long legs, heavy, sloping shoulders, thick neck. A hundred and fifty pounds, fifty-five, maybe. Good arms. No fat.

Dominic led him out to the corner of the gym where the mats were and threw him a pair of sixteen-ounce gloves. Charley came out to tie the laces for both of them.

"Let's see what you can do, kid," Dominic said. He put up his hands, lightly. Charley watched with interest.

The kid's hands were too low, naturally, and Dominic jabbed him twice with his left. But the kid kept swarming in.

After three minutes, Dominic dropped his hands and said, "Okay, that's enough." He had rapped the kid pretty hard a few times and had tied him up when he came in close, but with all that, the kid was awfully fast and the twice he had connected it had hurt. The kid was some kind of a fighter. Just what kind of fighter Dominic didn't know, but a fighter.

"Now listen, kid," Dominic said, as Charley undid the laces on his gloves, "this isn't a barroom. This is a gentlemen's club. The gentlemen don't come here to get hurt. They come to get some exercise while learning the manly art of self-defense. You come swinging in on them the way you did with me, you wouldn't last one day here."

"Sure," the kid said, "I understand. But I wanted to show you what I could do."

"You can't do much," Dominic said. "Yet. But you're fast and you move okay. Where you working now?"

"I was over in Brookline," the kid said. "In a garage. I'd like to find something where I can keep my hands clean."

"When you figure you could start in here?"

"Now. Today. I quit at the garage last week."

"How much you make there?"

"Fifty a week," the kid said.

"I think I can get you thirty-five here," Dominic said. "But you can rig up a cot in the massage room and sleep here. You'll have to help clean the swimming pool and vacuum the mats and stuff like that and check the equipment."

"Okay," the kid said.

"You got a job," Dominic said. "What's your name?"

"Thomas Jordache," the kid said.

"Just keep out of trouble, Tom," said Dominic.

He kept out of trouble for quite some time. He was quick and re-spectful and besides the work he had been hired to do, he cheerfully ran errands for Dominic and the members and made a point of smil-ing agreeably, at all times, with especial attention to the older men. The atmosphere of the club, muted, rich, and friendly, pleased him, and when he wasn't in the gym he liked to pass through the high-ceilinged, dark, wood-paneled reading and gaming rooms, with their deep leather armchairs and smoked-over oil paintings of Boston dur-ing the days of sailing ships. The work was undemanding, with long gaps in the day when he just sat around listening to Dominic reminisce about his years in the ring.

Dominic was not curious about Tom's past and Tom didn't bother to tell him about the months on the road, the flophouses in Cincinnati and Cleveland, and Chicago, about the jobs at filling sta-tions, or about the stretch as a bellboy in the hotel in Syracuse. He had been making good money at the hotel steering whores into guests' rooms until he had to take a knife out of a pimp's fist because the pimp objected to the size of the commission his girls were pass-ing on to the nice baby-faced boy they could mother when they weren't otherwise occupied. Thomas didn't tell Dominic, either, about the drunks he had rolled on the Loop or the loose cash he had stolen in various rooms, more for the hell of it than for the money, because he wasn't all that interested in money.

Dominic taught him how to hit the light bag and it was pleasant on a rainy afternoon, when the gym was empty, to tap away, faster and faster, at the bag, making the gym resound with the tattoo of the blows. Once in awhile, when he was feeling ambitious, and there were no members around, Dominic put on the gloves with him and taught him how to put together combinations, how to straighten out his right hand, how to use his head and elbows and slide with the punches, to keep up on the balls of his feet and how to avoid punches by ducking and weaving as he came in instead of falling back. Dominic still didn't allow him to spar with any of the members, because he wasn't sure about Thomas yet and didn't want any incidents. But the squash pro got him down to the courts and in just a few weeks made a fair player of him and when some of the lesser players of the club turned up without a partner for a game,

Thomas would go in there with them. He was quick and agile and he didn't mind losing and when he won he learned immediately not to make the win too easy and he found himself collecting twenty to thirty dollars a week extra in tips.

He became friendly with the cook in the club kitchen, mostly by finding a solid connection for buying decent marijuana and doing the cook's shopping for him for the drug, so before long he was getting all his meals free.

He tactfully stayed out of all but the most desultory conversations with the members, who were lawyers, brokers, bankers, and officials of shipping lines and manufacturing companies. He learned to take messages accurately from their wives and mistresses over the telephone and pass them on with no hint that he understood exactly what he was doing.

He didn't like to drink, and the members, as they downed their post-exercise whiskies at the bar, commented favorably on that, too.

There was no plan to his behavior; he wasn't looking for anything; he just knew that it was better to ingratiate himself with the solid citizens who patronized the club than not. He had knocked around too much, a stray in America, getting into trouble and always finishing in brawls that sent him on the road again. Now the peace and security and approval of the club were welcome to him. It wasn't a career, he told himself, but it was a good year. He wasn't ambitious. When Dominic talked vaguely of his signing up for some amateur bouts just to see how good he was, he put the old fighter off.

When he got restless he would go downtown and pick up a whore and spend the night with her, honest money for honest services, and no complications in the morning.

He even liked the city of Boston, or at least as much as he had ever liked any place, although he didn't travel around it much by daylight, as he was pretty sure that there was an assault and battery warrant out for him as a result of the last afternoon at the garage in Brookline, when the foreman had come at him with a monkey wrench. He had gone right back to his rooming house that afternoon and packed and got out in ten minutes, telling his landlady he was heading for Florida. Then he had booked into the Y.M.C.A. and lain low for a week, until he had seen the article in the newspaper about Dominic.

He had his likes and dislikes among the members, but was careful to be impartially pleasant to all of them. He didn't want to get involved with anybody. He had had enough involvements. He tried not to know too much about any of the members, but of course it was impossible not to form opinions, especially when you saw a man naked, his pot belly swelling, or his back scratched by some dame from his last go in bed, or taking it badly when he was losing a silly game of squash.

Dominic hated all the members equally, but only because they had money and he didn't. Dominic had been born and brought up in Boston and his *a* was as flat as anybody's, but in spirit he was still working by the day in a landlord's field in Sicily, plotting to burn down the landlord's castle and cut the throats of the landlord's family. Naturally, he concealed his dreams of arson and murder behind the most cordial of manners, always telling the members how well they looked when they came back after a vacation, marveling about how much weight they seemed to have lost, and being solicitous about aches and sprains.

"Here comes the biggest crook in Massachusetts," Dominic would whisper to Thomas, as an important-looking, gray-haired gentleman came into the locker room, and then, aloud, to the member, "Why, sir, it's good to see you back. We've missed you. I guess you've been working too hard."

"Ah, work, work," the man would say, shaking his head sadly.

"I know how it is, sir." Dominic would shake his head, too. "Come on down and I'll give you a nice turn on the weights and then you take a steam and a swim and a massage and you'll get all the kinks out and sleep like a babe tonight."

Thomas watched and listened carefully, learning from Dominic, useful dissembler. He liked the stony-hearted ex-pug, committed deep within him, despite all blandishments, to anarchy and loot.

Thomas also liked a man by the name of Reed, a hearty, easy-going president of a textile concern, who played squash with Thomas and insisted upon going onto the courts with him, even when there were other members hanging around waiting for a game. Reed was about forty-five and fairly heavy, but still played well and he and Thomas split their matches most of the time, Reed winning the early games and just losing out when he began to tire. "Young legs, young legs," Reed would say laughing, wiping the sweat off his face with a towel, as they walked together toward the showers after an hour on the courts. They played three times a week, regularly, and Reed always offered Thomas a Coke after they had cooled off and slipped him a five-dollar bill each time. He had one peculiarity. He always carried a hundred-dollar bill neatly folded in the right-hand pocket of his jacket. "A hundred-dollar bill saved my life once," Reed told Thomas. He had been caught in a dreadful fire one night in a nightclub, in which many people had perished. Reed had been lying under a pile of bodies near the door, hardly able to move, his throat too seared to cry out. He had heard the firemen dragging at the pile of bodies and with his last strength he had dug into his pants pocket, where he kept a hundred-dollar bill. He had managed to drag the bill out and work one arm free. His hand, waving feebly, with the bill clutched in it, had been seen. He had felt the money being taken from his grasp and then a fireman had moved the bodies lying on him and dragged him to safety. He had spent two weeks in the hospital, unable to talk, but he had survived, with a firm faith in the power of a single one-hundred-dollar bill. When possible, he advised Thomas, he should always try to have a hundred-dollar bill in a convenient pocket.

He also told Thomas to save his money and invest in the stock market, because young legs did not remain young forever.

The trouble came when he had been there three months. He sensed that something was wrong when he went to his locker to change after a late game of squash with Brewster Reed. There were no obvious signs, but he somehow knew somebody had been in there going through his clothes, looking for something. His wallet was half out of the back pocket of his trousers, as though it had been taken out and hastily stuffed back. Thomas took the wallet out and opened it. There had been four five-dollar bills in it and they were still there. He put the five-dollar bill Reed had tipped him into the wallet and slipped the wallet back in place. In the side pocket of his trousers there were some three dollars in bills and change, which had also been there before he had gone to the courts. A magazine which he had been reading and which he remembered putting front cover up on the top shelf was now spread open on the shelf.

For a moment Thomas thought of locking up, but then he thought, hell, if there's anybody in this club so poor he has to steal from me, he's welcome. He undressed, put his shoes in the locker, wrapped himself in a towel and went to the shower room, where Brewster Reed was already happily splashing around.

When he came back after the shower, there was a note pinned onto the inside of the locker door. It was in Dominic's handwriting and it read, "I want you in my office after closing time. D. Agostino."

The curtness of the message, the fact of its being written at all when he and Dominic passed each other ten times an afternoon, meant trouble. Something official, planned. Here we go again, he thought and almost was ready to finish dressing and quietly slip away, once and for all. But he decided against it, had his dinner in the kitchen, and afterward chatted unconcernedly with the squash pro and Charley in the locker room. Promptly at ten o'clock, when the club closed, he presented himself at Dominic's office.

Dominic was reading a copy of *Life*, slowly turning the pages on his desk. He looked up, closed the magazine and put it neatly to one side of the desk. He got up and looked out into the hall to make sure it was empty, then closed his office door. "Sit down, kid," he said.

Thomas sat down and waited while Dominic sat down opposite him behind the desk.

"What's up?" Thomas asked.

"Plenty," Dominic said. "The shit is hitting the fan. I've been getting reamed out all day."

"What's it got to do with me?"

"That's what I'm going to find out," Dominic said. "No use beatin' around the bush, kid. Somebody's been lifting dough out of people's wallets. Some smart guy who takes a bill here and there and leaves the rest. These fat bastards here're so rich most of 'em don't even know what they have in their pockets and if they do happen to miss an odd ten or twenty here or there, they think maybe they lost it or they made a mistake the last time they counted. But one guy is sure he don't make no mistakes. That bastard Greening. He says a ten-dollar bill was lifted from his locker while he was working out with me yesterday and he's been on the phone all day today talking to other members and now suddenly everybody's sure he's been robbed blind the last few months."

"Still, what's that got to do with me?" Thomas said, although he knew what it had to do with him.

"Greening figured out that it's only begun since you came to work here."

"That big shit," Thomas said bitterly. Greening was a cold-eyed man of about thirty who worked in a stock broker's office and who boxed with Dominic. He had fought light-heavy for some school out West and kept in shape and took no pity on Dominic, but went after him savagely for three two-minute rounds four times a week. After his sessions with Greening, Dominic, who didn't dare really to counter hard, was often bruised and exhausted.

"He's a shit all right," Dominic said. "He made me search your locker this afternoon. It's a lucky thing you didn't happen to have any ten-dollar bills there. Even so, he wants to call the police and have you booked on suspicion."

"What did you say to that?" Thomas asked.

"I talked him out of it," Dominic said. "I said I'd have a word with you."

"Well, you're having a word with me," Thomas said. "Now what?"

"Did you take the dough?"

"No. Do you believe me?"

Dominic shrugged warily. "I don't know. *Somebody* sure as hell took it."

"A lot of people walk around the locker room all day. Charley, the guy from the pool, the pro, the members, you . . ."

"Cut it out, kid," Dominic said. "I don't want no jokes."

"Why pick on me?" Thomas asked.

"I told you. It only started since you came to work here. Ah, Christ, they're talking about putting padlocks on all the lockers. Nobody's ever locked anything here for a hundred years. The way they talk they're in the middle of the biggest crime wave since Jesse James."

"What do you want me to do? Quit?"

"Naah." Dominic shook his head. "Just be careful. Keep in *somebody's* sight all the time." He sighed. "Maybe it'll all blow over. That bastard Greening and his lousy ten bucks . . . Come on out with me." He stood up wearily and stretched. "I'll buy you a beer. What a lousy day."

The locker room was empty when Thomas came through the door. He had been sent out to the post office with a package and he was in his street clothes. There was an interclub squash match on and everybody was upstairs watching it. Everybody but one of the members called Sinclair, who was on the team, but who had not yet played his match. He was dressed, ready to play, and was wearing a white sweater. He was a tall, slender young man who had a law degree from Harvard and whose father was also a member of the club. The family had a lot of money and their name was in the papers often. Young Sinclair worked in his father's law office in the city and Thomas had overheard older men in the club saying that young Sinclair was a brilliant lawyer and would go far.

But right now, as Thomas came down the aisle silently in his tennis shoes, young Sinclair was standing in front of an open locker and he had his hand in the inside pocket of the jacket hanging there and he was deftly taking out a wallet. Thomas wasn't sure whose locker it was, but he knew it wasn't Sinclair's, because Sinclair's locker was only three away from his own on the other side of the room. Sinclair's face, which was usually cheerful and ruddy, was pale and tense and he was sweating.

For a moment, Thomas hesitated, wondering if he could turn and get away before Sinclair saw him. But just as Sinclair got the wallet out, he looked up and saw Thomas. They stared at each other. Then it was too late to back away. Thomas moved quickly toward the man and grabbed his wrist. Sinclair was panting, as though he had been running a great distance.

"You'd better put that back, sir," Thomas whispered.

"All right," Sinclair said. "I'll put it back." He whispered, too.

Thomas did not release his wrist. He was thinking fast. If he denounced Sinclair, on one excuse or another he would lose his job. It would be too uncomfortable for the other members to be subjected daily to the presence of a lowly employee who had disgraced one of their own. If he didn't denounce him . . . Thomas played for time. "You know, sir," he said, "they suspect me."

"I'm sorry." Thomas could feel the man trembling, but Sinclair didn't try to pull away.

"You're going to do three things," Thomas said. "You're going to put the wallet back and you're going to promise to lay off from now on."

"I promise, Tom. I'm very grateful . . ."

"You're going to show just how grateful you are, Mr. Sinclair," Thomas said. "You're going to write out an IOU for five thousand dollars to me right now and you're going to pay me in cash within three days."

"You're out of your mind," Sinclair said, sweat standing out on his forehead.

"All right," Thomas said. "I'll start yelling."

"I bet you would, you little bastard," Sinclair said.

"I'll meet you in the bar of the Hotel Touraine, Thursday night at eleven o'clock," Thomas said. "Pay night."

"I'll be there." Sinclair's voice was so low that Thomas could barely hear it. He dropped the man's hand and watched as Sinclair put the wallet back into the jacket pocket. Then he took out a small notebook in which he kept a record of petty expenses he laid out on errands and opened it to a blank page and handed Sinclair a pencil.

Sinclair looked down at the open notebook thrust under his nose. If he could steady his nerves, Thomas knew, he could just walk away and if Thomas told anybody the story he could laugh it off. But never completely laugh it off. Anyway, his nerves were shot. He took the notebook, scribbled in it.

Thomas glanced at the page, put the notebook in his pocket and took back the pencil. Then he gently closed the locker door and went upstairs to watch the squash.

Fifteen minutes later Sinclair came onto the court and beat his opponent in straight games.

In the locker room later, Thomas congratulated him on his victory.

He got to the bar of the Touraine at five to eleven. He was dressed in a suit with a collar and tie. Tonight he wanted to pass for a gentleman. The bar was dark and only a third full. He carefully sat down at a table in a corner, where he could watch the entrance. When the waiter came over to him, he ordered a bottle of Budweiser. Five thousand dollars, he thought, five thousand . . . They had taken that amount from his father and he was taking it back from them. He wondered if Sinclair had had to go to *his* father to get the money and had had to explain why he needed it. Probably not. Probably Sinclair had so much dough in his own name he could lay his hands on five thousand cash in ten minutes. Thomas had nothing against Sinclair. Sinclair was a pleasant young man, with nice, friendly eyes and a soft voice and good manners who from time to time had given him some pointers on how to play drop shots in squash and whose life would be ruined if it became known he was a kleptomaniac. The system had just worked out that way.

He sipped at his beer, watching the door. At three minutes after eleven, the door opened and Sinclair came in. He peered around the dark room and Thomas stood up. Sinclair came over to the table and Thomas said, "Good evening, sir."

"Good evening, Tom," Sinclair said evenly and sat down on the banquette, but without taking off his topcoat.

"What are you drinking?" Thomas asked, as the waiter came over.

"Scotch and water, please," Sinclair said with his polite, Harvard way of talking.

"And another Bud, please," said Thomas.

They sat in silence for a moment, side by side on the banquette. Sinclair drummed his fingers briefly on the table, scanning the room. "Do you come here often?" he asked.

"Once in awhile."

"Do you ever see anybody from the Club here?"

"No."

The waiter came over and put down their drinks. Sinclair took a thirsty gulp from his glass. "Just for your information," Sinclair said, "I don't take the money because I need it."

"I know," Thomas said.

"I'm sick," Sinclair said. "It's a disease. I'm going to a psychiatrist."

"That's smart of you," Thomas said.

"You don't mind doing what you're doing to a sick man?"

"No," Thomas said. "No, sir."

"You're a hard little son of a bitch, aren't you?"

"I hope so, sir," said Thomas.

Sinclair opened his coat and reached inside and brought out a long, full envelope. He put it down on the banquette between himself and Thomas. "It's all there," he said. "You needn't bother to count it."

"I'm sure it's all there," Thomas said. He slipped the envelope into his side pocket.

"I'm waiting," Sinclair said. Thomas took out the IOU and put it on the table. Sinclair glanced at it, tore it up and stuffed the shreds into an ashtray. He stood up. "Thanks for the drink," he said. He walked toward the door past the bar, a handsome young man, the marks of breeding, gentility, education, and good luck clearly on him.

Thomas watched him go out and slowly finished his beer. He paid for the drinks and went into the lobby and rented a room for the night. Upstairs, with the door locked and the blinds down, he counted the money. It was all in hundred-dollar bills, all new. It occurred to him that they might be marked, but he couldn't tell.

He slept well in the big double bed and in the morning called the Club and told Dominic that he had to go to New York on family business and wouldn't be in until Monday afternoon. He hadn't taken any days off since he'd started working at the Club, so Dominic had to say okay, but no later than Monday.

It was drizzling when the train pulled into the station and the gray, autumnal drip didn't make Port Philip look any better as Thomas went out of the station. He hadn't brought his coat, so he put up the collar of his jacket to try to keep the rain from going down his neck.

The station square didn't look much different. The Port Philip House had been repainted and a big radio and television shop in a new, yellow-brick building was advertising a sale in portable radios. The smell of the river was still the same and Tom remembered it.

He could have taken a taxi, but after the years of absence he preferred to walk. The streets of his native town would slowly prepare him—for just what he was not quite sure.

He walked past the bus station. The last ride with his brother Rudolph. *You smell like a wild animal.*

He walked past Bernstein's Department Store, his sister's rendezvous point with Theodore Boylan. The naked man in the living room, the burning cross. Happy boyhood memories.

He walked past the public school. The returned malarial soldier and the samurai sword and the Jap's head spouting blood.

Nobody said hello. All faces in the mean rain looked hurried, closed, and unfamiliar. Return in Triumph. Welcome, Citizen.

He walked past St. Anselm's, Claude Tinker's uncle's church. *By the Grace of God, he was not observed.*

He turned into Vanderhoff Street. The rain was coming down more strongly. He touched the bulge in the breast of his jacket that concealed the envelope with the money in it. The street had changed. A square prisonlike building had been put up and there was some sort of factory in it. Some of the old shops were boarded up and there were names he didn't recognize on the windows of other shops.

He kept his eyes down to keep the rain from driving into them, so when he looked up finally he was stupidly puzzled because where the bakery had been, where the house in which he was born had stood, there was now a large supermarket, with three stories of apartments above it. He read the signs in the windows. Special Today, Rib Roast. Lamb Shoulder. Women with shopping bags were going in and out of a door which, if the Jordache house had been still there, would have opened onto the front hallway.

Thomas peered through the windows. There were girls making change at the front desks. He didn't know any of them. There was no sense in going in. He was not in the market for rib roasts or lamb shoulders.

Uncertainly, he continued down the street. The garage next door had been rebuilt and the name on it was a different one and he didn't recognize any of the faces there, either. But near the corner he saw that Jardino's Fruits and Vegetables was still where it always had been. He went in and waited while an old woman argued with Mrs. Jardino about string beans.

When the old woman had gone, Mrs. Jardino turned to him. She was a small, shapeless woman with a fierce, beaked nose and a wart on her upper lip from which sprang two long, coarse, black hairs. "Yes," Mrs. Jardino said. "What can I do for you?"

"Mrs. Jardino," Thomas said, putting down his coat collar to look more respectable, "you probably don't remember me, but I used to be a . . . well . . . a kind of neighbor of yours. We used to have the bakery. Jordache?"

Mrs. Jardino peered nearsightedly at him. "Which one were you?"

"The youngest one."

"Oh, yes. The little gangster."

Thomas tried a smile, to compliment Mrs. Jardino on her rough humor. Mrs. Jardino didn't smile back. "So, what do you want?"

"I haven't been here for awhile," Thomas said. "I've come back to pay a family visit. But the bakery isn't there any more."

"It's been gone for years," Mrs. Jardino said impatiently, arranging apples so that the spots wouldn't show. "Didn't your family tell you?"

"We were out of touch for awhile," Thomas said. "Do you know where they are?"

"How should I know where they are? They never talked to dirty Italians." She turned her back squarely on him and fussed with bunches of celery.

"Thank you very much, just the same," Thomas said and started out.

"Wait a minute," Mrs. Jardino said. "When you left, your father was still alive, wasn't he?"

"Yes," Thomas said.

"Well, he's dead," she said. There was a certain satisfaction in her voice. "He drowned. In the river. And then your mother moved away and then they tore the building down and now . . ." bitterly, "there's a supermarket there cutting our throats."

A customer came in and Mrs. Jardino began to weigh five pounds of potatoes and Thomas went out of the shop.

He went and stood in front of the supermarket for awhile, but it didn't tell him anything. He thought of going down to the river, but the river wasn't going to tell him anything, either. He walked back toward the station. He passed a bank and went in and rented a safety deposit box and put forty-nine hundred of the five thousand dollars in the box. He figured he might as well leave his money in

Port Philip as anywhere. Or throw it into the river in which his father had drowned.

He supposed he might be able to find his mother and brother by going to the post office, but he decided against the effort. It was his father he had come to see. And pay off.

Chapter 2

1950

Capped and gowned, Rudolph sat in the June sunlight, among the other graduates in rented black.

"Now, in 1950, at the exact mid-point of the century," the speaker was saying, "we Americans must ask ourselves several questions: What do we have? What do we want? What are our strengths and weaknesses? Where are we going?" The speaker was a cabinet member, up from Washington as a favor for the President of the college, who had been a friend of his at Cornell, a more illustrious place of learning.

Now at the exact mid-point of the century, Rudolph thought, moving restlessly on the camp chair set up on the campus lawn, what do I have, what do I want, what are my strengths and weaknesses, where am I going? I have a B.A., a debt of four thousand dollars, and a dying mother. I want to be rich and free and beloved. My strength—I can run the two-twenty in 23:8. My weakness? I am honest. He smiled inwardly, innocently regarding the Great Man from Washington. Where am I going? You tell me, brother.

The man from Washington was a man of peace. "The curve of military power is rising everywhere," he said in solemn tones. "The only hope for peace is the military might of the United States. To prevent war the United States needs a force so big and strong, so capable of counterattack as to serve as a deterrent."

Rudolph looked along the rows of his fellow graduates. Half of them were veterans of World War II, in college on the G.I. Bill of Rights. Many of them were married, their wives sitting with newly

set hair in the rows behind them, some of them holding infants in
their arms because there was nobody to leave them with in the
trailers and cluttered rented rooms which had been their homes
while their husbands had struggled for the degrees being awarded
today. Rudolph wondered how they felt about the rising curve of
military power.

Sitting next to Rudolph was Bradford Knight, a round-faced florid
young man from Tulsa, who had been a sergeant in the infantry in
Europe. He was Rudolph's best friend on the campus, an energetic,
overt boy, cynical and shrewd behind a lazy Oklahoma drawl. He
had come to Whitby because his captain had graduated from the
school and recommended him to the Dean of Admissions. He and
Rudolph had drunk a lot of beer together and had gone fishing together. Brad kept urging Rudolph to come out to Tulsa with him
after graduation and go into the oil business with him and his father.
"You'll be a millionaire before you're twenty-five, son," Brad had
said. "It's overflowin' country out there. You'll trade in your Cadillac
every time the ashtrays have to be emptied." Brad's father had been
a millionaire before he was twenty-five, but was in a low period now
("Just a little bad run of luck," according to Brad) and couldn't
afford the fare East at the moment for his son's graduation.

Teddy Boylan wasn't at the ceremony, either, although Rudolph
had sent him an invitation. It was the least he could do for the four
thousand dollars. But Boylan had declined. "I'm afraid I can't see
myself driving fifty miles on a nice June afternoon to listen to a
Democrat make a speech on the campus of an obscure agricultural
school." Whitby was not an agricultural school, although it did have
an important agricultural department, but Boylan still resented
Rudolph's refusal even to apply to an Ivy League university when he
had made his offer in 1946 to finance Rudolph's education. "However," the letter had gone on in Boylan's harsh, heavily accented
handwriting, "the day shall not go altogether uncelebrated. Come on
over to the house when the dreary mumblings are over, and we'll
break out a bottle of champagne and talk about your plans."

Rudolph had decided for several reasons to choose Whitby rather
than to take a chance on Yale or Harvard. For one, he'd have owed
Boylan a good deal more than four thousand dollars at the end, and
for another, with his background and his lack of money, he'd have
been a four-year outsider among the young lords of American society
whose fathers and grandfathers had all cheered at Harvard–Yale
games, who whipped back and forth to debutantes' balls, and most

of whom had never worked a day in their lives. At Whitby, poverty was normal. The occasional boy who didn't have to work in the summer to help pay for his books and clothes in the autumn was unusual. The only outsiders, except for an occasional stray like Brad, were bookish freaks who shunned their fellow students and a few politically minded young men who circulated petitions in favor of the United Nations and against compulsory military service.

Another reason that Rudolph had chosen Whitby was that it was close enough to Port Philip so that he could get over on Sundays to see his mother, who was more or less confined to her room and who, friendless, suspicious, and half mad, could not be allowed just to founder into absolute neglect. In the summer of his sophomore year, when he got the job after hours and on Saturdays at Calderwood's Department Store, he had found a cheap little two-room apartment with a kitchenette in Whitby and had moved his mother in with him. She was waiting for him there, now. She hadn't felt well enough to come to the graduation, she said, and besides, she would disgrace him, the way she looked. Disgrace was probably too strong a word, Rudolph thought, looking around at the neatly clothed, sober parents of his classmates, but she certainly wouldn't have dazzled anybody in the assemblage with her beauty or her style of dress. It was one thing to be a dutiful son. It was a very different thing not to face facts.

So—Mary Pease Jordache, sitting in a rocking chair at the window of the shabby apartment, cigarette ashes drifting down on her shawl, legs swollen and almost useless, was not there to see her son rewarded with his roll of imitation parchment. Among the other absentees—Gretchen, linked by blood, detained in New York by a crisis with her child; Julie, being graduated herself that day from Barnard; Thomas, more blood, address unknown; Axel Jordache, blood on his hands, sculling through eternity.

He was alone this day and it was just as well.

"The power of the military establishment is appalling," the speaker was saying, his voice magnified over the public address system, "but one great thing on our side is the wish of the ordinary man everywhere for peace."

If Rudolph was an ordinary man, the cabinet member was certainly speaking for him. Now that he had heard some of the stories about the war in bull sessions around the campus he no longer envied the generation before his which had stood on Guadalcanal and the sandy ridges of Tunisia and at the Rapido River.

The fine, intelligent, educated voice sang on in the sunny quadrangle of red-brick Colonial buildings. Inevitably, there was the salute to America, land of opportunity. Half the young men listening had had the opportunity to be killed for America, but the speaker was looking forward this afternoon, not toward the past, and the opportunities he mentioned were those of scientific research, public service, aid to those nations throughout the world who were not as fortunate as we. He was a good man, the cabinet member, and Rudolph was glad that such a man was near the seat of power in Washington, but his view of opportunity in 1950 was a bit lofty, evangelical, Washingtonian, all very well for a Commencement exercise, but not likely to coincide with the down-to-earth views of the three hundred or so poor men's sons who sat before him in black robes waiting to receive their degrees from a small, under-financed school known, if it was known at all, for its agricultural department, and wondering how they were going to start earning a living the next day.

Up front, in the section reserved for professors, Rudolph saw Professor Denton, the head of the History and Economics departments, squirming in his seat and turning to whisper to Professor Lloyd, of the English Department, sitting on his right. Rudolph smiled, guessing what Professor Denton's comments would be on the cabinet member's ritualistic pronouncements. Denton, a small, fierce, graying man, disappointed because by now he realized he would rise no higher in the academic world, was also a kind of outdated Midwestern Populist, who spent a good deal of his time in the classroom ranting about what he considered the betrayal of the American economic and political system, dating back to the Civil War, by Big Money and Big Business. "The American economy," he had said in class, "is a rigged crap table, with loaded dice. The laws are carefully arranged so that the Rich throw only sevens and everybody else throws only snake-eyes."

At least once a term he made a point of referring to the fact that in 1932, by his own admission before a congressional committee, J. P. Morgan had not paid a cent in income tax. "I want you gentlemen to keep this in mind," Professor Denton would declaim bitterly, "while also keeping in mind that in the same year, on a mere tutor's salary, I paid five hundred and twenty-seven dollars and thirty cents in tax to the Federal Government."

The effect on the class, as far as Rudolph could discern, was not the one Denton sought. Rather than firing the students up with indignation and a burning desire to rally forth to do battle for reform, most of the students, Rudolph included, dreamed of the time when they themselves could reach the heights of wealth and power, so that they, too, like J. P. Morgan, could be exempt from what Denton called the legal enslavement of the electorate body.

And when Denton, pouncing upon some bit of news in *The Wall Street Journal* describing some new wily tax-saving amalgamation or oil jobbing that kept millions of dollars immune from the federal treasury, Rudolph listened carefully, admiring the techniques that Denton lovingly dissected, and putting everything carefully down in his notebooks, against the blessed day when he perhaps might be faced with similar opportunities.

Anxious for good marks, not so much for themselves as for the possible advantages later, Rudolph did not let on that his close attention to Denton's tirades were not those of a disciple, but rather those of a spy in enemy territory. His three courses with Denton had been rewarded with three A's and Denton had offered him a teaching fellowship in the History Department for the next year.

Despite his secret disagreement with what he thought were Denton's naive positions, Denton was the one instructor Rudolph had come to like in all the time he had been in the college, and the one man he considered had taught him anything useful.

He had kept this opinion, as he had kept almost all his other opinions, strictly to himself, and he was highly regarded as a serious student and a well-behaved young man by the faculty members.

The speaker was finishing, with a mention of God in his last sentence. There was applause. Then the graduates were called up to receive their degrees, one by one. The President beamed as he bestowed the rolls of paper bedecked with ribbon. He had scored a coup getting the cabinet member to his ceremony. He had not read Boylan's letter about an agricultural school.

A hymn was sung, a decorous march played. The black robes filed down through the rows of parents and relatives. The robes dispersed under the summer foliage, of oak trees, mixing with the bright colors of women's dresses, making the graduates look like a flock of crows feeding in a field of flowers.

Rudolph limited himself to a few handshakes. He had a busy day and night ahead of him. Denton sought him out, shook his hand, a small, almost hunchbacked man with thick, silver-rimmed glasses. "Jordache," he said, his hand enthusiastic, "you will think it over won't you?"

"Yes, sir," Rudolph said. "It's very kind of you." Respect your elders. The academic life, serene, underpaid. A Master's in a year, a

Ph.D. a few years later, a chair perhaps at the age of forty-five. "I am certainly tempted, sir." He was not tempted at all.

He and Brad broke away to turn in their robes and go, as prearranged, to the parking lot. Brad had a pre-war Chevy convertible, and his bags, already packed, were in the trunk. Brad was ready to take off for Oklahoma, that overflowing country.

They were the first ones out of the parking lot. They did not look back. Alma Mater disappeared around a bend in the road. Four years. Be sentimental later. Twenty years from now.

"Let's go by the store for a minute," Rudolph said. "I promised Calderwood I'd look in."

"Yes, sir," Brad said, at the wheel. "Do I sound like an educated man?"

"The ruling class," Rudolph said.

"My time has not been wasted," Brad said. "How much do you think a cabinet member makes a year?"

"Fifteen, sixteen thousand," Rudolph hazarded.

"Chickenfeed," Brad said.

"Plus honor."

"That's another thirty bucks a year at least," Brad said. "Tax free. You think he wrote that speech himself?"

"Probably."

"He's overpaid." Brad began to hum the tune of "Everything's Up-to-Date in Kansas City." "Will there be broads there tonight?"

Gretchen had invited them both to her place for a party to mark the occasion. Julie was to come, too, if she could shake her parents.

"Probably," Rudolph said. "There're usually one or two girls hanging around."

"I read all that stuff in the papers," Brad said querulously, "about how modern youth is going to the dogs and how morality has broken down since the war and all, but I'm not getting any of that little old broken-down morality, that's for sure. The next time I go to college it's going to be coed. You're looking at a pure-bred, sex-starved Bachelor of Arts, and I ain't just talking." He hummed gaily.

They drove through the town. Since the war there had been a lot of new construction, small factories with lawns and flower-beds pretending to be places of recreation and gracious living, shop-fronts redone to look as though they were on eighteenth-century village streets in the English counties, a white clapboard building that had once been the town hall and was now a summer theater. People from New York had begun buying farmhouses in the adjoining countryside and came up for weekends and holidays. Whitby, in the four years that Rudolph had spent there, had grown visibly more prosperous with nine new holes added to the golf course and an optimistic real-estate development called Greenwood Estates, where you had to buy at least two acres of land if you wanted to build a house. There was even a small artists' colony and when the President of the university attempted to lure staff away from other institutions, he always pointed out that Whitby was situated in an up-and-coming town, improving in quality as well as size, and that it had a cultural atmosphere.

Calderwood's was a small department store on the best corner of the main shopping street of the town. It had been there since the 1890's, first as a kind of general store serving the needs of a sleepy college village with a back country of solid farms. As the town had grown and changed its character, the store had grown and changed accordingly. Now it was a long, two-story structure, with a considerable variety of goods displayed behind plate-glass windows. Rudolph had started as a stock boy in busy seasons, but had worked so hard and had come up with so many suggestions that Duncan Calderwood, descendant of the original owner, had had to promote him. The store was still small enough so that one man could do many different jobs in it, and by now Rudolph acted as part-time salesman, window dresser, advertising copy writer, adviser on buying, and consultant on the hiring and firing of personnel. When he worked full time in the summer, his salary was fifty dollars a week.

Duncan Calderwood was a spare, laconic Yankee of about fifty, who had married late and had three daughters. Aside from the store, he owned a good deal of real estate in and around the town. Just how much was his own business. He was a closemouthed man who knew the value of a dollar. The day before, he had told Rudolph to drop around after the graduation exercises were over, he might have an interesting proposition to put to him.

Brad stopped the car in front of the entrance to the store.

"I'll just be a minute," Rudolph said, getting out.

"Take your time," Brad said. "I've got my whole life ahead of me." He opened his collar and pulled his tie loose, free at last. The top of the car was down and he lay back and closed his eyes luxuriously in the sunlight.

As Rudolph went into the store, he glanced approvingly at one of the windows, which he had arranged three nights before. The window was devoted to carpentry tools and Rudolph had set them out so that they made a severe abstract pattern, uncluttered and gleaming. From time to time Rudolph went down to New York and studied the windows of the big stores on Fifth Avenue to pick up ideas for Calderwood's.

There was a comfortable, female hum of shopping on the main floor and a slight, typical odor of clothes and new leather and women's scents that Rudolph always enjoyed. The clerks smiled at him and waved hello as he went toward the back of the store, where Calderwood's private office was located. One or two of the clerks said, "Congratulations," and he waved at them. He was well liked, especially by the older people. They did not know that he was consulted on hiring and firing.

Calderwood's door was open, as it always was. He liked to keep an eye on what was happening in the store. He was seated at his desk, writing a letter with a fountain pen. He had a secretary, who had an office beside his, but there were some things about his business he didn't want even his secretary to know. He wrote four or five letters a day by hand and stamped them and mailed them himself. The door to the secretary's office was closed.

Rudolph stood in the doorway, waiting. Although he left the door open, Calderwood did not like to be interrupted.

Calderwood finished a sentence, reread it, then looked up. He had a sallow, smooth face with a long blade of a nose and receding black hair. He turned the letter face down on his desk. He had big farmer's hands and he dealt clumsily with frail things like sheets of paper. Rudolph was proud of his own slender, long-fingered hands, which he felt were aristocratic.

"Come in, Rudy," Calderwood said. His voice was dry, uninflected.

"Good afternoon, Mr. Calderwood." Rudolph stepped into the bare room in his good, blue, graduation suit. There was a giveaway Calderwood calendar on the wall, with a colored photograph of the store on it. Aside from the calendar the only other adornment in the room was a photograph of Calderwood's three daughters, taken when they were little girls, on the desk.

Surprisingly, Calderwood stood up and came around the desk and shook Rudolph's hand. "How did it go?" he asked.

"No surprises."

"You glad you did it?"

"You mean go to college?" Rudolph asked.

"Yes. Sit down." Calderwood went back behind his desk and sat on the straight-backed wooden chair. Rudolph seated himself on an-

other wooden chair on the right side of the desk. In the furniture department on the second floor there were dozens of upholstered
leather chairs, but they were for customers only.

"I suppose so," Rudolph said. "I suppose I'm glad."

"Most of the men who made the big fortunes in this country, who
are making them today," Calderwood said, "never had any real
schooling. Did you know that?"

"Yes," Rudolph said.

"They hire schooling," said Calderwood. It was almost a threat.
Calderwood himself had not finished high school.

"I'll try not to let my education interfere with my making a fortune," Rudolph said.

Calderwood laughed, dry, economical. "I'll bet you won't, Rudy,"
he said affably. He pulled open a drawer of the desk and took out a
jeweler's box, with the name of the store written in gilt script on the
velvet cover. "Here," he said, putting the box down on the desk.
"Here's something for you."

Rudolph opened the box. In it was a handsome steel Swiss wristwatch, with a black suede band. "It's very good of you, sir," Rudolph
said. He tried not to sound surprised.

"You earned it," Calderwood said. He adjusted his narrow tie in
the notch of his starched white collar, embarrassed. Generosity did
not come easily to him. "You put in a lot of good work in this store,
Rudy. You got a good head on your shoulders, you have a gift for
merchandising."

"Thank you, Mr. Calderwood." This was the *real* Commencement
address, none of that Washington stuff about the rising military
curve and aid to our less fortunate brothers.

"I told you I had a proposition for you, didn't I?"

"Yes, sir."

Calderwood hesitated, cleared his throat, stood up, walked toward
the calendar on the wall. It was as though before he took a stupen-
dous final plunge, he had to recheck his figures one last time. He was
dressed as always in a black suit with vest, and high-topped black
shoes. He liked full support for his ankles, he said. "Rudy," he
began, "how would you like to work for Calderwood's on a full-time
basis?"

"That depends," Rudolph said, carefully. He had expected this
and he had decided what terms he would accept.

"Depends on what?" Calderwood asked. He sounded pugnacious.

"Depends on what the job is," Rudolph said.

"The same as you've been doing," Calderwood said. "Only more so. A little bit of everything. You want a title?"

"That depends on the title."

"Depends, depends," Calderwood said. But he laughed. "Who ever made up that idea about the rashness of youth? How about Assistant Manager? Is that a good enough title for you?"

"For openers," Rudolph said.

"Maybe I ought to kick you out of this office," Calderwood said. The pale eyes iced up momentarily.

"I don't want to sound ungrateful," Rudolph said, "but I don't want to get into any dead ends. I have some other offers and . . ."

"I suppose you want to rush down to New York, like all the other young damn fools," Calderwood said. "Take over the city in the first month, get yourself invited to all the parties."

"Not particularly," Rudolph said. Actually he didn't feel ready for New York yet. "I like this town."

"With good reason," Calderwood said. He sat down behind his desk again, with a sound that was almost a sigh. "Listen, Rudy," he said, "I'm not getting any younger; the doctor says I've got to start taking it easier. Delegate responsibility, is the way he puts it, take holidays, prolong my life. The usual doctor's sales talk. I have a high cholesterol count. That's a new gimmick they got to scare you with, cholesterol count. Anyway, it makes sense. I have no sons . . ." He glared at the photograph of the three girl children on his desk, triply betrayed. "I've done the whole thing myself in here since my father died. Somebody's got to help take over. And I don't want any of those high-powered young snots from the business schools, changing everything and asking for a share in the shop after the first two weeks." He lowered his head and looked at Rudolph measuringly from under his thick black eyebrows. "You start at one hundred a week. After a year we'll see. Is that fair or isn't it fair?"

"It's fair," Rudolph said. He had expected seventy-five.

"You'll have an office," Calderwood said. "The old wrapping room on the second floor. Assistant Manager on the door. But I want to see you on the floor during store hours. We shake on it?"

Rudolph put out his hand. Calderwood's handshake was not that of a man with a high cholesterol count.

"I suppose you'll want to take some sort of holiday first," Calderwood said. "I don't blame you. What do you want—two weeks, a month?"

"I'll be here at nine o'clock tomorrow morning." Rudolph stood up.

Calderwood smiled, a flare of unconvincing dentures. "I hope I'm not making a mistake," he said. "I'll see you tomorrow morning."

He was turning over his unfinished letter and picking up his fountain pen with his big, square hand, as Rudolph left the office.

As he went through the store Rudolph walked slowly, looking around at the counters, the clerks, the customers, with a new, appraising, owning eye. At the doorway, he stopped, took off his cheap watch and put on the new one.

Brad was dozing at the wheel in the sunlight. He sat up as Rudolph got into the car. "Anything new?" he asked, as he started the engine.

"The old man gave me a present." Rudolph held up his hand to display the watch.

"He's got a soft heart," Brad said, as they pulled away from the curb.

"One hundred and fifteen dollars," Rudolph said, "at the watch counter. Fifty dollars wholesale." He didn't say anything about reporting to work at nine o'clock in the morning. Calderwood's was not overflowing country.

Mary Pease Jordache sat at the window looking down at the street, waiting for Rudolph. He had promised he'd come right home after the Commencement exercises to show her his degree. It would have been nice to arrange some sort of party for him, but she didn't have the energy. Besides, she didn't know any of his friends. It wasn't that he wasn't popular. The phone was always ringing and young voices would say, "This is Charlie," or, "This is Brad, is Rudy in?" But somehow he never seemed to bring any of them home. Just as well. It wasn't much of a home. Two dark rooms over a dry-goods store on a treeless, bare side street. She was doomed to live her life out over stores. And there was a Negro family living right smack across the street from them. Black faces at the window staring at her. Pickaninnies and rapists. She had learned all about *them* at the orphanage.

She lit a cigarette, her hand shaking, and brushed inaccurately at the ashes from former cigarettes on her shawl. It was a warm June day, but she felt better with her shawl.

Well, Rudolph had made it, despite everything. A college graduate, holding his head high, any man's match. Thank God for Theodore Boylan. She had never met him, but Rudolph had explained what an intelligent, generous man he was. It was no more than Rudolph deserved, though. With his manners and his wit. People *liked* to help him. Well, he was on his way now. Though when she'd asked him what he was going to do after college, he'd been vague. He had plans, though, she was sure. Rudolph was never without plans. As long as he didn't get caught up with some girl and get married. Mary Pease shivered. He was a good boy, you couldn't ask for a more thoughtful son; if it hadn't been for him God knows what would have happened to her since that night Axel disappeared. But once a girl came into the picture, boys became like wild animals, even the best of them, sacrificing everything, home, parents, career, for a pair of soft eyes and the promise under the skirt. Mary Pease Jordache had never met his Julie, but she knew she went to Barnard and she knew about Rudolph's trips to New York on Sundays, all those miles there and back, coming home at all hours, pale and dark under the eyes, restless and short of speech. Still, Julie had lasted over five years and he should be ready for someone else by now. She would have to talk to him, tell him now was the time to enjoy himself, take his time, there would be hundreds of girls who would be more than honored to throw themselves at his head.

She really ought to have done something special for this day. Baked a cake, gone down and bought a bottle of wine. But the effort of descending and climbing the stairs, making herself presentable for the neighbors . . . Rudolph would understand. Anyway, he was going to New York that afternoon to be with his friends. Let the old lady sit alone at the window, she thought with sudden bitterness. Even the best of them.

She saw the car turn the corner into the street, its tires squealing, going too fast. She saw Rudolph, his black hair blowing, young Prince. She saw well at a distance, better than ever, but close-up was another story. She had given up reading because it was too much of a strain, her eyes kept changing, no glasses seemed to help for more than a few weeks at a time, old eyes. She was under fifty, but her eyes were dying before her. She let the tears overflow.

The car stopped below her and Rudolph leaped out. Grace, grace. In a fine blue suit. He had a figure for clothes, slender, with wide shoulders and long legs. She pulled back from the window. He had never said anything, but she knew he didn't like her sitting at the window all day peering out.

She stood up, with an effort, dried her eyes with the edge of her shawl, and hobbled over to a chair near the table which they used for eating. She stubbed out her cigarette as she heard him bounding up the steps.

He opened the door and came in. "Well," he said, "here it is." He opened the roll of paper and spread it on the table in front of her. "It's in Latin," he said.

She could read his name, in Gothic script.

The tears came again. "I wish I knew your father's address," she said. "I'd like him to see this, see what you did without any help from him."

"Ma," Rudolph said gently, "he's dead."

"That's what he likes people to believe," she said. "I know him better than anybody. He's not dead, he escaped."

"Ma . . ." Rudolph said again.

"He's laughing up his sleeve right this minute," she said. "They never found the body, did they?"

"Have it your own way," Rudolph said. "I have to pack a bag. I'm staying in town overnight." He went into his room and started to throw some shaving things and a pair of pajamas and a clean shirt into a bag. "You got everything you need? Supper?"

"I'll open a can," she said. "You going to drive down with that boy in the car?"

"Yes," he said. "Brad."

"He's the one from Oklahoma? The Westerner?"

"Yes."

"I don't like the way he drives. He's reckless. I don't trust Westerners. Why don't you take the train?"

"What's the sense in spending money for the train?"

"What good will your money do you if you're killed, trapped under a car?"

"Ma . . ."

"And you'll make plenty of money now. A boy like you. With this." She smoothed the stiff paper with the Latin lettering. "Do you ever think of what would happen to me if anything happened to you?"

"Nothing will happen to me." He clipped the bag shut. He was in a hurry. She saw he was in a hurry. Leave her by the window.

"They will throw me on the garbage heap, like a dog," she said.

"Ma," he said, "this is a day for celebration. Rejoicing."

"I'll have this framed," she said. "Enjoy yourself. You earned it. Don't stay up too late. Where're you staying in New York? Do you have the phone number, in case there's an emergency?"

"There won't be any emergency."

"In case."

"Gretchen's," he said.

"The harlot," she said. They did not talk about Gretchen, although she knew he saw her.

"Oh, Christ," he said. She had gone too far, and she knew it, but she had to make her position clear.

He leaned over and kissed her to say goodbye and to make up for the "Oh, Christ." She held him. She had doused herself with the toilet water he had bought her for her birthday. She was afraid she smelled like an old woman. "You haven't told me what your plans were," she said. "Now your life is really beginning. I thought you would spare me a minute and sit down and tell me what to expect. If you want, I'll make you a cup of tea . . ."

"Tomorrow, Ma. I'll tell you everything tomorrow. Don't worry." He kissed her again and she released him and he was gone, light-footed, down the stairs. She got up and hobbled over to the window and sat down in her rocking chair, old lady at the window. Let him see her.

The car drove away. He never looked up.

They all leave. Every one of them. Even the best of them.

The Chevy labored up the hill and through the familiar stone gate. The poplar trees that lined the road leading to the house cast a funereal shade, despite the June sunshine. The house quietly decayed behind its unkempt flower borders.

"The Fall of the House of Usher," Brad said as he rounded the curve into the courtyard. Rudolph had been to the house so often that he no longer had an opinion of it. It was Teddy Boylan's house, that was all. "Who lives here—Dracula?"

"A friend," Rudolph said. He had never spoken about Boylan to Brad. Boylan belonged to another compartment of his life. "A friend of the family. He helped me through school."

"Dough?" Brad asked, stopping the car and staring critically at the stone pile of the building.

"Some," Rudolph said. "Enough."

"Can't he afford a gardener?"

"He's not interested. Come on in and meet him. There's some champagne waiting for us." Rudolph got out of the car.

"Should I button my collar?" Brad asked.

"Yes," Rudolph said. He waited while Brad struggled with his collar, and pulled up his tie. He had a thick, short, plebeian neck, Rudolph noticed for the first time.

They crossed the graveled courtyard to the heavy oak front doors. Rudolph rang the bell. He was glad he was not alone. He didn't want to be alone with Teddy Boylan with the news that he had for him. The bell rang in the muffled distance, a question in a tomb, *Are you alive?*

The door opened. Perkins stood there. "Good afternoon, sir," he said. There was the sound of the piano being played. Rudolph recognized a Schubert sonata. Teddy Boylan had taken him to concerts at Carnegie Hall and had played a great deal of music for him on his phonograph, pleased at Rudolph's pleasure in learning about it and his quick ability to tell good playing from bad, mediocre from great. "I was about to give up music before you arrived on the scene," Boylan had told him once. "I don't like to listen to it alone and I hate listening to it with people who are faking an interest in it."

Perkins led the two young men toward the living room. Even in taking five paces, Perkins suggested a procession. Brad straightened out of his usual slouch and walked more erectly, the great dark hall working on him.

Perkins opened the door to the living room. "Mr. Jordache and a friend, sir," he said.

Boylan finished the passage he was playing and stopped. There was a bottle of champagne in a bucket and two fluted glasses beside it.

Boylan stood up and smiled. "Welcome," he said, extending his hand to Rudy. "It's good to see you again." Boylan had been south for two months and he was very brown, his hair and straight eyebrows sun-bleached. There was some slight little difference in his face that Rudolph puzzled over momentarily, as he shook Boylan's hand. "May I present a friend of mine," Rudolph said. "Bradford Knight, Mr. Boylan. He's a classmate of mine."

"How do you do, Mr. Knight." Boylan shook Brad's hand.

"Happy to make your acquaintance, suh," Brad said, sounding more Oklahoman than usual.

"You're to be congratulated today, too, I take it," Boylan said.

"I reckon so. At least, that's the theory." Brad grinned.

"We'll need a third glass, Perkins." Boylan moved toward the champagne bucket.

"Yes, sir." Perkins, leading his lifelong imaginary procession, left the room.

"Was the Democrat edifying?" Boylan asked, twirling the bottle in the ice. "Did he mention malefactors of great wealth?"

"He talked about the bomb," Rudolph said.

"That Democratic invention," Boylan said. "Did he say whom we're going to drop it on next?"

"He didn't seem to want to drop it on anybody," Rudolph said. For some reason, Rudolph felt he had to defend the cabinet member. "Actually, he made a great deal of sense."

"Did he?" Boylan said, twirling the bottle again with the tips of his fingers. "Perhaps he's a secret Republican."

Suddenly Rudolph realized what was different about Boylan's face. There were no more bags under his eyes. He must have got a lot of sleep on his holiday, Rudolph thought.

"You've got yourself quite a fine little old place here, Mr. Boylan," Brad said. He had been staring around him frankly during the conversation.

"Conspicuous consumption," Boylan said carelessly. "My family was devoted to it. You're from the South, aren't you, Mr. Knight?"

"Oklahoma."

"I drove through it once," Boylan said. "I found it depressing. Do you plan to go back there now?"

"Tomorrow," Brad said. "I've been trying to get Rudy to go with me."

"Ah, have you?" Boylan turned to Rudolph. "Are you going?"

Rudolph shook his head.

"No," Boylan said. "I can't quite see you in Oklahoma."

Perkins came in with the third glass and set it down.

"Ah," said Boylan. "Here we are." He undid the wire around the cork, his hands working deftly as the wire came away. He twisted the cork gently and as it came out with a dry popping noise he poured the foam expertly into the glasses. Ordinarily, he allowed Perkins to open bottles. Rudolph realized that Boylan was making a special, symbolic effort today.

He handed a glass to Brad and one to Rudolph, then lifted his own. "To the future," he said. "That dangerous tense."

"This sure beats Coca-Cola," Brad said. Rudolph frowned slightly. Brad was being purposely bumpkinish, reacting unfavorably to Boylan's mannered elegance.

"Yes, doesn't it?" Boylan said evenly. He turned to Rudolph. "Why don't we go out into the garden and drink the rest of the bottle in the sunlight? It always seems more festive—drinking wine in the open."

"Well," Rudolph said, "we don't really have much time . . ."

"Oh?" Boylan raised his eyebrows. "I had thought we could have dinner together at the Farmer's Inn. You're invited, too, of course, Mr. Knight."

"Thank you, suh," Brad said. "But it's up to Rudy."

"There're some people expecting us in New York," said Rudolph.

"I see." Boylan said. "A party, no doubt. Young people."

"Something like that."

"Only natural," Boylan said. "On a day like this." He poured more champagne for the three of them. "Will you see your sister?"

"It's at her house." Rudolph lied to no man.

"Give her my best," said Boylan. "I must remember to send a gift for her child. What is it again?"

"A boy."

Rudolph had told him the day the child was born that it was a boy.

"A small piece of silver," Boylan said, "for it to eat its darling little porridge from. In my family," Boylan explained to Brad, "the custom was to give a newly born boy a block of stock. But that was in the family, of course. It would be presumptuous of me to do anything like that for Rudolph's nephew, although I'm very fond of Rudolph. For that matter, I'm quite attached to his sister, too, although we've allowed ourselves to drift apart in the last few years."

"When I was born my father put an oil well in my name," Brad said. "A dry hole." He laughed heartily.

Boylan smiled politely. "It's the thought that counts."

"Not in Oklahoma," Brad said.

"Rudolph," Boylan said, "I had thought we could discuss various matters quietly over dinner, but since you're busy, and I understand very well you want to be among young people your own age on a night like this, perhaps you could spare a minute or two now . . ."

"If you want," Brad said, "I'll take a little walk."

"You *are* sensitive, Mr. Knight," Boylan said, a knife-flick of mockery in his voice, "but there's nothing that has to be hidden between Rudolph and me. Is there, Rudolph?"

"I don't know," Rudolph said bluntly. He wasn't going to play whatever game Boylan was setting up.

"I'll tell you what I've done," Boylan said, businesslike now. "I've bought you a round-trip ticket on the *Queen Mary*. The sailing is in two weeks, so you'll have plenty of time to see your friends and get your passport and make whatever arrangements are necessary. I've drawn up a little itinerary of places I think you ought to see, London, Paris, Rome, the usual. Round off your education a bit. Education really begins *after* college. Don't you agree, Mr. Knight?"

"I can't do that," Rudolph said. He put his glass down.

"Why not?" Boylan looked surprised. "You're always talking about going to Europe."

"When I can afford it," Rudolph said.

"Oh, is that all?" Boylan chuckled tolerantly. "You misunderstand. It's a gift. I think it'll do you good. Rub off the provincial edges a bit, if you don't mind my saying so. I might even come over some time in August and join you in the south of France."

"Thanks, no, Teddy," Rudolph said. "I can't."

"I'm sorry." Boylan shrugged, dismissing the matter. "Wise men know when to accept gifts and when to turn them down. Even dry holes." With a nod for Brad. "Of course, if you have something better to do . . ."

"I have something to do," Rudolph said. Here it comes, he thought.

"May I inquire what it is?" Boylan poured himself more champagne, without attending to the other glasses.

"I'm starting work tomorrow at Calderwood's on a full-time basis," Rudolph said.

"Poor boy," Boylan said. "What a dreary summer lies ahead of you. I must say your tastes are curious. Preferring to sell pots and pans to sleazy small-town housewives to going to the south of France. Ah, well, if that's your decision, you must have your reasons. And after the summer—have you decided to go to law school as I suggested, or to make a stab at the Foreign Service examinations?"

For more than a year now, Boylan had on many occasions urged Rudolph to opt for one or another profession, with Boylan's preference for the law. "For a young man with no assets but his personality and his wits"—Boylan had written him—"the law is the way to power and preference. This is a lawyer's country. A good one often becomes indispensable to the companies which hire him. Frequently he finds himself in positions of command. We live in an intricate age, which is daily becoming more intricate. The lawyer, the good lawyer, finally is the only trusted guide through the intricacies and he is rewarded accordingly. Even in politics . . . Look at the percentage of lawyers in the Senate. Why shouldn't you crown your career that way? God knows the country could use a man of your intelligence and character instead of some of those dishonest clowns who bumble away on Capitol Hill. Or consider the Foreign Service. Whether we like it or not, we master the world, or should. We should put our best men in positions where they can influence our actions and the actions of our friends and enemies."

Boylan was a patriot. Out of the mainstream himself, through sloth or fastidiousness, he still had strong and virtuous opinions about the conduct of public life. The one man in Washington Rudolph had heard Boylan praise was James Forrestal, Secretary of the Navy. "If you were my own son"—Boylan had continued—"I wouldn't give you different advice. In the Foreign Service you wouldn't be highly paid, but you would live the life of a gentleman among gentlemen and you could do us all honor. And there would be nothing to prevent you from marrying well and moving on to an ambassadorship. Whatever help I could give you, I would give gladly. I would be rewarded enough if you invited me to the Embassy for lunch once every few months—and could say to myself that in a little way I made it possible."

Remembering all this, and remembering Calderwood glaring at the photograph of his three daughters that same afternoon, Rudolph thought, feeling oppressed, everybody is looking for a son. A son in some private, particular, impossible image.

"Well, Rudolph," Boylan was saying, "you haven't answered me. Which is it going to be?"

"Neither," Rudolph said. "I told Calderwood I'd stay on at the store for a year at least."

"I see," Boylan said flatly. "You don't aim very high, do you?"

"Yes, I do," Rudolph said. "In my own way."

"I'll cancel the booking for Europe," Boylan said. "I won't keep you from your friends any longer. It has been very nice having you here, Mr. Knight. If you ever happen to get away from Oklahoma again, you must come visit me again with Rudolph." He finished his champagne and went out of the room, his tweed jacket impeccably on his shoulders, the silk scarf a flash of color about his neck.

"Well . . ." Brad said. "What was that all about?"

"He once had something to do with my sister," Rudolph said. He started toward the door.

"Chilly bastard, isn't he?"

"No," Rudolph said. "Far from it. Let's get out of here."

As they drove through the gateway, Brad finally spoke. "There's something funny about the feller's eyes. What the hell is it? The skin looks as though—as though—" He puzzled for the exact words he wanted. "As though it's zippered up at the sides. Hey, you know something—I bet that feller just had his face lifted."

Of course, Rudolph thought. That was it. It wasn't all that sleep down South. "Maybe," he said. "Anything is possible with Teddy Boylan."

Who are all these people, she thought, looking around her own living room. "Drinks in the kitchen," she said gaily to a new couple who had just come through the open door. She'd have to wait till Willie came back to get the names. He had gone down to the bar on the corner for more ice. There always was enough Scotch, bourbon, gin, and red wine in half gallon jugs, but never enough ice.

There were at least thirty people in the room, about half of whom she knew, and more to come. How many more she never knew. Sometimes she had the feeling Willie just picked people up in the street and invited them. Mary Jane was in the kitchen, acting as barmaid. Mary Jane was getting over her second husband and you had to invite her to everything. Feeling herself an object of pity, Mary Jane tried to pay her way by helping out with the drinks, rinsing glasses, emptying ashtrays and taking lone stragglers home to bed with her. You needed *somebody* like that at a party.

Gretchen winced as she watched a Brooks Brothers type let ashes drop onto the floor and a moment later grind the stub of his cigarette into the carpet with his heel. The room looked so pretty when there was nobody in it, pale-rose walls, books in order on the shelves, curtains crisp, the hearth of the fireplace swept, cushions plumped, the wood polished.

She was afraid that Rudolph disapproved of the party, although there was nothing in his manner that showed that he did. As always, when he was in the same room with Johnny Heath, they were off in a corner together, Johnny doing most of the talking and Rudolph most of the listening. Johnny was only about twenty-five, but he was already a partner in a broker's office in Wall Street, and was reputed to have made a fortune on his own in the stock market. He was an engaging, soft-spoken young man, his face modest and conservative, his eyes quick. She knew that from time to time Rudolph came down to the city to have dinner with Johnny or go to a ball game with him. Whenever she happened to overhear what they were talking about, it was always the same thing—stock deals, mergers, new companies, margins, tax-shelters, all supremely boring to Gretchen, but seemingly fascinating to Rudolph, although he certainly wasn't in any position to deal in stock, merge with anybody, or form any kind of company.

Once, when she asked Rudolph why he had picked Johnny, of all the people he had met in her house, to latch onto, Rudolph replied, very seriously, "He's the only friend you have who can educate me."

Who could know her own brother? Still, she hadn't meant to have *this* kind of party for Rudolph's graduation night and Willie had agreed. But somehow, it always turned out to be the same kind of party. The cast changed somewhat, actors, actresses, young directors, magazine writers, models, girls who worked for Time, Inc., radio producers, an occasional man from an advertising agency who could not be insulted; women like Mary Jane who had just been divorced and told everybody that their husbands were fags, instructors at NYU or Columbia who were writing novels, young Wall Street men who looked as though they were slumming, a dazzlingly sensual secretary who would flirt with Willie after the third drink; an ex-pilot from Willie's war who would corner her to talk about London; somebody's discontented husband who would try to make a pass at her late in the evening, and who would probably slip out at the end with Mary Jane.

Even though the cast changed the activity remained almost the same. Arguments about Russia and Alger Hiss and Senator Joe McCarthy, intellectual girls with bangs praising Trotsky . . . ("Drinks in the kitchen," she said gaily to a new couple, sunburned, who had obviously been to the beach that day) . . . somebody who had just discovered Kierkegaard or who had met Sartre and had to tell about it, or who had just been to Israel or Tangier and had to tell about it. Once a month would have been fine. Or if they just didn't drop their ashes all over the room, even twice a month. They were by and large handsome and educated young people, all somehow with enough money to dress well and buy each other drinks and take a place in the Hamptons for the best part of the summer. Just the sort of people she had dreamed would be her friends when she was a girl in Port Philip. But she had been surrounded by them for nearly five years now. Drinks in the kitchen. The endless party.

Looking purposeful, she made her way to the staircase and started up toward the room under the roof where Billy slept. After Billy was born, they had moved to the top floor of an old brownstone on West Twelfth Street and had converted the attic into a large room and put in a skylight. Aside from Billy's bed and his toys, there was a big table on which Gretchen worked. There was a typewriter on it and it was piled with books and papers. She liked working in the same room with young Billy and the sound of her typing didn't bother him, but seemed to serve as a kind of clicking lullaby for him. A child for the machine age, soothed by Remington.

When she turned on the table lamp, she saw that he wasn't asleep now, though. He lay in the small bed in his pajamas, a cloth giraffe on the pillow beside him, his hands moving above his head slowly through the air, as though to make patterns in the cigarette smoke that drifted up from below. Gretchen felt guilty about the cigarette smoke but you couldn't ask people not to smoke because a four-year-old boy on another floor might not like it. She went over to the bed and leaned down and kissed Billy's forehead. There was the clean smell of soap from his bath and the sweet aroma of childish skin.

"When I grow up," he said, "I am not going to invite anybody."

Not your father's child, Gretchen thought. Even though he looked exactly like him, blond, serenely dimpled. No Jordache there at all. Yet. Unless her brother Thomas had looked like that as a child. She kissed him again, leaning low over the bed. "Go to sleep, Billy," she said.

She went over to the work table and sat down, grateful to be out of the chatter of the room below. She was sure nobody would miss her, even if she sat up there all night. She picked up a book that was lying on the table. Elementary psychology. She opened it idly. Two pages devoted to the blots of the Rorschach test. Know thyself. Know thine enemy. She was taking extension courses at NYU in the late afternoons and at night. If she stuck at it she would have her degree in two years. She had a nagging sense of inadequacy that made her shy with Willie's educated friends and sometimes with Willie himself. Besides, she liked classrooms, the unhurried sense that she was among people who were not merely interested in money or position or being seen in public.

She had slipped away from the theater after Billy was born. Later, she had told herself, when he's old enough not to need me all the time. By now she knew she would never try to act again. No loss. She had had to look for work that she could do at home and luckily she had found it, by the simplest of means. She had begun by helping Willie write his criticisms of radio and later television programs, whenever he was bored with them or busy doing something else or had a hangover. At first, he kept signing his name to her pieces, but then he was offered an executive job in the office of the magazine at a raise in pay and she had begun signing the pieces herself. The editor had told her privately that she wrote a lot better than Willie, but she had made her own judgment on Willie's writing. She had come across the first act of his play one day, while cleaning out a trunk. It was dreadful. What was funny and bright in Willie's speech turned arch on paper. She hadn't told him her opinion of his writing or that she had read his play. But she had encouraged him to take the executive job in the office.

She glanced at the sheet of yellow paper in the typewriter. She had penciled in a tentative title. "The Song of the Salesman." She glanced at random down the page. "The innocent air," she had written, "which theoretically is a national asset, the property of all Americans, has been delivered to merchants, so that they may beguile us or bully us into buying their products, whether the products are benevolent, needful, or dangerous to us. They sell us soup with laughter, breakfast food with violence, automobiles with *Hamlet*, purgatives with drivel . . ."

She frowned. Not good enough. And useless, besides. Who would listen, who would act? The American people were getting what they thought they wanted. Her guests downstairs were most of them in one way or another living off the thing their hostess was denouncing above their heads. The liquor they were drinking was bought with money earned by a man singing the salesman's song. She tore the sheet of paper from the machine and balled it up and threw it in the wastebasket. She would never get it printed, anyway. Willie would see to that.

She went over to the child's bed. He had fallen asleep, grasping the giraffe. He slept, miraculously complete. What are you going to buy, what are you going to sell when you are my age? What errors are ahead of you? How much of love will be wasted?

There was a tread on the stairs and she hurriedly bent over, pretending to be tucking in the child. Willie, provider of ice, opened the door. "I wondered where you were," he said.

"I was restoring my sanity," she said.

"Gretchen," he said reproachfully. He was a little flushed from drink and there were beads of perspiration on his upper lip. He had begun to bald, the forehead more Beethovenesque than ever, but somehow he still looked adolescent. "They're your friends, as well as mine."

"They're nobody's friends," Gretchen said. "They're drinkers, that's all." She was feeling bitchy. Rereading the lines from her article had crystallized the dissatisfaction that had sent her upstairs in the first place. And, suddenly, she was annoyed that the child resembled Willie so closely. I was there, too, she wanted to say.

"What do you want me to do," Willie said, "send them home?"

"Yes. Send them home."

"You know I can't do that," Willie said. "Come on down, honey. People'll begin to wonder what's wrong with you."

"Tell them I had a sudden wild urge to breast-feed," Gretchen said. "In some tribes they breast-feed children until the age of seven. They know everything down there. See if they know that."

"Honey . . ." He came over and put his arms around her. She could smell the gin. "Give a little. Please. You're getting awfully nervy."

"Oh. You noticed."

"Of course I noticed." He kissed her cheek. A nothing kiss, she thought. He hadn't made love to her in two weeks. "I know what's wrong," he said. "You're doing too much. Taking care of the kid, working, going to school, studying . . ." He was always trying to get her to drop her courses. "What're you proving?" he had asked. "You're the smartest girl in New York as it is."

"I'm not doing half enough," she said. "Maybe I'll go down and pick a likely candidate and go off and have an affair. For my nerves."

Willie dropped his arms from around her waist and stepped back, martinis receding. "Funny. Hah-hah," he said coldly.

"On to the cockpit," she said, putting out the lamp on the table. "Drinks are in the kitchen."

He grabbed her wrist in the dark. "What've I done wrong?" he demanded.

"Nothing," she said. "The perfect hostess and her mate will now rejoin the beauty and chivalry of West Twelfth Street." She pulled her arm away from his grasp and went down the stairs. A moment later Willie came down, too. He had stayed behind to plant a martini'd kiss on his son's forehead.

She saw Rudolph had quit Johnny Heath and was in a corner of the room talking earnestly to Julie, who must have come in while she was upstairs. Rudolph's friend, the boy from Oklahoma, Babbitt material, was laughing too hard over something that one of the executive secretaries had said. Julie had her hair up and was wearing a soft, black-velvet dress. "I am in a constant battle," Julie had confided to her, "to suppress the high-school cheerleader in me." This evening she had managed. Too well. She looked too sure of herself for a girl that young. Gretchen was certain that Julie and Rudolph had never slept with each other. After five years! Inhuman. There was something wrong with the girl, or Rudolph, or both.

She waved to Rudolph but she did not catch his eye and as she went toward him she was stopped by an advertising account executive, too beautifully dressed, and with a haircut that was too becoming. "Mine hostess," the man said, thin as an English actor. His name was Alec Lister. He had started as a page boy at CBS, but that was long behind him. "Let me congratulate you on an absolutely splendid do."

"Are you a likely candidate?" she asked, staring at him.

"What?" Lister transferred his glass uneasily from one hand to another. He was not used to being asked puzzling questions.

"Nothing," she said. "Train of thought, I'm glad you like the animals."

"I like them very much." Lister put his imprimatur firmly on the assemblage. "I'll tell you something else I like. Your pieces in the magazine."

"I will be known as the Samuel Taylor Coleridge of radio and television," she said. Lister was one of the guests who could not be insulted, but she was out after all scalps tonight.

"What was that?" He was puzzled for the second time in thirty seconds and he was beginning to frown. "Oh, yes, I get it." He didn't seem happy to have gotten it. "If I may make a comment, Gretchen," he said, knowing that anywhere between Wall Street and Sixtieth Street he could make whatever comment he pleased, "the pieces are excellent, but just a little bit too—well—biting, I find. There's a tone of hostility in them—it gives them a welcome tang, I have to admit—but there's a general underlying feeling of being against the whole industry . . ."

"Oh," she said calmly, "you caught that."

He stared at her evenly, all cordiality gone, his office face, cool and pitiless, replacing in a fraction of a second his tolerant English actor party face. "Yes, I caught it," he said. "And I'm not the only one. In today's atmosphere, with everybody being investigated, and advertisers being damn careful that they're not giving their good money to people whose motives might not be acceptable . . ."

"Are you warning me?" Gretchen asked.

"You might put it like that," the man said. "Out of friendship."

"It's good of you, dear," she touched his arm lightly, smiling tenderly at him, "but I'm afraid it's too late. I'm a red, raving Communist, in the pay of Moscow, plotting to destroy NBC and MGM and bring Ralston's Cereals crashing to the ground."

"She's putting on everyone tonight, Alec." Willie was standing next to her, his hand tightening on her elbow. "She thinks it's Halloween. Come on into the kitchen, I'll freshen your drink."

"Thanks, Willie," Lister said, "but I'm afraid I have to push on. I have two more parties I said I'd look in on tonight." He kissed Gretchen's cheek, a brush of ether on her skin. "Good night, sweets. I do hope you remember what I told you."

"Chiseled in stone," she said.

Expressionless, flat-eyed, he made his way toward the door, putting his glass down on a bookcase, where it would leave a ring.

"What's the matter?" Willie said in a low voice. "You hate money?"

"I hate *him*," she said. She pulled away from Willie and wove through the guests, smiling brightly, to where Rudolph and Julie were talking in the corner. They were talking in near whispers. There was an air of tension about them which built an invisible wall around them, cutting them off from all the laughter and conversation in the room. Julie seemed on the verge of tears and Rudolph looked concentrated and stubborn.

"I think it's terrible," Julie was saying. "That's what I think."

"You look beautiful tonight, Julie," Gretchen interrupted. "Very femme-fatalish."

"Well, I don't feel it." Julie's voice quavered.

"What's the matter?" Gretchen asked.

"You tell her," Julie said to Rudolph.

"Some other time," Rudolph said, lips tight. "This is a party."

"He's going to work permanently at Calderwood's," Julie said. "Starting tomorrow morning."

"Nothing is permanent," Rudolph said.

"Stuck away behind a counter for his whole life," Julie rushed on. "In a little one-horse town. What's the sense of going to college, if that's all you're going to do with it?"

"I told you I'm not going to be stuck anywhere all my life," Rudolph said.

"Tell her the rest," Julie said hotly. "I dare you to tell her the rest."

"What's the rest?" Gretchen asked. She, too, was disappointed, Rudolph's choice *was* inglorious. But she was relieved, too. Working at Calderwood's, he would continue to take care of their mother and she would not have to face the problem herself or ask for help from Willie. The sense of relief was ignoble, but there was no denying to herself that it existed.

"I've been offered the summer in Europe," Rudolph said evenly, "as a gift."

"By whom?" Gretchen asked, although she knew the answer.

"Teddy Boylan."

"I know my parents would let me go, too," Julie said. "We could have the best summer of our whole lives."

"I haven't got time for the best summer of our whole lives," Rudolph said, biting on the words.

"Can't you talk to him, Gretchen?" Julie said.

"Rudy," Gretchen said, "don't you think you owe yourself a little fun, after the way you've been working?"

"Europe won't go away," he said. "I'll go there when I'm ready for it."

"Teddy Boylan must have been pleased when you turned him down," Gretchen said.

"He'll get over it."

"I wish somebody would offer me a trip to Europe," Gretchen said. "I'd be on that boat so fast . . ."

"Gretchen, can you give us a hand?" One of the younger male guests had come over. "We want to play the phonograph and it seems to be kaput."

"I'll talk to you two later," Gretchen said to Rudolph and Julie. "We'll work something out." She went over to the phonograph with the young man. She bent down and fumbled for the plug. The colored maid had been in to clean that day and she always left the plug out after she vacuumed. "I bend enough," she had told Gretchen when Gretchen complained.

The phonograph warmed up with a hollow sound and then it began to play the first record from the album of *South Pacific*. Childish voices, sweet and American, far away on a make-believe warm island, piped the words to "Dites-moi." When Gretchen stood up she saw that Rudolph and Julie had gone. I'm not going to have a party in this place for a whole year, she decided. She went into the kitchen and had Mary Jane pour her a stiff drink of Scotch. Mary Jane had long, red hair these days and a great deal of blue eye shadow and long false eyelashes. From a distance she was a beauty but close up things came apart a little. Still, now, in the third hour of the party, with all the men passing through her domain and flattering her, she was at her peak for the day, flashing-eyed, her bright-red lips half open, avid and provocative. "What glory," she said, whiskey-hoarse. "This party. And that new man, Alec What's-his-name . . ."

"Lister," Gretchen said, drinking, noting that the kitchen was a mess and deciding that she'd do nothing about it till morning. "Alec Lister."

"Isn't he *dazzling?*" Mary Jane said. "Is he attached?"

"Not tonight."

"Blessings on him," Mary Jane said, "the dear fellow. He drowned the kitchen in charm when he was in here. And I've heard the most terrible things about him. He beats his women, Willie told me." She giggled. "*Isn't it exciting?* Did you notice, does he need a new drink? I'll appear at his side, goblet in hand, Mary Jane Hackett, the faithful cup-bearer."

"He left five minutes ago," Gretchen said, meanly pleased at being able to pass on the information to Mary Jane and wondering at the same time what women Willie was intimate enough with to hear from them that they had been beaten by Alec Lister.

"Ah, well," Mary Jane shrugged philosophically, "there are other fish in the sea."

Two men came into the kitchen and Mary Jane swung her red hair and smiled radiantly at them. "Here you are, boys," she said, "the bar never closes."

It was a cinch that Mary Jane had not gone two weeks without making love. What's so wrong with being divorced, Gretchen thought, as she went back into the living room.

Rudolph and Julie walked toward Fifth Avenue in the balmy June evening air. He did not hold her arm. "This is no place to talk seriously," he had said at the party. "Let's get out of here."

But it wasn't any better on the street. Julie strode along, careful not to touch him, the nostrils of her small nose tense, the full lips bitten into a sharp wound. As he walked beside her on the dark street he wondered if it wouldn't just be better to leave her then and there. It would probably come sooner or later anyway and sooner was perhaps to be preferred than later. But then he thought of never seeing her again and despaired. Still, he said nothing. In the battle that was being waged between them, he knew that the advantage would have to go to the one who kept silent longest.

"You have a girl there," she said finally. "That's why you're staying in the awful place."

He laughed.

"Your laughing doesn't fool me." Her voice was bitter, with no memory in it of the times they had sung together or the times she had said, I love you. "You're infatuated with some ribbon clerk or cashier or something. You've been sleeping with somebody there all this time. I know."

He laughed again, strong in his chastity.

"Otherwise you're a freak," she said harshly. "We've been seeing each other for five years and you say you love me and you haven't tried once to make love to me, really make love to me."

"I haven't been invited," he said.

"All right," she said. "I invite you. Now. Tonight. I'm in room 923 at the St. Moritz."

Wary of traps, fearful of helpless surrenders on a tumbled bed. "No," he said.

"Either you're a liar," she said, "or you're a freak."

"I want to marry you," he said. "We can get married next week."

"Where will we spend our honeymoon?" she asked. "In the garden-furniture department of Calderwood's Department Store? I'm offering you my pure-white, virgin body," she said mockingly. "Free and clear. No strings. Who needs a wedding? I'm a free, liberated, lustful, all-American girl. I've just won the Sexual Revolution by a score of ten to nothing."

"No," he said. "And stop talking like my sister."

"Freak," she said. "You want to bury me along with you forever in that dismal little town. And all this time, I've thought you were so smart, that you were going to have such a brilliant future. I'll marry you. I'll marry you next week. If you take the trip to Europe and start law school in the autumn. Or if you don't want to do that, if you just come down here to New York and work here. I don't care what you do here, I'll work, too. I *want* to work. What'll I do in Whitby? Spend my days deciding which apron to wear when you come home at night?"

"I promise you that in five years you can live in New York or anyplace you say."

"You promise," she said. "It's easy to promise. And I'm not going to bury myself for five years either. I can't understand you. What in God's name do you think you're getting out of it?"

"I'm starting two years ahead of anybody in my class," Rudolph said. "I know what I'm doing. Calderwood trusts me. He's got a lot more going for him than just his store. The store's just a beginning, a base. He doesn't know it yet, but I do. When I come down to New York I'm not going to be just another college graduate from a school nobody ever heard of, waiting in everybody's outer office, with his hat in his hand. When I come down, they're going to greet me at the front door. I've been poor a long time, Julie," he said, "and I'm going to do what I have to do never to be poor again."

"Boylan's baby," Julie said. "He's ruined you. Money! Does money mean that much to you? Just *money*?"

"Don't sound like Little Miss Rich Bitch," he said.

"Even if it does," she said, "if you went into law . . ."

"I can't wait," he said. "I've waited long enough. I've been in enough schoolrooms. If I need law, I'll hire lawyers." Echo of Duncan Calderwood, that hard-headed man. *They hire schooling.* "If you want to come along with me, fine. If not . . ." But he couldn't say it. "If not," he repeated lamely. "Oh, Julie, I don't know, I don't know. I think I know about everything else, but I don't know about you."

"I lied to my father and mother . . ." She was sobbing now. "So I could be alone with you. But it's not you. It's Boylan's doll. I'm going back to the hotel. I don't want to talk to you anymore." Weeping uncontrollably, she hailed a cab on the Avenue. It squealed to a halt and she opened the door and got in and slammed the door behind her.

He watched the cab roar away without moving. Then he turned and started back toward the party. He had left his bag there and Gretchen was going to make up a bed for him on the living room couch. 923, he remembered, the number of the hotel room.

Alimonied, Mary Jane did well for herself. Rudolph had never been in a wider or softer bed and in the glow of a lamp on the dressing table (Mary Jane insisted on keeping a light on) the large, warmly carpeted room, its walls pearl-gray silk, showed an expensive decorator's touch. Deep-green velvet curtains shut out the sounds of the city. The preliminaries (they had been brief) had taken place in the high-ceilinged living room furnished with gilt Directoire pieces and large, gold-tinted mirrors, in which the embracing couple were caught in a vague and metallic luminosity. "The main event takes place inside," Mary Jane had said, breaking away from a kiss, and without any further agreement from Rudolph had led him into the bedroom. "I'll get ready in the bathroom," she said, and kicked off her shoes and walked splendidly and almost steadily into the adjoining bathroom, from which had immediately come the sound of water running and the clink of bottles.

It was a little bit like being in a doctor's office while he prepared for a minor operation, Rudolph thought resentfully, and he had hesitated before getting undressed. When Mary Jane had asked him to take her home from the party, well after midnight, with only four or five guests still sprawled around, he had no idea that anything like this was going to happen. He felt a bit dizzy from all the drinking he had done and he was worried about what his head would feel like when he lay down. For a moment, he had considered stealing quietly out and through the front door, but Mary Jane, her intuition or her experience at work, had called out sunnily, "I'll just be a minute more, darling. Make yourself comfortable."

So Rudolph had undressed, putting his shoes soberly side by side under a chair and folding his clothes neatly on the seat of the chair. The bed was already made up for the night (lace-fringed pillows, he noticed, and pale-blue sheets) and he had slipped under the covers, shivering a little. This was one way of making sure he wouldn't be knocking on a hotel door that night. 923.

As he lay under the blankets, curious, a little fearful, he closed his eyes. It had to happen some day, he thought. What better day than this?

With his eyes closed, the room seemed to be dipping and wheeling around him and the bed under him seemed to move in an uneasy rhythm, like a small boat anchored in a chop. He opened his eyes just as Mary Jane came into the room, tall, naked, and superb, the long body with the small, round breasts and splendid hips and thighs unwearied by matrimony, unscarred by debauch. She stood over him, looking down at him with hooded eyes, veteran of many seasons, sweeper-up of stragglers, her red hair, dark in the glow of the lamp, swinging down toward him.

His erection was swift and sudden and huge, a pylon, a cannon barrel. He was torn between pride and embarrassment and almost asked Mary Jane to put out the light. But before he could say anything, Mary Jane bent and swept back the covers in a single tearing gesture.

She stood beside the bed, inspecting him, smiling softly.

"Little brother," she whispered, "little beautiful brother of the poor." Then, soft-handed, she touched him. He jumped convulsively.

"Lie still," she ordered. Her hands moved like small, expert animals on him, fur on damask. He quivered. "Lie still, I said," she said harshly.

It was over soon, shamefully soon, a fierce, arching jet and he heard himself sobbing. She knelt on the bed, kissed him on the mouth, her hands intolerable now, the smell of her hair, cigarette smoke and perfume smothering him.

"I'm sorry," he said, when she raised her head. "I just couldn't . . ."

She chuckled. "Don't be sorry. I'm flattered. I consider it a tribute." With a long graceful movement, she slid into bed beside him, pulled the covers over them, clamped him to her, her leg silken over his thighs, his semen oiling them both. "Don't worry, about any little thing, little brother," she said. She licked his ear and he was shaken once more by a quiver that started from her tongue and convulsed his body down to the tips of his toes, electrocution by lamp light. "I'm sure that in a very few minutes you'll be as good as new, little brother."

He wished she'd stop calling him little brother. He didn't want to be reminded of Gretchen. Gretchen had given him a peculiar look as he had left with Mary Jane.

Mary Jane's gift of prophecy in her chosen field had not deserted her. In less than a very few minutes her hands had awakened him once more and he did what Mary Jane had brought him to her bed to do. He plunged into her with all the hoarded strength of years of abstinence. "Oh, Christ, please, that's enough," she cried finally, and he let himself go in one great thrust, delivering them both.

Freak, he heard Julie's bitter voice, freak. Let her come to this room and this woman for testimony.

"Your sister said you were still a virgin," Mary Jane was saying.

"Let's not talk about it," he said shortly.

They were lying side by side now, on their backs, Mary Jane's leg, just a leg now, thrown lightly across his knee. She was smoking, inhaling deeply, and smoke drifting slowly up when she let it go from her lungs.

"I must discover me some more virgins," she said. "Is it true?"

"I said let's not talk about it."

"It is true."

"Not anymore, anyway."

"That's for fair," she said. "Why?"

"Why what?"

"A beautiful young man like you," she said. "The girls must be ravenous."

"They manage to restrain themselves. Let's talk about something else."

"How about that cute little girl you go around with?" Room 923. "What's her name?"

"Julie." He did not like saying Julie's name in this place.

"Isn't she after you?"

"We were supposed to get married."

"Were? And now?"

"I don't know," he said.

"She doesn't know what she's missing. It must come in the family," Mary Jane said.

"What do you mean by *that?*"

"Willie says your sister's absolutely delirious in the hay."

"Willie ought to learn to keep his mouth shut." Rudolph was shocked that Willie would say something like that to a woman, any woman, to *anybody* about his wife. He would never quite trust Willie again or completely like him again.

Mary Jane laughed. "We're in the big city now," she said, "where they burn the gas. Willie's an old friend of mine. I had an affair with him before he ever met your sister. And occasionally, when he's feeling down or needs a change of scenery, he still comes around."

"Does my sister know?" Rudolph tried to keep the sudden anger out of his voice. Willie, that drifting, frivolous man.

"I don't think so," Mary Jane said lightly. "Willie's awfully good at being vague. And nobody signs any affidavits. Did you ever lay her —Gretchen?"

"She's my sister, for Christ's sake." His voice sounded shrill in his ears.

"Big deal," Mary Jane said. "Sister. From what Willie says, it'd be worth the trouble."

"You're making fun of me." That was it, he told himself, the older, experienced woman amusing herself teasing the simple boy up from the country.

"Hell, no," Mary Jane said calmly. "My brother laid me when I was fifteen. In a beached canoe. Be a doll, honey, and get me a drink. The Scotch is on the table in the kitchen. Plain water. Never mind the ice."

He got out of bed. He would have liked to put on some clothes, a robe, his pants, wrap himself in a towel, anything to keep from parading around before those knowing, measuring, amused eyes. But he knew if he did anything to cover himself she would laugh. Damn it, he thought desperately, how did I ever let myself in for anything like this?

The room suddenly seemed cold to him and he felt the goose flesh prickle all over his body. He tried not to shiver as he walked toward the door and into the living room. Gold and shadowy in the metaled mirrors, he made his way soundlessly over the deep carpets toward the kitchen. He found the light and switched it on. Huge white refrigerator, humming softly, a wall oven, a mixer, a juicer, copper pans arranged on the white walls, steel double sink, a dish-washing machine, the bottle of Scotch in the middle of the red formica table, the domestic American dream in the bright white neon light. He took two glasses down from a cupboard (bone china, flowered cups, coffee pots, huge wooden pepper mills, housewifely accoutrements for the non-housewife in the bed in the other room). He ran the water until it was cold and first rinsed his mouth, spitting into the steel sink, xylophones of the night, then drank two long glasses of water. Into the other glass he poured a big slug of Scotch and half filled the glass with water. There was the ghost of a sound, a faint scratching and scurrying. At the back of the sink black insects, fat and armored, roaches, disappeared into cracks. Slob, he thought.

Leaving the light on in the kitchen, he carried the drink back to the mistress of the household in her well-used bed. We aim to serve.

"There's a doll," Mary Jane said, reaching up for the glass, long, pointed fingernails glinting crimson. She raised against the pillows, red hair wanton against the pale blue and lace, and drank thirstily. "Aren't you having one?"

"I've drunk enough." He reached down for his shorts and started to put them on.

"What're you doing?" she asked.

"I'm going home." He put on his shirt, relieved to be covered at last. "I've got to be at work at nine in the morning." He strapped on his new watch. A quarter to four.

"Please," she said, in a small, childish voice. "Please. Don't do that."

"I'm sorry," he said. He wasn't sorry. The thought of being out on the street, dressed, alone, was exhilarating to him.

"I can't stand being alone at night." She was begging now.

"Call up Willie," he said, sitting down and pulling on his socks and slipping into his shoes.

"I can't sleep, I can't sleep," she said.

He tied his shoelaces deliberately.

"Everybody leaves me," she said, "every goddamn sonofabitch leaves me. I'll do anything. Stay till six, until daylight, until five please, honey. I'll suck you, please . . ." She was crying now.

Tears all night, the world of women, he thought coldly, as he stood up, buttoned his shirt and did up his tie. The sobs echoed behind him as he stood before the mirror. He saw that his hair was mussed, plastered with sweat. He went into the bathroom. Dozens of bottles of perfume, bath-oil, Alka-seltzer, sleeping pills. He combed his hair carefully, erasing the night.

She had stopped crying when he went back into the bedroom. She was sitting up straighter, watching him coldly, her eyes narrowed. She had finished her drink but was still holding her glass.

"Last chance," she said harshly.

He put on his jacket.

"Good night," he said.

She threw the glass at him. He refused to duck. The glass hit him a glancing blow on the forehead, then shattered against the mirror over the mantelpiece of the white marble fireplace.

"Little shit," she said.

He went out of the room, crossed to the front hallway and opened the door. He stepped out through the doorway and closed the door silently behind him and rang for the elevator.

The elevator man was old, good only for short trips, late at night. He looked speculatively at Rudolph as they went down the whining shaft. Does he keep count of his passengers, Rudolph thought, does he make a neat record at dawn?

The elevator man opened the elevator door as they came to a halt. "You're bleeding, young man," he said. "Your head."

"Thank you," Rudolph said.

The elevator man said nothing as Rudolph crossed the hall and went out into the dark street. Once on the street and out of sight of those rheumy recording eyes, Rudolph took out his handkerchief and put it up to his forehead. The handkerchief came away bloody. There are wounds in all encounters. He walked, alone, his footsteps echoing on the pavement, toward the lights of Fifth Avenue. At the corner he looked up. The street sign read "63rd Street." He hesitated. The St. Moritz was on Fifty-ninth Street, along the Park. Room 923. A short stroll in the light morning air. Dabbing at his forehead again with his handkerchief he started toward the hotel.

He didn't know what he was going to do when he got there. Ask for forgiveness, swear, "I will do anything you say," confess, denounce, cleanse himself, cry love, reach out for a memory, forget lust, restore tenderness, sleep, forget . . .

The lobby was empty. The night clerk behind the desk looked at him briefly, incuriously, used to lone men late at night, wandering in from the sleeping city.

"Room 923," he said into the house phone.

He heard the operator ringing the room. After ten rings he hung up. There was a clock in the lobby. 4:35. The last bars in the city had been closed for thirty-five minutes. He walked slowly out of the lobby. He had begun and ended the day alone. Just as well.

He hailed a cruising taxi and got in. That morning, he was going to start earning one hundred dollars a week. He could afford a taxi. He gave Gretchen's address, but then as the taxi started south, he changed his mind. He didn't want to see Gretchen and he certainly didn't want to see Willie. They could send him his bag. "I'm sorry, driver," he said, leaning forward, "I want Grand Central Station."

Although he hadn't slept for twenty-four hours, he was wide-awake when he reported to work at nine o'clock in Duncan Calderwood's office. He did not punch the time clock, although his card was in its slot. He was through punching clocks.

Chapter 3

1950

Thomas twirled the combination of the padlock and threw open his locker. For many months now, every locker had been equipped with a padlock and members were requested to leave their wallets at the office, where they were put into sealed envelopes and filed in the office safe. The decision had been pushed through by Brewster Reed, whose talismanic hundred-dollar bill had been lifted from his pocket the Saturday afternoon of the weekend Thomas had gone down to Port Philip. Dominic had been pleased to announce this development the Monday afternoon when Thomas reported back to work. "At least," Dominic said, "now they know it isn't you and they can't blame me for hiring a thief, the bastards." Dominic had also pushed through a raise for Thomas of ten dollars and he was now getting forty-five dollars a week.

Thomas undressed and got into a clean sweatsuit and put on a pair of boxing shoes. He was taking over the five o'clock calisthenics class from Dominic and there were usually one or two members who asked him to spar a couple of rounds with them. He had learned from Dominic the trick of looking aggressive without inflicting any punishment whatever and he had learned enough of Dominic's phrases to make the members believe he was teaching them how to fight.

He hadn't touched the forty-nine hundred dollars in the safety deposit box in Port Philip and he still called young Sinclair sir when they met in the locker room.

He enjoyed the calisthenics classes. Unlike Dominic, who just called out the cadences, Thomas did all the exercises with the class, pushups, situps, bicycle riding, straddles, knee bending, touching the floor with the knees straight and the palms of the hand flat, and all the rest. It kept him feeling fit and at the same time it amused him to see all those dignified, self-important men sweating and panting. His voice, too, developed a tone of command that made him seem less boyish than before. For once, he began to wake up in the morning without the feeling that something bad, out of his control, was going to happen to him that day.

When Thomas went into the mat room after the calisthenics, Dominic and Greening were putting on the big gloves. Dominic had a cold and he had drunk too much the night before. His eyes were red and he was moving slowly. He looked shapeless and aging in his baggy sweatsuit and since his hair was mussed, his bald spot shone in the light from the big lamps of the room. Greening, who was tall for his weight, moved around impatiently, shuffling his boxing shoes against the mats with a dry, aggressive sound. His eyes seemed bleached in the strong light and his blond hair, crew-cut, almost platinum. He had been a captain in the Marines during the war and had won a big decoration. He was very handsome in a straight-nosed, hard-jawed, pink-cheeked way and if he hadn't come from a family that was above such things, he probably could have done well as a hero in Western movies. In all of the time since he had told Dominic that he thought Thomas had stolen ten dollars from his locker, he had never addressed a word to Thomas and now, as Thomas came into the mat room to wait for one of the members who had made a date to spar with him, Greening didn't even look Thomas's way.

"Help me with these, kid," Dominic said, extending his gloves. Thomas tied the laces. Dominic had already done Greening's gloves.

Dominic looked up at the big clock over the mat room door to make sure that he wouldn't inadvertently box more than two minutes without resting and put up his gloves and shuffled toward Greening, saying, "Whenever you're ready, sir."

Greening came at him fast. He was a straight-up, conventional, schooled kind of fighter who made use of his longer reach to jab at Dominic's head. His cold and his hangover made Dominic begin to breathe hard immediately. He tried to get inside the jab and put his head out of harm's way under Greening's chin while he punched away without much enthusiasm or power at Greening's stomach. Suddenly, Greening stepped back and brought up his right in an all-out uppercut that caught Dominic flush on the mouth.

The shit, Thomas thought. But he said nothing and the expression on his face didn't change.

Dominic sat on the mat pushing reflectively at his bleeding mouth with the big glove. Greening didn't bother to help him up, but stepped back and looked thoughtfully at him, his hands dangling. Still sitting, Dominic held out his gloves toward Thomas.

"Take 'em off me, kid," Dominic said. His voice was thick. "I've had enough exercise for today."

Nobody said anything as Thomas bent and unlaced the gloves and pulled them off Dominic's hands. He knew the old fighter didn't want to be helped up, so he didn't try. Dominic stood up wearily, wiping his mouth with the wrist band of his sweatsuit. "Sorry, sir," he said to Greening. "I guess I'm under the weather today."

"That wasn't much of a workout," Greening said. "You should have told me you weren't feeling well. I wouldn't have bothered getting undressed. How about you, Jordache?" he asked. "I've seen you in here a couple of times. You want to go a few minutes?"

Jordache, Thomas thought. He knows my name. He looked inquiringly over at Dominic. Greening was another story entirely from the pot-bellied, earnest, physical culture enthusiasts Dominic assigned him usually.

A flame of Sicilian hatred glowed momentarily in Dominic's hooded dark eyes. The time had come to burn down the landlord's mansion. "If Mr. Greening wants to, Tom," Dominic said mildly, spitting blood, "I think you might oblige him."

Thomas put on the gloves and Dominic laced them for him, his head bent, his eyes guarded, saying nothing. Thomas felt the old feeling, fear, pleasure, eagerness, an electric tingling in his arms and legs, his gut pulling in. He made himself smile boyishly over Dominic's bent head at Greening, who was watching him stonily.

Dominic stepped away. "Okay," he said.

Greening came right to Thomas, his long left out, his right hand under his chin. College man, Thomas thought contemptuously, as he picked off the jab and circled away from the right. Greening was taller than he but had only eight or nine pounds on him. But he was

faster than Thomas realized and the right caught him, hard, high up
on the temple. Thomas hadn't been in a real fight since the time
with the foreman at the garage in Brookline and the polite exercises
with the pacific gentlemen of the club membership had not prepared him for Greening. Greening feinted, unorthodoxly, with his
right, and crashed a left hook to Thomas's head. The sonofabitch
isn't fooling, Thomas thought, and went in low, looping a left to
Greening's side and following quickly with a right to the man's head.
Greening held him and battered at his ribs with his right hand. He
was strong, there was no doubt about it, very strong.

Thomas got a glimpse of Dominic and wondered if Dominic was
going to give him some sort of signal. Dominic was standing to one
side, placidly, giving no signals.

Okay, Thomas thought, deliciously, here it goes. The hell with
what happens later.

They fought without stopping for the usual two-minute break.
Greening fought controlledly, brutally, using his height and weight,
Thomas with the swift malevolence that he had carefully subdued
within himself all these months. Here you are, Captain, he was saying to himself as he burrowed in, using everything he knew, stinging,
hurting, ducking, here you are Rich-boy, here you are, Policeman, are
you getting your ten dollars' worth?

They were both bleeding from the nose and mouth, when Thomas
finally got in the one he knew was the beginning of the end. Greening stepped back, smiling foolishly, his hands still up, but feebly
pawing the air. Thomas circled him, going for the last big one, when
Dominic stepped between them.

"I think that's enough for the time being, gentlemen," Dominic
said. "That was a very nice little workout."

Greening recovered quickly. The blank look went out of his eyes
and he stared coldly at Thomas. "Take these off me, Dominic," was
all he said. He made no move to wipe the blood off his face.
Dominic unlaced the gloves and Greening walked, very straight, out
of the mat room.

"There goes my job," Thomas said.

"Probably," Dominic said, unlacing the gloves. "It was worth it.
For me." He grinned.

For three days, nothing happened. Nobody but Dominic, Greening,
and Thomas had been in the mat room and neither Thomas nor
Dominic mentioned the fight to any of the members. There was the

possibility that Greening was too embarrassed about being beaten by a twenty-year-old kid a lot smaller than he to make a fuss with the committee.

Each night, when they closed up, Dominic would say, "Nothing yet," and knock on wood.

Then, on the fourth day, Charley, the locker-room man, came looking for him. "Dominic wants to see you in his office," Charley said. "Right away."

Thomas went directly to Dominic's office. Dominic was sitting behind his desk, counting out ninety dollars in ten-dollar bills. He looked up sadly as Thomas came into the office. "Here's your two weeks' pay, kid," he said. "You're through as of now. There was a committee meeting this afternoon."

Thomas put the money in his pocket. And I hoped it was going to last at least a year, he thought.

"You should've let me get that last punch in, Dom," he said.

"Yeah," said Dominic, "I should've."

"Are you going to get into trouble, too?"

"Probably. Take care of yourself," Dominic said. "Just remember one thing—never trust the rich."

They shook hands. Thomas went out of the office to get his things out of the locker and went out of the building without saying good-bye to anyone.

Chapter 4

1954

He woke exactly at a quarter to seven. He never set the alarm. There was no need to.

The usual erection. Forget it. He lay quietly in bed for a minute or two. His mother was snoring in the next room. The curtains at the open window were blowing a little and it was cold in the room. A pale winter light came through the curtains, making a long, dark blur of the books on the shelves across from the bed.

This was not going to be an ordinary day. At closing the night before he had gone into Calderwood's office and laid the thick Manila envelope on Calderwood's desk. "I'd like you to read this," he said to the old man, "when you find the time."

Calderwood eyed the envelope suspiciously. "What's in there?" he asked, pushing gingerly at the envelope with one blunt finger.

"It's complicated," Rudolph said. "I'd rather we didn't discuss it until you've read it."

"This another of your crazy ideas?" Calderwood asked. The bulk of the envelope seemed to anger him. "Are you pushing me again?"

"Uhuh," Rudolph said, and smiled.

"Do you know, young man," Calderwood said, "my cholesterol count has gone up appreciably since I hired you? Way up."

"Mrs. Calderwood keeps asking me to try to make you take a vacation."

"Does she, now?" Calderwood snorted. "What she doesn't know is that I wouldn't leave you alone in this store for ten consecutive minutes. Tell her that the next time she tells you to try to make me take a vacation." But he had carried the thick envelope, unopened, home with him, when he left the store the night before. Once he started reading what was in it, Rudolph was sure he wouldn't stop until he had finished.

He lay still under the covers in the cold room, almost deciding not to get up promptly this morning, but lie there and figure out what to say to the old man when he came into his office. Then he thought, the hell with it, play it cool, pretend it's just another morning.

He threw back the covers, crossed the room quickly and closed the window. He tried not to shiver as he took off his pajamas and pulled on his heavy track suit. He put on a pair of woolen socks and thick, gum-soled tennis shoes. He put a plaid mackinaw on over the track suit and went out of the apartment, closing the door softly so as not to wake his mother.

Downstairs, in front of the house, Quentin McGovern was waiting for him. Quentin was also wearing a track suit. Over it he had a bulky sweater. A wool stocking hat was pulled down over his ears. Quentin was fourteen, the oldest son of the Negro family across the street. They ran together every morning.

"Hi, Quent," Rudolph said.

"Hi, Rudy," said Quentin. "Sure is cold. Mornings like this, my mother thinks we're out of our minds."

"She'll sing a different tune when you bring home a gold medal from the Olympics."

"I bet," Quentin said. "I can just hear her now."

They walked quickly around the corner. Rudolph unlocked the door of the garage where he rented space, and went to the motorcycle. Dimly, at the back of his mind, a memory lurked. Another door, another dark space, another machine. The shell in the warehouse, the smell of the river, his father's ropy arms.

Then he was back in Whitby again, with the boy in the track suit, in another place, with no river. He rolled out the motorcycle. He pulled on a pair of old wool-lined gloves and swung onto the machine and started the motor. Quentin got on the pillion and put his arms around him and they sped down the street, the cold wind making their eyes tear.

It was only a few minutes to the university athletic field. Whitby College was Whitby University now. The field was not enclosed but had a group of wooden stands along one side. Rudolph set up the motorcycle beside the stands and threw his mackinaw over the saddle of the machine. "Better take off your sweater," he said. "For later. You don't want to catch cold on the way back."

Quentin looked over the field. A thin, icy mist was ghosting up from the turf. He shivered. "Maybe my mother is right," he said. But he took off his sweater and they began jogging slowly around the cinder track.

While he was going to college, Rudolph had never had time to go out for the track team. It amused him that now, as a busy young executive, he had time to run half an hour a day, six days a week. He did it for the exercise and to keep himself hard, but he also enjoyed the early morning quiet, the smell of turf, the sense of changing seasons, the pounding of his feet on the hard track. He had started doing it alone, but one morning Quentin had been standing outside the house in his track suit and had said, "Mr. Jordache, I see you going off to work out every day. Do you mind if I tag along?" Rudolph had nearly said no to the boy. He liked being alone that early in the morning, surrounded as he was all day by people at the store. But Quentin had said, "I'm on the high-school squad. The four-forty. If I know I got to run seriously every morning, it's just *got* to help my time. You don't have to *tell* me anything, Mr. Jordache, just let me run along with you." He spoke shyly, softly, not asking for secrets, and Rudolph could see that he had had to screw up his courage to make a request like that of a grown-up white man who had only said hello to him once or twice in his life. Also, Quentin's father worked on a delivery truck at the store. Labor relations,

Rudolph thought. Keep the working man happy. All democrats together. "Okay," he said. "Come on."

The boy had smiled nervously and swung along down the street beside Rudolph to the garage.

They jogged around the track twice, warming up, then broke into a sprint for a hundred yards, then jogged once more, then went fast for the two-twenty, then jogged twice around the track and went the four-forty at almost full speed. Quentin was a lanky boy with long, skinny legs and a nice, smooth motion. It was good to have him along, since he pushed Rudolph to run harder than he would have alone. They finished by jogging twice more around the track, and finally, sweating, threw on their overclothes and drove back through the awakening town to their street.

"See you in the morning, Quent," Rudolph said as he parked the motorcycle along the curb.

"Thanks," Quentin said. "Tomorrow."

Rudolph waved and went into the house, liking the boy. They had conquered normal human sloth together on a cold winter's morning, had tested themselves together against weather, speed, and time. When the summer holidays came, he would find some sort of job for the boy at the store. He was sure Quentin's family could use the money.

His mother was awake when he came into the apartment. "How is it out?" she called.

"Cold," he said. "You won't miss anything if you stay home today." They continued with the fiction that his mother normally went out every day, just like other women.

He went into the bathroom, took a steaming-hot shower, then stood under an ice-cold stream for a minute and came out tingling. He heard his mother squeezing orange juice and making coffee in the kitchen as he toweled himself off, the sound of her movements like somebody dragging a heavy sack across the kitchen floor. He remembered the long-paced sprinting on the frozen track and thought, if I'm ever like that, I'll ask somebody to knock me off.

He weighed himself on the bathroom scale. One-sixty. Satisfactory. He despised fat people. At the store, without telling Calderwood his real reasons, he had tried to get rid of clerks who were overweight.

He rubbed some deodorant under his armpits before dressing. It was a long day and the store was always too hot in winter. He dressed in gray-flannel slacks, a soft blue shirt with a dark red tie, and put on a brown-tweed sports jacket, with no padding at the shoulders. For the first year as assistant manager he had dressed in sober, dark business suits, but as he became more important in the company's hierarchy he had switched to more informal clothes. He was young for his responsibilities and he had to make sure that he didn't appear pompous. For the same reason he had bought himself a motorcycle. Nobody could say as the assistant manager came roaring up to work, bareheaded, on a motorcycle, in all weathers, that the young man was taking himself too seriously. You had to be careful to keep the envy quotient down as low as possible. He could easily afford a car, but he preferred the motorcycle anyway. It kept his complexion fresh and made him look as though he spent a good deal of his time outdoors. To be tanned, especially in winter, made him feel subtly superior to all the pale, sickly looking people around him. He understood now why Boylan had always used a sun lamp. He himself would never descend to a sun lamp. It was deceitful and cheap, he decided, a form of masculine cosmetics and made you vulnerable to people who knew about sun lamps and saw through the artifice.

He went into the kitchen and kissed his mother good morning. She smiled girlishly. If he forgot to kiss her, there would be a long monologue over the breakfast table about how badly she had slept and how the medicines the doctor prescribed for her were a waste of money. He did not tell his mother how much money he earned or that he could very well afford to move them to a much better apartment. He didn't plan any entertainment at home and he had other uses for his money.

He sat down at the kitchen table and drank his orange juice and coffee and munched some toast. His mother just drank coffee. Her hair was lank and there were shocking, huge rings of purple sag under her eyes. But with all that, she didn't seem any worse to him than she had been for the last three years. She would probably live to the age of ninety. He did not begrudge her her longevity. She kept him out of the draft. Sole support of an invalid mother. Last and dearest maternal gift—she had spared him an icebound foxhole in Korea.

"I had a dream last night," she said. "About your brother, Thomas. He looked the way he looked when he was eight years old. Like a choirboy at Easter. He came into my room and said, Forgive me, forgive me . . ." She drank her coffee moodily. "I haven't dreamt about him in forever. Do you ever hear from him?"

"No," Rudolph said.

"You're not hiding anything from me, are you?" she asked.

"No. Why would I do that?"

"I would like to see him once more before I die," she said. "After all he is my own flesh and blood."

"You're not going to die."

"Maybe not," she said. "I have a feeling when spring comes, I'm going to feel much better. We can go for walks again."

"That's good news," Rudolph said, finishing his coffee and standing. He kissed her good-bye. "I'll fix dinner tonight," he said. "I'll shop on the way home."

"Don't tell me what it's going to be," she said coquettishly, "surprise me."

"Okay," he said, "I'll surprise you."

The night watchman was still on duty at the employees' entrance when Rudolph got to the store, carrying the morning papers, which he had bought on the way over.

"Good morning, Sam," Rudolph said.

"Hi, Rudy," the night watchman said. Rudolph made a point of having all the old employees, who knew him from his first days at the store, call him by his Christian name.

"You sure are an early bird," the night watchman said. "When I was your age you couldn't drag me out of bed on a morning like this."

That's why you're a night watchman at *your* age, Sam, Rudolph thought, but he merely smiled and went on up to his office, through the dimly lit and sleeping store.

His office was neat and bare, with two desks, one for himself and one for Miss Giles, his secretary, a middle-aged, efficient spinster. There were piles of magazines geometrically stacked on wide shelves, *Vogue, French Vogue, Seventeen, Glamour, Harper's Bazaar, Esquire, House and Garden,* which he combed for ideas for various departments of the store. The quality of the town was changing rapidly; the new people coming up from the city had money and spent it freely. The natives of the town were more prosperous than they had ever been and were beginning to imitate the tastes of the more sophisticated newer arrivals. Calderwood fought a stubborn rear guard action against the transformation of his store from a solid lower-middle-class establishment to what he called a grab bag of fads and fancy gewgaws, but the balance sheet could not be gainsaid as Rudolph pushed through one innovation after another, and each month it was becoming easier for Rudolph to put his ideas into practice. Calderwood had even agreed, after nearly a year of opposition, to wall off part of what had been an unnecessarily capacious delivery room and turn it into a liquor store, with a line of fine French wines that Rudolph, remembering what Boylan had taught him on the subject through the years, took pleasure in selecting himself.

He hadn't seen Boylan since the day of the Commencement exercises. He had called twice that summer to ask if Boylan was free for dinner and Boylan had said, "No," curtly, each time. Every month, Rudolph sent a hundred-dollar check to Boylan, toward repaying the four-thousand-dollar loan. Boylan never cashed the checks, but Rudolph made sure that if at any time Boylan decided to cash them all at once there would be enough money in the account to honor them. Rudolph didn't think about Boylan often, but when he did, he realized that there was contempt mixed with gratitude he felt for the older man. With all that money, Rudolph thought, all that freedom, Boylan had no right to be as unhappy as he was. It was a symptom of Boylan's fundamental weakness, and Rudolph, fighting any signs of weakness in himself, had no tolerance for it in anybody else. Willie Abbott and Teddy Boylan, Rudolph thought, there's a good team.

Rudolph spread the newspapers on his desk. There was the Whitby *Record*, and the edition of the New York *Times* that came up on the first train of the morning. The front page of the *Times* reported heavy fighting along the 38th parallel and new accusations of treason and infiltration by Senator McCarthy in Washington. The *Record*'s front page reported on a vote for new taxes for the school board (not passed) and on the number of skiers who had made use of the new ski area nearby since the season began. Every city to its own interests.

Rudolph turned to the inside pages of the *Record*. The half-page two-color advertisement for a new line of wool dresses and sweaters was sloppily done, with the colors bleeding out of register, and Rudolph made a note on his desk pad to call the paper that morning about it.

Then he opened to the Stock Exchange figures in the *Times* and studied them for fifteen minutes. When he had saved a thousand dollars he had gone to Johnny Heath and asked him, as a favor, to invest it for him. Johnny, who handled some accounts in the millions of dollars, had gravely consented, and worried over Rudolph's transactions as though Rudolph were one of the most important of his firm's customers. Rudolph's holdings were still small, but they were growing steadily. Looking over the Stock Exchange page, he was pleased to see that he was almost three hundred dollars richer this morning, on paper, than he had been the morning before. He breathed a quiet prayer of thanks to his friend Johnny Heath, and turned to the crossword puzzle and got out his pen and started on it. It was one of the pleasantest moments of the day. If he managed to finish the puzzle before nine o'clock, when the store opened, he started the day's work with a faint sense of triumph.

14 across. *Heep. Uriah,* he printed neatly.

He was almost finished with the puzzle, when the phone rang. He looked at his watch. The switchboard was at work early, he noted approvingly. He picked up the phone with his left hand. "Yes?" he said, printing *ubiquitous* in one of the vertical columns.

"Jordache? That you?"

"Yes. Who's this?"

"Denton, Professor Denton."

"Oh, how are you, sir?" Rudolph said. He puzzled over *Sober* in five letters, *a* the third letter.

"I hate to bother you," Denton said. His voice sounded peculiar, as though he were whispering and was afraid of being overheard. "But can I see you sometime today?"

"Of course," Rudolph said. He printed *staid* along the lowest line of the puzzle. He saw Denton quite often, when he wanted to borrow books on business management and economics at the college. "I'm in the store all day."

Denton's voice made a funny, sliding sound in the phone. "I'd prefer it if we could meet somewhere besides the store. Are you free for lunch?"

"I just take forty-five minutes . . ."

"That's all right. We'll make it someplace near you." Denton sounded gaspy and hurried. In class he was slow and sonorous. "How about Ripley's? That's just around the corner from you, isn't it?"

"Yes," Rudolph said, surprised at Denton's choice of a restaurant. Ripley's was more of a saloon than a restaurant and was frequented by workmen with a thirst rather than anybody who was looking for a decent meal. It certainly wasn't the sort of place you'd think an aging professor of history and economics would seek out. "Is twelve-fifteen all right?"

"I'll be there, Jordache. Thank you, thank you. It's most kind of you. Until twelve-fifteen, then," Denton said, speaking very quickly. "I can't tell you how I appreciate . . ." He seemed to hang up in the middle of his last sentence.

Rudolph frowned, wondering what was bothering Denton, then put the phone down. He looked at his watch. Nine o'clock. The doors were open. His secretary came into the office and said, "Good morning, Mr. Jordache."

"Good morning, Miss Giles," he said and tossed the *Times* into the wastebasket, annoyed. Because of Denton he hadn't finished the puzzle before nine o'clock.

He made his first round of the store for the day, walking slowly, smiling at the clerks, not stopping or seeming to notice when his eye caught something amiss. Later in the morning, back in his office, he would dictate polite memos to the appropriate department head that the neckties piled on the counter for a sale were not arranged neatly enough, that Miss Kale, in cosmetics, had on too much eye make-up, that the ventilation in the fountain and tea shop was not sufficient.

He looked with special interest at the departments that had not been there until he had induced Calderwood to put them in—the little boutique, which sold junk jewelry, Italian sweaters, French scarves, and fur hats and did a surprising amount of business; the fountain and tea shop (it was amazing how women never stopped eating all day), which not only showed a solid profit on its own but had become a meeting place for lunch for many of the housewives of the town who then rarely got out of the store without buying something; the ski shop, in a corner of the old sporting goods department, presided over by an athletically built young man named Larsen who dazzled the local girls on the nearby slopes on winter Sundays and who was being criminally underpaid considering how much trade he lured into the shop merely by sliding down a hill once a week. The young man had offered to teach Rudolph how to ski, but Rudolph had declined, with a smile. He couldn't afford to break a leg, he explained.

The record counter was his idea, too, and that brought in the young trade with their weirdly lavish allowances. Calderwood, who hated noise, and who couldn't stand the way most young people behaved (his own three daughters, two of them now young ladies and the third a pallid teen-ager, behaved with cowed Victorian decorum), had fought bitterly against the record counter. "I don't want to run a goddamn honky-tonk," he had said. "Deprave the youth of America with those barbaric noises that passes for music these days. Leave me in peace, Jordache, leave a poor old-fashioned merchant in peace."

But Rudolph had produced statistics on how much teen-agers in America spent on records every year and had promised to have soundproof booths put in and Calderwood as usual had capitulated. He often seemed to be irritated with Rudolph, but Rudolph was unfailingly polite and patient with the old man and in most things had learned how to manage him. Privately, Calderwood boasted about his pipsqueak of an assistant manager and how clever he himself had been in picking the boy out of the herd. He had also doubled his salary, with no urging from Rudolph, and had given him a bonus at Christmas of three thousand dollars. "He is not only modernizing the store," Calderwood had been heard to say, although not in Rudolph's presence, "the sonofabitch is modernizing me. Well, when it comes down to it, that's what I hired a young man for."

Once a month, Rudolph was invited to dinner at the Calderwoods' house, grim Puritanical affairs, at which the daughters spoke only when spoken to and nothing stronger than apple juice was served. The oldest daughter, Prudence, who was also the prettiest, had asked Rudolph to escort her to several of the country club dances, and Rudolph had done so. Once away from her father, Prudence did not behave with Victorian decorum, but Rudolph carefully kept his hands off her. He was not going to do anything as banal or as dangerous as marrying the boss's daughter.

He was not marrying anybody. That could come later. Three months ago, he had received an invitation to Julie's wedding. She was marrying a man called Fitzgerald in New York. He had not gone to the wedding and he had felt the tears come to his eyes when he had composed the telegram of congratulations. He had despised himself for the weakness and had thrown himself more completely into his work and almost managed to forget Julie.

He was wary of all other girls. He could tell as he walked through the store that there were girls who looked at him flirtatiously, who would be delighted to go out with him, Miss Sullivan, raven haired, in the Boutique; Miss Brandywine, tall and lithe, in the Youth Shop; Miss Soames, in the Record Shop, small, blonde, and bosomy, jiggling to the music, smiling demurely as he passed; maybe six or seven others. He was tempted, of course, but he fought the temptation down, and behaved with perfect, impersonal courtesy to everybody. There were no parties at Calderwood's, so there was no occasion on which, with the excuse of liquor and celebration, any real approach could be made.

The night with Mary Jane in New York and the forlorn telephone call in the deserted lobby of the St. Moritz Hotel had steeled him against the pull of his own desire.

Of one thing he was certain—the next time he asked a girl to marry him, he was going to be damn sure she would say yes.

As he repassed the record counter, he made a mental note to try to get some older woman in the store tactfully to suggest to Miss Soames that perhaps she ought to wear a brassiere under her sweater.

He was going over the drawings for the March window with Bergson, the young man who prepared the displays, when the phone rang.

"Rudy," it was Calderwood, "can you come down to my office for a minute?" The voice was flat, giving nothing away.

"I'll be right there, Mr. Calderwood," Rudolph said. He hung up. "I'm afraid these'll have to wait a little while," he said to Bergson. Bergson was a find. He had done the sets for the summer theater in Whitby. Rudolph liked them and had approached him about a job as window designer for Calderwood's during the winter. Until Bergson had come on the scene the windows had been done haphazardly, with the different departments fighting for space and then doing their own displays without any reference to what was being shown in any window besides their own. Bergson had changed all that. He was a small, sad young man who couldn't get into the scene designers' union in New York. He was grateful for the winter's work and put all his considerable talent into it. Used to working on the cheap for summer-theater productions, he made use of all sorts of unlikely inexpensive materials and did the art work himself.

The plans laid out on Rudolph's desk were on the theme of spring in the country and Rudolph had already told Bergson that he thought they were going to be the best set of windows Calderwood's had ever had. Glum as Bergson was, Rudolph enjoyed the hours he spent working with him, as compared with the hours he spent with the heads of departments and the head of Costs and Accounting. In an ideal scheme of things, he thought, he would never have to look at a balance sheet or go through a monthly inventory.

Calderwood's door was open and Calderwood saw him immediately and said, "Come in, Rudy, and close the door behind you." The papers that had been in the Manila envelope were spread over Calderwood's desk.

Rudolph sat down across from the old man and waited.

"Rudy," Calderwood said mildly, "you're the most astonishing young man I've ever come across."

Rudolph said nothing.

"Who else has seen all this?" Calderwood waved a hand over the papers on his desk.

"Nobody."

"Who typed them up? Miss Giles?"

"I did. At home."

"You think of everything, don't you?" It was not a reproach, but it wasn't a compliment, either.

Rudolph kept quiet.

"Who told you I owned thirty acres of land out near the lake?" Calderwood asked flatly.

The land was owned by a corporation with a New York address. It had taken all of Johnny Heath's cleverness to find out that the real owner of the corporation was Duncan Calderwood. "I'm afraid I can't say, sir," Rudolph said.

"Can't say, can't say." Calderwood accepted it, with a touch of impatience. "The feller can't say. The Silent Generation, like they say in *Time* magazine. Rudy, I haven't caught you in a lie since the first day I set eyes on you and I don't expect you to lie to me now."

"I won't lie to you, sir," Rudolph said.

Calderwood pushed at the papers on his desk. "Is this some sort of a trick to take me over?"

"No, sir," Rudolph said. "It's a suggestion as to how you can take advantage of your position and your various assets. To expand with the community and diversify your interests. To profit from the tax laws and at the same time protect your estate for your wife and children when you die."

"How many pages are there in this?" Calderwood said. "Fifty, sixty?"

"Fifty-three."

"Some suggestion." Calderwood snorted. "Did you think this up all by yourself?"

"Yes." Rudolph didn't feel he had to tell Calderwood that for months he had been methodically picking Johnny Heath's brain and that Johnny was responsible for the more involved sections of the overall plan.

"All right, all right," Calderwood grumbled. "I'll look into it."

"If I may make the suggestion, sir," Rudolph said, "I think you should talk this over with your lawyers in New York and your bankers."

"What do you know about my lawyers in New York?" Calderwood asked suspiciously.

"Mr. Calderwood," Rudolph said, "I've been working for you for a long time."

"Okay. Supposing, after studying this some more, I say Yes and do the whole goddamn thing the way you outline it—go public, float a stock issue, borrow from the banks, build the goddamn shopping center near the lake, with a theater, too, like an idiot, supposing I do all that, what's in it for you?"

"I would expect to be made chairman of the board, with you as president of the company, at an appropriate salary," Rudolph said, "and an option to buy a certain amount of stock in the next five years." Good old Johnny Heath. Don't niggle. Think big. "I would bring in an assistant to help take over here when I'm otherwise occupied." He had already written Brad Knight in Oklahoma about the job.

"You've got everything figured out, haven't you, Rudy?" Now Calderwood was frankly hostile.

"I've been working on this plan for more than a year," Rudolph said mildly. "I've tried to face all the problems."

"And if I just say no," Calderwood said, "if I just put all this pile of papers in a file and forget it, then what would you do?"

"I'm afraid I'd have to tell you I'm leaving at the end of the year, Mr. Calderwood," Rudolph said. "I'm afraid I'd have to look for something with more of a future for me."

"I got along without you for a long time," Calderwood said. "I could get along without you now."

"Of course you could," Rudolph said.

Calderwood looked down morosely at his desk, flicked out a sheet of paper from a pile, glared at it with especial distaste.

"A theater," he said angrily. "We already have a theater in town."

"They're tearing it down next year," Rudolph said.

"You sure do your homework, don't you?" Calderwood said. "They're not going to announce it until July."

"Somebody always talks," Rudolph said.

"So it seems. And somebody always listens, don't they, Rudy?"

"Yes, sir." Rudolph smiled.

Finally, Calderwood smiled, too. "What makes Rudy run, eh?" he said.

"That's not my style, at all," Rudolph said evenly. "You know that."

"Yes, I do," Calderwood admitted. "I'm sorry I said it. All right. Get back to work. You'll be hearing from me."

He was staring down at the papers on his desk as Rudolph left his office. Rudolph walked slowly among the counters, looking youthful and smiling benevolently as usual.

The plan that he had submitted to Calderwood was a complicated one and he had argued every point closely. The community was growing in the direction of the lake. What was more, the neighboring town of Cedarton, about ten miles away, was linked with Whitby by a new highway and was also growing in the direction of the lake. Suburban shopping centers were springing up all over America and people were becoming accustomed to doing the greater part of their shopping, for all sorts of things, in them. Calderwood's thirty acres were strategically placed for a market to siphon off trade from both towns and from the upper-middle-class homes that dotted the borders of the lake. If Calderwood didn't make the move himself, somebody or some corporation would undoubtedly seize the opportunity in the next year or two and besides profiting from the new trade would cut drastically into Calderwood's volume of business in the Whitby store. Rather than allow a competitor to undermine him, it was to Calderwood's advantage to compete, even partially, with himself.

In his plans Rudolph had argued for a place for a good restaurant, as well as the theater, to attract trade in the evenings as well. The theater, used for plays during the summer, could be turned into a movie house for the rest of the year. He also proposed building a middle-priced housing development along the lake, and suggested that the marshy and up to now unusable land at one end of Calderwood's holdings could be used for light industry.

Coached by Johnny Heath, Rudolph had meticulously outlined all the benefits the law allowed on enterprises of this kind.

He was sure that his arguments for making a public company out of the new Calderwood Association were bound to sway the old man. The real assets and the earning power, first of the store and then of the center, would insure a high price of issue for the stock. When Calderwood died, his heirs, his wife and three daughters, would not be faced with the possibility of having to sell the business itself at emergency prices to pay the inheritance taxes, but could sell off blocks of stock while holding onto the controlling interest in the corporation.

In the year that Rudolph had been working on the plan and digging into corporation and tax and realty laws, he had been cynically amused by the manner in which money protected itself legally in the American system. He had no moral feeling about trying to turn the law to his own advantage. The game had rules. You learned the rules and abided by them. If there were another set of rules you would abide by them.

Professor Denton was waiting for him, at the bar, uncomfortable and out of place among other patrons, none of whom looked as though he had ever been near a college.

"Good of you," Denton said, in a low, hurried voice, "good of you to come, Jordache. I'm drinking bourbon. Can I order you something?"

"I don't drink during the day," Rudolph said, then was sorry he said it, because it sounded disapproving of Denton, who was drinking at a quarter past noon.

"Quite right," Denton said, "quite right. Keep the head clear. Ordinarily, I wait until the day's work is over myself, but . . ." He took Rudolph's arm. "Perhaps we can sit down." He waved toward the last booth of the row that lined the wall opposite the bar. "I know you have to get back." He left some change on the bar for his drink, carefully counting it out, and still with his hand holding Rudolph's arm, guided him to the booth. They sat down facing each other. There were two greasy menus on the table and they studied them.

"I'll take the soup and the hamburger," Denton said to the waitress. "And a cup of coffee. How about you, Jordache?"

"The same," Rudolph said.

The waitress wrote the order down laboriously on her pad, illiteracy a family heritage. She was a woman of about sixty, gray haired and shapeless in an incongruously pert, revealing orange uniform with a coquettish, small, lace apron, age paying its iron debt to the ideal of youthful America. Her ankles were swollen and she shuffled flatly as she went back toward the kitchen. Rudolph thought of his mother, of her dream of the neat little candlelit restaurant that had never materialized. Well, she had been spared the orange uniform.

"You're doing well, Jordache," Denton said, hunched over the table, his eyes worried and magnified behind the thick, steel-rimmed glasses. He waved his hand impatiently, to ward off any contradiction. "I hear, I hear," he said. "I get reports from many sources. Mrs. Denton, for one. Faithful customer. She must be in the store three times a week. You must see her from time to time."

"I ran into her only last week," Rudolph said.

"She tells me the store is booming, booming, a new lease on life, she says. Very big-city. All sorts of new things. Well, people like to buy things. And everybody seems to have money these days. Except college professors." Indigence creased Denton's forehead briefly. "No matter. I didn't come here to complain. No doubt about it, Jordache, you did well to turn down the job in the department. The academic world," he said bitterly. "Rife with jealously, cabals, treachery, ingratitude, a man has to walk as if on eggs. Better the world of business. Give and take. Dog eat dog. Frankly. On the up and up."

"It isn't exactly like that," Rudolph said mildly. "Business."

"No, of course not," Denton said. "Everything is modified by character. It doesn't pay to ride a theory too hard, you lose sight of the reality, the living shape. At any rate, I'm gratified at your success, and I'm sure that there was no compromise of principle involved, none whatsoever."

The waitress appeared with their soup. Denton spooned it in. "Yes," he said, "if I had it to do all over again, I'd avoid the ivy-covered walls like the plague. It has made me what you see today, a narrow man, an embittered man, a failure, a coward . . ."

"I wouldn't call you any of those things," Rudolph said, surprised at Denton's description of himself. Denton had always seemed to Rudolph to be pleased with himself, enjoying acting out his visions of economic villainy before a captive audience of young people.

"I live in fear and trembling," Denton said through the soup. "Fear and trembling."

"If I can help you in any way," Rudolph began. "I'd . . ."

"You're a good soul, Jordache, a good soul," Denton said. "I picked you out immediately. Serious among the frivolous. Compassionate among the pitiless. On the search for knowledge where others were merely searching for advancement. Oh, I've watched you carefully through the years, Jordache. You're going to go far. Mark my words. I have been teaching young men for over twenty years, thousands of young men, they have no secrets from me, their future has no mysteries for me. Mark my words, Jordache."

Denton finished his soup and the waitress came and put down their hamburger steaks and coffee.

"And you won't do it by riding roughshod over your fellow men," Denton went on, darting at his hamburger with his fork. "I know your mind, I know your character, I observed you through the years. You have a code, a sense of honor, a fastidiousness of mind and body. These eyes don't miss much, Jordache, in class or out."

Rudolph ate silently, waiting for the spate of approval to die down, knowing that Denton must have a great favor to ask to be so effusive before making his demand.

"Before the war," Denton went on, chewing, "there were more young men of your mold, clear seeing, dependable, honorable. Most of them are dead now, killed in places whose names we have almost forgotten. This generation—" he shrugged despairingly. "Crafty, careful, looking to get something for nothing, hypocritical. You'd be astounded at the amount of cheating I find in each examination, term papers. Ah, if I had the money, I'd get away from it all, live on an island." He looked nervously at his watch. "Time, ever on the wing," he said. He peered around the dark bar conspiratorially. The booth next to theirs was empty and the four or five men hunched over the bar near the doorway were well out of earshot. "Might as well get to the nub of it." Denton dropped his voice and leaned forward over the table. "I'm in trouble, Jordache."

He's going to ask me for the name of an abortionist, Rudolph thought wildly. *Love on the Campus.* He saw the headlines. *History Professor Makes History by Moonlight with Coed. Doctor in Jail.* Rudolph tried to keep his face noncommittal and went on eating. The hamburger was gray and soggy and the potatoes were oily.

"You heard what I said?" Denton whispered.

"You're in trouble, you said."

"Exactly." There was a professorial tone of approval—the student had been paying attention. "*Bad* trouble." Denton sipped at his coffee, Socrates and hemlock. "They're out to get me."

"Who's out to get you?"

"My enemies." Denton's eyes scanned the bar, searching out enemies, disguised as workmen drinking beer.

"When I was in school," Rudolph said, "you seemed to be well liked everywhere."

"There are currents, currents," Denton said, "eddies and whirlpools that the undergraduate never has an inkling of. In the faculty rooms, in the offices of power. In the office of the President himself. I am too outspoken, it is a failing of mine. I am naive, I have believed in the myth of academic freedom. My enemies have bided their time. The vice-chairman of the department, I should have fired him years ago, a hopeless scholar; I restrained myself only out of pity, lamentable weakness. As I said, the vice-chairman, yearning for my job, has prepared a dossier, scraps of gossip over a drink, lines out of context, insinuations. They are preparing to offer me up as a sacrifice, Jordache."

"I think you'd better tell me specifically what's happening," Rudolph said. "Then perhaps I'd be able to judge if I could help."

"Oh, you could help, all right, no doubt about that." Denton pushed the half-eaten hamburger away from him. "They have found their witch," he said. "Me."

"I don't quite understand . . ."

"The witch hunt," Denton said. "You read the papers like everybody else. Throw the Reds out of our schools."

Rudolph laughed. "You're no Red, Professor, you know that," he said.

"Keep your voice low, boy." Denton looked around worriedly. "One does not broadcast on this subject."

"I'm sure you have nothing to worry about, Professor," Rudolph said. He decided to make it seem like a joke. "I was afraid it was something serious. I thought maybe you'd got a girl pregnant."

"You can laugh," Denton said. "At your age. Nobody laughs in a college or a university anymore. The wildest charges. A five-dollar contribution to an obscure charity in 1938, a reference to Karl Marx in a class, for God's sake, how is a man to teach the economic theories of the nineteenth century without mentioning Karl Marx! An ironic joke about prevalent economic practices, picked up by some stone-age moron in a class in American History and repeated to the moron's father, who is the Commander of the local American Legion Post. Ah, you don't know, boy, you don't know. And Whitby gets a yearly grant from the State. For the School of Agriculture. So some windbag of an upstate legislator makes a speech, forms a committee, demands an investigation, gets his name in the newspaper. Patriot, Defender of the Faith. A special board has been set up within the university, Jordache, don't mention it to a soul, headed by the President, to investigate charges against various members of the faculty. They hope to head off the State, throw them a few bodies, mine chief among them, not imperil the grant from the State. Does the picture grow clearer, Jordache?"

"Oh, Christ," Rudolph said.

"Exactly. Oh, Christ. I don't know what your politics are . . ."

"I don't have any politics," Rudolph said. "I vote independently."

"Excellent, excellent," Denton said. "Although it would have been better if you were a registered Republican. And to think that I voted for Eisenhower." He laughed hollowly. "My son was in Korea and he promised to end the war. But how to prove it. There is much to be said for public balloting."

"What do you want me to do, Professor?" Rudolph asked. "Specifically?"

"Now we come to it," Denton said. He finished his coffee. "The board meets to consider my case one week from today. Tuesday at two P.M. Mark the hour. I have only been allowed to see a general outline of the charges against me; contributions to Communist front organizations in the thirties, atheistic and radical utterances in the classroom, the recommendation of certain books for outside reading of a doubtful character. The usual academic hatchet job, Jordache, all too usual. With the temper of the country what it is, with that man Dulles roaring up and down the world, preaching nuclear destruction, with the most eminent men traduced and dismissed like errand boys in Washington, a poor teacher can be ruined by a whisper, the merest whisper. Luckily, they still have a sense of shame at the university, although I doubt it will last the year, and I am to have a chance to defend myself, bring in witnesses to vouch for me . . ."

"What do you want me to say?"

"Whatever you will, boy," Denton said, his voice broken. "I do not plan to coach you. Say what you think of me. You were in three of my classes, we had many instructive hours outside the courses, you have been to my house. You're a clever young man, you are not to be fooled. You know me as well as any man in this town. Say what you will. Your reputation is high, your record at the university was impeccable, not a blot on it, you are a rising young businessman, untainted, your testimony will be of the utmost value."

"Of course," Rudolph said. *Premonitions of trouble. Attacks. Calderwood's attitude. Dragging the store into politics on the Communist issue.* "Of course I'll testify," he said. This is the wrong day for something like this, he thought annoyedly. He suddenly and for the first time understood the exquisite pleasure that cowards must enjoy.

"I knew you would say that, Jordache." Denton gripped his hand emotionally across the table. "You'd be surprised at the refusals I've had from men who have been my friends for twenty years, the hedging, the pusillanimity. This country is becoming a haunt of whipped dogs, Jordache. Do you wish me to swear to you that I have never been a Communist?"

"Don't be absurd, Professor," Rudolph said. He looked at his watch. "I'm afraid I've got to get back to the store. When the board meets next Tuesday I'll be there." He dug into his pocket for his money clip. "Let me pay my share."

Denton stopped him with a gesture. "I invited you. You're my guest. Go ahead, boy, go ahead. I won't keep you." He stood up, looked around for a last time to see if anybody was making a point of watching them, then, satisfied, put out his hand and shook Rudolph's hand fervently.

Rudolph got his coat and went out of the bar. Through the fogged window he saw Denton stop and order a drink at the bar.

Rudolph walked slowly back toward the store, leaving his coat open, although the wind was keen and the day raw. The street looked as it always looked and the people passing him did not seem like whipped dogs. Poor Denton. He remembered that it was in Denton's classes that he had been given the first glimmerings of how to make himself successfully into a capitalist. He laughed to himself. Denton, poor bastard, could not afford to laugh.

He was still hungry after the disastrous meal, and once in the store, he went to the fountain in the basement and ordered a malted milk and drank it among the soprano twitterings of the lady shoppers all around him. Their world was safe. They would buy dresses at fifty dollars that afternoon, and portable radios and television consoles and frying pans and living room suites and creams for the skin and the profits would mount and they were happy over their club sandwiches and ice cream sodas.

He looked over the calm, devouring, rouged, spending, acquiring faces, mothers, brides, virgins, spinsters, mistresses, listened to the voices, breathed in the jumbled bouquet of perfumes, congratulated himself that he was not married and loved no one. He thought, I cannot spend my life serving these worthy women, paid for his malted milk, and went up to his office.

On his desk, there was a letter. It was a short one. "I hope you're coming to New York soon. I'm in a mess and I have to talk to you. Love, Gretchen."

He threw the letter in the wastebasket and said, "Oh, Christ," for the second time in an hour.

It was raining when he left the store at six-fifteen. Calderwood hadn't said a word since their talk in the morning. That's all I needed today, rain, he thought miserably, as he made his way through the streaming traffic on the motorcycle. He was almost home when he remembered that he had promised his mother that he would do the shopping for dinner. He cursed and turned the ma-

chine back toward the business section, where the stores remained
open until seven. A surprise, he remembered his mother saying. Your
loving son may be out on his ass in two weeks, Mother, will that be
surprise enough?

He did his shopping hastily, a small chicken, potatoes, a can of
peas, half an apple pie for dessert. As he pushed his way through the
lines of housewives he remembered the interview with Calderwood
and grinned sourly. The boy wonder financier, surrounded by admiring beauties, on his way to one of his usual elegantly prepared repasts
at the family mansion, so often photographed for *Life* and *House
and Garden*. At the last minute, he bought a bottle of Scotch. This
was going to be a night for whiskey.

He went to bed early, a little drunk, thinking, just before he dropped
off to sleep. The only satisfactory thing I did all day was run this
morning with Quentin McGovern.

The week was routine. When he saw Calderwood at the store, Calderwood made no mention of Rudolph's proposition, but spoke to
him of the ordinary business of the store in his usual slightly rasping
and irritable tone. There was no hint either in his manner or in what
he said of any ultimate decision.

Rudolph had called Gretchen on the phone in New York (from a
pay station—Calderwood did not take kindly to private calls on the
store's phones) and Gretchen had sounded disappointed when he
told her he couldn't get down to the city that week, but would try
the following weekend. She had refused to tell him what the trouble
was. It could wait, she said. If it could wait, he thought, it couldn't
be so bad.

Denton didn't call again. Perhaps he was afraid that if given a
chance at further conversation Rudolph would withdraw his offer
to speak in his behalf before the board next Tuesday afternoon.
Rudolph found himself worrying about his appearance before the
board. There was always the chance that some evidence would be
produced against Denton that Denton didn't know about or had
hidden that would make Rudolph seem like a confederate or a liar or
a dupe. What worried him more, though, was that the board was
bound to be hostile, prepared to do away with Denton, and antago-
nistic to anyone who stood in the way. All his life Rudolph had at-

tempted to get people, especially older people in authority, to like him. The thought of facing a whole room full of disapproving academic faces disturbed him.

Throughout the week he found himself making silent speeches to those imagined, unrelenting faces, speeches in which he defended Denton honorably and well while at the same time charming his judges. None of the speeches he composed seemed, in the end, worthwhile. He would have to go into the board as relaxed as possible, gauge the temper of the room and extemporaneously do the best he could for both Denton and himself. If Calderwood knew what he intended to do . . .

By the weekend he was sleeping badly, his dreams lascivious but unsatisfactory, images of Julie dancing naked before a body of water, Gretchen stretched out in a canoe, Mary Jane opening her legs in bed, then sitting up, her breasts bare, her face contorted, accusing him. A ship pulled away from a pier, a girl, her skirts blowing in the wind, smiled at him as he ran desperately down the pier to catch the ship, he was held back by unseen hands, the ship pulled away, open water . . .

Sunday morning, with church bells ringing, he decided he couldn't stay in the house all day, although he had planned to go over a copy of the papers he had given Calderwood and make some corrections and additions that had occurred to him during the week. But his mother was at her worst on Sundays. The bells made her mournful about her lost religion and she was apt to say that if only Rudolph would go with her, she would attend Mass, confess, take Communion. "The fires of hell are waiting for me," she said over breakfast, "and the church and salvation are only three blocks away."

"Some other Sunday, Mom," Rudolph said. "I'm busy today."

"I may be dead and in hell by some other Sunday," she said.

"We'll just have to take that chance," he said, getting up from the table. He left her weeping.

It was a cold, clear day, the sun a bright wafer in the pale winter sky. He dressed warmly, in a fleece-lined surplus Air Force jacket, a knitted wool cap, and goggles, and took the motorcycle out of the garage. He hesitated about which direction to take. There was nobody he wanted to see that day, no destination that seemed promising. Leisure, the burden of modern man.

He got on the motorcycle, started it, hesitated. A car with skis on its roof sped down the street, and he thought, why not, that's as good a place as any, and followed the car. He remembered that Larsen, the young man in the ski department, had told him that there was a barn near the bottom of the tow that could be converted into a shop for renting skis on the weekend. Larsen had said that there was a lot of money to be made there. Rudolph felt better as he followed the car with ski rack. He was no longer aimless.

He was nearly frozen when he got to the slope. The sun, reflected off the snow, dazzled him and he squinted at the brightly colored figures swooping toward him down the hill. Everybody seemed young, vigorous, and having a good time, and the girls, tight pants over trim hips and round buttocks, made lust a healthy outdoor emotion for a Sunday morning.

He watched, enjoying the spectacle for awhile, then became melancholy. He felt lonely and deprived. He was about to turn away and get his machine and go back to town, when Larsen came skimming down off the hill and made a dashing, abrupt stop in front of him, in a cloud of snow.

"Hi, Mr. Jordache," Larsen said. He had two rows of great shining white teeth and he smiled widely. Behind him two girls who had been following him came to a halt.

"Hello, Larsen," Rudolph said. "I came out to see that barn you told me about."

"Sure thing," Larsen said. Supple, in one easy movement, he bent over to free himself from his skis. He was bare headed and his longish, fine, blond hair fell over his eyes as he bent over. Looking at him, in his red sweater, with the two girls behind him, Rudolph was sure that Larsen hadn't dreamt about any boat pulling away from a pier the night before.

"Hello, Mr. Jordache," one of the girls said. "I didn't know you were a skier."

He peered at her and she laughed. She was wearing big green-tinted snow goggles that covered most of her small face. She pushed the goggles up over her red-and-blue woolen hat. "I'm in disguise," she said.

Now Rudolph recognized her. It was Miss Soames, from the Record Department. Jiggling, plump, blonde, fed by music.

"Good morning, good morning," Rudolph said, somehow flustered, noticing how small Miss Soames's waist was, and how well rounded her thighs and hips. "No, I'm not a skier. I'm a voyeur."

Miss Soames laughed. "There's plenty to voyeur about up here, isn't there?"

"Mr. Jordache . . ." Larsen was out of his skis by now, "may I present my fiancée? Miss Packard."

Miss Packard took off her goggles, too, and revealed herself to be as pretty as Miss Soames, and about the same age. "Pleasure," she said. Fiancée. People were still marrying.

"Be back in a half hour or so, girls," Larsen said. "Mr. Jordache and I have some business to transact." He stuck his skis and poles upright in the snow, as the girls, with a wave of their hands, skied off to the bottom of the lift.

"They look like awfully good skiers," Rudolph said as he walked at Larsen's side back toward the road.

"Mediocre," Larsen said carelessly. "But they have other charms." He laughed, showing the magnificent teeth in the brown face. He made sixty-five dollars a week, Rudolph knew. How could he be so happy on a Sunday morning on sixty-five dollars a week?

The barn was about two hundred yards away, and on the road, a big, solid structure, protected from the weather. "All you'd need," Larsen said, "is a big iron stove and you'd be plenty warm. I bet you could rent a thousand pairs of skis and two to three hundred pairs of boots out of this place a weekend, and then there're the Christmas and Easter vacations and other holidays. And you could get two college boys to run it for beans. It could be a gold mine. If we don't do it, somebody else sure as hell will. This is only the second year for this area, but it's catching on and somebody's bound to see the opportunity."

Rudolph recognized the argument, so much like the one he had used that week on Calderwood, and smiled. In business you sometimes were the pusher and sometimes the pushee. I'm a Sunday pushee, he thought. If we do it, I'll get Larsen a good hike in salary.

"Who owns this place?" Rudolph asked.

"Dunno," Larsen said. "It's easy enough to find out."

Poor Larsen, Rudolph thought, not made for business. If it had been my idea, I would have had an option to buy it before I said a word to anyone. "There's a job for you, Larsen," Rudolph said. "Find out who owns the barn, whether he'll rent it and for how much, or sell it and for how much. And don't mention the store. Say you're thinking of swinging it yourself."

"I get it, I get it," Larsen said, nodding seriously. "Keep 'em from asking too much."

"We can try," Rudolph said. "Let's get out of here. I'm freezing. Is there a place to get a cup of coffee near here?"

"It's just about time for lunch. There's a place a mile down the road that's not bad. Why don't you join me and the girls for lunch, Mr. Jordache?"

Automatically, Rudolph almost said no. He had never been seen outside the store with any of the employees, except once in awhile with one of the buyers or a head of a department. Then he shivered. He *was* awfully cold. He had to go in someplace. Dancy, dainty Miss Soames. What harm could it do? "Thanks, Larsen," he said. "I'd like that very much."

They walked back toward the ski tow. Larsen had a plowing, direct, uncomplicated kind of walk, in his heavy ski boots with their rubber bottoms. The soles of Rudolph's shoes were of leather and the way was icy and Rudolph had to walk delicately, almost mincingly, to keep from slipping. He hoped the girls weren't watching him.

The girls were waiting, their skis off, and Miss Soames was saying, "We're starrrving. Who's going to nourish the orphans?" even before Larsen had a chance to say anything.

"Okay, okay, girls," Larsen said commandingly, "we're going to feed you. Stop wailing."

"Oh, Mr. Jordache," Miss Soames said, "are you going to dine with us? What an honor." She dropped her lashes demurely over freckles, the mockery plain.

"I had an early breakfast," Rudolph said. Clumsy, he thought bitterly. "I could stand some food and drink." He turned to Larsen. "I'll follow you on the machine."

"Is that beautiful thing *yours*, Mr. Jordache?" Miss Soames waved toward where the motorcycle was parked.

"Yes," Rudolph said.

"I *yearn* for a ride," Miss Soames said. She had a gushy, cut-up manner of talking, as though confidences were being unwillingly forced from her. "Do you think you could find it in your heart to let me hang on?"

"It's pretty cold," Rudolph said stiffly.

"I have two pairs of long woolen underwear on," Miss Soames said. "I guarantee I'll be toasty. Benny," she said to Larsen, as though the matter were settled, "put my skis on your car, like a pal. I'm going with Mr. Jordache."

There was nothing Rudolph could do about it and he led the way to the machine while Larsen fixed the three pairs of skis on the rack on a brand-new Ford. How does he do it on sixty-five dollars a week?

Rudolph thought. For an unworthy moment he wondered if Larsen was honest with his accounts at the ski shop.

Rudolph got onto the motorcycle and Miss Soames swung lightly on behind him, putting her hands around his waist and holding on firmly. Rudolph adjusted his goggles and followed Larsen's Ford out of the parking lot. Larsen drove fast and Rudolph had to put on speed to keep up with him. It was much colder than before, and the wind cut at his face, but Miss Soames, holding on tighter than ever, shouted in his ear, "Isn't this *bliss?*"

The restaurant was large and clean and noisy with skiers. They found a table near a window and Rudolph took off his Air Force jacket while the others stripped themselves of their parkas. Miss Soames was wearing a pale-blue cashmere sweater, delicately shaped over her small, full breasts. Rudolph was wearing a sweater over a wool shirt, and a silk scarf, carefully arranged around his throat. Too fancy, he thought, memories of Teddy Boylan, and took it off, pretending it was warm in the restaurant.

The girls ordered Cokes and Larsen a beer. Rudolph felt he needed something more convincing and ordered an old-fashioned. When the drinks came, Miss Soames raised her glass and made a toast, clinking her glass against Rudolph's. "To Sunday," she said, "without which we'd all just *die.*" She was sitting next to Rudolph on the banquette and he could feel the steady pressure of her knee against his. He pulled his knee away, slowly, so as to make it seem merely a natural movement, but the girl's eyes, clear and cold blue, were amused and knowing over the rim of her glass as she looked at him.

They all ordered steaks. Miss Soames asked for a dime for the juke box and Larsen was faster out of his pocket than Rudolph. She took the dime from him and climbed over Rudolph to go to the machine, getting leverage by putting her hand on his shoulder, and walking across the room, her tight, lush bottom swinging and graceful, despite the clumsy boots on her feet.

The music blared out and Miss Soames came back to the table, doing little, playful dance steps as she crossed the floor. This time, as she climbed over Rudolph to her place, there was no doubt about what she was doing, and when she sat down, she was closer than before and the pressure of her knee was unmistakable against his. If he tried to move away now, everybody would notice, so he remained as he was.

He wanted wine with his steak, but hesitated to order a bottle because he was afraid the others might think he was showing off or being superior. He looked at the menu. On the back were listed a California red and a California white. "Would anybody like some wine?" he asked, putting the decision elsewhere.

"I would," Miss Soames said.

"Honey . . . ?" Larsen turned to Miss Packard.

"If everybody else does . . ." she said, being agreeable.

By the time the meal was over they had drunk three bottles of red wine among them. Larsen had drunk the most, but the others had done their fair share.

"What a story I'll have to tell the girls tomorrow at the store," Miss Soames, flushed rosy now, was saying, her knee and thigh rubbing cosily against Rudolph's. "I have been led astray on a Sunday by the great, unapproachable Mr. Frigidaire himself . . ."

"Oh, come on now, Betsy," Larsen said uneasily, glancing at Rudolph to see how he had taken the Mr. Frigidaire. "Watch what you're saying."

Miss Soames ignored him, sweeping her blonde hair loosely back from her forehead, with a little, plump, cushiony hand. "With his big-city ways and his dirty California wine, the Crown Prince lured me on to drunkenness and loose behavior in public. Oh, he's a sly one, our Mr. Jordache." She put a finger up to the corner of her eye and winked. "When you look at him you'd think he could cool a case of beer with one glance of his eyes. But come Sunday, aha, out comes the real Mr. Jordache. The corks pop, the wine flows, he drinks with the help, he laughs at Ben Larsen's corny old jokes, he plays footsy with the poor little shopgirls from the ground floor. My God, Mr. Jordache, you have bony knees."

Rudolph couldn't help laughing, and the others laughed with him. "Well, *you* don't, Miss Soames," he said. "I'm prepared to swear to that."

They all laughed again.

"Mr. Jordache, the daredevil motorcycle rider, the Wall of Death, sees all, knows all, feels all," Miss Soames said. "Oh, Christ, I can't keep on calling you Mr. Jordache. Can I call you Young Master? Or will you settle for Rudy?"

"Rudy," he said. If there had been nobody else there, he would have grabbed her, kissed that flushed small tempting face, the glistening, half mocking, half inviting lips.

"Rudy, it is," she said. "Call him Rudy, Sonia."

"Hello, Rudy," Miss Packard said. It didn't mean anything to her. She didn't work at the store.

"Benny," Miss Soames commanded.

Larsen looked beseechingly at Rudolph. "She's loaded," he began.

"Don't be silly, Benny," Rudolph said.

"Rudy," Larsen said reluctantly.

"Rudy, the mystery man," Miss Soames went on, sipping at her wineglass. "They lock him away at closing time. Nobody sees him except at work, no man, no woman, no child. Especially no woman. There are twenty girls on the ground floor alone who weep into their pillows nightly for him, to say nothing of the ladies in the other departments, and he passes them by with a cold, heartless smile."

"Where the hell did you learn to talk like that?" Rudolph asked, embarrassed, amused, and, at the same time, flattered.

"She's bookish," Miss Packard said. "She reads a book a day."

Miss Soames ignored her. "He is a mystery wrapped in an enigma, as Mr. Churchill said on another occasion. He has been reported running at dawn followed by a young colored boy. What is he running from? What message does the colored boy have for him? He is reported as having been seen in New York, in low neighborhoods. What sins does he commit in the big city? Why doesn't he commit his sins locally?"

"Betsy," Larsen said weakly. "Let's go skiing."

"Tune in on this same station next Sunday and perhaps all these questions will be answered," Miss Soames said. "You may now kiss my hand." She held out her hand, the wrist arched, and Rudolph kissed it, blushing a little.

"I've got to get back to town," he said. The check was on the table and he put down some bills. With tip, it came to fifteen dollars.

When they went outside, a light snow was falling. The mountain was bleak and dangerous looking, its outlines only suggested in the light swirl of snow.

"Thanks for the lunch, Mr. Jordache," Larsen said. One Rudy a week was enough for him. "It was great."

"I really enjoyed it, Mr. Jordache," Miss Packard said, practicing to be Larsen's wife. "I mean I really did."

"Come on, Betsy," Larsen said, "let's hit the slope, work off some of that wine."

"I am returning to town with my good and old friend, Rudy, on his death-defying machine," Miss Soames said. "Aren't I, Rudy?"

"It's an awfully cold ride," Rudolph said. She looked small and crushable in her parka, with her oversized goggles incongruously strapped onto her ski cap. Her head, especially with the goggles, seemed very large, a weighty frame for the small, wicked face.

"I will ski no more today," Miss Soames said grandly. "I am in the mood for other sports." She went over to the motorcycle. "Let us mount," she said.

"You don't have to take her if you don't want to," Larsen said anxiously, responsible.

"Oh, let her come," Rudolph said. "I'll go slow and make sure she doesn't fall off."

"She's a funny girl," Larsen said, still worried. "She doesn't know how to drink. But she doesn't mean any harm."

"She hasn't done any harm, Benny." Rudolph patted Larsen's thick, sweatered shoulder. "Don't worry. And see what you can find out about that barn." Back in the safe world of business.

"Sure thing, Mr. Jordache," Larsen said. He and Miss Packard waved as Rudolph gunned the motorcycle out of the restaurant parking lot, with Miss Soames clinging on behind him, her arms around his waist.

The snow wasn't thick, but it was enough to make him drive carefully. Miss Soames's arms around him were surprisingly strong for a girl so lightly made, and while she had drunk enough wine to make her tongue loose, it hadn't affected her balance and she leaned easily with him as they swept around curves in the road. She sang from time to time, the songs that she heard all day in the record department, but with the wind howling past, Rudolph could only hear little snatches, a phrase of melody in a faraway voice. She sounded like a child singing fitfully to herself in a distant room.

He enjoyed the ride. The whole day, in fact. He was glad his mother's talk about church had driven him out of the house.

At the outskirts of Whitby, as they were passing the university, he slowed down, to ask Miss Soames where she lived. It wasn't far from the campus and he zoomed down the familiar streets. It was still fairly early in the afternoon, but the clouds overhead were black and there were lights to be seen in the windows of the houses they passed. He had to slow down at a stop sign and as he did so, he felt Miss Soames's hand slide down from his waist, where she had been holding on, to his crotch. She stroked him there softly and he could hear her laughing in his ear.

"No disturbing the driver," he said. "State law."

But she only laughed and kept on doing what she had been doing.

They passed an elderly man walking a dog and Rudolph was sure the old man looked startled. He gunned the machine and it had some effect. Miss Soames just held on to the place she had been caressing.

He came to the address she had given him. It was an old, one-family clapboard house set on a yellowed lawn. There were no lights on in the house.

"Home," Miss Soames said. She jumped off the pillion. "That was a nice ride, Rudy. Especially the last two minutes." She took off her goggles and hat and put her head to one side, letting her hair swing loose over her shoulders. "Want to come inside?" she asked. "There's nobody home. My mother and father are out visiting and my brother's at the movies. We can go on to the next chapter."

He hesitated, looked at the house, guessed what it was like inside. Papa and Mama off on a visit but likely to return early. Brother perhaps bored with the movie and coming rattling in an hour earlier than expected. Miss Soames stood before him, one hand on her hip, smiling, swinging her goggles and ski cap in the other.

"Well?" she asked.

"Some other time, perhaps," he said.

"Scaredy-cat," she said, and giggled. Then she ran up the front walk toward the house. At the door she turned and stuck out her tongue at him. The dark building engulfed her.

Thoughtfully, he started the motorcycle and drove slowly toward the center of the town along the darkening streets. He didn't want to go home, so he parked the machine and went into a movie. He hardly saw the movie and would not have been able to tell what it was about when he got out.

He kept thinking about Miss Soames. Silly, cheap little girl, teasing, teasing, making fun of him. He didn't like the idea of seeing her in the store next morning. If it were possible he would have had her fired. But she would go to the union and complain and he would have to explain the grounds on which he had had her fired. "*She called me Mr. Frigidaire, then she called me Rudy and finally she held my cock on a public thoroughfare.*"

He gave up the idea of firing Miss Soames. One thing it all proved

—he had been right all along in having nothing to do with anybody from the store.

He had dinner alone in a restaurant and drank a whole bottle of wine by himself and nearly hit a lamp post on the way home.

He slept badly and he groaned at a quarter to seven Monday morning, when he knew he had to get up and run with Quentin McGovern. But he got up and he ran.

When he made his morning round of the store he was careful to avoid going near the record counter. He waved to Larsen in the ski shop and Larsen, red sweatered, said, "Good morning, Mr. Jordache," as though they had not shared Sunday together.

Calderwood called him into his office in the afternoon. "All right, Rudy," he said, "I've been thinking about your ideas and I've talked them over with some people down in New York. We're going down there tomorrow, we have a date at my lawyer's office in Wall Street at two o'clock. They want to ask you some questions. We'll take the 11:05 train down. I'm not promising anything, but the first time around, my people seem to think you got something there." Calderwood peered at him. "You don't seem particularly happy, Rudy," he said accusingly.

"Oh, I'm pleased, sir. Very pleased." He managed to smile. Two o'clock Tuesday, he was thinking, I promised Denton I'd go before the board two o'clock Tuesday. "It's very good news, sir." He smiled again, trying to seem boyish and naive. "I guess I just wasn't prepared for it—so soon, I mean."

"We'll have lunch on the train," Calderwood said, dismissing him.

Lunch on the train with the old man. That means no drink, Rudolph thought, as he went out of the office. He preferred to be gloomy about that than gloomy about Professor Denton.

Later in the afternoon, the phone rang in his office and Miss Giles answered. "I'll see if he's in," she said. "Who's calling please?" She put her hand over the mouthpiece and said, "Professor Denton."

Rudolph hesitated, then stretched out his hand for the phone. "Hello, Professor," he said heartily. "How're things?"

"Jordache," Denton said, his voice hoarse, "I'm at Ripley's. Can you come over for a few minutes? I've got to talk to you."

Just as well now as later. "Of course, Professor," he said. "I'll be right there." He got up from his desk. "If anybody wants me," he said to Miss Giles, "say I'll be back in a half hour."

When he came into the bar, he had to search to find Denton. Denton was in the last booth again, with his hat and coat on, hunched over the table, his hands cupped around his glass. He needed a shave and his clothes were rumpled and his spectacles clouded and smeared. It occurred to Rudolph that he looked like an old wino, waiting blearily on a park bench in the winter weather for a cop to come and move him on. The self-confident, loud, ironic man of Rudolph's classrooms, amused and amusing, had vanished.

"Hello, Professor." Rudolph slid into the booth opposite Denton. He hadn't bothered to put on a coat for the short walk from the store, "I'm glad to see you." He smiled, as though to reassure Denton that Denton was the same man he had always known, to be greeted in the usual manner.

Denton looked up dully. He didn't offer to shake hands. His face, ordinarily ruddy, was gray. Even his blood has surrendered, Rudolph thought.

"Have a drink." Denton's voice was thick. He had obviously already had a drink. Or several. "Miss," he called loudly to the lady in the orange uniform, who was leaning, like an old mare in harness, against the end of the bar. "What'll you have?" he asked Rudolph.

"Scotch, please."

"Scotch and soda for my friend, miss," Denton said. "And another bourbon for me."

After that, he sat silently for awhile, staring down at the glass between his hands. On the way over from the store, Rudolph had decided what he had to do. He would have to tell Denton that it was impossible for him to appear before the board the next day, but that he would offer to do so any other day, if the board would postpone. Failing that, he would go to see the President that night and say what he had to say. Or if Denton disapproved of that, he would write out his defense of Denton that night for Denton to read before the board when they considered his case. He dreaded the moment when he would have to make these proposals to Denton, but there was no question of not going down to New York with Calderwood on the 11:05 tomorrow morning. He was grateful that Denton kept silent, even for a moment, and he made a big business of stirring his drink when it came, the noise a little musical barrier against conversation for a few seconds.

"I hate to drag you away from your work like this, Jordache," Denton said, not lifting his eyes, and mumbling now. "Trouble makes a man egotistic. I pass a movie theater and I see people lined up to go in, to laugh at a comedy, and I say, 'Don't they know what's happening to me, how can they go to the movies?'" He laughed sourly. "Absurd," he said. "Fifty million people were being killed in Europe alone between 1939 and 1945, and I went to the movies twice a week." He took a thirsty gulp of his drink, bending low over the table and holding the glass with his two hands. The glass rattled as he put it down.

"Tell me what's happening," Rudolph said, soothingly.

"Nothing," Denton said. "Well, that's not true, either. A lot. It's over."

"What are you talking about?" Rudolph spoke calmly, but it was difficult to keep the excitement out of his voice. So, it was nothing, he thought. A storm in a teacup. People finally couldn't be *that* idiotic. "You mean they've dropped the whole thing?"

"I mean I've dropped the whole thing," Denton said flatly, lifting his head and looking out from under the brim of his battered brown felt hat at Rudolph. "I resigned today."

"Oh, no," Rudolph said.

"Oh, yes," Denton said. "After twelve years. They offered to accept my resignation and drop the proceedings. I couldn't face tomorrow. After twelve years. I'm too old, too old. Maybe if I were younger. When you're younger, you can face the irrational. Justice seems obtainable. My wife has been crying for a week. She says the disgrace would kill her. A figure of speech, of course, but a woman weeping seven days and seven nights erodes the will. So, it's done. I just wanted to thank you and tell you you don't have to be there tomorrow at two P.M."

Rudolph swallowed. Carefully, he tried to keep the relief out of his voice. "I would have been happy to speak up," he said. He would not have been happy, but one way or another he had been prepared to do it, and a more exact description of his feelings would do no good at the moment. "What are you going to do now?" he asked.

"I have been thrown a lifeline," Denton said dully. "A friend of mine is on the faculty of the International School at Geneva, I've been offered a place. Less money, but a place. They are not as maniacal, it seems, in Geneva. They tell me the city is pretty."

"But it's just a high school," Rudolph protested. "You've taught in colleges all your life."

"It's in Geneva," Denton said. "I want to get out of this goddamn country."

Rudolph had never heard anybody say this goddamn country about America and he was shocked at Denton's bitterness. As a boy in school he had sung "God shed his Grace on Thee" about his native land, along with the forty other boys and girls in the classroom, and now, he realized that what he had sung as a child he still believed as a grown man. "It's not as bad as you think," he said.

"Worse," Denton said.

"It'll blow over. You'll be asked back."

"Never," Denton said. "I wouldn't come back if they begged me on their knees."

"The Man Without a Country," Rudolph remembered from grade school, the poor exile being transferred from ship to ship, never to see the shores of the land where he was born, never to see the flag without tears. Geneva, that flagless vessel. He looked at Denton, exiled already in the back booth of Ripley's Bar, and felt a confused mixture of emotions, pity, contempt. "Is there anything I can do?" he asked. "Money?"

Denton shook his head. "We're all right. For the time being. We're selling the house. Real estate values have gone up since I bought it. The country is booming." He laughed drily. He stood up abruptly. "I have to go home now," he said. "I'm giving my wife French lessons every afternoon."

He allowed Rudolph to pay for the drinks. Outside on the street, he put his collar up, looking more like an old wino than ever, and shook Rudolph's hand slackly. "I'll write you from Geneva," he said. "Noncommittal letters. God knows who opens mail these days."

He shuffled off, a bent, scholarly figure among the citizens of his goddamn country. Rudolph watched him for a moment, then walked back to the store. He breathed deeply, feeling young, lucky, lucky.

He was in the line waiting to laugh, while the sufferers shuffled past. Fifty million dead, but the movies were always open.

He felt sorry for Denton, but overriding that, he felt joyous for himself. Everything from now on was going to be all right, everything was going to go his way. The sign had been made clear that afternoon, the omens were plain.

He was on the 11:05 the next morning with Calderwood, composed and optimistic. When they went into the dining car for lunch, he didn't mind not being able to order a drink.

Chapter 5

"Why do you have to come and wait for me?" Billy was complaining, as they walked toward home. "As though I'm a baby."

"You'll go around by yourself soon enough," she said, automatically taking his hand as they crossed a street.

"When?"

"Soon enough."

"When?"

"When you're ten."

"Oh, Christ."

"You know you mustn't say things like that."

"Daddy does."

"You're not Daddy."

"So do you sometimes."

"You're not me. And I shouldn't say it, either."

"Then why do you say it?"

"Because I get angry."

"I'm angry now. All the other kids don't have their mothers waiting for them outside the gate like babies. They go home by themselves."

Gretchen knew this was true and that she was being a nervous parent, not faithful to Spock, and that she or Billy or both of them would have to pay for it later, but she couldn't bear the thought of the child wandering by himself around in the doubtful traffic of Greenwich Village. Several times she had suggested to Willie that they move to the suburbs for their son's sake, but Willie had vetoed the idea. "I'm not the Scarsdale type," he said.

She didn't know what the Scarsdale type was. She knew a lot of people who lived in Scarsdale or in places very much like Scarsdale, and they seemed as various as people living anywhere else—drunks, wife-swappers, churchgoers, politicians, patriots, scholars, suicides, whatever.

"When?" Billy asked again, stubbornly, pulling away from her hand.

"When you're ten," she repeated.

"That's a whole year," he wailed.

"You'll be surprised how fast it goes," she said. "Now, button your coat. You'll catch cold." He had been playing basketball in the schoolyard and he was still sweating. The late-afternoon October air was nippy and there was a wind off the Hudson.

"A whole year," Billy said. "That's inhuman."

She laughed and bent and kissed the top of his head, but he pulled away. "Don't kiss me in public," he said.

A big dog came trotting toward them and she had to restrain herself from telling Billy not to pat him. "Old boy," Billy said, "old boy," and patted the dog's head and pulled his ears, at home in the animal kingdom. He thinks nothing living wishes him harm, Gretchen thought. Except his mother.

The dog wagged his tail, went on.

They were on their own street now, and safe. Gretchen allowed Billy to dawdle behind her, balancing on cracks in the pavement. As she came up to the front door of the brownstone in which she lived, she saw Rudolph and Johnny Heath standing in front of the building, leaning against the stoop. They each were holding a paper bag with a bottle in it. She had just put on a scarf over her head and an old coat and she hadn't bothered to change from the slacks she was wearing around the house when she had gone to fetch Billy. She felt dowdy as she approached Rudolph and Johnny, who were dressed like sober young businessmen and were even wearing hats.

She was used to seeing Rudolph in New York often. For the past six months or so, he had come to the city two or three times a week, in his young businessman's suits. There was some sort of deal being arranged, with Calderwood and Johnny Heath's brokerage house, although when she asked Rudolph about it, and he tried to explain, she never could quite grasp the details. It had something to do with setting up an involved corporation called Dee Cee Enterprises, after Duncan Calderwood's initials. Eventually, it was supposed to make Rudolph a wealthy man and get him out of the store, and for half the year, at least, out of Whitby. He had asked her to be on the lookout for a small furnished apartment for him.

Both Rudolph and Johnny looked somehow high, as though they had already done some drinking. She could see by the gilt paper sticking out of the brown paper bags that the bottles they were carrying contained champagne. "Hi, boys," she said. "Why didn't you let me know you were coming?"

"We didn't know we were coming," Rudolph said. "This is an impromptu celebration." He kissed her cheek. He had not been drinking.

"Hi, Billy," he said to the little boy.

"Hi," Billy said perfunctorily. The relationship between uncle and nephew was tenuous. Billy called his uncle Rudy. From time to time Gretchen tried to get the boy to be more polite and say Uncle Rudolph, but Willie backed up his son, saying, "Old forms, old forms. Don't bring up the kid to be a hypocrite."

"Come on upstairs," Gretchen said, "and we'll open these bottles."

The living room was a mess. She worked there now, having surrendered the upstairs room completely to Billy, and there were bits and pieces of two articles she had promised for the first of the month. Books, notes, and scraps of paper were scattered all over the desk and tables. Not even the sofa was immune. She was not a methodical worker, and her occasional attempts at order soon foundered into even greater chaos than before. She had taken to chain-smoking when she worked and ash trays full of stubs were everywhere. Willie, who was far from neat himself, complained from time to time. "This isn't a home," he said, "it's the goddamn city room of a small-time newspaper."

She noticed Rudolph's quick glance of disapproval around the room. Was he judging her now against the fastidious girl she had been at nineteen? She had an unreasonable flash of anger against her impeccable, well-pressed brother. I'm running a family, I'm earning a living, don't forget any of that, brother.

"Billy," she said, as she hung up her coat and scarf, with elaborate precision, to make up for the state of the room, "go upstairs and do your homework."

"Aah . . ." Billy said, more for form's sake than out of any desire to remain below with the grownups.

"Go ahead, Billy."

He went upstairs happily, pretending to be unhappy.

Gretchen got out three glasses. "What's the occasion?" she asked Rudolph, who was working on opening the bottle of champagne.

"We did it," Rudolph said. "Today we had the final signing. We can drink champagne morning, noon, and night for the rest of our lives." He got the cork out and let the foam splash over his hand as he poured.

"That's wonderful," Gretchen said mechanically. It was difficult for her to understand Rudolph's single-minded immersion in business.

They touched glasses.

"To Dee Cee Enterprises and the Chairman of the Board," Johnny said. "The Newest Tycoon of them all."

Both men laughed, nerves still taut. They gave Gretchen the curious impression of being survivors of an accident, almost hysterically congratulating themselves on their escape. What goes on in those offices downtown, Gretchen wondered.

Rudolph couldn't sit still. He prowled around the room, glass in hand, opening books, glancing at the confusion of her desk, ruffling the pages of a newspaper. He looked trained down and nervy, with very bright eyes and hollows showing in his cheeks.

By contrast, Johnny looked chubby, soft, smooth, unedged, and now that he had a glass in his hand, composed, almost sleepy. He was more familiar with money and its uses than Rudolph and was prepared for sudden strokes of fortune and misfortune.

Rudolph turned on the radio and the middle of the first movement of the *Emperor* Concerto blared out. Rudolph grinned. "They're playing Our Song," he said to Johnny. "Music to million by."

"Cut it out," Gretchen said. "You fellows are making me feel like a pauper."

"If Willie has any sense," Johnny said, "he'll beg, borrow, or steal to scrape up some dough and come in on the ground floor of Dee Cee Enterprises. I mean it. There's no limit to how high this stuff can go."

"Willie," Gretchen said, "is too proud to beg, too well known to borrow, and too cowardly to steal."

"You're talking about my friend," Johnny said, pretending to be shocked.

"He was once a friend of mine, too," Gretchen said.

"Have some more champagne," Johnny said, and poured.

Rudolph picked up a sheet of paper from her desk. "'The Age of Midgets,'" he read. "What sort of title is that?"

"It started out to be an article about the new television programs this season," Gretchen said, "and somehow I branched out. Last year's plays, this year's plays, a bunch of novels, Eisenhower's cabinet, architecture, public morality, education . . . I'm aghast at how Billy's being educated and maybe that really started me off."

Rudolph read the first paragraph. "You're pretty rough," he said.

"I'm paid to be a common scold," Gretchen said. "That's my racket."

"Do you really feel as black as you sound?" Rudolph asked.

"Yes," she said. She held out her glass toward Johnny.

The telephone rang. "Probably Willie saying he can't come home for dinner," Gretchen said. She got up and went to the telephone on the desk. "Hello," she said, her voice aggrieved in advance. She listened, puzzled. "One moment, please," she said, and handed the phone to Rudolph. "It's for you," she said.

"Me?" Rudolph shrugged. "Nobody knows I'm here."

"The man said Mr. Jordache."

"Yes?" Rudolph said into the phone.

"Jordache?" The voice was husky, secretive.

"Yes."

"This is Al. I put down five hundred for you for tonight. A good price. Seven to five."

"Wait a minute," Rudolph said, but the phone went dead. Rudolph stared at the instrument in his hand. "That was the queerest thing. It was a man called Al. He said he put down five hundred for me for tonight at seven to five. Gretchen, do you gamble secretly?"

"I don't know any Al," she said, "and I don't have five hundred dollars and besides, he asked for Mr. Jordache, not Miss Jordache." She wrote under her maiden name and was listed as G. Jordache in the Manhattan directory.

"That's the damnedest thing," Rudolph said. "Did I tell anyone I'd be at this number?" he asked Johnny.

"Not to my knowledge," Johnny said.

"He must have gotten the numbers mixed up," Gretchen said.

"That doesn't sound reasonable," Rudolph said. "How many Jordaches can there be in New York? Did you ever come across any others?"

Gretchen shook her head.

"Where's the Manhattan book?"

Gretchen pointed and Rudolph picked it up and opened it to the J's. "T. Jordache," he read, "West Ninety-third Street." He closed the book slowly and put it down. "T. Jordache," he said to Gretchen. "Do you think it's possible?"

"I hope not," Gretchen said.

"What's all this about?" Johnny asked.

"We have a brother named Thomas," Rudolph said.

"The baby of the family," Gretchen said. "Some baby."

"We haven't seen him or heard of him in ten years," Rudolph said.

"The Jordaches are an extraordinarily close-knit family," Gretchen said. After the work of the day, the champagne was beginning to take effect, and she lolled back on the couch. She remembered that she hadn't eaten any lunch.

"What does he do?" Johnny said. "Your brother?"

"I haven't the faintest idea," Rudolph said.

"If he's living up to his early promise," Gretchen said, "he is dodging the police."

"I'm going to find out." Rudolph opened the book again and looked up the number of T. Jordache on West Ninety-third Street. He dialed. The phone was answered by a woman, young from the sound of her voice.

"Good evening, madam," Rudolph said, impersonal, institutional. "May I speak to Mr. Thomas Jordache, please?"

"No, you can't," the woman said. She had a high, thin soprano voice. "Who's this?" Now she sounded suspicious.

"A friend of his," Rudolph said. "Is Mr. Jordache there?"

"He's sleeping," the woman said angrily. "He's got to fight tonight. He hasn't got time to talk to anybody."

There was the sound of the receiver slamming down.

Rudolph had been holding the receiver away from his ear and the woman had talked loudly, so both Gretchen and Johnny had heard every word of the conversation.

"Fighting tonight on the old camp grounds," Gretchen said. "Sounds like our Tommy."

Rudolph picked up the copy of the New York *Times* that was lying on a chair beside the desk and turned to the sports section. "Here it is," he said. "Main bout. Tommy Jordache versus Virgil Walters, middleweights, ten rounds. At the Sunnyside Gardens."

"It sounds bucolic," Gretchen said.

"I'm going," Rudolph said.

"Why?" Gretchen asked.

"He's my brother, after all."

"I've gotten along for ten years without him," Gretchen said. "I'm going to try for twenty."

"Johnny?" Rudolph turned to Heath.

"Sorry," Johnny said. "I'm invited to a dinner. Tell me how it works out."

The telephone rang again. Rudolph picked it up eagerly, but it was only Willie. "Hi, Rudy," Willie said. There were barroom noises behind him. "No, I don't have to speak to her," Willie said. "Just tell her I'm sorry, but I've got a business dinner tonight and I can't make it home until late. Tell her not to wait up."

Gretchen smiled, lying on the couch. "Don't tell me what he said."

"He's not coming home to dinner."

"And I'm not to wait up."

"Something along those lines."

"Johnny," Gretchen said, "don't you think it's time to open the second bottle?"

By the time they had finished the second bottle, Gretchen had called for a baby sitter and they had found out where Sunnyside Gardens was. She went in and took a shower, did her hair, and put on a dark-wool dress, wondering if it was comme il faut for prizefights. She had grown thinner and the dress was a little loose on her, but she caught the quick glances of approval of the two men at her appearance and was gratified by it. I must not let myself fall into slobhood, she thought. Ever.

When the baby sitter came, Gretchen gave her instructions and left the apartment with Rudolph and Johnny. They went to a nearby steak house. Johnny had a drink with them at the bar and was saying, "Thanks for the drink," and was preparing to leave when Rudolph said, "I only have five dollars." He laughed. "Johnny, be my banker for tonight, will you?"

Johnny took out his wallet and put down five ten-dollar bills. "Enough?" he said.

"Thanks." Rudolph put the bills carelessly in his pocket. He laughed again.

"What's so funny?" Gretchen asked.

"I never thought I'd like to see the day," Rudolph said, "when I didn't know exactly how much money I had in my pocket."

"You have taken on the wholesome and mind-freeing habits of the rich," Johnny said gravely. "Congratulations. I'll see you tomorrow at the office, Rudy. And I hope your brother wins."

"I hope he gets his head knocked off," Gretchen said.

A preliminary bout was under way as an usher led them to their seats three rows from ringside. Gretchen noted that there were few women present and that none of them was wearing a black-wool dress. She had never been to a prizefight before and she tuned out the television set whenever one was being shown. The idea of men beating each other senseless for pay seemed brutish to her and the faces of the men around her were just the sort of faces that one would expect at such an entertainment. She was sure she had never seen so many ugly people collected in one place.

The men in the ring did not appear to be doing much harm to each other and she watched with passive disgust as they clinched, wrestled, and ducked away from blows. The crowd, in its fog of tobacco smoke, was apathetic and only once in awhile, when there was the thud of a heavy punch, a sort of sharp, grunting, animal noise filled the arena.

Rudolph, she knew, went to prizefights from time to time and she had heard him discussing particular boxers like Ray Robinson enthusiastically with Willie. She looked surreptitiously over at her brother. He seemed interested by the spectacle in the ring. Now that she was actually seeing a fight, with the smell of sweat in her nostrils and the red blotches on pale skin where blows had landed, Rudolph's whole character, the subtle, deprecating air of educated superiority, the well-mannered lack of aggressiveness, seemed suddenly suspect to her. He was linked with the brutes in the ring, with the brutes in the rows around her.

In the next fight, one man was cut over the eye and the wound spurted blood all over him and his opponent. The roar of the crowd when they saw the blood sickened her and she wondered if she could sit there and wait for a brother to climb through the ropes to face similar butchery.

By the time the main bout came on, she was pale and sick and it was through a haze of tears and smoke that she saw a large man in a red bathrobe climb agilely through the ropes and recognized Thomas.

When Thomas's handlers took off his robe and threw it over his shoulders to put the gloves on over the bandaged hands, the first thing Rudolph noticed, with a touch of jealousy, was that Thomas had almost no hair on his body. Rudolph was getting quite hairy, with thick, tight, black curls on his chest and sprouting on his shoulders. His legs, too, were covered with dark hair, and it did not fit with the image he had of himself. When he went swimming in the summer, his hairiness embarrassed him and he felt that people were snickering at him For that reason he rarely sunbathed and put on a shirt as soon as he got out of the water.

Thomas, except for the ferocious, muscular, over-trained body, looked surprisingly the same. His face was unmarked and the expression was still boyish and ingratiating. Thomas kept smiling during the formalities before the beginning of the bout, but Rudolph could see him flicking the corner of his mouth nervously with his tongue. A muscle in his leg twitched under his shiny silk, purple trunks while the referee was giving the final instructions to the two men in the center of the ring. Except for the moment when he had been introduced (*In this corner, Tommy Jordache, weight one fifty-nine and a half*), and had raised his gloved hand and looked quickly up at the crowd, Thomas had kept his eyes down. If he had seen Rudolph and Gretchen, he made no sign.

His opponent was a rangy Negro, considerably taller than Tommy, and with much longer arms, shuffling dangerously in his corner in a little dance, nodding as he listened to the advice being whispered into his ear by his handler.

Gretchen watched with a rigid, painful grimace on her face, squinting through the smoke at her brother's powerful, destructive, bare figure. She did not like the hairless male body—Willie was covered with a comfortable reddish fuzz—and the ridged professional muscles made her shudder in primitive distaste. *Siblings, out of the same womb.* The thought dismayed her. Behind Thomas's boyish smile she recognized the sly malevolence, the desire to hurt, the pleasure in dealing pain, that had alienated her when they lived in the same house. The thought that it was her own flesh and blood exposed there under the bright lights in this dreadful ceremony was almost unbearable to her. Of course, she thought, I should have known; this is where he had to end. Fighting for his life.

The men were evenly matched, equally fast, the Negro less aggressive, but better able to defend himself with his long arms. Thomas kept burrowing in, taking two punches to get in one, slugging away at the Negro's body, making the Negro give ground and occasionally punishing him terribly when he got him in a corner against the ropes.

"Kill the nigger," a voice from the back of the arena cried out each time Thomas threw a volley of punches. Gretchen winced, ashamed to be there, ashamed for every man and woman in the place. Oh, Arnold Simms, limping, in the maroon bathrobe, saying, "You got pretty feet, Miss Jordache," dreaming of Cornwall, oh, Arnold Simms, forgive me for tonight.

It lasted eight of the ten rounds. Thomas was bleeding from the nose and from a cut above the eye, but never retreating, always shuffling in, with a kind of hideous, heedless, mechanical energy, slowly wearing his man down. In the eighth round, the Negro could hardly lift his hands and Thomas sent him to the canvas with a long, looping right hand that caught the Negro high on the forehead. The Negro got up at the count of eight, staggering, barely able to get his guard up, and Thomas, his face a bloody smear, but smiling, leapt after him mercilessly and hit him what seemed to Gretchen at least fifty times in the space of seconds. The Negro collapsed onto his face as the crowd yelled ear-splittingly around her. The Negro tried to get up, almost reached one knee. In a neutral corner, Thomas crouched alertly, bloody, tireless. He seemed to want his man to get up, to continue the fight, and Gretchen was sure there was a swift look of disappointment that flitted across his battered face as the Negro sank helplessly to the canvas and was counted out.

She wanted to vomit, but she merely retched drily, holding her handkerchief to her face, surprised at the smell of the perfume on it, among the rank odors of the arena. She sat huddled over in her seat, looking down, unable to watch any more, afraid she was going to faint and by that act announce to all the world her fatal connection to the victorious animal in the ring.

Rudolph had sat through the whole bout without uttering a sound, his lips twisted a little in disapproval at the clumsy blood-thirstiness, without style or grace, of the fight.

The fighters left the ring, the Negro, swathed in towels and robe, was helped through the ropes by his handlers, Thomas grinning, waving triumphantly, as people clapped him on the back. He left the ring on the far side, so that there was no chance of seeing his brother and sister as he made his way to the locker room.

The crowd began to drift out, but Gretchen and Rudolph sat side by side, without saying a word to each other, fearful of communicating after what they had seen. Finally Gretchen said, thickly, her eyes still lowered, "Let's get out of here."

"We have to go back," Rudolph said.

"What do you mean?" Gretchen looked up in surprise at her brother.

"We came," Rudolph said. "We watched. We have to see him."

"He's got nothing to do with us." As she said this, she knew she was lying.

"Come on." Rudolph stood up and took her elbow, making her

stand. He met all challenges, Rudolph, the cold, veray parfit gentil knight at Sunnyside Gardens.

"I won't, I won't . . ." Even as she was babbling this, she knew Rudolph would lead her inexorably to face Thomas, bloody, victorious, brutal, rancorous.

There were some men standing at the door of the dressing room, but nobody stopped Rudolph as he pushed the door open. Gretchen hung back. "I'd better wait outside," she said. "He may not be dressed."

Rudolph paid no attention to what she had said, but held her wrist and pulled her into the room after him. Thomas was sitting on a stained rubbing table with a towel around his middle and a doctor was sewing up the cut over his eye.

"It's nothing," the doctor was saying. "One more stitch and it's done."

Thomas had his eyes closed, to make it easier for the doctor to work. There was an orange stain of antiseptic above the eyebrow that gave him a clownish, lopsided air. He had obviously already taken his shower, as his hair was dark with water and plastered to his head, making him look like a print of an old-time bare-knuckle pugilist. Grouped around the table were several men, whom Rudolph recognized as having been in or near Thomas's corner during the fight. A curvy young woman in a tight dress kept making little sighing sounds each time the doctor's needle went into flesh. She had startling black hair and wore black nylon stockings over outlandishly shapely legs. Her eyebrows, plucked into a thin pencil line, high up, gave her a look of doll-like surprise. The room stank of old sweat, liniment, cigar smoke, and urine from the toilet visible through an open door leading off the dressing room. A bloodstained towel lay on the greasy floor, in a heap with the sweat-soaked purple tights and supporter and socks and shoes that Thomas had worn during the fight. It was sickeningly hot in the room.

What am I doing in a place like this, Gretchen thought. How did I get here?

"There we are," the doctor said, stepping back, his head cocked to one side, admiring his work. He put on a pad of gauze and a strip of adhesive tape over the wound. "You'll be able to fight again in ten days."

"Thanks, Doc," Thomas said and opened his eyes. He saw Rudolph and Gretchen. "Good Christ," he said. He smiled crookedly. "What the hell are you two doing here?"

"I have a message for you," Rudolph said. "A man called Al phoned me this afternoon and told me he'd put five hundred at seven to five for tonight."

"Good old Al," Thomas said. But he looked worriedly over at the curvy young woman with the black hair, as though he had wanted to keep this information from her.

"Congratulations on the fight," Rudolph said. He took a step forward and put out his hand. Thomas hesitated for a fraction of a second, then smiled again, and put out his swollen, reddened hand.

Gretchen couldn't get herself to congratulate her brother. "I'm glad you won, Tom," she said.

"Yeah. Thanks." He looked at her amusedly. "Let me introduce everybody to everybody," he said. "My brother, Rudolph; my sister, Gretchen. My wife, Teresa, my manager, Mr. Schultz, my trainer, Paddy, everybody . . ." He waved his hand vaguely at the men he hadn't bothered to introduce.

"Pleased to make your acquaintance," Teresa said. It was the suspicious voice of the telephone that afternoon.

"I didn't know you had family," Mr. Schultz said. He, too, seemed suspicious, as though having family was somehow perilous or actionable at law.

"I wasn't sure myself," Thomas said. "We have gone our separate ways, like they say. Hey, Schultzy, I must be getting to be one helluva draw at the gate if I even get my brother and sister to buy tickets."

"After tonight," Mr. Schultz said, "I can get you the Garden. It was a nice win." He was a small man with a basketball pouch under a greenish sweater. "Well, you people must have a lot to talk about, catch up with the news, as it were, we'll leave you alone. I'll drop in tomorrow sometime, Tommy, see how the eye's doing." He put on a jacket, just barely managing to button it over his paunch. The trainer gathered up the gear from the floor and put it into a bag. "Nice going, Tommy," he said, as he left with the doctor, the manager, and the others.

"Well, here we are," Thomas said. "A nice family reunion. I guess we ought to celebrate, huh, Teresa?"

"You never told me anything about a brother and sister," Teresa said aggrievedly, in her high voice.

"They slipped my mind for a few years," Thomas said. He jumped down off the rubbing table. "Now, if the ladies will retire, I'll put on some clothes."

Gretchen went out into the hall with her brother's wife. The hall

was empty now and she was relieved to get away from the stink and
heat of the dressing room. Teresa was putting on a shaggy red fox
coat with angry little movements of her shoulders and arms. "If the
ladies will retire," she said. "As though I never saw him naked before." She looked at Gretchen with open hostility, taking in the
black-wool dress, the low-heeled shoes, the plain, belted polo coat,
considering it, Gretchen could see, an affront to her style of living,
her dyed hair, her tight dress, her over-voluptuous legs, her marriage.
"I didn't know Tommy came from such a high-toned family," she
said.

"We're not so high-toned," Gretchen said. "Never fear."

"You never bothered to see him fight before tonight," Teresa said
aggressively, "did you?"

"I didn't know he was a fighter before today," said Gretchen. "Do
you mind if I sit down? I'm feeling very tired." There was a chair
across the hall and she moved away from the woman and sat down,
hoping to put an end to conversation. Teresa ruffled her shoulders irritably under the red fox, then began to walk peckishly up and down,
her high stiletto heels making a brittle, impatient sound on the concrete floor of the hallway.

Inside the dressing room Thomas was dressing slowly, turning away
modestly when he put on his shorts, occasionally wiping at his face
with a towel, because the shower had not completely broken the
sweat. From time to time he looked across at Rudolph and smiled
and shook his head and said, "Goddamn."

"How do you feel, Tommy?" Rudolph asked.

"Okay. But I'll piss blood tomorrow," Thomas said calmly. "He
got in a couple of good licks to the kidney, the sonofabitch. It was a
pretty good fight, though, wasn't it?"

"Yes," Rudolph said. He didn't have the heart to say that in his
eyes it had been a routine, ungraceful, second-rate brawl.

"I knew I could take him," Thomas said. "Even though I was the
underdog in the betting. Seven to five. That's a hot one. I made
seven hundred bucks on that bet." He sounded like a small boy
boasting. "Though it's too bad you had to say anything about it in
front of Teresa. Now she knows I have the dough and she'll be after
it like a hound dog."

"How long have you been married?" Rudolph asked.

"Two years. Legally. I knocked her up and I thought what the
hell." Thomas shrugged. "She's okay, Teresa, a little dumb, but okay.
The kid's worth it, though. A boy." He glanced maliciously over at
Rudolph. "Maybe I'll send him to his Uncle Rudy, to teach him

how to be a gentleman and not grow up to be a poor stupid pug, like his old man."

"I'd like to see him some day," Rudolph said stiffly.

"Any time. Come up to the house." Thomas put on a black turtle-neck sweater and his voice was muffled for a moment as he stuck his head into the wool. "You married yet?"

"No."

"Still the smart one of the family," Thomas said. "How about Gretchen?"

"A long time. She's got a son aged nine."

Thomas nodded. "She was bound not to hang around long. God, what a hot-looking dame. She looks better than ever, doesn't she?"

"Yes."

"Is she still as much of a shit as she used to be?"

"Don't talk like that, Tom," Rudolph said. "She was an awfully nice girl and she's grown into a very good woman."

"I guess I'll have to take your word for it, Rudy," Thomas said cheerfully. He was combing his hair carefully before a cracked mirror on the wall. "I wouldn't know, being on the outside the way I was."

"You weren't on the outside."

"Who you kidding, brother?" Thomas said flatly. He put the comb in his pocket, took a last critical look at his scarred, puffed face, with the diagonal white slash of adhesive tape above his eye. "I sure am a beauty tonight," he said. "If I'd known you were coming, I'd've shaved." He turned and put a bright-tweed jacket over the turtle-neck sweater. "You look as though you're doing all right, Rudy," he said. "You look like a goddamn vice-president of a bank."

"I'm not complaining," Rudolph said, not pleased with the vice-president.

"You know," Thomas said, "I went up to Port Philip a few years ago. For Auld Lang Syne. I heard Pop is dead."

"He killed himself," Rudolph said.

"Yeah, that's what the fruit-lady said." Thomas patted his breast pocket to make sure his wallet was in place. "The old house was gone. No light in the cellar window for the prodigal son," he said mockingly. "Only a supermarket. I still remember they had a special that day. Lamb shoulders. Mom alive?"

"Yes. She lives with me."

"Lucky you." Thomas grinned. "Still in Port Philip?"

"Whitby."

"You don't travel much, do you?"

"There's plenty of time." Rudolph had the uncomfortable feeling that his brother was using the conversation to tease him, undermine him, make him feel guilty. He was accustomed to controlling conversations himself by now and it took an effort not to let his irritation show. As he had watched his brother dress, watched him move that magnificent and fearsome body slowly and bruisedly, he had felt a huge sense of pity, love, a confused desire somehow to save that lumbering, brave, vengeful almost-boy from other evenings like the one he had just been through; from the impossible wife, from the bawling crowd, from the cheerful, stitching doctors, from the casual men who attended him and lived off him. He didn't want that feeling to be eroded by Thomas's mockery, by that hangover of ancient jealousy and hostility which by now should have long since subsided.

"Myself," Thomas was saying, "I been in quite a few places. Chicago, Cleveland, Boston, New Orleans, Philadelphia, San Francisco, Hollywood, Tia Juana. Name it and I've been there. I'm a man broadened by travel."

The door burst open and Teresa charged in, scowling under her pancake makeup. "You fellows going to talk in here all night?" she demanded.

"Okay, okay, honey," Thomas said. "We were just coming out. Do you want to come and have something to eat with us, you and Gretchen?" he asked Rudolph.

"We're going to eat Chinese," Teresa said. "I'm dying to eat Chinese."

"I'm afraid not tonight, Tom," Rudolph said. "Gretchen has to get home. She has to relieve the baby sitter." He caught the quick flicker of Thomas's eyes from him to his wife and then back again and he was sure Thomas was thinking, he doesn't want to be seen in public with my wife.

But Thomas shrugged and said amiably, "Well, some other time. Now we know we're all alive." He stopped abruptly in the doorway, as though he had suddenly thought of something. "Say," he said, "you going to be in town tomorrow around five?"

"Tommy," his wife said loudly, "are we going to eat or ain't we going to eat?"

"Shut up," Thomas said to her. "Rudy?"

"Yes." He had to spend the whole day in town, with architects and lawyers.

"Where can I see you?" Thomas asked.

"I'll be at my hotel. The Hotel Warwick on . . ."

"I know where it is," Thomas said. "I'll be there."

Gretchen joined them in the hallway. Her face was strained and pale, and for a moment Rudolph was sorry he had brought her along. But only for a moment. She's a big girl now, he thought, she can't duck *everything*. It's enough that she has so gracefully managed to duck her mother for ten years.

As they passed the door to another dressing room, Thomas stopped again. "I just have to look in here for a minute," he said, "say hello to Virgil. Come on in with me, Rudy, tell him you're my brother, tell him what a good fight he put up, it'll make him feel better."

"We'll never get out of this goddamn place tonight," Teresa said.

Thomas ignored her and pushed open the door and motioned for Rudolph to go first. The Negro fighter was still undressed. He was sitting, droop-shouldered, on the rubbing table, his hands hanging listlessly between his legs. A pretty young colored girl, probably his wife or sister, was sitting quietly on a camp chair at the foot of the table and a white handler was gently applying an icebag to a huge swelling on the fighter's forehead. Under the swelling the eye was shut tight. In a corner of the room an older, light-colored Negro with gray hair, who might have been the fighter's father, was carefully packing away a silk robe and trunks and shoes. The fighter looked up slowly with his one good eye as Thomas and Rudolph came into the room.

Thomas put his arm gently around his opponent's shoulders. "How you feeling, Virgil?" he asked.

"I felt better," the fighter said. Now Rudolph could see that he couldn't have been more than twenty years old.

"Meet my brother, Rudy, Virgil," Thomas said. "He wants to tell you what a good fight you put up."

Rudolph shook hands with the fighter, who said, "Glad to meet you, sir."

"It was an awfully good fight," Rudolph said, although what he would have liked to say was, Poor young man, please never put on another pair of gloves again.

"Yeah," the fighter said. "He awful strong, your brother."

"I was lucky," Thomas said. "Real lucky. I got five stitches over my eye."

"It wasn't a butt, Tommy," Virgil said. "I swear it wasn't a butt."

"Of course not, Virgil," Thomas said. "Nobody said it was. Well, I just wanted to say hello, make sure you're all right." He hugged the boy's shoulders again.

"Thanks for comin' by," Virgil said. "It's nice of you."

"Good luck, kid," Thomas said. Then he and Rudolph shook hands gravely with all the other people in the room and left.

"It's about time," Teresa said as they appeared in the hall.

I give the marriage six months, Rudolph thought as they went toward the exit.

"They rushed that boy," Thomas said to Rudolph as they walked side by side. "He had a string of easy wins and they gave him a main bout. I watched him a couple of times and I knew I could take him downstairs. Lousy managers. You notice, the bastard wasn't even there. He didn't even wait to see if Virgil ought to go home or to the hospital. It's a shitty profession." He glanced back to see if Gretchen objected to the word, but Gretchen seemed to be moving in a private trance of her own, unseeing and unhearing.

Outside, they hailed a taxi and Gretchen insisted upon sitting up front with the driver. Teresa sat in the middle on the back seat, between Thomas and Rudolph. She was overpoweringly perfumed, but when Rudolph put the window down she said, "For God's sake, the wind is ruining my hair," and he said, "I'm sorry," and wound the window up again.

They drove back to Manhattan in silence, with Teresa holding Thomas's hand and occasionally bringing it up to her lips and kissing it, marking out her possessions.

When they came off the bridge, Rudolph said, "We'll get out here, Tom."

"You're sure you don't want to come with us?" Thomas said.

"It's the best Chinese food in town," Teresa said. The ride had been neutral, she no longer felt in danger of being attacked, she could afford to be hospitable, perhaps in the future there was an advantage there for her. "You don't know what you're missing."

"I have to get home," Gretchen said. Her voice was quivering, on the point of hysteria. "I just must get home."

If it hadn't been for Gretchen, Rudolph would have stayed with Thomas. After the noise of the evening, the public triumph, the battering, it seemed sad and lonely to leave Thomas merely to go off to supper with his twittering wife, anonymous in the night, unsaluted, uncheered. He would have to make it up to Thomas another time.

The driver stopped the car and Gretchen and Rudolph got out. "Good-bye for now, in-laws," Teresa said, and laughed.

"Five o'clock tomorrow, Rudy," Thomas said and Rudolph nodded.

"Good night," Gretchen whispered. "Take care of yourself, please."

The taxi moved off and Gretchen gripped Rudolph's arm, as though to steady herself. Rudolph stopped a cruising cab and gave the driver Gretchen's address. Once in the darkness of the cab, Gretchen broke down. She threw herself into Rudolph's arms and wept uncontrollably, her body racked by great sobs. The tears came to Rudolph's eyes, too, and he held his sister tightly, stroking her hair. In the back of the dark cab, with the lights of the city streaking past the windows, erratically illuminating, in bursts of colored neon, the contorted, lovely, tear-stained face, he felt closer to Gretchen, bound in stricter love, than ever before.

The tears finally stopped. Gretchen sat up, dabbed at her eyes with a handkerchief. "I'm sorry," she said. "I'm such a hateful snob. That poor boy, that poor, poor boy . . ."

The baby sitter was asleep on the couch in the living room when they came into the apartment. Willie hadn't come home yet. There had been no calls, the baby sitter said. Billy had read himself to sleep quietly and she had gone up and turned off his light without awakening him. She was a girl of about seventeen, a high-school student, bobby-soxed, pretty, in a snub-nosed, shy way, and embarrassed at being caught asleep. Gretchen poured two Scotches and soda. The baby sitter had straightened out the room and the newspapers, which had been strewn around, were now in a neat pile on the window sill and the cushions were plumped out.

There was only one lamp lit and they sat in shadow, Gretchen with her feet curled up under her on the couch, Rudolph in a large easy chair. They drank slowly, exhausted, blessing the silence. They finished their drinks and silently Rudolph rose from his chair and refilled the glasses, sat down again.

An ambulance siren wailed in the distance, somebody else's accident.

"He *enjoyed* it," Gretchen said finally. "When that boy was practically helpless and he hit him so many times. I always thought— when I thought anything about it—that it was just a man earning a living—in a peculiar way—but just that. It wasn't like that at all tonight, was it?"

"It's a curious profession," Rudolph said. "It's hard to know what really must be going on in a man's head up there."

"Weren't you *ashamed*?"

"Put it this way," Rudolph said. "I wasn't happy. There must be at least ten thousand boxers in the United States. They have to come from *somebody's* family."

"I don't think like you," Gretchen said coldly.

"No, you don't."

"Those sleazy purple trunks," she said, as though by finding an object on which she could fix her revulsion, she could exorcise the complex horror of the entire night. She shook her head against memory. "Somehow I feel it's our fault, yours, mine, our parents', that Tom was up there in that vile place."

Rudolph sipped at his drink in silence. *I wouldn't know,* Tom had said in the dressing room, *being on the outside the way I was.* Excluded, he had reacted as a boy in the most simple, brutal way, with his fists. Older, he had merely continued. They all had their father's blood in them, and Axel Jordache had killed two men. As far as Rudolph knew, Tom at least hadn't killed anybody. Perhaps the strain was ameliorating.

"Ah, what a mess," Gretchen said. "All of us. Yes, you, too. Do you enjoy *anything,* Rudy?"

"I don't think of things in those terms," he said.

"The commercial monk," Gretchen said harshly. "Except that instead of the vow of poverty, you've taken the vow of wealth. Which is better in the long run?"

"Don't talk like a fool, Gretchen." Now he was sorry he had come upstairs with her.

"And the two others," she continued. "Chastity and obedience. Chaste for our Virgin Mother's sake—is that it? Obedience to Duncan Calderwood, the Pope of Whitby's Chamber of Commerce?"

"That's all going to change now," Rudolph said, but he was unwilling to defend himself further.

"You're going to go over the wall, Father Rudolph? You're going to marry, you're going to wallow in the fleshpots, you're going to tell Duncan Calderwood to go fuck himself?"

Rudolph stood up and went over and poured some more soda into his glass, biting back his anger. "It's silly, Gretchen," he said, as calmly as possible, "to take tonight out on me."

"I'm sorry," she said, but her voice was still hard. "Ah—I'm the worst of the lot. I live with a man I despise, I do work that's mean-spirited and piddling and useless, I'm New York's easiest lay . . . Do I shock you, brother?" she said mockingly.

"I think you're giving yourself a title you haven't earned," Rudolph said.

"Joke," Gretchen said. "Do you want a list? Beginning with Johnny Heath? Do you think he's been so good to you because of your shining bright eyes?"

"What does Willie think about all this?" Rudolph asked, ignoring the jibe. No matter how it had started and for whatever reasons, Johnny Heath was now his friend.

"Willie doesn't think about anything but infesting bars and occasionally screwing some drunken broad and getting by in this world with as little work and as little honor as possible. If he somehow was given the original stone tablets of the Ten Commandments, his first thought would be which sponsor he could sell it to at the highest price to advertise vacation tours to Mount Sinai."

Rudolph laughed and despite herself Gretchen had to laugh, too. "There's nothing like a failing marriage," she said, "to bring out flights of rhetoric."

Rudolph's laughter was part relief. Gretchen had switched targets and he no longer was under attack.

"Does Willie know what your opinion is of him?" he asked.

"Yes," Gretchen said. "He agrees with it. That's the worst thing about him. He says there's not a man or a woman or a *thing* in this world that he admires, especially himself. He'd be deeply dissatisfied with himself, he told me, if he was anything but a failure. Beware romantic men."

"Why do you live with him?" Rudolph asked bluntly.

"Do you remember the note I sent you saying I was in a mess and I wanted to see you?"

"Yes." Rudolph remembered it very well, remembered that whole day very well. When he had come down to New York the next week and asked Gretchen what the trouble was she had said, "Nothing. It's blown over."

"I'd more or less decided I wanted to ask Willie for a divorce," Gretchen said, "and I wanted your advice."

"What changed your mind?"

Gretchen shrugged. "Billy got sick. Nothing. For a day the doctor thought it was appendicitis, but it wasn't. But Willie and I stayed up with him all night and as I looked at him lying all white faced and in pain on the bed and Willie hovering over him, so obviously loving him, I couldn't bear the thought of making him another one of those poor forlorn statistics—child of a broken marriage, permanently homesick, preparing for the psychiatrist's couch. Well . . ." her voice hardened, "that charming fit of maternal sentimentality has passed on. If our parents had divorced when I was nine, I'd be a better woman than I am today."

"You mean you want a divorce now?"

"If I get custody of Billy," she said. "And that's one thing he won't give me."

Rudolph hesitated, took a long drink of his whiskey. "Do you want me to see what I can do with him?" He wouldn't have offered to interfere if it hadn't been for the tears in the taxicab.

"If it'll do any good," Gretchen said. "I want to sleep with one man, not ten, I want to be honest, do something useful, finally. God, I should like *The Three Sisters*. Divorce is my Moscow. Give me one more drink, please." She held out her glass.

Rudolph went over to the bar and filled both their glasses. "You're running low on Scotch," he said.

"I wish that were true," she said.

There was the sound of an ambulance siren again, wailing, diminishing, a warning as it approached, a lament as it departed. The Doppler phenomenon. Was it the same accident, completing the round trip? Or one of an endless series, limitless blood on the avenues of the city?

Rudolph handed her her drink and she sat curled up on the couch, staring at it.

A clock chimed somewhere. One o'clock.

"Well," Gretchen said, "I guess they're finished eating Chinese by now, Tommy and that lady. Is it possible that he has the only happy marriage in the history of the Jordaches? Do they love, honor and cherish each other as they eat Chinese and warm the bosomy marriage bed?"

There was the sound of a key in the front door lock. "Ah," Gretchen said, "the veteran is returning home, wearing his medals."

Willie came into the room, walking straight. "Hi, darling," he said, and went over and kissed Gretchen's cheek. As always, when he hadn't seen Willie for some time, Rudolph was surprised at how short he was. Perhaps that was his real flaw—his size. He waved at Rudolph. "How's the merchant prince tonight?" he said.

"Congratulate him," Gretchen said. "He signed that deal today."

"Congratulations," Willie said. He squinted around the room. "God, it's dark in here. What've you two been talking about—death, tombs, foul deeds done by night?" He went over to the bar and poured the last of the whiskey. "Darling," he said, "we need a fresh bottle."

Automatically, Gretchen stood up and went into the kitchen.

Willie looked after her anxiously. "Rudy," he whispered, "is she sore at me for not coming home to dinner?"

"No, I don't think so."

"I'm glad you're here," Willie said. "Otherwise, I'd be getting Lecture Number 725. Thanks, darling," he said as Gretchen came into the room carrying a bottle. He took the bottle from her, opened it, and strengthened his drink. "What'd you kids do tonight?" he asked.

"We had a family reunion," Gretchen said, from her place on the couch. "We went to a prize fight."

"What?" Willie said puzzledly. "What is she talking about, Rudy?"

"She can tell you about it later." Rudolph stood up, leaving most of his last whiskey undrunk. "I've got to be moving along. I have to get up at the crack of dawn." He felt uncomfortable sitting there with Willie, pretending that this night was no different from others, pretending he had not heard what Gretchen had said about him and about herself. He bent over and kissed Gretchen and Willie accompanied him to the door.

"Thanks for coming by and keeping the old girl company," Willie said. "It makes me feel like less of a shit, leaving her alone. But it was unavoidable."

It wasn't a butt, Tommy, Rudolph remembered, *I swear it wasn't a butt.* "You don't have to make any excuses to me, Willie," he said.

"Say," Willie said, "she was joking, wasn't she? That stuff about the prize fight? What is it—a kind of riddle, or something?"

"No. We went to a fight."

"I'll never understand that woman," Willie said. "When I want to watch a fight on television, I have to go to somebody else's house. Ah, well, I suppose she'll tell me about it." He pressed Rudolph's hand warmly and Rudolph went out the door. He heard Willie locking it securely behind him and fixing the anti-burglar chain. The danger is inside, Willie, Rudolph wanted to say. You are locking it in with you. He went down the stairs slowly. He wondered where he would be tonight, what evasions he would be offering, what cuckoldry and dissatisfaction would have been in the air, if that night in 1950, room 923 in the St. Moritz Hotel had answered?

If I were a religious man, he thought, going out into the night, I would believe that God was watching over me.

He remembered his promise to try to do what he could to get

Gretchen a divorce, on her terms. There was the logical first step to be taken and he was a logical man. He wondered where he could find a reliable private detective. Johnny Heath would know. Johnny Heath was made for New York City. Rudolph sighed, hating the moment ahead of him when he would enter the detective's office, hating the detective himself, still unknown to him, preparing, all in the week's work, to spy on the breakdown and end of love.

Rudolph turned and took a last look at the building he had just left and against which he was sworn to conspire. He knew he'd never be able to mount those steps again, shake that small, desperate man's hand again. Duplicity, too, must have its limits.

Chapter 6

I

He had pissed blood in the morning, but not very much and he wasn't hurting. The reflection of his face in the train window when they went through a tunnel was a little sinister, because of the slash of bandage over his eye, but otherwise, he told himself, he looked like anybody else on the way to the bank. The Hudson was cold blue in the October sun and as the train passed Sing Sing he thought of the prisoners peering out at the broad river running free to the sea, and he said, "Poor bastards," aloud.

He patted the bulge of his wallet under his jacket. He had collected the seven hundred dollars from the bookie on the way downtown. Maybe he could get away with giving Teresa just two hundred of it, two fifty if she made a stink.

He pulled the wallet out. He had been paid off in hundreds. He took out a bill and studied it. Founding father, Benjamin Franklin, stared out at him, looking like somebody's old mother. Lightning on a kite, he remembered dimly; at night all cats are gray. He must have been a tougher man than he looked to get his picture on a bill that size. Did he once say, Gentlemen we must hang together or we will hang separately? I should have at least finished high school, Thomas thought, vague in the presence of one hundred dollars' worth of history. *This note is legal tender for all debts, public and private and is redeemable in lawful money at the United States Treasury or at any Federal Reserve Bank*. If this wasn't lawful money, what the hell was? It was signed in fancy script by somebody called Ivy Baker Priest, Treasurer of the United States. It took a someone with a name like that to give out with double talk about debts and money and get away with it.

Thomas folded the bill neatly and slipped it by itself in a side pocket, to be put with the other hundred-dollar bills, reposing in the dark vault for just such a day as this.

The man on the seat in front of him was reading a newspaper, turned to the sports page. Thomas could see that he was reading about last night's fight. He wondered what the man would say if he tapped him on the shoulder and said, "Mister, I was there, how would you like an account of the battle right from the middle of the ring?" Actually, the reports of the fight in the papers had been pretty good and there had been a picture on the back page of the *News* of Virgil trying to get up the last time and himself in a neutral corner. One newspaperman had even said the fight had raised him into the ranks of the contenders for the title and Schultzy had called him all excited, right before he left the house, to say that a promoter over from England had seen the fight and was offering them a bout in London in six weeks. "We're going international," Schultzy had said excitedly. "We can fight all over the Continent. And you'll knock 'em dead. They ain't got anybody half as good even as Virgil Walters in England at your weight. And the guy said he'd give us some of the purse under the table and we won't have to declare it to the goddamn income tax."

So, all in all, he should have been feeling pretty good, sitting there in the train, with the prison falling away behind him, full of a lot of guys who probably were a damn sight smarter than he was and maybe less guilty of one thing and another, too. But he wasn't feeling good. Teresa had given him a load of grief about not telling her about the bet and about his la-di-da family, as she called them. She was sore because he'd never said anything about them, as though he was hiding some fucking treasure or something.

"That sister of yours looked at me like I was dirt," Teresa had said. "And your fancy brother opened the window as though I smelled like horseshit and he pulled away to his side of the cab like if he happened to touch me for a second he'd catch the clap. And after not seeing their brother for ten years they were just too fine even to come and have a cup of coffee with him, for God's sake. And you, the big fighter, you never said a word, you just took it all."

This had been in bed, after the restaurant, where she had eaten in sullen silence. He had wanted to make love to her, as he always did after a fight, because he didn't touch her for weeks before a fight and his thing was so hard you could knock out fungoes to the outfield with it, but she had closed down like a stone and wouldn't let him near her. For Christ's sake, he thought, I didn't marry her for her conversation. And it wasn't as though even in her best moments Teresa was so marvelous in bed. If you mussed her hair while you were going at it hammer and tongs, she'd complain bloody murder, and she was always finding excuses to put it off till tomorrow or next week or next year and when she finally opened her legs it was like a tollgate being fed a counterfeit coin. She came from a religious family, she said, as though the Angel Michael with his sword was standing guard over all Catholic cunts. He'd bet his next purse his sister Gretchen, with her straight hair and her no make-up and her black dress and that ladylike don't-you-dare-touch-the-hem-of-my-garment look would give a man a better time in one bang than Teresa in twenty ten-minute rounds.

So he'd slept badly, his wife's words ringing in his ears. The worst of it was that what she said was true. Here he was a big grown man, and all his brother and sister had to do was come into the room and he felt just the way they had made him feel when he was a kid— slimy, stupid, useless, suspect.

Go win fights, have your picture in the papers, piss blood, go have people cheer you and clap you on the back and ask you to appear in London; two snots you thought you'd never see or hear from again show up and say hello, just hello, and everything you are is nothing. Well, his goddamn brother, momma's pet, poppa's pet, blowing his golden horn, opening taxi windows, was going to be in for a shock from his nothing pug brother today.

For a crazy moment he thought maybe he wouldn't get off the train, he'd go on to Albany and make the change and arrive in Elysium, Ohio, and go to the one person in the whole world who had touched him with love, who had made him feel like a whole man, when he was just a kid of sixteen. Clothilde, servant to his uncle's bed. St. Sebastian, in the bathtub.

But when the train pulled into Port Philip, he got off and went to the bank, just as he had planned.

II

She tried not to show her impatience as Billy played with his lunch. Superstitiously (children sensed things that transcended the years) she had not dressed yet for the afternoon ahead of her, but was sitting with him in her work clothes, slacks and a sweater. She picked at her food, without appetite, trying not to scold the boy as he pushed bits of lamb chop and lettuce around his plate.

"Why do I have to go to the Museum of Natural History?" Billy demanded.

"It's a treat," she said, "a special treat."

"Not for me. Why do I have to go?"

"The whole class is going."

"They're dopes. Except for Conrad Franklin they're all dopes." Billy had had the same morsel of lamb chop in his mouth for what seemed like five minutes. Occasionally, he would move it symbolically from one side of his mouth to the other. Gretchen wondered if, finally, she should hit him. The clock in the kitchen suddenly ticked louder and louder and she tried not to look at it, but couldn't resist. Twenty to one. She was due uptown at a quarter to two. And she had to take Billy to school, hurry back, bathe and dress, carefully, carefully, and then make sure not to arrive panting as though she had just run a marathon.

"Finish your lunch," Gretchen said, marveling at the motherly calmness of her voice, on this afternoon when she felt anything but motherly. "There's Jello for dessert."

"I don't like Jello."

"Since when?"

"Since today. And what's the sense in going to see a lot of old stuffed animals? At least if they want us to look at animals we could go see some live ones."

"On Sunday," Gretchen said, "I'll take you to the zoo."

"I told Conrad Franklin I'd go over to his house on Sunday," Billy said. He reached into his mouth and took out the piece of lamb chop and put it on his plate.

"That's not a polite thing to do," Gretchen said, as the clock ticked.

"It's tough."

"All right," Gretchen said, reaching for his plate. "If you're through, you're through."

Billy held onto the plate. "I haven't finished my salad." Deliberately, he cut a lettuce leaf into geometric forms with his fork.

He is asserting his personality, Gretchen made herself think, to keep from hitting him. It bodes well for his future.

Unable to bear watching his measured game with the lettuce, she got up and took a cup of Jello out of the refrigerator.

"Why're you so nervous today?" Billy asked. "Jumping around."

Children and their goddamn intuition, Gretchen thought. Not in utter nakedness, but trailing clouds of radar do we come. She put the Jello down on the table. "Eat your dessert," she said, "it's getting late."

Billy folded his arms and leaned back. "I told you I don't like Jello."

She was tempted to say that he'd eat his Jello or he'd sit there all day. Then she had the dark suspicion that that was exactly what Billy wanted her to say. Was it possible that in that mysterious pool of emotion, love, hate, sensuality, greed, that lay within a child, somehow he knew what her errand uptown was going to be and that in his own instinctive way he was defending himself, defending his father, guarding the unity of the home in which he felt himself, with casual childish arrogance, the center?

"Okay," she said. "No Jello. Let's go."

Billy was a good winner. No smile of triumph lit his face. Instead, he said, "Why do I have to go see a lot of old dead stuffed animals?"

She was hot and panting as she unlocked the door. She had practically run all the way from the school gates, after depositing Billy. The phone was ringing, but she let it ring as she hurried into the bathroom, stripping off her clothes. She took a warm shower, looked briefly and critically at her body in the long mirror as she stood there, glistening wetly, before she toweled herself off. I could have gone either way, she thought, plump or thin. Thank God I went thin. But not too. My body, the luring, damp house of my soul. She laughed and went naked into the bedroom and took out the diaphragm which she kept hidden under a pile of scarves. *Oh, well-used device.* She put it in carefully, sinning. One day they have to invent something better than a piece of machinery.

As she touched herself, she remembered the curious flush of desire that had come over her the night before when she had finally gone to bed. The images of the fighters, white and black, that had sickened her while she was in the arena, suddenly became the inspirers of desire, the magnificent, harsh bodies tumbled around her. Sex for a woman was in a demonstrable way an intrusion, a profound invasion of privacy, as was a blow given by one man to another. In the uneasy, early-morning bed, after the disturbing night, the lines crossed, blows became caresses, caresses blows, and she turned, aroused, under the covers. If Willie had come into her bed she would have welcomed him ardently. But Willie was sleeping, on his back, snoring softly from time to time.

She had gotten up and taken a pill to sleep.

During the morning, she had put it all from her mind, the shame of the night covered with the innocent mask of daylight.

She shook her head, opened a drawer full of panties and brassieres. When she thought about it, "panties" seemed a hypocritically innocuous word, falsely childish, to cover such desperate territory. Girdle was a better word, though it was from more melodious periods of language, and she didn't wear girdles. Boylan's teaching.

The phone rang again, persistently, but she ignored it as she dressed. She stared for a moment at the clothes hanging in the closet, then chose a simple, severe blue suit. No advertising the mission. The emergent rosy body better appreciated later for having been concealed before. She brushed her dark hair, straight and long to her shoulders, the broad, low forehead clear, serene, unwrinkled, concealing all betrayals, all doubts.

She couldn't find a taxi so she took the Eighth Avenue subway uptown, remembering to get on the Queens train that crossed over to the East Side on Fifty-third Street. Persephone, coming from the underground in the flowertime of love.

She got out at the Fifth Avenue exit and walked in the windy autumn sunshine, her demure navy-blue figure reflected in the glitter of shop windows. She wondered how many of the other women she passed were, like her, briefly parading the avenue, drifting cunningly through Saks, diaphragms in place.

She turned east on Fifty-fifth Street, past the entrance of the St. Regis, remembered a wedding party on a summer evening, a white veil, a young lieutenant. There were only a certain number of streets in the city. One could not avoid them all. The echoes of urban geography.

She looked at her watch. Twenty to two. Five full minutes, in which to walk slowly, to arrive cool, controlled.

Colin Burke lived on Fifty-sixth between Madison and Park. Another echo. On that street there had once been a party from which she had turned away. When renting an apartment, a man could not be blamed for not picking through his future lover's memories before putting down the first month's rent.

She went into the familiar white vestibule, rang the bell. How many times, on how many afternoons, had she rung that bell? Twenty? Thirty? Sixty? Some day she would make the count.

The buzzer hummed at the doorlatch and she went in and took the small elevator up to the fourth floor.

He was standing at the door, in pajamas and a robe, his feet bare. They kissed briefly, no rush, no rush.

There were breakfast things on the coffee table in the big, disordered living room, and a half-finished cup of coffee, among piles of leatherette-bound scripts. He was a director in the theater and he kept theatrical hours, rarely going to bed before five in the morning.

"Can I give you a cup of coffee?" he asked.

"No, thanks," she said. "I've just had lunch."

"Ah, the orderly life," he said. "So to be envied." The irony was gentle.

"Tomorrow," she said, "you can come down and feed Billy a lamb chop. Envy me later."

Burke had never seen Billy, had never met her husband, or been to their home. She had met him at a luncheon with one of the editors of a magazine for which she did occasional pieces. The idea was that she was to do an article on him, because she had praised a play he had directed. At the luncheon she hadn't liked him, had thought him cocky, theory ridden, too confident of himself. She hadn't written the article, but three months later, after several scattered meetings, she had gone to bed with him, out of lust, revenge, boredom, hysteria, indifference, accident . . . She no longer probed her reasons.

He sipped at his coffee, standing up, watching her over the cup, his dark-gray eyes tender under thunderous black eyebrows. He was thirty-five years old, a short man, shorter than she (*Am I doomed all my life to small men?*) but there was a thin intensity about his face, dark-stubbled with beard now, a strained intellectual rigor, an impression of directness and strength, that made one forget his size. In his profession he was used to ordering complex and difficult people about and the look of command was on him. He was moody and sometimes sharply spoken, even to her, tortured by failures in excellence in himself and others, easily scornful, given sometimes to disappearing without a word for weeks at a time. He was divorced and was reputed to be a ladies' man and in the beginning, last year, she felt that he was using her for the simplest and most obvious of reasons, but now, standing across the room from him, watching the slim, barefooted, small man in the soft, navy-blue bathrobe (happy matching of afternoon colors) she was sure she loved him and that she wanted none else but him and would make great sacrifices to remain at his side for her entire life.

She was talking about Burke when she had said last night to her brother that she wanted to sleep with one man, not ten. And in fact, since the beginning of their affair she had made love with no one else but him, except for the infrequent times when Willie had come to her bed, in nostalgic moments of tenderness; unhappy, fleeting reconciliations; the almost forgotten habits of marriage.

Burke had asked if she still slept with her husband and she had told him the truth. She had also confessed that it gave her pleasure. She had no need to lie to him and he was the one man she had ever known to whom she could say anything that came to her mind. He had told her that since their first meeting he had not slept with another woman and she was sure that this was so.

"Beautiful Gretchen," he said, taking the cup from his lips, "bounteous Gretchen, glorious G. Oh, to have you come in every morning with the breakfast tray."

"My," she said, "you're in a good mood today."

"Not really," he said. He put down the cup and came over and they slipped their arms around each other. "I have a disastrous afternoon ahead of me. My agent called me an hour ago and I have to go to the Columbia office at two-thirty. They want me to go out West and do a movie. I called you a couple of times, but there was no answer."

The phone had rung as she had entered the apartment, again as she had dressed. Love me tomorrow, not today, courtesy of American Tel and Tel. But tomorrow, there was no trip to the museum for Billy's class, freeing her until five o'clock. She would have to be at the school gate at three. Passion by children's hours.

"I heard the phone ring," she said, moving away from him, "but I didn't answer it." Abstractedly, she lit a cigarette. "I thought you had a play to do this year," she said.

"Throw away that cigarette," Burke said. "Whenever a bad director wants to show unspoken tension between two characters, he has
them lighting a cigarette."

She laughed, stubbing it out.

"The play isn't ready," Burke said, "and the way the rewrite's
going it won't be ready for another year. And everything else that
I've been offered is junk. Don't look so sad."

"I'm not sad," she said. "I'm horny and unlaid and disappointed."

It was his turn to laugh. "The vocabulary of Gretchen," he said.
"Always to be trusted. Can't you make it this evening?"

"Evenings're out. You know that. That would be flaunting it. And
I'm not a flaunter." There was no telling with Willie. He might
come home for dinner, whistling cheerfully, two weeks in a row. "Is
it a good picture?"

"It can be." He shrugged, rubbing the blue-black stubble of his
beard. "The whore's cry," he said. "It can be. Frankly, I need the
money."

"You had a hit last year," she said, knowing she shouldn't push
him, but pushing him nevertheless.

"Between Uncle Sam and the alimony, my bank is howling." He
grimaced. "Lincoln freed the slaves in 1863, but he overlooked the
married men."

Love, like almost everything else these days, was a function of the
Internal Revenue Service. We embrace between tax forms. "I ought
to introduce you," she said, "to Johnny Heath and my brother. They
swim like fish among the deductions."

"Businessmen," he said. "They know the magic. When my tax
man sees my records he puts his head in his hands and weeps. No
use crying over spilt money. On to Hollywood. Actually, I look forward to it. There's no reason these days why a director shouldn't do
movies as well as plays. That old idea that there's something holy
about the theater and eternally grubby about film is just snobbism
and it's as dead as David Belasco. If you asked me who was the
greatest dramatic artist alive today I'd say Federico Fellini. And
there hasn't been anything better on the stage in my time than *Citizen Kane* and that was pure Hollywood. Who knows—I may be the
Orson Welles of the fifties."

Burke was walking back and forth as he spoke and Gretchen could
tell that he meant what he was saying, or at least most of it, and was
eager to take up the new challenge in his career. "Sure, there're
whores in Hollywood, but nobody would seriously claim that

Shubert Alley is a cloister. It's true I need money and I'm not averse
to the sight of the dollar, but I'm not hunting it. Yet. And I hope
never. I've been negotiating with Columbia for more than a month
now and they're giving me an absolute free hand—the story I want,
the writer I want, no supervision, the whole thing shot on location,
final cut, everything, as long as I stay within the budget. And the
budget's a fair one. If it's not as good as anything I've done on
Broadway, the fault'll be mine and nobody else's. Come to the opening night. I will expect you to cheer."

She smiled, but it was a dutiful smile. "You didn't tell me you
were so far along. More than a month . . ."

"I'm a secretive bastard," he said. "And I didn't want to say anything until it was definite."

She lit a cigarette, to give her something to do with her hands and
her face. The hell with directors' clichés of tension. "What about
me? Back here?" she asked, through smoke, knowing again she
shouldn't ask it.

"What about you?" He looked at her thoughtfully. "There are always planes."

"In which direction?"

"In both directions."

"How long do you think we'd last?"

"Two weeks." He flipped his finger against a glass on the coffee
table and it tinkled faintly, a small chime marking a dubious hour.
"Forever."

"If I were to come out West," she said evenly, "with Billy, could
we live with you?"

He came over to her and kissed her forehead, holding her head
with his two hands. She had to bend a little for the kiss. His beard
scraped minutely against her skin. "Ah, God," he said softly, then
pulled back. "I have to shave and shower and dress," he said. "I'm
late as it is."

She watched him shave, shower and dress, then drove with him in
a taxi to the office on Fifth Avenue where he had the appointment.
He hadn't answered her question, but he asked her to call him later
so that he could tell her what the people at Columbia had said.

She got out of the taxi with him and spent the afternoon shopping, idly, buying a dress and a sweater, both of which she knew she
would return later in the week.

At five o'clock, dressed once more in slacks, and wearing her old
tweed coat, she was at the gates of Billy's school, undiaphragmed,

waiting for the class to come back from the Museum of Natural History.

III

By the end of the afternoon he was tired. There had been lawyers all morning and lawyers, he had discovered, were the most fatiguing group of people in the world. At least for him. Even the ones who were working for him. The constant struggle for advantage, the ambiguous, tricky, indigestible language, the search for loopholes, levers, profitable compromises, the unashamed pursuit of money, was abhorrent to him, even while he was profiting from it all. There was one good thing about dealing with lawyers—it reassured him a hundred times over that he had acted correctly in refusing Teddy Boylan's offer to finance him through law school.

Then there had been the architects in the afternoon, and they had been trying, too. He was working on the plans for the center and his hotel room was littered with drawings. On Johnny Heath's advice, he had chosen a firm of young architects who had already won some important prizes, but were still hungry. They were eager and talented, there was no doubt about that, but they had worked almost exclusively in cities and their ideas ran to glass and steel or poured cement, and Rudolph, knowing that they considered him hopelessly square, insisted upon traditional forms and traditional materials. It was not exactly his own taste, but he felt it would be the taste best appreciated by the people who would come to the center. And it certainly would be the only thing that Calderwood might approve of. "I want it to look like a street in an old New England village," Rudolph kept saying, while the architects groaned. "White clapboard and a tower over the theater so that you can mistake it for a church. It's a conservative rural area and we're going to be catering to conservative people in a country atmosphere and they will spend their money more easily in an ambience that they feel happy and at home in."

Again and again the architects had almost quit, but he had said, "Do it this way this time, boys, and the next time it'll be more your way. This is only the first of a chain and we'll get bolder as we go along."

The plans they had sketched for him were still a long way from what he wanted, but as he looked at the last rough drawings they had shown him that day, he knew they would finally surrender.

His eyes ached and he wondered if he needed glasses as he made some notes on the plans. There was a bottle of whiskey on the bureau and he poured himself a drink, topping it off with water from the tap in the bathroom. He sipped at the drink as he spread the sheets of stiff paper out on the desk. He winced at the drawing of a huge sign, CALDERWOOD'S, that the architects had sketched in at the entrance to the center. It was to be outlined in flashing neon at night. In his old age, Calderwood sought renown, immortality in flickering multicolored glass tubing, and all Rudolph's tactful intimations about keeping a single modest style for the center had fallen on deaf ears.

The telephone rang, and Rudolph looked at his watch. Tom had said he would come by at five and it was almost that now. He picked up the phone, but it wasn't Tom. He recognized the voice of Johnny Heath's secretary on the phone. "Mr. Jordache? Mr. Heath calling."

He waited, annoyed, for Johnny to get on the phone. In his organization, he decided, when anybody made a call, whoever was making it would have to be ready to speak when the phone was answered. How many slightly angered clients and customers there must be each day in America, hung up on a secretary's warning trill, how many deals lost, how many invitations refused, how many ladies who, in that short delay, had decided to say, No.

When Johnny Heath finally said, "Hello, Rudy," Rudolph concealed his irritation.

"I have the information you asked me for," Johnny said. "Have you got a pencil and a piece of paper?"

"Yes."

Johnny gave him the name and address of a detective agency. "I hear they're very dependable," Johnny said. He didn't inquire why Rudolph needed a private detective, although there must have been some guessing going on in his mind.

"Thanks, Johnny," Rudolph said, after he had written down the name and address. "Thanks for your trouble."

"It was nothing," Johnny said. "You free for dinner tonight?"

"Sorry," Rudolph said. He had nothing on for the evening and if Johnny's secretary had not kept him waiting he would have said yes.

After he hung up, he felt more tired than ever and decided to postpone calling the detective agency until the next day. He was surprised that he felt tired. He didn't remember ever feeling tired at five o'clock in the afternoon.

But he was tired now, no doubt about it. Age? He laughed. He was twenty-seven years old. He looked at his face in the mirror. No gray hairs in the even, smooth blackness. No bags under the eyes. No signs of debauchery or hidden illness in the clear, olive skin. If he had been overworking, it did not show in that youthful, contained, unwrinkled face.

Still, he was tired. He lay, fully clothed, on the bed, hoping for a few minutes of sleep before Tom arrived. But he could not sleep. His sister's contemptuous words of the night before kept running through his mind, as they had been all day, even when he was struggling with lawyers and architects. "Do you enjoy *anything?*" He hadn't defended himself, but he could have pointed out that he enjoyed working, that he enjoyed going to concerts, that he read enormously, that he went to the theater, prizefights, art galleries, that he enjoyed running in the morning, riding a motorcycle, he enjoyed, yes, seeing his mother sitting across from him at the table, unlovely, unlovable, but alive, and *there*, by his efforts, not in a grave, or a pauper's hospital bed.

Gretchen was sick with the sickness of the age. Everything was based on sex. The pursuit of the sacred orgasm. She would say love, he supposed, but sex would do as a description as far as he was concerned. From what he had seen, what happiness lay there was bought at too high a price, tainting all other happiness. Having a sleazy woman clutch you at four in the morning, trying to claim you, hurling a glass at you with murderous hatred because you'd had enough of her in two hours, even though that had been the implicit bargain to begin with. Having a silly little girl taunt you in front of her friends, making you feel like some sort of frozen eunuch, then grabbing your cock disdainfully in broad daylight. If it was sex or even anything like love that had brought his mother and father together originally, they had wound up like two crazed animals in a cage in the zoo, destroying each other. Then the marriages of the second generation. Beginning with Tom. What future faced him, captured by that whining, avaricious, brainless, absurd doll of a woman? And Gretchen, herself, superior and scathing in her helpless sensuality, hating herself for the beds she fell into, adrift from a worthless and betrayed husband. Who was immersing himself in the ignominy of detectives, keyhole-peeping, lawyers, divorce—he or she?

Screw them all, he thought. Then laughed to himself. The word was ill chosen.

The telephone rang. "Your brother is in the lobby, Mr. Jordache," the clerk said.

"Will you send him up, please?" Rudolph swung off the bed, straightened out the covers. For some reason, he didn't want Tom to see that he had been lying down, with its implication of luxury and sloth. Hurriedly, he stuffed all the architects' drawings into a closet. He wanted the room to look bare, without clues. He did not want to seem important, engrossed in large affairs, when his brother appeared.

There was a knock on the door and Rudolph opened it. At least he's wearing a tie, Rudolph thought meanly, for the opinion of the clerks and bellboys in the lobby. He shook Thomas's hand and said, "Come on in. Sit down. Want a drink? I have a bottle of Scotch, but I can ring down if you'd like something else."

"Scotch'll do." Thomas sat stiffly in an armchair, his already-gnarled hands hanging down, his suit bunched up around his great shoulders.

"Water?" Rudolph said. "I can call down for soda if you . . ."

"Water's fine."

I sound like a nervous hostess, Rudolph thought, as he went into the bathroom and poured water out of the tap into Thomas's drink.

Rudolph raised his glass. "Skoal."

"Yeah," Thomas said. He drank thirstily.

"There were some good write-ups this morning," Rudolph said.

"Yeah," Thomas said. "I read the papers. Look, there's no sense in wasting any time, Rudy." He dug into his pocket and brought out a fat envelope. He stood up and went over to the bed and opened the envelope flap and turned it upside down. Bills showered over the bedspread.

"What the hell are you doing, Tom?" Rudolph asked. He did not deal in cash—he rarely had more than fifty dollars in his pocket—and the scattering of bills on the hotel bed was vaguely disquieting to him, illicit, like the division of loot in a gangster movie.

"They're hundred-dollar bills." Thomas crumpled the empty envelope and tossed it accurately into the wastebasket. "Five thousand dollars' worth. They're yours."

"I don't know what you're talking about," Rudolph said. "You don't owe me anything."

"There's your goddamn college education that I did you out of," Thomas said. "Paying off those crooks in Ohio. I tried to give it to Pa, but he happened to be dead that day. Now it's yours."

"You work too hard for your money," Rudolph said, remembering the blood of the night before, "to throw it away like this."

"I didn't work for this money," Thomas said. "I got it easy—the way Pa lost his—by blackmail. A long time ago. It's been in a vault for years, waiting. Feel free, brother. I didn't take any punishment for it."

"It's a stupid gesture," Rudolph said.

"I'm a stupid man," Thomas said. "I make stupid gestures. Take it. Now I'm rid of you." He turned away from the bed and finished his drink in one gulp. "I'll be going now."

"Wait a minute. Sit down." Rudolph pushed at his brother's arms, feeling, even at that hurried touch, the ferocious power in them. "I don't need it. I'm doing great. I just made a deal that's going to make me a rich man, I . . ."

"I'm happy to hear it, but it's beside the point." Stonily, Thomas remained standing. "I want to pay off our fucking family and this does it."

"I won't take it, Tom. Put it in the bank for your kid, at least."

"I'll take care of my kid my own way, don't you worry about that." Now he sounded dangerous.

"It's not mine," Rudolph said helplessly. "What the hell am I going to do with it?"

"Piss on it. Blow it on dames. Give it to your favorite charity," Thomas said. "I'm not walking out of this room with it."

"Sit down, for Christ's sake." This time Rudolph pushed hard at his brother, edging him toward the armchair, risking the blow that could come at any moment. "I have to talk to you."

Rudolph refilled Thomas's glass and his own and sat across from his brother on a straight wooden chair. The window was open a little and the city wind entered in little gusts. The bills on the bed fluttered a little, like a small, complicated animal, shuddering. Both Thomas and Rudolph sat as far away from the bed as possible, as though the first one inadvertently to touch a bill would have to claim them all.

"Listen, Tom," Rudolph began, "we're not kids anymore, sleeping in the same bed, getting on each other's nerves, competing with each other, whether we knew it or not. We're two grown men and we're brothers."

"Where were you for ten years, Brother, you and Princess Gretchen?" Thomas said. "Did you ever send a postcard?"

"Forgive me," Rudolph said. "And if you talk to Gretchen, she'll ask you to forgive her, too."

"If I see her first," Thomas said, "she'll never get a chance to get close enough to me to say hello."

"Last night, watching you fight, made us realize," Rudolph persisted. "We're a family, we owe each other something . . ."

"I owed the family five thousand bucks. There it is, on the bed. Nobody owes anybody anything." Thomas kept his head down, his chin almost on his chest.

"Whatever you say, whatever you think about the way I behaved all this time," Rudolph said, "I want to help you now."

"I don't need any help." Thomas drank most of his whiskey.

"Yes, you do. Look, Tom," Rudolph said, "I'm no expert, but I've seen enough fights to have an idea of what to expect from a fighter. You're going to get hurt. Badly. You're a club fighter. It's one thing to be the champ of the neighborhood, but when you go up against trained, talented, ambitious men—and they're going to get better each time now for you—because you're still on the way up—you're going to get chopped to pieces. Aside from the injuries—concussions, cuts, kidneys—"

"I only have half hearing in one ear," Thomas volunteered, surprisingly. The professional talk had drawn him out of his shell. "For more than a year now. What the hell, I'm not a musician."

"Aside from the injuries, Tom," Rudolph went on, "there's going to come the day when you've lost more than you've won, or you're suddenly all worn out and some kid will drop you. You've seen it dozens of times. And that'll be the end. You won't get a bout. How much money will you have then? How will you earn your living then, starting all over at thirty, thirty-five, even?"

"Don't hex me, you sonofabitch," Thomas said.

"I'm being realistic." Rudolph got up and filled Thomas's glass again, to keep him in the room.

"Same old Rudy," Thomas said mockingly. "Always with a happy, realistic word for his kid brother." But he accepted the drink.

"I'm at the head of a large organization now," Rudolph said, "I'm going to have a lot of jobs to fill. I could find a place in it for you, a permanent place . . ."

"Doing what? Driving a truck at fifty bucks a week?"

"Better than that," Rudolph said. "You're no fool. You could wind up as a manager of a branch or a department," Rudolph said, wondering if he was lying. "All it takes is some common sense and a willingness to learn."

"I have no common sense and I'm not willing to learn anything," Thomas said. "Don't you know that?" He stood up. "I've got to get going now. I have a family waiting for me."

Rudolph shrugged, looked across at the bills fluttering gently on the bedspread. He stood up, too.

"Have it your own way," he said. "For the time being."

"There ain't no time being." Thomas moved toward the door.

"I'll come and visit you and see your kid," Rudolph said. "Tonight? I'll take you and your wife to dinner tonight. What do you say to that?"

"I say balls to that." Thomas opened the door, stood there. "Come and see me fight sometime. Bring Gretchen. I can use fans. But don't bother to come back to the dressing room."

"Think everything over. You know where you can reach me," Rudolph said wearily. He was unused to failure and it exhausted him. "Anyway, you might come up to Whitby and say hello to your mother. She asks about you."

"What does she ask—have they hung him yet?" Thomas grinned crookedly.

"She says she wants to see you at least once more before she dies."

"Maestro," Thomas said, "the violins, please."

Rudolph wrote down the Whitby address and the telephone number. "Here's where we live, in case you change your mind."

Thomas hesitated, then took the slip of paper and jammed it carelessly into his pocket. "See you in ten years, brother," he said. "Maybe." He went out and closed the door behind him. The room seemed much larger without his presence.

Rudolph stared at the door. How long can hatred last? In a family, forever, he supposed. Tragedy in the House of Jordache, now a supermarket. He went over to the bed and gathered up the bills and put them carefully into an envelope and sealed it. It was too late in the afternoon to put the money in the bank. He'd have to lock it in the hotel safe overnight.

One thing was certain. He was not going to use it for himself. Tomorrow he'd invest it in Dee Cee stock in his brother's name. The time would come, he was sure, when Thomas could use it. And it would be a lot more than five thousand dollars by then. Money did not negotiate forgiveness, but it could be depended upon, finally, to salve old wounds.

He was bone tired, but sleep was out of the question. He got out the architect's drawings again, grandiose imaginings, paper dreams, the hopes of years, imperfectly realized. He stared at the pencil lines that would be transformed within six months into the neon of the name of Calderwood, against the northern night. He grimaced unhappily.

The phone rang. It was Willie, buoyant but sober. "Merchant Prince," Willie said, "how would you like to come down here and have dinner with the old lady and me? We'll go to a joint in the neighborhood."

"I'm sorry, Willie," Rudolph said. "I'm busy tonight. I have a date."

"Put it in once for me, Prince," Willie said lightly. "See you soon."

Rudolph hung up slowly. He would not see Willie soon, at least not for dinner.

Look behind you, Willie, as you pass through doors.

Chapter 7

I

"My dear son," he read, in the round schoolgirlish handwriting, "your brother Rudolph was good enough to provide me with your address in New York City and I am taking the opportunity to get in touch with my lost boy after all these years."

Oh, Christ, he thought, another county heard from. He had just come in and had found the letter waiting for him on the table in the hallway. He heard Teresa clanging pots in the kitchen and the kid making gobbling sounds.

"I'm home," he called and went into the living room and sat down on the couch, pushing a toy fire engine out of the way. He sat there, on the orange-satin couch Teresa had insisted upon buying, holding the letter dangling from his hand, trying to decide whether or not to throw it away then and there.

Teresa came in, in an apron, a little sweat glistening on her make-up, the kid crawling after her.

"You got a letter," she said. She was not very friendly these days, ever since she had heard about his going to England and leaving her behind.

"Yeah."

"It's a woman's handwriting."

"It's from my mother, for Christ's sake."

"You expect me to believe that?"

"Look." He shoved the letter under her nose.

She squinted to read. She was very nearsighted but refused to wear glasses. "It's awful young handwriting for a mother," she said, retreating reluctantly. "A mother, now. Your family is growing in leaps and bounds."

She went back to the kitchen, picking up the kid, who was squalling that he wanted to stay where he was.

To spite Teresa, Thomas decided to read the letter and see what the old bitch had to say.

"Rudolph described the circumstances of your meeting"—he read —"and I must say I was more than a little shocked at your choice of a profession. Although I shouldn't be surprised, considering your father's nature and the example he set you with that dreadful punching bag hanging out in the back yard all the time. Still, it's an honest living, I suppose, and your brother says you seem to have settled down with a wife and a child and I hope you are happy.

"Rudolph did not describe your wife to me, but I hope that your family life is happier than your father's and mine. I don't know whether Rudolph mentioned it to you but your father just vanished one fine night, with the cat.

"I am not well and I have the feeling my days are numbered. I would like to come to New York City and see my son and my new grandson, but traveling is very difficult for me. If Rudolph saw fit to buy an automobile instead of the motorcycle he charges around town on perhaps I could manage the trip. He might even be able to drive me to church one Sunday, so I could begin to make up for the years of paganism your father forced me to endure. But I guess I shouldn't complain. Rudolph has been very kind and takes good care of me and has got me a television set which makes the long days bearable. He seems to be so busy on his own projects that he barely comes home to sleep. From what I can tell, especially from the way he dresses, he is doing quite well. But he was always a good dresser and always managed to have money in his pocket.

"I cannot honestly say that I would like to see the entire family reunited, as I have crossed your sister from my heart, for good and sufficient reason, but seeing my two sons together again would bring tears of joy to my eyes.

"I was always too tired and overworked and struggling to meet your father's drunken demands to show the love I felt for you, but maybe now, in my last days, we can have peace between us.

"I gathered from Rudolph's tone that you were not very friendly with him. Perhaps you have your reasons. He has turned into a cold man although a thoughtful one. If you do not wish to see him, I could let you know when he is out of the house, which happens more and more often, for days on end, and you and I could visit with each other undisturbed. Kiss my grandson for me. Your loving Mother."

Holy God, he thought, voices from the tomb.

He sat there, holding the letter, staring into space, not hearing his wife scolding the kid in the kitchen, thinking of the years over the bakery, years when he had been more thoroughly exiled although he lived in the same house than when he had been sent away and told never to show his face again. Maybe he would go to visit the old lady, listen to the complaints, so late in coming, about her beloved Rudolph, her fair-haired boy.

He would borrow a car from Schultzy and ride her over to church, that's what he would do. Let the whole goddamn family see how wrong they were about him.

II

Mr. McKenna went out of the hotel room, aldermanic, benign, ex-cop on pension now pursuing private crime, having taken the report from a neat, black-seal briefcase and laid it on Rudolph's desk. "I am quite certain this will provide all the information you need about the individual in question," Mr. McKenna had said, kindly, plump, rubbing his bald head, his sober, gray-felt hat, neatly rimmed, on the desk beside him. "Actually, the investigation was comparatively simple, and unusually short for such complete results." There had been a note of regret in Mr. McKenna's voice at Willie's artless simplicity, which had required so little time, so little professional guile to investigate. "I think the wife will find that any competent lawyer can get her a divorce with no difficulty under the laws of the State of New York dealing with adultery. She is very clearly the injured party, very clearly indeed."

Rudolph looked at the neatly typed report with distaste. Tapping telephone wires, it seemed, was as easy as buying a loaf of bread. For five dollars, hotel clerks would allow you to attach a microphone to a wall. Secretaries would fish out torn love letters from wastebaskets and piece them together carefully for the price of a dinner. Old girls, now rejected, would quote chapter and verse. Police files were open, secret testimony before committees was available, nothing was unpleasant enough to be disbelieved. Communication, despite what poets were saying at the moment, was rife.

He picked up the phone and asked for Gretchen's number. He listened as the operator dialed. The busy signal, that snarling sound, came over the wire. He hung up and went over to the window and parted the curtains and looked out. The afternoon was cold and gray. Down below pedestrians leaned against the wind, hurrying for shelter, collars up. It was an ex-policeman's kind of day.

He went back to the phone, asked for Gretchen's number again. Once more, he heard the busy signal. He slammed down the instrument, annoyed. He wanted to get this miserable business over with as quickly as possible. He had spoken to a lawyer friend, without mentioning names, and the lawyer friend had advised him that the injured party should move out of the communal habitation with the child before bringing any action, unless there was some way of keeping the husband out of the apartment completely from that moment on. Under no conditions should the injured party sleep one night more under the same roof with the defendant-to-be.

Before he called Willie and confronted him with the detective's report, he had to tell Gretchen this and tell her also that he intended to speak to Willie immediately.

But again the phone rang busy. The injured party was having a chatty afternoon. With whom was she talking—Johnny Heath, quiet, bland lover, constant guest, or one of the other ten men she had said she no longer wanted to sleep with? The easiest lay in New York. Sister mine.

He looked at his watch. Five minutes to four. Willie would undoubtedly be back in his office by now, happily dozing off the prelunch martinis.

Rudolph picked up the phone and called Willie's number. Two secretaries in Willie's office wafted him along, disembodied sweet voices, electric with public relations charm. "Hi, Merchant Prince," Willie said, when he came on the line. "To what do I owe the honor?" It was a three-martini voice this afternoon.

"Willie," Rudolph said, "you have to come over here to my hotel right away."

"Listen, kid, I'm sort of tied up here and . . ."

"Willie, I warn you, you'd better come over here this minute."

"Okay," Willie said, his voice subdued. "Order me a drink."

Drinkless, Willie sat in the chair the ex-policeman had used earlier, and carefully read the report. Rudolph stood at the window, looking out. He heard the rustle of paper as Willie put the report down.

"Well," Willie said, "it seems I've been a very busy little boy. What're you going to do with this now?" He tapped the report.

Rudolph reached over and picked up the clipped-together sheets of paper and tore them into small pieces and dropped the pieces into the wastebasket.

"What does that mean?" Willie asked.

"It means that I can't go through with it," Rudolph said. "Nobody's going to see it and nobody's going to know about it. If your wife wants a divorce, she'll have to figure out another way to get it."

"Oh," Willie said. "It was Gretchen's idea?"

"Not exactly. She said she wanted to get away from you, but she wanted to keep the kid, and I offered to help."

"Blood is thicker than marriage. Is that it?"

"Something like that. Only not *my* blood. This time."

"You came awfully close to being a shit, Merchant Prince," Willie said, "didn't you?"

"So I did."

"Does my beloved wife know you have this on me?"

"No. And she's not going to."

"In days to come," Willie said, "I shall sing the praises of my shining brother-in-law. Look, I shall tell my son, look closely at your noble uncle and you will be able to discern the shimmer of his halo. Christ, there must be one drink somewhere in this hotel."

Rudolph brought out the bottle. With all his jokes, if ever a man looked as though he needed a drink, it was Willie at this moment. He drank off half of the glass. "Who's picking up the tab for the research?" he asked.

"I am."

"What does it come to?"

"Five hundred and fifty dollars."

"You should've come to me," Willie said. "I'd've given you the information for half the price. Do you want me to pay you back?"

"Forget it," Rudolph said. "I never gave you a wedding present. Consider this my wedding present."

"Better than a silver platter. I thank you, brother-in-law. Is there more in that bottle?"

Rudolph poured. "You'd better keep sober," he said. "You're going to have some serious conversation ahead of you."

"Yeah." Willie nodded. "It was a sorrowful day for everybody when I bought your sister a bottle of champagne at the Algonquin bar." He smiled wanly. "I loved her that afternoon and I love her now and there I am in the trash basket." He gestured to where the shreds of the detective's report lay scattered in the tin bucket, decorated with a hunting print, riders with bright-red coats. "Do you know what love is?"

"No."

"Neither do I." Willie stood up. "Well, I'll leave you. Thanks for an interesting half hour."

He went out without offering to shake hands.

III

He was incredulous when he came to the house. He looked again at the piece of paper Rudolph had given him to make sure that he was at the right address. Still over a store. And in a neighborhood that was hardly any better than the old one in Port Philip. Seeing Rudolph in that fancy room at the Hotel Warwick and hearing him talk you'd think that he was just rolling in dough. Well, if he was, he wasn't wasting any of it on rent.

Maybe he just kept the old lady in this joint and had a rich pad for himself in some other part of town. He wouldn't put it past the bastard.

Thomas went into the dingy vestibule, saw the name Jordache printed next to a bell, rang. He waited, but the buzzer remained silent. He had called and told his mother he was coming to visit today, and she said she'd be home. He couldn't make it on a Sunday, because when he suggested it to Teresa, she'd started to cry. Sunday was her day, she wept, and she wasn't going to be done out of it by an old hag who hadn't even bothered to send a card when her grandson was born. So they'd left the kid with a sister of Teresa's up in the Bronx and they'd gone to a movie on Broadway and had dinner at Toots Shor's, where a sportswriter recognized Thomas, which made Teresa's day for her and maybe it was worth the twenty bucks the dinner had cost.

Thomas pushed the bell again. Still, there was no response. Probably, Thomas thought bitterly, at the last minute Rudolph called and said he wanted his mother to come down to New York and shine his shoes or something, and she'd rushed off, falling all over herself with joy.

He started to turn away, half relieved that he didn't have to face her. It hadn't been such a hot idea to begin with. Let sleeping mothers lie. He was just about out of the door when he heard the buzzer. He went back, opened the door and went up the steps.

The door opened at the first floor landing and there she was, looking a hundred years old. She took a couple of steps toward him and he understood why he had had to wait for the buzzer. The way she walked it must take her five minutes to cross the room. She was crying already and had her arms outstretched to embrace him.

"My son, my son," she cried, as her arms, thin sticks, went around him. "I thought I'd never see your face again."

There was a strong smell of toilet water. He kissed her wet cheek gently, wondering what he felt.

Clinging to his arm, she led him into the apartment. The living room was tiny and dark and he recognized the furniture from the apartment on Vanderhoff Street. It had been old and worn-out then. Now it was practically in ruins. Through an open door he could look into an adjoining room and see a desk, a single bed, books everywhere.

If he can afford to buy all those books, Thomas thought, he sure can afford to buy some new furniture.

"Sit down, sit down," she said excitedly, guiding him to the one threadbare easy chair. "What a wonderful day." Her voice was thin, made reedy by years of complaint. Her legs were swollen, shapeless, and she wore wide, soft, invalid's shoes, like a cripple. She moved as though she had been broken a long time ago in an accident. "You look splendid. Absolutely splendid." He remembered those words she used, out of *Gone With the Wind*. "I was afraid my little boy's face would be all battered, but you've turned out handsomely. You resemble my side of the family, that's plain to see, Irish. Not like the other two." She moved in a slow awkward flutter before him as he sat stiffly in the chair. She was wearing a flowered dress that blew loosely about her thin body. Her thick legs stuck out below her skirt like an error in engineering, another woman's limbs. "That's a lovely gray suit," she said, touching his sleeve. "A gentleman's suit. I was afraid you'd still be in a sweater." She laughed gaily, his childhood already a romance. "Ah, I knew Fate couldn't be so unkind," she said, "not letting me see my child's face before I die. Now let me see my grand-son's face. You must have a picture. I'm sure you carry one in your wallet, like all proud fathers."

Thomas took out a picture of his child.

"What's his name?" his mother asked.

"Wesley," Thomas said.

"Wesley Pease," his mother said. "It's a fine name."

Thomas didn't bother to remind her that the boy's name was Wesley Jordache, nor did he tell her that he had fought Teresa for a week to try to get her to settle for a less fancy name. But Teresa had wept and carried on and he'd given in.

His mother stared at the photograph, her eyes dampening. She kissed the snapshot. "Dear little beautiful thing," she said.

Thomas didn't remember her ever kissing *him* as a child.

"You must take me to see him," she said.

"Sure."

"Soon."

"When I come back from England," he said.

"England! We've just found each other again and you're leaving for the other side of the earth!"

"It's only for a couple of weeks."

"You must be doing very well," she said, "to be able to afford va-cations like that."

"I have a job to do there," he said. He was reluctant to use the word fight. "They pay my way." He didn't want her to get the idea that he was rich, which he wasn't, by a long shot. In the Jordache family, it was safer to cry poverty. One woman grabbing at every cent that came into the house was enough for one family.

"I hope you're saving your money," she said. "In your profes-sion . . ."

"Sure," he said. "Don't worry about me." He looked around him. "It's a cinch Rudy's saving his money."

"Oh," she said. "The apartment. It's not very grand, is it? But I can't complain. Rudy pays for a woman to come in and clean every day and do the shopping for me the days I can't make the stairs. And he says he's looking for a bigger place. On the ground floor somewhere, so it'll be easier for me, without steps. He doesn't talk to me much about his work, but there was an article last month in the paper all about how he was one of the up-and-coming young busi-nessmen in town, so I suppose he's doing well enough. But he's right to be thrifty. Money was the tragedy of the family. It made an old woman of me before my time." She sighed, self-pitying. "Your father was demented on the subject. I couldn't get ten dollars from him for the barest necessities of life without a pitched battle every time. When you're in England you might make some confidential inquiries, find out if anyone has seen him there. He's liable to be *anyplace*, that man. After all, he was European, and it would be the most natural thing in the world for him to go back there to hide out."

Off her rocker, he thought. Poor old lady. Rudy hadn't prepared him for this. But he said, "I'll ask around when I get over there."

"You're a good boy," she said. "I always knew deep down that you were essentially a good boy, but swayed by bad companions. If I had had the time to be a proper mother to my family, I could have saved you from so much trouble. You must be strict with your son. Loving, but strict. Is your wife a good mother to him?"

"She's okay," he said. He preferred not to talk about Teresa. He looked at his watch. The conversation and the dark apartment were depressing him. "Look," he said, "it's nearly one o'clock. Why don't I take you out to lunch? I have a car downstairs."

"Lunch? In a restaurant. Oh, wouldn't that be lovely," she said, girlishly. "My big strong son taking his old mother out to lunch."

"We'll go to the best place in town," he said.

On his way home, driving Schultzy's car down toward New York late in the afternoon, he thought about the day, wondering if he would ever make the trip again.

The image of his mother formed in adolescence, that of a scolding, perpetually disapproving hard woman, fanatically devoted to one son, to the detriment of another, was now replaced by that of a harmless and pitiful old lady, pathetically lonely, pleased by the slightest attention, and anxious to be loved.

At lunch he had offered her a cocktail and she had grown a little tipsy, had giggled and said, "Oh, I do feel naughty." After lunch he had driven her around town and was surprised to see that most of it was entirely unknown to her. She had lived there for years, but had seen practically nothing of it, not even the university from which her son had been graduated. "I had no idea it was such a beautiful place," she kept saying over and over again, as they passed through neighborhoods where comfortable, large houses were set among trees and wintry lawns. And when they passed Calderwood's, she said, "I had no idea it was so big. You know, I've never been in there. And to think that Rudy practically runs it!"

He had parked the car and had walked slowly with her along the ground floor and insisted upon buying her a suede handbag for fifteen dollars. She had had the salesgirl wrap up her old bag and carried the new one proudly over her arm as they left the store.

She had talked a great deal in the course of the afternoon, telling him for the first time about her life in the orphanage ("I was the brightest girl in the class. They gave me a prize when I left."), about working as a waitress, being ashamed of being illegitimate, about going to night school in Buffalo to improve herself, about not ever letting a man even kiss her until she married Axel Jordache, about only weighing ninety-two pounds on the day of her wedding, about how beautiful Port Philip was the day she and Axel came down to inspect the bakery, about the white excursion boat going by up the river, with the band playing waltzes on the deck, about how nice the neighborhood was when they first came there and her dream of starting a cosy little restaurant, about her hopes for her family. . . .

When he took her back to the apartment she asked him if she could have the photograph of his son to frame and put on the table in her bedroom and when he gave it to her, she hobbled into her room and came back with a photograph of herself, yellowed with age, taken when she was nineteen, in a long, white dress, slender, grave, beautiful. "Here," she said, "I want you to have this."

She watched silently as he put it carefully in his wallet in the same place that he had kept his son's picture.

"You know," she said, "I feel closer to you somehow than to anybody in the whole world. We're the same kind of people. We're simple. Not like your sister and your brother. I love Rudy, I suppose, and I should, but I don't understand him. And sometimes I'm just afraid of him. While you . . ." She laughed. "Such a big, strong young man, a man who makes his living with his fists. . . . But I feel so at home with you, almost as though we were the same age, almost as though I had a brother. And today . . . today was so wonderful. I'm a prisoner who has just come out from behind the walls."

He kissed her and held her and she clutched at him briefly.

"Do you know," she said, "I haven't smoked a single cigarette since you arrived."

He drove down slowly through the dusk, thinking about the afternoon. He came to a roadhouse and went in and sat at the empty bar and had a whiskey. He took out his wallet and stared at the young girl who had turned into his mother. He was glad he had come to see her. Perhaps her favor wasn't worth much, but in the long race for that meager trophy he had finally won. Alone in the quiet bar he enjoyed an unaccustomed tranquillity. For an hour, at least, he was at peace. Today, there was one less person in the world that he had to hate.

PART
THREE

Chapter 1

1960

The morning was a pleasant one, except for the smog that lay cupped, a thin, metallic soup, in the Los Angeles basin. Barefooted, in her nightgown, Gretchen went through the open French windows, sliding between the still curtains, out onto the terrace, and looked down from her mountain top at the stained but sunlit city and the distant flat sea below her. She breathed deeply of the September morning air, smelling of wet grass and opening flowers. No sound came from the city and the early silence was broken only by the calls of a covey of quail crossing the lawn.

Better than New York, she thought for the hundredth time, much better than New York.

She would have liked a cup of coffee, but it was too early for Doris, the maid, to be up, and if she went into the kitchen to make the coffee herself, Doris would be awakened by the sound of running water and clinking metal and would come fussing out, apologizing but aggrieved at being deprived of rightful sleep. It was too early to awake Billy, too, especially with the day he had ahead of him, and she knew better than to rouse Colin, whom she had left sleeping in the big bed, flat on his back, frowning, his arms crossed tightly, as though in his dreams he was watching a performance of which he could not possibly approve.

She smiled, thinking of Colin, sleeping, as she sometimes told him, in his important position. His other positions, and she had told him about them in detail, were amused, vulnerable, pornographic, and horrified. She had been awakened by a thin shaft of sunlight coming through a rift in the curtains and had been tempted to reach for him and unfold those clenched arms. But Colin never made love in the morning. Mornings were for murder, he said. Used to New York theatrical hours, he had never taken kindly to the matinal necessities of the studios, and was, as he freely admitted, a savage before noon.

She went around to the front of the house, padding happily through the dewy grass with her bare feet, her transparent cotton nightgown blowing around her body as she walked. They had no neighbors and the chance of any cars passing by at this hour was almost nil. Anyway, in California, nobody cared how you dressed. She often sunbathed naked in the garden and her body was a deep brown after the summer. Back East she had always been careful to stay out of the sun, but if you weren't brown in California people assumed that you were either ill or too poor to take a holiday.

The newspaper was lying in the front driveway, folded and bound by a rubber band. She opened it up and glanced at the headlines as she walked slowly back around the house. Nixon and Kennedy had their pictures on the front page and they were promising everybody everything. She mourned briefly for Adlai Stevenson and wondered if it was morally right for somebody as young and as good looking as John Fitzgerald Kennedy to run for the Presidency. "Charm boy," Colin called him, but Colin had charm thrown at him every day by actors and its effect on him was almost invariably negative.

She reminded herself to make sure to apply for absentee ballots for herself and Colin, because they were going to be in New York in November and every vote against Nixon was going to be precious. Although now that she no longer wrote for magazines she didn't get too worked up about politics. The McCarthy period had disillusioned her with the value of private righteousness and alarmed public utterance. Her love for Colin, whose politics were, to say the least, capricious, had led her to abandon old attitudes along with old friends. Colin described himself at various times as a socialist without hope, a nihilist, a single-taxer, and a monarchist, depending upon whom he was arguing with at the moment, although he usually wound up voting for Democrats. Neither he nor Gretchen was involved in the passionate political activities of the movie colony, the feting of candidates, the signing of advertisements, the fund-raising cocktail parties. In fact, they hardly went to any parties at all. Colin didn't like to drink much and he found the boozy, aimless conversation of the usual Hollywood gatherings intolerable. He never flirted, so the presence of battalions of pretty ladies available at the functions of the rich and famous had no attraction for him. After the loose, gregarious years with Willie, Gretchen welcomed the domestic days and quiet nights with her second husband.

Colin's refusal to "go public," as he phrased it, had not damaged his career. As he said, "Only people without talent have to play the Hollywood game." He had asserted his talent with his first picture, confirmed it with his second, and now, with his third picture in five years in the final cutting and mixing stage, was established as one of the most gifted directors of his generation. His only failure had come when he had gone back to New York, after completing his first picture, to put on a play that closed after only eight performances. He had disappeared for three weeks after that. When he returned he was morose and silent and it had been months before he felt he was ready to go to work again. He was not a man designed for failure and he had made Gretchen suffer along with him. It had not helped, either, that Gretchen had told him in advance that she didn't think the play was ready for production. Still, he always asked for her opinions on every aspect of his work and demanded absolute frankness, which she gave him. Right now she was troubled by a sequence in his new film, which they had seen together in rough cut at the studio the night before. Only Colin, she, and Sam Corey, the cutter, had seen it. She had felt there was something wrong, but couldn't give coherent reasons why. She hadn't said anything after the running, but she knew he would question her at breakfast. As she went back into the bedroom, where Colin was still sleeping in his important position, she tried to remember the sequence of the film, frame by frame, so that she could make sense when she spoke about it.

She looked at the bedside clock and saw that it was still too early to wake Colin. She put on a robe and went into the living room. The desk in the corner of the room was strewn with books and manuscripts and reviews of novels torn out of the Sunday *Times Book Review* section and *Publisher's Weekly* and the London newspapers. The house was not a large one and there was no other place for the never-diminishing pile of print that they both attacked methodically, searching for possible ideas for films.

Gretchen took a pair of glasses off the desk and sat down to finish the newspaper. They were Colin's glasses, but they fitted her well enough so that she didn't bother to go back into the bedroom to get her own. Matched imperfections.

On the theater page there was a review from New York of a new play that had just opened, with a rave for a young actor whom nobody had ever heard of before and she made a note to get tickets for the play for herself and Colin as soon as she got into the city. In the listing of movies for Beverly Hills she saw that Colin's first picture was being revived over the weekend and she neatly tore out the listing to show it to him. It would make him less savage at breakfast.

She turned to the sports section to see what horses were running at Hollywood Park that afternoon. Colin loved the races and was a not inconsiderable gambler and they went as often as they could. The last time they had gone he had won enough to buy her a lovely spray brooch. There didn't seem to be any jewelry on today's card and she was about to put the paper down when she saw a photograph of two boxers sparring in training. Oh, God, she thought, there he is again. She read the caption under the photograph. "Henry Quayles with Sparmate Tommy Jordache at Las Vegas in workout for middle-weight fight next week."

She hadn't seen or heard from her brother since that one night in New York and she knew almost nothing about boxing, but she knew enough to understand that if he was working as somebody's sparring partner Thomas had gone downhill since the winning bout in Queens. She folded the paper neatly, hoping that Colin would over-look the photograph. She had told him about Thomas, as she told him about everything, but she didn't want Colin's curiosity to be aroused and perhaps insisting on meeting Thomas and seeing him fight.

There were sounds from the kitchen now and she went into Billy's room to wake him. He was sitting cross-legged in his pajamas on the bed, silently fingering chords on his guitar. Pure blond hair, grave, thoughtful eyes, fuzzed pink cheeks, nose too big for the un-developed face, skinny, young boy's neck, long, coltish legs, concen-trated, unsmiling, dear.

His valise, with the lid up, was on the chair, packed. Neatly packed. Somehow Billy, despite his parents, or perhaps because of his parents, had grown up with a passion for order.

She kissed the top of his head. No reaction. No hostility, but no love. He fingered a final chord.

"You all ready?" she asked.

"Uhuh." He uncurled the long legs, slid off the bed. His pajama top was open. Skinny, long torso, ribs countable, close to the skin, skin California summer color, days on the beach, body-surfing, girls and boys together on the hot sand, salt and guitars. As far as she knew he was still a virgin. Nothing had been said.

"You all ready?" he asked.

"Bags all packed," she said. "All I have to do is lock them." Billy had an almost pathological fear of being late for anything, school, trains, planes, parties. She had learned to be well in advance for anything she had to do with him.

"What do you want for breakfast?" she asked, prepared to feast him.

"Orange juice."

"That all?"

"I better not eat. I puke on planes."

"Remember to take your Dramamine."

"Yeah." He stripped off the top of his pajamas and went into the bathroom to brush his teeth. After she had moved in with Colin, Billy had suddenly refused to be seen naked in front of her. Two theories about that. She knew that Billy admired Colin, but she also knew that the boy admired her less for having lived with Colin before they were married. The strict, painful conventions of childhood.

She went to wake Colin. He was talking in his sleep and moving uneasily on the bed. "All that blood," he said.

War? Celluloid? It was impossible to tell with a movie director.

She woke him with a kiss under his ear. He lay still, staring blackly up at the ceiling. "Christ," he said, "it's the middle of the night."

She kissed him again. "Okay," he said, "morning." He rumpled her hair. She was sorry she had gone in to see Billy. One morning, on a national or religious holiday perhaps, Colin would finally make love to her. This might have been the morning. Non-coordinated rhythms of desire.

With a groan he tried to lift himself from the bed, fell back. He extended his hand. "Give a poor old man a lift," he said. "Out of the depths."

She grasped his hand and pulled. He sat on the edge of the bed rubbing his eye with the back of his hand, regretting daylight.

"Say," Colin stopped rubbing his eye and looked at her alertly, "last night, at the running, in the next to the last reel, there was something you thought was lousy . . ."

He didn't even wait for breakfast, she thought. "I didn't say anything," she said.

"You don't have to *say* anything. All you have to do is *breathe*."

"Don't be sure a naked nerve," she said, stalling for time. "Especially before you've had your coffee."

"Come on."

"All right," she said. "There was something I didn't like, but I didn't figure out why I didn't like it."

"And now?"

"I think I know."

"What is it?"

"Well, the sequence after he gets the news and he believes it's his fault . . ."

"Yes," Colin said impatiently. "It's one of the key scenes in the picture."

"You have him going around the house, looking at himself in one mirror after another, in the bathroom, in the full-length mirror on the closet wall, in the dark mirror in the living room, in the magnifying shaving mirror, at his own reflection in the puddle on the front porch . . ."

"The idea's simple enough," Colin said irritably, defensively. "He's examining himself—okay, let's be corny—he's looking into his soul in various lights, from different angles, to discover . . . Okay, what do you think is wrong about it?"

"Two things," she said calmly. Now she realized she had been gnawing at the problem subconsciously ever since she had come out of the projection room—in bed before falling asleep, on the terrace looking out over the smoggy city, while going through the newspaper in the living room. "Two things. First, the tempo. Everything in the whole picture has moved fast up to then, it's the style of the whole work, and then, suddenly, as though to show the audience that a Big Moment has arrived, you slow it down to a drag. It's too obvious."

"That's me," he said, biting his words. "Obvious."

"If you're going to get angry, I'll shut up."

"I'm already angry and don't shut up. You said two things. What's the other thing?"

"You have all those big close-ups of him, going on forever and I'm supposed to be seeing that he's tortured, doubtful, confused."

"Well, at least you got that, for Christ's sake . . ."

"Do you want me to go on or should we go in and have breakfast?"

"The next dame I marry," he said, "is not going to be so goddamn smart. Go on."

"Well, you may think that he's showing that he's tortured and doubtful and confused," she said, "and *he* may think he's showing that he's tortured and doubtful and confused, but all I get out of it is a handsome young man admiring himself in a mirror and wondering if the lighting is doing all it can for his eyes."

"Shit," he said, "you are a bitch. We worked four days on that sequence."

"I'd cut it if I were you," she said.

"The next picture," he said, "you go on the set and I'll stay home and do the cooking."

"You asked me," she said.

"I'll never learn." He jumped up off the bed. "I'll be ready for breakfast in five minutes." He stumped off toward the bathroom. He slept without the tops of his pajamas and the sheets had made pink ridges on the skin of his neatly muscled, lean back, small welts after the night's faint flogging. At the door, he turned. "Every other dame I ever knew thought everything I did was glorious," he said, "and I had to go and marry you."

"They didn't think," she said sweetly. "They *said*."

She went over to him and he kissed her. "I'm going to miss you," he whispered. "Hideously." He pushed her away roughly. "Now go see that the coffee's *black*."

He was humming as he went in to shave, an unusually merry thing for him to be doing at that time of day. She knew that he had been worried by the sequence, too, and was relieved now that he believed he knew what was wrong with it and that in the cutting room that morning he was going to have the exquisite pleasure of throwing away four days' hard work, representing forty thousand dollars of the studio's money.

They reached the airport early and the lines of worry on Billy's forehead vanished as he saw his and his mother's bags disappear across the counter. He was dressed in a gray-tweed suit and buttoned-down pink shirt, with a blue tie, for traveling, and his hair was neatly brushed and there were no adolescent pimples on his chin. Gretchen thought he looked very grown-up and handsome, much more than his fourteen years. He was already as tall as she, taller than Colin, who had driven them to the airport and was making an admirable effort to hide his impatience to get to the studio and back to work. Gretchen had had to control herself on the trip to the airport, because Colin's driving made her nervous. It was the one thing she thought he did badly, sometimes mooning along slowly, thinking about other things, then suddenly becoming fiercely competitive and cursing out other drivers as he spurted ahead of them or tried to prevent them from passing him. When she couldn't resist from warning him about near-misses, he would snarl at her, "Don't be the All-American wife." He was convinced he drove superbly. As he pointed out to her, he had never had an accident, although he had been caught several times for speeding, incidents that had been discreetly kept off his record by the studio fixers, those valuable, doubtful gentlemen.

As other passengers came up to the counter with their bags, Colin said, "We've got lots of time. Let's go get a cup of coffee."

Gretchen knew that Billy would have preferred to go stand at the gate so that he could be the first to board the plane. "Look, Colin," she said, "you don't have to wait. Good-byes're such a bore anyway . . ."

"Let's get a cup of coffee," Colin said. "I'm still not awake yet."

They walked across the hall toward the restaurant, Gretchen between her husband and her son, conscious of their beauty and her own, and happy about it as she caught people staring at the three of them. Pride, she thought, that delicious sin.

In the restaurant, she and Colin had coffee and Billy had a Coca-Cola, with which he washed down his dose of Dramamine.

"I used to puke on buses until I was eighteen," Colin said, watching the boy swallow the pills. "Then I had my first girl and I stopped puking."

There was a quick, judging flick of Billy's eyes. Colin spoke in front of Billy as he did to any grown-up. Sometimes Gretchen wondered if it was altogether wise. She didn't know whether the boy loved his stepfather, merely endured him, or hated him. Billy was not one to volunteer information about his emotions. Colin did not seem to make any extra effort to win the boy over. He was sometimes brusque with him, sometimes deeply interested and helpful with his work at school, sometimes playful and charming, sometimes distant. Colin made no concessions to his audience, but what was admirable in his work, Gretchen thought, was not necessarily healthy in the case of a withdrawn only child living with a mother who had left his father for a temperamental and difficult lover. She and Colin had had their fights, but never on the subject of Billy, and Colin was paying for the boy's education because Willie Abbott had fallen upon hard times and could not afford to. Colin had forbidden Gretchen to tell the boy where the money was coming from, but Gretchen was sure Billy guessed.

"When I was just your age," Colin was saying, "I was sent off to school. I cried the first week. The first year I hated school. The second year I endured it. The third year I edited the school newspaper and I had my first taste of the pleasures of power and although I didn't admit it to anybody, even to myself, I liked it. My last year I wept because I had to leave."

"I don't mind going," Billy said.

"Good," Colin said. "It's a good school, if any school these days can be said to be good, and at the very worst you'll come out of it knowing how to write a simple declarative sentence in the English language. Here." He produced an envelope and gave it to the boy. "Take this and never tell your mother what's in it."

"Thank you," Billy said. He put the envelope in the inside pocket of his jacket. He looked at his watch. "Don't you think we'd better be going?"

They walked three abreast toward the gate, Billy carrying his guitar. Briefly, Gretchen worried about how the school, which was old New England Presbyterian Respectable, would react to the guitar. Probably no reaction at all. By this time they must be prepared for anything from fourteen-year-old boys.

The plane was just beginning to load when they reached the gate. "Go ahead on board, Billy," Gretchen said. "I want to say good-bye to Colin."

Colin shook Billy's hand and said, "If there's anything you need, call me. Collect."

Gretchen searched his face as he spoke to her son. The tenderness and caring were real on the sharp, thin features, and the dangerous eyes under the heavy black brows were gentle and loving. I didn't make a mistake, she thought, I didn't.

Billy smiled gravely, en route from father to father, disturbing journey, and went aboard, guitar held like an infantryman's gun on patrol.

"He'll be all right," Colin said as the boy went through the gate and out onto the tarmac where the big jet waited.

"I hope so," Gretchen said. "There was money in that envelope, wasn't there?"

"A few bucks," Colin said carelessly. "Buffer money. Ease the pain. There are moments when a boy can't survive education without an extra milkshake or the latest issue of *Playboy*. Willie meeting you at Idlewild?"

"Yes."

"You taking the kid up to the school together?"

"Yes."

"I suppose you're right," Colin said flatly. "Parents should be present in twos at the ceremonies of adolescents." He looked away from her, staring at the passengers going through the gate. "Every time I see one of those ads for airlines with pictures of people smiling broadly as they climb the steps getting onto a plane, I realize what a lying society we inhabit. Nobody's happy getting onto a plane. Are you going to sleep with ex-husband Willie tonight?"

"Colin!"

"Ladies have been known to. Divorce, the final aphrodisiac."

"Goddamn you," she said. She started toward the gate.

He put out his hand and held her back, gripping her arm.

"Forgive me," he said. "I am a dark, self-destructive, happiness-doubting, unforgivable man." He smiled, sadly, pleadingly. "Just one thing—don't talk to Willie about me."

"I won't." She had already forgiven him and was facing him, close to him. He kissed her lightly. The public address system was announcing the last call for the flight.

"See you in New York in two weeks," Colin said. "Don't enjoy the city until I get there."

"Not to worry," she said. She brushed his cheek with her lips and he turned abruptly and strode away, walking, as always, in a way that made her smile secretly to herself, as though he were on his way to a dangerous encounter from which he was determined to emerge the victor.

She watched him for a moment, then went through the gate.

Despite the Dramamine, Billy threw up as they were approaching Idlewild for the landing. He did it neatly and apologetically into the bag provided for the purpose, but the sweat stood out on his forehead and his shoulders heaved uncontrollably. Gretchen stroked the back of Billy's neck, helplessly, knowing that it wasn't serious, but racked, just the same, by her inability at such a moment to stand between her son and pain. The irrationality of mothering.

When he had finished retching, Billy neatly closed the bag and went down the aisle to the toilet to dispose of the bag and rinse out his mouth. He was still white when he came back. He had wiped the sweat off his face and seemed composed, but as he seated himself next to Gretchen, he said, bitterly, "Goddamn, I'm such a *baby*."

Willie was wearing sunglasses as he stood in the small crowd that awaited the passengers from Los Angeles. The day was gray and humid and even before she was close enough to say hello to him, Gretchen knew that he had been drinking the night before and that the sunglasses were meant to hide the evidence of bloodshot eyes from her and his son. At least one night, just before he greets a son he hasn't seen for months, she thought, he might have kept sober. She fought down her annoyance. Friendliness and serenity between divorced parents in the presence of offspring. The necessary hypocrisy of divided love.

Billy saw his father and hurried through the lines of debarking passengers toward him. He put his arms around his father and kissed his cheek. Gretchen purposely walked more slowly, not to interfere. Together, father and son were plainly linked. Although Billy was taller than his father and better looking than Willie ever could have been, their blood connection was absolutely clear. Once again, Gretchen felt her old irritation that her contribution to the genetic make-up of the child was nowhere in evidence.

Willie was smiling widely (fatuously?) at his son's demonstration of affection, as Gretchen finally approached him. He kept his arm around Billy's shoulder and said, "Hello, dear," to Gretchen and leaned forward to kiss her cheek. Two similar kisses, on the same day, on two sides of the continent, departing and arriving. Willie had been wonderful about the divorce and about Billy, and she couldn't deny him the "dear" or the rueful kiss. She didn't say anything about the dark glasses or the unmistakable aroma of alcohol on Willie's breath. He was dressed neatly, soberly proper, just the costume for taking a son to introduce him to the headmaster of a good New England school. Somehow, she would keep him from drinking when they drove up to the school the next day.

She sat alone in the small living room of the hotel suite, the lights of evening New York outside the windows, the growl of the city, familiar and exciting, rising from the avenues. Foolishly, she had expected Billy to stay with her that night, but in the rented car driving into the city from Idlewild, Willie had said to Billy, "I hope you don't mind sleeping on the couch. I've only got one room, but there's a couch. A couple of springs're busted, but at your age I imagine you'll sleep all right."

"That's great," Billy said, and there was no mistaking his tone. He hadn't even turned around to look questioningly at his mother. Even if he had appealed to her, what could she have said?

When Willie had asked her where she was staying, and she had told him, "The Algonquin," he had raised his eyebrows sardonically.

"Colin likes it," she said defensively. "It's near the theater district and it saves him a lot of time being able to walk to rehearsals and to the office."

When Willie stopped the car in front of the Algonquin to let her out, he said, not looking either at her or at Billy, "I once bought a girl a bottle of champagne in this hotel."

"Call me in the morning, please," Gretchen said. "As soon as you wake up. We ought to get to the school before lunch."

Billy was on the far side of the front seat as she got out on the sidewalk and the porter took her bags, so she didn't get to kiss him good-bye and it was just with a little wave of her hand that she had sent him off to dinner with his father and the broken couch for the night in his father's single room.

There had been a message waiting for her at the desk when she registered. She had wired Rudolph that she was arriving in New York and had asked him to have dinner with her. The message had been from Rudolph, saying that he couldn't meet her that night, but would call her in the morning.

She went up to the suite, unpacked, took a bath, and then hesitated about what to wear. Finally she just threw on a robe, because she didn't know what she was going to do with the evening. All the people she knew in New York were Willie's friends, or her ex-lovers, or people she had met briefly with Colin when she had been in the city three years ago for the play that was a disaster, and she wasn't going to call any of them. She wanted a drink badly, but she couldn't go down to the bar and sit there by herself and get drunk. That miserable Rudolph, she thought, as she stood at the window, looking down at the traffic on Forty-fourth Street below her, can't even spare one night from his gainful activities for his sister. Rudolph had come out to Los Angeles twice during the years on business and she had shepherded him around every free minute. Wait till he gets out there again, she promised herself. There'll be a hot message waiting for *him* at his hotel when he arrives.

She almost picked up the telephone to call Willie. She could pretend that she wanted to find out if Billy was feeling all right after his sickness on the plane and perhaps Willie would ask her to have dinner with them. She even went over to the phone, but with her hand reaching out to pick it up, she halted herself. Keep female tricks to an absolute minimum. Her son deserved at least one complete, unemotional evening with his father, unwatched by mother's jealous eye.

She prowled back and forth in the small, old-fashioned room. How happy she had been once to arrive in New York, how wide open and inviting the city had seemed to her. When she was young, poor, and alone, it had welcomed her, and she had moved about its streets freely and without fear. Now, wiser, older, richer, she felt a prisoner in the room. A husband three thousand miles away, a son a few blocks away, put invisible restrictions on her behavior. Well, at least she could go downstairs and have dinner in the hotel's dining room. Another lonely lady, with her half-bottle of wine, sitting at a small table, trying not to hear the conversation of other diners, growing slightly tipsy, talking too much and too brightly to the headwaiter. Christ, what a bore it was sometimes to be a woman.

She went into the bedroom and pulled out her plainest dress, a black concoction that had cost too much and that she knew Colin didn't like, and started to dress. She was careless with her make-up and hardly bothered to brush her hair and was just going out the door when the telephone rang.

She almost ran back into the room. If it's Willie, she thought, no matter what, I'll have dinner with them.

But it wasn't Willie. It was Johnny Heath. "Hi," Johnny said. "Rudolph said you'd be here and I was just passing by and I thought I'd take a chance . . ."

Liar, she thought, nobody just is passing by the Algonquin at a quarter to nine in the evening. But she said, happily, "Johnny! What a nice surprise."

"I'm downstairs," Johnny said, echoes of other years in his voice, "and if you haven't eaten yet . . ."

"Well," she said, sounding reluctant, and despising herself for the ruse, "I'm not dressed and I was just about to order dinner up here. I'm exhausted from the flight and I have to get up early tomorrow and . . ."

"I'll be in the bar," Johnny said, and hung up.

Smooth, confident Wall Street sonofabitch, she thought. Then she went in and changed her dress. But she made him wait twenty full minutes before she went down to the bar.

"Rudolph was heartbroken that he couldn't come down and see you tonight," Johnny Heath was saying, across the table from her.

"I bet," Gretchen said.

"He was. Honestly. I could tell over the phone that he was really upset. He made a special point of calling me to ask me to fill in for him and explain why . . ."

"May I have some more wine, please," Gretchen said.

Johnny signaled to the waiter, who refilled the glass. They were eating in a small French restaurant in the fifties. It was almost empty. Discreet, Gretchen thought. The sort of place you were not likely to meet anyone you knew. Good for dining out with married ladies you were having an affair with. Johnny probably had a long list of similar places. The Quiet Philanderer's Guide for Dining in New York. Put it between covers and you'd probably have a big bestseller. The headwaiter had smiled warmly when they had come in and had placed them at a table in a corner, where nobody could overhear what they were saying.

"If he possibly could have made it," Johnny persisted, excellent go-between in times of stress for friends, enemies, lovers, blood relations, "he'd have come. He's deeply attached to you," said Johnny, who had never been deeply attached to anyone. "He admires you more than any woman he's ever met. He told me so."

"Don't you boys have anything better to chat about on the long winter nights?" Gretchen took a sip from her glass. At least she was getting a good bottle of wine out of the evening. Maybe she would get drunk tonight. Make sure she'd get some sleep before tomorrow's ordeal. She wondered if Willie and her son were also dining in a discreet restaurant. Do you hide a son, too, with whom you had once lived?

"In fact," Johnny said, "I think it's a lot your fault that Rudy's never been married. He admires you and he hasn't found anybody yet who lives up to his idea of you and . . ."

"He admires me so much," Gretchen said, "that after not seeing me for nearly a year he can't take a night off to come and see me."

"He's opening a new center at Port Philip next week," Johnny Heath said. "One of the biggest so far. Didn't he write you?"

"Yes," she admitted. "I guess I didn't pay attention to the date."

"There's a million last-minute things he has to do. He's working twenty hours a day. It was just physically impossible. You know how he is when it comes to work."

"I know," Gretchen said. "Work now, live later. He's demented."

"What about your husband? Burke?" Johnny demanded. "Doesn't he work? I imagine he admires you, too, but I don't notice that he took time off to come to New York with you."

"He's arriving in two weeks. Anyway, it's a different kind of work."

"I see," Johnny said. "Making movies is a sacred enterprise and a woman is ennobled when she's sacrificed to it. While running a big business is sordid and crass and a man ought to be delighted to get away from all that filth and run down to New York to meet his lonely, innocent, purifying sister at the plane and buy her dinner."

"You're not defending Rudolph," Gretchen said. "You're defending yourself."

"Both," Johnny said. "Both of us. And I don't feel I have to defend anybody. If an artist wants to feel that he's the only worthwhile creature spewed up by modern civilization, that's his business. But to expect poor, money-soiled slobs like myself to agree with him is idiotic. It's a great line with the girls and it gets a lot of half-baked painters and would-be Tolstoys into some pretty fair beds, but it doesn't wash with me. I bet that if I worked in a garret in Greenwich Village instead of in an air-conditioned office in Wall Street, you'd have married me long before you ever met Colin Burke."

"Guess again, brother," Gretchen said. "I'd like some more wine." She extended her glass.

Johnny poured the wine, almost filling her glass, then signaled to the waiter, who was out of earshot, for another bottle. He sat in silence, immobile, brooding. Gretchen was surprised at his outburst. It wasn't like Johnny at all. Even when they had been making love, he had seemed cool, detached, as technically expert at that as he was at everything he undertook. By now, the last roughnesses, physical and mental, seemed to have been planed away from the man. He was like a highly polished, enormous, rounded stone, an elegant weapon, siege ammunition.

"I was a fool," he said, finally, his voice low, without timbre. "I should have asked you to marry me."

"I was married at the time. Remember?"

"You were married at the time you met Colin Burke, too. Remember?"

Gretchen shrugged. "It was in a different year," she said. "And he was a different man."

"I've seen some of his pictures," Johnny said. "They're pretty good."

"They're a lot more than that."

"The eyes of love," Johnny said, pretending to smile.

"What're you trying to do, Johnny?"

"Nothing," he said. "Ah, hell. I guess what I'm doing is being bitchy because I made such poor use of my time. Unmanly fellow. I now brighten up and ask polite questions of my guest, ex-wife of one of my best friends. I suppose you're happy."

"Very."

"Good answer." Johnny nodded approvingly. "Very good answer. Lady found fulfillment, long denied, in fulfilling second marriage to short but active artist of the silver screen."

"You're still being bitchy. If you want, I'll get up and leave."

"There's dessert coming." He put out his hand and touched hers. Smooth, fleshed, round fingers, soft palm. "Don't leave. I have other questions. A girl like you, so *New York*, so busy with a life of your own—what the hell do you do with yourself day after day in that goddamn place?"

"Most of the time," she said, "I spend thanking God I'm no longer in New York."

"And the rest of the time? Don't tell me you like just sitting there and being a housewife, waiting for Daddy to come home from the studio and tell you what Sam Goldwyn said at lunch."

"If you must know," she said, stung, "I do very little just sitting around, as you put it. I'm part of the life of a man I admire and can help, and it's a lot better than what I had here, being important and snotty, secretly screwing, and getting my name in magazines and living with a man who had to be dragged up from the bottom of a bottle three times a week."

"Ah—the new female revolution—" Johnny said. "Church, children, kitchen. Jesus, you were the last woman in the world I'd've thought . . ."

"Leave out the church," Gretchen said, "and you've got a perfect description of my life, okay?" She stood up. "And I'll skip dessert. Those short, active artists of the silver screen like their women skinny."

"Gretchen," he called after her, as she strode out of the restaurant. His voice had the ring of innocent surprise. Something had just happened to him that had never happened before, that was unimaginable within the rules of the nicely regulated games he played. Gretchen didn't look back, and she went out the door before any of the flunkeys in the restaurant had time to push it open for her.

She walked quickly toward Fifth Avenue, then slackened her pace as her anger cooled. She was silly to have become so upset, she decided. Why should she care what Johnny Heath thought about what she was doing with her life? He pretended he liked what he considered free women because that meant he could be free with them. He

had been turned away from the banquet and he was trying to make
her pay for it. What could he know of what it was like for her to
wake up in the morning and see Colin lying beside her? She wasn't
free of her husband and he wasn't free of her and they were both
better and more joyous human beings because of it. What crap people believed freedom to be.

She hurried to the hotel and went up to her room and picked up
the phone and asked the operator for her own number in Beverly
Hills. It was eight o'clock in California and Colin ought to be home
by now. She had to hear his voice, even though he detested talking
on the phone and was most often sour and brusque on it, even with
her, when she called him. But there was no answer and when she
called the studio and asked them to ring the cutting room, she was
told that Mr. Burke had left for the night.

She hung up slowly, paced the room. Then she sat down at the
desk and drew out a sheet of paper and began to write: "Dear Colin,
I called and you weren't home and you weren't at the studio and I
am sad and a man who once was my lover said some untrue things
that bothered me and New York is too warm and Billy loves his father more than he does me and I am very unhappy without you and
you should have been home and I am thinking unworthy thoughts
about you and I am going down to the bar to have a drink or two
drinks or three drinks and if anybody tries to pick me up I am going
to call for the police and I don't know how I'm going to live the two
weeks before I see you again and I hope I didn't sound like a con-
ceited know-it-all about the mirror sequence and if I did forgive me
and I promise not to change or reform or keep my mouth shut on
the condition that you promise not to change or reform or keep your
mouth shut and your collar was frayed when you took us to the airport and I am a terrible housewife, but I am a housewife, housewife,
housewife, a wife in your house, the best profession in the whole
world and if you're not home the next time I call you God knows
what revenge I shall prepare for you. Love, G."

She put the letter into an airmail envelope without rereading it
and went down into the lobby and had it stamped and put it into
the slot, connected by paper and ink and night-flying planes to the
center of her life three thousand miles away across the dark great
continent.

Then she went into the bar and nobody tried to pick her up and
she drank two whiskies without talking to the bartender. She went
up and undressed and got into bed.

When she woke the next morning, it was the phone ringing that awoke her and Willie was speaking, saying, "We'll be over to pick you up in a half hour. We've already had breakfast."

Ex-husband, ex-airman Willie drove swiftly and well. The first leaves were turning toward autumn on the small lovely hills of New England as they approached the school. Willie was wearing his dark glasses again, but today against the glare of the sun on the road, not because of drink. His hands were steady on the wheel and there was none of the tell-tale shiftiness in his voice that came after a bad night. They had to stop twice because Billy got carsick, but aside from that the trip was a pleasant one, a handsome, youngish American family, comfortably off, driving in a shining new car through some of the greenest scenery in America on a sunny September day.

The school was mostly red-brick Colonial, with white pillars here and there and a few old wooden mansions scattered around the campus as dormitories. The buildings were set among old trees and widespread playing fields. As they drove up to the main building, Willie said, "You're enrolling in a country club, Billy."

They parked the car and went up the steps to the big hall of the main building in a bustle of parents and other schoolboys. A smiling middle-aged lady was behind the desk, set up for signing in the new students. She shook their hands, said she was glad to see them, wasn't it a beautiful day, gave Billy a colored tag to put through his lapel, and called out, "David Crawford," toward a group of older boys with different-colored tags in their lapels. A tall, bespectacled boy of eighteen came briskly over to the desk. The middle-aged lady made introductions all around and said, "William, this is David, he'll settle you in. If you have any problems today or any time during the school year, you go right to David and pester him with them."

"That's right, William," Crawford said. Deep, responsible Sixth Former voice. "I am at your service. Where's your gear? I'll show you to the room." He led the way out of the building, the middle-aged lady already smiling behind him at another family trio at the desk.

"William," Gretchen whispered as she walked behind the two boys with Willie. "For a minute I didn't know whom she was talking to."

"It's a good sign," Willie said. "When I went to school everybody called everybody by their last names. They were preparing us for the Army."

Crawford insisted upon carrying Billy's bag and they crossed the campus to a three-story red-brick building that was obviously newer than most of the other structures surrounding it.

"Sillitoe Hall," Crawford said, as they went in. "You're on the third floor, William."

There was a plaque just inside the doorway announcing that the dormitory was the gift of Robert Sillitoe, father of Lieutenant Robert Sillitoe, Jr., Class of 1938, fallen in the service of his country, August 6th, 1944.

Gretchen was sorry she had seen the plaque, but took heart from the sound of young male voices singing from other rooms and the pounding of jazz groups from phonographs, all very much alive, as she climbed the stairs behind Crawford and Billy.

The room assigned to Billy wasn't large, but it was furnished with two cots, two small desks, and two wardrobes. The small trunk they had sent ahead with Billy's belongings was under one of the cots and there was another trunk tagged Fournier next to the window.

"Your roommate's already here," Crawford said. "Have you met him yet?"

"No," Billy said. He seemed very subdued, even for him, and Gretchen hoped that Fournier, whoever he was, would not turn out to be a bully or a pederast or a marijuana smoker. She felt suddenly helpless—a life was out of her hands.

"You'll see him at lunch," Crawford said. "You'll hear the bell any minute now." He smiled his sober responsible smile at Willie and Gretchen. "Of course, all parents are invited, Mrs. Abbott."

She caught the agonized glance from Billy, saying plainly, Not now, *please!* and she checked the correction before it crossed her lips. Time enough for Billy to explain that his father was Mr. Abbott but his mother was called Mrs. Burke. Not the first day. "Thank you, David," she said, her voice unsteady in her own ears. She looked at Willie. He was shaking his head. "It's very kind of the school to invite us," she said.

Crawford gestured at the bare, unmade cot. "I advise you to get three blankets, William," he said. "The nights up here get beastly cold and they're Spartan about heat. They think freezing is good for our unfolding characters."

"I'll send you the blankets from New York today," Gretchen said. She turned toward Willie. "Now about lunch . . ."

"You're not hungry, are you, dear?" Willie's voice was pleading, and Gretchen knew that the last thing Willie wanted was to eat lunch in a school dining room, without a drink in sight.

"Not really," Gretchen said, pitying him.

"Anyway, I have to get back to town by four o'clock," Willie said. "I have an appointment that's very . . ." His voice trailed off unconvincingly.

There was a booming of bells and Crawford said, "There it is. The dining room is just behind the desk where you signed in, William. Now if you'll excuse me, I have to wash up. And remember—anything you need." Upright and gentlemanly in his blazer and scuffed white shoes, a credit to the three years of schooling behind him, he went into the corridor, still resounding with the clashing melodies from three different phonographs, Elvis Presley's wail, frantic and forlorn, dominating.

"Well," Gretchen said, "he does seem like an awfully nice boy, doesn't he?"

"I'll wait and see what he's like when you're not around," Billy said, "and tell you."

"I guess you'd better get over for your lunch," Willie said. Gretchen could tell he was panting for the first drink of the day. He had been very good about not suggesting stopping at any of the roadhouses they had passed on the way up and he had been a proper father all morning. He had earned his martini.

"We'll walk you over to the dining room," Gretchen said. She wanted to cry, but of course she couldn't, in front of Billy. She looked erratically around the room. "When you and your roommate do a little decorating here," she said, "this place ought to be very cosy. And you do have a pretty view." Abruptly, she led the way into the hall.

They crossed the campus, along with other small groups converging on the main building. Gretchen stopped some distance from the steps. The moment had come to say good-bye and she didn't want to have to do it in the middle of the herd of boys and parents at the foot of the steps.

"Well," she said, "we might as well do it here."

Billy put his arms around her and kissed her brusquely. She managed a smile. Billy shook his father's hand. "Thanks for driving me up," he said evenly, to both of them. Then, dry-eyed, he turned and walked, not hurrying, toward the steps, joining in the stream of students, lost, gone, a thin, gangling, childish figure departed irrevocably for that budding company of men where mothers' voices which had comforted and lullabyed and admonished were now and forever heard only from afar.

Through a haze of tears she watched him vanish through the white pillars, the open doors, out of sunlight into shadow. Willie put his arm around her and, grateful for the touch of each other's body, they walked toward the car. They drove down the winding drive, along a tree-shaded street that bordered the school's playing fields, deserted now of athletes, goals undefended, base paths clear of runners.

She sat in the seat beside Willie staring straight ahead. She heard a curious sound from Willie's side of the car and he stopped the car under a tree. Willie was sobbing uncontrollably and now she couldn't hold it back any more and she clutched him and, their arms around each other, they wept and wept, for Billy, and the life ahead of him, for Robert Sillitoe, Jr., for themselves, for love, for Mrs. Abbott, for Mrs. Burke, for all the whiskey, for all their mistakes, for the flawed life behind them.

"Just don't pay any attention to me," the girl with the cameras was saying to Rudolph as Gretchen and Johnny Heath got out of the car and walked across the parking lot to where Rudolph was standing under the huge sign that traced the name of Calderwood against the blue September sky. It was the opening day of the new shopping center on the northern outskirts of Port Philip, a neighborhood that Gretchen knew well, because it was on the road that led, a few miles farther on, to the Boylan estate.

Gretchen and Johnny had missed the opening ceremony because Johnny couldn't break loose from his office until lunchtime. Johnny had been apologetic about that, as he had been apologetic about his conversation at dinner two nights before, and the drive up had been a friendly one. Johnny had done most of the talking, but not about himself or Gretchen. He had spent the time explaining, admiringly, the mechanics of Rudolph's rise as an entrepreneur and manager. According to Johnny, Rudolph understood the complexities of modern business better than any man his age Johnny had ever come across. When Johnny tried to explain what a brilliant coup Rudolph had pulled off last year in getting Calderwood to agree to buy a firm that had shown a two-million-dollar loss in the last three years, she had to admit to him that he had finally taken her beyond her intellectual depth, but that she would accept his opinion of the deal on faith.

When Gretchen came to where Rudolph was standing, making notes on a pad on a clipboard he was carrying, the photographer was crouched a few feet in front of him, shooting upward, to get the Calderwood sign in behind him. Rudolph smiled widely when he saw her and Johnny and moved toward them to greet them. Dealer in millions, juggler with stock options, disposer of risk capital, he merely looked like her brother to Gretchen, a well-tanned, handsome young man in a nicely tailored, unremarkable suit. She was struck once again by the difference between her brother and her husband. From what Johnny had told her she knew that Rudolph was many times wealthier than Colin and wielded infinitely more real power over a much greater number of people, but nobody, not even his own mother, would ever accuse Colin of being modest. In any group, Colin stood out, arrogant and commanding, ready to make enemies. Rudolph blended into groups, affable and pliant, certain to make friends.

"That's good," the crouching girl said, taking one picture after another. "That's very good."

"Let me introduce you," Rudolph said. "My sister, Mrs. Burke, my associate, Mr. Heath. Miss . . . uh . . . Miss . . . I'm terribly sorry."

"Prescott," the girl said. "Jean will do. Please don't pay any attention to me." She stood up and smiled, rather shyly. She was a small girl, with straight, long, brown hair, caught in a bow at the nape of her neck. She was freckled and unmade-up and she moved easily, even with the three cameras hanging from her, and the heavy film case slung from her shoulder.

"Come on," Rudolph said, "I'll show you around. If you see old man Calderwood, make admiring noises."

Wherever they went, Rudolph was stopped by men and women who shook his hand and said what a wonderful thing he had done for the town. While Miss Prescott clicked away, Rudolph smiled his modest smile, said he was glad they were enjoying themselves, remembered an amazing number of names.

Among the well-wishers, Gretchen didn't recognize any of the girls she had gone to school with or had worked with at Boylan's. But all of Rudolph's schoolmates seemed to have turned out to see for themselves what their old friend had done and to congratulate him, some sincerely, some with all too obvious envy. By a curious trick of time, the men who came up to Rudolph with their wives and children, and said, "Remember me? We graduated in the same class?" seemed older, grosser, slower, than her unmarried, unimpeded brother. Success had put him in another generation, a slimmer, quicker, more elegant generation. Colin, too, she realized, seemed much younger than he was. The youth of winners.

"You seem to have the whole town here today," Gretchen said.

"Just about," Rudolph said. "I even heard that Teddy Boylan put in an appearance. We'll probably bump into him." Rudolph looked over at her carefully.

"Teddy Boylan," she said flatly. "Is he still alive?"

"So the rumor goes," Rudolph said. "I haven't seen him for a long time, either."

They walked on, a small, momentary chill between them. "Wait a minute for me here," Rudolph said. "I want to talk to the band leader. They're not playing enough of the old standards."

"He sure likes to keep everything under control, doesn't he?" Gretchen said to Johnny, as she watched Rudolph hurry toward the bandstand, followed, as ever, by Miss Prescott.

When Rudolph came back to them, the band was playing "Happy Days Are Here Again," and he had a couple in tow, a slender, very pretty blonde girl in a crisp, white-linen dress, and a balding, sweating man somewhat older than Rudolph, wearing a wrinkled seersucker suit. Gretchen was sure she had seen the man somewhere before, but for the moment she couldn't place him.

"This is Virginia Calderwood, Gretchen," Rudolph said. "The boss's youngest. I've told her all about you."

Miss Calderwood smiled shyly. "He has, indeed, Mrs. Burke."

"And you remember Bradford Knight, don't you?" Rudolph asked.

"I drank you dry the night of the graduation party in New York," Bradford said.

She remembered then, the ex-sergeant with the Oklahoma accent, hunting girls in the apartment in the Village. The accent seemed to have been toned down somewhat and it was too bad he was losing his hair. She remembered now that Rudolph had coaxed him to come back to Whitby a few years ago and was grooming him to be an assistant manager. Rudolph liked him, she knew, although looking at the man she couldn't tell just why. Rudolph had told her he was shrewd, behind his Rotarian front, and was wonderful at getting along with people while carrying out instructions to the letter.

"Of course, I remember you, Brad," Gretchen said. "I hear you're invaluable."

"I blush, ma'am," Knight said.

"We're all invaluable," Rudolph said.

"No," the girl said. She spoke seriously, keeping her eyes fixed, in a way that Gretchen recognized, on Rudolph.

They all laughed. Except for the girl. Poor thing, Gretchen thought. Better learn to look at another man that way.

"Where *is* your father?" Rudolph asked. "I want to introduce my sister to him."

"He went home," the girl said. "He got angry at something the Mayor said, because the Mayor kept talking about you and not about him."

"I was born here," Rudolph said lightly, "and the Mayor wants to take credit for it."

"And he didn't like *her* taking pictures of you all the time." She gestured at Miss Prescott, who was focusing on the group from a few feet away.

"Hazards of the trade," Johnny Heath said. "He'll get over it."

"You don't know my father," the girl said. "You'd better give him a ring later," she said to Rudolph, "and calm him down."

"I'll give him a ring later," Rudolph said, carelessly. "If I have the time. Say, we're all going to have a drink in about an hour. Why don't you two join us?"

"I can't be seen in bars," Virginia said. "You know that."

"Okay," Rudolph said. "We'll have dinner instead. Brad, just wander around and break up anything that looks as if it's getting rough. And later on, the kids're bound to start dancing. Make them keep it clean, in a polite way."

"I'll insist on minuets," Knight said. "Come on, Virginia, I'll treat you to a free orange pop, courtesy of your father."

Reluctantly, the girl allowed herself to be pulled away by Knight.

"He is not the man of her dreams," Gretchen said, as they started walking again. "That's plain."

"Don't tell Brad that," Rudolph said. "He has visions of marrying into the family and starting an empire."

"She's nice," Gretchen said.

"Nice enough," said Rudolph. "Especially for a boss's daughter."

A heavy-set woman, rouged and eye-shadowed, wearing a turbanlike hat that made her look like something from a movie of the 1920's, stopped Rudolph, winking and working her mouth coquettishly. "*Eh bien, mon cher Rudolph,*" she said, her voice high with a desperate attempt at girlishness, "*tu parles français toujours bien?*"

Rudolph bowed gravely, taking his cue from the turban. "*Bonjour, Mlle. Lenaut,*" he said, "*je suis très content de vous voir.* May I present my sister, Mrs. Burke. And my friend, Mr. Heath."

"Rudolph was the brightest pupil I ever taught," Miss Lenaut said, rolling her eyes. "I was certain that he would rise in the world. It was plain in everything he did."

"You are too kind," Rudolph said, and they walked on. He grinned. "I used to write love letters to her when I was in her class. I never sent them. Pop once called her a French cunt and slapped her face."

"I never heard that story," Gretchen said.

"There're a lot of stories you never heard."

"Some evening," she said, "you've got to sit down and tell me the history of the Jordaches."

"Some evening," Rudolph said.

"It must give you an awful lot of satisfaction," Johnny said, "coming back to your old town on a day like this."

Rudolph reflected for an instant. "It's just another town," he said offhandedly. "Let's go look at the merchandise."

He led them on a tour of the shops. Gretchen's acquisitive instinct was, as Colin had once told her, subnormal, and the gigantic assembly of things to buy, that insensate flood of *objects* which streamed inexorably from the factories of America saddened her.

Everything, or almost everything that most depressed Gretchen about the age in which she lived, was crammed into this artfully rustic conglomeration of white buildings, and it was her brother, whom she loved, and who softly and modestly surveyed this concrete, material proof of his cunning, who had put it all together. When he told her the history of the Jordaches, she would reserve one chapter for herself.

After the shops, Rudolph showed them around the theater. A touring company from New York was to open that night in a comedy and a lighting rehearsal was in progress when they went into the auditorium. Here, old man Calderwood's taste had not been the deciding factor. Dull-pink walls and deep-red plush on the chairs softened the clean severity of the interior lines of the building and Gretchen could tell, from the ease with which the director was getting complicated lighting cues, that no expense had been spared on the board backstage. For the first time in years she felt a pang of regret that she had given up the theater.

"It's lovely, Rudy," she said.

"I had to show you *one* thing of which you could approve," he said quietly.

She reached out and touched his hand, begging forgiveness with the gesture for her unspoken criticism of the rest of his accomplishment.

"Finally," he said, "we're going to have six theaters like this around the country and we're going to put on our own plays and run them at least two weeks in each place. That way each play will be guaranteed a run of three months at a minimum and we won't have to depend upon anybody else. If Colin ever wants to put on a play for me . . ."

"I'm sure he'd love to work in a place like this," Gretchen said. "He's always grumbling about the old barns on Broadway. When he gets to New York I'll bring him up to see it. Though maybe it's not such a good idea . . ."

"Why not?" Rudolph asked.

"He sometimes gets into terrible fights with the people he works with."

"He won't fight with me," Rudolph said confidently. He and Burke had liked each other from their first meeting. "I am deferential and respectful in the presence of artists. Now for that drink."

Gretchen looked at her watch. "I'm afraid I'll have to skip it. Colin's calling me at the hotel at eight o'clock and he fumes if I'm not there when the phone rings. Johnny, do you mind if we leave now?"

"At your service, ma'am," Johnny said.

Gretchen kissed Rudolph good-bye and left him in the theater, his face glowing in the light reflected from the stage, with Miss Prescott changing lenses and clicking away, pretty, agile, busy.

Johnny and Gretchen passed the bar going toward the car and she was glad they hadn't gone in because she was sure that the man she glimpsed, in the dark interior, bent over a drink, was Teddy Boylan, and even after fifteen years she knew he had the power to disturb her. She didn't want to be disturbed.

The phone was ringing when she opened the door to her room. The call was from California, but it wasn't Colin. It was the head of the studio and he was calling to say that Colin had been killed in an automobile accident at one o'clock that day. He had been dead all afternoon and she hadn't known it.

She thanked the man on the phone calmly for his muted words of sympathy and hung up and for a long while sat alone in the hotel room without turning on the light.

Chapter 2

The bell rang for the last round of the sparring session and Schultzy called, "See if you can crowd him more, Tommy." The boxer Quayles was going to meet in five days was a crowder and Thomas was supposed to imitate his style. But Quayles was a hard man to crowd, a dancer and jabber, quick and slippery on his feet and with fast hands. He never hurt anybody much, but he had come a long way with his cleverness. The bout was going to be nationally televised and Quayles was getting twenty thousand dollars for his end. Thomas, on the supporting card, was going to get six hundred. It would have been less if Schultzy, who handled both fighters, at least for the record, hadn't held out for the money with the promoters. There was Mafia money behind the fight and those boys didn't go in for charity.

The training ring was set up in a theater and the people who came to watch the sessions sat in the orchestra seats in their fancy Las Vegas shirts and canary-yellow pants. Thomas felt more like an actor than a fighter up there on the stage.

He shuffled toward Quayles, who had a mean flat face and dead-cold pale eyes under the leather headguard. When Quayles sparred with Thomas, there was always a little derisive smile on his lips, as though it was absurd for Thomas to be in the same ring with him. He made a point of never talking to Thomas, not as much as a good morning, even though they were both in the same stable. The only satisfaction Thomas got out of Quayles was that he was screwing Quayles's wife and one day he was going to let Quayles know it.

Quayles danced in and out, tapping Thomas sharply, slipping Thomas's hooks easily, showing off for the crowd, letting Thomas swing at him in a corner and just bobbing his head, untouched, as the crowd yelled.

Sparring partners were not supposed to damage main-eventers, but this was the last round of the training schedule and Thomas attacked doggedly, ignoring punishment, to get just one good one in, set the bastard down on the seat of his fancy pants. Quayles realized what Thomas was trying to do and the smile on his face became loftier than ever as he flicked away, danced in and out, picked off punches in mid-air. He wasn't even sweating at the end of the round and there wasn't a mark on his body, although Thomas had been hacking away trying to reach him there, for a solid two minutes.

When the bell rang, Quayles said, "You ought to pay me for a boxing lesson, you bum."

"I hope you get killed Friday, you cheap ham," Thomas said, then climbed down and went into the showers, while Quayles did some rope skipping and calisthenics and worked on the light bag. He never got tired, the bastard, and he was a glutton for work, and would probably wind up middleweight champion, with a million bucks in the bank.

When Thomas came back out after his shower, his skin reddened under the eyes by Quayles's jabs, Quayles was still at it, showing off, shadow boxing, with the hicks in the crowd in their circus clothes oh-ing and ah-ing.

Schultzy gave him the envelope with the fifty bucks in it for his two rounds and he walked quickly through the crowd and out into the glare of the searing Las Vegas afternoon. After the air-conditioned theater the heat seemed artificial and malevolent, as though the entire town were being cooked by some diabolical scientist who wanted to destroy it in the most painful way possible.

He was thirsty after the workout and went across the blazing street to one of the big hotels. The lobby was dark and cold. The expensive hookers were on patrol and the old ladies were playing the slot machines. The crap and roulette tables were in action as he passed them on his way to the bar. Everybody in the whole stinking town was loaded with money. Except him. He had lost over five hundred dollars, almost all the money he had earned, at the crap tables in the last two weeks.

He felt the envelope with Schultzy's fifty in his pocket and fought back the urge to try the dice. He ordered a beer from the barman. His weight was okay and Schultzy wasn't there to bawl him out. Anyway, Schultzy didn't much care what he did any more, now that he had a contender in the stable. He wondered how much of Schultzy's end of the purse he had to give to the gunslingers.

He drank a second beer, paid the barman, started out, stopped for a moment to watch the crap game. A guy who looked like a small-town undertaker had a pile of chips about a foot high in front of him. The dice were hot. Thomas took out the envelope and bought chips. In ten minutes he was down to ten dollars and he had sense enough to hold onto that.

He got the doorman to beg a ride for him from a guest to his hotel downtown, so he wouldn't have to pay taxi fare. His hotel was a grubby one, with a few slot machines and one crap table. Quayles was staying at the Sands, with all the movie stars. And his wife. Who lay around the pool all day getting stoned on Planter's Punches when she wasn't sneaking down to Thomas's hotel for a quick one. She had a loving nature, she said, and Quayles slept alone, in a separate room, being a serious fighter with an important bout coming up. Thomas wasn't a serious fighter any more and there were no more important bouts for him so it didn't make much difference what he did. The lady was active in bed and some of the afternoons were really worth the trouble.

There was a letter at the desk for him. From Teresa. He didn't even bother to open it. He knew what was in it. Another demand for money. She was working now and making more money than he did, but that didn't stop her. She had gone to work as a hatcheck and cigarette girl in a nightclub, wiggling her ass and showing her legs as high up as the law allowed and raking in the tips. She said she was bored just hanging around the house with the kid, with him away so much of the time and she wanted to have a career. She thought being a hatcheck girl was some sort of show business. The kid was stashed away with her sister in the Bronx and even when Thomas was in town Teresa came in at all hours, five, six in the morning, with her purse stuffed with twenty-dollar bills. God knows what she did. He didn't care any more.

He went up to his room and lay down on his bed. That was one way to save money. He had to figure how to get from today to Friday on ten bucks. The skin under his eyes smarted where Quayles had peppered him. The air conditioning in the room was almost useless and the desert heat made him sweat.

He closed his eyes and slept uneasily, dreaming. He dreamt of France. It had been the best time of his life and he often dreamt about the moment on the shore of the Mediterranean, although it had been almost five years ago now, and the dreams were losing their intensity.

He woke, remembering the dream, sighed as the sea and the white buildings disappeared and he was surrounded once more by the cracked Las Vegas walls.

He had gone down to the Côte d'Azur after winning the fight in London. It had been an easy victory and Schultzy had gotten him another bout in Paris a month later, so there was no sense in going back to New York. Instead he had picked up one of those wild London girls. She had said she knew a great little hotel in Cannes and since Thomas was rolling in money for once and it looked as though he could beat everybody in Europe with one hand tied behind him, he had taken off for the weekend. The weekend had stretched into ten days, with frantic cables from Schultzy. Thomas had lain on the beach and eaten two great, heavy meals a day, developed a taste for vin rosé, and had put on fifteen pounds. When he finally got to Paris, he had just managed to make the weight the morning of the fight and the Frenchman had nearly killed him. For the first time in his life he had been knocked out and suddenly there were no more bouts in Europe. He had blown most of his money on the English girl, who happened to like jewelry, aside from her other attractions, and Schultzy hadn't talked to him all the way back to New York.

The Frenchman had taken something out of him and nobody was writing that he should be considered for a shot at the title anymore. The time between bouts became greater and greater and the purses smaller and smaller. Twice he had to take a dive for walking-around money and Teresa closed him off entirely and if it hadn't been for the kid he'd have just gotten up and left.

Lying in the heat on the wrinkled bed, he thought of all these things and remembered what his brother had told him that day at the Hotel Warwick. He wondered if Rudolph had followed his career and was saying, to his snooty sister, "I told him it would happen."

Screw his brother.

Well, maybe on Friday night, there'd be some of the old juice in him and he'd score spectacularly. People would start hanging around him again and he'd make a comeback. Plenty of fighters—older than he—had made comebacks. Look at Jimmy Braddock, down to being a day laborer and then beating Max Baer for the heavyweight championship of the world. Schultzy just had to pick his opponents for him more carefully—keep him away from the dancers, give him somebody who came to fight. He'd have to have a talk with Schultzy. And not only about that. He had to get some money in advance, before Friday, to keep alive in this lousy town.

Two, three good wins and he could forget all this. Two, three good wins and they'd be asking for him in Paris again and he'd be down on the Côte sitting at a sidewalk café, drinking vin rosé and looking out at the masts of the boats anchored in the harbor. With real luck he might even get to rent one of them, sail around, out of reach of everybody. Maybe only two, three fights a year just to keep the bank balance comfortable.

Just thinking about it made him cheerful again and he was just about to go downstairs and put his ten bucks on the come at the crap table when the phone rang.

It was Cora, Quayles's wife and she sounded demented, screaming and crying into the phone. "He's found out, he's found out," she kept saying. "Some lousy bellboy got to him. He nearly killed me just now. I think he broke my nose, I'm going to be a cripple the rest of my life . . ."

"Go easy now," Thomas said. "What has he found out?"

"You know what he found out. He's on his way right now to . . ."

"Wait a minute. What did you tell him?"

"What the hell do you think I told him?" she screamed. "I told him no. Then he clouted me across the face. I'm blood all over. He doesn't believe me. That lousy bellboy in your hotel must've had a telescope or something. You'd better get out of town. This minute. He's on his way over to see you, I tell you. Christ knows what he'll do to you. And later on, to me. Only I'm not waiting. I'm going to the airport right now. I'm not even packing a bag. And I advise you to do the same. Only stay away from me. You don't know him. He's a murderer. Just get on something and get out of town. Fast."

Thomas hung up on the terrified, high-pitched babble. He looked at his one valise in a corner of the room, then stood up and went to the window and peered out through the Venetian blinds. The street was empty in the four o'clock afternoon desert glare. Thomas went over to the door and made sure it was unlocked. Then he moved the one chair to a corner. He didn't want to get charged and sent backward over the chair in the first rush.

He sat on the bed, smiling a little. He had never run away from a fight and he wasn't going to run away from this one. And this one might be the most enjoyable fight of his entire career. The small hotel room was no place for jabbers and dancers.

He got up and went over to the closet and took out a leather windjacket and put it on, zipping it up high and turning the collar up to protect his throat. Then he sat on the edge of the bed again, waiting placidly, hunched over a little, his hands hanging loose between his legs. He heard a car screech to a halt in front of the hotel, but he didn't move. One minute later there were steps outside in the hall and then the door was flung open and Quayles came into the room, stopping just inside the doorway.

"Hi," Thomas said. He stood up slowly.

Quayles closed the door behind him and turned the key in the lock.

"I know all about it, Jordache," Quayles said.

"About what?" Thomas asked mildly, keeping his eyes on Quayles's feet for the first hint of movement.

"About you and my wife."

"Oh, yes," Thomas said. "I've been screwing her. Did I forget to mention it?"

He was ready for the leap and almost laughed when he saw Quayles, that dandy and stylist of the ring, lead with a blind long right, a sucker's punch if ever there was one. Because he was ready, Thomas went inside it easily, tied Quayles up, held onto him, with no referee to part them, and clubbed at Quayles's body, with delicious, pent-up ferocity. Then, old street fighter with all the tricks, he rushed Quayles to the wall, ignoring the man's attempt to writhe out of his grasp, stepped back just far enough to savage Quayles with an uppercut, then closed, wrestled, hit, held, used his elbows, his knee, butted Quayles's forehead with his head, wouldn't let him drop, but kept him up against the wall with his left hand around Quayles's throat, and pounded at his face with one brutal right hand after another. When he stepped back, Quayles crumpled onto the blood-stained rug and lay there on his face, out cold.

There was a frantic knocking on the door and he heard Schultzy's voice in the hall. He unlocked the door and let Schultzy in.

Schultzy took the whole thing in with one glance.

"You stupid bastard," he said, "I saw that bird-brained wife of his and she told me. I thought I'd get here in time. You're a great indoor fighter, aren't you, Tommy? You can't beat your grandmother for dough, but when it comes to fighting for nothing you're the all-time beauty." He knelt beside Quayles, motionless on the rug. Schultzy turned him over, examined the cut on Quayles's forehead, ran his hand alongside Quayles's jaw. "I think you broke his jaw. Idiots. He won't be able to fight this Friday or a month of Fridays. The boys're going to like that. They're going to like it a lot. They've got a big investment tied up in this horse's ass—" He prodded the inert Quayles fiercely. "They're going to be just overjoyed you took him apart. If I was you I'd start going right now, before I get this—this *husband* out of the room and into a hospital. And I'd keep on going until I got to an ocean and then I'd cross the ocean and if I wanted to stay alive I wouldn't come back for ten years. And don't go by plane. By the time the plane comes down anywhere, they'll be waiting for you and they won't be waiting for you with roses in their hands."

"What do you want me to do," Thomas asked, "walk? I got ten bucks to my name."

Schultzy looked worriedly down at Quayles, who was beginning to stir. He stood up. "Come on out into the hall." He took the key out of the lock and when they were both outside, he locked the door.

"It would serve you right if they filled you full of holes," Schultzy said. "But you've been with me a long time . . ." He looked nervously up and down the hallway. "Here," he said, taking some bills out of his wallet. "All I got. A hundred and fifty. And take my car. It's downstairs, with the key in the ignition. Leave it in Reno in the airport parking lot and bus East from there. I'll tell 'em you stole the car. Don't get in touch with your wife, whatever you do. They'll be after her. I'll get in touch with her and tell her you're running and not to expect to hear from you. Don't go in a straight line anywhere. And I'm not kidding when I tell you to get out of this country. Your life isn't worth two cents anywhere in the United States." He wrinkled his seamy brow, concentrating. "The safest thing is getting a job on a ship. When you get to New York go to a hotel called the Aegean. It's on West Eighteenth Street. It's full of Greek sailors. Ask for the manager. He's got a long Greek name, but everybody calls him Pappy. He handles jobs for freighters that don't fly the American flag. Tell him I sent you and I want you out of the country fast. He won't ask questions. He owes me a favor from when I was in the Merchant Marine during the war. And don't be a wise guy. Don't think you can pick up a few bucks fighting anywhere, even in Europe or Japan, under another name. As of this minute you're a sailor and nothing else. Do you hear that?"

"Yes, Schultzy," Thomas said.

"And I never want to hear from you again. Got that?"

"Yes." Thomas made a move toward the door of his room.

Schultzy stopped him. "Where do you think you're going?"

"My passport's in there. I'll be needing it."

"Where is it?"

"In the top dresser drawer."

"Wait here," Schultzy said. "I'll get it for you." He turned the key in the lock and went into the room. A moment later he was back in

the hall with the passport. "Here." He slapped the booklet into
Thomas's hand. "And from now on try to think with your head instead of your cock. Now breeze. I got to start putting that bum together again."

Thomas went down the steps, into the lobby, past the crap game.
He didn't say anything to the clerk, who looked at him curiously, because there was blood on his windjacket. He went out to the street.
Schultzy's car was parked right behind Quayles's Cadillac. Thomas
got in, started the motor and slowly drove toward the main highway.
He didn't want to be picked up this afternoon for a traffic violation
in Las Vegas. He could wash the windjacket later.

Chapter 3

The date was for eleven o'clock, but Jean had phoned to say that she
would be a few minutes late and Rudolph had said that was all right,
he had a few calls to make, anyway. It was Saturday morning. He
had been too busy to telephone his sister all week and he felt guilty
about it. Since he had flown back from the funeral, he had usually
managed at least two or three calls a week. He had suggested to
Gretchen that she come East and stay with him in his apartment,
which would mean that she would have the place to herself more
often than not. Old man Calderwood refused to move the central
office down to the city, so Rudolph couldn't count on more than ten
days a month in New York. But Gretchen had decided she wanted
to stay in California, at least for awhile. Burke had neglected to leave
a will, or at least one that anyone could find, and the lawyers were
squabbling and Burke's ex-wife was suing for the best part of the estate and trying to evict Gretchen from the house, among other unpleasant legal maneuvers.

It was eight o'clock in the morning in California, but Rudolph
knew that Gretchen was an early riser and that the ringing of the
phone wouldn't awaken her. He placed the call with the operator
and sat down at the desk in the small living room and tried to finish

a corner of the *Times* crossword puzzle that had stumped him when he had tried it at breakfast.

The apartment had come furnished. It was decorated with garish solid colors and spiky metal chairs, but Rudolph had only taken it as a temporary measure and it did have a good small kitchen with a refrigerator that produced a lot of ice. He often liked to cook and eat by himself, reading at the table. That morning he had made the toast, orange juice, and coffee for himself early. Sometimes Jean would come in and fix breakfast for both of them, but she had been busy this morning. She refused to stay overnight, although she had never explained why.

The phone rang and Rudolph picked it up, but it wasn't Gretchen. It was Calderwood's voice, flat and twangy and old. Saturdays and Sundays didn't mean much to Calderwood, except for the two hours on Sunday morning he spent in church. "Rudy," Calderwood said, as usual without any polite preliminaries, "you going to be up here this evening?"

"I hadn't planned to, Mr. Calderwood, I have some things to do here over the weekend and there's a meeting scheduled downtown for Monday and . . ."

"I'd like to see you as soon as can be, Rudy." Calderwood sounded testy. As he had grown older he had become impatient and bad tempered. He seemed to resent his increasing wealth and the men who had made it possible, as he resented the necessity of depending more and more upon dealing with financial and legal people in New York for important decisions.

"I'll be in the office on Tuesday morning, Mr. Calderwood," Rudolph said. "Can't it wait until then?"

"No, it can't wait until then. And I don't want to see you in the office. I want you to come to the house." The voice on the telephone was grating and tense. "I'll wait until tomorrow night after supper, Rudy."

"Of course, Mr. Calderwood," Rudy said.

The phone clicked, as Calderwood hung up, without saying good-bye.

Rudolph frowned at the phone as he put it down. He had tickets for the Giant game at the Stadium for himself and Jean Sunday afternoon and Calderwood's summons meant he'd have to miss it. Jean had had a boy friend on the team when she went to Michigan and she knew a surprising amount about football so it was always fun to go to a game with her. Why didn't the old man just lie down and die?

The phone rang again and this time it was Gretchen. Ever since Burke's death, something had gone out of her voice, a sharpness, an eagerness, a quick music that had been special to her ever since she was a young girl. She sounded pleased to hear Rudolph, but dully pleased, like an invalid responding to a visit in her hospital bed. She said she was all right, that she was being kept busy going through Colin's papers and sorting them and answering letters of condolence that still came drifting in and conferring with lawyers about the estate. She thanked him for the check he had mailed her the week before, saying that when the estate was finally settled she would pay back all the money he had sent her.

"Don't worry about that," Rudolph said. "Please. You don't have to pay back anything."

She ignored that. "I'm glad you called," she said. "I was going to call you myself and ask for another favor."

"What is it?" he asked, then said, "Hold on a second," because the bell was ringing on the intercom from downstairs. He hurried over to the box and pushed the button.

"There's a Miss Prescott in the lobby, Mr. Jordache." It was the doorman, protecting him.

"Send her up, please," Rudolph said, and went back to the phone. "I'm sorry, Gretchen," he said, "what were you saying?"

"I got a letter from Billy from school yesterday," she said, "and I don't like the way it sounds. There's nothing that you can grasp in it, but that's the way he is, he never really tells you what's bothering him, but somehow I have the feeling he's in despair. Do you think you could find the time to go and visit him and see what's wrong?"

Rudolph hesitated. He doubted that the boy liked him enough to confide in him and he was afraid he might do more harm than good by going to the school. "Of course I'll go," he said, "if you want. But don't you think it might be better if his father went?"

"No," Gretchen said. "He's a bungler. If there's a wrong word to be said, he'll say it."

The front door was ringing now. "Hold on again, Gretchen," Rudolph said. "There's somebody at the door." He hurried over to the door and threw it open. "I'm on the phone," he said to Jean and trotted back into the room. "Back again, Gretchen," he said, using his sister's name to show Jean he wasn't talking to another lady. "I tell you what I'll do—I'll drive up to the school tomorrow morning and take him to lunch and see what's up."

"I hate to bother you," Gretchen said. "But the letter was so—so *dark*."

"It's probably nothing. He came in second in a race or he flunked an algebra exam or something like that. You know how kids are."

"Not Billy. I tell you, he's in despair." She sounded unlike herself, near tears.

"I'll call you tomorrow night, after I see him," Rudolph said. "Will you be home?"

"I'll be home," she said.

He put down the phone slowly, thinking of his sister alone, waiting for a telephone call, in the isolated house on the mountain crest, overlooking the city and the sea, going over her dead husband's papers. He shook his head. He would worry about her tomorrow. He smiled across the room at Jean, sitting neatly on a straight-backed wooden chair, wearing red-woolen stockings and moccasins, her hair brushed and bright and pulled together low on the nape of her neck in a black-velvet bow, and falling down her back freely below the bow. Her face, as always, looked scrubbed and schoolgirlish. The slender, beloved body was lost in a floppy camel's-hair polo coat. She was twenty-four years old, but at moments like this she seemed no more than sixteen. She had been out on a job and she had her camera equipment with her, which she had dumped carelessly on the floor next to the front door.

"You look as though I ought to offer you a glass of milk and a cookie," he said.

"You can offer me a drink," she said. "I've been on the streets since seven this morning. Not too much water."

He went over to her and kissed her forehead. She smiled, rewarding him. Young girls, he thought, as he went into the kitchen and got a pitcher of water.

While she drank the bourbon, she checked the list of art galleries in last Sunday's *Times*. When he was free on Saturdays they usually made the rounds of galleries. She worked as a free-lance photographer and many of her assignments were for art magazines and catalogue publishers.

"Put on comfortable shoes," she said. "We're in for a long afternoon." She had a surprisingly low voice, with husky overtones, for such a small girl.

"Where you walk," he said, "I shall follow."

They were just going out the door when the phone rang again. "Let it ring," he said. "Let's get out of here."

She stopped in the doorway. "Do you mean to say you can hear a telephone ring and not answer it?"

"I certainly can."

"I never could. It might be something absolutely wonderful."

"Nothing wonderful has ever happened to me over the phone. Let's get out of here."

"Answer it. It'll bother you all day if you don't."

"No, it won't."

"It'll bother me. *I'll* answer it." She started back into the room.

"All right, all right." He pushed past her and picked up the phone.

It was his mother, calling from Whitby. From the tone in which she said, "Rudolph," he knew the conversation was not going to be wonderful.

"Rudolph," she said, "I don't want to interfere with your holiday—" It was his mother's fixed conviction that he left Whitby for New York only for unseemly, secret pleasures. "But the heating's gone off and I'm freezing in this drafty old place—" Rudolph had bought a fine old low-ceilinged eighteenth-century farmhouse on the outskirts of town three years before, but his mother referred to it at all times as this crumbling dark hole or this drafty old place.

"Can't Martha do anything about it?" Rudolph asked. Martha was the live-in maid who kept the house, cooked, and took care of his mother, a job for which Rudolph felt she was grossly underpaid.

"Martha!" his mother snorted. "I'm tempted to fire her on the spot."

"Mom . . ."

"When I told her to go down to look at the furnace, she flatly refused." His mother's voice rose a half octave. "She's afraid of cellars. She said for me to put on a sweater. If you weren't so lenient with her, she wouldn't be so free with her advice about putting on sweaters, I guarantee. She's so fat, swilling down our food, she wouldn't feel cold at the North Pole. When you get back home, if you ever do deign to come back home, I implore you to have a word with that woman."

"I'll be home tomorrow afternoon and I'll talk to her," Rudolph said. He was aware of Jean smiling maliciously at him. Her parents lived somewhere in the Midwest and she hadn't seen them for two years. "In the meanwhile, Mom, call the office. Get Brad Knight. He's on today. Tell him I told you to ask him to send one of our engineers."

"He'll think I'm an old crank."

"He won't think anything. Do as I say, please."

"You have no idea how cold it is up here. The wind just howls under the windows. I don't know why we can't live in a decent new house like everybody else."

This was an old song and Rudolph ignored it. When his mother had finally realized that Rudolph was making a good deal of money she had suddenly developed a gluttonous taste for luxury. Her charge account at the store made Rudolph wince every month when the bills came in.

"Tell Martha to build a fire in the living room," Rudolph said, "and close the door and you'll be warm in no time."

"Tell Martha to build a fire," his mother said. "If she'll condescend. Will you be home in time for dinner tomorrow night?"

"I'm afraid not," he said. "I have to see Mr. Calderwood." It wasn't quite a lie. He wasn't going to dine with Calderwood, but he *was* going to see him. In any case, he didn't want to have dinner with his mother.

"Calderwood, Calderwood," his mother said. "Sometimes I think I'll scream if I ever hear that name again."

"I have to go now, Mom. Somebody's waiting for me."

He heard his mother begin to cry as he hung up. "Why can't old ladies just lie down and die?" he said to Jean. "The Eskimos do it better. They expose them. Come on, let's get out of here before anybody else calls."

As they went out the door he was glad to see that Jean was leaving her camera equipment in the flat. That meant she'd have to come back with him that afternoon to pick it up. She was unpredictable in that department. Sometimes she'd come in with him when they'd been out together as though it were inconceivable that she could do anything else. Other times, without any explanation, she'd insist on getting into a taxi and going downtown alone to the apartment she shared with another girl. Then, on several occasions, she had merely appeared at his door, on the off chance that he'd be home.

She went her own way, Jean, and pleased her own appetites. He had never even seen the place she lived. She always met him at his apartment or in a bar uptown. She didn't explain this, either. Young as she was, she seemed self-reliant, confident. Her work, as Rudolph had seen when she came up to Whitby with the proofs after the opening of the Port Philip center, was highly professional, surprisingly bold for a girl who had seemed so young and shy when he had first met her. She wasn't shy in bed, either, and however she behaved and for whatever reasons, she was never coy. She never complained that because of his work in Whitby there were long periods when he couldn't see her, two weeks at a time. It was Rudolph who complained of their separations, and he found himself plotting all sorts of stratagems, unnecessary appointments in the city, merely for an evening with Jean.

She was not one of those girls who lavished a full autobiography on her lover. He learned little about her. She came from the Midwest. She was on bad terms with her family. She had an older brother who was in the family firm, something to do with drugs. She had finished college at the age of twenty. She had majored in sociology. She had been interested in photography ever since she was a child. To get anywhere, you had to start in New York, so she had come to New York. She liked the work of Cartier-Bresson, Penn, Capa, Duncan, Klein. There was room among those names for a woman's name. Perhaps, eventually, it would be hers.

She went out with other men. Not described. In the summer she sailed. Names of craft unmentioned. She had been to Europe. A Yugoslavian island to which she would like to return. She was surprised that he had never been out of the United States.

She dressed youthfully, with a fresh eye for colors that at first glance seemed to clash, but then, after a moment, subtly complemented each other. Her clothes, Rudolph could see, were not expensive and after the first three times he had gone out with her, he was fairly certain he was familiar with her entire wardrobe.

She did the Sunday New York *Times* crossword puzzle faster than he did. Her handwriting was without frills, like a man's. She liked new painters whose work Rudolph couldn't appreciate or understand. "Keep looking," she said, "and then one day, a door will open, you will suddenly cross the barrier."

She never went to church. She never cried at sad movies. She never introduced him to any of her friends. She was unimpressed by Johnny Heath. She didn't mind getting her hair wet in the rain. She never complained about the weather or traffic jams. She never said, "I love you."

"I love you," he said. They were lying close together in bed, his hand on her breast, the covers pulled up under their chins. It was seven o'clock in the evening and the room was dark. They had strolled through twenty galleries. He had crossed no barriers. They had had lunch in a small Italian restaurant, where the proprietors had no objection to girls with red-wool stockings. He had told her at lunch that he couldn't take her to the game tomorrow and told her why. She wasn't disturbed. He had given her the tickets. She said she would take a man she knew who had once played tackle for Columbia. She ate heartily.

They had been cold when they came in from their wanderings around the city, because the December afternoon had turned bitter early, and he had made them both hot tea spiked with rum.

"It would be nice if we had a fire," she said, curled up on the sofa, her moccasins kicked off on the floor.

"The next apartment I rent," he said.

When they kissed they both tasted of rum, perfumed with lemon. They had made love unhurriedly, completely.

"This is what a Saturday afternoon in New York in the winter should be like," she said, when they had finished and were lying together quietly. "Art, spaghetti, rum, and lust."

He laughed, pressed her closer. He regretted his years of abstinence. Then he wasn't so sure. Perhaps it was because of the abstinence that he was ready for her, free for her.

"I love you," he said. "I want to marry you."

She lay still for a moment, then moved away, threw the covers back, started to dress in silence.

I have ruined everything, he thought. "What's the matter?"

"It's a subject I never discuss naked," she said gravely.

He laughed again, but was not happy. How many times had this beautiful, assured girl, with her own mysterious rules of behavior, discussed marriage, and with how many men? He had never been jealous before. Unprofitable emotion.

He watched the slender shadow move around the dark room, heard the rustle of cloth over skin. She went into the living room. Bad sign? Good sign? Would it be better just to lie here as he was, not go after her? He hadn't planned on saying either "I love you" or "I want to marry you."

He got out of bed and dressed quickly. She was sitting in the living room, other people's furniture, fiddling with the radio. Announcers' voices, honeyed and smooth, voices you would never believe if they said, "I love you."

"I want a drink," she said, without turning around, still fiddling with the dials.

He poured them both some bourbon and water. She drank like a man. What previous lover had taught her that?

"Well?" he said. He stood before her, feeling at a disadvantage, pleading. He hadn't put on his shoes or his jacket and tie. Barefooted and in his shirtsleeves he felt he wasn't properly dressed for the occasion.

"Your hair is mussed," she said. "You look much better with your hair mussed."

"Maybe my language is mussed," he said. "Maybe you didn't understand what I said in the bedroom."

"I understood." She turned the radio off, sat down in an easy chair, holding the glass of bourbon in her two hands. "You want to marry me."

"Exactly."

"Let's go to the movies," she said. "There's a picture I want to see just around the corner . . ."

"Don't be flip."

"It's only on till tomorrow night and you won't be here tomorrow night."

"I asked you a question."

"Am I supposed to be flattered?"

"No."

"Well, I *am* flattered. Now let's go to the movies . . ." But she didn't make any move to get up from the chair. Sitting there, half in shadow, because the one lamp that was lit threw its light obliquely from the side, she was fragile, vulnerable. Looking at her he knew that he had been right to say what he had in bed, that he hadn't spoken just from a flicker of tenderness on a cold afternoon, but from a deep and abiding need.

"I will be broken," he said, "if you say no."

"Do you believe that?" She was looking down into her glass, swirling the drink around now with a finger. He could see only the top of her head, her loose hair gleaming in the lamplight.

"Yes."

"Tell the truth."

"Partially," he said. "I partially believe it. Partially broken."

It was her turn to laugh. "At least you'll make somebody an honest husband," she said.

"Well?" he demanded. He stood above her and put his hand under her chin and made her look up at him. Her eyes seemed doubtful, frightened, the small face pale.

"The next time you come to town, give me a ring," she said.

"That's no answer."

"In a way, it is," she said. "The answer is I want time to think."

"Why?"

"Because I've done something I'm not particularly proud of," she said, "and I want to figure out how I can be proud of myself again."

"What've you done?" He didn't know whether he wanted to know or not.

"I've overlapped," Jean said. "It's a female disease. I was having an affair with a boy when I started with you and I haven't broken it off. I'm doing something I thought I'd never do in my whole life. I'm sleeping with two men at once. And he wants to marry me, too."

"Lucky girl," Rudolph said bitterly. "Is he the girl roommate you share your apartment with?"

"No. The girl is an authentic girl. I'll produce her for you if you want."

"Is that why you never let me come to your place? He's there?"

"No, he's not there."

"But he *has* been there." With surprise, Rudolph realized that he had been wounded, deeply wounded, and worse yet, that he himself was intent on turning the knife in the wound.

"One of the most attractive things about you," Jean said, "was that you were too sure of yourself to ask questions. If love is going to make you unattractive, forget love."

"What a goddamn afternoon," Rudolph said.

"I guess that wraps it up." Jean stood up, put her glass down carefully. "No movies tonight."

He watched her put on her coat. If she walks out now, like this, he thought, I'll never see her again. He went over to her and put his arms around her and kissed her.

"You're all wrong," he said. "There'll be movies tonight."

She smiled at him, but tremulously, as though it cost her an effort. "You'd better finish getting dressed," she said. "I hate to miss the beginning of a picture."

He went into the bedroom, combed his hair, put on a tie and got into his shoes. He looked briefly at the tumbled bed, now a confused battlefield, as he put on his jacket.

When he came out into the living room again, he saw that she had slung her camera equipment around her. He tried to argue but she insisted upon taking the stuff with her.

"I've been in this place enough," she said, "for one Saturday."

As he drove along the rain-drenched highway the next morning on the way to Billy's school, through sparse early traffic, he was thinking about Jean, not about Billy. They had gone to the movie, which was disappointing, had eaten supper afterward in a joint on Third Avenue, had talked about things that hardly mattered to either of them, the movie they had seen, other movies, plays they had seen, books and magazine articles they had read, rumors from Washington. The conversation of strangers. They had avoided mentioning marriage or overlapping lovers. They were both unaccountably weary, as though a great physical effort had drained them earlier. They drank more than they usually did. If this had been the first time they had gone out together, they would have thought each other dull. When they had finished their steaks, in the emptying restaurant, and had a cognac apiece, he was relieved to be able to put her into a taxi, walk home alone and turn the key behind him in the silent apartment, although the raw colors of the décor and the arty spikiness of the furniture made it look like an abandoned float from last year's Mardi Gras. The bed now was just messy, the neglected tangle of a slatternly housewife, not the warm abode of love. He slept heavily and when he awoke in the morning and remembered the night before and his errand for the day, the sooty December rain outside his window seemed the appropriate weather for the weekend.

He had called the school and left a message for Billy that he would be there around twelve-thirty to take him to lunch, but he arrived earlier than he expected, a little after noon. Even though the rain had stopped and a faint cold sun was filtering through the clouds in the south, there was no one to be seen on the campus, coming or going into any of the buildings. From what Gretchen had told him about the school, in fine weather and a more clement season it was a place of beauty, but under the wet sky, seemingly abandoned, there was something forbiddingly prisonlike about the cluster of buildings and the muddy lawns. He drove up to what was obviously the main building and got out uncertainly, not knowing where to find Billy. Then, from the chapel a hundred yards away he heard young voices singing strongly, "Onward Christian Soldiers."

Sunday. Compulsory services, he thought. They still do that in schools. Christ. When he was a boy Billy's age, all he had to do was salute the flag every morning and pledge allegiance to the United States of America. The advantages of public education. Separation of Church and State.

A Lincoln Continental drove up to the steps and stopped. It was a richly endowed school. Future rulers of America. He himself drove a Chevrolet. He wondered what would have been said at faculty teas if he had arrived on his motorcycle, which he still owned, though he now seldom used it. An important-looking man in a smart raincoat got out of the Lincoln, leaving a lady in the car. Parents. Occasional faint weekend communication with a future ruler of America. From his manners, the man had to be at least the president of a company, ruddy and brisk, well exercised. By now Rudolph could spot the type.

"Good morning, sir," Rudolph said, in his automatic speaking-to-company-presidents' voice. "I wonder if you could tell me where Sillitoe Hall is?"

The man smiled widely, showing five thousand dollars' worth of exquisite dental work. "Good morning, good morning. Yes, of course. My boy was there last year. In some ways the best house on the campus. It's just over there." He pointed. The building was four hundred yards away. "You can drive there if you want. Just down this driveway and around."

"Thank you," Rudolph said.

The hymn rang out from the chapel. The parent cocked an ear. "They're still praising God," he said. "All in favor of it. We could stand more of it."

Rudolph got into his Chevrolet and drove to Sillitoe Hall. He looked at the plaque commemorating Lieutenant Sillitoe as he went into the silent building. A girl of about four, in blue overalls, was pedaling a three-wheeler around the cluttered common room on the ground floor. A large setter in the room barked at him. Rudolph was a little disconcerted. He hadn't expected four-year-old girls in a boys' school.

A door opened and a chubby, pleasant-faced young woman in slacks came into the room and said, "Shut up, Boney," to the dog. She smiled at Rudolph. "He's harmless," she said.

Rudolph didn't know what she was doing there, either.

"Are you a father?" the woman asked, grabbing the dog by the collar and half strangling him, while he wagged his tail madly, full of love.

"Not exactly," Rudolph said. "I'm Billy Abbott's uncle. I called this morning."

A curious little expression—concern? suspicion? relief?—shadowed the pleasant, chubby, young face. "Oh, yes," the woman said. "He expects you. I'm Mollie Fairweather. I'm the housemaster's wife."

That explained the child, the dog, herself. Whatever was wrong with Billy, Rudolph decided instantly, it wasn't the fault of this healthy, agreeable woman.

"The boys'll be back from chapel any minute now," the woman said. "Don't you want to come into our place and have a drink, perhaps, while you're waiting?"

"I don't want to put you to any trouble," Rudolph said, but didn't protest further, as Mrs. Fairweather waved him in.

The room was large, comfortable, the furniture well worn, the books many. "My husband's at chapel, too," Mrs. Fairweather explained. "But I do think we have some sherry." A child cried from another room. "My youngest," Mrs. Fairweather said, "making an announcement." She poured the sherry hurriedly and said, "Excuse me," and went off to see what announcement her child was making. The cries stopped immediately. She came back, smoothing her hair, poured herself a sherry, too. "Do sit down, please."

There was an awkward pause. It occurred to Rudolph as he sat down that this woman, who had only met Billy a few months ago, must know him much better than himself, who was on a mission, unbriefed and flying blind, to rescue the boy. He should have asked Gretchen to read the letter that disturbed her so to him over the phone.

"He's a very nice boy," Mrs. Fairweather said, "Billy. So handsome and well behaved. We do get some wild ones, Mr. . . ." she hesitated.

"Jordache," Rudolph said.

"So we appreciate the ones who know their manners." She sipped at her sherry. Looking at her, Rudolph decided that Mr. Fairweather was a lucky man.

"His mother is worried about him," Rudolph said.

"Is she?" The response was too quick. Gretchen wasn't the only one who had noticed something.

"She got a letter from him this week. She said—well, of course, mothers are prone to exaggeration—but she said it sounded as though Billy is in despair." There was no sense in not revealing to this obviously level-headed and well-meaning woman what his errand was. "The word seems a little strong to me," he said, "but I've come to see what can be done. His mother's in California. And . . ." He was a little embarrassed now. "She remarried."

"That's not so uncommon around here," Mrs. Fairweather said. She laughed. "I don't mean about parents living in California. I mean the remarried."

"Her husband died several months ago," Rudolph said.

"Oh," Mrs. Fairweather said. "I'm so sorry. Perhaps that's why Billy—" She left the sentence unfinished.

"Have you observed anything in particular?" Rudolph asked.

The woman pushed at her short hair uncomfortably. "I'd prefer it if you talked to my husband. It's really his department."

"I'm certain you wouldn't say anything that your husband wouldn't agree to," Rudolph said. Without meeting the husband, he was sure that the wife would be less guarded, less defensive about the school, if indeed the school was at fault.

"Your glass is empty," Mrs. Fairweather said. She took it from him and refilled it.

"Is it his marks?" Rudolph asked. "Are any of the boys bullying him for some reason?"

"No." Mrs. Fairweather handed him the tiny glass of sherry. "His marks are fine and he doesn't seem to have any trouble keeping up. And we don't allow any bullying here." She shrugged. "He's a puzzling boy. I've talked it over several times with my husband and we've tried to sound him out. Without success. He—he's remote. He doesn't seem to connect with anybody. Not with any of the other boys. Or any of his teachers. His roommate has asked to be transferred to another house . . ."

"Do they fight?"

She shook her head. "No. The roommate says Billy just doesn't talk to him. Ever. About anything. He does his share of housekeeping neatly, he studies at the proper hours, he doesn't complain, but he barely answers yes or no when he's spoken to. Physically he's a strong boy, but he doesn't join in any of the games. He doesn't even throw a football around and during this season there're always dozens of boys playing pickup touch tackle games or just passing the ball back and forth in front of the house. And on Saturdays when we play other schools and the whole school is in the stands, he stays in his room and reads." As she spoke, her voice sounded just as troubled as Gretchen's when she had spoken over the phone about Billy.

"If he were a grown man, Mr. Jordache," Mrs. Fairweather said, "I'd be inclined to say he was suffering from melancholy. I know that's not very helpful . . ." She smiled apologetically. "It's a description, not a diagnosis. But it's the best my husband and I have been able to come up with. If you can find out anything specific, anything the school can do, we'll be most grateful."

The bells of the chapel were ringing far away across the campus and Rudolph could see the first boys crossing from the chapel porch.

"I wonder if you could tell me where Billy's room is," Rudolph said. "I'll wait for him there." Perhaps there would be some clues there that would prepare him for his meeting with the boy.

"It's on the third floor," Mrs. Fairweather said. "All the way down the corridor, the last door to the left."

Rudolph thanked her and left her with the two children and the setter. What a nice woman, he thought as he mounted the steps. There certainly had been nobody as good as that connected with his education. If she was worried about Billy, there was something to be worried about.

The door, like most of the doors along the corridor, was open. The room seemed to be divided by an invisible curtain. On one side the bed was rumpled and strewn with phonograph records. Books were piled on the floor beside the bed and there were pennants and pictures of girls and athletes torn from magazines pinned to the wall. On the other side, the bed was tightly made and there were no decorations on the wall. The only photographs on that side were on the neatly ordered small desk. They were separate ones of Gretchen and Burke. Gretchen was sitting in a deck chair in the garden of the house in California. The portrait of Burke was one that had been published in a magazine. There was no picture of Willie Abbott.

One book, open and face down, lay on the bed. Rudolph leaned over to see what it was. *The Plague*, by Camus. Peculiar reading for a fourteen-year-old boy and hardly designed to rescue him from melancholy.

If excessive neatness was a symptom of adolescent neurosis, Billy was neurotic. But Rudolph remembered how neat he had been at the same age and no one had considered him abnormal.

Somehow, though, the room oppressed him, and he didn't want to have to meet Billy's roommate, so he went downstairs and waited in front of the door. The sun was stronger now, and with the groups of boys, all shined up for chapel, advancing across the campus, the place no longer seemed prisonlike. Most of the boys were tall, much taller than the boys Rudolph had gone to school with. Increasing America. Everybody took it for granted that it was a good thing. But was it? The better to look down upon you, my dear.

He saw Billy at a distance. He was the only boy walking alone. He walked slowly, naturally, with his head up, nothing hangdog about him. Rudolph remembered how he had practiced walking himself at that age, keeping his shoulders still, trying to glide, making himself seem older, more graceful than his comrades. He still walked that way, but out of habit, not thinking about it.

"Hello, Rudy," Billy said, without smiling, as he came up to the front of the building. "Thanks for coming to visit me."

They shook hands. Billy had a strong, quick grasp. He still didn't have to shave, but his face was not babyish and his voice had already changed.

"I have to be up in Whitby this evening," Rudolph said, "and since I was going to be on the road anyway, I thought I'd drop in and have lunch with you. It's only a couple of hours out of the way. Not even that."

Billy eyed him levelly and Rudolph was sure that the boy knew that the visit wasn't as off-hand as all that.

"Is there a good restaurant around here?" Rudolph asked, quickly. "I'm starving."

"My father took me to lunch at a place that wasn't too bad," Billy said, "when he was up here the last time."

"When was that?"

"A month ago. He was going to come up last week, but he wrote that the man who was going to lend him the car had to go out of town at the last minute."

Rudolph wondered if originally Willie Abbott's picture had been on the neat desk, next to the photographs of Gretchen and Colin Burke and had been put away after that last letter.

"Do you have to do anything in your room or tell anybody you're going out to lunch with your uncle?"

"I have nothing to do," Billy said. "And I don't have to tell anybody anything."

Rudolph suddenly became conscious as they stood there, with boys passing them in a steady stream, laughing and fooling around and talking loudly, that Billy hadn't said hello to a single one of them and that no one had come up to him. It's as bad as Gretchen feared, he thought. Or worse.

He put his arm briefly around Billy's shoulder. There was no reaction. "Let's be off," he said. "You show me the road."

As he drove through the lovely school grounds, with the somber boy beside him, past the handsome buildings and playing fields, so intelligently and expensively designed to prepare young men for useful and happy lives, so carefully staffed with devoted men and women of the caliber of Mrs. Fairweather, Rudolph wondered how anyone dared to try to educate anybody.

"I know why the man didn't lend my father the car last week," Billy was saying as he went at his steak. "He backed into a tree getting out of the parking lot here when we had lunch together and crushed the fender. He had three martinis before lunch and a bottle of wine and two glasses of brandy after lunch."

The censorious young. Rudolph was glad he wasn't drinking anything but water.

"Maybe he was unhappy about something," he said. He was not there to destroy the possibility of love between father and son.

"I guess so. He's unhappy a lot of the time." Billy went on eating. Whatever he was suffering from had not impaired his appetite. The food was hearty American, steaks, lobster, clams, roast beef, hot biscuits, served by pretty waitresses in modest uniforms. The room was large and rambling, the tables were covered with red-checkered cloths and there were many groups from the school, five or six boys at a table with the parents of one of the students, who had invited his friends to take advantage of the parental visit. Rudolph wondered if one day he would claim a son of his own from a school and take him and his friends out for a similar lunch. If Jean said yes and married him, perhaps in fifteen years. What would he be like in fifteen years, what would she be like, what would his son be like? Withdrawn, taciturn, troubled, like Billy? Or open and gay, as the boys at the other tables seemed to be? Would schools like this still exist, meals like this still be served, fathers still drunkenly ram into trees at two o'clock in the afternoon? What risks the gentle women and comfortable fathers sitting proudly at table with their sons had run fifteen years ago, with the war just over and the atomic cloud still drifting across the skies of the planet.

Maybe, he thought, I will tell Jean I have reconsidered.

"How's the food at school?" he asked, just to break the long silence.

"Okay," Billy said.

"How're the boys?"

"Okay. Ah—not so okay. There's an awful lot of talk about what bigshots their fathers are, how they have lunch with the President and tell him how to run the country, how they go to Newport for the summertime, how they have horses at home, and how their sisters have debutante parties that cost twenty-five thousand dollars."

"What do you say when they talk like that?"

"I keep quiet." Billy's glance was hostile. "What am I supposed to say? My father lives in one room and he's been fired from three jobs in two years? Or should I tell them what a great driver he is after lunch?" Billy said all this in an even, uninflected conversational tone, alarmingly mature.

"What about your stepfather?"

"What about him? He's dead. And even before he died, there weren't six boys in the school who ever heard of him. They think people who do plays and make movies are some kind of freak."

"What about the teachers?" Rudolph asked, desperate to find one thing at least that the boy approved of.

"I don't have anything to do with them," Billy said, putting more butter on his baked potato. "I do my work and that's all."

"What's wrong, Billy?" It was time now to be direct. He did not know the boy well enough to be indirect.

"My mother asked you to come here, didn't she?" Billy looked at him shrewdly, challengingly.

"If you must know—yes."

"I'm sorry if I worried her," Billy said. "I shouldn't have sent that letter."

"Of course, you should have sent the letter. What is it, Billy?"

"I don't know." The boy had stopped eating by now and Rudolph could see that he was fighting to control his voice. "Everything. I feel like I am going to die if I have to stay here."

"Of course you won't die," Rudolph said sharply.

"No, I guess not. I just *feel* as though I am." Billy was petulant, juvenile, for a moment. "That's a whole different thing, isn't it? But feeling is real, too, isn't it?"

"Yes, it is," Rudolph admitted. "Come on. Talk."

"This is no place for me," Billy said. "I don't want to be trained to grow up into what all these fellows are going to grow up into. I see their fathers. A lot of them went to this same school twenty-five years ago. They're like their kids, only older, telling the President what to do, not knowing that Colin Burke was a great man, not even knowing he's dead. I don't belong here, Rudy. My father doesn't belong here. Colin Burke wouldn't have belonged here. If they keep me here, by the end of four years they'll make me belong here and I don't want that. I don't know . . ." He shook his head despondently, his fair hair swinging over the high forehead he had inherited from his father. "I guess you think I'm just not making any sense. I guess you think I'm just another homesick kid griping because he wasn't elected captain of the team or something . . ."

"I don't think that at all, Billy. I don't know whether you're right or not, but you certainly have figured out your reasons." Homesick, he thought. The word had reared up from the sentence. Which home?

"Compulsory chapel," Billy said. "Making believe I'm a Christian seven times a week. I'm no Christian, Mom isn't a Christian, my father's not a Christian, Colin wasn't a Christian, why do I have to take the rap for the whole family, listen to all those sermons? Be upright, have clean thoughts, don't think about sex. Our Lord Jesus died to cleanse our sins. How would you like to sit through crap like that seven times a week?"

"Not much." The boy certainly had a point there. Atheists did have a religious responsibility toward their children.

"And money," Billy said, his voice low but intense, as a waitress passed nearby. "Where's the money going to come for my big fat education now that Colin's dead?"

"Don't worry about that," Rudolph said. "I've told your mother I'd take care of it."

Billy looked at him malevolently, as though Rudolph had just confessed that he had been plotting against him. "I don't like you enough, Uncle Rudy," he said, "to take that from you."

Rudolph was shaken, but he managed to speak calmly. After all, Billy was only fourteen, only a child. "Why don't you like me well enough?"

"Because you belong here," Billy said. "Send your own son here."

"I won't comment on that."

"I'm sorry I said it. But I meant it." There was a pressure of tears in the long-lashed, blue, Abbott eyes.

"I admire you for saying it," Rudolph said. "By the time boys reach your age they usually have learned to dissemble for rich uncles."

"What am I doing here, on the other side of the country, when my mother is sitting alone, all by herself, night after night, crying?" Billy went on, in a rush. "A man like Colin is killed and what am I supposed to be doing—cheering at a silly football game or listening to some Boy Scout in a black suit telling us Jesus saves. I'll tell you something—" The tears were rolling down his cheeks now and he was mopping them with a handkerchief, but speaking fiercely at the same time. "If you don't get me out of here, I'm going to run away. And, somehow, I'm going to turn up in that house where my mother is, and any way I can help her I'm going to help her."

"All right," Rudolph said. "We can stop talking about it. I don't know what I can do, but I promise you I'll do something. Fair enough?"

Billy nodded miserably, mopped some more, put the handkerchief away.

"Now let's finish our lunch," Rudolph said. He didn't eat much more, but watched Billy clean his plate, then order apple pie à la mode and clean that plate. Fourteen was an all-absorbing age. Tears, death, pity, apple pie, and ice cream mingled without shame.

After lunch, in the car driving over to the school, Rudolph said,

"Go up to your room. Pack a bag. Then come down and wait for me in the car."

He watched the boy go into the building, neat in his Sunday go-to-chapel suit, then got out of the car and followed. Behind him, a touch-tackle game was in progress on the drying lawn, boys crying, "Throw it to me, throw it to me," in one of the hundreds of games of their youth that Billy never joined.

The Common Room off the hallway was full of boys playing Ping-Pong, sitting over chess boards, reading magazines, listening to the Giant game on a transistor radio. From upstairs came the roar of a folk-singing group from another radio. Politely, the boys around the Ping-Pong table made way for him, older man, as he walked across the room, toward the doorway of the Fairweathers' apartment. They seemed like fine boys, good looking, healthy, well mannered, content, the hope of America. If he were a father he would have been happy to see his own son in this company this Sunday afternoon. But among them, his nephew, misfitted, felt that he was going to die. The Constitutional right to be a misfit.

He rang the bell to the Fairweather apartment and the door was opened by a tall, slightly stooping man, with a lock of hair hanging over his forehead, a healthy complexion, a ready and welcoming smile. What nerves a man must have to be able to live in a house full of boys like this.

"Mr. Fairweather?" Rudolph said.

"Yes?" Amiable, easy.

"I hate to disturb you, but I'd like to talk to you for a moment. I'm Billy Abbott's uncle. I was . . ."

"Oh, yes," Fairweather said. He extended his hand. "My wife told me you paid her a visit before lunch. Won't you please come in?" He led the way down a book-lined hallway into the book-lined living room, the noise from the Common Room miraculously extinguished with the closing of the door. Sanctuary from youth. Insulation from the young by books. Rudolph wondered if perhaps when Denton had offered him the post at the college, the book-lined life, he had made the wrong choice.

Mrs. Fairweather was sitting on the couch, drinking a cup of coffee, her child sitting on the floor leaning against her knee, turning the pages of a picture book, the setter sprawled, asleep, against her. Mrs. Fairweather smiled at him, raised her cup in greeting.

They can't be *that* happy, Rudolph thought, conscious of jealousy.

"Please sit down," Fairweather said. "Would you like some coffee?"

"No, thank you, I've just had some. And I can only stay a minute." Rudolph sat, stiffly, feeling awkward because he was an uncle, not a father.

Fairweather sat comfortably next to his wife. He was wearing green-stained tennis shoes and a wool shirt, making the most of Sunday afternoon. "Did you have a good talk with Billy?" he asked. There was a little pleasant holdover of the South in his voice, gentlemanly Tidewater Virginia.

"I had a talk," Rudolph said. "I don't know how good it was. Mr. Fairweather, I want to take Billy away with me. For a few days at least. I think it's absolutely necessary."

The Fairweathers exchanged glances.

"It's as bad as that, is it?" the man said.

"Pretty bad."

"We've done everything we can," Fairweather said, but without apology.

"I realize that," Rudolph said. "It's just that Billy's a certain kind of boy, certain things have happened to him—in the past, recently . . ." He wondered if the Fairweathers had ever heard of Colin Burke, mourned the vanished talent. "There's no need to go into it. A boy's reasons can be fantasy, but his feelings can be horribly real."

"So you want to take Billy away?" Mr. Fairweather said.

"Yes."

"When?"

"In ten minutes."

"Oh, dear," Mrs. Fairweather said.

"For how long?" Fairweather asked calmly.

"I don't know. A few days. A month. Perhaps permanently."

There was an uncomfortable silence. From outside the window, thinly, came the sound of a boy calling signals in the touch-tackle game, 22, 45, 38, *Hut!* Fairweather stood up and went over to the table where the coffee pot was standing and poured himself a cup. "You're sure you don't want some, Mr. Jordache?"

Rudolph shook his head.

"The Christmas holidays come in just two and a half weeks," Fairweather said. "And the term-end examinations begin in a few days. Don't you think it would be wiser to wait until then?"

"I don't think it would be wise for me to leave here this afternoon without Billy," Rudolph said.

"Have you spoken to the headmaster?" Fairweather asked.

"No."

"I think it would be advisable to consult with him," Fairweather said. "I don't really have the authority to . . ."

"The less fuss we make, the fewer the people who talk to Billy," Rudolph said, "the better it will be for the boy. Believe me."

Again the Fairweathers exchanged glances.

"Charles," Mrs. Fairweather said to her husband, "I think we could explain to the headmaster."

Fairweather sipped thoughtfully at his coffee, still standing at the table. A ray of pale sunlight came through the windows, outlining him against the bookshelves behind him. Healthy, pondering man, head of family, doctor of young souls.

"I suppose we could," he said. "I suppose we could explain. You *will* call me in the next day or two and tell me what's been decided, won't you?"

"Of course."

Fairweather sighed. "There're so many defeats in this quiet profession, Mr. Jordache," he said. "Tell Billy he's welcome to come back any time he wishes. He's bright enough to make up any time he's lost."

"I'll tell him," Rudolph said. "Thank you. Thank you both for everything."

Fairweather escorted him back along the hallway, opened the door into the turmoil of boys, didn't smile as he shook Rudolph's hand and closed the door behind him.

As Rudolph drove away from the school, Billy, in the front seat beside him, said, "I never want to see this place again." He didn't ask where they were going.

It was half-past five when they got to Whitby and the street lights were on in the wintry darkness. Billy had slept a good deal of the way. Rudolph dreaded the moment when he would have to introduce his mother to her grandson. "Spawn of the harlot," might not be beyond the powers of his mother's rhetoric. But he had the appointment with Calderwood after the Calderwood Sunday supper, which would be over by seven, and it would have been impossible to take Billy back to New York and then arrive in Whitby on time. And even if he had had the time to drive the boy down to the city, to whom could he have turned him over? Willie Abbott? Gretchen had asked him to bypass Willie in the matter and he had done so and there was no having it both ways. And after what Billy had said about his father at lunch, being put in Willie's alcoholic care could hardly have seemed like much of an improvement over staying in school.

Briefly, Rudolph had considered putting Billy in a hotel, but had discarded the idea as too cold-blooded. This was no night for the boy to spend alone in a hotel. Also, it would have been cowardly. He would have to face the old lady down.

Still, when he awakened the boy as he stopped the car in front of the house, and led him through the door, he was relieved to see that his mother was not in the living room. He looked down the hallway and saw that her door was closed. That meant she had probably had a fight with Martha and was sulking. He could confront her alone and prepare her for her first meeting with her grandson.

He went into the kitchen with Billy. Martha was sitting at the table reading a newspaper and there was a smell of something cooking coming from the oven. Martha was not fat, as his mother spitefully described her, but in fact was an angular, virginal, gaunt woman of fifty, sure of the world's displeasure, anxious to give back as good as she got.

"Martha," he said, "this is my nephew, Billy. He's going to stay with us for a few days. He's tired and he needs a bath and some hot food. Do you think you can give him a hand? He'll sleep in the guest room, next to mine."

Martha smoothed out the newspaper on the kitchen table. "Your mother said you weren't going to be in for dinner."

"I'm not. I'm going out again."

"Then there'll be enough for him," Martha said. "She—" with a savage gesture of the head toward the part of the house inhabited by his mother—"she didn't say nothing about no nephews."

"She doesn't know yet," Rudolph said, trying to make his voice sound cheery, for Billy's sake.

"That'll make her day," Martha said. "Finding out about nephews."

Billy stood quietly to one side, testing the atmosphere, not liking it.

Martha stood up, her face no more disapproving, really, than usual, but how could Billy know that? "Come on, young man," Martha said. "I guess we can make room for a skinny little thing like you."

Rudolph was surprised at what was, in Martha's vocabulary, practically a tender invitation.

"Go ahead, Billy," he said. "I'll be up to see you in a little while."

Billy followed Martha out of the kitchen, hesitantly. Attached now to his uncle, any separation was full of risk.

Rudolph heard their footsteps going up the stairs. His mother would be alerted that someone strange was in the house. She recognized his tread and invariably called out to him when he was on his way to his room.

He got some ice out of the refrigerator. He needed a drink after the almost teetotaling day and before the meeting with his mother. He carried the ice out into the living room and was pleased to find that the living room was warm. Brad must have sent over an engineer yesterday for the furnace. His mother's tongue would at least not be honed by cold.

He made himself a bourbon and water, with plenty of ice, sank into a chair, put his feet up, and sipped at his drink, enjoying it. He was pleased with the room, not too heavily furnished, with modern, leather chairs, globular glass lamps, Danish wood tables and simple, neutral-colored curtains, all of it making a carefully thought-out contrast with the low-beamed ceiling and the small eighteenth-century, square-paned windows. His mother complained that it looked like a dentist's waiting room.

He finished his drink slowly, in no hurry for the scene ahead of him. Finally, he pushed himself up out of the chair, went down the hallway, and knocked on the door. His mother's bedroom was on the ground floor so that she wouldn't have to manage the stairs. Although, now, since the two operations, one for phlebitis, the second for cataracts, she got around fairly well. Complainingly, but well.

"Who is it?" The voice was sharp behind the closed door.

"It's me, Mom," Rudolph said. "You asleep?"

"Not any more," she said.

He pushed the door open.

"Not with people tramping up and down like elephants all over the house," she said from the bed. She was propped up against lacy pillows, wearing a pink bed jacket that was trimmed with what seemed to be some kind of pinkish fur. She was wearing the thick glasses that the doctor had prescribed for her after the operation. They permitted her to read, watch television, and go to the movies, but they gave a wild, blank, soulless stare to her hugely magnified eyes.

Doctors had done wonders for her since they had moved to the new house. Before that, when they were still living over the store, although Rudolph had pleaded with his mother to undergo the various operations he was sure she needed, she had adamantly refused. "I will be nobody's charity patient," she had said, "being experimented on by interns who shouldn't be allowed to put a knife to a dog." Rudolph's protestations had fallen then on deaf ears. While they lived in the poor apartment nothing could convince her that she was not poor and doomed to suffer the fate of the poor once confided to the cold care of an institution. But once they made the move and Martha read the write-ups in the newspapers about Rudy's successes to her and she had ridden in the new car that Rudy had bought, she went boldly into surgery, after ascertaining that the men who treated her were the best and most expensive available.

She had been literally rejuvenated, resuscitated, brought back from the lip of the grave, by her belief in money. Rudy had thought that decent medical care would make his mother's last years a little more comfortable. Instead, they had almost made her young. With Martha glooming at the wheel, she now went out in Rudy's car whenever it was free; she frequented beauty parlors (her hair was almost blue and waved); patronized the town's movie houses; called for taxis; attended Mass; played bridge with newly found church acquaintances twice a week; fed priests on nights when Rudy was not at home; had bought a new copy of Gone With the Wind, as well as all the novels of Frances Parkinson Keyes.

A wide variety of clothes and hats for all occasions were stored in the wardrobe in her room, which was as full of furniture as a small antique shop, gilt desks, a chaise longue, a dressing table with ten different flasks of French perfume on it. For the first time in her life her lips were heavily rouged. She looked ghastly, Rudolph thought, with her painted face and gaudy dresses, but she was infinitely more alive than before. If this was the way she was making up for the dreadful years of her childhood and the long agony of her marriage, it was not up to him to deprive her of her toys.

He had played with the idea of moving her to an apartment of her own in town, with Martha to tend her, but he could not bear the thought of the expression on her face at the moment when he would take her through the door of the house for the last time, stricken by the ingratitude of a son whom she had loved above all things in her life, a son whose shirts she had ironed at midnight after twelve hours on her feet in the store, a son for whom she had sacrificed youth, husband, friends, her other two children.

So she stayed on. Rudolph was not one to miss payment on his debts.

"Who is it upstairs? You've brought a woman into the house," she said accusingly.

"I've never brought a woman into the house, as you put it, Mom," Rudolph said, "although if I wanted to, I don't see why I shouldn't."

"Your father's blood," his mother said. Dreadful charge.

"It's your grandson. I brought him home from school."

"That was no six-year-old boy going up the staircase," she said. "I have ears."

"It isn't Thomas's son," Rudolph said. "It's Gretchen's son."

"I will not hear that name," she said. She put her hands to her ears. Television-watching had left its mark on her gestures.

Rudolph sat on the edge of his mother's bed and gently took her hands down, holding them. I have been lax, he thought. This conversation should have been held years ago.

"Now listen to me, Mom," he said. "He's a very good boy and he's in trouble and . . ."

"I won't have that whore's brat in my house," she said.

"Gretchen is not a whore," Rudolph said. "Her son is not a brat. And this is not your house."

"I was waiting for the day you would finally say those words," she said.

Rudolph ignored the invitation to melodrama. "He's going to stay only a few days," he said, "and he needs kindness and attention and I'm going to give it to him and Martha's going to give it to him and you're going to give it to him."

"What will I ever tell Father McDonnell?" His mother looked, eyes magnified and blank, up toward Heaven, before whose gates stood, theoretically, Father McDonnell.

"You're going to tell Father McDonnell that you have finally learned the virtue of Christian charity," Rudolph said.

"Ah," she said, "you're a fine one to talk about Christian charity. Have you ever seen the inside of a church?"

"I haven't got time to argue," Rudolph said. "Calderwood is expecting me any minute now. I'm telling you how you're going to behave with the boy."

"I will not allow him in my presence," she said, quoting from some portion of her favorite reading. "I will close my door and Martha will serve my meals on a tray."

"You can do that if you want, Mom," Rudolph said quietly. "But if you do, I'm cutting you off. No more car, no more bridge parties, no more charge accounts, no more beauty parlors, no more dinners for Father McDonnell. Think about it." He stood up. "I've got to go now. Martha's prepared to give Billy dinner. I suggest you join them."

Tears as he closed his mother's bedroom door. What a cheap way to threaten an old lady, he thought. Why didn't she just die? Gracefully, unwaved, unrinsed, unrouged.

There was a grandfather's clock in the hallway and he saw that he had time to phone Gretchen if he made an immediate connection to California. He put in the call and made himself another drink while waiting for the call to come through. Calderwood might smell the liquor on his breath and disapprove, but he was past that, too. As he sipped his drink he thought of what he had been doing the day before at just this hour. Entwined in twilit warmth in the soft bed, the red-wool stockings strewn on the floor, the sweet warm breath mingled with his, rum and lemon. Had his mother once lain sweetly in a lover's arms on a cold December afternoon, clothes carelessly discarded in lover's haste? The image refused to materialize. Would Jean, old, one day lie in a fussed-up bed, eyes staring behind thick glasses, old lips rouged in scorn and avarice? Better not to think about it.

The phone rang and it was Gretchen. He explained the afternoon as quickly as he could and said that Billy was safely with him and that if she thought best he would put Billy on a plane to Los Angeles in two or three days, unless, of course, she wanted to come East.

"No," she said. "Put him on a plane."

A tricky little sense of pleasure. An excuse to get to New York on Tuesday or Wednesday. Jean.

"I don't have to tell you how grateful I am, Rudy," Gretchen said.

"Nonsense," he said. "When I have a son I will expect you to take care of him. I'll let you know what plane he's on. And maybe one day soon, I'll come out and visit you."

The lives of others.

Calderwood himself answered the door when Rudolph rang. He was dressed for Sunday, even though his Sabbath duties were behind him, dark suit with vest, white shirt, somber tie, his high, black shoes. There never was enough light in the frugal Calderwood house and it was too dark for Rudolph to see what sort of expression Calderwood had on his face as he said, neutrally, "Come in, Rudy. You're a little late."

"Sorry, Mr. Calderwood," Rudolph said. He followed the old man, who walked heavily now, a certain measured number of steps between him and the grave, to be economized, doled out.

Calderwood led him into the somber oak-paneled room he called his study, with a big mahogany desk and cracked oak and leather easy chairs. The glassed bookcases were filled with files, records of bills paid, twenty-year-old transactions that Calderwood still didn't trust putting in the modest basement vaults where the ordinary business files were kept, open to any clerk's prying eye.

"Sit down." Calderwood gestured toward one of the leather and oak easy chairs. "You've been drinking, Rudy," he said mournfully. "My sons-in-law, I regret to say, are also drinkers." Calderwood's two older daughters had married some time before, one a man from Chicago, another a man from Arizona. Rudolph had the feeling that the girls had picked their mates not out of love, but geography, to get away from their father.

"That isn't what I brought you here to talk about though," Calderwood said. "I wanted to speak to you man-to-man, when Mrs. Calderwood and Virginia were not on the premises. They have gone to the movie show and we can speak freely." It was not like the old man to indulge in elaborate preliminaries. He seemed ill at ease, which also was not like him.

Rudolph waited, conscious that Calderwood was fiddling with objects on his desk, a paper opener, an old-fashioned inkstand.

"Rudolph . . ." Calderwood cleared his throat portentously. "I'm surprised at your behavior."

"My behavior?" For a wild instant Rudolph thought that Calderwood had somehow found out about himself and Jean.

"Yes. It's not like you at all, Rudy." The tone was sorrowful now. "You've been like a son to me. Better than a son. Truthful. Open. Trustworthy."

The old Eagle Scout, covered with merit badges, Rudolph thought, waiting, wary.

"Suddenly something has come over you, Rudy," Calderwood continued. "You have been operating behind my back. With no apparent reason. You know you could have come to the door of my house and rung my bell and I would have been glad to welcome you."

"Mr. Calderwood," Rudolph said, thinking, old age here, too. "I don't know what you're talking about."

"I am talking about the affections of my daughter Virginia, Rudy. Don't deny."

"Mr. Calderwood . . ."

"You have been tampering with her affections. Gratuitously. You have stolen where you could have demanded." There was anger in the voice now.

"I assure you, Mr. Calderwood, that I haven't . . ."

"It's not like you to lie, Rudy."

"I'm not lying. I don't know . . ."

"What if I told you the girl has confessed everything?" Calderwood boomed.

"There's nothing to confess." Rudolph felt helpless, and at the same time like laughing.

"Your story differs from my daughter's. She has told her mother that she is in love with you and that she intends to go to New York City to learn to be a secretary to be free to see you."

"Holy God!" Rudolph said.

"We do not use the name of God in vain in this house, Rudy."

"Mr. Calderwood, the most I've ever done with Virginia," Rudolph said, "is buy her a lunch or an ice cream soda when I've bumped into her at the store."

"You've bewitched her," Calderwood said. "She's in tears five times a week about you. A pure young girl doesn't indulge in antics like that unless she's been led on artfully by a man."

The Puritan inheritance has finally exploded, Rudolph thought. Land on Plymouth Rock, hang around for a couple of centuries in the bracing air of New England, prosper, and go crackers. It was all too much for one day—Billy, the school, his mother, now this.

"I want to know what you intend to do about it, young man." When Calderwood said young man, he was apt to be dangerous. Instantaneously, Rudolph's mind flashed over the possibilities—he was well entrenched, but the final power in the business lay with Calderwood. There could be a fight, but in the long run Calderwood could get him out. That silly bitch Virginia.

"I don't know what you want me to do, sir." He was stalling for time.

"It's very simple," Calderwood said. Obviously he had been thinking about the problem ever since Mrs. Calderwood had come to him with the happy news about their daughter's shame. "Marry Virginia. But you must promise not to move down to New York." He was demented about New York City, Rudolph decided. Haunt of evil. "I will make you a full partner with me. Upon my death, after I make adequate provisions for my daughters and Mrs. Calderwood, you will get the bulk of my shares. You will have voting control. I shall never bring up this conversation again and there will be no reproaches. In fact, I shall put it out of my mind forever. Rudy, I couldn't be happier than to have a boy like you in the family. It has been my fondest wish for years and both Mrs. Calderwood and I were disappointed when we invited you to partake of the hospitality of our home that you seemed to take no interest in any of our daughters, although they are all pretty, in their way, and well brought up, and if I may say so, independently wealthy. I have no idea why you thought you couldn't approach me directly when you had made your choice."

"I haven't made any choice," Rudolph said distractedly. "Virginia's a charming girl, and she'll make the best of wives, I'm sure. I had no inkling she had any interest in me whatever . . ."

"Rudy," Calderwood said sternly. "I've known you a long time. You're one of the smartest men I've ever met. And you have the nerve to sit there and tell me . . ."

"Yes, I do." The hell with the business. "I'll tell you what I'll do. I'll sit right here with you and wait until Mrs. Calderwood and Virginia come home and I'll ask her point-blank in front of both of you whether I've ever made any advances to her, if I've ever as much as tried to kiss her." It was all pure farce but he had to go on with it. "If she says yes, she's lying, but I don't care. I'll walk out right now and you can do whatever you want with your goddamn business and your goddamn stocks and your goddamn daughter."

"Rudy!" Calderwood's voice was shocked, but Rudolph could see that he had suddenly become uncertain of his ground.

"If she'd had the sense to tell me long ago that she loved me," Rudolph went on swiftly pressing his advantage, reckless now, "maybe something would have come of it. I *do* like her. But it's too late now. Yesterday evening, if you must know, in New York City, I asked another girl to marry me."

"New York City," Calderwood said, resentfully. "Always New York City."

"Well, do you want me to sit here and wait until the ladies come home?" Rudolph crossed his arms menacingly.

"This could cost you a lot of money, Rudy," Calderwood said.

"Okay, it could cost me a lot of money." Rudolph said it firmly, but he could feel the sick quiver inside his stomach.

"And this—this lady in New York," Calderwood said, sounding plaintive. "Has she accepted you?"

"No."

"Love, by God!" The insanity of the tender emotion, the cross-purposes of desire, the sheer anarchy of sex, was too much for Calderwood's piety. "In two months you'll forget her and then maybe you and Virginia . . ."

"She said no for yesterday," Rudolph said. "But she's thinking it over. Well, should I wait for Mrs. Calderwood and Virginia?" He still had his arms crossed. It kept his hands from trembling.

Calderwood pushed the inkstand irritably back to the edge of the desk. "Obviously you're telling the truth, Rudy," Calderwood said. "I don't know what possessed my foolish daughter. Ah—I know what my wife will say—I brought her up all wrong. I made her shy. I overprotected her. If I were to tell you some of the arguments I've had with that woman in this house. It was different when I was a boy, I'll tell you that. Girls didn't go around telling their mothers they were in love with people who never even looked at them. The damned movies. They rot women's brains. No, you don't have to wait. I'll handle it alone. Go ahead. I have to compose myself."

Rudolph stood up and Calderwood with him. "Do you want some advice?" Rudolph asked.

"You're always giving me advice," Calderwood said petulantly. "When I dream it's always about you whispering in my ear. For years. Sometimes I wish you'd never showed up that summer at the store. What advice?"

"Let Virginia go down to New York and learn to be a secretary and leave her alone for a year or two."

"Great," Calderwood said bitterly. "You can say that. You have no daughters. I'll see you to the door."

At the door, he put his hand on Rudolph's arm. "Rudy," he said, pleading, "if the lady in New York says no, you'll think about Virginia, won't you? Maybe she's an idiot, but I can't stand to see her unhappy."

"Don't worry, Mr. Calderwood," Rudolph said ambiguously, and went down to his car.

Mr. Calderwood was still standing in the open doorway, lit by the frugal hall light, as Rudolph drove away.

He was hungry, but decided to wait before going to a restaurant for dinner. He wanted to return to the house and see how Billy was doing. He also wanted to tell him that he had talked to Gretchen and that he would be going out to California in two or three days. The boy would sleep better after hearing that news, the specter of the school no longer hanging over him.

When he opened the front door with his key he heard voices in the kitchen. He went silently through the living and dining rooms and listened outside the kitchen door. "There's one thing I like to

see in a growing boy—" Rudolph recognized his mother's voice—
"and that's a good appetite. I'm happy to see you appreciate food,
Billy. Martha, give him another slice of meat and some more salad.
No back talk, Billy, about not eating salad. In my house, all children
eat salad."

Holy God! Rudolph thought.

"There's another thing I like to see in a boy, Billy," his mother
went on. "Old as I am, and I should be beyond such feminine
weaknesses—and that's good looks combined with good manners."
The voice was coquettish, cooing. "And you know whom you remind
me of—and I never said so to his face for fear of spoiling him—
there's nothing worse than a vain child—you remind me of your
Uncle Rudolph and he was by common agreement the handsomest
boy in town and he grew up into the handsomest young man."

"Everybody says I look like my father," Billy said, with the
bluntness of his fourteen years, but not aggressively. From his tone
he was obviously feeling at home.

"I have not had the good fortune ever to meet your father," the
mother said, a slight chill in her speech. "No doubt there must be a
certain resemblance here and there, but fundamentally you resemble
my branch of the family, especially Rudolph. Doesn't he, Martha?"

"I can see some signs," Martha said. She was not out to give the
mother a perfect Sunday night supper.

"Around the eyes," the mother said. "And the intelligent mouth.
In spite of the difference in the hair. I never think hair makes too
much difference. There's not much character in hair."

Rudolph pushed the door and went into the kitchen. Billy was
seated at one end of the table, flanked by the two women. Hair flattened down wet after his bath, Billy looked shining clean and smiling as he packed into his food. The mother had put on a sober-
brown dress and was consciously playing grandmother. Martha
looked less grumpy than usual, her mouth less thin, welcoming a bit
of youth into the household.

"Everything all right?" Rudolph asked. "They giving you enough
to eat?"

"The food's great," Billy said. There was no trace of the agony of
the afternoon in his face.

"I do hope you like chocolate pudding for dessert, Billy," the
mother said, hardly looking up for a moment at Rudolph, standing
at the door. "Martha makes the most delicious chocolate pudding."

"Yeah," Billy said. "I really like it."

"It was Rudolph's favorite dessert, too. Wasn't it, Rudolph?"

"Uhuh," he said. He didn't remember ever getting it more than once a year and he certainly didn't remember ever remarking on it, but this was not the night to halt the flights of his mother's fancy. She had even refrained from putting on rouge, the better to play the role of grandmother and she deserved some marks for that, too.

"Billy," Rudolph said, "I spoke to your mother."

Billy looked at him gravely, fearing a blow. "What did she say?"

"She's waiting for you. I'm going to put you on a plane Tuesday or Wednesday. As soon as I can break away from the office here and take you down to New York."

The boy's lips trembled, but there was no fear that he was going to cry. "How did she sound?" he asked.

"Delighted that you're coming out," Rudolph said.

"That poor girl," his mother said. "The life she's led. The blows of fortune."

Rudolph didn't allow himself to look at her.

"Though it's a shame, Billy," she continued, "that now that we've found each other you can't spend a little time with your old grandmother. Still, now that the ice has been broken, perhaps I can come out and visit you. Wouldn't that be a nice idea, Rudolph?"

"Very nice."

"California," she said. "I've always wanted to see it. The climate is kind to old bones. And from what I hear, it's a virtual paradise. Before I die . . . Martha, I think Billy is ready for the chocolate pudding."

"Yes, ma'am," Martha said, rising from the table.

"Rudolph," the mother said, "don't you want a bite? Join the happy family circle?"

"No, thanks." The last thing he wanted was to join the happy family circle. "I'm not hungry."

"Well, I'm off to bed," she said. She stood up heavily. "Must get my beauty sleep at my age, you know. But before you go upstairs to sleep you'll come in and give your grandmother a great big goodnight kiss, won't you, Billy?"

"Yes, ma'am," Billy said.

"Grandma."

"Grandma," Billy said obediently.

She swept out of the room. One last triumphant glare at Rudolph. Lady Macbeth, the blood behind her, undetected, now splendidly running a nursery for precocious children in a warmer country than Scotland.

Mothers should not be exposed, Rudolph thought, as he said, "Good night, Mom, sleep well." They should be shot out of hand.

He left the house, ate dinner at a restaurant, tried to call Jean in New York to find out what night she could see him, Tuesday or Wednesday. There was no answer at her apartment.

Chapter 4

Draw the curtains at sunset. Do not sit in the evenings and look out at the lights of the city spread below you. Colin did so, with you at his side, because he said it was the view he liked most in the world, America at its best at night.

Do not wear black. Mourning is a private matter.

Do not write emotional letters in answer to letters of condolence from friends or from strangers using words like genius or unforgettable or generous or strength of character. Answer promptly and politely. No more.

Do not weep in front of your son.

Do not accept invitations to dinner from friends or colleagues of Colin who do not wish you to suffer alone.

When a problem comes up do not reach for the phone to call Colin's office. The office is closed.

Resist the temptation to tell the people who are now in charge of finishing Colin's last picture how Colin wanted it to be done.

Give no interviews, write no articles. Do not be a source of anecdote. Do not be a great man's widow. Do not speculate on what he would have done had he lived.

Commemorate no birthdays or anniversaries.

Discourage retrospective showings, festivals, laudatory meetings to which you have been invited.

Attend no previews or opening nights.

When planes fly low overhead, leaving the airport, do not remember voyages you have taken together.

Do not drink alone or in company, whatever the temptation. Avoid sleeping pills. Bear in unassuaged silence.

Clear the desk in the living room of its pile of books and scripts. They are now a lie.

Refuse, politely, the folios of clippings, reviews of plays and films your husband has directed, which the studio has kindly had made up in tooled-leather covers. Do not read the eulogies of critics.

Leave only one hasty snapshot of husband on view in house. Pack all other photographs in a box and put them away in the cellar.

Do not, when thinking about preparing dinner, arrange a menu that would please husband. (Stone crabs, chili, piccata of veal piz-zaiola.)

When dressing, do not look at the clothes hanging in the closet and say, "He likes me in that one."

Be calm and ordinary with your son. Do not overreact when he gets into trouble at school, when he is robbed by a group of hood-lums or comes home with a bloody nose. Do not cling to him or allow him to cling to you. When he is invited with friends to go swimming or to a ball game or to a movie, tell him, "Of course. I have an awful lot of things to do about the house and I'll get them done faster if I'm alone."

Do not be a father. The things your son must do with men let him do with men. Do not try to entertain him, because you fear it must be dull for him living alone with a grieving woman on top of a hill far away from the centers where boys amuse themselves.

Do not think about sex. Do not be surprised that you do think about it.

Be incredulous when ex-husband calls and emotionally suggests that he would like to remarry you. If the marriage that was founded on love could not last, the marriage based on death would be a dis-aster.

Neither avoid nor seek out places where you have been happy to-gether.

Garden, sunbathe, wash dishes, keep a neat house, help son with homework, do not show that you expect more of him than other par-ents expect of other sons. Be prompt to take him to the corner where he picks up the school bus, be prompt to meet the bus when it re-turns. Refrain from kissing him excessively.

Be understanding about your own mother, whom son now says he wishes to visit during the summer vacation. Say, "Summer is a long time off."

Be careful about being caught alone with men whom you have admired or Colin has admired and who admire you and have been known to admire many other women in this town of excess women, and whose sympathy will skillfully turn into something else in three or four sessions and who will then try to lay you and will probably succeed. Be careful about being caught alone with men who have admired Colin or Colin had admired and whose sympathy is genuinely only that but who will eventually want to lay you, too. They, too, will probably succeed.

Do not build your life on your son. It is the most certain way to lose him.

Keep busy. But at what?

"Are you sure you've looked everywhere, Mrs. Burke?" Mr. Greenfield asked. He was the lawyer Colin's agent had sent her to. Or rather, one of a huge battery of lawyers, all of whose names were on the door of the suite of offices in the elegant building in Beverly Hills. All of the names on the door seemed equally concerned with her problem, equally intelligent, equally well dressed, equally urbane, smiling, and sympathetic, equally costly, and equally helpless.

"I've turned the house upside down, Mr. Greenfield," Gretchen said. "I've found hundreds of scripts, hundreds of bills, some of them unpaid, but no will."

Mr. Greenfield almost sighed, but refrained. He was a youngish man in a button-down collar, to show that he had gone to law school in the East, and a bright bow tie, to show that he now lived in California. "Do you have any knowledge of any safety deposit boxes that your husband might have had?"

"No," she said. "And I don't believe he had any. He was careless about things like that."

"I'm afraid he was careless about quite a few things," Mr. Greenfield said. "Not leaving a will . . ."

"How did he know he was going to die?" she demanded. "He never had a sick day in his life."

"It makes it easier if one thinks about all the possibilities," Mr. Greenfield said. Gretchen was sure he had been drawing up wills for himself since he was twenty-one. Mr. Greenfield finally permitted himself the withheld sigh. "For our part, we've explored every avenue. Incredibly enough, your husband never employed *any* lawyer. He allowed his agent to draw up his contracts and from what his agent said, most of the time he hardly bothered to read them. And when he allowed the ex-Mrs. Burke to divorce him, he permitted *her* lawyer to write the divorce settlement."

Gretchen had never met the ex-Mrs. Burke, but now, after Colin's death, she was beginning to get to know her very well. She had been an airline hostess and a model. She had an abiding fondness for money and believed that to work for it was unfeminine and repugnant. She had been getting twenty thousand dollars a year as alimony and at the time of Colin's death had been starting proceedings to get it raised to forty thousand dollars a year because Colin's income had risen steeply since he had come to Hollywood. She was living with a young man, in places like New York, Palm Beach, and Sun Valley, when she wasn't traveling abroad, but sensibly refused to marry the young man, since one of the clauses that Colin *had* managed to insert in the divorce settlement would cut off the alimony on her remarriage. She or her lawyers seemed to have a wide knowledge of the law, both State and Federal, and immediately after the funeral, which she had not attended, she had had Colin's bank deposits impounded and had secured an injunction against the estate to prevent Gretchen from selling the house.

Since Gretchen had had no separate bank account and had merely asked Colin for money when she needed it and allowed his secretary at the office to pay the bills, she found herself without any cash and had to depend upon Rudolph to keep her going. Colin had left no insurance because he thought insurance companies were the biggest thieves in America, so there was no money there, either. As the accident had been his fault alone, with no one else involved (he had hit a tree and the County of Los Angeles was preparing to sue the estate for damage to the tree), there was nobody against whom Gretchen could press claims for compensation.

"I have to get out of that house, Mr. Greenfield," Gretchen said. The evenings were the worst. Whispers in shadowy corners of rooms. Half expecting the door to open at any moment and Colin to come in, cursing an actor or a cameraman.

"I quite understand," Mr. Greenfield said. He really was a decent man. "But if you don't remain in possession, physical possession, Mr. Burke's ex-wife might very possibly find legal grounds for moving in. Her lawyers are very good, very good indeed—" The professional admiration was ungrudging, all the names on one door of an elegant building paying sincere tribute to all the names on the door of another elegant building just a block away. "If there's a loophole, they'll find it. And in law, if one looks long enough, there is almost always a loophole."

"Except for me," Gretchen said despairingly.

"It's a question of time, my dear Mrs. Burke." Just the gentlest of rebukes at a layman's impatience. "There's nothing clear-cut about this case, I regret to say. The house was in your husband's name, there is a mortgage on it, payments to be made. The size of the estate is undetermined and may remain undetermined for many years. Mr. Burke had a percentage, quite a large percentage of the three films he directed and a continuing interest in stock and foreign royalties and possible movie sales of quite a number of the plays he was connected with." The enumeration of these splendid difficulties that remained to be dealt with before the file of Colin Burke could be marked "Closed" obviously brought Mr. Greenfield an elegiac pleasure. If the law were not as complicated as it was he would have sought another and more exigent profession. "There will have to be expert opinions, the testimony of studio officials, a certain amount of give and take between parties. To say nothing of the possibility of other claims against the estate. Relatives of the deceased, for example, who have a habit of cropping up in cases like this."

"He only has one brother," Gretchen said. "And he told me he didn't want anything." The brother had come to the cremation. He was a taut young colonel in the Air Force who had been a fighter pilot in Korea and who had crisply taken charge of everything, even putting Rudolph on the sidelines. It was he who had made sure there were no religious services and who had told her that when Colin and he had spoken about death, they had each promised the other unceremonious burning. The day after the cremation, Colin's brother had hired a private plane, had flown out to sea and strewn Colin's ashes over the Pacific Ocean. He had told Gretchen if there was anything she needed to call on him. But short of strafing the ex-Mrs. Burke or bombing her lawyer's offices, what could a straightforward colonel in the Air Force do to help his brother's widow, enmeshed in the law?

Gretchen stood up. "Thank you for everything, Mr. Greenfield," she said. "I'm sorry I've taken so much of your time."

"Not at all." Mr. Greenfield stood, legally courteous. "I'll keep you informed, naturally, of all developments."

He escorted her to the door of his office. Although his face showed nothing, she was sure he disapproved of the dress she was wearing, which was pale blue.

She went down a long aisle flanked by rows of desks at which secretaries typed rapidly, without looking up, deeds, wills, com-

plaints, summonses, contracts, bankruptcy petitions, transfers, mort-
gages, briefs, enjoinders, writs of replevin.

They are typing away the memory of Colin Burke, she thought.
Day after day after day.

Chapter 5

It was cold up in the bow of the ship, but Thomas liked it up there
alone, staring out at the long, gray swells of the Atlantic. Even when
it wasn't his watch, he often went up forward and stood for hours, in
all weathers, not saying anything to the man whose watch it happened to be, just standing there silently, watching the bow plunge
and come up in a curl of white water, at peace with himself, not
thinking consciously of anything, not wanting or needing to think
about anything.

The ship flew the Liberian flag, but in two voyages he hadn't come
close to Liberia. The man called Pappy, the manager of the Aegean
Hotel, had been as helpful as Schultzy had said he would be. He had
fitted him out with the clothes and seabag of an old Norwegian seaman who had died in the hotel and had gotten him the berth on the
Elga Andersen, Greek ownership, taking on cargo at Hoboken for
Rotterdam, Algeciras, Genoa, Piraeus. Thomas had stayed in his
room in the Aegean all the time he was in New York, eight days, and
Pappy had brought him his meals personally, because Thomas had
said he didn't want any of the help to see him and start asking questions. The night before the *Elga Andersen* was due to sail Pappy had
driven him over to the pier in Hoboken himself and watched while
he signed on. The favor that Pappy owed Schultzy from Schultzy's
days in the Merchant Marine during the war must have been a big
one.

The *Elga Andersen* had sailed at dawn the next day and anybody
who was looking for Tommy Jordache was going to have a hard time
finding him.

The *Elga Andersen* was a Liberty ship, ten thousand tons. It had been built in 1943 and had seen better days. It had gone from owner to owner, for quick profits, and nobody had done more to maintain it than was absolutely necessary to keep it afloat and moving. Its hull was barnacled, its engines wheezed, it hadn't been painted in years, there was rust everywhere, the food was miserable, the captain an old religious maniac who knelt on the bridge during storms and who had been beached during the war for Nazi sympathies. The officers had papers from ten different countries and had been dismissed from other berths for drunkenness or incompetence or theft. The men in the crew were from almost every country with a coast on the Atlantic or the Mediterranean, Greeks, Yugoslavs, Norwegians, Italians, Moroccans, Mexicans, Americans, most of them with papers that could not stand inspection. There were fights almost every day in the mess room, where a poker game was always in progress, but the officers carefully refrained from interfering.

Thomas kept out of the poker game and the fights and spoke only when necessary and answered no questions and was at peace. He felt that he had found his place on the planet, plowing the wide waters of the world. No women, no worrying about weight, no pissing blood in the morning, no scrambling for money at the end of every month. Someday, he'd pay Schultzy back the one fifty he had given him in Las Vegas. With interest.

He heard steps behind him, but didn't turn around.

"We're in for a rough night," said the man who had joined him in the bow. "We're going right into a storm."

Thomas grunted. He recognized the voice. A young guy named Dwyer, a kid from the Middle West who somehow managed to sound like a fag. He was rabbit-toothed and was nicknamed Bunny.

"It's the skipper," Dwyer went on. "Praying on the bridge. You know the saying—you have a minister on board, watch out for lousy weather."

Thomas didn't say anything.

"I just hope it's not a big one," Dwyer said. "Plenty of these Liberty ships have just broke in half in heavy seas. And the way we're loaded. Did you notice the list to port we got?"

"No."

"Well, we got it. This your first voyage?"

"Second."

Dwyer had signed on in Savannah, where the *Elga Andersen* had put in after Thomas's first return voyage on her.

"It's a hell hole," Dwyer said. "I'm only on it for the opportunity."

Thomas knew Dwyer wanted him to ask what opportunity but just stood there staring out at the darkening horizon.

"You see," Dwyer went on, when he realized Thomas wasn't going to talk, "I've got my third mate's papers. On American ships I might have to wait years before I move up top. But on a tub like this, with the kind of scum we got as officers, one of them's likely to fall overboard drunk or get picked up by the police in port and then it'd be my opportunity, see?"

Thomas grunted. He had nothing against Dwyer, but he had nothing for him, either.

"You planning to try for mate's papers, too?" Dwyer asked.

"Hadn't thought about it." Spray was coming over the bow now as the weather worsened and he huddled into his pea jacket. Under the jacket he had a heavy turtle-neck blue sweater. The old Norwegian who had died in the Hotel Aegean must have been a big man, because his clothes fit Thomas comfortably.

"The only thing to do," Dwyer said. "I saw that the first day I set foot on the deck of my first ship. The ordinary seaman or even the A.B. winds up with nothing. Lives like a dog and winds up a broken old man at fifty. Even on American ships, with the union and everything and fresh fruit. Big deal. Fresh fruit. The thing is to plan ahead. Get some braid on you. The next time I'm back I'm going up to Boston and I'm going to take a shot at second mate's papers."

Thomas looked at him curiously. Dwyer was wearing a gob's white hat, pulled down all around a yellow sou'wester and solid new rubber-soled, high, working shoes. He was a small man and he looked like a boy dressed up for a costume party, with the new, natty, seagoing clothes. The wind had reddened his face but not like an outdoor man's face, rather like a girl's who is not used to the cold and has suddenly been exposed to it. He had long, dark eyelashes over soft, black eyes and he seemed to be begging for something. His mouth was too large and too full and too busy. He kept moving his hands in and out of his pockets restlessly.

Christ, Thomas thought, is that why he's come up here to talk to me and he always smiles at me when he passes me? I better put the bastard straight right now. "If you're such an educated hotshot," he said roughly, "with mate's papers and all, what're you doing down here with all of us poor folks? Why aren't you dancing with some heiress on a cruise ship in your nice white officer's suit?"

"I'm not trying to be superior, Jordache," Dwyer said. "Honest I'm not. I like to talk to somebody once in awhile and you're about my age and you're American and you got dignity, I saw that right away, dignity. Everybody else on this ship—they're animals. They're always making fun of me, I'm not one of them, I've got ambition, I won't play in their crooked poker games. You must've noticed."

"I haven't noticed anything," Thomas said.

"They think I'm a fag or something," Dwyer said. "You didn't notice that?"

"No, I didn't." Except for meals, Thomas stayed out of the mess room.

"It's my curse," Dwyer said. "That's what happens when I apply for third mate anywhere. They look at my papers, my recommendations, then they talk to me for awhile and look me over in that queer way and they tell me there's no openings. Boy, I can see that look coming from a mile off. I'm no fag, I swear to God, Jordache."

"You don't have to swear anything for me," Thomas said. The conversation made him uncomfortable. He didn't want to be let in on anybody's secrets or troubles. He wanted to do his job and go from one port to another and sail the seas in solitude.

"I'm engaged to be married, for Christ's sake," Dwyer cried. He dug into the back pocket of his pants and brought forth a wallet and took out a photograph. "Here, look at this." He thrust the snapshot in front of Thomas's nose. "That's my girl and me. Last summer on Narragansett Beach." A very pretty, full-bodied young girl, with curly blonde hair, in a bathing suit, and beside her, Dwyer, small but trim and well muscled, like a bantamweight, in a tightly fitting pair of swimming trunks. He looked in good enough shape to go into the ring, but of course that meant nothing. "Does that look like a fag?" Dwyer demanded. "Does that girl look as though she was the type to marry a fag?"

"No," Thomas admitted.

The spray coming over the bow sprinkled the photograph. "You better put the picture away," he said. "The water'll ruin it."

Dwyer took out a handkerchief and dried the snapshot and put it back in his wallet. "I just wanted you to know," he said, "that if I like to talk to you from time to time it's nothing like that."

"Okay," Thomas said. "Now I know it."

"As long as we have matters on a firm basis," Dwyer said, almost belligerently. "That's all." Abruptly, he turned away and made his way along the temporary wooden cat track built over the oil drums stowed as deck cargo forward.

Thomas shook his head, feeling the sting of spray on his face. Everybody has his troubles. A boatload of troubles. If everybody on the whole goddamn ship came up and told you what was bothering him, you'd want to jump overboard there and then.

He crouched in the bow, to escape the direct blows of spray, only occasionally lifting his head to do his job, which was to see what was ahead of the *Elga Andersen* on his watch.

Mate's papers, he thought. If you were going to make your living out of the sea, why not? He'd ask Dwyer, offhandedly, later, how you went about getting them. Fag or no fag.

They were in the Mediterranean, passing Gibraltar, but the weather, if anything, was worse. The captain no doubt was still praying to God and Adolf Hitler on the bridge. None of the officers had gotten drunk and fallen overboard and Dwyer still hadn't moved up top. He and Thomas were in the old naval gun crew's quarters at the stern, seated at the steel table riveted to the deck in the common room. The anti-aircraft guns had long since been dismounted, but nobody had bothered to dismantle the crew's quarters. There were at least ten urinals in the head. The kids of the gun crew must have pissed like mad, Thomas thought, every time they heard a plane overhead.

The sea was so rough that on every plunge the screw came out of the water and the entire stern shuddered and roared and Dwyer and Thomas had to grab for the papers and books and charts spread on the table to keep them from sliding off. But the gun crew's quarters was the only place they could get off alone and work together. They got in at least a couple of hours a day and Thomas, who had never paid any attention at school, was surprised to see how quickly he learned from Dwyer about navigation, sextant reading, star charts, loading, all the subjects he would have to have at his fingertips when he took the examination for third mate's papers. He was also surprised how much he enjoyed the sessions. Thinking about it in his bunk, when he was off watch, listening to the other two men in the cabin with him snore away, he felt he knew why the change had come about. It wasn't only age. He still didn't read anything else, not even the newspapers, not even the sporting pages. The charts, the pamphlets, the drawings of engines, the formulas, were a way out. Finally, a way out.

Dwyer had worked in the engine rooms of ships, as well as on deck, and he had a rough but adequate grasp of engineering problems and Thomas's experience around garages made it easier to understand what Dwyer was talking about.

Dwyer had grown up on the shores of Lake Superior and had sailed small boats ever since he was a kid and as soon as he had finished high school he had hitchhiked to New York, gone down to the Battery to see the ships passing in and out of port, and had got himself signed on a coastal oil tanker as a deckhand. Nothing that had happened to him since that day had diminished his enthusiasm for the sea.

He didn't ask any questions about Thomas's past and Thomas didn't volunteer any information. Out of gratitude for what Dwyer was teaching him, Thomas was almost beginning to like the little man.

"Some day," Dwyer said, grabbing for a chart that was sliding forward, "you and I will both have our own ships. Captain Jordache, Captain Dwyer presents his compliments and asks if you will honor him and come aboard."

"Yeah," Thomas said. "I can just see it."

"Especially if there's a war," Dwyer said. "I don't mean a great big one, like World War II, where if you could sail a rowboat across Central Park Lake, you could get to be skipper of *some* kind of ship. I mean even a little one like Korea. You have no idea how much money guys come home with, with combat zone pay, stuff like that. And how many guys who didn't know their ass from starboard came out masters of their own ships. Hell, the United States has got to be fighting somewhere soon and if we're ready, there's no telling how high we can go."

"Save your dreams for the sack," Thomas said. "Let's get back to work."

They bent over the chart.

It was in Marseilles that the idea hit Thomas. It was nearly midnight and he and Dwyer had had dinner together at a seafood place on the Vieux Port. Thomas remembered that this was the south coast of France and they had drunk three bottles of vin rosé between them because they were on the south coast of France, even though Marseilles hardly could be considered a tourist resort. The *Elga Andersen* was due to lift anchor at 5 A.M. and as long as they got back on board before that, they were okay.

After dinner they had walked around, stopping in several bars and now they were at what was going to be their last stop, a small dark bar off the Canebiere. A juke box was playing and a few fat whores at the bar were waiting to be asked if they wanted a drink. Thomas wouldn't have minded having a girl, but the whores were sleazy and probably had the clap and didn't go with his idea of the kind of lady you ought to have on the south coast of France.

Drinking, a little blearily, at a table along the wall, looking at the girls, fat legs showing under loud, imitation silk dresses, Thomas remembered ten of the best days in his life, the time in Cannes with the wild English girl who liked jewelry.

"Say," he said to Dwyer, sitting across from him, drinking beer, "I got an idea."

"What's that?" Dwyer was keeping a wary eye on the girls, fearful that one of them would come over and sit down next to him and put her hand on his knee. He had offered earlier in the evening to pick up a prostitute to prove, once and for all, to Thomas that he wasn't a fag, but Thomas had said it wasn't necessary, he didn't care whether he was a fag or not and anyway it wouldn't prove anything because he knew plenty of fags who also screwed.

"What's what?" Thomas asked.

"You said you had an idea."

"An idea. Yeah. An idea. Let's skip the fucking ship."

"You're crazy," Dwyer said. "What the hell'll we do in Marseilles without a ship? They'll put us in jail."

"Nobody'll put us in jail," Thomas said. "I didn't say for good. Where's the next port she puts into? Genoa. Am I right?"

"Okay. Genoa," Dwyer said reluctantly.

"We pick her up in Genoa," Thomas said. "We say we got drunk and we didn't wake up until she was out of the harbor. Then we pick her up in Genoa. What can they do to us? Dock us a few days' pay, that's all. They're shorthanded as it is. After Genoa, the ship goes straight back to Hoboken, right?"

"Yeah."

"So we don't lose any shore time, them keeping us on board in a port. I don't want to sail on that lousy tub any more, anyway. We can always pick up something better in New York."

"But what'll we do between now and Genoa?" Dwyer asked worriedly.

"We tour. We make the grand tour," Thomas said. "We get on the train and we go to Cannes. Haunt of millionaires, like they say in the papers. I been there. Time of my life. We lay on the beach, we find ourselves some dames. We got our pay in our pocket . . ."

"I'm saving my money," Dwyer said.

"Live a little, live a little," Thomas said impatiently. By now it was inconceivable to him that he could go back to the gloom of the ship, stand watches, chip paint, eat the garbage they handed out, with Cannes so close by, available, waiting.

"I don't even have my toothbrush on me," Dwyer said.

"I'll buy you a toothbrush," Thomas said. "Say, you're always telling me what a great sailor you are, how you sailed a dory all over Lake Superior when you were a kid . . ."

"What's Lake Superior got to do with Cannes?"

"Sailor boy . . ." It was one of the whores from the bar, in a spangled dress showing most of her bosom. "Sailor boy, want to buy nize lady nize little drink, have good time, wiz ozzer lady later?" She smiled, showing gold teeth.

"Get outa here," Thomas said.

"*Salaud*," the woman said amiably, and spangled over to the juke box.

"What's Lake Superior got to do with Cannes?" Thomas said. "I'll tell you what Lake Superior's got to do with Cannes. You're a hot small boat sailor on Lake Superior . . ."

"Well, I . . ."

"Are you or aren't you?"

"For Christ's sake, Tommy," Dwyer said, "I never said I was Christopher Columbus or anybody like that. I said I sailed a dory and some small power boats when I was a kid and . . ."

"You know how to handle boats. Am I right in supposing that or ain't I right?"

"Sure, I can handle small boats," Dwyer admitted. "I still don't see . . ."

"On the beach at Cannes," Thomas said, "they got sailboats you can rent by the hour. I want to see with my own eyes how you rate. You're big on theory, with charts and books. All right, I want to see you actually get a boat in and out of some place. Or do I have to take that on faith, too, like your not being a fag?"

"Tommy!" Dwyer said, hurt.

"You can teach me," Thomas said. "I want to learn from an expert. Ah—the hell with it—if you're too yellow to come with me, I'll do it myself. Go on back to the boat, like a nice little boy."

"Okay," Dwyer said. "I never did anything like this before. But I'll do it. The hell with the ship." He drained his beer.

"The grand tour," Thomas said.

It wasn't as good as he'd remembered it, because he had Dwyer with him, not that wild English girl. But it was good enough. And it certainly was a lot better than standing watches on the *Elga Andersen* and eating that slop and sleeping in the same stinking hole with two snoring Moroccans.

They found a cheap little hotel that wasn't too bad behind the rue d'Antibes and went swimming off the beach, although it was only springtime and the water was so cold you could only stay in a little while. But the white buildings were the same, the pink wine was the same, the blue sky was the same, the great yachts lying in the harbor were the same. And he didn't have to worry about his weight or fighting some murderous Frenchman when the holiday was over.

They rented a little sailboat by the hour and Dwyer hadn't been lying, he really knew how to handle small boats. In two days he had taught Thomas a great deal and Thomas could slip a mooring and come up to it dead, with the sail rattling down, nine times out of ten.

But most of the time they spent around the harbor, walking slowly around the quays, silently admiring the sloops, the schooners, the big yachts, the motor cruisers, all still in the harbor and being sanded down and varnished and polished up for the season ahead.

"Christ," Thomas said, "would you believe there's so much money in the world and we don't have any of it."

They found a bar on the Quai St. Pierre frequented by the sailors and captains working on pleasure craft. Some of them were English and many of the others could speak a little and they got into conversations with them whenever they could. None of the men seemed to work very hard and the bar was almost always at least half full at all hours of the day. They learned to drink pastis because that was what everybody else drank and because it was cheap. They hadn't found any girls and the ones who accosted them from cars on the Croisette or back behind the port asked too much money. But for once in his life Thomas didn't mind going without a woman. The harbor was enough for him, the vision of the life based on it, of grown men living year in and year out on beautiful ships was enough for him. No boss to bother about nine months of the year, and then in the summer being a big shot at the wheel of a hundred-thousand-dollar craft, going to places like St. Tropez and Monte Carlo and Capri, coming into harbor with girls in bathing suits draped all over the decks. And they all seemed to have money. What they didn't earn in salary they got in kickbacks from ship chandlers and boatyards and rigged expense accounts. They ate and drank like kings and some of the older ones weren't sober from one day to the next.

"These guys," Thomas said, after they had been in town for four days, "have solved the problems of the universe."

He even thought of skipping the *Elga Andersen* for good and trying to get a job on one of the yachts for the summer, but it turned out that unless you were a skipper you most likely only got hired for three or four months, at lousy pay, and you were let go for the rest of the year. Much as he liked Cannes, he couldn't see himself starving eight months a year just to be there.

Dwyer was just as dazzled as he was. Maybe even more so. He hadn't even been in Cannes before but had admired and had been around boats all his life. What was an adult discovery for Thomas was a reminder for Dwyer of the deepest pleasures of his boyhood.

There was one Englishman in the bar, a dark-brown colored little man with white hair, named Jennings, who had been in the British navy during the war and who owned, actually *owned*, his boat, a sixty-footer with five cabins. It was old and cranky, the Englishman told them, but he knew it like his own mother, and he coaxed her all around the Med, Malta, Greece, Sicily, everywhere, as a charter captain during the summer. He had an agent in Cannes who booked his charters for him, for ten per cent. He had been lucky, he said. The man who had owned the boat and for whom he had worked, had hated his wife. When he died, out of spite, he had left the boat to Jennings. Well, you couldn't bank on things like that.

Jennings sipped complacently at his pastis. His motor yacht, the *Gertrude II*, stubby, but clean and comfortable looking, was moored for the winter across the street, just in front of the bar, and as he drank Jennings could look fondly at it, all good things close at hand. "It's a lovely life," he said. "I fair have to admit it, Yanks. Instead of fighting for a couple of bob a day, hauling cargo on the docks of Liverpool or sweating blood oiling engines in some tub in the North Sea in a winter's gale. To say nothing of the climate and taxes." He waved largely toward the view of the harbor outside the bar where the mild sun tipped the gently bobbing masts of the boats moored side by side at the quay. "Rich man's weather," Jennings said. "Rich man's weather."

"Let me ask you a question, Jennings," Thomas said. He was paying for the Englishman's drinks and he was entitled to a few questions. "How much would it cost to get a fair-sized boat, say one like yours, and get into business?"

Jennings lit a pipe and pulled at it reflectively. He never did anything quickly, Jennings. He was no longer in the British navy, or on the docks, there was no foreman or mate to snarl at him, he had time for everything. "Ah, that's a hard question to answer, Yank," he said. "Ships are like women—some come high and some come cheap, but the price you pay has little to do with the satisfaction you get from them." He laughed appreciatively at his own worldliness.

"The minimum," Thomas persisted. "The absolute minimum?"

Jennings scratched his head, finished his pastis. Thomas ordered another round.

"It's a matter of luck," Jennings said. "I know men put down a hundred thousand pounds, cash on the barrelhead, ships designed by the fanciest naval architects, built in the best shipyards in Holland or Britain, steel hulls, teak decks, every last little doodad on board, radar, electric toilets, air conditioning, automatic pilot, and they cursed the day the bloody thing was put in the water and they would have been glad to get rid of it for the price of a case of whiskey, and no takers."

"We don't have any hundred thousand pounds," Thomas said shortly.

"We?" Dwyer said bewilderedly. "What do you mean, *we?*"

"Shut up," Thomas said. "*Your* boat never cost any hundred thousand pounds," he said to Jennings.

"No," Jennings said. "I don't pretend it ever did."

"I mean something *reasonable*," Thomas said.

"Reasonable aren't a word you use about boats," Jennings said. He was beginning to get on Thomas's nerves. "What's reasonable for one man is pure lunacy for another, if you get my meaning. It's a matter of luck, like I was saying. For example, a man has a nice snug little ship, cost him maybe twenty, thirty thousand pounds, but maybe his wife gets seasick all the time, or he's had a bad year in business and his creditors are panting on his traces and it's been a stormy season for cruising and maybe the market's been down and it looks as though the Communists're going to take over in Italy or France or there's going to be a war or the tax people're after him for some hanky-panky, maybe he didn't tell them he paid for the ship with money he had stowed away quiet-like in some bank in Switzerland, so he's pressed, he's got to get out and get out fast and suddenly nobody wants to buy boats that week . . . You get my drift, Yank?"

"Yeah," Thomas said. "You don't have to draw a map."

"So he's desperate," Jennings went on. "Maybe he needs five thousand guineas before Monday or the house falls in on his head. If you're there and you have the five thousand guineas . . ."

"What's a guinea?" Dwyer asked.

"Five thousand guineas is fifteen thousand bucks," Thomas said. "Isn't it?"

"Give or take a few bob," Jennings said. "Or you hear about a naval vessel that's up for auction or a vessel that's been confiscated by the Customs for smuggling. Of course, it needs refitting, but if you're clever with your hands and don't pay these pirates in the shipyards around here to do your work for you—never trust a Frenchman on the Côte, especially along the waterfront, he'll steal the eyes right out of your head—why, maybe, playing everything close and counting your money every night, maybe with luck, and getting some people to trust you till the end of the season for gear and provisions, you're in the water and ready for your first charter for as little as eight, ten thousand pounds."

"Eight, ten thousand pounds," Dwyer said. "It might as well be eight, ten million dollars."

"Shut up," Thomas said. "There're ways of making money."

"Yeah?" Dwyer said. "How?"

"There're ways. I once made three thousand bucks in one night."

Dwyer took in a deep breath. "How?"

It was the first time Thomas had given anybody a clue to his past since he had left the Hotel Aegean, and he was sorry he had spoken. "Never mind how," he said sharply. He turned to Jennings. "Will you do me a favor?"

"Anything within my power," Jennings said. "As long as it don't cost me no money." He chuckled softly, boat owner, sitting on top of the system, canny graduate of the Royal Navy, survivor of war and poverty, pastis drinker, wise old salt, nobody's fool.

"If you hear of anything," Thomas said. "Something good, but cheap, get in touch with us, will you."

"Happy to oblige, Yank," Jennings said. "Just write the address down."

Thomas hesitated. The only address he had was the Hotel Aegean and the only person he had given it to was his mother. Before the fight with Quayles, he had visited her fairly regularly, when he was sure he wouldn't run into his brother Rudolph. Since then he had written her from the ports he had touched at, sending her folders of postcards and pretending he was doing better than he was doing. When he had come back from his first voyage there had been a bundle of letters from her waiting for him at the Aegean. The only trouble with her letters was that she kept asking to see her grandson and he didn't dare get in touch with Teresa even to see the boy. It was the one thing he missed about America.

"Just write the address down, lad," Jennings repeated.

"Give him your address," Thomas said to Dwyer. Dwyer got his mail at the headquarters of the National Maritime Union in New York. Nobody was looking for *him*.

"Why don't you stop dreaming?" Dwyer said.

"Do like I say."

Dwyer shrugged, wrote out his address, and gave it to Jennings. His handwriting was clear and straight. He would keep a neat log, Third Mate Dwyer. If he ever got the chance.

The old man put the slip of paper into an old, cracked, leather wallet. "I'll keep my eyes peeled and my ears open," he promised.

Thomas paid the bill and he and Dwyer started along the quay, examining all the boats tied up there, as usual. They walked slowly and silently. Thomas could feel Dwyer glancing at him uneasily from time to time.

"How much money you got?" Thomas asked, as they reached the foot of the harbor, where the fishing boats, with their acetylene lamps, were tied up, with the nets laid out along the pavement, drying.

"How much money I got?" Dwyer said querulously. "Not even a hundred bucks. Just enough to buy one-millionth of an ocean liner."

"I don't mean how much money you got *on* you. I mean altogether. You keep telling me you save your dough."

"If you think I've got enough for a crazy scheme like . . ."

"I asked you how much money you got. In the bank?"

"Twenty-two hundred dollars," Dwyer said reluctantly. "In the bank. Listen, Tommy, stop jerking off, we'll never . . ."

"Between us," Thomas said, "you and me, one day, we're going to have our own boat. Right here. In this port. Rich man's weather, like the Englishman said. We'll get the money somehow."

"I'm not going to do anything criminal." Dwyer sounded scared. "I never committed a crime in my life and I'm not going to start now."

"Who said anything about committing a crime?" Thomas said. Although the thought had crossed his mind. There had been plenty of what Dwyer would call criminals hanging around during his years in the ring, in two-hundred-dollar suits and big cars, with fancy broads hanging on their arms, and everybody being polite and glad to see them, cops, politicians, businessmen, movie stars. They were just about like everybody else. There was nothing so special about them. Crime was just another way of earning a buck. Maybe an easier way. But he didn't want to scare Dwyer off. Not yet. If it ever came off, he'd need Dwyer to handle the boat. He couldn't do it alone. Yet. He wasn't that much of an idiot.

Somehow, he told himself, as they passed the old men playing boules on the quay-side, with the harbor behind them, the protected sheet of water crowded with millions of dollars worth of pleasure craft, shining in the sun. The one time he had been here before, he had sworn he'd come back. Well, he had come back. And he was going to come back again. SOMEHOW.

The next morning, early, they caught the train on the way to Genoa. They gave themselves an extra day, because they wanted to stop off and see Monte Carlo. Maybe they'd have some luck at the Casino.

If he had been at the other end of the platform he'd have seen his brother Rudolph getting out of one of the sleeping cars from Paris, with a slender, pretty, young girl and a lot of new luggage.

Chapter 6

When they walked through the exit gate of the station, they saw the Hertz sign and Rudolph said, "There's the man with our car." The concierge at the hotel in Paris had taken care of everything. As Jean had said, after the concierge had arranged for tickets to the theater, for a limousine to tour the chateaux of the Loire, for tables at ten

restaurants, for places at the Opera and Longchamps, "Every marriage should have its own private Paris concierge."

The porter trundled their luggage over to the car, said *merci* for
the tip and smiled, although they were plainly American. According
to the newspapers back home Frenchmen were not smiling at Americans this year. The man from the Hertz agency started to talk in
English but Rudolph showed off with his French, mostly to amuse
Jean, and the remaining formalities for renting the Peugeot convertible were concluded in the language of Racine. Rudolph had bought
a Michelin map of the Alpes-Maritimes in Paris, and after consulting
it, with the car top down, and the soft Mediterranean morning sun
shining on their bare heads, they drove through the white town and
then along the edge of the sea, through Golfe Juan, where Napoleon
had landed, through Juan-les-Pins, its big hotels still in their pre-
season sleep, to the Hotel du Cap, shapely, cream colored and splendid on its gentle hill among the pines.

As the manager showed them up to their suite, with a balcony
overlooking the calm, blue sea below the hotel park, Rudolph said,
coolly, "It's very nice, thank you." But it was only with the greatest
difficulty that he kept from grinning idiotically at how perfectly the
manager, himself, and Jean were playing their roles in his ancient
dream. Only it was better than the dream. The suite was larger and
more luxuriously furnished; the air was sweeter; the manager was
more of a manager than anyone could imagine; he himself was richer
and cooler and better dressed than he had been in his poor-boy rev-
erie; Jean, in her slim Paris suit, was more beautiful than the imaginary girl who had walked out onto the balcony overlooking the sea
and kissed him in his fantasy.

The manager bowed himself out, the porters finished placing the
bags on folding stools around the gigantic bedroom. Solid, real, with
a solid, real wife, he said, "Let's go out on the balcony."

They went out on the balcony and kissed in the sunlight.

They nearly hadn't married at all. Jean had hesitated and hesitated,
refusing to say yes or no and for awhile he was on the brink of
delivering an ultimatum to her every time he saw her, which was
tantalizingly seldom. He was kept in Whitby and Port Philip a great
deal of the time by work and then, when he did get to New York it
was often only to find a message with his answering service from
Jean telling him that she was out of town on a job. One night, he
had seen her in a restaurant after the theater with a small, beady-

eyed young man with matted long hair and a week-old growth of dark stubble on his jaws. The next time he saw her he asked her who the young man was and she admitted it still was the same one, the one she was overlapping with. When he asked her if she was still sleeping with him, she answered that it was none of his business.

He had felt humiliated that he was in competition with anyone that unsavory looking and it didn't make him feel any better to be told by Jean that the man was one of the most famous fashion photographers in the country. He had walked out on her that time and waited for her to get in touch with him, but she never called him and finally he couldn't bear it any longer and called her, swearing to himself that he would screw her but he'd be damned if he ever would marry her.

His whole conception of himself was damaged by her treatment of him and it was only in bed, where she delighted him and seemed to be delighted by him that he found any relief from his brooding feeling that he was being debased by the entire affair. All the men he knew assured him that all the girls *they* knew did nothing but plot constantly to get married. What sensational lack was there in his character or his lovemaking or general desirability that had made the only two girls he had asked to marry reject him?

Virginia Calderwood hadn't helped matters either. Old man Calderwood had followed Rudolph's advice about allowing his daughter to come down to New York and live alone and take a secretarial course. But if she was learning typing and stenography, Virginia must have done it at very odd hours indeed, because almost every time Rudolph went to his New York apartment, he would spot her, lurking in a doorway across the street or pretending just to be walking by. She would telephone in the middle of the night, sometimes three or four times, to say, "Rudy, I love you, I love you. I want you to fuck me."

To avoid her, he took to staying in different hotels when he came to New York, but for some prudish reason, Jean refused to visit him in a hotel and even the pleasures of the bed were denied him. Jean still wouldn't let him call for her at her apartment and he had never seen the place where she lived or met her roommate.

Virginia sent him long letters, horrifyingly explicit about her sensual longings for him, the language straight out of Henry Miller, whom Virginia must have studied assiduously. The letters were sent to his home at Whitby, to his apartment, to the main office at the store, and all it would take would be for one careless secretary to

open any one of them and he doubted if old man Calderwood would
ever talk to him again.

When he told Jean about Virginia, she just laughed and said,
"Oh, you poor attractive man." Mischievously, one night, when they
came back late to his apartment and he spotted Virginia in the shadows across the street, Jean wanted to go over and invite the girl up
for a drink.

His work suffered and he found that he had to read simple reports
over three and four times before they registered on his brain. He
slept restlessly and awoke weary. For the first time in his life he had
a rash of pimples on his chin.

At a party in New York he met a bosomy blond lady who seemed
to have three men around her at all times during the evening, but
who made it plain to him that she wanted to go home with him. He
took her to her apartment in the East Eighties, off Fifth Avenue,
learned that she was rich, that she was divorced, that she was lonely,
that she was tired of the men who pursued her around New York,
that she found him ravishingly sexy (he wished she had found another style of expressing herself). They went to bed together after
one drink and he was impotent and he left on a volley of coarse
laughter from the useless bed.

"The unluckiest day of my life," he told Jean, "was the day you
came up to Port Philip to take those pictures."

Nothing that happened made him stop loving her or wanting to
marry her and live with her for the rest of his life.

He had called her all day, ten times, a dozen times, but there never
was any answer. One more time, he decided, sitting disconsolately in
the living room of his apartment, I'll try one more goddamn time
and if she's not home I will go out and get roaring drunk and pick
up girls and fight in bars and if Virginia Calderwood is outside the
door when I come home I will bring her up here and screw her and
then call the men with the straitjacket and tell them to come and
take us both away.

The phone rang and rang and he was just about to put it down
when it was picked up and Jean said, "Hello," in the hushed, childish little way she had.

"Has your phone been out of order?" he asked.

"I don't know," she said. "I've been out all day."

"Are you going to be out all night?"

There was a pause. "No," she said.

"Do we meet?" He was ready to slam the phone down if she said no. He had once told her that he only had two alternating emotions about her—rage and ecstasy.

"Do you want to meet?"

"Eight o'clock?" he said. "I'll give you a drink here." He had looked out the window and had not spotted Virginia Calderwood.

"I have to take a bath," she said, "and I don't feel like hurrying. Why don't you come down here and I'll give *you* a drink."

"I hear the sound of cymbals and trumpets," he said.

"Stop trying to sound educated," she said, but she chuckled.

"What floor?"

"Fourth," she said. "No elevator. Be careful of your heart." She hung up.

He went in and showered and shaved. His hand wasn't steady and he cut himself badly on the chin. The cut wouldn't stop bleeding for a long time and he didn't ring the bell of her apartment on East Fortieth Street until five minutes past eight.

The door was opened by a girl in blue jeans and a sweater whom he had never seen before, who said, "Hi, I'm Florence," and then called, "Jeanny, the man's here."

"Come in, Rudy." Jean's voice floated out of an open door leading off the foyer. "I'm making up."

"Thanks, Florence," Rudolph said and went into Jean's room. She was seated naked at a table in front of a small mirror putting mascara on her eyelashes. He hadn't realized before that she used mascara. But he didn't say anything about the mascara. Or her being naked. He was too busy looking around the room. Almost every inch of wall space was taken up with photographs of himself, smiling, frowning, squinting, writing on the clip board. Some of the photographs were small, others were immense blow-ups. All of them were flattering. It's over, he thought gratefully, it's all over. She's decided.

"I know that man from somewhere," he said.

"I thought you'd recognize him," Jean said. Pink, firm, and dainty, she went on putting on mascara.

Over dinner, they talked about the wedding. By the time dessert came, they nearly called it off.

"What I like," Rudolph said bitterly, "is a girl who knows her own mind."

"Well, I know mine," Jean said. She had grown sullen as Rudolph had argued with her. "I think I know what I'm going to do with my weekend," she said. "I'm going to stay home and tear down every one of those photographs and whitewash the walls."

To begin with, she was grimly devoted to secrecy. He wanted to let everybody know immediately, but she shook her head. "No announcements," she said.

"I have a sister and a mother," Rudolph said. "Actually, I have a brother, too."

"That's the whole idea. I've got a father and a brother. And I can't stand either of them. If they find out that you told your family and I didn't tell them, there'll be thunder from the West for ten years. And after we're married I don't want to have anything to do with your family and I don't want you to have anything to do with mine. Families're out. Thanksgiving dinners at the old homestead. Christ!"

Rudolph had given in on that without too much of a fight. His wedding couldn't be a gloriously happy occasion for Gretchen, with Colin dead just a few months. And the thought of his mother blubbering away in some horrible concoction of a church-going dress was not an appealing one. He could also easily do without the scene Virginia Calderwood would make upon hearing the news. But not telling Johnny Heath or Calderwood or Brad Knight would lead to complications around the office, especially if he wanted to leave immediately after the wedding on the honeymoon. The points that Jean and he *had* agreed upon were that there was to be no party, that they would get out of New York promptly, that they would not be married in church, and that they would go to Europe on the honeymoon.

They had not agreed upon what they would do when they returned from Europe. Jean refused to stop working and she refused to live in Whitby.

"Damn it," Rudolph said, "here we're not even married yet and you've got me down as a part-time husband."

"I'm not domestic," Jean had said stubbornly. "I don't like small towns. I'm on my way up in this city. I'm not going to give it all up just because a man wants to marry me."

"Jean . . ." Rudolph said warningly.

"All right," she said. "Just because I want to marry a man."

"That's better," he said.

"You've said yourself, the office rightly ought to be in New York."

"Only it's not in New York," he said.

"You'll like me better if you don't see me all the time."

"No, I won't."

"Well, I'll like *you* better."

He had given in on that, too. But without grace. "That's my last surrender," he said.

"Yes, dear," she said, mock demurely, fluttering her eyelashes. She stroked his hand exaggeratedly on the table. "I do admire a man who knows how to assert himself."

Then they had both laughed and everything was all right and Rudolph said, "There's one sonofabitch that's going to get an announcement and that's that slimy photographer and if he wants to come to the wedding tell him he's welcome, but he's got to shave."

"Fair enough," Jean said, "if I can send an announcement to Virginia Calderwood."

Cruel and happy, hand in hand, they left the restaurant and went into bar after bar on Third Avenue secretly and lovingly and finally, drunkenly, to toast the years ahead of them.

The next day he bought a diamond engagement ring at Tiffany's, but she made him take it back. "I hate the trappings of wealth," she said. "Just make sure to show up at City Hall on the day with a nice simple gold band."

It was impossible, finally, not to tell Calderwood and Brad and Johnny Heath that he was going to be away for at least a month and why. Jean conceded the point, but on condition that he swear them to secrecy, which he did.

Calderwood was mournful. Rudolph couldn't tell whether it was because of his daughter or because he didn't like the idea of Rudolph being away from the business for a month. "I hope you're not being rash," Calderwood said. "I remember the girl. She seemed like a poor little thing to me. I'll bet she doesn't have a dime."

"She works," Rudolph said defensively.

"I don't approve of wives working," Calderwood said. He shook his head. "Ah, Rudy—and you could have had everything."

Everything, Rudolph thought. Including crazy Virginia Calderwood and her pornographic letters.

Neither Brad nor Johnny Heath was wildly enthusiastic, but he wasn't marrying to please them. Enthusiastic or not, they both came to the wedding at City Hall and drove out to the airport with the bride and groom and Florence.

Rudolph's first husbandly moment came when they checked in

and Jean's luggage was nearly a hundred pounds overweight. "Good Lord," he said, "what have you got in there?"

"A change of clothes," Jean said. "You don't want your wife to walk around naked in front of all those Frenchmen, do you?"

"For a girl who doesn't like the trappings of luxury," he said, as he wrote out the check for the overweight, "you sure carry around a lot of supplies." He tried to make it sound light, but he had a moment of foreboding. The long years of having to pinch pennies had made him fitfully careful about money. Extravagant wives had ruined men many times wealthier than he. Unworthy fear. I'll handle her, if necessary, he thought. Today he felt he could handle anything. He took her hand and led the way toward the bar.

They had time for two bottles of champagne before they took off and Johnny Heath promised to call Gretchen and Rudolph's mother and tell them the news once the plane was off the ground.

The days grew warmer. They lazed in the sun. They became dark brown and Jean's hair turned almost blond, bleached by the sun and salt water. She gave him tennis lessons on the courts of the hotel and said that he had talent for the game. She was very serious about the lessons and spoke sharply to him when he didn't hit out correctly. She taught him how to water ski. She kept amazing him with the number of things she could do well.

They had lunch brought to them at their cabana overlooking the speed-boat mooring. They ate cold langouste and drank white wine and after lunch they went up to their rooms to make love, with the windows shuttered against the afternoon sun.

He didn't look at any of the girls lying almost naked around the hotel pool and on the rocks next to the diving board, although two or three of the girls well deserved to be looked at.

"You're unnatural," Jean said to him.

"Why am I unnatural?"

"Because you don't ogle."

"I ogle you."

"Keep it up," she said.

They found new restaurants and ate bouillabaisse on the *terrasse* of Chez Felix, where you could look through the arch of the rampart at the boats in the harbor of Antibes. When they made love later they both smelled of garlic and wine, but they didn't mind.

They took excursions to the hill towns and visited the Matisse chapel and the pottery works at Vallauris and ate lunch on the terrace of the Colombe d'Or at St.-Paul-de-Vence, in the white flutter of doves' wings. They learned with regret that the flock was kept white because the white doves drove off pigeons of any other color. When occasionally the doves did tolerate their impure fellows, the proprietor killed them off himself.

Wherever they went, Jean took her cameras along, and took innumerable pictures of him against backgrounds of masts, ramparts, palms, waves. "I am going to make you into the wallpaper for our bedroom in New York," she said.

He no longer bothered to put on a shirt when he came out of the water. Jean said she liked the hair on his chest and the fuzz on his shoulders.

They planned a trip to Italy when they got tired of the Cap d'Antibes. They got out a map and circled the towns of Menton, San Remo, Milano for the Last Supper, Rappallo, Santa Margherita, Firenze, for Michelangelo and the Botticellis, Bologna, Siena, Assisi, Rome. The names were like little bells chiming in sunshine. Jean had been everywhere. Other summers. It would be a long time before he learned everything about her.

They didn't get tired of the Cap d'Antibes.

One day, he took a set from her in tennis. She fought off set point three times, but he finally won. She was furious. For two minutes.

They sent a cable to Calderwood to say that they weren't coming back for awhile.

They didn't speak to anyone at the hotel except an Italian movie actress who was so beautiful that you had to speak to her. Jean spent a morning taking photographs of the Italian movie actress and sent them to *Vogue* in New York. *Vogue* cabled back that they were going to run a set in their September issue.

Nothing could go wrong that month.

Although they still were not tired of the Cap d'Antibes, they got into the car and started driving south to visit the towns they had circled on the map. They were disappointed nowhere.

They sat in the cobbled square of Portofino and ate chocolate ice cream, the best chocolate ice cream in the world. They watched the women selling postcards and lace and embroidered tablecloths from their stands to tourists and they eyed the yachts moored in the harbor.

There was one slender, white yacht, about fifty feet long, with racy, clean Italian lines and Rudolph said, "That's what machinery is all about. When it comes out like that."

"Would you like to own it?" Jean asked, scooping up her chocolate ice cream.

"Who wouldn't like to own it?" he said.

"I'll buy it for you," she said.

"Thanks," he said. "And how about a Ferrari and a mink-lined overcoat and a forty-room house on the Cap d'Antibes, too, while you're at it?"

"No," she said, still eating her ice cream. "I really mean it. If you really want it."

He examined her closely. She was calm and serious. "Wait a minute," he said. "*Vogue* isn't paying you *that* much for those pictures."

"I don't depend on *Vogue*," she said. "I'm *awfully* rich. When my mother died she left me an obscene amount of stocks and bonds. Her father owned one of the biggest drug companies in the United States."

"What's the name of the company?" Rudolph asked suspiciously.

Jean told him the name of the company.

Rudolph whistled softly and put down his spoon.

"It's all in a trust fund that my father and brother control until I'm twenty-five," Jean said, "but even now my income is at least three times the size of yours. I hope I haven't spoiled your day."

Rudolph burst into a roar of laughter. "Christ," he said. "What a honeymoon!"

She didn't buy him a yacht that afternoon, but as a compromise, she bought him a shocking-pink shirt in a faggy shop alongside the harbor.

Later on, when he asked why she hadn't told him before, she was evasive. "I hate talking about money," she said. "That's all they ever talked about in my family. By the time I was fifteen I came to the belief that money degrades the soul if you think about it all the time. I never went home a single summer after the age of fifteen. Since I got out of college I never used a cent of the money my mother left me. I let my father and brother put it back into the business. They want me to let them keep using the income when the trust expires, but they're in for a big surprise. They'll cheat me if they can and I'm not out to be cheated. Especially not by them."

"Well, what *are* you going to do with it?"

"You're going to handle it for me," she said. "I'm sorry. For *us*. Do whatever you think best. Just don't talk to me about it. And don't use it to make us lead soggy, fancy, useless lives."

"We've been leading pretty fancy lives these past few weeks," Rudolph said.

"We've been spending your money and you worked for it," Jean said. "Anyway, this is a honeymoon. It isn't for real."

When they got to the hotel in Rome there was a cable waiting for Rudolph. It was from Bradford Knight and it read, "Your mother in hospital Stop Doctor fears end is near Stop Believe you should return soonest."

Rudolph handed the cable to Jean. They were still in the lobby and had just handed over their passports to the clerk at the desk. Jean read the cable silently, gave it back to him. "I suppose we ought to see if there's a plane out tonight," she said. It had been nearly five o'clock in the afternoon when they drove up to the hotel.

"Let's go upstairs," Rudolph said. He didn't want to have to think about what to do about his mother's dying in a crowded Roman hotel lobby.

They went up in the elevator and watched while the clerk who had accompanied them opened the shutters and let in the late sunlight and the roar of Rome.

"I hope you enjoy your stay," the clerk said, and left.

They watched the porters come in and arrange their luggage. The porters went and they stared at the unopened bags. They had planned to stay in Rome at least two weeks.

"No," Rudolph said. "We're not going to see if there's a plane tonight. The old lady is not going to do me out of Rome completely. We'll leave tomorrow. I'll take one day for you and me. She'll be alive when I get there. She wouldn't do herself out of the pleasure of dying before my eyes for anything in the world. Unpack."

Chapter 7

I

As soon as he got back on board the *Elga Andersen* in Genoa, he knew he was in for trouble with Falconetti. Falconetti was the bully of the ship, a huge, ham-handed man, with a small turnip-shaped head, who had been in jail for armed robbery. He cheated at cards, but the one time he had been called on it by an oiler from the engine room he had nearly strangled the oiler before he was pulled away from the man's throat by the rest of the men in the mess room. He was free and dangerous with his fists. At the beginning of each voyage he made a point of picking fights with four or five men and beating them up brutally, so that there would be no doubt about his position below decks. When he was in the mess room, no one else dared touch the radio there and everybody listened to the programs of Falconetti's choice, whether they liked it or not. There was one Negro on board by the name of Renway, and when Falconetti came into the mess room he slipped away. "I don't sit in any room with a nigger," Falconetti had announced the first time he saw the man in the mess room. Renway hadn't said anything, but he hadn't moved, either.

"Nigger," Falconetti said, "I guess you didn't hear me." He strode over to where the man was sitting at the table, grabbed him under the armpits, carried him to the door and hurled him against the bulkhead. Nobody said or did anything. You took care of yourself on the *Elga Andersen*, and the next man took care of himself.

Falconetti owed money to half the crew. Theoretically they were loans, but nobody expected to see his money again. If you didn't lend Falconetti a five- or ten-dollar bill when he asked for it, he wouldn't do anything about it at the time, but two or three days later, he would pick a fight with you and there would be black eyes and broken noses and teeth to spit out.

Falconetti hadn't tried anything with Thomas, although he was much larger than Thomas. Thomas was not looking for trouble and stayed out of Falconetti's way, but even though he was taciturn and pacific and kept to himself, there was something about Thomas's manner that made Falconetti pick on easier targets.

But the first night out of Genoa, Falconetti, who was dealing a poker hand in the mess room, said, when Thomas and Dwyer came in together, "Ah, here come the lovebirds," and made a wet, kissing noise. The men at the table laughed, because it was dangerous not to laugh at Falconetti's jokes. Dwyer turned red, but Thomas calmly poured himself a cup of coffee and picked up a copy of the Rome *Daily American* that was lying there, and began to read it.

"I'll tell you what, Dwyer," Falconetti said, "I'll be your agent. It's a long way home and the boys could use a nice piece of ass to while away the lonely hours. Couldn't you, boys?"

There were little embarrassed murmurs of assent from the men around the table.

Thomas read his paper and sipped his coffee. He knew that Dwyer was trying to catch his eye, pleading, but until it got much worse he wasn't going to get into a brawl.

"What's the sense in giving it away free like you do, Dwyer," Falconetti said, "when you could make a fortune and distribute happiness at the same time just by setting yourself up in business with my help. What we have to do is fix a scale—say five bucks for buggering, ten bucks for sucking. I'll just take my ten per cent, like a regular Hollywood agent. What do you say, Dwyer?"

Dwyer jumped up and fled. The men at the table laughed. Thomas read his paper, although his hands were trembling. He had to control himself. If he beat up on a big thug like Falconetti, who had terrorized whole shiploads of men for years, somebody would begin to wonder who the hell he was and what made him so tough and it wouldn't take too long for somebody to recognize his name or remember that he had seen him fight somewhere. And there were mob members or hangers-on everywhere along the waterfront, just waiting to rush to some higher-up with the news that he'd been spotted.

Read your goddamn newspaper, Thomas said to himself, and keep your mouth shut.

"Hey, lover." Falconetti made the wet kissing noise again. "You going to let your boy friend cry himself to sleep all by his little itsy-bitsy self?"

Methodically, Thomas folded the paper, put it down. He walked slowly across the room, carrying his coffee cup. Falconetti looked at him from across the table, grinning. Thomas threw the coffee into Falconetti's face. Falconetti didn't move. There was dead silence at the table.

"If you make that noise once more," Thomas said, "I'll slug you every time I pass you on this ship from here to Hoboken."

Falconetti stood up. "You're for me, lover," he said. He made the kissing noise again.

"I'll be waiting for you on deck," Thomas said. "And come alone."

"I don't need no help," Falconetti said.

Thomas wheeled and went out onto the stern deck. There would be room to move around there. He didn't want to have to tangle with a man Falconetti's size in close quarters.

The sea was calm, the night balmy, the stars bright. Thomas groaned. My goddamn fists, he thought, always my goddamn fists.

He wasn't worried about Falconetti. That big fat gut hanging over his belt wasn't made for punishment.

He saw the door open onto the deck, Falconetti's shadow thrown on the deck by the light in the gangway. Falconetti stepped on deck. He was alone.

Maybe I'm going to get away with it, Thomas thought. Nobody's going to see me take him.

"I'm over here, you fat slob," Thomas called. He wanted Falconetti to rush him, not take the chance of going in on him and perhaps being grappled by those huge arms and wrestled down. It was a cinch Falconetti wasn't going to fight under Boxing Commission rules. "Come on, Fatso," Thomas called. "I haven't got all night."

"You asked for it, Jordache," Falconetti said and rushed at him, flailing his fists, big round house swings. Thomas stepped to one side and put all his strength into the one right hand to the gut. Falconetti sounded as though he was strangling, teetered back. Thomas stepped in and hit him again in the gut. Falconetti went down and lay writhing on the deck, a gurgling noise bubbling up from his throat. He wasn't knocked out and his eyes were glaring up at Thomas as Thomas stood over him, but he couldn't say anything.

It had been neat and quick, Thomas thought with satisfaction, and there wasn't a mark on the man and if he didn't say anything none of the crew would ever know what happened out on the deck. It was a cinch Thomas wasn't going to do any talking. Falconetti had learned his lesson and it wouldn't do *his* reputation any good to pass the news around.

"All right, slob," Thomas said. "Now you know what it's all about. Now you'll keep that toilet of a mouth of yours shut."

Falconetti made a sudden move and Thomas felt the big hand gripping at his ankle, bringing him down. There was a gleam in Falconetti's other hand and Thomas saw the knife there. He gave suddenly and dropped onto Falconetti's face with his knees, hard, grabbing at the hand with the knife, twisting. Falconetti was still fighting for his breath and the fingers holding the knife handle weakened quickly. Thomas, now with his knees pinning Falconetti's arms to the deck, reached the knife, pushed it away. Then he methodically chopped at Falconetti's face for two minutes.

Finally, he stood up. Falconetti lay inert on the deck, the blood black on the starlit deck around his head. Thomas picked up the knife and threw it overboard.

With a last look at Falconetti, he went in. He was breathing hard, but it wasn't from the exertion of the fight. It was exultation. God-damn it, he thought, I enjoyed it. I'm going to wind up a crazy old man fighting orderlies in the Old Folks' Home.

He went into the mess room. The poker game had stopped, but there were more men in there than before, as the players who had seen the clash between Thomas and Falconetti had gone to tell their bunkmates and bring them back to the mess room to get the dope on the action. The room had been alive with talk, but when Thomas came in, calmly, breathing normally now, no one said a word.

Thomas went over to the coffee pot and poured himself a cup. "I wasted half the last cup," he said to the men in the mess room.

He sat down and unfolded the paper again and continued reading.

He walked down the gangplank with his pay in his pocket and the dead Norwegian's seabag over his shoulder. Dwyer followed him. Nobody had said good-bye. Ever since Falconetti had jumped over-board at night, in the middle of a storm, they had given him the si-lent treatment on the ship. The hell with them. Falconetti had it coming to him. He had stayed away from Thomas, but when his face had healed, he'd begun to take it out on Dwyer when Thomas wasn't around. Dwyer reported that Falconetti made the kissing sound every time he saw him and then one night, just as he was com-ing off his watch, Thomas heard screams from Dwyer's cabin. The door was unlocked and when Thomas went in, Dwyer was on the floor and Falconetti was pulling his pants off. Thomas slugged Fal-conetti across the nose and kicked him in the ass as he went through the door. "I warned you," he said. "You better stay out of sight. Be-cause you're going to get more of the same every time I lay eyes on you on this ship."

"Jesus, Tommy," Dwyer said, his eyes wet, as he struggled back into his pants, "I'll never forget what you've done for me. Not in a million years, Tommy."

"Stop bawling," Thomas said. "He won't bother you any more."

Falconetti didn't bother anyone any more. He did his best to avoid Thomas, but at least once a day, they'd run across each other. And each time, Thomas would say, "Come over here, slob," and Fal-conetti would shamble over, his whole face twitching, and Thomas would punch him hard in the gut. Thomas made a point of doing it when there were other crewmen around, although never in front of an officer. He had nothing to hide any more; after one look at what

Thomas had done to Falconetti's face that night on the deck, the men in the crew had caught on. In fact, a deckhand by the name of Spinelli had said to Thomas, "I been puzzling ever since I set eyes on you where I seen you before."

"You never saw me before," Thomas said, but he knew it was no use.

"Yeah, yeah," Spinelli said. "I saw you knock out a nigger five, six years ago, one night in Queens."

"I never been in Queens in my whole life," Thomas said.

"Have it your own way." Spinelli spread his hands pacifically. "It ain't none of my business."

Thomas knew that Spinelli would spread the news around that he was a pro and that you could look up his record in *Ring Magazine*, but while they were still at sea, there was nothing anybody could do about it. When they landed, he'd have to be careful. But meanwhile he had the pleasure of grinding Falconetti down to nothing. The curious thing, though, was that the men on the crew whom Falconetti had terrorized, and whom the crew now treated with contempt, hated Thomas for what he was doing. Somehow, it made them all seem ignoble in their own eyes, for having submitted to a big bag of wind who had been deflated in ten minutes by a man who was smaller than many of them and who hadn't even raised his voice on two voyages.

Falconetti tried to stay out of the mess room when he knew Thomas would be there. The one time he got caught there, Thomas didn't hit him but said, "Stay there, slob. I got company for you."

He went down the gangway to Renway's cabin. The Negro was sitting alone, on the edge of his bunk. "Renway," Thomas said, "come on with me."

Frightened, Renway had followed him back to the mess room. He had tried to pull back when he saw Falconetti sitting there, but Thomas pushed him into the room. "We're just going to sit down like gentlemen," Thomas said, "next to this gentleman here, and enjoy the music." The radio was playing.

Thomas sat down on one side of Falconetti and Renway on the other. Falconetti didn't move. He just sat with his eyes lowered, his big hands flat on the table in front of him.

When Thomas said, "Okay, that's enough for tonight. You can go now, slob," Falconetti had stood up, not looking at any of the men in the room who were watching him, and had gone out on deck and thrown himself overboard. The second mate, who was on deck at the time, had seen him, but was too far away to stop him. The ship had swung around and they had made a halfhearted search, but the seas were mountainous, the night black, and there wasn't a chance.

The captain had ordered an inquiry, but not one of the crew had volunteered information. Suicide, causes unknown, the captain had put down in his report to the owners.

Thomas and Dwyer found a taxi near the pier and Thomas said, "Broadway and Ninety-sixth Street," to the driver. He had said the first thing that came to his mind, but as they drove toward the tunnel, he realized that Broadway and Ninety-sixth Street was near where he had lived with Teresa and the kid. He didn't care if he never saw Teresa again in his whole life, but the ache in him to see his son had subconsciously made him direct the driver to the old neighborhood, just on the chance.

As they drove up Broadway, Thomas remembered that Dwyer was going to stay at the Y.M.C.A. on Sixty-second Street, and to wait there for word from Thomas. Thomas had not told Dwyer about the Hotel Aegean.

The driver stopped the cab at Sixty-second Street and Thomas said to Dwyer, "Okay, you get out here."

"I'll be hearing from you soon, won't I, Tommy?" Dwyer said anxiously, as he descended from the cab.

"That depends." Thomas closed the cab door. He didn't want to be bothered with Dwyer and his slobbering gratitude.

When they reached Ninety-sixth Street, Thomas asked the driver to wait. He got out of the cab to discover there were other children at Broadway and Ninety-sixth Street but no Wesley. Back in the cab, he ordered the driver to go to Ninety-sixth Street and Park.

At Ninety-sixth and Park, he got out of the cab, made sure the man drove off, then hailed another cab and told the driver, "Eighteenth Street and Fourth Avenue." When they got there, he walked west one block, turned the corner and came back and walked to the Aegean Hotel.

Pappy was behind the desk, but didn't say anything, just gave him a key. There were three seamen arguing in the lobby next to the one potted palm that was the sole adornment in what was really just a narrow hall, with a bulge in it for the desk. The seamen were talking in a language Thomas couldn't understand. Thomas didn't wait for them to get a good look at him. He walked quickly past them and up the two floors to the room whose number was on the key. He went in, threw the bag down, and lay down on the lumpy bed, with a mustard-colored spread, and stared up at the cracks of the ceiling. The shade had been down when he came into the room and he didn't bother to pull it up.

Ten minutes later, there was a knock on the door. Pappy's knock. Thomas got off the bed and let him in.

"You hear anything?" Thomas demanded.

Pappy shrugged. You couldn't tell what his expression was behind the dark glasses he wore night and day. "Somebody knows you're here," he said. "Or at least that when you're in New York you're here."

They were closing in. His throat felt dry. "What're you talking about, Pappy?" he said.

"A guy was in the hotel seven, eight days ago," Pappy said, "wanting to know if you were registered."

"What'd you say?"

"I said I never heard of you."

"What'd he say?"

"He said he knew you came here. He said he was your brother."

"What did he look like?"

"Taller than you, slim, maybe one-fifty-five, one-sixty, black hair cut short, greenish eyes, darkish complexion, sunburned, good suit, college-boy talk, manicured nails . . ."

"That's my fucking brother," Thomas said. "My mother must've given him the address. I made her swear not to tell anybody. Not anybody. I'm lucky it's not all over town. What'd my brother want?"

"He wanted to talk to you. I said if anybody by your name happened in here, I'd pass on the message. He left a telephone number. In a place called Whitby."

"That's him. I'll call him when I'm good and ready. I got other matters on my mind. I never heard any good news from him yet. There're some things I want you to do for me, Pappy."

Pappy nodded. At his prices he was happy to be of service.

"First—get me a bottle," Thomas said. "Second—get me a gun. Third—get hold of Schultzy for me and find out if the heat is still on. And if he thinks I can take a chance seeing my kid. Fourth—get me a girl. In that order."

"One hundred dollars," Pappy said.

Thomas took out his wallet and gave Pappy two fifties, from his pay. Then he gave him the wallet. "Put it in the safe." He didn't want to have a pocket full of cash with him drunk and some strange broad in the room, going through his clothes.

Pappy took the wallet and went out of the room. He didn't talk more than was necessary. He did all right, not talking. He had two diamond rings on his fingers and he wore alligator shoes. Thomas locked the door behind him and didn't get up until Pappy came back with the bottle and three cans of beer, a plate of ham sandwiches, and a Smith and Wesson British army revolver, with the serial number filed off. "I happened to have it in the house," Pappy said as he gave Thomas the gun. He had a lot of things in the house. "Don't use it on the premises, that's all."

"I won't use it on the premises." Thomas opened the bottle of bourbon and offered it to Pappy. Pappy shook his head. "I don't drink. I got a delicate stomach."

"Me, too," Thomas said and took a long gulp from the bottle.

"I bet," Pappy said, as he went out.

What did Pappy know? What did anyone know?

The bourbon didn't help, although he kept swigging at the bottle. He kept remembering the silent men standing along the rail watching him and Dwyer go down the gangplank, hating him. Maybe he didn't blame them. Putting a loudmouth ex-con in his place was one thing. Putting the boots to him so hard that he killed himself was another. Somewhere, Thomas realized, a man who considered himself a human being should know where to stop, leave another man a place to live in. Sure, Falconetti was a pig and deserved a lesson, but the lesson should have ended somewhere else than in the middle of the Atlantic.

He drank some more whiskey to try to help him forget the look on Falconetti's face when Thomas had said, "You can go now, slob," and Falconetti had got up from the table and walked out of the mess room with everybody watching him.

The whiskey didn't help.

He had been bitter when Rudolph had called him a wild animal when they were kids, but would he have the right now to be bitter if somebody said it to him today? He really believed that if people would leave him alone he would leave them alone. He yearned for peace. He had felt that the sea had finally relieved him of his burden of violence; the future he and Dwyer hoped for for themselves was harmless and unobjectionable, on a mild sea, among mild men. And here he was, with a death on his conscience, hiding away with a gun in a crumbling hotel room, exiled in his own country. Christ, he wished he could cry.

Half the bottle was empty when Pappy knocked on the door again.

"I talked to Schultzy," Pappy said. "The heat's still on. You better ship out again as soon as you can."

"Sure," Thomas nodded, maudlin, bottle in hand. The heat was still on. The heat had been on all his life. There had to be people like that. If only for the sake of variety. "Did Schultzy say there was any chance of sneaking a look at my kid?"

"He advised against it," Pappy said. "This trip."

"He advised against it. Good old Schultzy. It's not his kid. You hear anything else about me?"

"There's a Greek from the *Elga Andersen* just checked in," Pappy said. "He's talking in the lobby. About how you killed a certain individual called Falconetti."

"When they have it in for you," Thomas said, "they don't lose any time, do they?"

"He knows you fought as a pro. You better stick close to this room until I get you a berth."

"I'm not going anywhere," Thomas said. "Where's that dame I asked for?"

"She'll be here in an hour," Pappy said. "I told her your name was Bernard and she won't ask any questions."

"Why Bernard?" Thomas asked irritably.

"I had a friend once by that name." Pappy left lightly, on his wary alligator feet.

Bernard, Thomas thought, what a name!

He hadn't been out of the room all week. Pappy had brought him six bottles of whiskey. No more girls. He had lost his taste for whores. He had started to grow a moustache. The trouble was it came out red. With his blond hair it looked more like a disguise than a false moustache. He practiced loading and unloading the revolver. He tried not to think about the look on Falconetti's face. He paced up and down all day like a prisoner. Dwyer had lent him one of his books on navigation and he managed a couple of hours a day on that. He felt he could plot a course from Boston to Johannesburg. But he didn't dare go downstairs and buy himself a newspaper. He made his bed and cleaned his room himself, to keep out the chambermaid. He was paying Pappy ten bucks a day, everything included, except the booze, of course, and his money was running low. He yelled at Pappy because Pappy didn't come up with a berth, but Pappy only shrugged and said it was a slack time and to have patience. Pappy came and went, a free man. It was easy for him to have patience.

It was three o'clock in the afternoon when he heard Pappy's knock. It was a strange hour for him to come up. Usually, he only came in three times a day, with the meals.

Thomas unlocked the door. Pappy came in, light on his feet, expressionless behind his dark glasses.

"You got something for me?" Thomas asked.

"Your brother was at the desk a few minutes ago," Pappy said.

"What'd you tell him?"

"I said maybe I knew a place where I could get hold of you. He's coming back in a half hour. You want to see him?"

Thomas thought for a moment. "Why not?" he said. "If it'll make the sonofabitch happy."

Pappy nodded. "I'll bring him up when he comes," he said.

Thomas locked the door behind him. He felt the stubble of his moustache, decided to shave. He looked at his face in the peeling mirror in the grimy little bathroom. The moustache was ridiculous. His eyes were bloodshot. He lathered up, shaved. He needed a haircut. He was balding on the top of his head, but his hair hung halfway down over his ears and over the collar of his shirt in back. Pappy was useful in many ways but he didn't give haircuts.

The half hour took a long time passing.

The knock on the door was not Pappy's. "Who's there?" Thomas whispered. He was uncertain about the tone of his voice after not talking to anyone but Pappy for a week. And you didn't hold long conversations with Pappy.

"It's me. Rudy."

Thomas unlocked the door. Rudolph came into the room and Thomas locked the door before they shook hands. Thomas didn't ask him to sit down. Rudolph didn't need a haircut, he wasn't going bald and he was wearing a pressed seersucker country-gentleman kind of suit because the weather had turned warm. He must have a laundry bill a yard long, Thomas thought.

Rudolph smiled tentatively. "That man downstairs is pretty mysterious about you," he said.

"He knows what he's doing."

"I was here about two weeks ago."

"I know," Thomas said.

"You didn't call."

"No."

Rudolph looked curiously around the room. The expression on his face was peculiar, as though he didn't quite believe what he saw. "I suppose you're hiding from somebody," he said.

"No comment," Thomas said. "Like they say in the newspapers."

"Can I help you?"

"No." What could he say to his brother? Go look for a man called Falconetti, longitude 26.24, latitude 38.31, depth ten thousand feet? Go tell some gangster in Las Vegas with a sawed-off shotgun in the trunk of his car he was sorry he'd beaten up Gary Quayles, he wouldn't do it again?

"I'm glad to see you, Tom," Rudolph said, "although this isn't exactly a social visit."

"I gathered that."

"Mom is dying," Rudolph said. "She wants to see you."

"Where is she?"

"In the hospital at Whitby. I'm on my way there now and if you . . ."

"What do you mean dying? Dying today or dying next week or dying in a couple of years?"

"Dying any minute," Rudolph said. "She's had two heart attacks."

"Oh, Christ." It had never occurred to Thomas that his mother could die. He even had a scarf that he'd bought for her in Cannes, in his seabag. The scarf had an old map of the Mediterranean on it, in three colors. People you were bringing presents to didn't die.

"I know you've seen her from time to time," Rudolph said, "and that you've written her letters. She turned religious, you know, and she wants to make her peace with everybody before she goes. She asked for Gretchen, too."

"She doesn't have to make her peace with me," Thomas said. "I got nothing against the old lady. It wasn't her fault. I gave her a rough time. And what with our goddamn father . . ."

"Well," Rudolph said, "do you want to come with me? I have the car downstairs in front of the door."

Thomas nodded.

"You'd better pack some things in a bag," Rudolph said. "Nobody knows exactly how long . . ."

"Give me ten minutes," Thomas said. "And don't wait in front of the door. Drive around for awhile. Then in ten minutes come up

Fourth Avenue going north. I'll be walking that way, near the curb. If you don't see me, go back two blocks below here and drive up Fourth Avenue again. Make sure the door on the right side isn't locked. Go slow. What kind of car you got?"

"A Chevrolet, 1960. Green."

Thomas unlocked the door. "Don't talk to anybody on the way out."

When he'd locked the door again, he threw some things into his shaving kit. He didn't have a valise, so he stuffed two shirts and some underwear and socks and the scarf, wrapped in tissue paper, into the bag in which Pappy had brought the last bottle of bourbon. He took a gulp of bourbon to steady his nerves. He decided that he might need the whiskey on the trip, so he put the half-empty bottle in another bag.

He put on a tie and the blue suit which he had bought in Marseilles. If your mother was dying you had to be dressed for the occasion. He took the Smith and Wesson out of the dresser drawer, checked the safety, stuck it in his belt, under his jacket, and unlocked the door. He peeked out. There was nobody in the hallway. He went out, locked the door and dropped the key into his pocket.

Pappy was behind the desk but didn't say anything when he saw Thomas going through the lobby carrying the shaving kit under his left arm and the paper bags in his left hand. Thomas blinked as the sun hit him outside the hotel. He walked quickly, but not as though he was trying to get away from anything, toward Fourth Avenue.

He had only walked a block and a half up the Avenue when the Chevy drew up alongside. He took one last look around and jumped inside.

Once they got out of the city he began to enjoy the trip. The breeze was cool, the countryside light green. Your mother was dying and you were sorry about that, but your body didn't know anything about mothers dying, it just knew it liked to be cool and moving and out of prison and breathing country air. He took the bottle out of the bag and offered it to Rudolph, but Rudolph shook his head. They hadn't talked much. Rudolph had told him that Gretchen had remarried and that her husband had been killed not long ago. He also told Thomas that he had just gotten married. The Jordaches never learn, Thomas thought.

Rudolph drove fast and he concentrated on the road. Thomas took a swig from the bottle from time to time, not enough to start getting drunk, just enough to keep him feeling good.

They were going seventy when they heard the siren behind them. "Damn it," Rudolph said, as he pulled over to the side.

The State trooper came up to them and said, "Good afternoon, sir." Rudolph was the sort of man cops said, "Good afternoon, sir," to. "Your license, please," the trooper said, but he didn't examine the license until he'd taken a good look at the bottle on the front seat between Rudolph and Thomas. "You were going seventy in a fifty-mile zone," he said, staring coldly at Thomas, with his wind-beaten face, busted nose, and his Marseilles blue suit.

"I'm afraid I was, officer," Rudolph said.

"You fellas've been drinking," the trooper said. It was not a question.

"I haven't touched a drop," Rudolph said, "and I'm driving."

"Who's he?" The trooper pointed with the hand holding Rudolph's license at Thomas.

"He's my brother," Rudolph said.

"You got any identification?" The trooper's voice was hard and suspicious as he spoke to Thomas.

Thomas dug into his pocket and produced his passport. The trooper opened it as though it were loaded. "What're you doing carrying your passport around?"

"I'm a seaman."

The trooper gave Rudolph his license, but put Thomas's passport in his pocket. "I'll hold onto this. And I'll take that." He gestured toward the bottle and Rudolph gave it to him. "Now turn around and follow me."

"Officer," Rudolph said, "why don't you just give me the ticket for speeding and let us go on our way. It's absolutely imperative for us to . . ."

"I said turn around and follow me," the trooper said. He strode back to his car, where another trooper was sitting at the wheel.

They had to drive back more than ten miles the way they had come, to the State Troopers' barracks. Thomas managed to get the pistol out from under his belt and slide it under the seat without Rudolph's noticing it. If the cops searched the car, it would be six months to a year, at least. Concealed weapon. No permit. The trooper who arrested them explained to a sergeant that they had been speeding and that they had committed a further violation by having an opened bottle of liquor in a moving vehicle and that he wanted a sobriety test run on them. The Sergeant was impressed by Rudolph and was apologetic, but he smelled both their breaths and made them take a breathing test and he made Thomas piss in a bottle.

It was dark by the time they got out of the building, without the whiskey, but with a ticket for speeding. The Sergeant had decided neither of them was drunk, but Thomas saw that the trooper who had arrested them took a long hard look at his passport before he gave it back to him. Thomas was unhappy about it, because there were plenty of cops who traded with the gangs, but there was nothing he could do about it.

"You should've known better than to offer me a ride," Thomas said when they were back on the road. "I get arrested for breathing."

"Forget it," Rudolph said shortly and stepped on the gas.

Thomas felt under the seat. The gun was still there. The car hadn't been searched. Maybe his luck was changing.

They got to the hospital a little after nine but the nurse at the entrance stopped Rudolph and whispered to him for awhile. Rudolph said, "Thank you," in a funny voice, then came over to Thomas and said, "Mom died an hour ago."

II

"The last thing she said," Gretchen was saying, "was, 'You tell your father, wherever he is, that I forgave him.' Then she went into a coma and never came out of it."

"She was nutty on the subject," Thomas said. "She asked me to be on the lookout for him in Europe."

It was late that night and the three of them were sitting in the living room of the house that Rudolph had shared with his mother for the last few years. Billy was asleep upstairs and Martha was weeping in the kitchen for the woman who had been her daily opponent and tormentor. Billy had begged to be allowed to come East to see his grandmother for one last time and Gretchen had decided that death was a part of a child's education, too, and brought him along. Her mother had forgiven Gretchen, too, before they had put her in the oxygen tent for the last time.

Rudolph had already made the arrangements for the funeral. He had spoken to Father McDonnell and consented to the whole rigamarole, as he had told Jean when he had called her in New York. Eulogy, Mass, the whole thing. But he stopped at having the windows of the house closed and the blinds drawn. He was only going to coddle his mother up to a certain point. Jean had said morosely she'd come up if he wanted but he had said there was no sense in that.

The cable in Rome had had an unsettling effect on her. "Families," she said. "Always goddamn families." She had drunk a great deal that night and all the way back on the plane. If he hadn't held her he was sure she would have fallen going down the steps from the plane. When he left her in New York she was in bed, looking frail and worn out. Now, facing his brother and sister in the hushed house he had shared with the dead woman, Rudolph was thankful his wife was not with him.

"After all this time," Thomas said, "when your mother dies you're pissing in a bottle for a cop." Thomas was the only one drinking, but he was sober.

Gretchen had kissed him at the hospital, and held him close and in her grief she wasn't the snooty, superior woman, looking down her nose at him, that he had remembered, but warm, loving, familiar. Thomas felt there was a chance they would forget the past and be reconciled finally. He had enough enemies in the world as it was, without keeping up a running battle with his family.

"I dread the funeral," Rudolph said. "All those old ladies she used to play bridge with. And what the hell will that idiot McDonnell have to say?"

"She was broken in spirit by poverty and lack of love and she was devoted to God," Gretchen said.

"If I can keep him to that," Rudolph said.

"Excuse me," Thomas said. He went out of the room and to the guest bedroom he was sharing with Billy. Gretchen was in the second extra room. Nobody had gone into their mother's room yet.

"He seems different, doesn't he?" Gretchen said, when she and Rudolph were alone.

"Yeah."

"Subdued. Beaten, somehow."

"Whatever it is," Rudolph said, "it's an improvement."

They heard Thomas's footsteps coming down the stairs and they broke off the conversation. Thomas came into the room, carrying something soft wrapped in tissue paper. "Here," he said, handing it to Gretchen, "here's something for you."

Gretchen unwrapped the gift, spread out the scarf with the old map of the Mediterranean on it in three colors. "Thank you," she said. "It's lovely." She got up and kissed him. For some reason the kiss unnerved him. He felt he might do something crazy, like breaking down and crying or smashing furniture or going up and getting the Smith and Wesson and shooting out the window at the moon. "I bought it in Cannes," Thomas said, "for Mom."

"Cannes?" Rudolph said. "When were you in Cannes?"

Thomas told him and they figured out that they must have been there at the same time, at least one day. "That's terrible," Rudolph said. "Brothers just passing each other by like that. From now on, Tom, we've got to keep in touch with each other."

"Yeah," Thomas said. He knew he wanted to keep seeing Gretchen, but Rudolph was another matter. He had suffered too much at Rudolph's hands. "Yeah," Thomas said. "I'll have my secretary send you a copy of my itinerary in the future." He stood up. "I'm going to bed. I've had a long day."

He went up the stairs. He wasn't all that tired. He just didn't want to be in the same room with Rudolph. If he'd known where the funeral home was, he'd have slipped out of the house and gone there and sat up all night with the body of his mother.

He didn't want to wake Gretchen's kid, asleep in blue pajamas in the other bed, so he didn't turn on the light as he undressed, but just left the door open a little so that enough light came in from the hallway to see what he was doing. He didn't have any pajamas and he wondered if the kid would comment on his sleeping in his shorts when he woke in the morning. Probably not. The kid seemed like a nice boy and he wouldn't know automatically that he was supposed to have a low opinion of his uncle. The kid smelled clean, soapy. He had tried to comfort Gretchen at the hospital, hugging her, both of them crying. He didn't remember ever having hugged his mother.

Looking at the kid made him think about Wesley. He had to see him. He had to do something about him. He couldn't let him be brought up all his life by a tramp like Teresa.

He closed the door and got into the soft, clean bed. Rudolph slept in a bed like this every night of his life.

III

Teddy Boylan was at the funeral. So were a great many other people. The newspapers in Whitby and Port Philip had considered the news of the death of the mother of that leading citizen Rudolph Jordache important enough to display the obituary prominently. There wasn't much to say about Mary Jordache, but the newspapers made up for it with descriptions of Rudolph's honors and accomplishments,

Chairman of the Board of Dee Cee Enterprises, President Junior Chamber of Commerce of Whitby, graduate *cum laude*, Whitby University, Member of the Board of Trustees, Whitby University, Member Town Planning Committee of both Whitby *and* Port Philip, bold and forward-looking merchant and real-estate developer. There was even a mention of the fact that Rudolph had run the two twenty for the Port Philip track team and that he had played the trumpet in a jazz combination called the River Five in the middle 1940's.

Poor Mom, Rudolph thought, as he surveyed the crowded church, she would have enjoyed seeing so many people come out for a ceremony in her honor.

Father McDonnell was worse and longer than Rudolph feared and he tried not to listen to the lies spoken above the flower-banked coffin. He hoped Gretchen wasn't taking it too hard, remembering the other coffin in the crematorium in California. He glanced at her. There was no sign on her face that she was remembering anything.

The birds were singing in the cemetery trees, pleased with the onset of summer. At the grave, as the coffin was being lowered, to the sobs of the bridge ladies, Rudolph and Thomas and Gretchen stood side by side, Gretchen holding Billy by the hand.

Boylan caught up with them as they walked away from the grave toward the line of waiting black limousines. "I don't want to intrude," he said, as they halted, "Gretchen, Rudolph—I just wanted to say how sorry I was. Such a young woman."

For a moment, Rudolph was confused. His mother had looked ancient to him, *was* ancient. She had been old at thirty, had started dying before that. For the first time her real age made a conscious impression on him. Fifty-six. Just about Boylan's age. No wonder Boylan said, "Such a young woman."

"Thank you, Teddy," Rudolph said. He shook hands with Boylan. Boylan didn't look ready for the grave. His hair was the same color as always, his face was tanned and unlined, his carriage was as erect, his shoes were as well shined as ever.

"How've you been, Gretchen?" Boylan asked. The mourners had stopped behind the group, not wishing to push past them on the narrow graveled walk between the gravestones. As usual, Boylan accepted without thinking about it the fact that others waited on his pleasure.

"Very well, thank you, Teddy," Gretchen answered.

"I take it this is your son." Boylan smiled at Billy, who stared at him soberly.

"Billy, this is Mr. Boylan," Gretchen said. "He's an old friend."

"How do you do, Billy." Boylan shook the boy's hand. "I hope we meet again on a happier occasion."

Billy said nothing. Thomas was regarding Boylan through narrowed eyes, hiding, Rudolph thought, what could only have been a desire to laugh under the lowered lids. Was Thomas remembering the night he had seen Boylan parading naked around the house on the hill, preparing a drink to take to Gretchen, in bed upstairs? Graveyard thoughts.

"My brother, Thomas," Rudolph said.

"Oh, yes," Boylan said. He didn't offer to shake hands. He spoke to Rudolph. "If you have the time, Rudy," he said, "with all your multifarious activities, perhaps you could give me a ring and we could get together for dinner sometime. I want to confess that I was wrong and you were right about your choice of career. And bring Gretchen along, if she's available. Please."

"I'm leaving for California," Gretchen said.

"What a pity. Well, I won't keep you any longer." He made a little bow and stepped back, a slender, expensively maintained figure, brilliantly out of place, even in his dark suit, in the drab march of small-town mourners.

As they walked toward the first limousine, from which Rudolph had steadfastly barred Father McDonnell, Gretchen realized, with a little shock, how much alike Rudolph and Boylan were, not in looks, of course, and she hoped not in character, but in attitudes, turns of speech, gestures, choice of clothes, manner of moving. She wondered if Rudolph knew how much he owed to the man and whether he would be pleased if she pointed it out to him.

She thought about Boylan on the trip back to Rudolph's house. She supposed she ought to think about her mother, whose grave was being filled with earth at that moment in the sunny cemetery, full of the summery sound of birds. But she thought about Boylan. There was no sense of loving or desire, but no feeling, either, of distaste or hatred or wish for revenge. It was like taking an old girlhood toy, a special doll, out of a forgotten trunk and holding it curiously, trying to remember how you felt when it meant something to you and not succeeding and deciding to throw it away or give it to some later child down the block. First love. Be my Valentine.

When they got to the house they all decided they needed a drink. Billy, who looked pale and drawn, complained that he had a headache and went upstairs and lay down. Martha, despite her unceasing flow of tears, went into the kitchen to prepare a cold lunch.

Rudolph made martinis for Gretchen and himself and gave some bourbon over ice to Thomas, who had taken off his coat, which was uncomfortably tight across his massive shoulders. He had unbuttoned his collar, too, and was sitting hunched forward on a straight-backed wooden chair, his elbows resting on his thighs, his hands hanging between his legs. He makes every place he sits look like a stool in the corner of a ring, Rudolph thought, as he gave him the drink.

They raised their glasses, although they did not mention their mother.

They had decided to leave for New York all together after lunch, because they didn't want to be in the house for the calls of condolence. Great heaps of flowers had been delivered, but Rudolph had instructed Martha to send all but one bunch to the hospital where his mother had died. The flowers he had kept, daffodils, made a little yellow explosion on the coffee table in front of the couch. The windows were open and the sun streamed in, a smell of warm grass came in from the lawn. The low-beamed eighteenth-century room was handsome, subdued and orderly, not quaint or cluttered, not aggressively modern, Rudolph's taste.

"What are you going to do with the house?" Gretchen asked. "Now?"

Rudolph shrugged. "Keep it, I suppose. I still have to be up here a good part of the time. Although, it's a lot too big for me now. Would you like to come and live here?"

Gretchen shook her head. The debates with the lawyers went on and on. "I'm committed to California."

"What about you?" Rudolph asked Thomas.

"Me?" Thomas said, surprised. "What the hell would I do here?"

"You'd find something." Rudolph was careful not to say, "I'll find you something." He sipped at the martini, grateful for it. "You must admit it's an improvement on where you stay in New York."

"I don't plan to stay there long. Anyway, this is no place for me. The people here look at me as though I'm an animal in the zoo."

"You're exaggerating," Rudolph said.

"Your friend Boylan wouldn't shake my hand at the cemetery. If you don't shake a man's hand in a cemetery, where the hell would you shake his hand?"

"He's a special case."

"He sure is." Thomas began to laugh. The laughter wasn't loud, but it was somehow alarming in the atmosphere.

"What're you laughing about?" Rudolph asked as Gretchen looked at Thomas puzzledly.

"The next time you see him," Thomas said, "tell him he was right not to shake my hand."

"What're you talking about, Tom?"

"Ask him if he remembers the night of VE Day. The night they burned a cross on his property and there was the fire."

"What're you saying?" Rudolph asked sharply. "That you did it?"

"Me and a friend." Thomas stood up and went over to the sideboard and refilled his glass.

"Why did you do it?" Gretchen asked.

"Boyish high spirits," Thomas said, as he put in some more ice. "We just won the war."

"But why did you pick on *him?*" Gretchen asked.

Thomas fiddled with his drink, pushing the ice down, his back to Gretchen. "He happened to be involved with a lady I knew at the time," he said. "I didn't approve of the involvement. Should I mention the lady's name?"

"There's no need," Gretchen said quietly.

"Who was the friend?" Rudolph asked.

"What difference does it make?"

"It was that Claude, Claude What's-his-name that you used to hang around with, wasn't it?"

Thomas smiled, but didn't answer. He drank standing up, leaning against the sideboard.

"He disappeared right after that," Rudolph said. "I remember now."

"He sure did," said Thomas. "And I disappeared right after him, if you remember *that.*"

"Somebody knew you boys had done it," Rudolph said.

"Somebody." Thomas nodded ironically.

"You're lucky you didn't go to jail," Gretchen said.

"That's what Pa was intimating," said Thomas. "When he kicked me out of town. Well, there's nothing like a funeral to get people to remembering the good old days, is there?"

"Tom," Gretchen said, "you're not like that *any more,* are you?"

Thomas crossed over to where Gretchen was sitting on the couch and bent over and kissed her forehead gently. "I hope I'm not," he said. Then he straightened up and said, "I'll go up and see how the kid's doing. I like him. He'll probably feel better if he's not alone."

He took his drink with him as he went upstairs.

Rudolph mixed two more martinis for himself and Gretchen. He was glad to have something to do with his hands. His brother was not a comfortable man to be with. Even after he went out of a room, he left an air of tension, of anguish.

"God," Gretchen said finally, "it doesn't seem possible that we all have the same genes, does it?"

"The runt of the litter," Rudolph said. "Who is it—you, me—him?"

"We were awful, Rudy, you and I," Gretchen said.

Rudolph shrugged. "Our mother was awful. Our father was awful. You knew why they were awful, or at least you thought you knew why—but that didn't change matters. I *try* not to be awful."

"You're saved by your luck," Gretchen said.

"I worked pretty hard," Rudolph said defensively.

"So did Colin. The difference is, you'll never run into a tree."

"I'm terribly sorry, Gretchen, that I'm not dead." He couldn't hide the hurt in his voice.

"Don't take it the wrong way, please. I'm *glad* that there's somebody in the family who'll never run into a tree. It's certainly not Tom. And I know it isn't me. I'm the worst, maybe. I carried the luck of the whole family. If I hadn't been on a certain road at lunchtime near Port Philip one Saturday afternoon, all our lives would've been completely different. Did you know that?"

"What're you talking about?"

"Teddy Boylan," she said matter-of-factly. "He picked me up. I am what I am today largely because of him. I've slept with the men I've slept with because of Teddy Boylan. I ran away to New York because of Teddy Boylan. I met Willie Abbott because of Teddy Boylan and despised him finally because he wasn't different enough from Teddy Boylan and I loved Colin because he was the opposite of Teddy Boylan. All those scolding articles I wrote that everybody thought were so smart, were digs at America because it produced men like Teddy Boylan and made life easy for men like Teddy Boylan."

"That's maniacal. . . . The luck of the family! Why don't you go consult the gypsies and wear an amulet and be done with it?"

"I don't need any gypsies," Gretchen went on. "If I hadn't met Teddy Boylan and laid him, do you think Tom would have burned a cross on his hill? Do you think he'd have been sent away like a criminal if there'd never been a Teddy Boylan? Do you think he'd be just what he is today if he'd stayed in Port Philip with his family around him?"

"Maybe not," Rudolph admitted. "But there would've been something else."

"Only there wasn't anything else. There was Teddy Boylan, screwing his sister. As for you—"

"I know all I have to know about me," Rudolph said.

"You do? You think you'd have gone to college without Teddy Boylan's money? You think you'd dress the way you do or be so interested in success and money and how to get there the fastest way possible without Teddy Boylan? Do you think somebody else would have sought you out and taken you to concerts and art galleries and pampered you through school, and given you all that lordly confidence in yourself, if it hadn't been Teddy Boylan?" She finished her second martini.

"Okay," Rudolph said, "I'll build a monument in his honor."

"Maybe you should. You certainly can afford it now, with your wife's money."

"That's below the belt," Rudolph said angrily. "You know I didn't have the faintest idea . . ."

"That's what I was talking about," Gretchen said. "Your Jordache awfulness is turned into something else by your luck."

"How about *your* Jordache awfulness?"

Gretchen's entire tone changed. The sharpness went out of her voice, her face became sad, soft, younger. "When I was with Colin I wasn't awful," she said.

"No."

"I don't think I'm ever going to find a Colin again."

Rudolph reached out and touched her hand, his anger blunted by his sister's continuing sorrow. "You wouldn't believe me," Rudolph said, "if I told you I think you will."

"No," she said.

"What're you going to do? Just sit and mourn forever?"

"No."

"What're you going to do?"

"I'm going back to school."

"School?" Rudolph said incredulously. "At your age?"

"Postgraduate school," Gretchen said. "At UCLA. That way I can live at home and take care of Billy, all at the same time. I've been to see them and they've agreed to take me."

"To study what?"

"You'll laugh."

"I'm not laughing at anything today," Rudolph said.

"I got the idea from the father of a boy in Billy's class," Gretchen said. "He's a psychiatrist."

"Oh, Christ," Rudolph said.

"That's more of your luck," Gretchen said. "To be able to say, Oh, Christ, when you hear the word psychiatrist."

"Sorry."

"He works part time at a clinic. With lay analysts. They're people who aren't M.D.'s, but who've studied analysis, who've been analyzed, and are licensed to treat cases that don't call for deep analysis. Group therapy, intelligent children who refuse to learn how to read or write or are wilfully destructive, kids from broken homes who have retreated into themselves, girls who have been made frigid by their religion or by some early sexual trauma, and who are breaking up with their husbands, Negro and Mexican children who start school far behind the others and never catch up and lose their sense of identity . . ."

"So," Rudolph said. He had been listening impatiently. "So, you're going to go out and solve the Negro problem and the Mexican problem and the religious problem all on your own, armed with a piece of paper from UCLA, and . . ."

"I will try to solve one problem," Gretchen said, "or maybe two problems, or maybe a hundred problems. And I'll be solving my own problem at the same time. I'll be busy and I'll be doing something useful."

"Not something useless like your brother," Rudolph said, stung. "Is that what you're trying to say?"

"Not at all," Gretchen said. "You're being useful in your own way. Let me be useful in mine, that's all."

"How long is all this going to take?"

"Two years, minimum, for the degree," Gretchen said. "Then finishing the analysis . . ."

"You'll never finish," he said. "You'll find a man and . . ."

"Maybe," Gretchen said. "I doubt it, but maybe . . ."

Martha came in, red eyed, and said that lunch was ready on the dining-room table. Gretchen went upstairs to get Billy and Thomas and when they came down the entire family went into the dining room and had lunch, everybody being polite to everybody else, saying, "Please pass the mustard," and "Thanks," and "No, I think that's enough for me right now."

After lunch, they got into the car and drove out of Whitby for New York, leaving their dead behind them.

They reached the Hotel Algonquin at a little after seven. Gretchen and Billy were staying there, because there was no room for them in Rudolph's one-bedroom apartment, where Jean was waiting for him. Rudolph asked Gretchen if she and Billy wanted to have dinner with him and Jean, but Gretchen said this was no day to meet a new sister-in-law. Rudolph invited Thomas, too, but Thomas, who was sitting low in the front seat, said, "I have a date."

When Billy got out of the car, Thomas got out too, and put his arm around the boy's shoulders. "I have a son, too, Billy," Thomas said. "A lot younger than you. If he grows up anything like you, I'll be a proud father."

For the first time in three days, Billy smiled.

"Tom," Gretchen said, standing under the hotel's canopy, "am I ever going to see you again?"

"Sure," Thomas said. "I know where to reach you. I'll call you."

Gretchen and her son went into the hotel, a porter carrying the two bags.

"I'll get a cab from here, Rudy," Thomas said. "You must be anxious to get home to your wife."

"I'd like a drink," Rudolph said. "Let's go in the bar here and . . ."

"Thanks. I'm pressed for time," Thomas said. "I got to be on my way." He kept peering over Rudolph's shoulder at the traffic on Sixth Avenue.

"Tom," Rudolph insisted, "I have to talk to you."

"I thought we were all talked out," Thomas said. He tried to hail a cab, but the driver was off duty. "You got nothing more to say to me."

"No?" Rudolph said savagely. "Don't I? What if I told you you're worth about sixty thousand dollars as of the close of the market today? Would that make you change your mind?"

"You're a great little old joker, aren't you, Rudy?" Thomas said.

"Come on in to the bar. I'm not joking."

Thomas followed Rudolph into the bar.

The waiter brought them their whiskies and then Thomas said, "Let's hear."

"That goddamn five thousand dollars you gave me," Rudolph said. "You remember that?"

"Blood money," Thomas said. "Sure I remember."

"You said to do anything I wanted with it," Rudolph said. "I think I recall your exact words, 'Piss on it, blow it on dames, give it to your favorite charity . . .'"

"That sounds like me." Thomas grinned.

"Well, what I wanted to do with it was invest it," Rudolph said.

"Always a head for business," Thomas said. "Even as a kid."

"I invested it in your name, Tom," Rudolph said deliberately. "In my own company. There haven't been much in the way of dividends so far, but what there've been I've plowed back. But the stock has been divided four times and it's gone up and up. I tell you, you have about sixty thousand dollars in shares that you own outright."

Thomas gulped down his drink. He closed his eyes and pushed at his eyeballs with his fingers.

"I tried to get hold of you time and time again in the past two years," Rudolph said. "But the phone company said your phone was disconnected and when I sent letters to your old address, they always came back with a stamp on them saying 'Unknown at this address.' And Ma never told me she was in touch with you until she went to the hospital. I read the sports pages, but you seemed to have dropped out of sight."

"I was campaigning in the West," Thomas said, opening his eyes. The room looked blurry now.

"Actually, I was just as glad I couldn't find you," Rudolph said, "because I knew the stock would keep going up and I didn't want you to be tempted to sell prematurely. In fact, I don't think you ought to sell now."

"You mean I can go somewhere tomorrow," Thomas asked, "and just say I got some stock I want to sell and somebody'll give me sixty thousand dollars, *cash?*"

"I told you I don't advise you to . . ."

"Rudy," Thomas said, "you're a great guy and all that and maybe I take back a lot of what I've been thinking about you all these years, but right now I ain't listening to any advice. All I want is for you to give me the address of the place where that man is waiting to give me that sixty thousand dollars cash."

Rudolph gave up. He wrote out Johnny Heath's office address, and gave it to Thomas. "Go to this place tomorrow," he said, "I'll call Heath and he'll be expecting you. Please, Tom, be careful."

"Don't worry about me, Rudy. From now on I'll be so careful, you won't even recognize me." Thomas ordered another round of drinks. When he lifted his arm to call the waiter, his jacket slipped back and Rudolph saw the pistol stuck in the belt. But he didn't say anything. He had done what he could for his brother. He could do no more.

"Wait a minute for me here, will you?" Thomas said. "I have to make a phone call."

He went into the lobby and found a booth and looked up the number of TWA. He dialed the number and asked about flights the next day to Paris. The girl at TWA told him there was a flight at eight P.M. and asked him if he wished to make a reservation. He said, "No thank you," and hung up, then called the Y.M.C.A. and asked for Dwyer. It was a long time before Dwyer came to the phone and Thomas was just about ready to hang up the phone and forget him.

"Hello," Dwyer said, "who's this?"

"Tom. Now listen to . . ."

"Tom!" Dwyer said excitedly. "I've been hanging around and hanging around waiting to hear from you. Jesus, I was worried. I thought maybe you were dead . . ."

"Will you stop running off at the mouth?" Thomas said. "Listen to me. There's a TWA plane leaving Idlewild for Paris tomorrow night at eight o'clock. You be there at the Reservations Counter at six-thirty. All packed."

"You mean you got reservations? On a *plane?*"

"I don't have them yet," Thomas said, wishing Dwyer wasn't so excitable. "We'll get them there. I don't want my name on any lists all day."

"Oh, sure, sure, Tom, I understand."

"Just be there. On time."

"I'll be there. Don't you worry."

Thomas hung up.

He went back to the bar and insisted on paying for the drinks.

Outside, on the sidewalk, just before he got into the cab, that drew up next to the curb, he shook hands with his brother.

"Listen, Tom," Rudolph said, "let's have dinner this week. I want you to meet my wife."

"Great idea," Thomas said. "I'll call you Friday."

He got into the cab and told the driver, "Fourth Avenue and Eighteenth Street."

He settled back in the cab luxuriously, holding on to the paper bag with his belongings. When you had sixty thousand dollars everybody invited you to dinner. Even your brother.

PART
FOUR

Chapter 1

It was raining when she drove up to the house, the torrential, tropical rain of California that flattened flowers, bounced off the tiles of roofs, like ricocheting silvery bullets and sent bulldozed hillsides sliding down into neighbors' gardens and swimming pools. Colin had died two years ago but she still automatically looked into the open garage to see if his car was there.

She left her books in the 1959 Ford and hurried to the front door, her hair soaking, even though it was only a few yards. Once inside she took off her coat and shook her wet hair. It was only four-thirty in the afternoon, but the house was dark and she turned on the front hall light. Billy had gone off on a camping trip to the Sierras with friends for the weekend and she hoped that the weather was better up in the mountains than down on the coast.

She reached into the mailbox. There were some bills, some circulars, a letter from Venice, in Rudolph's handwriting.

She went into the living room, turning on lights as she went. She kicked off her wet shoes, made herself a Scotch and soda, and seated herself on the couch, her legs curled up under her, pleased with the warmly lit room. There were no whispers in the shadows anymore. She had won the battle with Colin's ex-wife and she was going to stay in the house. The judge had awarded her a temporary allowance from the estate, against a final settlement, and she didn't have to depend upon Rudolph anymore.

She opened Rudolph's letter. It was a long one. When he was in America, he preferred to phone, but now that he was wandering around Europe, he used the mails. He must have had a lot of time on his hands, because he wrote often. She had had letters from him from London, Dublin, Edinburgh, Paris, St.-Jean-de-Luz, Amsterdam, Copenhagen, Geneva, Florence, Rome, Ischia, Athens, and from little inns in towns that she had never heard of where he and Jean stopped en route for the night.

"Dear Gretchen"—she read—"It's raining in Venice and Jean is out in it taking pictures. She says it's the best time to get the quality of Venice, water on water. I'm snug in my hotel, undriven by art. Jean also likes to take pictures of people for the series she's doing under the worst possible circumstances. Hardship and age, she tells me, preferably the two together, tell more about the character of a people and a country than anything else. I do not attempt to argue with her. I prefer handsome young people in sunshine, myself, but I am only her Philistine husband.

"I am enjoying to the utmost the glorious fruits of sloth. Within me, after all the years of hustle and toil, I have discovered a happy, lazy man, content to look at two masterpieces a day, to lose myself in a foreign city, to sit for hours at a cafe table like any Frenchman or Italian, to pretend I know something about art and haggle in galleries for paintings by new men whom nobody ever heard about and whose works will probably make my living room in Whitby a chamber of horrors when I eventually get back there.

"Curiously enough, with all our traveling, and despite the fact that Pa came from Germany and probably had as much German in him as American, I have no desire to visit the country. Jean has been there, but isn't anxious to go back. She says it's too much like America, in all essential ways. I'll have to take her opinion on the subject.

"She is the dearest woman alive and I am terribly uxorious and find myself carting her cameras around so as not to miss a moment with her. Except when it rains, of course. She has the sharpest of eyes and I have seen and understood more about Europe in six months with her than I would in sixty years alone. She has absolutely no literary sense and never reads a newspaper and the theater bores her, so I fill in that section of our communal life. She also drives our little Volkswagen very well, so I get a chance to moon and sightsee and enjoy things like the Alps and the valley of the Rhone without worrying about falling off the road. We have a pact. She drives in the morning and drinks a bottle of wine at lunch and I drive in the afternoon, sober.

"We don't stay in the fancy places, as we did on our honeymoon, because as Jean says, now it's for real. We do not suffer. She talks freely to everybody and with my French and her Italian and everybody's English, we find ourselves striking up friendships with the widest variety of people—a wine-grower from Burgundy, a masseur on the beach at Biarritz, a rugby player from Lourdes, a non-objective painter, priests galore, fishermen, a bit-part actor in the French movies, old English ladies on bus tours, ex-commandos in the British army, GI's based in Europe, a representative in the Paris Chamber of Deputies who says the only hope for the world is John Fitzgerald Kennedy. If you happen to bump into John Fitzgerald Kennedy, pass the word on to him.

"The people it is almost impossible not to love are the English. Except for other English. The English are dazed, although it doesn't do to tell them so. Somehow, all the wheels of power went wrong, and after winning the war with their last ounce of blood and courage, they gave the whole thing away to the Germans. I don't want the Germans, or anybody, to starve, but the English had a right to expect that they could live in a world at least approximately as comfortable as the old enemy once the guns fell silent. Chalk one up against us, I'm afraid.

"Whatever you do, you must make sure that Billy gets a good dose of Europe before he's twenty, while it's still Europe and before it becomes Park Avenue and the University of Southern California and Scarsdale and Harlem and the Pentagon. All those things, or at least some of them, may be good for us, but it would be sad to see it happen to places like Rome and Paris and Athens.

"I have been to the Louvre, to the Rijks-museum in Amsterdam, to the Prado, and I have seen the lions at Delos and the gold mask in the museum in Athens, and if I had seen nothing else and had been deaf and mute and unloved, these things alone would have been worth much more than the six months of my life I have been away."

The phone rang and Gretchen put the letter down and got up and answered. It was Sam Corey, the old cutter who had worked with Colin on the three pictures he had made. Sam called faithfully, at least three times a week, and occasionally she would go with him to the showing of a new film at the studio that he thought would interest her. He was fifty-five years old, solidly married, and was comfortable to be with. He was the only one of the people who had been around Colin that she had kept up with.

"Gretchen," Sam said, "we're running one of the *Nouvelle Vague* pictures that just came in from Paris tonight. I'll take you to dinner after."

"Sorry, Sam," Gretchen said. "Somebody, one of the people from my classes, is coming over to work with me."

"School days, school days," Sam croaked, "dear old golden rule days." He had left school in the ninth grade and was not impressed with higher education.

"We'll do it some other night, eh, Sam?"

"Sure thing," he said. "Your house wash down the hill yet?"

"Just about."

"California," Sam said.

"It's raining in Venice, too," Gretchen said.

"How do you get top-secret information like that?"

"I'm reading a letter from my brother Rudolph. He's in Venice. And it's raining."

Sam had met Rudolph when Rudolph and Jean had come out to stay with her for a week. After they had left Sam had said Rudolph was okay, but he was crazy about his wife.

"When you write him back," said Sam, "ask him if he wants to put five million dollars in a little low-budget picture I would like to direct."

Sam, who had been around enormously wealthy people for so long in Hollywood, believed that the sole reason for the existence of a man who had more than a hundred thousand dollars in the bank was to be fleeced. Unless, of course, he had talent. And the only talents Sam recognized were those involved in making films.

"I'm sure he'll be delighted to," Gretchen said.

"Keep dry, Baby," Sam said, and hung up.

Sam was the calmest man she knew. In the storms of temperament that he had been through in the years in the studios, he had survived serenely, knowing what he knew, running a hundred thousand miles of film through his hands, catching mistakes, patching up other men's blunders, never flattering, doing the utmost with the material he was handed, walking off pictures when the people making them became insufferable, going through one style after another with imperturbable efficiency, something of an artist, something of a handyman, loyal to the few directors, who, despite failures, were always what Sam considered pros, committed to their craft, painstaking, perfectionist. Sam had seen Colin's plays and when Colin had come to Hollywood had sought Colin out and said he wanted to work with him, modest, but secure enough in what he did to know that the new director would be grateful for his experience and that their collaboration would be fruitful.

After Colin died, Sam had a long talk with Gretchen and had warned her that if she just was going to hang around Hollywood, doing nothing, just being a widow, she would be miserable. He had seen her with Colin enough in the course of the three films Colin had made, with Sam as the cutter, to understand that Colin had depended upon her, and with reason. He had offered to take her in with him, teach her what he knew about the business. "For a lone woman in this town," he had said, "the cutting room is the best place. She isn't on her own, she isn't flinging her sex around, she isn't challenging anybody's ego, she has something methodical and practical to do, like baking a cake, every day."

Gretchen had said, "Thank you, no," at the time, because she didn't want to profit, even by that much, on Colin's reputation, and had opted for the graduate course. But every time she talked to Sam she wondered if she hadn't said no too quickly. The people around her in school were too young, moved too fast, were interested in things that seemed useless to her, learned and discarded huge gobs of information in hours while she still was painfully struggling with the same material for weeks and weeks.

She went back to the couch and picked up Rudolph's letter again. Venice, she remembered, Venice. With a beautiful young wife who, just by chance, happened to turn out to be rich. Rudolph's luck.

"There are murmurs of unrest from Whitby,"—she read.—"Old man Calderwood is taking very unkindly to my prolonged version of the Grand Tour and even Johnny, who has a Puritan conscience under that egg-smooth debauchee face, hints delicately to me that I have vacationed long enough. In fact, I don't even see it as a vacation, although I have never enjoyed anything more. It is the continuation of my education, the continuation that I was too poor to pay for when I got out of college and went to work full time in the store.

"I have many things to solve when I get back, which I am slowly turning over in my mind even as I look at a Titian in the Doges' Palace or drink an espresso at a table in the Piazza San Marco. At the risk of sounding grandiose, what I have to decide is what to do with my life. I am thirty-five years old and I have enough money, both capital and yearly income, so that I can live extremely well for the rest of my life. Even if my tastes were wildly extravagant, which they're not, and even if Jean were poor, which she isn't, this would still be true. Once you are rich in America, it takes genius or over-powering greed to fall back into poverty. The idea of spending the rest of my life buying and selling, using my days to increase my wealth, which is already more than sufficient, is distasteful to me. My acquisitive instinct has been deadened by acquisition. The satis-faction I might get by opening new shopping centers throughout the country, under the Calderwood sign, and gaining control of still more companies, is minimum. A commercial empire, the prospects of which enchant men like Johnny Heath and Bradford Knight, has small charms for me and running one seems to me to be the drab-best kind of drudgery. I like travel and would be desolate if I were told that I could not come here ever again, but I cannot be like the characters in Henry James, who, in the words of E. M. Forster, land in Europe and look at works of art and at each other and that is all. As you can tell, I've used my new-found leisure to do some reading.

"Of course, I could set myself up as a philanthropist and dole out sums to the deserving poor or deserving artists or deserving scientists and scholars, but although I give, I hope generously, to many causes, I can't see putting myself into the position of arbiter in such matters. It certainly is not a full-time vocation, at least not for me.

"It must seem funny to you, as it does to me, for anyone in the Jordache family to be worrying so because he has money, but the swings and turns of American life are so weird that here I am doing just that.

"Another complication. I love the house in Whitby and I love Whitby itself. I do not, really, want to live anywhere else. Jean, too, sometime ago, confessed that she liked it there, and said that if we ever had children she would prefer bringing them up there than in the city. Well, I shall see to it that she'll have children, or at least a child, to bring up. We can always keep a small apartment in New York for when we want a bit of worldly excitement or when she has work to do in the city. But there is nobody in Whitby who just does nothing. I would be immediately branded as a freak by my neigh-bors, which wouldn't make the town as attractive to me as it now is. I don't want to turn into a Teddy Boylan.

"Maybe when I get back to America, I'll buy a copy of the *Times* and look through the want-ads.

"Jean has just come in, soaked and happy and a little drunk. The rain drove her into a cafe and two Venetian gentlemen plied her with wine. She sends her love.

"This has been a long, egotistical letter. I expect one of equal length, equally egotistical, from you. Send it to the American Express in Paris. I don't know just when we'll be in Paris, but we'll be there sometime in the next couple of weeks and they'll hold the letter for me. Love to you and Billy, Rudolph. P.S. Have you heard from Tom? I haven't had a word from him since the day of Mom's funeral."

Gretchen put down the flimsy sheets of air-mail stationery, covered densely with her brother's firm, clearly formed handwriting. She finished her drink and decided against another one. She got up and went to the window and looked out. The rain was pouring down. The city below her was erased by water.

She mused over Rudolph's letter. They were friendlier through the mails than when they saw each other. In writing, Rudolph showed a hesitant side, a lack of pride and confidence, that was endearing and that he somehow hid at other times. When they were together, at one moment or another, the urge to wound him swept over her. His letters showed a largeness of spirit, a willingness to forgive that was the sweeter because it was tacit and he never showed any signs that he knew that there was anything that needed forgiving. Billy had told her about his assault on Rudolph at the school and Rudolph had never even mentioned it to her and had been warm and thoughtful with the boy every time he saw him. And the letters were always signed "Love to you and Billy."

I must learn generosity, she thought, staring out at the rain.

She didn't know what to do about Tom. Tom didn't write her often, but he kept her abreast of what he was doing. But as he had done with his mother, he made her promise to say nothing of his whereabouts to Rudolph. Right now, right this day, Tom was in Italy, too. On the other side of the peninsula, it was true, and farther south, but in Italy. She had received a letter from him just a few days before, from a place called Porto Santo Stefano, on the Mediterranean, above Rome. Tom and a friend of his called Dwyer had finally found the boat they were looking for at a price they could manage and had been working on it in a shipyard there all autumn and winter, to get it ready for service by June first. "We do everything ourselves,"—Tom had written in his large, boyish handwriting, on ruled paper.—"We took the Diesels apart piece by piece and we put them together again, piece by piece and they're as good as new. We've rewired the entire boat, calked and scraped the hull, trued the propellers, repaired the generator, put in a new galley, painted the hull, painted the cabins, bought a lot of second hand furniture and painted that. Dwyer turns out to be quite an interior decorator and I'd love you to see what he's done with the saloon and the cabins.

We've been putting in a fourteen-hour day seven days a week, but it's worth it. We live on board, even though the boat is up on blocks on dry land, and save our money. Neither Dwyer or me can cook worth a damn, but we don't starve. When we go out on charter we'll have to find somebody who can cook to crew with us. I figure we can make do with three in crew. If Billy would like to come over for the summer we have room for him on board and plenty of work. When I saw him he looked as though a summer's hard work out in the open might do him a lot of good.

"We plan to put the boat in the water in ten days. We haven't decided on a name yet. When we bought it it was called the *Penelope II*, but that's a little too fancy for an ex-pug like me. Talking about that—nobody hits anybody here. They argue a lot, or at least they talk loud, but everybody keeps his hands to himself. It's restful to go into a bar and be sure you won't have to fight your way out. They tell me it's different south of Naples, but I wouldn't know.

"The man who runs the shipyard here is a good guy and from what I gather, asking around, he is giving us a very good deal on everything. He even found us two charters already. One in June and one in July and he says more will be coming up. I had some run-ins with certain Italians in the U.S., but these Italians are altogether different. Nice people. I am learning a few words in Italian, but don't ask me to make a speech.

"When we get into the water, my friend Dwyer will be the skipper, even though it was my money that bought the boat. He's got third mate's papers and he knows how to handle a boat. But he's teaching me. The day I can get into a harbor on my own without busting into anything, I am going to be the skipper. After expenses, we're splitting on everything, because he's a pal and I couldn't have done it without him.

"Again, I got to remind you of your promise not to tell Rudy anything. If he hears I did something crazy like buying a leaky old boat on the Mediterranean with the money he made for me, he'll split a gut. His idea of money is something you hide in the bank. Well, everybody to his own pleasure. When I have the business on a good, solid, paying basis, I'll write and tell him and invite him to come on a cruise with us, with his wife. Free. Then he can see for himself just how dumb his brother is.

"You don't write much, but in your letters I get the impression things aren't so hot with you. I'm sorry. Maybe you ought to change whatever it is you're doing and do something else. If my friend

Dwyer wasn't so close to being a fag as to make no difference, I'd ask you to marry him, so you could be the cook. Joke.

"If you have any rich friends who like the idea of a Mediterranean cruise this coming summer, mention my name. No joke.

"Maybe it seems gaga to you and Rudy, your brother's being a yacht captain but I figure it must be in the blood. After all Pa sailed the Hudson in his own boat. One time too many. Not such a joke.

"The boat is painted white, with blue trim. It looks like a million dollars. The shipyard owner says we could sell it like it is right now and make 10,000 dollars profit. But we're not selling.

"If you happen to go East you could do me a favor. See if you can find out where my wife is and what she's doing and how the kid is. I don't miss the flag and I don't miss the bright lights, but I sure miss him.

"I am writing such a long letter because it is raining like crazy here and we can't finish the second coat of the deck house (blue). Don't believe anybody who tells you it doesn't rain on the Mediterranean.

"Dwyer is cooking and he is calling me to come eat. You have no idea how awful it smells. Love and kisses, Tom."

Rain in Porto Santo Stefano, rain in Venice, rain in California. The Jordaches weren't having much luck with the weather. But two of them, at least, were having luck with everything else, if only for one season. "Five o'clock in the afternoon is a lousy time of day," Gretchen said aloud. To stave off self-pity, she drew the curtains and made herself another drink.

It was still raining at seven o'clock, when she got into the car and went down to Wilshire Boulevard to pick up Kosi Krumah. She drove slowly and carefully down the hill, with the water, six inches deep, racing ahead of her, gurgling at the tires. Beverly Hills, city of a thousand rivers.

Kosi was taking his master's in sociology and was in two of her courses and they sometimes studied together, before examinations. He had been at Oxford and was older than the other students and more intelligent, she thought. He was from Ghana and had a scholarship. The scholarship, she knew, was not a lavish one, so when they worked together, she tried to arrange to give him dinner first at the house. She was sure he wasn't getting quite enough to eat, although he never talked about it. She never dared to go into restaurants too far off campus with him, as you never knew how headwaiters would behave if a white woman came in with a black man,

no matter how properly dressed he was and regardless of the fact
that he spoke English with a pure Oxford accent. In class there never
was any trouble and two or three of the professors seemed even un-
duly to defer to him when he spoke. With her, he was polite but invariably distant, almost like a teacher with a student. He had never
seen any of Colin's movies. He didn't have the time to go to movies,
he said. Gretchen suspected he didn't have the money. She never
saw him with girls and he didn't seem to have made any friends except for herself. If she was his friend.

Her practice was to pick him up at the corner of Rodeo and
Wilshire in Beverly Hills. He didn't have a car, but he could take
the bus along Wilshire from Westwood, where he lived, near the
university campus. As she came along Wilshire, peering through the
spattered windshield, the rain so dense that the wipers couldn't work
fast enough to clear the glass, she saw him standing on the corner,
with no raincoat, with not even the collar of his jacket turned up for
protection. His head was up and he was looking out at the stream of
traffic through his blurred glasses as though he were watching a parade.

She stopped and opened the door for him and he got in leisurely,
water dripping from his clothes and forming an immediate pool on
the floor around his shoes.

"Kosi!" Gretchen said. "You're drowning. Why didn't you wait in
a doorway, at least?"

"In my tribe, my dear," he said, "the men do not run from a little
water."

She was furious with him. "In my tribe," she mimicked him, "in
my tribe of white weaklings, the men have sense enough to come in
out of the rain. You . . . you . . ." She racked her brain for an
epithet. "You *Israeli!*"

There was a moment of stunned silence. Then he laughed, uproar-
iously. She had to laugh with him. "And while you're at it," she said,
"you might as well wipe your glasses, tribesman."

Obediently, he dried off his glasses.

When they got home, she made him take off his shirt and jacket
and gave him one of Colin's sweaters to wear. He was a small man,
just about Colin's size, and the sweater fit him. She hadn't known
what to do with Colin's things, so they just lay in the drawers and
hung in the closets, where he had left them. Every once in a while
she told herself that she should give them to the Red Cross or some
other organization, but she never got around to it.

They ate in the kitchen, fried chicken, peas, salad, cheese, ice cream, and coffee. She opened a bottle of wine. Kosi had once told her he had gotten used to drinking wine with his meals at Oxford.

He always protested that he wasn't hungry and that she needn't have bothered, but she noticed that he ate every morsel she put before him, even though she wasn't much of a cook and the food was just passable. The only difference in their eating habits was that he used his fork with the left hand. Another thing he had learned in Oxford. He had gone through Oxford on a scholarship, too. His father kept a small cotton-goods shop in Accra, and without the scholarship there never would have been enough money to educate the brilliant son. He hadn't been home in six years, but planned to go back and settle in Accra and work for the government as soon as he had written his thesis.

He asked where Billy was. Usually, they all ate together. When Gretchen said that Billy was away for the weekend, he said, "Too bad. I miss the little man."

Actually, Billy was taller than he, but Gretchen had become accustomed to Kosi's speech, with its "my dears" and its "little men."

The rain drummed on the flagstones of the patio outside the window. They dawdled over dinner and Gretchen opened another bottle of wine.

"To tell you the truth," she said, "I don't feel like working tonight."

"None of that, now," he said reprovingly. "I didn't make that fearful journey in a flood just to eat."

They finished the wine as they did the dishes, Gretchen washing and Kosi wiping. The dishwasher had been broken for six months, but there wasn't much need for it, as there were never more than three people for any one meal and fiddling with the machine was more trouble than it was worth for so few dishes.

She carried the pot of coffee into the living room with her and they each had two cups as they went over the week's work. He had a quick, agile mind, by now severely trained, and he was impatient with her slowness.

"My dear," he said, "you're just not concentrating. Stop being a dilettante."

She slammed the book shut. It was the third or fourth time he had reprimanded her since they had sat down at the desk together. Like a—like a governess, she thought, a big black mammy governess. They were working on a course on statistics and statistics bored her to stupefaction. "Not everyone can be as goddamn clever as you," she said. "I was never the brightest student in Accra, I never won a scholarship to . . ."

"My dear Gretchen," he said quietly, but obviously hurt, "I never claimed to be the brightest student anywhere . . ."

"Never claimed, never claimed," she said, thinking, hopelessly, I'm being shrill. "You don't have to claim. You just sit there being superior. Or stand out in the rain like some idiotic tribal god, looking down on the poor, cowardly white folk slinking past in their decadent Cadillacs."

Kosi stood up, stepped back. He took off his glasses and put them in his pocket. "I'm sorry," he said. "This relationship doesn't seem to be working out . . ."

"This relationship," she taunted him. "Where did you learn to talk like that?"

"Good night, Gretchen," he said. He stood there, his mouth tight, his body taut. "If you'll just give me the time to change back into my shirt and jacket . . . I won't be a minute."

He went into the bathroom. She heard him moving around in there. She drank what was left in her cup. The coffee was cold and the sugar at the bottom of the cup made it too sweet. She put her head in her hands, her elbows on the desk, above the scattered books, ashamed of herself. I did it because of Rudolph's letter this afternoon, she thought. I did it because of Colin's sweater. Because of nothing to do with that poor young man with his Oxford accent.

When he came back, wearing his shirt and jacket, still shapeless and damp, she was standing, waiting for him. Without his glasses his close-cropped head was beautiful, the forehead wide, the eyelids heavy, the nose sharply cut, the lips rounded, the ears small and flat against the head. All done in flawless, dark stone, and all somehow pitiful and defeated.

"I shall be leaving you now, my dear," he said.

"I'll take you in the car," she said, in a small voice.

"I'll walk, thank you."

"It's still pouring," she said.

"We Israelis," he said somberly, "do not pay attention to the rain."

She essayed a laugh, but there was no answering glint of humor.

He turned toward the door. She reached out and seized his sleeve. "Kosi," she said. "Please don't go like that."

He stopped and turned back toward her. "Please," she said. She put her arms loosely around him, kissed his cheek. His hands came up slowly and held her head between them. He kissed her gently.

Then not so gently. She felt his hands sliding over her body. Why not? she thought, why not, and pressed him to her. He tried to pull away and move her toward the bedroom, but she dropped onto the couch. Not in the bed in which she and Colin had lain together.

He stood over her. "Undress," he said.

"Put out the lights."

He went over to the switch on the wall and the room was in darkness. She heard him undressing as she took off her clothes. She was shivering when he came to her. She wanted to say, "I have made a mistake, please go home," but she was ashamed to say it.

She was dry and unready but he plunged into her at once, hurting her. She moaned, but the moan was not one of pleasure. She felt as though she were being torn apart. He was rough and powerful and she lay absolutely still, absorbing the pain.

It was over quickly, without a word. He got up and she heard him feeling his way across the room toward the light switch. She jumped up and ran into the bathroom and locked the door. She washed her face repeatedly in cold water and stared at her reflection in the mirror above the basin. She wiped off what was left of her lipstick which had smeared around her mouth. She would have liked to take a hot shower, but she didn't want him to hear her doing it. She put on a robe and waited as long as she dared, hoping he would be gone when she went out. But he was still there, standing in the middle of the living room, dressed, impassive. She tried to smile. She had no idea of how it came out.

"Don't you ever do anything like that again to anybody, my dear," he said evenly. "And certainly not to me. I will not be tolerated. I will not be condescended to. I will not be part of anybody's program of racial integration."

She stood with her head lowered, unable to speak.

"When you get your degree," he went on in the same flat, malevolent tone, "you can play Lady Bountiful with the poor bastards in the charity clinics, the beautiful, rich white lady proving to all the little niggers and all the little greasers how democratic and generous this wonderful country is and how loving and Christian educated beautiful white ladies who don't happen to have husbands can be. I won't be here to see it. I'll be back in Africa, praying that the grateful little niggers and the grateful little greasers are getting ready to slit your throat."

He went out silently. There was only the smallest sound as the front door closed.

After a while, she cleared the desk they had been working on. She put the cups and saucers and the coffee pot in the sink in the kitchen and piled the books on one side of the desk. I'm too old for school books, she thought. I can't cope. Then, walking painfully, she went around and locked up. Arnold Simms, in your maroon bathrobe, she thought as she switched off the lights, rest easy. I have paid for you.

In the morning, she didn't attend her two Saturday classes, but called Sam Corey at the studio and asked if she could come over and talk to him.

Chapter 2

1964

Even pregnant as she was, Jean insisted upon coming down and having breakfast with him every day. "At the end of the day," she said, "I want to be as tired as you. I don't want to be one of those American women who lie around all day and then when their husbands come home, drag the poor beasts out every evening, because they're bursting with unused vigor. The energy gap has ruined more marriages by half than adultery."

She was nearly at term and even under the loosely flowing nightgown and robe she was wearing, the bulge was huge and clumsy. Rudolph had a pang of guilt when he watched her. She had had such a neat delicate way of walking and now she was forced to balance herself painfully, belly protruding, pace careful, as she went from room to room. Nature has provided women with a kind of necessary lunacy, he thought, for them to desire to bring children into the world.

They sat in the dining room, with the pale April sun streaming through the windows, while Martha brought them fresh coffee. Martha had changed miraculously since his mother's death. Although she ate no more than before, she had filled out and was now matronly and comfortable. The sharp lines of her face had disappeared and the everlasting downward twitch of her mouth had been replaced by something that might even have been a smile. Death has its uses, Rudolph thought, watching her gently place the coffee pot in front of Jean. In the old days she would have banged it down on the table, her daily accusation against Fate.

Pregnancy had rounded Jean's face and she no longer looked like a schoolgirl fiercely determined to get the best marks in the class. Placid and womanly, her face glowed softly in the sunlight.

"This morning," Rudolph said, "you look saintly."

"You'd look saintly, too," Jean said, "if you hadn't had any sex for two months."

"I hope the kid turns out to be worth all this," Rudolph said.

"He'd better."

"How is it this morning?"

"Okay. He's marching up and down wearing paratroop boots, but otherwise okay."

"What if it's a girl?" Rudolph asked.

"I'll teach her not to overlap," Jean said. They both laughed.

"What have you got to do this morning?" he asked.

"There's a nurse coming to be interviewed, and the furniture's coming for the nursery and Martha and I have to put it in place and I have to take my vitamins and I have to weigh myself," Jean said. "A big morning. How about you?"

"I have to go to the university," Rudolph said. "There's a board of trustees' meeting. Then I ought to look in at the office . . ."

"You're not going to let that old monster Calderwood nag at you again, are you?"

Ever since Rudolph had told Calderwood he intended to retire from the business in June, Calderwood had argued with him almost every time he saw him. "Who retires at the age of thirty-six, for the Lord's sake?" Calderwood kept repeating.

"I do," Rudolph had once replied, but Calderwood had refused to believe him. Suspicious, as always, Calderwood felt that Rudolph was really maneuvering for more control and had hinted that if Rudolph would stay he would give it to him. Calderwood had even offered to move the main office down to New York, but Rudolph said he no longer wanted to live in New York. Jean now shared his attachment to the old farmhouse in Whitby and was poring over plans with an architect to enlarge it.

"Don't worry about Calderwood," Rudolph said, standing. "I'll be home for lunch."

"That's what I like," Jean said. "A husband who comes home for lunch. I'll make love to you after lunch."

"You'll do nothing of the kind." He leaned over to kiss the dear, smiling face.

It was early and he drove slowly, enjoying the town. Small children in bright-colored parkas were riding tricycles on the sidewalks or played on the drying lawns, burgeoning with the first frail green of spring. A young woman in slacks pushed a baby carriage in the sunshine. An old dog dozed on the warm steps of a big gingerbread house, painted white. Hawkins, the mailman, waved at him and he waved back. Slattery, standing beside his prowl car and talking to somebody's gardener, saluted him with a smile; two professors from the biology department, walking toward the university deep in conversation, looked up long enough to indicate a mild hello. This part of town, with its trees and large wooden houses and quiet streets, had an innocent nineteenth-century neighborly air, before the wars, before booms and depressions. Rudolph wondered how he ever had been anxious to get away from the town, where he was known and greeted at every turn, for the anonymous uncertainties and stony hostility of New York.

He had to pass the athletic field on the way to the Administration Building and he saw Quentin McGovern in a gray suit, jogging along the track. He stopped the car and got out and Quentin came over to him, a tall, serious young man, his skin gleaming with the sweat of his exercise. They shook hands. "I don't have my first class till eleven," Quentin said. "And it was a nice day for running, after being indoors on the boards all winter."

They didn't run in the morning anymore. Since his marriage, Rudolph had taken up tennis, for Jean's sake. Anyway, it was too Spartan a deed to make himself get up every morning at seven o'clock in all weathers from the bed of his bride to pound around a track for three-quarters of an hour, trying to keep pace with a young athlete at the top pitch of his form. Besides, it made him feel old. There was time enough for that bit.

"How's it going, Quentin?" Rudolph asked.

"Not bad. I'm twenty-two eight for the two twenty and the Coach says he's going to run me in the four forty and the relay as well."

"What does your mother say now?"

Quentin smiled, remembering the cold winter mornings. "She says for me not to get too swell-headed. Mothers don't change."

"How about your work in school?"

"They must have made a mistake at the office," Quentin said. "They put me on the Dean's List."

"What does your mother say about *that?*"

"She says it's because I'm colored and they want to show how liberal they are." Quentin smiled faintly.

"If you have any further trouble with your mother," Rudolph said, "tell her to call me."

"I'll do that, Mr. Jordache."

"Well, I've got to be going. Give my regards to your father."

"My father's dead, Mr. Jordache," Quentin said quietly.

"I'm sorry." Rudolph got back into his car. Christ, he thought. Quentin's father must have worked at least twenty-five years at Calderwood's. You'd think somebody would have had the sense to pass the word around.

The morning was no longer as pure and pleasurable as it had been before his conversation with Quentin.

All the parking places were taken in front of the Administration Building and Rudolph had to leave his car almost five hundred yards away. Everything is turning into a parking lot, he thought irritably, as he locked the car. The radio had been stolen out of it some time before, in New York, and Rudolph now locked the car wherever he left it, even if he was only going to be five minutes. He had had a mild argument with Jean on the subject, because she refused to lock the car at any time and even left the front door of the house open when she was home alone. You could love your neighbor, he had told her, but it was foolish to ignore the larceny in his heart.

As he was testing the door, he heard his name called. "Hey, Jordache!" It was Leon Harrison, who was also on the board of trustees and was on his way to the meeting. Harrison was a tall, portly man of about sixty, with senatorial white hair and a misleading heartiness of manner. He was the publisher of the local newspaper, which he had inherited from his father, along with a great deal of real estate in and around Whitby. The newspaper was not doing very well, Rudolph knew. He wasn't sorry about it. It was badly run by a small, underpaid, drunken, broken-down staff of men who had been thrown off other papers all across the country. Rudolph made a point in not believing anything he read in Harrison's paper, even reports on the weather.

"How are you, boy," Harrison said, putting his arm around Rudolph's shoulder as they walked toward the Administration Building. "All prepared to put a fire under us old fogies again this morning?" He laughed loudly, to show his lack of malice. Rudolph had

had many dealings with Harrison, not all of them agreeable, about the Calderwood advertising in his paper. Harrison had started out calling him boy, then Rudy, then Jordache, and by now was back to boy, Rudolph noted.

"Just the same routine suggestions," Rudolph said. "Like burning down the Science Building to get rid of Professor Fredericks." Fredericks was the head of the department and Rudolph was sure that it was safe to say that the science courses were the worst in any university the size of Whitby north of the Mason-Dixon Line. Fredericks and Harrison were cronies and Fredericks often wrote scientific articles for Harrison's paper, articles that made Rudolph blush with shame for the university. At least three times a year Fredericks would write an article acclaiming a new cure for cancer that would appear on the editorial page of the Whitby *Sentinel*.

"You businessmen," Harrison said largely, "you never can appreciate the role of pure science. You want to see a return on your investment every six months. You expect to see the simoleons come pouring out of every test tube."

When it suited his convenience, Harrison, with his acres of choice downtown property and his interest in a bank, was very much the hard-headed businessman. At other times, publisher that he was, immersed in printer's ink, he was a literary figure, decrying the elimination of Latin as a required subject for graduation or inveighing against a new English syllabus because it did not include enough of the works of Charles Dickens.

He tipped his hat grandly to a woman instructor in the psychology department who crossed their path. He had old-fashioned manners and up-to-date hatreds, Harrison. "I hear there're some interesting things going on down at Dee Cee," he said.

"There are always interesting things going on at Dee Cee," Rudolph said.

"More interesting than usual," said Harrison. "There's a rumor that you're going to step down."

"I never step down," Rudolph said and then was sorry he said it. The man brought out the worst in him.

"If you *do* happen to step down," Harrison persisted, "who's the next in line? Knight?"

"The matter hasn't come up," Rudolph said. Actually, the matter had come up, between him and Calderwood, but no decision had been reached. He didn't like to lie, but if you didn't lie to a man like Harrison you would deserve canonization.

"Dee Cee means a lot to this town," Harrison said, "largely thanks to you, and you know I'm not a man who indulges in flattery, and my readers have a right to know what's going on behind the scenes." The words were banal and innocuous, but there was a threat there, and both Harrison and Rudolph understood it.

"If anything happens," Rudolph said, "your readers will be the first to know."

As he went up the steps of the Administration Building, with Harrison at his side, Rudolph couldn't help but feel that the morning was deteriorating rapidly.

The President of the university was a new, youngish, brisk man from Harvard, by the name of Dorlacker, who stood for no nonsense from his board. He and Rudolph were friendly and he came over to the house quite often with his wife and talked freely, mostly about getting rid of the majority of the board of trustees. He detested Harrison.

The meeting ran along familiar lines. The finance committee chairman reported that although endowments were going up, costs were going up even faster and advised raising the price of tuition and putting a freeze on the number of scholarships. The motion was tabled for further study.

The board was reminded that the new wing for the library would be ready for the fall term and had not yet been given a name. It was recalled from the last meeting that Mr. Jordache had suggested that it be called the Kennedy Wing, or even better, have the whole building, now merely called the Memorial Library, be renamed the Kennedy Library.

Harrison protested that the late President had been a controversial figure, and had represented only half the country and that a university campus was no place to introduce divisive politics. On a vote, it was decided to call the new wing the Kennedy Wing, leaving the entire building under its old title, the Memorial Library. The President drily appointed Mr. Harrison to find out for the board what or whom the library was in memory of.

Another member of the board, who also had had to park at some distance from the Administration Building, said that he thought there ought to be a strict rule that no students be allowed to own automobiles. Impossible to enforce, Dorlacker said, therefore unwise. Perhaps a new parking lot could be built.

Harrison was disturbed by an editorial in the student newspaper, calling for a ban-the-bomb demonstration. The editor should be disciplined for introducing politics to the campus and for disrespect for the government of the United States. Dorlacker explained that it was his opinion that a university was not the place to put down freedom of speech in America. On a vote, it was decided not to discipline the editor.

"This board," Harrison growled, "is running away from its responsibilities."

Rudolph was the youngest member of the board and he spoke softly and deferentially. But because of his alliance with Dorlacker and his ability to dig up endowments from alumni and foundations (he had even got Calderwood to donate fifty thousand dollars toward the new library wing) and his close knowledge of the town and its inter-relation with the university, he was the most influential member of the board and he knew it. What had started as almost a hobby and a mild boost to his ego had become a ruling interest in his life. It was with pleasure that he dominated the board and pushed one project after another down the throats of the die-hards like Harrison on the board. The new wing on the library, the expanded courses in sociology and foreign affairs, the introduction of a resident artist and the expansion of the Art School, the donation for two weeks a year of the theater at the Shopping Center to the Drama Department had all been his ideas. Remembering Boylan's sneer, Rudolph was resolved that before he got through, nobody, not even a man like Boylan, could call Whitby an agricultural school.

As an added satisfaction, he could at the end of each year deduct a good part of his travel expenses, both in the United States and abroad, from his income tax, as he made it a point to visit schools and universities wherever he went, as part of his duties as a trustee of the university. The training he had received at the hands of Johnny Heath had made this almost automatic. "The amusements of the rich," Johnny called the game with the Internal Revenue Service.

"As you know," Dorlacker was saying, "at this meeting we are to consider new appointments to the faculty for the next school year. There is one department post that will be open—the head of the department of economics. We have inspected the field and conferred with the members of the department and we would like to offer for your approval the name of an ex-head of what used to be the combined departments of history and economics here, a man who has been gaining valuable experience in Europe for the past few years, Professor Lawrence Denton." As he spoke the name, Dorlacker casually turned toward Rudolph. There was the barest hint of a wink. Rudolph had exchanged letters with his old teacher and knew that

Denton wanted to come back to America. He was not made to be a man without a country, Denton had written, and his wife had never gotten over being homesick. Rudolph had told Dorlacker all about Denton and Dorlacker had been sympathetic. Denton had helped his own case by using the time in Europe to write a book about the rebirth of the German economy, which had gotten respectful reviews.

Denton's resurrection was only poetic justice, Rudolph thought. He had not testified in his old friend's behalf at a time when it might have helped. But if he *had* testified the chances were that he never would have been elected to the board of trustees and been able to politick for Denton's reinstatement. There was something pleasingly ironic about the situation that made Rudolph smile to himself as Dorlacker spoke. He knew that between them Dorlacker and he had canvassed enough votes to put Denton across. He sat back comfortably, in silence, allowing Dorlacker to make the necessary moves.

"Denton," Harrison said. "I remember the name. He got kicked out for being a Red."

"I've looked into the record thoroughly, Mr. Harrison," Dorlacker said, "and I've found that there never was any kind of accusation against Professor Denton or any formal investigation. Professor Denton resigned to work in Europe."

"He was a Red of some kind," Harrison said doggedly. "We have enough wild men as it is on this campus without importing any new ones."

"At the time," Dorlacker said gently, "the country was under the McCarthy cloud and a great number of estimable people were made to suffer groundlessly. Fortunately, that is far behind us, and we can judge a man by his abilities alone. I, for one, am happy to be able to demonstrate that Whitby is guided only by strict scholastic standards."

"If you put that man in here," Harrison said, "my paper will have something to say about it."

"I consider your remark unseemly, Mr. Harrison," Dorlacker said, without heat, "and I'm certain that upon reflection you will think better of it. Unless somebody else has more to add, I believe it is time to put the appointment to a vote."

"Jordache," Harrison said, "I don't suppose you had anything to do with this?"

"Actually, I did," Rudolph said. "Professor Denton was the most interesting teacher I had when I was an undergraduate here. I also found his recent book most illuminating."

"Vote, vote," Harrison said. "I don't know why I bother to come to these meetings."

His was the only vote against Denton and Rudolph planned to send a cable to the exile in Geneva as soon as the meeting was over.

There was a knock on the door and Dorlacker said, "Come in."

His secretary entered. "I'm sorry to disturb you, sir," she said to Dorlacker, "but there's a call for Mr. Jordache. I said that he was in a meeting, but . . ."

Rudolph was out of his chair and walking toward the secretary's phone in the anteroom.

"Rudy," Jean said. "I think you'd better come here. Quick. The pains are starting." She sounded happy and unworried.

"I'll be right there," he said. "Make my excuses to President Dorlacker and the members of the board, please," he said to the secretary. "I have to take my wife to the hospital. And will you please call the hospital and tell them to get in touch with Dr. Levine and say that Mrs. Jordache will be there in about a half hour."

He ran out of the office and all the way to where his car was parked. He fumbled with the lock, cursing whoever had stolen the radio in New York City, and for a wild moment looked in the car parked next to his to see if by chance the keys were in the ignition. They weren't. He went back to his own car. This time the lock turned and he jumped in and sped through the campus and down the quiet streets toward home.

Waiting all through the long day, holding Jean's hand, Rudolph didn't know how she could stand it. Dr. Levine was calm. It was normal, he said, for a first birth. Dr. Levine's calmness made Rudolph nervy. Dr. Levine just dropped in casually from time to time during the day, as though it were just a routine social call. When he suggested that Rudolph go down to the hospital cafeteria to have some dinner, Rudolph had been shocked that the doctor could think he could leave his suffering wife and gorge himself, abandoning her to her agony. "I'm a father," he said, "not an obstetrician."

Dr. Levine had laughed. "Fathers have been known to eat, also," he had said. "They have to keep their strength up."

Materialistic, casual bastard. If ever they were crazy enough to have another baby, they'd hire somebody who wasn't a machine.

The child was born just before midnight. A girl. When Dr. Levine came out of the delivery room for a minute to tell Rudolph the news that mother and child were fine, Rudolph wanted to tell Dr. Levine that he loved him.

He walked beside the rolling bed on which Jean was being taken back to her room. She looked flushed and small and exhausted and when she tried to smile up at him the effort was too much for her.

"She's going to sleep now," Dr. Levine said. "You might as well go home."

But before he went out of the room, she said, in a surprisingly strong voice, "Bring my Leica tomorrow, Rudy, please. I want to have a record of her first day."

Dr. Levine took him to the nursery to see his daughter, asleep with five other infants, behind glass. Dr. Levine pointed her out. "There she is."

All six infants looked alike. Six in one day. The endless flood. Obstetricians must be the most cynical men in the world.

The night was cold outside the hospital. It had been warm that morning when he left the house and he hadn't taken a coat. He shivered as he walked toward his car. This time he had neglected to lock the doors, but the new radio was still there.

He knew he was too excited to sleep and he would have liked to call someone and have a drink in celebration of fatherhood, but it was past one o'clock now and he couldn't awaken anybody.

He turned the heater on in the car and was warm by the time he stopped the car in his driveway. Martha had left the lights on to guide him home. He was crossing the front lawn when he saw the figure move in the shadow of the porch.

"Who's there?" he called sharply.

The figure came slowly into the light. It was Virginia Calderwood, a scarf over her head, in a fur-trimmed gray coat.

"Oh, Christ, Virginia," he said, "what are you doing here?"

"I know all about it." She came up and stood close to him, staring at him, her eyes large and dark in her pale, thin, pretty face. "I kept calling the hospital for news. I said I was your sister. I know everything. She's had the child. *My* child."

"Virginia, you'd better go home." Rudolph stepped back a little, so that she couldn't touch him. "If your father finds out that you've been hanging around here like this, he'll . . ."

"I don't care what anyone finds out," Virginia said. "I'm not ashamed."

"Let me drive you home," Rudolph said. Let her own family cope with her madness, not him. And not on a night like this. "What you need is a good night's sleep and you'll . . ."

"I have no home," Virginia said. "I belong in your arms. My father doesn't even know I'm in town. I'm here, with you, where I belong."

"You don't belong here, Virginia," Rudolph said despairingly. Devoted to sanity himself, he was helpless in the face of aberration. "I live here with my wife."

"She lured you away from me," Virginia said. "She came between one true love and another. I prayed for her to die in the hospital today."

"Virginia!" He had not been really shocked by anything she had said or done before. He had been annoyed or amused or pitying, but this was beyond annoyance or amusement or pity. For the first time it occurred to him that she might be dangerous. He would call the hospital as soon as he got into the house and warn them to keep Virginia Calderwood away from the nursery or his wife's room. "I'll tell you what," he said soothingly, "get in my car and I'll take you home."

"Don't treat me like a child," she said. "I'm no child. And I have my own car parked down the block. I don't need anyone to drive me anyplace."

"Virginia," he said, "I'm awfully tired and I really have to get some sleep. If there's anything you really have to talk to me about, call me in the morning."

"I want you to make love to me," she said, standing there, staring at him, her hands sunk in the pockets of her coat, looking normal, everyday, neatly dressed. "I want you to make love to me tonight. I know you want to do it. I've seen it in your eyes from the beginning." She spoke in a rushed, flat whisper. "It's just that you haven't dared. Like everybody else, you're afraid of my father. Come on. I'm worth trying. You keep thinking of me as a little girl, like when you first saw me in my father's house. Well, I'm nobody's little girl, don't worry about that. I've been around. Maybe not as much as your precious wife with her photographer friend—oh, you're surprised I know about that—I made it my business to know, I tell you, and I could tell you plenty more if you want to hear."

But by this time, he had opened the door and slammed and locked it behind him, leaving her raving there on the porch and beating with her fists on the door. He went to all the doors of the house and the windows on the ground floor and made sure they were locked. When he came back to the front door the hammering of small, mad, feminine fists had stopped. Luckily, Martha had slept through it all. He turned the light out on the porch, from inside. After he had called the hospital, he climbed wearily to the bedroom he shared with Jean.

Happy birthday, daughter, in this quiet, respectable town, he thought, just before he fell asleep.

It was Saturday afternoon in the country club bar, but early, and the bar was empty because most of the members were still out on the golf course and on the tennis courts. Rudolph had the bar to himself, as he drank his beer. Jean was still in the women's locker room getting dressed. She had only been out of the hospital five weeks, but she had beaten him in two straight sets. Rudolph smiled as he remembered how gleeful she had been as she came off the court, victorious.

The clubhouse was a low, nondescript, rambling clapboard structure. The club was always on the point of going into bankruptcy and accepted anyone who paid the low initiation fees and had summer memberships for the people who came up only for the season. The bar was adorned with the faded photographs of people in long, flannel pants who had won club tournaments thirty years ago and a fly-specked photograph of Bill Tilden and Vincent Richards, who had once played an exhibition match on the club courts.

While waiting for Jean, Rudolph picked up the weekend edition of the Whitby *Sentinel* and was immediately sorry he had done so. On the front page there was an article about the hiring of Professor Denton by the college, with all the old insinuations and made-up quotes from unidentified sources which expressed concern that the impressionable youth of the college were going to be exposed to such a doubtful influence. "That sonofabitch Harrison," Rudolph said.

"You want something, Mr. Jordache?" asked the bartender, who was reading a magazine at the other end of the bar.

"Another beer, please, Hank," Rudolph said. He tossed the paper aside. At that moment, he decided that if he could swing it, he was going to buy Harrison's paper. It would be the best thing he could do for the town. And it shouldn't be too difficult to do. Harrison hadn't shown a profit on it for at least three years and if he didn't know that it was Rudolph who was after it, he probably would be willing to let it go at a fair price. Rudolph resolved to talk to Johnny Heath about procedure on Monday.

He was sipping his beer, trying to forget about Harrison until Monday, when Brad Knight came in from the golf course with the other three men in his foursome. Rudolph winced at the orange pants that Brad was wearing. "You entered in the Ladies' Handicap Cup?" he asked Brad as the men came up to the bar and Brad slapped him on the back.

Brad laughed. "Male plumage, Rudy," he said. "In nature always more brilliant than the female's. On weekends, I'm the natural man. This round is on me, Hank, I'm the big winner."

The men ordered and went over their cards. Brad and his partner had won close to three hundred dollars. Brad was one of the best golfers in the club and played a hustler's game, often starting badly and then getting his opponents to double bets. Well, that was his business. If people could lose nearly a hundred and fifty dollars apiece on a Saturday afternoon, Rudolph supposed they could afford it. But it made him uneasy to listen to men taking that much of a loss so lightly. He was not a born gambler.

"I saw Jean on the court with you," Brad said. "She looks just great."

"She comes from tough stock," Rudolph said. "Oh, by the way, thanks for the present for Enid." Jean's mother's maiden name had been Enid Cunningham and as soon as Jean had been strong enough to talk lucidly, she had asked Rudolph if he minded naming the child after her mother. "We're rising in the world, we Jordaches," Rudolph had said. "We are moving into three-name, ancestral territory." There had been no christening ceremony and there would be none. Jean shared his atheism, or as he himself preferred to think of it, his agnosticism. He had merely written the name in on the birth certificate, thinking as he did so that Enid Cunningham Jordache was a lot of letters for a seven-pound child to start life with. Brad had sent a sterling silver porringer with matching saucer and pusher for the baby. They now had eight sterling silver porringers in the house. Brad was not terribly original. But he had also started a savings account for the child with a deposit of five hundred dollars. "You never know," Brad had said when Rudolph had protested at the size of the gift, "when a girl has to pay for an abortion, fast."

One of the men Brad had been playing with was the chairman of the greens committee, Eric Sunderlin, and he was talking about his pet project, lengthening and improving the course. There was a large parcel of abandoned farm and timber land adjoining the course and Sunderlin was circulating a petition among the club members to float a loan and buy it. "It would put us in the big time," Sunderlin was saying. "We could even have a stab at a PGA tournament. We'd double our membership."

Everything in America, Rudolph thought resentfully, has a built-in tendency to double itself and move into the big time. He himself didn't play golf. Still, he was grateful that they were talking about golf at the bar and not about the article in the *Sentinel*.

"What about you, Rudy?" Sunderlin asked, finishing his Tom Collins. "Are you going to sign up with the rest of us?"

"I haven't given it much thought," Rudolph said. "Give me a couple of weeks to think it over."

"What's there to think over?" Sunderlin asked aggressively.

"Good old Rudy," Brad said. "No snap decisions. He thinks it over for two weeks if he has to have a haircut."

"It would help if a man of your stature was behind us," Sunderlin said. "I'll be after you."

"I'm sure you will, Eric," Rudy said. Sunderlin laughed at this tribute to him and he and the two other men went off to the showers, their spiked golf shoes clattering on the bare wooden floor. It was a club rule that spikes were not to be worn in the bar or restaurant or card room, but nobody paid any attention to it. If we ever move into the big time, Rudolph thought, you will have to take off your shoes.

Brad remained at the bar and ordered another drink. He always had a high flush on his face, but it was impossible to tell whether it was from the sun or from drink.

"A man of your stature," Brad said. "Everybody in this town always talks about you as though you're ten feet tall."

"That's why I stick to this town," Rudolph said.

"You going to stay here when you quit?" Brad didn't look at Rudolph while he spoke, but nodded at Hank as Hank put his glass in front of him on the bar.

"Who said anything about quitting?" Rudolph had not talked to Brad about his plans.

"Things get around."

"Who told you?"

"You *are* going to quit, aren't you?"

"Who told you?"

"Virginia Calderwood," Brad said.

"Oh."

"She overheard her father talking to her mother."

Spy, information gatherer, demented night-lurker, on quiet feet, Virginia Calderwood, listening in and out of shadows.

"I've been seeing her the last couple of months," Brad said. "She's a nice girl."

Student of character, Bradford Knight, originally from Oklahoma, open Western plains, where things were what they seemed to be.

"Uhuh," Rudolph said.

"Have you and the old man discussed who's going to take your place?"

"Yes, we've discussed it."

"Who's it going to be?"

"We haven't decided yet."

"Well," Bradford said, smiling, but more flushed than ever, "give an old college chum at least ten minutes notice before it's announced, will you?"

"Yes. What else has Miss Calderwood told you?"

"Nothing much," Brad said offhandedly. "That she loves me. Stuff like that. Have you seen her recently?"

"No." Rudolph hadn't seen her since the night Enid was born. Six weeks wasn't recently.

"We've had some laughs together," Brad said. "Her appearance is deceptive. She's a fun girl."

New aspects of the lady's character. Given to laughter. A fun girl. Merriment on porches at midnight.

"Actually," Brad said, "I'm considering marrying her."

"Why?" Rudolph asked. Although he could guess why.

"I'm tired of whoring around," Brad said. "I'm getting on toward forty and it's becoming wearing." Not the whole answer, friend, Rudolph thought. Nowhere nearly the whole answer.

"Maybe I'm impressed with your example," Brad said. "If marriage is good enough for a man of your stature—" He grinned, burly and red. "It ought to be good enough for a man of mine. Conjugal bliss."

"You didn't have much conjugal bliss the last time."

"That's for sure," Brad said. His first marriage, to the daughter of an oil man, had lasted six months. "But I was younger then. And I wasn't married to a decent girl like Virginia. And maybe my luck's changed."

Rudolph took a deep breath. "Your luck hasn't changed, Brad," he said quietly. Then he told Brad about Virginia Calderwood, about the letters, the phone calls, the ambushes in front of his apartment, the last crazy scene just six weeks ago. Brad listened in silence. All he said, at the end, was, "It must be plain glorious to be as wildly desirable as you, kid."

Jean came up then, shining from her shower, her hair tied back in a velvet bow, her brown legs bare in moccasins. "Hi, Mom," Brad

said, getting off his bar stool and kissing her. "Let me buy everybody
a drink."

They talked about the baby and golf and tennis and the new play
that was going into the Whitby Theater, which was opening for the
season next week. Virginia Calderwood's name wasn't mentioned,
and after he had finished his drink, Brad said, "Well, me for a
shower," and signed for the drinks and ambled off, a thickening,
aging man in orange pants, his expensive golf shoes making a peck-
ing noise with their spikes on the scarred wooden floor.

Two weeks later, the invitation to the wedding of Miss Virginia
Calderwood to Mr. Bradford Knight was in the morning mail.

The organ struck up the wedding march and Virginia came down
the aisle on her father's arm. She looked pretty, delicate, fragile, and
composed, in her bridal white. She did not look at Rudolph as she
passed him, although he was standing in a front pew, with Jean beside him. Bradford Knight, bridegroom, sweating a little and flushed
in the June heat, was waiting at the altar, with Johnny Heath, best
man, both of them in striped pants and Prince Alberts. People had
been surprised that Rudolph hadn't been chosen as best man, but
Rudolph had not been surprised.

It's my doing, Rudolph thought, as he half listened to the service.
I brought him here from Oklahoma, I took him into the business, I
refused the bride. It's my doing, am I responsible?

The wedding lunch was held at the Country Club. The buffet was
laid on a long table under an awning and tables were set all around
the lawn, under brightly colored umbrellas. A band played on the
terrace, where the bride and bridegroom, now dressed for traveling,
had led the first dance, a waltz. Rudolph had been surprised at how
well Brad, who did not seem like a graceful man, had danced.

Rudolph had kissed the bride dutifully. Virginia had smiled at him
with exactly the same smile she had given everybody else. Maybe,
Rudolph thought, it's all over, she's going to be all right.

Jean had insisted upon dancing with him, although he had protested, "How can you dance in the middle of the day?"

"I love weddings," Jean said, holding him close. "Other people's."
Then, maliciously, "Shouldn't you get up and make a toast to the
bride? You might mention what a loyal friend she is—waiting outside your door night after night to make sure you got home safely

and calling you at all hours to see if you were afraid in the dark and offering to keep you company in your poor lonely bed?"

"Sssh," Rudolph said, looking around apprehensively. He hadn't told her about the night of the hospital.

"She does look beautiful," Jean said. "Are you sorry about your choice?"

"In despair," he said. "Now, dance."

The boys in the band were a combination from the college and Rudolph was saddened by how well they played. He remembered his days with the trumpet when he was about their age. The young did everything so much better these days. The boys on the Port Philip track team were running the two twenty, his old distance, at least two seconds faster than he had ever run it. "Let's get off this damned floor," he said. "I feel crowded."

They went over and had a glass of champagne and talked to Brad's father, who had come from Tulsa for the occasion, wearing a wide-brimmed Stetson hat. He was weatherbeaten and thin and had deep sun-creases in the back of his neck. He didn't look like a man who had won and lost fortunes, but rather like a small-part player in the movies, hired to play the sheriff in a Western.

"Brad sure has talked enough about you, sir," old man Knight said to Rudolph. "And about your beautiful young bride." He raised his glass gallantly to Jean, who had taken off her hat and who now looked not bridal, but coeducational. "Yes, sir, Mister Jordache," old man Knight went on, "my son Brad is eternally in your debt, and don't think he don't know it. He was turning on his own tail out there in Oklahoma, hardly knowing where his next square meal was coming from when he got the call from you to come East. And I was in mighty poor straits myself at the time, I don't mind telling you, and I couldn't raise the price of a broken-down oil rig to help my boy. I'm proud to say I'm back on my own two feet again, now, but for awhile there it really looked like poor old Pete Knight was finally ready to be put to rest. Me and Brad were living in one room and eating chili three times a day for sustenance when like a bolt from the blue, the call came from his friend Rudy. I told him when he came home from the service, now you see here, Brad, you take the offer of the United States Government, and you get yourself to a college with that old GI Bill of Rights, from now on a man ain't going to be worth spit in this country if he ain't been to college. He's a good boy, Brad, and he had the sense to listen to his pa, and now look at him." He beamed across the dance floor to where his son and Virginia and Johnny Heath were drinking champagne among a group of the younger guests. "All dressed up, drinking champagne, with all the future in the world, married to a beautiful young heiress. And if ever he says he doesn't owe it all to his friend Rudy, his pa'll be the first to call him a liar."

Brad and Virginia came over with Johnny to pay their respects to Knight and the old man took Virginia onto the floor to dance with her, while Brad danced with Jean.

"You're not celebrating much today, are you, Rudy?" Johnny asked. Nothing escaped those sleepy eyes in that smooth round face.

"The bride is pretty, the champagne plentiful, the sun is shining, my friend thinks he's got it made for life," Rudolph said. "Why shouldn't I be celebrating?"

"As I said," Johnny said.

"My glass is empty," said Rudolph. "Let's get some more wine." He started toward the end of the buffet table under the awning, where the bar had been set up.

"We're going to have an answer on Monday from Harrison," Johnny said. "I think he's going to go for the deal. You'll have your toy."

Rudolph nodded. Although it annoyed him when Johnny, who didn't see how any real money could ever be made out of the *Sentinel*, called it a toy. Whatever his feelings were, Johnny, as usual, had come through. He had found a man called Hamlin, who was putting together a chain of small-town newspapers, to act as the buyer of record. He was contracted to sell out his interest to Rudolph three months later. Hamlin was a hard dealer and he had demanded three percent of the purchase price for his services, but he had beaten down Harrison's first demands so far that it was worthwhile to meet his conditions.

At the bar, Rudolph was clapped on the back by Sid Grossett, who had been Mayor of Whitby until the last election, and who was sent every four years as a delegate to the Republican convention. He was a hardy, friendly man, a lawyer by profession, who had successfully squashed rumors that he had taken bribes while he was in office, but had chosen not to run at the last election. Wisely, people said. The present mayor of the town, a Democrat, was at the other end of the bar, equally drinking Calderwood's champagne. Everybody had turned out for the wedding.

"Hi, young man," Grossett said. "I've been hearing about you."

"Good or bad?" Rudolph asked.

"Nobody ever hears anything bad about Rudolph Jordache," Grossett said. He wasn't a politician for nothing.

"Hear, hear," Johnny Heath said.

"Hi, Johnny." A handshake for everybody. There was always another election. "I got it from the horse's mouth," Grossett said. "You're quitting Dee Cee at the end of the month."

"Who's the horse this time?"

"Mr. Duncan Calderwood."

"The emotions of the day must have gone to the poor old man's head," Rudolph said. He didn't want to talk about his business to Grossett, or answer questions about what he was going to do next. There was plenty of time for that later.

"The day any emotions go to Duncan Calderwood's head," Grossett said, "you call me. I'll come running. He tells me he doesn't know what your future plans are. In fact, he said, he didn't know if you *had* any plans. But just in case you're open to suggestions—" He swiveled around, sniffing the air for possible Democrats. "Maybe we could talk in a day or two. Maybe you could come around to my office some afternoon next week."

"I'm going to be in New York next week."

"Well, there's no sense beating about the bush," Grossett said. "Have you ever thought you'd like to go into politics?"

"When I was twenty," Rudolph said. "Now that I'm old and wise . . ."

"Don't give me that," Grossett said roughly. "Everybody thinks about going into politics. Especially somebody like you. Rich, popular, with a big success behind you, a beautiful wife, looking for new worlds to conquer."

"Don't tell me you want to run me for President, now that Kennedy's dead," Rudolph said.

"I know that's a joke," Grossett said earnestly. "But who knows if it'll still be a joke ten years, twelve years from now? No. You got to start politics on a local level, Rudy, and right here in this town you're everybody's fair-haired boy. Am I right, Johnny." He turned, pleadingly, to the best man.

"Everybody's fair-haired boy." Johnny nodded.

"Up from poverty, went to college right here, handsome, educated, public-spirited."

"I've always felt I was actually private spirited," Rudolph said, to cut off the praise.

"Okay, be smart. But just look at all the goddamn committees you're on. And you haven't got an enemy in the world."

"Don't insult me, Sid." Rudolph was enjoying baiting the insistent little man, but he was listening more closely than he seemed to be.

"I know what I'm talking about."

"You don't even know whether I'm a Democrat or a Republican," Rudolph said. "Ask Leon Harrison and he'll tell you I'm a Communist."

"Leon Harrison is an old fart," Grossett said. "If I had my way I'd take up a collection to buy his paper away from him."

Rudolph couldn't refrain from winking at Johnny Heath.

"I know what you are," Grossett went plugging on. "You're a Kennedy-type Republican. It's a winning model. Just what the old Party needs."

"Now that you've got the pin in me, Sid," Rudolph said, "mount me and put me in a glass case." He disliked being categorized, no matter what the category.

"The place I want to put you is in the Whitby Town Hall," Grossett said. "As Mayor. And I bet I can do it. How do you like that? And from then on, up the ladder, up the ladder. I suppose you wouldn't like to be a Senator, the Senator from New York, I suppose that rubs you the wrong way, doesn't it?"

"Sid," Rudolph said gently, "I've been teasing you. I'm flattered, really I am. I'll be in next week to see you, I promise. Now, let's remember this is a wedding, not a smoke-filled hotel room. I'm off to dance with the bride."

He set down his glass and gave Grossett's shoulder a friendly pat, then went looking for Virginia. He hadn't danced with her yet and if he didn't go around the floor at least once with her, there would undoubtedly be talk. It was a small town and there were sharp eyes and tongues everywhere.

Good Republican, potential Senator, he approached the bride where she stood, demure and gay, under an awning, her hand light and loving on her new husband's arm. "May I have the honor?" Rudolph asked.

"Anything I have is yours," Brad said. "You know that."

Rudolph swung Virginia onto the floor. She danced bridally, her hand cool in his, her touch on his back feathery, her head thrown back proudly, conscious of being watched by girls who wished they were in her place today, by men who wished they were in her husband's.

"All happiness," Rudolph said. "Many, many years of happiness."

She laughed softly. "I'll be happy," she said, her thighs touching his. "Never fear. I'll have Brad for a husband and you for a lover."

"Oh, Christ," Rudolph said.

With the tip of a finger she touched his lips to silence him, and they finished the dance. As he walked her back to where Brad was standing, he knew that he had been too optimistic. Things were not going to work out all right. Never in a million years.

He did not throw rice along with the other guests as the newlyweds drove off in Brad's car to begin their honeymoon. He was on the front steps of the club, next to Calderwood. Calderwood didn't throw any rice either. The old man was frowning, but it was hard to tell whether it was because of something he was thinking or because the sun was in his eyes. As the guests drifted back for one last glass of champagne, Calderwood remained on the steps, looking into the shimmering summer afternoon distance in which his last daughter had disappeared with her husband. Earlier, Calderwood had said to Rudolph that he wanted to talk to him so Rudolph gave a sign to Jean that he would meet her later and she left the two men alone.

"What do you think?" Calderwood said finally.

"It was a beautiful wedding."

"Not about that."

Rudolph shrugged. "Who knows how a marriage is going to turn out?"

"He expects he's going to get your job now."

"That's normal," Rudolph said.

"I wish to God it was you riding off down to New York with her this afternoon."

"Life doesn't work out that neatly most of the time," Rudolph said.

"It certainly doesn't." Calderwood shook his head. "I don't trust him completely," he said. "I hate to say that about any man who's worked loyally for me the way he has and who's married my daughter, but I can't hide it from myself."

"He's never made a wrong move since he came here," Rudolph said. Except one, he thought. Not believing what I told him about Virginia. Or worse, believing it and marrying her anyway. But he couldn't tell Calderwood that.

"I know he's your friend," Calderwood said, "and he's smart as a fox and you've known him a long time and you had enough confidence in him to bring him here and give him a big load of responsibility, but there's something about him—" Calderwood shook his big, sallow, death-marked head again. "He drinks, he's a whoremonger—don't contradict me, Rudy, I know what I know—he gambles, he comes from Oklahoma . . ."

Rudolph chuckled.

"I know," Calderwood said. "I'm an old man and I have my prejudices. But there they are. I guess I've been spoiled by you, Rudy. I never dealt with a man in my whole life I knew I could trust the way I trust you. Even when you talked me into acting against my better judgment—and you'd be surprised how many times that's happened —I knew you'd never do anything that you thought was against my interests or was underhanded or would reflect against my reputation."

"Thank you, Mr. Calderwood," Rudolph said.

"Mr. Calderwood, Mr. Calderwood," the old man said peevishly. "Are you still going to be calling me Mr. Calderwood on my death bed?"

"Thank you, Duncan." It was an effort to say Duncan.

"To turn the whole damn shebang over to that man." There was a cranky, aged complaint in Calderwood's voice. "Even if it's after I die. I don't feel like doing it. But if you say so . . ." He trailed off unhappily.

Rudolph sighed. There is always someone to betray, he thought. "I don't say so," he said quietly. "There's a young lawyer in our legal department by the name of Mathers . . ."

"I know him," Calderwood said. "Light-complected fellow with glasses and two kids. From Philadelphia."

"He has a degree from the Wharton School of Business that he took before he went to Harvard Law. He's been with us more than four years. He knows every department. He asks all the right questions. He's been in and out of my office. He could earn a lot more than he does here in any one of a dozen law firms in New York, but he likes living here."

"Okay," Calderwood said. "Tell him tomorrow."

"I would prefer it if you told him, Duncan." Second Duncan in his life.

"As usual," Calderwood said. "I don't like to do what you're telling me to do, and I know you're right. I'll tell him. Now let's go back and drink some more of that champagne. I paid enough for it, God knows, I might as well drink it."

The new appointment was announced the day before the newlyweds were due back from the honeymoon.

Brad took it calmly, like a gentleman, and never queried Rudolph about who had made the decision. But three months later he quit his job and he and Virginia went out to Tulsa, where Brad's father had made a place for him in his oil business. On Enid's first birthday, he sent a check for five hundred dollars to the bank to be deposited in Enid's savings account.

Brad wrote regularly, jovial, breezy, friendly letters. He was doing very well, he wrote, and was making more money than he ever had before. He liked Tulsa, where the golf bets were on a generous Western scale and on three successive Saturdays he had won more than a thousand dollars a round. Virginia was liked by everyone and had made dozens of friends. She had taken up golf. Brad invited Rudolph to invest with him—"It's like picking money off a tree," was the way he put it. He said he wanted somehow to pay back all that Rudolph had done for him, and this was one way of doing it.

Out of a sense of guilt—he could not forget the moment on the steps of the Country Club with Duncan Calderwood—Rudolph started taking shares in wells that Brad prospected, drilled, and managed. Besides, as Johnny Heath pointed out, for a man in his income bracket, considering the twenty-seven-per-cent depletion tax allowance that the oil industry enjoyed, it was more than worth the gamble. Johnny checked on the credit rating of Peter Knight and son, found it was A one, then matched Rudolph's investments dollar for dollar.

Chapter 3

1965

Thomas squatted on the forward deck, whistling tunelessly, polishing the bronze spool of the anchor winch. Although it was only early June, it was already warm and he worked barefooted and stripped to the waist. His torso was dark brown from the sun, as dark as the skin of the swarthiest Greeks or Italians on any of the ships in the harbor of Antibes. His body wasn't as hard as it had been when he was fighting. The muscles didn't stand out in ridges as they had then, but were smoother, not as heavy. When he was wearing something to cover his small bald spot, as he was now, he looked younger than he had two years ago. He tilted the white American gob's hat, which he wore with the rim turned down all around, over his eyes, to protect him from the glare of the sun off the water.

From the engine room below there was the sound of hammering. Pinky Kimball was down there with Dwyer, working on a pump. The first charter of the year began tomorrow and the port engine had overheated on a trial run. Pinky, who was the engineer on the Vega, the biggest ship in the harbor, had volunteered to come over and take a look at it. Dwyer and Thomas could handle simple repairs themselves, but when it came to anything really complicated they had to ask for help. Luckily, Thomas had struck up a friendship with Kimball during the winter and Kimball had given them a hand on various things as they got the Clothilde into shape for the summer. Thomas had not explained to Dwyer why he had decided to call the ship the Clothilde when they changed it from the Penelope at Porto Santo Stefano. To himself, he had said, a ship had to be called by a woman's name, why not Clothilde? He certainly wasn't going to call it Teresa.

He was happy on the Clothilde, although even in his own eyes it wasn't one of the smartest craft on the Mediterranean. He knew its superstructure was a little topheavy and presented too much surface to the wind and its top speed was only twelve knots, cruising speed ten knots, and it rolled alarmingly in certain seas. But everything that two determined men, working month after month, could do to make a craft snug and seaworthy had been done to the peeling hulk they had bought at Porto Santo Stefano two and a half years before. They had had two good seasons, and while neither of them had gotten rich off the boat, they both had some money in the bank, in case of trouble. The season coming up looked as though it was going to be even better than the first two and Thomas felt a calm pleasure as he burnished the bronze spool and saw it reflect the sun from its surface. Before taking to sea he would never have thought that a simple, brainless act like polishing a piece of metal could give him pleasure.

It was the same with everything on the ship. He loved to stroll from bow to stern and back again, touching the hand rails, pleased to see the lines curled into perfect spiral patterns on the calked, pale, teak deck, admiring the polished brass handles on the old-fashioned wheel in the deck house and the perfectly arranged charts in their slots and the signal flags tightly rolled in their pigeonholes. He, who had never washed a dish in his life, spent long hours in the galley scrubbing pans until they shone and making sure that the icebox was immaculate and fresh smelling, the range and oven scrubbed. When there was a charter on board he and Dwyer and whoever they signed on as a cook dressed in tan drill shorts and immaculate white cotton T-shirts with *Clothilde* printed across the chest in blue. In the evenings, or in cold weather, they wore identical heavy navy-blue sailor's sweaters.

He had learned to mix all sorts of drinks and serve them frosty and cold in good glasses, and there was one party, Americans, who swore they only took the ship for his Bloody Marys. A pleasure craft on the Mediterranean, going between one country and another, could be a cheap holiday for a drunkard, because you could take on case after case of duty-free liquor and you could buy gin and whiskey for about a dollar and a half a bottle. He rarely drank anything himself, except for a little pastis and an occasional beer. When charters came aboard he wore a peaked captain's cap, with the gilt anchor and chain. It made his clients' holidays more seagoing, he felt.

He had learned a few words of French and Italian and Spanish, enough to go through harbor-master formalities and do the shopping, but too little to get into arguments. Dwyer picked up the languages quickly and could rattle away with anybody.

Thomas had sent a photograph of the *Clothilde*, spraying through a wave, to Gretchen and Gretchen had written back that she kept it on the mantelpiece of her living room. One day, she wrote, she would come over and take a trip with him. She was busy, she wrote, doing some sort of job at a movie studio. She said that she had kept her promise and had not told Rudolph where he was or what he was doing. Gretchen was his one link with America and the times when he felt lonely or missed the kid, he wrote to her. He had asked Dwyer to write his girl in Boston, whom Dwyer still said he was going to marry, to try to go down to the Aegean Hotel when she had the time and talk to Pappy, but the girl hadn't replied yet.

Some year soon, no matter what, he was going to go to New York and try to find his kid.

He hadn't had a single fight since Falconetti. He still dreamed about Falconetti. He wasn't sentimental about him, but he was sorry Falconetti was dead and the passage of time hadn't persuaded him that it wasn't his fault that the man had thrown himself overboard.

He finished with the winch and stood up. The deck was promisingly warm under his bare feet. As he went aft, running his hands along the newly varnished mahogany-colored rails, the hammering below stopped and Kimball's flaming red hair appeared, as he came out of the saloon and onto the deck. To get to the engine room, you had to pick up sections of the floor from the saloon. Dwyer appeared after Kimball. They were both wearing oil-stained green overalls, because there was no keeping clean in the confined space of the engine room. Kimball was wiping his hands on a piece of waste, which he threw overboard. "That ought to do it, mate," Kimball said. "Why don't we give it a spin?"

Thomas went into the pilot house and started the engines while Dwyer and Pinky cast off from the dock and clambered forward to bring up the hook, Dwyer working the winch and cleaning off the harbor muck from the chain with the hose before it dropped into the well. They had a lot of chain out, for stability, and the *Clothilde* was almost in the middle of the harbor before Pinky gave the sign that they were clear and helped Dwyer bring the hook on board with the gaff.

By now Thomas was skilled at handling the ship and only when he was coming into a very crowded harbor, with a bad wind blowing, did he hand over the wheel to Dwyer. Today, he turned the bow toward the harbor entrance and, keeping the speed down until they were outside, chugged beyond the fishermen with their rods at the end of the rampart and around the buoy before he increased speed, turning toward the Cap d'Antibes, leaving the fortress of the Vieux Carré on its hill, behind them. He watched the gauges of both engines and was relieved to see that the port engine wasn't heating up. Good old Pinky. Through the winter he must have saved them at least a thousand dollars. The ship he was on, the V*ega*, was so new and so pampered that there was almost nothing for him to do when they were in port. He was bored on it and delighted to be able to putter about in the *Clothilde*'s cluttered, hot engine room.

Kimball was a knotty Englishman whose freckled face never got tan, but remained a painful hot pink all summer. He had a problem with the drink, as he put it. When he drank he became pugnacious and challenged people in bars. He quarreled with his owners and rarely stayed on one ship more than a year, but he was so good at his job that he never had any trouble finding other berths quickly. He only worked on the very big yachts, because his skill would be wasted on smaller craft. He had been raised in Plymouth and had been on the water all his life. He was amazed that somebody like Thomas had wound up the owner-skipper of a ship like the *Clothilde* in Antibes harbor, and was making a go of it. "Yanks," Kimball said, shaking his head. "They're fucking well capable of anything. No wonder you own the world."

He and Thomas had been friendly from the beginning, greeting each other as they passed on the quay or buying each other beers in the little bar at the entrance to the port. Kimball had guessed that Thomas had been in the ring and Thomas had told him about some of his fights and what it was like and about the win in London and the later two dives he had had to take and even about the last fight in the hotel room with Quayles in Las Vegas, which had especially delighted Kimball's belligerent heart. Thomas had not told him about Falconetti and Dwyer knew enough to keep quiet on that subject.

"By God, Tommy," Kimball said, "if I knew I could fight like that I would clean out every bar from Gib to Piraeus."

"And get a knife between your ribs in the process," Thomas said.

"No doubt you're right," Kimball agreed. "But man, the pleasure before!"

When he got very drunk and saw Thomas he would pound the bar and shout, "See that man? If he wasn't a friend of mine, I'd drive him into the deck." Then loop an affectionate tattooed arm around Thomas's neck.

Their friendship had been cemented one night in a bar in Nice. They hadn't gone to Nice together, but Dwyer and Thomas had wandered into the bar, near the port, by accident. There was a cleared space around the bar and Kimball was holding forth, loudly, to a group that included some French seamen and three or four flashily dressed but dangerous-looking young men of a type that Thomas had learned to recognize and avoid—small-time hoodlums and racketeers, doing odd jobs along the Côte for the chiefs of the *milieu* with headquarters in Marseilles. His instinct told him that they were probably armed, if not with guns, certainly with knives.

Pinky Kimball spoke a kind of French and Thomas couldn't understand him, but he could tell from the tone of Kimball's voice and the grim looks on the faces of the other patrons of the bar that Kimball was insulting them. Kimball had a low opinion of the French when he was drunk. When he was drunk in Italy, he had a low opinion of Italians. When he was drunk in Spain, he had a low opinion of the Spanish. Also, when he was drunk, he seemed to forget how to count and the fact that he was alone and outnumbered at least five to one only spurred him on to greater feats of scornful oratory.

"He's going to get himself killed here tonight," Dwyer whispered, understanding most of what Kimball was shouting. "And us, too, if they find out we're his friends."

Thomas grasped Dwyer's arm firmly and took him with him to Kimball's side, at the bar.

"Hi, Pinky," he said cheerfully.

Pinky swung around, ready for new enemies. "Ah," he said. "I'm glad you're here. I'm telling these *maquereaux* a few home truths for their own good."

"Knock it off, Pinky," Thomas said. Then, to Dwyer. "I'm going to say a few words to these gentlemen. I want you to translate. Clearly and politely." He smiled cordially at the other men in the bar, arranged now in an ominous semicircle. "As you see, gentlemen," he said, "this Englishman is my friend." He waited while Dwyer nervously translated. There was no change in the expression of the faces lined up around him. "He is also drunk," Thomas said. "Naturally, a man does not like to see a friend damaged, drunk or sober. I will try to prevent him from making any more speeches here, but no matter what he says or has said, there will be no trouble here tonight. I am the policeman tonight in this bar and I am keeping the peace. Please translate," he said to Dwyer.

As Dwyer was translating, haltingly, Pinky said, disgustedly, "Shit, mate, you're lowering the flag."

"What is further," Thomas went on, "the next round of drinks is on me. Barman." He was smiling as he spoke, but he could feel the muscles tightening in his arms and he was ready to spring on the biggest one of the lot, a heavy-jawed Corsican in a black leather jacket.

The men looked at each other uncertainly. But they hadn't come into the bar to fight and while they grumbled a little among themselves they each came up to the bar and accepted the drinks that Thomas had bought for them.

"Some fighter," Pinky sneered. "Every day is Armistice day with you, Yank." But he allowed himself to be led safely out of the bar ten minutes later. When he came over to the *Clothilde* the next day, he brought a bottle of pastis with him and said, "Thanks, Tommy. They'd have kicked in my skull in the next two minutes if you hadn't come along. I don't know what it is comes over me when I have a few. And it's not as though I ever *win*. I've got scars from head to toe in tribute to my courage." He laughed.

"If you've got to fight," Thomas said, remembering the days when he felt he had to fight, no matter whom and for no matter what reason, "fight sober. And pick on one man at a time. And don't take me along. I've given all that up."

"What would you have done, Tommy, boy," Pinky said, "if they'd jumped me?"

"I'd have created a diversion," Thomas said, "just long enough for Dwyer to get you out of the saloon, and then I'd have run for my life."

"A diversion," Pinky said. "I'd pay a couple of bob to have seen that diversion."

Thomas didn't know what it was in Pinky Kimball's life that changed him from a friendly, amiable, if profane man, into a suicidal, fighting animal when he got a few drinks in him. Sometime, perhaps, he'd have it out with him.

Pinky came into the pilot house, looked at the gauges, listened critically to the throb of the Diesels. "You're ready for the summer, lad," he said. "On your own craft. And I envy you."

"Not quite ready," Thomas said. "We're missing one in crew."

"What?" Pinky asked. "Where's that Spaniard you hired last week?"

The Spaniard had come well recommended as a cook and steward and he hadn't asked for too much money. But one night, when he was leaving the ship to go ashore, Thomas had seen him putting a knife into his shoe, alongside his ankle, hidden by his pants.

"What's that for?" Thomas had asked.

"To make respect," the Spaniard said.

Thomas had fired him the next day. He didn't want anybody aboard who had to keep a knife in his shoe to make respect. Now he was short-handed.

"I put him ashore," Thomas said to Pinky, as they crossed outside the bay of La Garoupe. He explained why. "I still need a cook-steward. It doesn't make much difference the next two weeks. My charter just wants the boat during the day and they bring their own food aboard. But I'll need somebody for the summer."

"Have you ever thought about hiring a woman?" Pinky asked.

Thomas grimaced. "There's a lot of heavy work beside the cooking and stuff like that," he said.

"A *strong* woman," Pinky said.

"Most of the trouble in my life," Thomas said, "came because of women. Weak and strong."

"How many days a summer do you lose," Pinky asked, "with your charters grousing that they're wasting their valuable time, waiting in some godforsaken port just to get their washing and ironing done?"

"It *is* a nuisance," Thomas agreed. "You got somebody in mind?"

"Righto," Pinky said. "She works as a stewardess on the *Vega* and she's pissed off with her job. She's crazy about the sea and all she sees all summer long is the inside of the laundry."

"Okay," Thomas said, reluctantly. "I'll talk to her. And tell her to leave her knives at home."

He didn't need a woman aboard as a *woman*. There were plenty of girls to be picked up around the ports. You had your fun with them, spent a few bucks on them for a dinner and maybe a night club and a couple of drinks and then you moved on to the next port, without complications. He didn't know what Dwyer did for sex and thought it better not to ask.

He turned the *Clothilde* around, to go back to the harbor. She was ready. There was no sense in using up fuel. He was paying for his own fuel until tomorrow, when the first charter began.

At six o'clock he saw Pinky coming down the quay with a woman. The woman was short and a little thick in the body and wore her hair in two plaits on either side of her head. She had on a pair of denim pants, a blue sweater, and espadrilles. She kicked off her espadrilles before she came up the gangplank in the stern of the ship. In the Mediterranean harbors most of the time you tied up stern to the quay, unless there was room to come alongside, which there rarely was.

"This is Kate," Pinky said. "I told her about you."

"Hello, Kate." Thomas put out his hand and she shook it. She had soft hands for a girl who worked in the laundry room and could do heavy work on deck. She was English, too, and came from Southampton and looked about twenty-five. She spoke in a low voice when she talked about herself. She could cook, as well as do laundry, she said, and she could make herself useful on deck, and she spoke French and Italian, "not mightily," she said, with a smile, but she could understand the météo on the radio in both languages and could follow a charted course and stand watches, and drive a car if ever that was necessary. She would work for the same salary as the Spaniard with the knife. She wasn't really pretty, but healthy and buxom in a small, brown way, with a direct manner of looking at the person she was talking to. In the winter, if she was laid off, she went back to London and got a job as a waitress. She wasn't married, and she wasn't engaged and she wanted to be treated like any member of the crew, no better and no worse.

"She's a wild English rose," Pinky said. "Aren't you, Kate?"

"None of your jokes, Pinky," the girl said. "I want this job. I'm tired of going from one end of the Med to the other all dressed up in a starched uniform with white cotton stockings, like a nurse, and being called Miss or Mademoiselle. I've been taking a glance at your ship, Tom, from time to time, as I've passed by, and it's pleased me. Not so big to be hoity-toity and British Royal Yacht Club. It's nice and clean and friendly looking. And it's a dead sure thing there won't be many ladies coming aboard that need to have their ball-gowns pressed all one hot steaming afternoon in Monte Carlo harbor for a ball at the Palace that night."

"Well," Thomas said, defending the elegance of his clientele, "we don't exactly cater to paupers."

"You know what I mean," the girl said. "I'll tell you what. I don't want you to take a pig in a poke. Have you had your dinner yet?"

"No." Dwyer was down in the galley messing around desolately with some fish he'd bought that morning, but Thomas could tell by the sounds coming from the galley that nothing of any importance had as yet been done.

"I'll cook you a dinner," the girl said. "Right now. If you like it, you take me on, I'll go back to the *Vega* and clear out my things to-night and come aboard. If you don't like it, what have you lost? If you're hungry the restaurants in town keep open late. And Pinky, you can stay and eat with us."

"Okay," Thomas said. He went down to the galley and told Dwyer to get out of there, they had a cook from the Cordon Bleu, at least for a night. The girl looked around the galley, nodded approvingly, opened the icebox, opened drawers and cupboards to see where everything was, looked at the fish that Dwyer had bought and said he didn't know how to buy fish, but that they'd do in a pinch. Then she told them both to get out of there, she'd call them when dinner was ready. All she wanted was to have somebody to go into Antibes to get some fresh bread and two ripe Camembert cheeses.

They ate on the after deck, behind the pilot house, instead of in the little dining alcove forward of the saloon that they would have used if there had been clients aboard. Kate had set the table and somehow it looked better than when Dwyer did it. She had put two bottles of wine in an icebucket, uncorked them, and put the bucket on a chair.

She had made a stew of the fish, with potatoes, garlic, onions, tomatoes, thyme, a lot of rock salt and pepper, and a little white wine and diced bacon. It was still light when they sat down at the table, with the sun setting in the cloudless, greenish-blue sky. The three men had washed, shaved, and put on fresh clothes and had had two pastis apiece while sitting on deck, sniffing the aromas coming from the galley. The harbor itself was quiet, with just the sound of little ripples lapping at hulls to be heard.

Kate brought up a big tureen with the stew in it. Bread and butter were already on the table, next to a big bowl of salad. After she served them all, she sat down with them, unhurried and calm. Thomas, as captain, poured the wine.

Thomas took a first bite, chewed it thoughtfully. Kate, her head down, also began to eat. "Pinky," Thomas said, "you're a true friend. You're plotting to make me a fat man. Kate, you're hired."

She looked up and smiled. They raised their glasses to the new member of the crew.

Even the coffee tasted like coffee.

After dinner, while Kate was doing the dishes, the three men sat out in the silent evening, smoking cigars that Pinky had produced, watching the moon rise over the mauve hills of the Alpes Maritimes.

"Bunny," Thomas said, leaning back in his chair and spreading his legs in front of him, "this is what it's all about."

Dwyer did not contradict him.

Later, Thomas went with Kate and Pinky to where the Vega was berthed. It was late and the ship was almost dark, with very few lights showing, but Thomas waited some distance away while Kate went on board to collect her things. He didn't want to get into an argument with the skipper, if he happened to be awake and angry about losing a hand on five minutes' notice.

A quarter of an hour later Thomas saw Kate coming noiselessly down the gangplank, carrying a valise. They walked together, along the fortress wall, past the boats moored one next to another to where the Clothilde was tied up. Kate stopped for a moment, looked gravely at the white-and-blue boat, groaning a little with the pull of the water against the two lines that made it fast to the quay. "I'm going to remember this evening," she said, then kicked off her espadrilles and, holding them in her hand, went barefooted up the gangplank.

Dwyer was waiting up for them. He had made up the extra bunk in Thomas's cabin for himself and put clean sheets for Kate on the bunk in the other cabin that he had been living in alone. Thomas snored, because of his broken nose, but Dwyer was going to have to get used to it. At least for awhile.

A week later, Dwyer moved back to his own cabin, because Kate moved into Thomas's. She said she didn't mind Thomas's snoring.

The Goodharts were an old couple who stayed at the Hotel du Cap every June. He owned cotton mills in North Carolina, but had handed over the business to a son. He was a tall, erect, slow-moving heavy man with a shock of iron-gray hair and looked like a retired colonel in the Regular Army. Mrs. Goodhart was a little younger than her husband, with soft white hair. Her figure was good enough so that she could get away with wearing slacks. The Goodharts had chartered the *Clothilde* for two weeks the year before and had liked it so much that they had arranged a similar charter with Thomas for this year by mail early in the winter.

They were the least demanding of clients. Each morning at ten, Thomas anchored as close inshore as he could manage opposite the row of the hotel's cabanas and the Goodharts came out in a speed-boat. They came with full hampers of food, prepared in the hotel kitchen, and baskets of wine bottles wrapped in napkins. They were both over sixty and if the water was at all rough the transfer could be tricky. On those days, their chauffeur would drive them down to the *Clothilde* in Antibes harbor. Sometimes there would be other couples, always old, with them, or they would tell Thomas that they were to pick up some friends in Cannes. Then they'd chug out to the straits between the Isles de Lérins, lying about four thousand yards off the coast, and anchor there for the day. It was almost always calm there and the water was only about twelve feet deep and brilliantly clear so that you could see the seagrass waving on the bottom. The Goodharts would put on bathing suits and lie on mattresses in the sun, reading or dozing, and occasionally dive in for a swim.

Mr. Goodhart said that he felt safer about Mrs. Goodhart's swimming when Thomas or Dwyer swam beside her. Mrs. Goodhart, who was a robust woman with full shoulders and young, strong legs, swam perfectly well, but Thomas knew that it was Mr. Goodhart's way of telling him that he wanted Thomas and anybody else on the boat to feel free to enjoy the clear, cool water between the islands whenever they felt like taking a dip.

Sometimes, if they had guests, Thomas would spread a blanket for them on the after deck and they would play a few rubbers of bridge.

Both Mr. and Mrs. Goodhart were soft-spoken and enormously polite with each other and everybody else.

Promptly at one-thirty every day, they were ready for the first drink, invariably a Bloody Mary, which Thomas made for them. After that, Dwyer unrolled the awning and in its shade they ate the food they had brought with them from the hotel. On the table there would be cold langouste, cold roast beef, fish salad or cold loup de mer with a green sauce, melon with prosciutto, cheese, and fruit. They always brought along so much food, even when they had friends with them, that there was plenty left over for the crew, not only for lunch, but for dinner, too. With their meal they each had a bottle of white wine apiece.

The only thing Thomas had to worry about was the coffee and now with Kate aboard that was no problem. The first day of the charter she came up from the galley with the coffee pot, dressed in white shorts and the white T-shirt with the legend *Clothilde* stretched tightly across her plump bosom and when Thomas introduced her, Mr. Goodhart nodded approvingly and said, "Captain, this ship is improving every year."

After lunch, Mr. and Mrs. Goodhart went below for their siesta. Quite often, Thomas heard muffled sounds that could only come from lovemaking. Mr. and Mrs. Goodhart had told Thomas they had been married more than thirty-five years and Thomas marveled that they still did it and still so obviously enjoyed it. The Goodharts shook his entire conception of marriage.

Around about four o'clock, the Goodharts would reappear on deck, grave and ceremonious, as usual, in their bathing suits, and would swim for another half hour, with either Dwyer or Thomas accompanying them. Dwyer swam poorly and there were one or two times when Mrs. Goodhart was more than a hundred yards away from the *Clothilde* that Thomas thought there was a good chance she'd have to tow Dwyer back to the boat.

At five o'clock promptly, showered, combed, and dressed in cotton slacks, white shirt, and a blue blazer, Goodhart would come up on deck from below and say, "Don't you think it's time for a drink, Captain?" and, if there were no guests aboard, "I'd be honored if you'd join me."

Thomas would prepare two Scotch and sodas and give the signal to Dwyer, who would start the engines and take the wheel. With Kate handling the anchor up forward, they would start back toward the Hotel du Cap. Seated on the aft deck Mr. Goodhart and

Thomas would sip at their drinks as they pulled out of the straits and went around the island, with the pink-and-white towers of Cannes across the water on their port side.

On one such afternoon, Mr. Goodhart said, "Captain, are there many Jordaches in this part of the world?"

"Not that I know of," Thomas said. "Why?"

"I happened to mention your name to the assistant manager of the hotel yesterday," Mr. Goodhart said, "and he said that a Mr. and Mrs. Rudolph Jordache were sometimes guests at the hotel."

Thomas sipped at his whiskey. "That's my brother," he said. He could feel Mr. Goodhart glancing at him curiously, and could guess what he was thinking. "We've gone our different ways," he said shortly. "He was the smart one of the family."

"I don't know." Mr. Goodhart waved his glass to take in the boat, the sunlight, the water churning away from the bows, the green and ochre hills of the coast. "Maybe you were the smart one. I worked all my life and it was only when I became an old man and retired that I had the time to do something like this two weeks a year." He chuckled ruefully. "And I was considered the smart one of *my* family."

Mrs. Goodhart came up then, youthful in slacks and a loose sweater and Thomas finished his drink and went and got a whiskey for her. She matched her husband drink for drink, day in and day out.

Mr. Goodhart paid two hundred and fifty dollars a day for the charter, plus fuel, and twelve hundred old francs a day for food for each of the crew. After the charter the year before he had given Thomas five hundred dollars as a bonus. Thomas and Dwyer had tried to figure out how rich a man had to be to afford two weeks at that price, while still paying for a suite at what was probably one of the most expensive hotels in the world. They had given up trying. "Rich, that's all, rich," Dwyer had said. "Christ, can you imagine how many hours thousands of poor bastards in those mills of his in North Carolina have to put in at the machines, coughing their lungs out, so that he can have a swim every day?" Dwyer's attitude toward capitalists had been formed young by a Socialist father who worked in a factory. All workers, in Dwyer's view of labor, coughed their lungs out.

Until the Goodharts, Thomas's feeling about people with a great deal of money, while not quite as formally rigid as Dwyer's, had been composed of a mixture of envy, distrust, and the suspicion that whenever possible a rich man would do whatever harm he could to anyone within his power. His uneasiness with his brother, which had begun when they were boys, for other reasons, had been compounded by Rudolph's rise to wealth. But the Goodharts had shaken old tenets of faith. They had not only made him reflect anew on the subject of marriage, but about old people as well, and the rich, and even about Americans in general. It was too bad that the Goodharts came so early in the season, because after them, it was likely to be downhill until October. Some of the other charter parties they took on more than justified Dwyer's darkest strictures on the ruling classes.

On the last day of the charter, they started back toward the hotel earlier than usual because the wind had sprung up and the sea beyond the islands was full of whitecaps. Even between the islands the *Clothilde* was rolling and pulling at her chain. Mr. Goodhart had drunk more than usual, too, and neither he nor his wife had gone below for their siesta. When Dwyer upped anchor they were still in their bathing suits, with sweaters, against the spray. But they stayed out on deck, like children at a party that was soon to end, hungry for the last drop of joy from the declining festival. Mr. Goodhart was even a little curt with Thomas when Thomas didn't automatically produce the afternoon whiskies.

Once they were out of the lee of the islands it was too rough to use the deck chairs and the Goodharts and Thomas had to hold onto the after rail while they drank their Scotch and sodas.

"I think it's going to be impossible to get the dinghy into the hotel landing," Thomas said. "I'd better tell Dwyer to go around the point and into Antibes."

Mr. Goodhart put out his hand and held Thomas's arm as Thomas started toward the pilot house. "Let's just take a look," Mr. Goodhart said. His eyes were a little bloodshot. "I like a little rough weather from time to time."

"Whatever you say, sir," Thomas said. "I'll go tell Dwyer."

In the pilot house, Dwyer was already fighting the wheel. Kate was seated on the bench that ran along the rear of the structure, munching a roast beef sandwich. She had a hearty appetite and was a good sailor in all seas.

"We're in for a blow," Dwyer said. "I'm going around the point."

"Go to the hotel," Thomas said.

Kate looked over her sandwich at him in surprise.

"Are you crazy?" Dwyer said. "All the speedboats must have gone back to the harbor hours ago, with this wind. And we'll never get the dinghy in."

"I know," Thomas said. "But they want to take a look."

"It's a pure waste of time," Dwyer grumbled. They had a new charter beginning the next morning at St. Tropez and they had planned to start immediately after discharging the Goodharts. Even with a calm sea and no wind, it would have been a long day, and they would have had to prepare the ship for the new clients en route. The wind was from the north, the mistral, and they would have to hug the coast for protection, which made the voyage much longer. They would also have to reduce speed to keep the hull from pounding too badly. And there would be no question, in this weather, of doing any work below while they were moving.

"It's only a few more minutes," Thomas said soothingly. "They'll see it's impossible and we'll make for Antibes."

"You're the captain," Dwyer said. He pulled viciously at the wheel as a wave quartered against their port side and the *Clothide* yawed.

Thomas stayed in the pilot house, keeping dry. The Goodharts remained out on deck, soaked by spray, but seeming to enjoy it. There were no clouds and the high afternoon sun shone brightly and when the spray swept over the deck, the two old people shimmered in brief rainbows.

As they passed Golfe Juan, far off to port, with the boats at anchor in the little harbor already bobbing, Mr. Goodhart signaled to Thomas that he and Mrs. Goodhart wanted another drink.

When they got within five hundred yards of the palisade on which the cabanas stood, they saw that the waves were breaking over the little concrete dock to which the speedboats were usually tied. The speedboats, as Dwyer had predicted, were all gone. At the regular swimming place farther along the cliff, the red flag was up and the chain was across the swimming ladder below the restaurant of Eden Roc. The waves went crashing in high over the steps, then pulled back, frothing and green-white, leaving the ladder uncovered down to the last rung before the next wave roared in.

Thomas left the shelter of the pilot house and went out on deck. "I'm afraid I was right, sir," he said to Mr. Goodhart. "There's no getting a boat in with this sea. We'll have to go into port."

"You go into port," Mr. Goodhart said calmly. "My wife and I have decided we'll swim in. Just get the ship in as close as you can without endangering her."

"The red flag's up," Thomas said. "Nobody's in the water."

"The French," Mr. Goodhart said. "My wife and I have swum in surf twice as bad as this at Newport, haven't we, dear?"

"We'll send the car around to the harbor to pick up our things later, Captain," Mr. Goodhart said.

"This isn't Newport, sir," Thomas said, making one last attempt. "It's not a sandy beach. You'll get thrown against the rocks if you . . ."

"Like everything in France," Mr. Goodhart said, "it looks worse than it is. Just pull in as close to shore as you think is wise and we'll do the rest. We both feel like a swim."

"Yes, sir," Thomas said. He went back into the pilot house, where Dwyer was spinning the wheel, first revving up one engine, then another, to make tight circles that brought the ship at its closest about three hundred yards from the ladder. "Bring her in another hundred yards," Thomas said. "They're going to swim for it."

"What do they want to do," Dwyer asked, "commit suicide?"

"It's their bones," Thomas said. Then, to Kate, "Put on your bathing suit." He himself was wearing swimming trunks and a sweater.

Without a word, Kate went below for her bathing suit.

"As soon as we're off," Thomas said to Dwyer, "pull away. Get well off the rocks. When you see we've made it, head for port. We'll get a ride in a car and join you. One trip in this stuff is enough. I don't want to swim back."

Kate came up in two minutes, in an old, bleached, blue suit. She was a strong swimmer. Thomas took off his sweater and they both went out on deck. The Goodharts had taken off their sweaters and were waiting for them. In his long, flowered swimming trunks, Mr. Goodhart was massive and tanned by his holiday. His muscles were old muscles, but he must have been powerful in his prime. The little wrinkles of age showed in the skin of Mrs. Goodhart's still shapely legs.

The swimming raft, anchored midway between the *Clothilde* and the steps, was dancing in the waves. When a particularly large one hit it it would go up on end and stand almost perpendicularly for a moment.

"I suggest we make for the raft first," Thomas said, "so we can take a breather before we go in the rest of the way."

"We?" Mr. Goodhart said. "What do you mean, we?" He was definitely drunk. And so was Mrs. Goodhart.

"Kate and I decided we'd like a swim this afternoon, too," Thomas said.

"As you wish, Captain," Mr. Goodhart said. He climbed over the rail and dove in. Mrs. Goodhart followed. Their heads, gray and white, bobbed up and down in the dark green, frothing water.

"You stick with her," Thomas said to Kate. "I'll go with the old man."

He dove overboard and heard Kate splash in just after him.

Getting to the raft wasn't too difficult. Mr. Goodhart swam an old-fashioned trudgeon stroke and kept his head out of the water most of the time. Mrs. Goodhart swam an orthodox crawl and when Thomas turned to look at her she seemed to be swallowing water and breathing hard. But Kate was close beside her at all times. Mr. Goodhart and Thomas climbed onto the raft, but it was too rough to stand up on and they stayed on their knees as they helped pull Mrs. Goodhart up. She was gasping a little and she looked as though she was going to be sick.

"I think we ought to stay here for awhile," Mrs. Goodhart said, trying to keep her balance on the wet cord surface of the heaving raft. "Until it calms down a little."

"It's going to get worse, Mrs. Goodhart," Thomas said. "In a few minutes you won't have a chance of getting in."

Dwyer, worried about being too close to shore, had gone out another five hundred yards and was circling there. Anyway, there was no chance of getting Mrs. Goodhart up on the rolling boat in that sea without hurting her badly.

"You'll just have to come in with us right now," Thomas said to Mrs. Goodhart.

Mr. Goodhart didn't say anything. He was sober now.

"Nathaniel," Mrs. Goodhart said to her husband, "will you tell him I'm going to stay here until the sea calms a bit."

"You heard what he said," Mr. Goodhart said. "You wanted to swim in. Swim in." He toppled into the water.

By now there were at least twenty people clustered on the rocks, safely out of reach of the spume, watching the group on the raft.

Thomas took Mrs. Goodhart's hand and said, "In we go. Together." He stood up shakily and brought her to her feet and they jumped in, holding hands. Once in the sea, Mrs. Goodhart was less frightened and they swam side by side toward the ladder. As they came closer to the rocks, they felt themselves being swept forward by a wave, then sucked back as it broke against the rocks and receded. Thomas trod water and shouted, to be heard above the noise of the sea. "I'll go in first. Then Mrs. Goodhart. Watch how I do it. I'll go in on a wave and catch onto the railing and hold on. Then, I'll give you the signal when to start. Swim as hard as you can. I'll grab you when you get to the ladder. Just hold onto me. You'll be all right." He wasn't sure that anybody would be all right, but he had to say something.

He waited, looking over his shoulder at the oncoming waves. He saw a big one, thrashed hard with his arms, rode it in, smashed against the steel of the ladder, grabbed the railing, hung on against the pull away. Then he stood up, faced seaward. "Now!" he shouted at Mrs. Goodhart, and she came in fast, high above him for an instant, then breaking down. He grabbed her, held her tight, just managing to keep her from sliding back. Hurriedly, he pushed her up the ladder. She stumbled, but got to the safety of the rock platform before the next wave crashed in.

Mr. Goodhart, when he came in, was so heavy that, for a moment, Thomas lost his grip and he thought they were both going to be washed back. But the old man was strong. He swung in the water and grabbed the other pipe, holding onto Thomas at the same time. He didn't need any help up the ladder, but climbed it decorously, looking coldly at the silent group of spectators above him, as though he had caught them prying into some intensely private affair of his own.

Kate came in lightly and she and Thomas climbed the ladder together.

They got towels from the locker room attendant and dried themselves off, although there was nothing to do about their wet suits.

Mr. Goodhart called the hotel for his car and chauffeur and merely said, "That was very well done, Captain," when the car came down for Thomas and Kate. He had borrowed terrycloth robes for himself and Mrs. Goodhart and had ordered them all drinks at the bar while Kate and Thomas were drying themselves off. As he stood there, in the long robe, like a toga, you'd never think that he had been drinking all afternoon and had nearly got them all drowned just fifteen minutes before.

He held the door of the car open for Kate and Thomas. As Thomas got in, Mr. Goodhart said, "We have to settle up, Captain. Will you be in the harbor after dinner?"

Thomas had planned to set out for St. Tropez before sunset, but he said, "Yes, sir. We'll be there all evening."

"Very good, Captain. We'll have a farewell drink aboard." Mr. Goodhart closed the car door and they drove up the driveway, with the pines along its borders thrashing their branches about in the increasing wind.

When Thomas and Kate got out of the car on the quay they left two wet spots on the upholstery where they had been sitting in their bathing suits. The *Clothilde* hadn't come into the harbor yet and they sat with towels wrapped around their shoulders on an overturned dinghy on the quay and shivered.

Fifteen minutes later the *Clothilde* came into port. They grabbed the lines from Dwyer, made her fast, jumped on board, and rushed to put on dry clothes. Kate made a pot of coffee and as they drank it in the pilot house, with the wind whistling through the rigging, Dwyer said, "The rich. They always find a way of making you pay." Then he got out the hose, attached it to a water line on the quay and they all three of them began to scrub down the ship. There was salt crusted everywhere.

After dinner, which Kate prepared from the food left over from the Goodharts' lunch, she and Dwyer went into Antibes with the week's sheets, pillowcases, and towels. Kate did all the personal laundry, but the heavy items had to be done ashore. The wind had died down as suddenly as it had risen, and while the sea was still thundering at the harbor walls outside, the port itself was calm and the *Clothilde*'s buffers were merely nudging gently at the boats on either side from time to time.

It was a clear, warm night, and Thomas sat on the afterdeck, smoking a pipe, admiring the stars, waiting for Mr. Goodhart. He had made up the bill and it was in an envelope in the pilot house. It didn't amount to very much—just fuel, laundry, a few bottles of whiskey and vodka, ice and the twelve hundred francs a day for food for himself and the two others. Mr. Goodhart had given him a check for the charter itself the first day he had come aboard. Before going ashore, Kate had packed the Goodharts' belongings, extra bathing suits, clothes, shoes, and books, in two of the hotel baskets. The baskets were on deck, near the after rail.

Thomas saw the lights of Mr. Goodhart's car coming up to the quay. He stood up as the car stopped and Mr. Goodhart got out and came up the gangplank. He was dressed for the evening, in a gray suit and white shirt and dark silk tie. Somehow he looked older and frailer in his city clothes.

"May I offer you something to drink?" Thomas asked.

"A whiskey would be nice, Captain," Mr. Goodhart said. He was absolutely sober now. "If you'll join me." He sat down in one of the folding canvas-and-wood chairs while Thomas went to the saloon for the drinks. On his way up, he went into the pilot house and got the envelope with the bill.

"Mrs. Goodhart has a slight chill," Mr. Goodhart said, as Thomas gave him the glass. "She's gone to bed for the night. She especially commanded me to tell you how much she enjoyed these two weeks."

"That's very kind of her," Thomas said. "It was a pleasure having her with us." If Mr. Goodhart wasn't going to mention the afternoon's adventure, he wasn't going to say a word about it, either. "I made up the bill, sir," he said. He gave the envelope to Mr. Goodhart. "If you want to go over it and . . ."

Mr. Goodhart waved the envelope negligently. "I'm sure it's in order," he said. He took the bill out, squinted at it briefly in the light of the quay lamppost. He had a checkbook with him and he wrote out a check and handed it to Thomas. "There's a little something extra there for you and the crew, Captain," he said.

Thomas glanced at the check. Five-hundred-dollar bonus. Like last year. "It's most generous of you, sir." Oh, for summers of Goodharts!

Mr. Goodhart waved off gratitude. "Next year," he said, "perhaps we can make it a full month. There's no law that says that we have to spend the whole summer in the house in Newport, is there?" He had explained that ever since he was a boy he had spent July and August in the family house in Newport and now his married son and two daughters and their children spent their holidays there with Mrs. Goodhart and himself. "We could give the house over to the younger generation," Mr. Goodhart went on, as though trying to convince himself. "They could have orgies or whatever the younger generation has these days when we're not around. Maybe we could steal a grandchild or two and go on a real cruise with you." He settled comfortably back in his chair, sipping at his drink, playing with this new idea. "If we had a month, where could we go?"

"Well," Thomas said, "the party we're picking up tomorrow at St. Tropez, two French couples, are only taking the boat for three weeks and with any break in the weather, we can go down the coast of Spain, the Costa Brava, Cadaques, Rosas, Barcelona, then across to the Balearics. And after them, we come back here and there's an English family who want to go south—that's another three week cruise—the Ligurian coast, Portofino, Porto Venere, Elba, Porto Ercole, Corsica, Sardinia, Ischia, Capri . . ."

Mr. Goodhart chuckled. "You're making Newport sound like Coney Island, Captain. Have you been to all those places?"

"Uhuh."

"And people pay you for it?"

"A lot of them make you earn your money, and more," Thomas said. "Not everybody's like you and Mrs. Goodhart."

"Old age has sweetened us, perhaps," Mr. Goodhart said slowly. "In some ways. Do you think I might have another drink, Captain?"

"If you don't plan to do any more swimming tonight," Thomas said, rising and taking Mr. Goodhart's glass.

Mr. Goodhart chuckled. "That was a horse's ass thing to do today, wasn't it?"

"Yes, sir, it was." Thomas was surprised at Mr. Goodhart's using an expression like that. He went below and mixed two more drinks. When he came back on deck, Mr. Goodhart was stretched out in his chair, his long legs crossed at the ankles, his head back, looking up at the stars. He took the glass from Thomas's hand without changing his position.

"Captain," he said, "I've decided to pamper myself. And my wife. I'll make a firm commitment with you right now. Starting June first next year we'll take the *Clothilde* for six weeks and go south to all those pretty names you were reeling off. I'll give you a deposit to-night. And when you say no swimming, nobody will swim. How does that strike you?"

"It would be fine for me, but . . ." Thomas hesitated.

"But what?"

"The *Clothilde*'s all right for you using it during the day the way you do, going to the islands . . . but for six weeks, living aboard . . . I don't know. For some people it's fine, but for others, who are used to luxury . . ."

"You mean for spoiled old crocks like my wife and myself," Mr. Goodhart said, "it's not grand enough, is that it?"

"Well," Thomas said uncomfortably, "I wouldn't like you not to enjoy yourselves. The *Clothilde* rolls quite a bit in rough weather and it's pretty stuffy down below when we're under way, because we have to close all the portholes, and there's no proper bath, just showers, and . . ."

"It'll do us good. We've had it too easy all our lives. Oh, it's ridiculous, Captain." Mr. Goodhart sat up. "You make me ashamed of myself. To have you feel as though going around the Mediterranean on a boat as nice as this one is roughing it for me and my wife. God, it sends cold shivers down my spine to think of the opinion people must have of us."

"People get used to living in different ways," Thomas said.

"You've lived yours the hard way, haven't you?" Mr. Goodhart said.

"No worse than a lot of others."

"You don't seem any the worse for it," Mr. Goodhart said. "In fact, if I may say so, if my son had turned out like you, I'd be more pleased with him than I am now. Considerably more pleased."

"It's hard to know," Thomas said neutrally. If he knew about Port Philip, he thought, burning the cross on VE day, and hitting my father, and taking money for screwing married ladies in Elysium, Ohio, if he knew about blackmailing Sinclair in Boston, and throwing fights, and about Quayles and Quayles's wife in Las Vegas, and about Pappy and Teresa and Falconetti, maybe he wouldn't be sitting there being friendly, with a glass in his hand, wishing his son was more like me. "There's a lot of things I've done I'm not so goddamn proud of," he said.

"That doesn't make you any different from the rest of us, Captain," Goodhart said quietly. "And while we're on the subject—forgive me for this afternoon. I was drunk and I had had two weeks of watching three splendid young people happily working together, moving around like graceful animals, and I felt old and I didn't want to feel old and I wanted to prove that I wasn't all that old and I risked all our lives. Knowingly, Captain, knowingly. Because I was sure you weren't going to let us make that swim alone."

"It's better not to talk about it, sir," Thomas said. "Anyway, no harm was done."

"Old age is an aberration, Tom," Mr. Goodhart said bitterly. "A terrible, perverted aberration." He stood up and put his glass down carefully. "I'd better be getting back to the hotel and see how my wife is doing," he said. He extended his hand and Thomas shook it. "Until next June first," he said and strode off the ship, carrying the two baskets with him.

When Kate and Dwyer came back, with the freshly laundered linen, all Thomas said was that Mr. Goodhart had been and gone and that they had their first charter, six weeks, for the following year.

Dwyer had a letter from his girl. She had been down to the Aegean Hotel, but she had no information for Tom, she said, because Pappy was dead. He had been found, knifed and with a gag in his mouth, in his room, the new man at the desk had told her. Three months ago.

Thomas listened to the news without surprise. That was the kind of business Pappy had run and he had finally paid his dues.

There was something else in the letter that was obviously bothering Dwyer, but he didn't tell the others what it was, although Thomas could guess. Dwyer's girl didn't want to wait any more and she wouldn't leave Boston and if Dwyer wanted to marry her he'd have to go back to America. He hadn't asked Thomas's advice yet, but if he had, Thomas would have told him that no dame was worth it.

They went to bed early, because they were going to set out for St. Tropez at four in the morning, before the wind sprang up.

Kate had made up the big bed in the master cabin for herself and Thomas for the night, because there were no clients on board. It was the first time they had a chance to make love in comfort and Kate said she wasn't going to miss it. In the cabin they shared forward, they had two narrow bunks, one above the other.

Kate's stocky, solid, full-breasted body was not made for showing off clothes, but her skin was wonderfully soft and she made love with gentle avidity and as Thomas lay later, with her in his arms in the big bed, he was grateful that he was not old, that his girl was not in Boston, that he had allowed himself to be persuaded by Pinky to have a woman on board.

Before she went to sleep, Kate said, "Dwyer told me tonight that when you bought the boat you changed the name. Who was Clothilde?"

"She was a queen of France," Thomas said. He pulled her closer to him. "She was somebody I knew as a boy. And she smelled like you."

The cruise to Spain wasn't bad, although they hit some weather off Cap Cruz and had to stay in port for five days at a stretch. The French couples consisted of two paunchy Parisian businessmen and two young women who were definitely not their wives. There was some trading going on between the couples in the after cabins, but Thomas hadn't come to the Mediterranean to teach French businessmen how to behave. As long as they paid their bills and kept the two ladies from walking around in high heels and poking holes in the deck, he wasn't going to interfere with their fun. The ladies also lay on deck with the tops of their bikinis off. Kate took a poor view of that, but one of the ladies had really sensational tits and it didn't interfere with the navigation too much, although if there had been any reefs on the course while Dwyer was at the wheel, Dwyer would have most likely run them aground. That particular lady also made it clear to Thomas that she wouldn't mind sneaking up on deck in the middle of the night to have a go with him while her Jules was snoring away below. But Thomas told her he didn't come with the charter. You got into enough complications with clients without any of that.

Because of the delay caused by the storm, the two French couples got off at Marseilles, to catch the train up to Paris. The two businessmen had to meet their wives in Paris to go to Deauville for the rest of the summer. When they paid Thomas off at the dock in front of the Mairie in the Vieux Port, the two Frenchmen gave Thomas fifty thousand francs as a tip, which wasn't bad, considering they were Frenchmen. After they had gone, Thomas took Kate and Dwyer to the same restaurant that Dwyer and Thomas had eaten at when they first came to Marseilles on the *Elga Andersen*. It was too bad that the *Elga Andersen* wasn't in port. It would have been satisfying to sail across her rusty bows in the shining white-and-blue *Clothilde* and dip the flag in salute to the old Nazi captain.

They had three days before picking up the next charter in Antibes, and again Kate made up the big bed in the master cabin for herself and Thomas. She had had the portholes and the doors wide open all evening to get out the smell of perfume.

"That *poule*," Kate said as they lay in the darkness. "Parading around naked. You had a hard on for three weeks running."

Thomas laughed. There were times when Kate talked like any sailor.

"I don't like the way you laugh," Kate said. "Let me warn you—if I ever catch you grabbing any of that stuff, I'm going to go out and jump into the kip with the first man I see as I walk off the boat."

"There's one sure way," Thomas said, "that you can keep me honest."

Kate then made sure that he was going to be honest. That night, anyway. As she lay in his arms he whispered, "Kate, every time I make love to you I forget one more bad thing in my life." A moment later he could feel her tears on his shoulders.

Luxuriously, they slept late the next morning and when they sailed out of the harbor in the sunlight, they even took time off to do a little sight-seeing. They went out to the Château d'If and walked around the fortress and saw the dungeon where the Count of Monte Cristo was supposed to have been chained. Kate had read the book and Thomas had seen the movie. Kate translated the signs that told how many Protestants had been imprisoned in the place before being sent to the galleys.

"There's always somebody sitting on somebody else's back," Dwyer said. "If it's not the Protestants sitting on the Catholics, it's the Catholics sitting on the Protestants."

"Shut up, you Communist," Thomas said.

"Are you a Protestant?" he asked Kate.

"Yes."

"I'm going to imprison you in my galley," he said.

By the time they got back onto the *Clothilde* and started East, the last whiff of perfume had vanished from the main cabin.

They sailed without stopping, with Dwyer taking eight full hours at night at the wheel so that Thomas and Kate could sleep. They reached Antibes before noon. There were two letters waiting for Thomas, one from his brother, and one in a handwriting he didn't recognize. He opened the letter from Rudolph first.

"Dear Tom,"—he read,—"I finally got news of you after all this time and I must say it sounds as if you're doing all right for yourself. A few days ago I received a call at my office from a Mr. Goodhart, who told me he had been on your boat, or ship, as I believe you fellows like to call it. It turns out that we have done some business with his firm, and I guess he was curious to see what your brother looked like. He invited Jean and myself over for a drink and he and his wife turned out to be charming old people, as you must know. They were most enthusiastic about you and about your ship and the life you lead. Maybe you've made the best investment of the century with the money you made on Dee Cee. If I weren't so busy (it looks as though I'm going to allow myself to be talked into running for mayor of Whitby this fall!), I'd take a plane with Jean immediately and come over to sail the deep blue sea with you. Maybe next year. In the meantime, I've taken the liberty of suggesting renting the *Clothilde* (as you see the Goodharts were most explicit about everything) to a friend of mine who is getting married and would like to spend his honeymoon on the Mediterranean. Perhaps you remember him—Johnny Heath. If he bothers you, put him adrift in a raft.

"But seriously, I am very happy for you and I'd like to hear from you and if there's anything I can do for you, please don't hesitate to let me know what it is. Love, Rudolph."

Thomas scowled as he read the letter. He didn't like to be reminded that it was because of Rudolph that he now owned the *Clothilde*. Still, the letter was so friendly, the weather was so fine, and the summer was going so well, it was silly to spoil things by remembering old grudges. He folded the letter carefully and put it in his pocket. The other letter was from Rudolph's friend and asked if he could charter the *Clothilde* from September fifteenth to the thirtieth. It was the end of the season, and they had nothing on the books, and it would be found money. Heath said he only wanted to sail up and down the coast between Monte Carlo and St. Tropez, and with only two people on board and very little mileage to cover, it would be a lazy way to end the season.

Thomas sat down and wrote a letter to Heath, telling him he'd meet him either at the Nice airport or the Antibes station on the fifteenth.

He told Kate about the new charter and how it was his brother who had arranged it, and she made him write a letter of thanks to Rudolph. He had signed it and was just going to seal the envelope, when he remembered that Rudolph had written him that if there was anything he could do for him not to hesitate to let him know what it was. Well, why not, he thought. It couldn't do any harm. In a P.S. he wrote, "There's one thing you can do for me. For various reasons I haven't been able to come back to New York so far but maybe those reasons don't hold any more. I haven't had any news of my kid for years and I don't know where he is or whether I'm still married or not. I'd like to come over and see him and if possible take him back here with me for awhile. Maybe you remember the night you and Gretchen came back after my fight in Queens, there was my manager, a man I introduced you to called Schultzy. Actually his name is Herman Schultz. The last address I had for him is the Bristol Hotel on Eighth Avenue, but maybe he doesn't live there any more. But if you ask somebody in the Garden office if they know where you can lay your hands on Schultzy they're bound to know if he's still alive and in town. He's likely to have some news about Teresa and the kid. Just don't tell him where I am for the time being. But ask him if the heat's still on. He will understand. Let me know if you find him and what he says. This will be a real good turn and I will be really grateful."

He air-mailed the two letters at the Antibes post office and then went back to the ship to get it ready for the English party.

Chapter 4

I

Nobody had remembered Herman Schultz at the Bristol Hotel, but somebody in the publicity department at Madison Square Garden had finally come up with the address of a rooming house on West Fifty-third Street. Rudolph was getting to know Fifty-third Street very well. He had been there three times in the last four weeks, on every trip he had made to New York in the month of August. Yes, the man at the rooming house said, Mr. Schultz stayed there when he was in New York, but he was out of town. He didn't know where out of town. Rudolph left his telephone number with him, but Schultz never called him. Rudolph had to suppress a quiver of distaste every time he rang the bell. It was a decaying building in a dying neighborhood, inhabited, you felt, only by doomed old men and derelict young men.

A shuffling, bent old man with a twisted hair piece opened the peeling door, the color of dried blood. From the gloom of the hall-way he peered nearsightedly at Rudolph standing on the stoop in the hot September sun. Even with the distance between them, Rudolph could smell him, mildew and urine.

"Is Mr. Schultz at home?" Rudolph asked.

"Fourth floor back," the old man said. He stepped aside to allow Rudolph to enter.

As he climbed the steps, Rudolph realized that it wasn't only the old man who smelled like that, it was the entire house. A radio was playing Spanish music, a fat man, naked to the waist, was sitting at the head of the second flight of steps, his head in his hands. He didn't look up as Rudolph squeezed past him.

The door to the fourth floor back was open. It was stifling hot, under the roof. Rudolph recognized the man he had been introduced to as Schultzy in Queens. Schultzy was sitting on the edge of an un-made bed, grayish sheets, staring at the wall of the room, three feet across from him.

Rudolph knocked on the framework of the doorway. Schultzy turned his head slowly, painfully.

"What do you want?" Schultz said. His voice was reedy and hostile.

Rudolph went in. "I'm Tom Jordache's brother." He extended his hand.

Schultz put his right hand behind his back. He was wearing a sweat-stained skivvy shirt. He still had the basketball of a stomach. He moved his mouth uneasily, as though he was wearing plates that fit badly. He was pasty and totally bald. "I don't shake hands," Schultz said. "It's the arthritis." He didn't ask Rudolph to sit down. There was no place to sit down except on the bed, anyway.

"That sonofabitch," Schultz said. "I don't want to hear his name."

Rudolph took out his wallet and extracted two twenty-dollar bills. "He asked me to give you this."

"Put it on the bed." Schultz's expression, snakelike and livid, did not change. "He owes me one fifty."

"I'll have him send the rest over tomorrow," Rudolph said.

"It's about fucking well time," Schultz said. "What does he want now? Did he put the boots to somebody else again?"

"No," Rudolph said, "he's not in trouble."

"I'm sorry to hear it," Schultz said.

"He asked me to ask you if the heat's still on." The words sounded strange to him as they came off his tongue.

Schultz's face became sly, secretive, and he looked sideways at Rudolph. "You sure he's going to give me the rest of the money tomorrow?"

"Positive," Rudolph said.

"Nah," Schultz said. "There's no more heat. There's no more anything. That bum Quayles never had a good night again after your shitty brother got through with him. The one chance I ever had to make a real buck. Not that they left me much of a share, the dagoes. And I was the one who discovered Quayles and brought him along. No, there's no heat. Everybody's dead or in jail. Nobody remembers your goddamn brother's name. He can walk down Fifth Avenue at the head of the Columbus Day Parade and nobody'd raise a finger. Tell him that. Tell him that's worth a lot more than one fifty."

"I will, Mr. Schultz," Rudolph said, trying to sound as though he knew what the old man was talking about. "And then there's another question . . ."

"He wants a lot of answers for his money, don't he?"

"He wants to know about his wife."

Schultz cackled. "That whore," he said, pronouncing the word in two syllables. "She got her picture in the papers. In the *Daily News*. Twice. She got picked up twice for soliciting in bars. She said her name was Theresa Laval in the papers. French. But I recognized the bitch. Some French. They're all whores, every last one of them. I could tell you stories, mister . . ."

"Do you know where she lives?" Rudolph didn't relish the thought of spending the afternoon in the sweltering, evil-smelling room listening to Schultz's opinions of the female sex. "And where the boy is?"

Schultz shook his head. "Who keeps track? I don't even know where *I* live. Theresa Laval. French." He cackled again. "Some French."

"Thank you very much, Mr. Schultz," Rudolph said. "I won't trouble you any more."

"Ain't no trouble. Glad for a little conversation. You for sure going to send over that money tomorrow?"

"I guarantee."

"You're wearing a good suit," Schultz said. "But that ain't no guarantee."

Rudolph left him sitting on the bed, his head nodding in the heat. He went down the steps quickly. Even West Fifty-third Street looked good to him when he put the rooming house behind him.

II

He had Rudolph's cable in his pocket when he got off the plane at Kennedy and went with hundreds of other passengers through the Health and Immigration formalities. The last time he had been at the airport it had been called Idlewild. Taking a bullet through your head was an expensive way of getting an airport named after you.

The big Irishman with the Immigration badge looked at him as though he didn't like the idea of letting him back into the country. And he thumbed through a big, black book, full of names, hunting for Jordache, and seemed disappointed that he couldn't find it.

He went into the Customs hall to wait for his bag. The whole population of America seemed to be coming back from a holiday in Europe. Where did all the money come from?

He looked up at the glass-enclosed balcony where people were lined up two and three deep waving at relatives down below that they had come to meet. He had cabled Rudolph his flight number and time of arrival, but he couldn't pick him out in the crowd behind the glass window. He had a moment of irritation. He didn't want to go wandering around New York hunting for his brother.

The cable had been waiting for him for a week when he came back to Antibes after the charter with Heath and his wife. "Dear Tom," the cable read, "Everything OK for you here Stop Believe will have sons address soonest Love Rudolph."

He finally saw his bag in the bin and grabbed it and went and stood in line to go through the Customs counter. Some idiot from Syracuse was sweating and telling a long story to the inspector about where he had gotten two embroidered dirndls and whom they were for. When it was his turn, the inspector made him open his bag and went through everything. He had no gifts for anyone in America, and the inspector passed him through.

He said no to a porter who wanted to carry his bag and carried it through the exit doors himself. Standing bareheaded among the crowd, looking cooler than anybody else in a pair of slacks and a lightweight jacket, Rudolph waved at him. They shook hands and Rudolph tried to take the bag from him, but Thomas wouldn't let him.

"Have a good trip?" Rudolph asked him as they walked out of the building.

"Okay."

"I've got my car parked near here," Rudolph said. "Wait here. I'll just be a minute."

As he went for the car, Thomas noted that Rudolph still walked in that peculiar gliding way, not moving his shoulders.

He opened his collar and pulled his tie down. Although it was the beginning of October, it was stinking hot, wet smoggy heat, smelling of burned kerosene. He had forgotten the climate of New York. How did anyone live here?

Five minutes later Rudolph drove up in a blue Buick coupe. Thomas threw his bag in the back and got in. The car was air-conditioned, which was a relief. Rudolph drove at just the legal speed and Thomas remembered being picked up by the state troopers with the bottle of bourbon and the Smith and Wesson in the car on the way to his mother's deathbed. Times had changed. For the better.

"Well?" Thomas said.

"I found Schultz," Rudolph said. "That's when I sent you the wire. He said the heat's off. Everybody's dead or in jail, he said. I didn't inquire what that meant."

"What about Teresa and the kid?"

Rudolph fiddled with the air-conditioning levers, frowning. "Well, it's a little hard to begin."

"Come on. I'm a big, strong fella."

"Schultz didn't know where either of them was. But he said he saw your wife's picture in the newspapers. Twice."

"What the hell for?" For a moment, Thomas was rattled. Maybe the crazy dame had finally made it on the stage or in a nightclub.

"She was arrested for soliciting in a bar. Twice," Rudolph said. "I hate to be the one who has to tell you this, Tom."

"Forget it," Thomas said roughly. "It figured."

"Schultz said she was using another name, but he recognized her," Rudolph said. "I checked. It was her. The police gave me her address."

"If I can afford her prices," Thomas said, "maybe I'll go around and give her a screw. Maybe she's learned how to do it by now." He saw the pained expression on Rudolph's face, but he hadn't crossed the ocean to be polite. "How about the kid?"

"He's up at a military school near Poughkeepsie," Rudolph said. "I just found out two days ago."

"Military school," Thomas said. "Christ. Do the officers get to bang his mother on maneuvers?"

Rudolph drove without speaking, allowing Thomas to get his bitterness out.

"That's just what I want my kid to be," Thomas said. "A soldier. How did you get all this good news?"

"A private detective."

"Did he talk to the bitch?"

"No."

"So nobody knows I'm here?"

"Nobody," Rudolph said. "Except me. I did one other thing. I hope you won't mind."

"What's that?"

"I talked to a lawyer friend of mine. Without mentioning any names. You can get a divorce and custody without any trouble. Because of the two convictions."

"I hope they put her in jail and throw away the key."

"Just overnight each time. And a fine."

"They got some great lawyers in this city, don't they?" He remembered his days in the jail in Elysium. Two out of three in the family.

"Look," Rudolph said, "I have to get back to Whitby tonight. You can come with me if you want. Or you can stay in the apartment. It's empty. There's a maid comes in every morning to clean up."

"Thanks. I'll take you up on the apartment. I want to see that lawyer you talked to first thing in the morning. Can you fix it?"

"Yes."

"You got her address and the name of the school and all that?"

Rudolph nodded.

"That's all I need," Thomas said.

"How long do you plan to stay in New York?"

"Just long enough to make sure of the divorce and go up and get the kid and take him back to Antibes with me."

Rudolph didn't say anything for awhile and Thomas looked out the window to his right at the boats moored in Flushing Bay. He was glad the *Clothilde* was in Antibes harbor and not in Flushing Bay.

"Johnny Heath wrote me that he had a wonderful trip with you," Rudolph said. "He said his bride loved it."

"I don't know when she had the time to love anything," Thomas said. "She was going up and down the ladder changing her clothes every five minutes. She must have had thirty bags with her. It was lucky there were only two of them. We filled two empty cabins with her luggage."

Rudolph smiled. "She comes from a very rich family."

"It sticks out all over her. He's okay, though. Your friend. Didn't mind rough weather and asked so many questions by the end of the two weeks he could have sailed the *Clothilde* by himself right to Tunis. He said he was going to ask you and your wife to come with him on a cruise next summer."

"If I have the time," Rudolph said quickly.

"What's this about your running for mayor of that little one-horse town?" Thomas asked.

"It's far from a one-horse town," Rudolph said. "Don't you think it's a good idea?"

"I wouldn't wipe my feet on the best politician in the country," Thomas said.

"Maybe I'll make you change your mind," Rudolph said.

"They had one good man," Thomas said, "so naturally they shot him."

"They can't shoot all of them."

"They can try," Thomas said. He leaned over and turned on the radio. The roar of a crowd filled the car and then an excited announcer's voice, saying, ". . . a clean line drive into center field, the runner is rounding second, it's going to be close, close, he goes into his slide. Safe! Safe!" Thomas turned the radio off.

"The World Series," Rudolph said.

"I know. I get the Paris *Herald Tribune.*"

"Tom," Rudolph said, "don't you ever miss America?"

"What's America done for me?" Thomas said. "I don't care if I never see it again after this time."

"I hate to hear you talk like that."

"One patriot in the family is enough," Thomas said.

"What about your son?"

"What about him?"

"How long are you figuring you'll keep him in Europe?"

"Forever," Thomas said. "Maybe when you get elected President and straighten out the whole country and put all the crooks and generals and policemen and judges and congressmen and high-priced lawyers in jail and if they don't shoot you maybe I'll send him over on a visit."

"What about his education?" Rudolph persisted.

"There're schools in Antibes. Better than a crappy military academy."

"But he's an American."

"Why?" Thomas asked.

"Well, he's not a Frenchman."

"He won't be a Frenchman either," Thomas said. "He'll be Wesley Jordache."

"He won't know where he belongs."

"Where do you think *I* belong? Here?" Thomas laughed. "My son'll belong on a boat in the Mediterranean, sailing from one country where they make wine and olive oil to another country where they make wine and olive oil."

Rudolph quit then. They drove the rest of the way in silence to the building on Park Avenue where Rudolph had an apartment. The doorman double-parked the car for him when he said he'd only be a few minutes. The doorman gave a queer look at Thomas, with his collar open and his tie loose and his blue, wide-trousered suit and green fedora hat with the brown band that he had bought in Genoa.

"Your doorman doesn't approve of my clothes," Thomas said as they went up in the elevator. "Tell him I buy my clothes in Marseilles and everybody knows Marseilles is the greatest center of *haute couture* for men in Europe."

"Don't worry about the doorman," Rudolph said as he led Thomas into the apartment.

"Not a bad little place you have here," Thomas said, standing in the middle of the large living room, with its fireplace and long, straw-colored corduroy couch, with two winged easy chairs on each side of it. There were fresh flowers in vases on the tables, a pale-beige wall-to-wall carpet, and bright, non-objective paintings on the dark-green walls. The room faced west and the afternoon sun streamed in through the curtained windows. The air-conditioning was on, humming softly, and the room was comfortably cool.

"We don't get down to the city as much as we'd like," Rudolph said. "Jean's pregnant again and she's having a bad couple of months just now." He opened a cupboard. "Here's the bar," he said. "There's ice in the refrigerator. If you want to eat here, just tell the maid when she gets in in the morning. She's a pretty good cook." He led Thomas into the spare room, which Jean had made over to look exactly like the guest room in the farmhouse in Whitby, countrified and delicate. Rudolph couldn't help but notice how out of place his brother looked in the neat, feminine room, with its four-poster twin beds and patchwork quilts.

Thomas threw his battered valise and his jacket and hat on one of the beds and Rudolph tried not to wince. On his boat, Johnny Heath had written, Tom was a stickler for neatness. Obviously, he did not carry his seagoing habits with him when he went ashore.

Back in the living room Rudolph poured a whiskey and soda for Thomas and himself and while they drank, got out the papers he had collected from the Police Department and the report from the private detective and gave them to Thomas. He called the lawyer's office and made an appointment for Thomas for the next morning at ten.

"Now," he said, as they finished their drinks, "is there anything else you need? Do you want me to go with you when you go up to the school?"

"I'll handle the school on my own," Thomas said. "Don't worry."

"How are you fixed for money?"

"I'm rolling," Thomas said. "Thanks."

"If anything comes up," Rudolph said, "call me."

"Okay, mayor," Thomas said.

They shook hands and Rudolph left his brother standing next to the table on which lay the reports from the Police Department and the detective. Thomas was picking them up to read as Rudolph went out the front door.

Teresa Jordache, Thomas read from the police file, alias Theresa Laval. Thomas grinned. He was tempted to call her up and ask her to come over. He'd disguise his voice. "Apartment 14B, Miss Laval. It's on Park Avenue between Fifty-seventh and Fifty-eighth street." Even the most suspicious whore wouldn't think there'd be any trouble at an address like that. He would love to see her face when she rang the bell and he opened the door. He nearly went to the phone to dial the last number the detective had ferreted out, then stopped. It would be almost impossible not to give her the beating she deserved and that wasn't what he had come to America for.

He shaved and showered, using the perfumed soap in the bathroom, and had another drink and put on a clean shirt and the blue Marseilles suit, then went down in the elevator and walked over to Fifth Avenue in the dusk. On a side street he saw a steak place and went in and had a steak with half a bottle of wine and apple pie à la mode, to salute his native country. Then he strolled over to Broadway. Broadway was worse than ever, with noise coming out of the music shops and bigger and uglier signs than he remembered and the people pushing and sick looking, but he enjoyed it. He could walk anywhere, go to any bar, any movie.

Everybody was dead or in jail. Music.

The Hilltop Military Academy was on top of a hill and it was military. A high, gray, stone wall enclosed it, like a prison, and when Thomas drove through the front gate in the car he had rented, he could see boys in blue-gray uniforms doing close-order drill on a dusty field. The weather had turned cooler and some of the trees on the grounds had begun to change color. The driveway passed close to the parade grounds and Thomas stopped the car and watched. There were four separate groups wheeling and marching on different parts of the field. The group of boys nearest to him, perhaps thirty of them, were between twelve and fourteen, just about Wesley's age. Thomas stared at them as they passed him, but if Wesley was among them he didn't recognize him.

He started the car again and went up the driveway to a stone building that looked like a small castle. The grounds were well kept, with flower beds and closely mown lawns and the other buildings were large and solidly built, of the same stone as the little castle.

Teresa must get a fancy price for her services, Thomas thought, to afford a place like this for the kid.

He got out of the car and went into the building. The granite hallway was dark and chilly. It was lined with flags, sabers, crossed rifles, and marble lists of the names of graduates who had been killed in the Spanish-American War, the Mexican Expedition, the First World War, the Second World War, and the war in Korea. It was like the head office of a company, with a display advertising their product. A boy with close-cropped hair and a lot of fancy chevrons on his arm was coming down the steps, and Thomas asked him, "Son, where's the main office here?"

The boy came to attention, as though Thomas were General MacArthur, and said, "This way, sir." They obviously taught respect to the older generation at Hilltop Military Academy. Maybe that was why Teresa had sent the kid here. She could use all the respect going.

The boy opened the door to a big office. Two women were working at desks behind a small fence. "Here you are, sir," the boy said, and clicked his heels before turning smartly back into the hallway. Thomas went over toward the nearest desk behind the fence. The woman there looked up from papers she was making checks on and said, "May I help you, sir?" She was not in uniform and she didn't click her heels.

"I have a son in the school," Thomas said. "My name is Jordache. I'd like to speak to whoever is in charge here."

The woman gave him a peculiar look, as though the name meant something not particularly pleasant to her. She stood up and said, "I'll tell Colonel Bainbridge you're here, sir. Won't you please take a seat." She indicated a bench along the wall and waddled off to a door on the other side of the office. She was fat and about fifty and her stockings were crooked. They were not tempting the young soldiers with too much sex at the Hilltop Military Academy.

After a little while she came out of the door and opened a gate in the little fence and said, "Colonel Bainbridge will see you now, sir. Thank you for waiting." She led Thomas to the rear of the room and closed the door after him as he went into Colonel Bainbridge's office. There were more flags there and photographs of General Patton and General Eisenhower and of Colonel Bainbridge looking fierce in a combat jacket and pistol and helmet, with binoculars hanging around his neck, taken during World War Two. Colonel Bainbridge himself, in a regular U.S. Army uniform, was standing behind his desk to greet Thomas. He was thinner than in the photograph, with almost no hair, and he was wearing silver-rimmed glasses and no weapons or binoculars and he looked like an actor in a war play.

"Welcome to Hilltop, Mr. Jordache," Colonel Bainbridge said. He was not standing at attention but he gave the impression that he was. "Won't you sit down?" His expression was peculiar, too, a little like the doorman's at Rudolph's building.

If I stay in America much longer, Thomas thought as he sat down, I guess I'll have to change my tailor.

"I don't want to take up much of your time, Colonel," Thomas said. "I just came up here to see my son, Wesley."

"Yes, of course, I understand," Bainbridge said. He was stumbling a little over his words. "There's a games period shortly and we'll have him sent for." He cleared his throat embarrassedly. "It's a pleasure to have a member of the young man's family finally visit the school. I am correct in assuming that you *are* his father, am I not?"

"That's what I told the lady outside," Thomas said.

"I hope you'll forgive me for the question, Mr. . . . Mr. Jordache," Bainbridge said, looking distractedly at General Eisenhower on the wall, "but in Wesley's application it was clearly stated that his father was dead."

The bitch, Thomas thought, oh, the stinking, miserable bitch. "Well," he said, "I'm not dead."

"I can see that," Bainbridge said nervously. "Of course I can see that. It must be a clerical error of some kind, although it's hard to understand how . . ."

"I've been away a few years," Thomas said. "My wife and I are not on friendly terms."

"Even so." Bainbridge's hand fluttered over a small model brass cannon on his desk. "Of course, one doesn't meddle in intimate family matters . . . I've never had the honor of meeting Mrs. Jordache. Our communication was entirely by mail. It *is* the same Mrs. Jordache, isn't it?" Bainbridge said desperately. "In the antique business in New York?"

"She may handle some antiques," Thomas said. "I wouldn't know. Now, I want to see my son."

"They'll be finished with drill in five minutes," Bainbridge said. "I'm sure he'll be happy to see you. Very happy. Seeing his father may just be what he needs at this particular moment . . ."

"Why? What's the matter with him?"

"He's a difficult boy, Mr. Jordache, very difficult. We have our problems with him."

"What problems?"

"He's extraordinarily . . . uh . . . pugnacious." Bainbridge seemed happy to have found the word. "He's constantly getting into fights. With everyone. No matter what age or size. On one occasion last term he even hit one of the instructors. General science. The instructor missed a whole week of classes. He's very . . . adept . . . shall we say, with his fists, young Wesley. Of course, we like a boy to show a normal amount of aggressiveness in a school of this nature, but Wesley . . ." Bainbridge sighed. "His disagreements are not ordinary schoolboy fights. We've had to hospitalize boys, upperclassmen . . . To be absolutely frank with you, there's a kind of, well, the only word is adult, adult *viciousness* about the boy that we on the staff consider very dangerous."

Jordache blood, Thomas thought bitterly, fucking Jordache blood.

"I'm afraid I have to tell you, Mr. Jordache, that Wesley is on probation this term, with no privileges," Bainbridge said.

"Well, Colonel," Thomas said, "I have some good news for you. I'm going to do something about Wesley and his problems."

"I'm glad to hear that you propose to take the matter in hand, Mr. Jordache," Bainbridge said. "We've written innumerable letters to his mother but she seems to be too busy even to reply."

"I propose to take him out of school this afternoon," Thomas said. "You can stop worrying."

Bainbridge's hand trembled on the brass cannon on his desk. "I wasn't suggesting anything as drastic as that, sir," he said. His voice quavered a little. The battlefields of Normandy and the Rhine basin were far behind him and he was an old man, dressed up like a soldier.

"Well, *I'm* suggesting it, Colonel."

Bainbridge stood up too, behind his desk. "I'm afraid it's most . . . most irregular," he said. "We would have to have his mother's written permission. After all, all our dealings have been with her. She has paid the tuition for the entire school year. We would have to authenticate your relationship with the boy."

Thomas took out his wallet and drew his passport from it and put it on the desk in front of Bainbridge. "Who does this look like?" he asked.

Bainbridge opened the little green book. "Of course," he said, "your name is Jordache. But otherwise . . . Really, sir, I must get in touch with the boy's mother . . ."

"I don't want to waste any more of your time, Colonel," Thomas said. He dug into his inside pocket once more and brought out the Police Department report on Teresa Jordache, alias Theresa Laval. "Read this, please," he said, handing the paper to the Colonel.

Bainbridge glanced at the report, then took off his glasses and rubbed his eyes wearily. "Oh, dear," he said. He handed the paper back to Thomas, as though he were afraid that if it lay around his office one moment more it would go permanently into the files of the school.

"Do you still want to keep the kid?" Thomas asked brutally.

"Of course, this alters things," Bainbridge said. "Considerably."

A half hour later, they drove out the gate of the Hilltop Military Academy. Wesley's footlocker was on the back seat and Wesley, still in uniform, was up front beside Thomas. He was big for his age, sallow skinned and pimpled, and around his sullen eyes and wide, set mouth, he resembled, as a son does his father, Axel Jordache. He had not been effusive when he was brought in to see Thomas and had seemed neither glad nor sorry when he was told he was being taken from the school and he hadn't asked where Thomas was taking him.

"Tomorrow," Thomas said, as the school disappeared behind them, "you're going to get some decent clothes. And you've had your last fight."

The boy was silent.

"Did you hear me?"

"Yes, sir."

"Don't call me sir. I'm your father," Thomas said.

Chapter 5

1966

For a few minutes at a time, while she was working, Gretchen forgot that it was her fortieth birthday. She sat on the high steel stool in front of the moviola, pushing the levers, gazing intently into the glass screen. She ran film and sound track together, her hands in dirty white-cotton gloves, emulsion stained. The spoor of film. She made swift marks in soft red pencil, giving the strips to her assistant to splice and file. From adjacent cutting rooms on the floor in the building on Broadway, where other companies rented rooms, came scraps of voices, screeches, explosions, orchestral passages, and the shrill gabble as track was run backward at high speed. Engrossed in her own labor she hardly noticed the noise. It was part of the furniture of a cutting room, with the clacking machines, the distorted sounds, the round tins of film stacked on the shelves.

This was her third picture as a head cutter. Sam Corey had taught her well as his assistant and then, after praising her highly to directors and producers, had sent her off on her own, to get her first independent job. Skilled and imaginative, with no ambition to become a director herself that would arouse jealousy, she was in great demand and could pick and choose among the jobs offered her.

The picture she was working on now was being shot in New York and she found the city's impersonal variety exhilarating after the inbred, ambiguously jovial, big-family atmosphere of Hollywood, where everybody lived in everyone else's pocket. In her free hours she tried to continue with the political activities that had taken up a great deal of her time in Los Angeles since Colin's death. With her assistant, Ida Cohen, she went to meetings where people made speeches about the war in Viet Nam and school busing. She signed dozens of petitions and tried to get the important people in the movie business to sign them, too. All this helped her assuage her sense of guilt about having given up her studies in California. Also, Billy was now of a draftable age, and the thought of her one son being killed in Viet Nam was intolerable to her. Ida had no sons but was even more intense about the meetings, demonstrations, and petitions than Gretchen. They both wore Ban the Bomb buttons on their blouses and on their coats.

When she wasn't going to meetings in the evenings, Gretchen went as often as she could to the theater, with a renewed appetite for it, after the years of being away. Sometimes she went with Ida, a small, dowdy, shrewd woman of about her own age, with whom she had developed a steady friendship, sometimes she went with Evans Kinsella, the director of the picture, with whom she was having an affair, sometimes with Rudolph and Jean, when they were in town, or with one or another of the actors she met when she visited the locations on which they were shooting.

The images passed before her on the glass screen and she grimaced. The way Kinsella had done the shooting made it difficult to get the tone that she felt the sequence needed. If she couldn't somehow correct it by more ingenious cutting, or if Kinsella himself couldn't come up with some ideas on it, she knew that eventually the whole scene would have to be reshot.

She stopped for a cigarette. The film tins she and Ida used for ash trays were always brimming with butts. Here and there stood empty coffee containers, lipstick stained.

Forty years old, she thought, inhaling.

Nobody today had as yet congratulated her. With good reason. Although she had looked for a telegram, at least, in her box at the hotel, from Billy. There had been no telegram. She hadn't told Ida, now rewinding long strips of film on spools out of a big canvas basket. Ida was past forty herself, why drive in another spike? And she certainly hadn't told Evans. He was thirty-two. A forty-year-old woman did not remind a thirty-two-year-old lover of her birthday.

She thought of her dead mother, forty years ago today. First born, a girl, to a girl scarcely more than twenty herself. If Mary Pease Jordache had known that day what words were going to pass between herself and the new infant in her arms, what tears would she have shed? And Billy . . . ?

The door opened and Evans Kinsella came in. He was wearing a white, belted raincoat over his corduroy slacks and red polo shirt and cashmere sweater. He made no sartorial concessions to New York. His raincoat was wet. She hadn't looked out the window for hours and didn't know it was raining.

"Hi, girls," Evans said. He was a tall, thin man with tousled black hair and a blue-black beard that made him look as if he needed a shave at all times. His enemies said he looked like a wolf. Gretchen varied between thinking he was alertly handsome and Jewishly ugly, although he was not a Jew. Kinsella was his real name. He had been in analysis for three years. He had already made six pictures, three of which had been very successful. He was a lounger. As soon as he entered a room he leaned against something or sat on a desk, or if there were a couch handy lay down and put his feet up. He was wearing suede desert boots.

He kissed Ida on the cheek, then Gretchen. He had made one picture in Paris and had learned to kiss everybody there. The picture had been disastrous. "A foul day," he said. He swung himself up on one of the high, metal cutting benches. He made a point of seeming at home wherever he was. "We got in two set-ups this morning and then the rains came. Just as well. Hazen was drunk by noon." Richard Hazen was the male star of the picture. He was always drunk by noon. "How's it going here?" Evans asked. "We ready to run?"

"Just about," Gretchen said. She was sorry she hadn't realized how late it was. She would have done something about her hair and put on fresh make-up to be ready for Evans. "Ida," she said, "will you take the last sequence with you and tell Freddy to run it after the rushes?"

They went down the hall to the small projection room at the end of the corridor. Evans pinched her arm secretly. "Gretchen," he said, "beautiful toiler in the vineyards."

They sat in the darkened projection room and watched the rushes of the day before, the same scene, from different angles, done over and over again, that would one day, they hoped, be arranged into one harmonious flowing entity and be shown on huge screens in theaters throughout the world. As she watched, Gretchen thought again how Evans' talent, kinky and oblique, showed in every foot of film he shot. She made mental notes of how she would make the first cut of the material. Richard Hazen had been drunk before noon yesterday, too, she saw. In two years nobody would give him a job.

"What do you think?" Evans asked, when the lights went up.

"You might as well quit every morning by one," Gretchen said, "if Hazen's working."

"It shows, eh?" Evans was sitting slouched low in his chair, his legs over the back of the chair in front of him.

"It shows," Gretchen said.

"I'll talk to his agent."

"Try talking to his bartender," Gretchen said.

"Drink," Evans said, "Kinsella's curse. When drunk by others."

The room went dark again and they watched the sequence Gretchen had been working on all day. Projected that way, it seemed even worse to Gretchen than it had been on the moviola. But when it was over and the lights went up again, Evans said, "Fine. I like it."

Gretchen had known Evans for two years and had already done a picture with him before this one and she had come to recognize that he was too easily pleased with his own work. Somewhere in his analysis he had come to the conclusion that arrogance was good for his ego and it was dangerous to criticize him openly. "I'm not so sure," Gretchen said. "I'd like to fiddle with it some more."

"A waste of time," Evans said. "I tell you it's okay."

Unlike most directors he was impatient in the cutting room and careless about details.

"I don't know," Gretchen said. "It seems to me to drag."

"That's just what I want right there," Evans said. "I *want* it to drag." He argued like a stubborn child.

"All those people going in and out of doors," Gretchen persisted, "with those ominous shadows with nothing ominous happening . . ."

"Stop trying to make me into Colin Burke." Evans stood up abruptly. "My name is Evans Kinsella, in case it slipped your mind, and Evans Kinsella it will remain. Please remember that."

"Oh, stop being an infant," Gretchen snapped at him. Sometimes the two functions she served for Evans became confused.

"Where's my coat? Where did I leave my goddamn coat?" he said loudly.

"You left it in the cutting room."

They went back to the cutting room together, Evans allowing her to carry the cans of film they had just run and which she picked up from the projectionist. Evans put on his coat, roughly. Ida was making out the sheet for the film they had handled that day. Evans started out of the door, then stopped and came back to Gretchen. "I had intended to ask you to have dinner with me and take in a movie," he said. "Can you make it?" He smiled placatingly. He dreaded the thought of being disliked, even for a moment.

"I'm sorry," Gretchen said. "My brother's coming to pick me up. I'm going up to his place for the weekend."

Evans looked forlorn. He was capable of sixty moods a minute. "I'm free as a bird this weekend. I'd hoped we could . . ." He looked over at Ida, as though he wished she were out of the room. Ida continued working stolidly on her sheets.

"I'll be back Sunday night in time for dinner," Gretchen said.

"Okay," Evans said. "I suppose I'll have to settle for that. Give my regards to your brother. And congratulate him for me."

"For what?"

"Didn't you see his picture in *Look?* He's famous all over America. This week."

"Oh, that," Gretchen said. The magazine had run a piece under the title "Ten Political Hopefuls Under Forty," and there had been two photographs of Rudolph, one with Jean in the living room of their house, one at his desk in the town hall. Rising fast in Republican councils, the article had said about handsome young Mayor with beautiful, rich young wife. Moderate liberal thinker, energetic administrator. Was not just another theoretical politician; had met a payroll all his life. Had streamlined town government, integrated housing, cracked down on industrial pollution, jailed former police chief and three patrolmen for accepting bribes, raised a bond issue for new schools; as influential trustee of Whitby University had been instrumental in making it a co-educational institution; far-seeing town-planner, had experimented with closing off center of town to traffic on Saturday afternoons and evenings so that people could stroll about in a neighborly fashion while they did their shopping; had used the Whitby *Sentinel*, of which he was the publisher, as a platform for hard-hitting articles on honest government, both local and national, and had won awards for newspapers in cities of under fifty thousand population; had made a forceful speech at a convention of mayors in Atlantic City and had been enthusiastically applauded; had been invited to the White House for thirty minutes with a select committee of other mayors.

"Reading that piece," Gretchen said, "you'd think he's done everything but raise the dead in Whitby. It must have been written by a lady journalist who's wildly in love with him. He knows how to turn on the charm, my brother."

Evans laughed. "You don't let emotional attachments cloud your opinions of your near and dear ones, do you?"

"I just hope my near and dear ones don't believe all the gush people write about them."

"The barb has found its mark, sweetie," Evans said. "I now am going home to burn all my scrapbooks." He kissed Ida good-bye first, then Gretchen, and said, "I'll pick you up at your hotel at seven Sunday night."

"I'll be there," Gretchen said.

"Out into the lonely night," Evans said, as he left, pulling the belt of his white raincoat tight around his slim waist, young double agent playing his dangerous game in a low-budget movie.

Gretchen had an idea of just how lonely the night and the weekend were likely to be. He had two other mistresses in New York. That she knew of.

"I can never make up my mind," Ida said, "whether he's a jerk or a genius."

"Neither," Gretchen said and began putting the sequence that displeased her on the moviola again, to see if there was anything she could do with it.

Rudolph came into the cutting room at six-thirty, looking politically hopeful in a dark-blue raincoat and a beige cotton rain hat. Next door a train was going over a trestle on the sound track and farther down the hall an augmented orchestra was playing the 1812 Overture. Gretchen was rewinding the sequence she was working on and the dialogue was coming out in whistling, loud, incomprehensible gibberish.

"Holy man," Rudolph said. "How can you stand it?"

"The sounds of honest labor," Gretchen said. She finished rewinding and gave the spool to Ida. "Go home immediately," she said to her. If you didn't watch her, and if she didn't have a meeting to go to, Ida would stay every night until ten or eleven o'clock, working. She dreaded leisure, Ida.

Rudolph didn't say Happy Birthday when they went down in the elevator and out onto Broadway. Gretchen didn't remind him. Rudolph carried the small valise Gretchen had packed in the morning for the weekend. It was still raining and there wasn't a cab to be had, so they started walking in the direction of Park Avenue. It hadn't been raining when she had come to work and she didn't have an umbrella. She was soaked by the time they reached Sixth Avenue.

"This town," Rudolph said, "needs ten thousand more taxis. It's insane, what people will put up with to live in a city."

"Energetic administrator," Gretchen said. "Moderate liberal thinker, far-seeing town-planner."

Rudolph laughed. "Oh, you read that article. What crap." But she thought he sounded pleased.

They were on Fifty-second Street and the rain was coming down harder than ever. In front of Twenty-One he stopped her and said, "Let's duck in here and have a drink. The doorman'll get us a taxi later."

Gretchen's hair was lank with the rain and the backs of her stockings were splattered and she didn't relish the idea of going into a place like Twenty-One looking bedraggled and wearing a Ban the Bomb button on her coat, but Rudolph was already pulling her to the door.

Inside, four or five different door guarders, hatcheck girls, managers, and head waiters said, "Good evening, Mr. Jordache," and there was considerable handshaking. There was nothing much that Gretchen could do to repair the ruin of her hair and stockings, so she didn't bother to go to the ladies' room, but went into the bar with Rudolph. Because they weren't having dinner, they didn't ask for a table, but went to the far corner of the bar, which was empty. Near the entrance there were people grouped three deep, men with booming advertising and oil voices who almost certainly did not want to ban the bomb, and women who had obviously just come from Elizabeth Arden and who always found taxis. The lighting was low and artful and was designed to make it worthwhile for women to spend the afternoon getting their hair done and their faces massaged at Elizabeth Arden.

"This'll destroy your reputation in this place," Gretchen said. "Coming in with someone who looks the way I look tonight."

"They've seen worse," Rudolph said. "Much worse."

"Thanks, brother."

"I didn't mean it the way it sounded," Rudolph said. "Actually, you're beautiful."

She didn't feel beautiful. She felt wet and shabby and old and tired and lonely and wounded. "This is my night for self-pity," she said. "Pay no heed.

"How's Jean?" Gretchen asked. Jean had had a miscarriage with her second child and had taken it hard and the times Gretchen had seen her she had seemed remote and subdued, dropping suddenly out of conversations or getting up in the middle of a sentence and walking off into another room. She had quit her photography and when Gretchen had asked her once when she was going back to it she had merely shaken her head.

"Jean?" Rudolph said shortly. "She's improving."

A barman came up and Rudolph ordered a Scotch and Gretchen a martini.

Rudolph lifted his glass to her. "Happy birthday," he said.

He had remembered. "Don't be nice to me," she said, "or I'll cry."

He took an oblong jeweler's box from his pocket and put it on the bar in front of her. "Try it on for size," he said.

She opened the box, which had Cartier inscribed on it. Inside was a beautiful gold watch. She took off the heavy steel watch she was wearing and clipped on the slim gold band. Time, jeweled and fleeing, exquisitely. The day's one gift. She kissed Rudolph's cheek, managed not to cry. I must make myself think better of him, she thought. She ordered another martini.

"What other loot did you get today?" Rudolph asked.

"Nothing."

"Did Billy call?" He said it too casually.

"No."

"I ran into him two days ago on the campus and reminded him," Rudolph said.

"He's awfully busy," Gretchen said defensively.

"Maybe he resented my telling him about it and suggesting he call you," Rudolph said. "He's not too fond of his Uncle Rudolph."

"He's not too fond of anybody," Gretchen said.

Billy had matriculated at Whitby because when he finished high school in California he said he wanted to go East to college. Gretchen had hoped he would go to UCLA or the University of Southern California, so that he could still live at home, but Billy had made it clear that he didn't want to live at home any more. Although he was very intelligent, he didn't work, and his marks weren't good enough to get him into any of the prestige schools in the East. Gretchen had asked Rudolph to use his influence to have him accepted at Whitby. Billy's letters were rare—sometimes she wouldn't hear from him for two months at a time. And when they did come they were short and consisted mostly of lists of courses he was taking and projects for the summer holidays, always in the East. She had been working more than a month now in New York, just a few hours away from Whitby, but he hadn't come down once. Until this weekend she had been too proud to go up to see him but she finally couldn't bear it any longer.

"What is it with that kid?" Rudolph said.

"He's making me suffer," Gretchen said.

"What for?"

"For Evans. I tried to be as discreet as possible—Evans never stayed overnight at the house and I always came home to sleep, myself, and I never went on weekends with him, but, of course, Billy caught on right away and the freeze was on. Maybe women ought to have fits of melancholy when they *have* babies, not when they lose them."

"He'll get over it," Rudolph said. "It's a kid's jealousy. That's all."

"I hope so. He despises Evans. He calls him a phoney."

"Is he?"

Gretchen shrugged. "I don't think so. He doesn't measure up to Colin, but then, neither did I."

"Don't run yourself down," Rudolph said gently.

"What better occupation could a lady find on her fortieth birthday?"

"You look thirty," Rudolph said. "A beautiful, desirable thirty."

"Dear brother."

"Is Evans going to marry you?"

"In Hollywood," Gretchen said, "successful directors of thirty-two don't marry widows of forty, unless they're famous or rich or both. And I'm neither."

"Does he love you?"

"Who knows?"

"Do you love him?"

"Same answer. Who knows? I like to sleep with him, I like to work for him, I like to be attached to him. He fulfills me. I have to be attached to a man and feel useful to him and somehow Evans turned out to be the lucky man. If he asked me to marry him, I'd do it like a shot. But he won't ask."

"Happy days," Rudolph said thoughtfully. "Finish your drink. We'd better be getting on. Jean's waiting for us in the apartment."

Gretchen looked at her watch. "It's now exactly eighteen minutes past seven, according to Mr. Cartier."

It was still raining outside, but a taxi drove up and a couple got out and the doorman protected Gretchen with a big umbrella as she ran for the cab. Outside Twenty-One, you'd never guess that the city needed ten thousand more taxis.

When Rudolph let them into the apartment, they heard the violent sound of metal on metal. Rudolph ran into the living room with Gretchen on his heels. Jean sat on the floor, in the middle of the room, with her legs spread apart, like a child playing with blocks. She had a hammer in her hand and she was methodically destroying a pile of cameras and lenses and camera equipment that lay between her knees. She was wearing a pair of slacks and a dirty sweater and her unwashed hair hung down, masking her face, as she bent over her work.

"Jean," Rudolph said, "what the hell are you doing?"

Jean looked up, peering slyly through her hair. "His Honor the Mayor wants to know what his beautiful, rich young wife is doing. I'll tell his Honor the Mayor what his beautiful, rich young wife is doing. She is making a junk pile." Her speech was thick and she was drunk. Jean smashed the hammer down on a big wide-angle lens and splintered it.

Rudolph grabbed the hammer from her. She did not struggle. "His Honor the Mayor now has taken the hammer from his beautiful rich young wife's hand," Jean said. "Don't worry, little junk pile. There are other hammers. You'll grow up and one day you'll be one of the biggest, most beautiful junk piles in the world and his Honor the Mayor will claim it as a public park for the citizens of Whitby."

Still holding the hammer, Rudolph glanced over at Gretchen. There was a shamed, frightened look in his eyes. "Christ, Jean," he said to his wife, "there's at least five thousand dollars' worth of stuff there."

"Her Honor the Mayor's wife doesn't need cameras," Jean said. "Let people take pictures of *me*. Let poor people take pictures. Talented people. Hoopla!" She made a spreading, gay ballet gesture with her arms. "Bring on the hammers. Rudy, darling, don't you think you ought to give your beautiful rich young wife a drink?"

"You've had enough to drink."

"Rudolph," Gretchen said, "I'd better be off. We're not going to Whitby tonight."

"Beautiful Whitby," Jean said. "Where the beautiful rich young wife of his Honor the Mayor smiles at Democrats and Republicans alike, where she opens charity bazaars and appears faithfully at her husband's side at banquets and political meetings, where she is to be seen at Commencements and Fourth of July celebrations and the home games of the Whitby University football team and the dedication of new science laboratories and the ground-breaking ceremonies for housing projects with real toilets for colored folk."

"Cut it out, Jean!" Rudolph said harshly.

"Really, I think I'd better go," Gretchen said. "I'll call you in . . ."

"Sister of his Honor the Mayor, what's your rush to leave?" Jean said. "Who knows, one day he may need your vote. Stay and we'll have a nice cosy little family drink. Maybe if you play your cards right, he may even marry you. Stay and listen. It may be in . . . instructive." She stumbled on the word. "How to be an appendage, in a hundred easy lessons. I'm having visiting cards printed up. Mrs. Rudolph Jordache, ex-career girl, now in the appendage business. One of the ten most hopeful appendages in the United States. Parasitism and hypocrisy a specialty. Courses given in appendaging." She giggled. "Any true-blue American girl guaranteed a diploma."

Rudolph didn't try to stop Gretchen as she went out of the room and into the hallway, leaving him standing in his raincoat, the hammer in his hand, staring down at his drunken wife.

The elevator door opened directly into the apartment and Gretchen had to wait in the hallway and she heard Jean say, in a childish, aggrieved voice, "People are always taking away my hammers," before the elevator door opened and she could flee.

When she got back to the Algonquin she called Evans's hotel, but there was no answer from his apartment. She left a message with the operator that Mrs. Burke had not left for the weekend and could be reached all night at her hotel. Then she took a hot bath and changed her clothes and went down to the hotel dining room and had dinner.

Rudolph called at nine the next morning. She was alone. Evans hadn't called. Rudolph said that Jean had gone to sleep after Gretchen had left and had been contrite and ashamed when she woke up and was all right now and they were going to Whitby after all and they'd wait for Gretchen in the apartment.

"You're sure you don't think it's wiser to spend the day alone with her?" Gretchen asked.

"It's better when we're not alone," Rudolph said. "You left your bag here, in case you think you've lost it."

"I remember," Gretchen said. "I'll be up at your place by ten."

As she dressed she puzzled over the scene the night before and remembered Jean's less violent, but almost equally strange behavior at other times. Now it all added up. She had managed to hide it from Gretchen until now, because Gretchen hadn't seen her all that often. But it was plain now—Jean was an alcoholic. Gretchen wondered if Rudolph realized it, and what he was going to do about it.

By a quarter to ten Evans hadn't called, and Gretchen went down in the elevator and into the sun of Forty-fourth Street, a slender, tall woman, with fine legs, her hair soft and black, her skin unblemished and pale, her tweed suit and jersey blouse exactly right for a gracious country weekend. Only the Ban the Bomb button, worn like a brooch on the well-tailored lapel, might indicate to the passerby that not everything was as it seemed on that sunny American spring morning of 1966.

The debris of the cameras had been cleared away from the living room. Rudolph and Jean were listening to a Mozart piano concerto on the radio when Gretchen came in. Rudolph seemed unruffled and although Jean was pale and a little shaky when she stood up to kiss Gretchen hello, she, too, seemed to have recovered from the night before. She gave Gretchen a quick glance, that perhaps asked for pity and understanding, but after that, in her normal, quick, low-timbred voice, with a hint of gaiety that didn't seem forced, she said, "Gretchen, don't you look smashing in that suit. And tell me where I can get one of those buttons. The color goes with my eyes."

"Yes," Rudolph said. "I'm sure it'll make a big hit the next time we have to go down to Washington." But his voice was tender and he laughed, relaxed.

Jean held his hand, like a child on an outing with a father, as they went downstairs and waited for the man from the garage to bring the car. Her hair was washed and shone chestnut brown, and she had it tied in back with a bow and she was wearing a very short skirt. Her legs, without stockings, were lovely, slender, straight, and already tanned. As usual, she looked no more than eighteen.

While they were waiting for the car, Rudolph said to Gretchen, "I called my secretary and told her to get in touch with Billy and tell him we were expecting him for lunch at our place."

"Thank you, Rudy," Gretchen said. She hadn't seen Billy in so long that for their first meeting it would be much better if there were others around.

When the car came, the two women sat in front with Rudolph. He turned on the radio. Mozart, unworried and spring-like, accompanied them as far as the Bronx.

They drove through dogwood and tulips and skirted fields where men and boys were playing baseball. Mozart gave way to Loesser on the radio, and Ray Bolger sang, irresistibly, "Once in love with Amy, Always in love with Amy," and Jean sang along with the radio, in a low, true, sweet voice. They all remembered Bolger in the show and how much pleasure he had given them. By the time they reached the farmhouse in Whitby, where the first twilight-colored lilacs were budding in the garden, the night before was almost as if it had never happened. Almost.

Enid, now two, blonde and round, was waiting for them. She leaped at her mother and they embraced and kissed each other again and again. Rudolph carried Gretchen's bag as he and Gretchen went up the stairs to the guest room. The room was crisp and sparkling, full of flowers.

Rudolph put her bag down and said, "I think you have everything you need."

"Rudy," Gretchen said, keeping her voice low, "we ought to skip drinks today."

"Why?" He sounded surprised.

"You mustn't tempt her. Jean. Even if she doesn't take any herself —seeing others drink . . ."

"Oh," Rudolph said negligently, "I wouldn't worry about that. She was just a little upset last night . . ."

"She's an alcoholic, Rudy," Gretchen said gently.

Rudolph made a dismissive, light gesture. "You're being melodramatic," he said. "It's not like you. Every once in a while she goes on a little bender, that's all. Even as you and I."

"Not even as you and I," Gretchen said. "She shouldn't touch one drop. Not even a sip of beer. And as much as possible, she should be kept away from people who drink. Rudy, I know. Hollywood is full of women like her. In the beginning stages, like her, and in later stages, horrible stages, the way she's liable to be. You've got to protect her."

"Nobody can say I don't protect her." There was a thin edge of anger in his voice.

"Rudy, lock up every bottle of liquor in this house," Gretchen said.

"Calm yourself," Rudolph said. "This isn't Hollywood."

The phone was ringing downstairs and then Jean called up and said, "Gretchen, it's Billy, for you. Down here."

"Please listen to me," Gretchen said.

"Go talk to your son," Rudolph said coldly.

On the phone, Billy's voice was very grown-up. "Hello, Mother. It's wonderful that you could come up." He had begun calling her Mother when Evans had appeared on the scene. Before that it had been Mummy. She had thought it childish for a boy as big and as old as he, but now, on the phone, she longed for the Mummy. "Say, I'm awfully sorry," Billy said. "Will you make my excuses to Rudolph? He invited me to come to lunch, but there's a softball game on here at one o'clock and I'm pitching, so I'm afraid I'll have to ask for a raincheck."

"Yes," Gretchen said. "I'll make your excuses. When will I see you?"

"Well, it's a little difficult to say." Billy sounded honestly perplexed. "There's a kind of giant beer-fest after the game at one of the houses and . . ."

"Where're you playing?" Gretchen said. "I'll come down and watch you. We can visit between the innings."

"Now you sound sore."

"I'm not sore, as you put it. Where're you playing?"

"There's a whole bunch of fields on the east side of the campus," Billy said. "You can't miss it."

"Good-bye, Billy," Gretchen said, and hung up. She went out of the hall where the phone was and into the living room. Jean was on the couch, cradling Enid and rocking her back and forth. Enid was making small cooing noises. Rudolph was shaking up Daiquiris.

"My son sends his regrets," Gretchen said. "He has weighty affairs that will detain him all afternoon. He cannot lunch."

"That's too bad," Rudolph said. But his mouth hardened for a moment. He poured the cocktails for himself and Gretchen. Jean, occupied with her child, said she was not drinking.

After lunch, Gretchen borrowed the car and drove to the Whitby University campus. She had been there before but now she was struck afresh by the quiet, countrified beauty of the place, with its homely old buildings spread out haphazardly on acres of green, its wandering graveled walks, the tall oaks and elms. Because it was Saturday afternoon there were few students about and the campus dozed in a peaceful sunny trance. It was a place to look back upon, she thought, an image for later nostalgia. If a university was a place that prepared young people for life, these peaceful lawns, these unpretentious welcoming halls and classrooms might be found wanting. The life Whitby's graduates would have to face in the last third of the twentieth century was almost certainly not going to be anything like this.

There were three desultory baseball games in progress on the playing fields. The most desultory, in which almost half the players were girls, was the one in which Billy was playing. The girl who was in the field had a book with her. She sat on the grass reading it and only looked up and ran after a ball when her teammates shouted at her. The game must have been going on for some time, because as Gretchen came up behind the first-base line there was a mild argument between the first-baseman and some of the members of the opposing team who were sprawled on the grass awaiting their turn at bat, about whether the score was nineteen to sixteen or eighteen to fifteen. It could hardly have made any difference to anyone whether or not Billy had played.

Dressed in fringed blue jeans stained with bleach, and a gray T-shirt, Billy was pitching, just lobbing it up to the girls, but throwing the ball hard to the boys when they came to bat. Billy didn't see Gretchen immediately and she watched him, tall and moving lazily and gracefully, his hair too long over the face that was a beautiful, improved version, sensual, strong, dissatisfied, of Willie Abbott's face, the forehead as broad and high, the eyes deeper set and darker, the nose longer, with tense, wide nostrils, a single asymmetrical dimple in the right cheek when he smiled, his teeth pure, youthful white.

If only he will live up to his face, Gretchen thought, as her son tossed the ball up to a pretty, chubby girl, who swung and missed and cried, in mock despair, "I'm *hopeless!*"

It was the third out of the inning and Billy saw Gretchen standing behind first base and came over to her and said, "Hi, Mother," and kissed her. There was a little crinkle of amusement around his eyes as he glanced at the Ban the Bomb button. "I told you you'd find us without trouble."

"I hope I'm not interfering," she said. The wrong tone, she knew. Love me, I'm your mother.

"No, of course not," he said. "Say, kids," he called, "somebody bat for me. I have a visitor. I'll see you all later at the house." He didn't introduce her to anyone. "Why don't we take a little walk? I'll show you around."

"Rudolph and Jean were disappointed you couldn't come for lunch," Gretchen said, as they walked away from the game. Wrong tone again.

"Were they?" Billy said evenly. "I'm sorry."

"Rudolph says he's invited you over again and again and you never come."

Billy shrugged. "You know how it is," he said. "Something's always coming up."

"I'd feel better if you went there once in awhile," Gretchen said.

"I'll go. Sometime. We can discuss the generation gap. Or how everybody on the campus smokes pot. His newspaper's great on those subjects."

"Do *you* smoke pot?"

"Mother, darling, come into the twentieth century."

"Don't condescend to me," she said sharply.

"It's a nice day," he said. "I haven't seen you for a long time. Let's not argue. That building over there is the dormitory where I lived when I was a freshman."

"Was your girl there in that game?" He had written her that he was interested in a girl in one of his classes.

"No. Her mother and father are here for the weekend and she has to pretend I don't exist. Her father can't stand me and I can't stand him. I'm an immoral, depraving influence, her father says. He's Neanderthal."

"Have you got a good word to say for anybody?"

"Sure. Albert Camus. But he's dead. That reminds me. How's that other poet, Evans Kinsella?"

"He's alive," Gretchen said.

"That's great news," said Billy. "That's really sensational news."

If Colin hadn't died he wouldn't be like this, Gretchen thought. He would be completely different. An absent-minded, busy man gets behind the wheel of a car and hits a tree and the impact spreads and spreads, never stopping, through the generations.

"Do you ever come down to New York?" she asked.

"Once in awhile."

"If you'll let me know, the next time you're coming," she said, "I'll get tickets for a show. Bring your girl, if you want. I'd like to meet her."

"She's nothing much," Billy said.

"Anyway, let me know."

"Sure."

"How are you doing in your work?" she asked.

Billy made a face.

"Rudolph says you're not doing very well. He says there's a chance that you'll be dropped from school."

"Being Mayor of this burg must be an easy job," Billy said, "if he has time to check up on how many classes I cut a semester."

"If you get kicked out, you'll be drafted. Do you want that?"

"Who cares?" Billy said. "The Army can't be more boring than most of the courses around here."

"Do you ever think about me?" Immensely wrong. Classically wrong. But she had said it. "How do you think I'd feel if you were sent to Viet Nam?"

"Men fight and women weep," Billy said. "Why should you and I be different?"

"Do you do anything about trying to change things? About stopping the war, for example? A lot of students all over the country are working day and night to . . ."

"Kooks," Billy said. "Wasting their time. The war's too good a racket for too many big shots. What do they care what a few spastic kids do? If you want, I'll take your button and wear it. Big deal. The Pentagon will quake when they hear that Billy Abbott is protesting against the bomb."

"Billy," Gretchen stopped walking and faced him, "are you interested in *anything*?"

"Not really," he said calmly. "Is there something wrong with that?"

"All I hope," Gretchen said, "is that it's a pose. A silly, adolescent pose."

"It's not a pose," he said. "And I'm not an adolescent, in case you haven't noticed. I'm a big, grown man and I think everything stinks. If I were you, I'd forget about me for awhile. If it's any hardship to you to send me the money to keep me in school, don't send it. If you don't like the way I am and you're blaming yourself for the way I turned out, maybe you're right, maybe you're not. I'm sorry to have to talk this way, but there's one thing I know I don't want to be and that's a hypocrite. I think you'll be happier if you don't have to worry about me, so you go back to my dear Uncle Rudolph and to your dear Evans Kinsella and I'll go back to my ball game." He turned and strode away, along the path toward the playing fields.

Gretchen watched him until he was just a small blue-and-gray figure in the distance, then walked slowly, heavily, toward where she had parked Rudolph's car.

There was no sense in staying for the whole weekend anymore. She had a quiet dinner with Rudolph and Jean and took the morning train down to New York.

When she got back to her hotel, there was a message from Evans saying that he couldn't have dinner with her that night.

Chapter 6

1967

On the plane down to Dallas, Johnny Heath, sitting next to him, was going through a briefcase full of papers. Rudolph was going through his own briefcase full of papers. He had to submit the budget for the next year to the town council and he frowned as he went over the thick booklet which contained the Comptroller's estimates. The price of everything was going up, the police and fire departments, the public school staffs, and the clerical employees were all due for a raise in salary; there was an alarming increase in the number of welfare recipients, especially in the Negro section of town; a new sewage-disposal plant was on the books; everybody was fighting tax increases; state and federal aid were being kept at their old levels. Here I am, he thought, at thirty thousand feet, worrying about money again.

Johnny Heath was worrying about money in the seat next to his, too, but at least it was his own money, and Rudolph's. Brad Knight had moved his office from Tulsa to Dallas after his father had died, and the purpose of their trip was to confer with Brad about their investments in the Peter Knight and Son Oil Company. Suddenly, Brad had seemed to have lost his touch, and they had found themselves investing in one dry hole after another. Even the wells that had come in had suffered from a series of disasters; salt water, collapsing shale, unpredictable, expensive formations to drill through. Johnny Heath had made some quiet investigations and was sure Brad had been rigging his report and was stealing from them and had been doing so for some time. The figures Johnny had come up with looked conclusive, but Rudolph refused to move against Brad until they had had it out in person. It seemed impossible to him that a man he had known so long and so well could turn like that. Despite Virginia Calderwood.

When the plane landed, Brad wasn't at the airport to greet them. Instead, he had sent an assistant, a burly, tall man in a brown straw hat, a string tie, and a madras jacket, who made Mr. Knight's excuses (he was tied up in a meeting, the assistant said) and drove with them in an air-conditioned Cadillac along a road that throbbed in heat mirages, to the hotel in the center of Dallas where Brad had rented a suite with a salon and two bedrooms for Johnny and Rudolph.

The hotel was brand new and the rooms were decorated in what the decorator must have thought was a Lone Star improvement of Second Empire. On a long table against the wall were ranged six bottles of bourbon, six of Scotch, six of gin and vodka, plus a bottle of vermouth, a filled ice bucket, dozens of bottles of Coke and soda water, a basket of lemons, a huge bowl of oversized fruit, and an array of glasses of all sizes.

"You'll find beer and champagne in the refrigerator in the closet," the assistant said. "If that's your pleasure. You're the guests of Mr. Knight."

"We're only staying overnight," Rudolph said.

"Mr. Knight told me to make you gentlemen comfortable," the assistant said. "You're in Texas now."

"If they had all this stuff at the Alamo," Rudolph said, "they'd still be holding out."

The assistant laughed politely and said that Mr. Knight was almost sure to be free by five P.M. It was a little past three now. "Remember," he said, as he left, "if you gentlemen need anything, you call me at the office, hear?"

"Window dressing," Johnny said, with a gesture for the suite and the table loaded with drink.

Rudolph felt a twinge of irritation with Johnny and his automatic reflex of suspicion in all situations.

"I have some calls to make," Rudolph said. "Let me know when Brad arrives." He went into his own room and closed the door.

He called his home first. He tried to call Jean at least three times each day. He had finally taken Gretchen's advice and there was no liquor in the house, but Whitby was full of liquor stores and bars. No worry today. Jean was cheerful and bright. It was raining in Whitby. She was taking Enid to her first children's party. Two months before, she had had an accident while driving drunk with Enid in the rear seat. The car had been demolished but aside from a few scratches neither of them had been hurt.

"What's it like in Dallas?" she asked.

"All right for Texans, I suppose," Rudolph said. "Intolerable for the rest of the human race."

"When will you be back?"

"As soon as possible."

"Hurry," she said. He hadn't told her why he and Johnny had had to come to Texas. Sober, she was depressed by duplicity.

He then called his office at the Town Hall and got his secretary on the phone. His secretary was a young man, a little effeminate, but usually serene. He wasn't serene this afternoon. There had been a demonstration of students that morning in front of the offices of the *Sentinel* because of an editorial in favor of the continued existence of the ROTC at the university. Rudolph had approved the editorial himself, as it was moderate and had not advocated compulsory military training but said it should be open to those students who felt that they wanted a career in the armed forces or even those students who felt that in case of need they would like to be ready to defend their country. The sweet voice of reason had not helped to mollify the demonstrators. A rock had been thrown through a plate-glass window and the police had had to be called. President Dorlacker, of the university, had phoned, in a black mood, the secretary said, and had said, quote, If he's the Mayor, why isn't he at his desk?

Unquote. Rudolph had not deigned to tell the secretary the nature of his business. Police Chief Ottman had been into the office, looking harassed. Something very, *very* important, Ottman had said. The Mayor was to get back to him soonest. Albany had telephoned twice. A Black delegation had presented a petition about something to do with a swimming pool.

"That's enough, Walter," Rudolph said, wearily. He hung up the phone and lay back on the baby-blue, slippery silk bedspread. He got ten thousand dollars a year for being Mayor of Whitby. And he donated the entire amount to charity. Public service.

He got up from the bed, maliciously pleased to see that his shoes had left a stain on the silk, and went into the living room. Johnny was sitting at a huge desk, going over his papers in his shirt sleeves. "There's no doubt about it, Rudy," Johnny said, "the sonofabitch has taken us for a ride."

"Later, please," Rudolph said. "I'm busy being a devoted and self-sacrificing public servant at the moment." He poured a Coke over some ice and went to the window and looked out at Dallas. Dallas glittered in the baking sun, rising from its desolate plain like a senseless eruption of metal and glass, the result of a cosmic accident, inorganic and arbitrary.

Rudolph went back into his bedroom, and gave the number of the office of the Chief of Police in Whitby to the telephone operator. While waiting for the call to come through he looked at himself in the mirror. He looked like a man who needed a vacation. He wondered when he was going to have his first heart attack. Although in America only businessmen were supposed to have heart attacks, and theoretically he had abandoned all that. Professors lived forever, he had read somewhere, and most generals.

When he got Ottman on the phone, Ottman sounded mournful. But he always sounded mournful. His *métier*, which was crime, offended him. Bailey, the former Chief of Police, whom Rudolph had put in jail, had been a hearty and happy man. Rudolph often regretted him. The melancholy of integrity.

"We've opened up a can of worms, Mr. Mayor," Ottman said. "Officer Slattery picked up a Whitby freshman at eight-thirty this morning in a diner, smoking a marijuana cigarette. At eight-thirty in the morning!" Ottman was a family man who kept regular hours, and the mornings were precious to him. "The boy had one and one-third ounces of the drug on him. Before we booked him he talked and talked. He says in his dormitory there are at least fifty kids who smoke hash and marijuana. He says if we go there we'll find a pound of the stuff, at least. He's got a lawyer and he'll be out on bail by this evening, but by now the lawyer must have told a few people and what am I supposed to do? President Dorlacker called me a little while ago and told me to stay away from the campus, but it's bound to be all over town and if I stay away from the campus what does that make me look like? Whitby University isn't Havana or Buenos Aires, for Christ's sake, it's within the city limits and the law's the law, for Christ's sake."

I picked a great day to come to Dallas, Rudolph thought. "Let me think for a minute, Chief," he said.

"If I can't go in there, Mr. Mayor," Ottman said, "you can have my resignation as of this minute."

Oh, God, Rudolph thought, honest men! Some day he was going to try marijuana himself and see what all the fuss was about. Maybe it would be just the thing for Jean.

"The lawyer for the kid is Leon Harrison's lawyer, too," Ottman said. "Harrison's already been in here and asked what I intend to do. He's talking about calling a special meeting of the board of trustees."

"All right, Chief," Rudolph said. "Call Dorlacker and tell him you've spoken to me and that I've ordered a search for eight o'clock tonight. Get a warrant from Judge Satterlee and tell your men to leave their clubs at home. I don't want anybody hurt. The news'll get around and maybe the kids'll have the sense to get rid of the stuff before you hit the dormitory."

"You don't know kids these days, Mr. Mayor," Ottman said sorrowfully. "They ain't got the sense to wipe their ass."

Rudolph gave him the number of the hotel in Dallas and told him to get back to him after the raid that evening. He hung up and finished his Coke. The lunch on the plane coming down had been dreadful and he had heartburn. He had foolishly drunk the two Manhattans the stewardess had plunked down on his tray. For some reason he drank Manhattans when he was in the air. Never on the ground. What significance there?

The phone rang. He waited for Johnny to pick it up in the other room, but it wasn't ringing in the other room. "Hello," he said.

"Rudy?" It was Gretchen's voice.

"Yes." There had been a coolness between them since she had told him that Jean was an alcoholic. Gretchen had been right, but that only made the coolness more pronounced.

"I called Jean at your house," Gretchen said, "and she told **me** where you are. I hope I'm not disturbing you." She sounded disturbed herself.

"No, no," Rudolph lied. "I'm just dawdling idly in that well-known holiday spot, Dallas Les Bains. Where are you anyway?"

"Los Angeles. I wouldn't have called you, but I'm out of my mind."

Depend upon families to pick the right time and place to be out of their minds.

"What is it?" Rudolph asked.

"It's Billy. Did you know he dropped out of school a month ago?"

"No," Rudolph said. "He hardly ever whispered his secrets to me, you know."

"He's down in New York, living with some girl . . ."

"Gretchen, darling," Rudolph said, "there are probably half a million boys Billy's age in New York right this minute living with some girl. Be thankful he isn't living with some boy."

"Of course it isn't that," Gretchen said. "He's being drafted, now that he's not a student anymore."

"Well, it might do him some good," Rudolph said. "A couple of years in the Army might make a man of him."

"You have a baby daughter," Gretchen said bitterly. "You can talk like that. I have one son. I don't think a bullet through his head is going to make a man of my son."

"Now, Gretchen," Rudolph said, "don't make it so automatic. Induct the boy and two months later send the corpse home to mother. There are an awful lot of boys who serve their time and come home without a scratch."

"That's why I'm calling you," Gretchen said. "I want you to make sure that he comes home without a scratch."

"What can I do?"

"You know a lot of people in Washington."

"Nobody can keep a kid out of the draft if he's goofed school and he's in good health, Gretchen. Not even in Washington."

"I'm not so sure about that, either," Gretchen said, "from some of the things I've heard and read. But I'm not asking you to try to keep Billy out of the Army."

"Then what *are* you trying to get me to do?"

"Use your connections to make sure that once Billy is in, he doesn't ever get sent to Viet Nam."

Rudolph sighed. The truth was that he did know some people in Washington who could most probably do it and who would most probably do it if he asked them. But it was just the sort of petty, privileged, inside politicking that he despised the most. It offended his sense of rectitude and cast a shadow on his entire reason for going into public life. In the world of business it was perfectly normal for a man to come to you and ask you to place a nephew or a cousin in some favored position. Depending upon how much you owed the man or how much you expected to get from him in the future, or even how much you liked him, you helped the nephew or cousin, if you could, without thinking twice about it. But to use the power you had gained by the votes of people to whom you had promised impeccable representation and the sternest respect for the law to deliver your sister's son from the threat of death while actively or tacitly approving of sending thousands of other boys the same age to their destruction was another thing.

"Gretchen," he said over the slight buzz of wire between Dallas and Los Angeles, "I wish you could figure out some other way . . ."

"The only other person I know who might be able to do something," Gretchen said, her voice rising, "is Colin Burke's brother. He's a general in the Air Force. He's in Viet Nam right now. I bet he'd just fall all over himself with eagerness to keep Billy from hearing a shot fired."

"Not so loud, Gretchen," Rudolph said, holding the phone away from his ear. "I hear you perfectly well."

"I'm going to tell you something." She was shouting hysterically now. "If you don't help, I'm coming to New York and I'm taking Billy with me to Canada or Sweden. And I'm going to make one hell of a loud noise about why I'm doing it."

"Christ, Gretchen," Rudolph said, "what's wrong with you—are you approaching the menopause or what?"

He heard the phone slam at the other end. He got up slowly and went over to the window and looked out at Dallas. It didn't look any better from the bedroom than it had from the salon.

Family, he thought. Without reasoning it out, he had always been the one to try to protect his family. He was the one who helped his father at the ovens and made the deliveries for the bakery; he was the one who had kept his mother alive. He was the one who had had the shabby dealings with detectives and the painful scene with Willie Abbott and had helped Gretchen with her divorce and befriended her second husband. He was the one who had made the money for Tom, so that he could escape the savage life he had fallen into. He was the one who had gone to Colin Burke's funeral on the

other edge of the continent to comfort his sister at the worst moments of her sorrow. He was the one who had taken the responsibility of taking Billy, ungrateful and derisive as he was, out of his
school when Billy was suffering there; he was the one who had gotten Billy into Whitby, when the boy's marks were hardly good
enough to get him into a trade school. He was the one who had
hunted down Tom at the Aegean Hotel, for his mother's sake, and
had learned all about West Fifty-third Street and put up the money
for Schultz and made the arrangement with the lawyer for Tom's reunion with his son and his divorce from a prostitute . . .

He had not asked for gratitude and, he thought wryly, he had gotten damn little for it. Well, he hadn't done it for gratitude. He was
honest with himself. He was conscious of the duties owed to himself
and others and wouldn't have been able to live comfortably with
himself if he hadn't fulfilled them.

Duties never end. It is their essential characteristic.

He went over to the phone and asked for Gretchen's number in
California. When she answered, he said, "All right, Gretchen. I'll
stop over in Washington on the way North and see what I can do. I
think you can stop worrying."

"Thank you, Rudy," Gretchen said in a small voice. "I knew you'd
come through."

Brad arrived at the suite at five-thirty. Texas sun and Texas liquor
had made him ruddier than ever. Also heavier and more expansive.
He was wearing a dark, summer-weight, striped suit and a ruffled
blue shirt with huge pearl cufflinks. "Sorry I couldn't meet you at
the airport, but I hope my boy treated you all right." He poured himself a slug of bourbon over ice and beamed at his friends. "Well, it's
about time you fellas came down and paid me a visit and took a look
for yourselves at where your money's coming from. We're bringing
in a new well and maybe tomorrow I'll hire a plane and we'll fly over
and take a look at how it's doing. And I've got tickets on the fifty-
yard line for Saturday. The big game of the season. Texas against
Oklahoma. This town's got to be seen to be believed on that weekend. Thirty thousand happy drunks. I'm sorry Virginia's not here to
welcome you. She'll be heartbroken when she hears you've been and
gone. But she's up North visiting her Pappy. I hear he's not too well.
I hope it's nothing serious. I'm real fond of the old critter."

It was too painful, the Western heartiness, the lush hospitality,
the desperate rush of Southern blarney. "Cut it out, please, Brad,"

Rudolph said. "For one thing, we know why Virginia's not here. And it isn't to visit her Pappy, as you describe him." Two weeks ago Calderwood had come to Rudolph's office and had told him that Virginia had left Brad for good because Brad had taken up with some movie actress in Hollywood and was commuting between Dallas and Hollywood three times a week and was having money troubles. It was after Calderwood's visit that Rudolph had begun to suspect something and had called Johnny.

"Pardner," Brad said, drinking, "I don't know what all you're talking about. I just talked to my wife and she said she expected to be coming home any day now and . . ."

"You didn't just talk to your wife and she's not coming home, Brad," Rudolph said. "And you know it."

"And you know a lot of other things, too," Johnny said. He was standing between Brad and the door, almost as if he expected Brad to make a sudden run for it. "And so do we."

"By God," Brad said, "if you fellas weren't my lifelong buddies, I'd swear you sounded hostile." He was sweating, despite the air-conditioning and his blue shirt was darkly stained. He filled his glass again. His stubby, manicured fingers were shaking as he fumbled with the ice.

"Come clean, Brad," Johnny said.

"Well . . ." Brad laughed, or tried to laugh. "Maybe I've been stepping out a little on my wife, here and there. You know how I am, Rudy, I don't have the strength of character you have, I can't resist a little bit of soft, cuddly poontang when it's waved in my face. But Virginia's taking it too big, she . . ."

"We're not interested in you and Virginia," Johnny said. "We're interested in where our money's gone to."

"You get a statement every month," Brad said.

"We sure do," Johnny said.

"We've run into a little hard luck recently." Brad wiped his face with a large, monogrammed, linen handkerchief. "Like my Pappy, bless his soul, used to say about the oil business, if you don't like the waves, don't go in the water."

"We've been doing some checking," Johnny said, "and we figure that in the last year you've stolen roughly seventy thousand dollars apiece from me and Rudy."

"You fellas must be kidding," Brad said. His face was almost purple now and his smile was fixed, as though it were permanently ironed on the florid, stretched skin over the damp collar. "You *are* kidding, aren't you? This is some kind of practical joke. Jesus, a hundred and forty thousand dollars!"

"Brad . . ." Rudolph said warningly.

"Okay," Brad said. "I guess you're not kidding." He sank down heavily on the flowered couch, a thick, round-shouldered weary man against the gay colors of the best piece of furniture in the best suite of the best hotel in Dallas, Texas. "I'll tell you how it happened."

The way it happened was that Brad had met a starlet by the name of Sandra Dilson a year before when he had gone out to Hollywood to scout around for more investors. "A sweet, innocent young thing," were Brad's words for Miss Dilson. He'd gone ape for her, he said, but it was a long time before she'd let him touch her. To impress her he'd started buying her jewelry. "You have no idea what they charge for stones out there in that town," Brad said. "It's as though they printed their own money." And to impress her further, he'd bet heavily when they went to the races. "If you want to know the truth," Brad said, "that girl is walking around with about four hundred thousand dollars' worth of jewelry on her back that I paid for. And there were times in bed with her," he said defiantly, "that I felt it was worth it, every cent of it. I love her and I lost my head over her and in a way I'm proud of it and I'm willing to take the consequences."

To find the money, Brad had started to falsify the monthly statements. He had reported prospecting and drilling for oil in holes that had been abandoned as dry or worthless years before and had hiked up the cost of equipment ten or even fifteen times what the actual price would have been. There was a bookkeeper in his office who was in on it, but whom he paid to keep quiet and to work with him. There had been some ominous inquiries from other people who invested with him, but up to now he had been able to fend them off.

"How many investors have you got backing you at this moment?" Johnny asked.

"Fifty-two."

"Fifty-two idiots," Johnny said bitterly.

"I never did anything like this before," Brad said ingenuously. "My reputation in Oklahoma and Texas is as clean as a hound's tooth. You ask anyone. People trusted me. And they had a right to."

"You're going to go to jail, Brad," Rudolph said.

"You wouldn't do that to me, to your old friend, Brad, who sat next to you the day you graduated from college, would you, Rudy?"

"I certainly would," Rudolph said.

"Wait a minute, wait a minute," Johnny said, "before we start talking about jail. I'm more interested in seeing if we can get our money back than in sending this moron to jail."

"That's it," Brad said eagerly, "that's the way to talk. Sensibly."

"What have you got in the way of assets?" Johnny asked. "Right now?"

"That's it," repeated Brad. "Now we're talking business. It's not as though I'm wiped out. I still have credit."

"When you walk out of this room, Brad," Rudolph said, "you won't be able to borrow ten cents from any bank in the country. I'll see to that." He found it hard not to show his disgust.

"Johnny . . ." Brad appealed to Heath. "He's vindictive. Talk to him. I can understand he's a little sore, but to be vindictive like that . . ."

"I asked you about your assets," Johnny said.

"Well," Brad said, "on the books, it's not so . . . so optimistic." He grinned, hopefully. "But from time to time, I've been able to accumulate a little cash. For a rainy day, you might say. I've got it in safety-deposit boxes here and there. It's not enough to pay off everybody, of course, but I could go pretty far toward paying you fellas back."

"Is it Virginia's money?" Rudolph asked.

"Virginia's money!" Brad snorted. "Her old man tied up the money he gave her so tight, I couldn't buy a hot dog with any of it if I was dying of hunger in a ballpark."

"He was a lot smarter than we were," Rudolph said.

"Jesus, Rudolph," Brad complained, "you don't have to keep rubbing it in. I feel bad enough as it is."

"How much is there in cash?" Johnny asked.

"You understand, Johnny," Brad said, "it's not on the company's books anywhere or anything like that."

"I understand," Johnny said. "How much?"

"Close to a hundred thousand. I could give each of you nearly fifty thousand dollars on account. And I'd personally guarantee to pay the rest back later."

"How?" Rudolph asked brutally.

"Well, there's still some wells being dug . . ." Rudolph could tell he was lying. "And then I could go to Sandra and explain how I'm in a little hole for the time being and ask her to give me back the jewelry, and . . ."

Rudolph shook his head, wonderingly. "You really believe she'd do that?"

"She's a fine little girl, Rudy. I have to introduce her to you sometime."

"Oh, grow up, for Christ's sake," Rudolph said.

"You wait here," Johnny said to Brad. "I want to talk to Rudy alone." He ostentatiously took the papers he had been working on with him as he went toward Rudolph's bedroom door.

"You fellas don't mind if I mix myself a little drink while I'm waiting, do you?" Brad said.

Johnny closed the door behind them when he and Rudolph were in the bedroom. "We have a decision to make," he said. "If as he says he's got close to a hundred thousand cash, we can take it and cut our losses. That is, about twenty thousand give or take a few dollars in one way or another. If we don't take it, we have to report it and ask for a creditors' meeting and probably put him through bankruptcy. If we don't start criminal proceedings. All his creditors would have an equal shot at the money, or at least pro rata, according to the size of their investments and the amount he actually owes them."

"Does he have the right to pay us off like that, preferentially?"

"Well, he isn't in bankruptcy yet," Johnny said. "I think it would stand up in a court of law."

"Nothing doing," Rudolph said. "Let him throw it into the pot. And let's get the safety-deposit box keys from him tonight, so he can't lift the money before we can stop him."

Johnny sighed. "I was afraid you'd say that," he said. "When knighthood was in flower."

"Just because he's a crook," Rudolph said, "doesn't mean that I'm going to be a crook to cut my losses, as you say."

"I said I thought it would probably stand up in a court of law," Johnny said.

"Not good enough," Rudolph said. "Not good enough for me."

Johnny looked speculatively at Rudolph. "What would you do if I went to him and said, okay, I'll take my half, and drop out of the rest of it?"

"I'd report it at the creditors' meeting," Rudolph said evenly, "and make a motion to sue you for recovery."

"I surrender, dear," Johnny said. "Who can stand up to an honest politician?"

They went back into the living room. Brad was standing at the window, a full glass in hand, tickets at the fifty yard line for the big game of the season in his wallet, gazing out at the rich, friendly city of Dallas. Johnny explained what they had decided. Brad nodded, numbly, not quite understanding.

"And we want you back here tomorrow morning at nine o'clock," Rudolph said. "Before the banks open. We'll go around with you to those safety-deposit boxes you spoke about and we'll take care of the money for you. We'll give you a receipt for your files. If you're not here by one minute before nine, I'll call the police and make out a complaint for fraud."

"Rudy . . ." Brad said plaintively.

"And if you want to hold onto those fancy, pearl cufflinks," Rudolph said, "you'd better hide them someplace, because by the end of the month the sheriff is going to come around to seize your property, every bit of property you own, including that pretty, frilled shirt you're wearing, to satisfy your debts."

"You guys," Brad said brokenly. "You guys . . . you don't know what it's like. You're rich, you've got wives with millions, you've got everything you want. You don't know what it's like to be somebody like me."

"Don't break our hearts," Rudolph said roughly. He had never been as angry with anyone in his whole life. He had to restrain himself from jumping on the man and trying to strangle him. "Just be here at nine o'clock."

"Okay. I'll be here," Brad said. "I don't suppose you want to have dinner with me . . . ?"

"Get out of here before I kill you," Rudolph said.

Brad went to the door. "Well," he said, "have a good time in Dallas. It's a great city. And remember . . ." He gestured for the suite, the liquor. "All this on my bill."

Then he went out.

Rudolph didn't have time to call home the next morning. Brad came over at nine o'clock, as ordered, red eyed and looking as though he hadn't slept all night, with a collection of keys for safety-deposit boxes in various Dallas banks. Ottman hadn't called the night before, although Rudolph and Johnny had dined in the hotel to be ready for his call. Rudolph took it as a sign that all had gone smoothly on the Whitby campus and that Ottman's fears had been exaggerated.

Rudolph and Johnny, with Brad in tow, went to the office of a lawyer whom Johnny knew. There, the lawyer drew up a power of attorney, for Johnny to act as Rudolph's representative. Johnny was going to stay in Dallas to sort out the mess. Then, with a clerk from the lawyer's office as a witness, they went from bank to bank and watched as Brad, not wearing his pearl cufflinks, opened the boxes and took out neat packages of cash. All four men counted the bills methodically, before the clerk made out a receipt, which Rudolph and Johnny signed, acknowledging that they had received the sum from Bradford Knight, and the date. The lawyer's clerk would then duly witness the slip of paper, after which they would all go up to the main floor from the bank's vault and deposit the money in a joint account in Rudolph's and Johnny's names, all withdrawals to be made on presentation of *both* signatures. Rudolph and Johnny had planned the procedure the night before, knowing that from now on anything to do with Bradford Knight would have to stand up to scrutiny.

After the last box had been emptied, the final figure stood at ninety-three thousand dollars. Brad had been almost accurate in his estimate of what he had hidden away for what he had called a rainy day. Neither Johnny nor Rudolph asked him where the money had come from. That would be somebody else's job.

The visit to the lawyer's office and the round of the banks had taken up most of the morning and Rudolph had to hurry to catch his plane, which was to leave Dallas for Washington at noon. As he rushed out of the suite, carrying his bag and small briefcase, he saw that the only bottles of the array in the salon that had been opened had been the one Coke he had taken himself and the fifth of bourbon that Brad had drunk from.

Brad had offered him the use of his car to take him to the airport. "This morning, anyway," he had said, trying to smile, "I still got my Cadillac. Might as well enjoy it." But Rudolph had refused and called for a taxi. As he climbed into the taxi he asked Johnny to telephone his office in Whitby and tell his secretary that he couldn't get home tonight, but would be staying over at the Mayflower Hotel in Washington.

On the plane he did not eat the lunch nor drink the two Manhattans. He got the Comptroller's estimates out of his briefcase and tried to work, but he couldn't concentrate on the figures before him. He kept thinking about Brad, doomed, branded, bankrupt, with a jail sentence hanging over his head. Ruined for what? For a money-digging Hollywood tart. It was sickening. He loved her, Brad had said, it had been worth it. Love, the Fifth Horseman of the Apocalypse. At least in Texas. It was almost impossible to associate Brad with the emotion. He was a man born, Rudolph saw now, for saloons and brothels. Maybe he had known it all the time and had refused to acknowledge it. Still, it was always difficult to believe in the existence of the love of others. Perhaps his refusal to accept the fact that Brad actually was capable of love was condescension on his part. He himself loved Jean, he thought, but would he face ruin for her? The answer had to be no. Was he then more superficial than the blubbering, sweating man in the ruffled shirt? And was he responsible in some way for the hideous day his friend was passing through now and the even more hideous days to come? When he had killed Brad's chances with Calderwood on the steps of the Country Club, the afternoon of the wedding, had he subconsciously prepared Brad's fate for him? When he had invested in Brad's business, out of guilt, hadn't he really known that one day Brad would revenge himself, and in the only way possible to Brad, by cheating? And had he not, in fact, wanted it to happen to rid himself finally of Brad because Brad had not believed him about Virginia? And even more disturbingly, if he had succumbed to Virginia Calderwood's proposals and slept with her, would she have married Brad, and in marrying him, carried her husband out of the area of his friend's protection? For there was no doubt about it—he had protected Brad through the years, first in calling him East for a job that dozens of other men could initially have done better, then in training him carefully (and overpaying him in the process) so that in Brad's mind at least the idea of being awarded the top post in the firm was a reasonable one. At what point was it moral to stop protecting a friend? Never?

It would have been easier to allow Johnny Heath to go down to Dallas and handle the matter alone. Johnny had been Brad's friend, too, and the best man at his wedding, but it had never been the same thing as between Rudolph and Brad. Somehow, it had been more hurtful to Brad to have to answer to Rudolph, face to face. God knows, it would have been easy for Rudolph to have pleaded pressure of work in Whitby and sent Johnny off on his own. He had considered it, but rejected it as cowardly. He had made the trip to maintain his own self-esteem. Self-esteem might be another way of saying vanity. Had his continued success dulled his sensibilities, led him into complacency and self-righteousness?

When the bankruptcy was finally settled, he decided, he would somehow pension Brad off. Five thousand dollars a year, paid secretly, so that neither Brad's creditors nor the government could touch it? Would the money, which Brad would so desperately need and have to accept, pay for the sting of having to accept it from a man who had turned his back on him?

The seat-belt sign went on. They were making the approach for the landing. Rudolph put the papers back into his briefcase, sighed, and hooked up his belt.

When he got to the Mayflower there was a message waiting for him from his secretary. It was urgent, the message read, for him to call his office as soon as possible.

He went up to his room, where nobody had bothered to supply any liquor, and called his office. Twice, the line was busy, and he nearly decided to abandon the attempt to reach his office and get in touch with the Senator who was most likely to help him in keeping Billy Abbott out of harm's way in the United States Army. It was not something that could be arranged over the phone and he hoped to make an appointment for lunch the next day and then take an afternoon plane for New York.

On the third try, he got his secretary. "I'm terribly sorry, Mr. Mayor," Walter said, sounding exhausted, "but I'm afraid you'd better get up here right away. After the office closed last night and I'd gone home, all hell broke loose, I just found out about it this morning or I'd have tried to get through to you sooner."

"What is it? What is it?" Rudolph asked impatiently.

"It's all terribly confused and I'm not sure that I have the sequence of events all straight," Walter said. "But when Ottman tried to go into the dormitory last night, they had it barricaded, the students, I mean, and they wouldn't let the police in. President Dorlacker tried to get Ottman to call the police off, but Ottman refused. Then when they tried to get in again, the students began to throw things. Ottman got hit in the eye with a stone, nothing serious, they say, but he's in the hospital, and the police gave up, at least for last night. Then other students organized a mass march and I'm afraid they demonstrated in front of your house. I went out to your house just awhile ago and the lawn is in frightful condition. Mrs. Jordache is under sedation and . . ."

"You can tell me the rest of the story when I get there," Rudolph said. "I'm getting the first plane out of Washington."

"I thought that's what you would do," Walter said, "and I took the liberty of sending Scanlon down with your car. He'll be waiting at La Guardia."

Rudolph picked up his bags and hurried down to the lobby and checked out. Billy Abbott's military career would have to hang in abeyance for awhile.

Scanlon was a fat man who wheezed when he talked. He was on the police force, but was nearly sixty years old and was scheduled for retirement. He suffered from rheumatism and it was almost as an act of mercy that he had been assigned as chauffeur to Rudolph. As an object lesson in civic economy Rudolph had sold the former mayor's car, which had been owned by the town, and used his own car.

"If I had it to do all over again," Scanlon said breathily, "I swear to God I'd never sign on any police force in a town where there was college students or niggers."

"Scanlon, please," Rudolph said. He had been trying to correct Scanlon's vocabulary since the first day, with little success. He was sitting up front with the old patrolman, who drove at a maddeningly slow pace. But he would have been offended if Rudolph took the wheel.

"I mean it, sir," Scanlon said. "They're just wild animals. With no more respect for the law than a pack of hyenas. As for the police—they just laugh at us. I don't like to tell you your business, Mr. Mayor, but if I was you, I'd go right to the Governor and ask for the Guard."

"There's time enough for that," Rudolph said.

"Mark my words," said Scanlon. "It'll come to it. Look what they've done down in New York and out in California."

"We're not New York or California," Rudolph said.

"We got students and niggers," Scanlon said stubbornly. He drove silently for awhile. Then he said, "You shoulda been at your house last night, Mr. Mayor, then maybe you'd know what I was talking about."

"I heard about it," Rudolph said. "They trampled the garden."

"They did a lot more than that," Scanlon said. "I wasn't there myself, but Ruberti was there, and he told me." Ruberti was another policeman. "It was sinful what they did, Ruberti told me, sinful. They kept calling for you and singing dirty-minded songs, young girls, using the dirtiest language anybody ever heard, and they pulled up every plant in your garden and then when Mrs. Jordache opened the door . . ."

"She opened the door?" Rudolph was aghast. "What did she do that for?"

"Well, they started throwing things at the house. Clods of dirt, beer cans, and yelling, 'Tell that motherfucker to come out.' They meant you, Mr. Mayor, I'm ashamed to say. There was only Ruberti and Zimmermann there, the whole rest of the force was up at the college, and what could just two of them do against those howling wild Indians, maybe three hundred of them. So like I said, Mrs. Jordache opened the door and yelled at them."

"Oh, Jesus," Rudolph said.

"You might as well hear it now from me as later from somebody else," Scanlon said. "When Mrs. Jordache opened the door, she was drunk. And she was stark naked."

Rudolph made himself stare straight ahead at the tail lights of the cars ahead of him and into the blinding beams of light of the cars going the other way.

"There was a kid photographer there, from the school paper," Scanlon went on, "and he took some flashlight pictures. Ruberti went for him, but the other kids made a kind of pocket and he got away. I don't know what use they think they're going to make of the pictures, but they got them."

Rudolph ordered Scanlon to drive directly to the university. The main administration building was brilliantly floodlit and there were students at every window, throwing out thousands of pieces of paper from the files and shouting at the line of policemen, alarmingly few, but armed with their clubs now, who cordoned off the building. As he drove up to where Ottman's car was parked under a tree, Rudolph saw what use had been made of the photograph of his wife taken naked the night before. It had been enormously blown up and it was hanging from a first-story window. In the glare of the floodlights, the image of Jean's body, slender and perfect, her breasts full, her fists clenched and threatening, her face demented, hung, a mocking banner, over the entrance of the building, just above the words carved in the stone, "Know the truth and the truth shall make ye free."

When Rudolph got out of the car, some of the students at the windows recognized him and greeted him with a wild, triumphant howl. Somebody leaned out the window and shook Jean's picture, so that it looked as though she were doing an obscene dance.

Ottman was standing beside his car, a big bandage over one eye, making his cap sit on the back of his head. Only six of the policemen had helmets. Rudolph remembered vetoing a request from Ottman for two dozen more helmets six months before, because it had seemed an unnecessary expense.

"Your secretary told us you were on your way," Ottman said, without any preliminaries, "so we held off on any action until you got here. They have Dorlacker and two professors locked in there with them. They only took the building at six o'clock tonight."

Rudolph nodded, studying the building. At a window on the ground floor he saw Quentin McGovern. Quentin was a graduate student now and had a job as an assistant in the chemistry department. Quentin was grinning down at the scene. Rudolph was sure that Quentin saw him and he felt that the grin was directed, personally, at him.

"Whatever else happens tonight, Ottman," Rudolph said, "I want you to arrest that black man there, the third window from the left on the ground floor. His name is McGovern and if you don't get him here get him at his home."

Ottman nodded. "They want to talk to you, sir. They want you to go in there and discuss the situation with them."

Rudolph shook his head. "There's no situation to be discussed." He wasn't going to talk to anybody under the photograph of his naked wife. "Go in and clear the building."

"It's easier said than done," Ottman said. "I've already called on them three times to come out. They just laugh."

"I said clear the building." Rudolph was raging, but cold. He knew what he was doing.

"How?" Ottman asked.

"You've got weapons."

"You don't mean you want us to use guns?" Ottman said incredulously. "As far as we know, none of them is armed."

Rudolph hesitated. "No," he said. "No guns. But you've got clubs and you've got tear gas."

"You sure you don't want us just to sit tight and wait till they get tired?" Ottman said. He sounded more tired himself than any of the students in the building would ever be. "And if things don't improve, ask for the Guard, maybe?"

"No, I don't want to sit and wait." Rudolph didn't say it, but he knew that Ottman knew he wanted that picture down immediately. "Tell your men to start with the grenades."

"Mr. Mayor," Ottman said slowly, "you'll have to put that in writing for me. Signed."

"Give me your pad," Rudolph said.

Ottman gave him the pad, and Rudolph used the fender of Ottman's car to steady it and wrote out the order, making sure that his handwriting was clear and legible. He signed his name and gave the pad back to Ottman, who tore off the top sheet on which Rudolph had written and carefully folded the piece of paper and put it in the pocket of his blouse. He buttoned the pocket of the blouse and then went along the line of police, some thirty strong, the town's entire force, to give his orders. As he passed them, the men began to put on their gas masks.

The line of police moved slowly across the lawn toward the building, their shadows, in the blaze of the floodlights, intense on the brilliant green grass. They did not keep a straight line, but wavered uncertainly, and they looked like a long, wounded animal, searching not to do harm, but to find a place to hide from its tormentors. Then the first grenade was shot off through one of the lower windows and there was a shout from within. Then more grenades were sent through other windows and the faces that had been there disappeared and one by one the policemen, helping each other, began to climb through the windows into the building.

There hadn't been enough police to send around to the back of the building, and most of the students escaped that way. The acrid smell of the gas drifted out toward where Rudolph was standing, looking up toward where Jean's picture was still hanging. A policeman appeared at the window above and ripped it away, taking it in with him.

It was all over quickly. There were only about twenty arrests. Three students were bleeding from scalp wounds and one boy was carried out with his hands up to his eyes. A policeman said he was blinded but that he hoped it was only temporary. Quentin McGovern was not among the group arrested.

Dorlacker came out with his two professors, their eyes tearing. Rudolph went over to him. "Are you all right?" he asked.

Dorlacker squinted to see who was addressing him. "I'm not talking to you, Jordache," he said. "I'm making a statement to the press tomorrow and you can find out what I think of you if you'll buy your own paper tomorrow night." He got into somebody's car and was driven away.

"Come on," Rudolph said to Scanlon. "Drive me home."

As they drove away from the campus, ambulances passed them, their sirens going. A school bus, for the students who had been arrested, lumbered past them.

"Scanlon," Rudolph said, "as of tonight, I'm no longer Mayor of this town, am I?"

Scanlon didn't answer for a long time. He scowled as he watched the road and he wheezed like an old man when he had to turn a corner. "No, Mr. Jordache," he finally said, "I wouldn't think you were."

Chapter 7

1968

I

This time, when he got off the plane at Kennedy, there was nobody there to greet him. He was wearing dark glasses and he moved uncertainly. He hadn't written Rudolph that he was coming because he knew from Gretchen's letters that Rudolph had enough to think about without bothering with a half-blind brother. While he was working on the boat in the Antibes harbor during the winter, a line had snapped and whipped across his face and the next day he had started having dizzy spells and suffering from double vision. He had pretended nothing was wrong, because he didn't want Kate and Wesley to worry about him. He had written Mr. Goodhart for the name of an eye specialist in New York and when he received Goodhart's answer had announced to Kate that he was going to New York to arrange finally about his divorce. Kate had been after him to marry her and he didn't blame her. She was pregnant and was due to have the child in October and it was the middle of April already.

She had made him buy a new suit and he was ready to face any lawyer or doorman now. He was wearing the dead Norwegian's pea jacket because it was still in good condition and there was no sense in throwing money away.

A planeload of people who had been on a ski holiday had landed just before him and the baggage hall was full of skis and tanned, healthy-looking, fancily dressed men and women, many of them loud and more or less drunk. He tried not to be anti-American as he searched for his bag.

He took a cab, although it was expensive, because he felt he couldn't cope with getting on and off the airport bus and fiddling with his bag again and struggling to find a taxi in New York.

"The Paramount Hotel," he said to the taxi driver and settled back wearily on the seat, closing his eyes.

When he had checked in and gone up to his room, which was small and dark, he called the doctor. He would have liked to go over right away, but the nurse said that the doctor couldn't see him before eleven o'clock the next day. He undressed and got into bed. It was only six o'clock New York time, but it was eleven o'clock Nice time and he had taken the plane at Nice. His body felt as though he hadn't slept for forty-eight hours.

"The retina is partially detached," the doctor said. The examination had been slow and thorough and painful. "I'm afraid I'll have to turn you over to a surgeon."

Thomas nodded. Another wound. "How much is it going to cost?" he asked. "I'm a working man and I can't pay Park Avenue prices."

"I understand," the doctor said. "I'll explain to Dr. Halliwell. The nurse has your telephone number, hasn't she?"

"Yes."

"She'll call you and tell you when to report to the hospital. You'll be in good hands." He smiled reassuringly. His own eyes were large and clear, unscarred, without lesions.

Three weeks later he was out of the hospital. His face was drained and pale and the doctor had warned him that he was to avoid any sudden movements or strenuous exertion for a long time. He had lost about fifteen pounds and his collar swam around his neck and his clothes hung loosely from his shoulders. But he wasn't seeing double any more and he wasn't attacked by dizzy spells when he turned his head.

The whole thing had cost him a little over twelve hundred dollars, but it was worth it.

He checked in again at the Paramount Hotel and called the number of Rudolph's apartment. Rudolph answered himself.

"Rudy," Thomas said, "how are you?"

"Who is this?"

"Tom."

"Tom! Where are you?"

"Right here. In New York. At the Hotel Paramount. Can I see you sometime soon?"

"You certainly can." Rudolph sounded genuinely pleased. "Come on right over. You know where it is."

When he arrived at Rudolph's building, he was stopped by the doorman, new suit or no new suit. He gave his name and the doorman pressed a button and said, "Mr. Jordache, there's a Mr. Jordache to see you."

Thomas heard his brother say, "Please tell him to come up," and crossed the marbled lobby to the elevator, thinking, With all that protection, he still got hurt.

Rudolph was standing in the hallway when the elevator door opened. "Lord, Tom," he said, as they shook hands, "I was surprised to hear your voice." Then he stepped back and regarded Thomas critically. "What's happened to you?" he asked. "You look as though you've been sick."

Thomas could have said that he didn't think that Rudolph looked so hot, himself, but he didn't say it. "I'll tell you all about it," he said, "if you give me a drink." The doctor had said to go easy on the drink, too.

Rudolph let him into the living room. It looked just about the same as it had the last time Thomas had been there, comfortable, spacious, a place for comfortable small events, not decorated for failure.

"Whiskey?" Rudolph asked, and when Thomas nodded, poured one for Thomas and one for himself. He was fully dressed, with collar and tie, as though he were in an office. Thomas watched him as he picked up the bottles from the sideboard and hit the ice in the bucket with a small silver hammer. He looked much older than when Thomas had seen him last, with lines deep around his eyes and in his forehead. His movements were hesitant, tentative. Finding the tool to open the soda water bottle was a problem. He didn't seem to be certain about how much soda water he should put in each glass. "Sit down, sit down," he said. "Tell me what brings you here. How long have you been in New York?"

"About three weeks." He took the glass of whiskey and sat down on a wooden chair.

"Why didn't you call me?" He sounded hurt by the delay.

"I had to go to the hospital for an operation," Thomas said. "On my eyes. When I'm sick I like to be alone."

"I know," Rudolph said, sitting across from him in an easy chair. "I'm the same way myself."

"I'm okay now," Thomas said. "I have to take it easy for a little while, that's all. Cheers." He raised his glass. Between Pinky Kimball and Kate he had learned to say cheers before drinking.

"Cheers," Rudolph said. He stared soberly at Thomas. "You don't look like a fighter, any more, Tom," he said.

"You don't look like a mayor any more," Thomas said, and regretted having said it, immediately.

But Rudolph laughed. "Gretchen told me she wrote you all about it," he said. "I had a little bad luck."

"She wrote me you sold the house in Whitby," Thomas said.

"There wasn't much sense in trying to hang on." Rudolph swished the ice in his drink around the glass thoughtfully. "This place is enough for us now. Enid's out in the park with her nurse. She'll be back in a few minutes. You can say hello to her. How's your boy?"

"Fine," Thomas said. "You ought to hear him talk French. And he handles the boat better than I do. And nobody's making him do close-order drill in the afternoons."

"I'm glad it turned out well," Rudolph said. He sounded as if he meant it. "Gretchen's boy—Billy—is in the Army in Brussels, at NATO."

"I know. She wrote me that, too. And she wrote me you arranged it."

"One of my last official acts," Rudolph said. "Or maybe I should say, semiofficial acts." He had a hushed, quiet way of talking now, as though he didn't want to make any statements too positively.

"I'm sorry the way things happened, Rudy," Thomas said. For the first time in his life he pitied his brother.

Rudolph shrugged. "It could have been worse," he said. "That kid could have been killed instead of just blinded."

"What're you going to do now?"

"Oh, I keep myself busy, one way and another," Rudolph said. "New York's a great place to be a gentleman of leisure in. When Jean gets back maybe we'll do a bit of traveling. Maybe even visit you."

"Where is she?"

"In a home upstate," Rudolph said, making noise with the ice in his glass. "Not a home, really—more of a clinic—a drying-out place. They have a remarkable record of cures. This is the second time she's been there. After the first time, she didn't touch a drop for nearly six months. I'm not supposed to go up there and visit her—some goddamn doctor's theory—but I hear from the man who runs the place and he says she's doing very well. . . ." He swallowed some whiskey the wrong way and coughed a little. "Maybe I can use a little cure myself," he said, smiling, when the coughing fit had passed. "Now," he said, brightly, "now that the eye is all right, what are your plans?"

"I've got to get a divorce, Rudy," Thomas said. "And I thought maybe you could help me."

"That lawyer I sent you to said there wouldn't be any problem. You should've done it then."

"I didn't have the time," Thomas said. "I wanted to get Wesley out of the country as quick as possible. And in New York, I'd have to come out with the reason. I don't want Wesley to find out I got a divorce from his mother because she's a whore. And even if I did get the divorce in New York, it would take too long. I'd have to hang around here and I'd miss a good part of my season and I can't afford that. And I have to be divorced by October at the latest."

"Why?"

"Well . . . I'm living with a woman. An English girl. A wonderful girl. And she's going to have a baby in October."

"I see," Rudolph said. "Congratulations. The increasing tribe of Jordaches. Maybe the line can stand some English blood. What do you want me to do?"

"I don't want to have to talk to Teresa," Thomas said. "If I see her, I'm afraid of what I'll do to her. Even now. If you or somebody could talk to her and get her to go out to Reno or a place like that . . ."

Rudolph put his glass down neatly. "Sure," he said. "I'll be glad to help." There was a noise at the door. "Ah, here's Enid." He called, "Come here, baby." Enid came bouncing in, dressed in a red coat. She stopped short when she saw the strange man in the room with her father. Rudolph picked her up, kissed her. "Say hello to your Uncle Thomas," he said. "He lives on a boat."

Three mornings later, Rudolph called Thomas and made a date for lunch with him at P. J. Moriarty's, on Third Avenue. The atmosphere there was male and plain and not likely to make Thomas feel ill at ease or give him the idea that Rudolph was showing off.

Thomas was waiting for him at the bar when he came in, a drink in front of him. "Well," Rudolph said, as he sat down on the stool next to his brother's, "the lady's on her way to Nevada."

"You're kidding," Thomas said.

"I drove her to the airport myself," Rudolph said, "and watched the plane take off."

"Christ, Rudy," Thomas said, "you're a miracle worker."

"Actually, it wasn't so hard," Rudolph said. He ordered a martini, to get over the effects of a whole morning with Teresa Jordache. "She's thinking of remarrying, too, she says." This was a lie, but Rudolph said it convincingly. "And she saw the wisdom of not dragging her good name, as she calls it, through the courts in New York."

"Did she hit you for dough?" Thomas asked. He knew his wife.

"No," Rudolph lied again. "She says she makes good money and she can afford the trip."

"It doesn't sound like her," Thomas said doubtfully.

"Maybe life has mellowed her." The martini was sustaining. He had argued with the woman for two whole days and had finally agreed to pay for her round-trip fare, first class, her hotel bill in Reno for six weeks, plus five hundred dollars a week, for what Teresa had described as loss of trade. He had paid her half in advance and would pay her the rest when she came back and gave him the papers that formally ended her marriage.

They had a good, solid lunch, with two bottles of wine, and Thomas became a little maudlin and kept telling Rudy how grateful he was and how stupid he had been all these years not to realize what a great guy he had for a brother. Over cognacs, he said, "Look, the other day you said you were going to do some traveling when your wife got out of the clinic. The first two weeks in July I haven't got a charter. I'll keep it open and you and your wife can come on board, as my guests, and we'll do a little cruising. And if Gretchen can come, bring her along, too. You've got to meet Kate. Christ, the divorce'll be final by then and you can come to my wedding. Come on, Rudy, I won't take no for an answer."

"It depends upon Jean," Rudolph said. "How she feels . . ."

"It'll be the best thing in the world for her," Thomas said. "There won't be a bottle of liquor on board. Rudy, you just got to do it."

"Okay," Rudy said. "The first of July. Maybe it'll do us both good to get out of this country for awhile."

Thomas insisted upon paying for the lunch. "It's the least I can do," he said. "I got a lot to celebrate. I got back an eye and got rid of a wife all in the same month."

II

The Mayor was wearing a sash, the bride was dressed in cornflower blue and did not look pregnant. Enid was wearing white gloves and was holding her mother's hand and was frowning a little at the mysterious games the grown-ups were playing in a language she did not understand. Thomas was brown and healthy again. He had put back the weight he had lost and his muscular neck bulged at the collar of the white shirt he was wearing. Wesley stood just behind his father, a tall, graceful boy of fifteen in a suit whose sleeves were too short for him, his face deeply tanned, and his blond hair bleached by the Mediterranean sun. They were all tanned because they had been cruising for a week and had only come back to Antibes for the ceremony. Gretchen, Rudolph thought, looked superb, her dark hair with just a little animal sheen of gray in it, severely drawn around the bony, wide-eyed, magnificent face. Queenlike, Rudolph thought, nobly tragic. Rhetoric went with weddings. Rudolph knew that the single week on the sea had made him look years younger than when he had stepped off the plane at Nice. He listened, amused, to the Mayor, who was describing, in a rich Midi accent, full of rolling hard g's, the duties expected of the bride. Jean understood French, too, and they exchanged little smiles as the Mayor went on. Jean hadn't had a drink since she had come down from the clinic and she looked dear and beautifully fragile in the room full of Thomas's friends from the harbor, with their weather-worn, strong, dark faces, above unaccustomed neckties and jackets. There was an aura of voyages in the sunny, flower-bedecked Mayor's office, Rudolph thought, a tang of salt, the flavors of a thousand ports.

Only Dwyer seemed sad, touching the white carnation in his buttonhole. Thomas had told Rudolph Dwyer's story and Rudolph thought perhaps the sight of his friend's happiness made Dwyer regret the girl in Boston he had foresworn for the *Clothilde*.

The Mayor was robust and obviously liked this part of his job. He was as sun-darkened as the seamen around him. When I was the mayor of another town, Rudolph thought, I didn't spend much time in the sun. He wondered if the Mayor was worried about kids smoking pot in dormitories and whether or not to order the police to use tear gas. Whitby, too, at certain seasons, looked idyllic.

When he had first met Kate, Rudolph had been disappointed in his brother's choice. He was partial to pretty women and Kate, with her flat, dark, humble face, and her stubby body, was certainly not pretty in any conventional terms. She reminded him of some of the native women in Gauguin's Tahitian paintings. *Vogue* and *Harper's Bazaar*, he thought, have much to answer for. With all those long, slender beauties, they have tuned us out from simpler and more primitive appeals.

Kate's speech, shy, uneducated, and Liverpudlian, had jarred on his ears in the beginning, too. It was curious, Rudolph thought, how Americans, with their ideas of the English formed by visiting actors and lecturers, were more snobbish about British accents than those of their own countrymen.

But after a day or two of watching Kate with Tom and Wesley, uncomplainingly doing all sorts of chores on board the ship, handling the man and the boy with the most transparent, undemonstrative love and trust, he had felt ashamed of his first reactions to the woman. Tom was a lucky man, and he told him so and Tom had soberly agreed.

The Mayor came to the end of his speech, rings were exchanged, bride and groom kissed each other. The Mayor kissed the bride, beaming, as though he had brilliantly performed some extraordinarily delicate bureaucratic function.

The last wedding Rudolph had attended had been that of Brad Knight and Virginia Calderwood. He preferred this one.

Rudolph and Gretchen signed the register, after the newlyweds. Rudolph hesitantly kissed the bride. There were finger-mangling handshakes all around, and the entire party trooped out into the sunlight of the town that had been founded more than two thousand years ago by men who must have looked very much like the men who accompanied his brother in the wedding procession.

There was champagne waiting for them at Chez Felix au Port and melon and bouillabaisse for lunch. An accordionist played, the Mayor toasted the bride, Pinky Kimball toasted the bridegroom in Southampton French, Rudolph toasted the couple in French that made the guests gaze at him with wonder and got him a great round of applause when he finished. Jean had brought along a camera and took roll after roll of photographs to commemorate the occasion. It was the first time since the night she had broken her cameras that she had taken any pictures. And Rudolph hadn't suggested it. She had suggested it herself.

The lunch broke up at four o'clock and all the guests, some of them weaving now, paraded the bridal couple back to where the *Clothilde* lay at the quay. On the after deck there was a big crate tied up in red ribbon. It was Rudolph's wedding gift and he had arranged for it to be put aboard during the festivities. He had had it shipped over from New York to Thomas's agent, with instructions to hold it until the wedding day.

Thomas read the card. "What the hell is this?" he asked Rudolph.

"Open it and find out."

Dwyer went to get a hammer and chisel and the bridegroom stripped down to the waist and with all the guests crowding around, broke open the crate. Inside it was a beautiful Bendix radar set and scanner. Before leaving New York, Rudolph had spoken to Mr. Goodhart and asked him what Thomas would like best for the *Clothilde* and Mr. Goodhart had suggested the radar.

Thomas held the set up triumphantly, and the guests applauded Rudolph again, as though he personally had invented and manufactured the machine with his own hands.

There were tears in Thomas's eyes, a little drunken, to be sure, as he thanked Rudolph. "Radar," he said. "I've been wanting this for years."

"I thought it made a fitting wedding present," Rudolph said. "Mark the horizon, recognize obstacles, avoid wrecks."

Kate, sea-going wife, kept touching the machine as though it were a delightful young puppy.

"I tell you," Thomas said, "this is the greatest goddamn wedding anybody ever had."

The plan was to set sail that afternoon for Portofino. They would stay along the coast past Monte Carlo, Menton, and San Remo, then cross the Gulf of Genoa during the night and make a landfall on the Italian mainland some time the next morning. The *météo* was good and the entire voyage, according to Thomas, shouldn't take more than fifteen hours.

Dwyer and Wesley wouldn't allow Thomas or Kate to touch a line, but made them sit enthroned on the after deck while they got the *Clothilde* under way. As the anchor finally came up and the ship turned its nose seaward, from various boats in the harbor there came the sound of horns, in salute, and a fishing boat full of flowers accompanied them to the buoy, with two men strewing the flowers in their wake.

As they hit the gentle swell of open water they could see the white towers of Nice far off across the Baie des Anges.

"What a place to live," Rudolph said. "France."

"Especially," Thomas said, "if you're not a Frenchman."

III

Gretchen and Rudolph sat in deck chairs near the stern of the *Clothilde*, watching the sun begin to set behind them. They were just opposite the Nice airport and could watch the jets swoop in, one every few minutes. Coming in, their wings gleamed in the level sunlight and nearly touched the silvery sea as they landed. Taking off, they climbed above the escarpment of Monaco, still brightly sunlit to the east. How pleasant it was to be moving at ten knots, Rudolph thought, and watch everybody else going at five hundred.

Jean was below putting Enid to bed. When she was on deck Enid wore a small orange life-jacket and she was attached by a line around her waist to a metal loop on the pilot house to make sure she wasn't lost overboard. The bridegroom was forward sleeping off his champagne. Dwyer was with Kate in the galley preparing dinner. Rudolph had protested about this and had invited them all to dinner in Nice or Monte Carlo, but Kate had insisted. "I couldn't think of a better thing to do on my wedding night," Kate had said. Wesley, in a blue turtle-neck sweater, because it was getting cool, was at the wheel. He moved around the boat, barefooted and sure handed, as though he had been born at sea.

Gretchen and Rudolph were wearing sweaters, too. "What a luxury it is," Rudolph said, "to be cold in July."

"You're glad you came, aren't you?" Gretchen asked.

"Very glad," Rudolph said.

"The family restored," Gretchen said. "No, not even that. *Assembled*, for the first time. And by Tom, of all people."

"He's learned something we never quite learned," Rudolph said.

"He certainly has. Have you noticed—wherever he goes, he moves in an atmosphere of love. His wife, Dwyer, all those friends at the wedding. Even his own son." She laughed shortly.

She had talked to Rudolph about her visit with Billy in Brussels before she had come down to Antibes to join them, so Rudolph knew what was behind the laugh. Billy, safe in an Army office as a typist and clerk, was, she had told Rudolph, cynical, ambitionless, sweating out his time, mocking of everything and everybody, including his mother, incurious about the wealth of the Old World around him, shacking up with silly girls in Brussels and Paris, one after the other, smoking marijuana, if he wasn't going in for stronger stuff, risking jail with the same lack of interest that he had risked getting kicked out of college, unwavering in his icy attitude toward his mother. At their last dinner in Brussels, Gretchen had reported, when the subject of Evans Kinsella had finally come up, Billy had been savage. "I know all about people your age," he had said. "Big phoney ideals, going into raptures about books and plays and politicians that just make people my age horse laugh, out saving the world and going from one crap-talking artist to another to pretend you're still young and the Nazis have just been licked and the brave new world is just around the corner or at the next bar or in the next bed."

"In a way," Gretchen had told Rudolph, "maybe he's right. Hateful but right. When he says the word phoney. You know better than anyone about me. When the time came I didn't tell him, 'Go to prison,' or 'Desert.' I just called my influential brother and saved my son's miserable skin and let other mothers persuade their sons to go to prison or desert or march on the Pentagon, or go die in the jungle someplace. Anyway, I've signed my last petition."

There was nothing much Rudolph could say to that. He had been the necessary accomplice. They were both guilty as charged.

But the week on the sea had been so healing, the wedding so gay and optimistic, that he had consciously put it all from his mind. He was sorry that the sight of Wesley at the wheel, brown and agile, had made them both, inevitably, think about Billy.

"Look at him," Gretchen was saying, staring at Wesley. "Brought up by a whore. With a father who never got past the second year in high school, who hasn't opened a book since then and who's been beaten and hunted and knocked down and lived ever since he was sixteen with the scum of the earth. And no questions asked. When Tom decided the time was right he got his kid and took him to another country and made him learn another language and threw him in with a whole group of ruffians who can barely read and write. And he's made him go to work at an age when Billy was still asking for two dollars on Saturday night to go to the movies. As for the amenities of family life." She laughed. "That boy sure has his share of elegant privacy, living in the next room to a little English peasant girl who's his father's mistress, with his father's illegitimate child in her belly. And what's the result? He's healthy and useful and polite. And he's so devoted to his father Tom doesn't ever have to raise his voice to him. All he has to do is *indicate* what he wants the boy to do and the boy does it. Christ," she said, "we'd better start rewriting all those books on child care. And one thing that boy is sure of. No draft board is going to send *him* to Viet Nam. His father will see to that. I'll tell you something—if I were you, as soon as Enid is big enough to walk around this boat without falling overboard, I'd send her over here to let Tom bring her up for you. Lord, I could use a drink. Tom must have one bottle of something stashed away on this Woman's Christian Temperance Union vessel."

"I imagine he has," Rudolph said. "I'll ask." He got up from his chair and went forward. It was getting dark and Wesley was putting the running lights on. Wesley smiled at him as he passed him. "I guess the excitement was too much for the old man," he said. "He hasn't even been up to check whether I'm heading into the Alps or not."

"Weddings don't happen every day," Rudolph said.

"They sure don't," Wesley said. "It's a lucky thing for Pa they don't. His constitution couldn't stand it."

Rudolph went through the saloon to the galley. Dwyer was washing lettuce in the sink and Kate, no longer dressed for celebration, was basting a roast in the oven. "Kate," Rudolph said, "has Tom got a bottle hidden away down here somewhere?"

Kate closed the oven door and stood up and looked troubledly at Dwyer. "I thought he promised you we'd be bone dry all the time you were on board," she said.

"That's all right, Kate," Rudolph said. "Jean's in the cabin with the kid. It's for Gretchen and me. We're up on deck and it's getting nippy."

"Bunny," Kate said to Dwyer, "go get it."

Dwyer went up forward to his cabin and came back with a bottle of gin. Rudolph poured the gin into two glasses and put some tonic in with it.

When he returned to Gretchen and gave her her glass, she made a face. "Gin and tonic. I hate it."

"If Jean happens to come up on deck, we can pretend it's just plain tonic. It disguises the smell of the gin."

"You hope," Gretchen said.

They drank. "It's Evans's favorite drink," Gretchen said. "Among our many points of difference."

"How's it going?"

"The same," she said carelessly. "A little worse each year, but the same. I suppose I ought to quit him, but he needs me. He doesn't want me so damned much, but he needs me. Maybe needing is better than wanting at my age."

Jean came on deck, in tight, low-waisted pink denim pants and a pale-blue cashmere sweater. She glanced at the glasses in their hands but didn't say anything.

"How's Enid?" Rudolph asked.

"Sleeping the sleep of the just. She asked if Kate and Uncle Thomas got to keep the rings they gave each other." She shivered. "I'm cold," she said and snuggled up against Rudolph's shoulder. He kissed her cheek.

"Fee-fie-fo-fum," Jean said. "I smell the blood of an Englishman." The tonic hadn't fooled her. Not for an instant.

"One drop," she said.

Rudolph hesitated. If he had been alone, he would have held onto his glass. But Gretchen was there, watching them. He couldn't humiliate his wife in front of his sister. He gave Jean the glass. She took a tiny sip, then handed the glass back to him.

Dwyer came out on deck and began to set the table for dinner, putting out little weighted brass hurricane lamps with candles in them. The table was always tastefully set on board, with the candles at night and straw place mats and a little bowl of flowers and a wooden salad bowl. Somehow, Rudolph thought, watching Dwyer work, neat in his pressed chino pants and blue sweater, somehow among the three of them they have developed a sense of style. The candles winked in their glasses, like captured fireflies, making small, warm pools of light in the center of the big, scrubbed table.

Suddenly, there was a dull, thudding noise against the hull and a chattering under the stern. The boat throbbed unevenly and there was a clanking below decks before Wesley could cut the engines. Dwyer ran to the after rail and peered at the wake, pale in the dark sea.

"Damn it," he said, pointing, "we hit a log. See it?"

Rudolph could see a dim shadow floating behind him, just a bare two or three inches protruding from the water. Thomas came running out, barefooted and bare chested, but clutching a sweater. Kate was on his heels.

"We hit a log," Dwyer said to him. "One or maybe both of the screws."

"Are we going to sink?" Jean asked. She sounded frightened. "Should I get Enid?"

"Leave her alone, Jean," Thomas said calmly. "We're not going to sink." He pulled on his sweater and went into the pilot house and took the wheel. The ship had lost way and was swinging a little in the light wind, bobbing against the swell. Thomas started the port engine. It ran normally and the propeller turned smoothly. But when he started the starboard engine there was a metallic clanking below and the *Clothilde* throbbed irregularly. Thomas cut the starboard engine and they moved forward slowly. "It's the starboard propeller. And maybe the shaft, too," he said.

Wesley was near tears. "Pa," he said, "I'm sorry. I just didn't see it."

Thomas patted the boy's shoulder. "It's not your fault, Wes," he said. "Really not. Look into the engine room and see if we're taking any water in the bilge." He cut the port engine and in a moment they were drifting again. "A wedding present from the Med," he said, but without bitterness. He filled a pipe and lighted it and put his arm around his wife and waited for Wesley to come up on deck.

"Dry," Wesley said.

"She's solid," Thomas said. "The old *Clothilde*." Then he noticed the glasses in Rudolph's and Gretchen's hands. "We continuing the celebration?" he asked.

"Just one drink," Rudolph said.

Thomas nodded. "Wesley," he said, "take the wheel. We're going back to Antibes. On the port engine. Keep the revs low and watch the oil and water gauges. If the pressure drops or it begins to heat up, cut it right away."

Rudolph could sense that Thomas would have preferred to take the wheel himself, but he wanted to make sure that Wesley didn't feel guilty about the accident.

"Well, folks," Thomas said as Wesley started the engine and slowly swung the *Clothilde*'s bow around, "I'm afraid there goes Portofino."

"Don't worry about us," Rudolph said. "Worry about the boat."

"There's nothing we can do tonight," Thomas said. "Tomorrow morning, we'll put on the masks and go down and take a look. If it's what I think it is, it'll mean waiting for a new screw and maybe a new shaft and putting her up on land to fit them. I could go on to Villefranche, but I get a better deal from the yard in Antibes."

"That's all right," Jean said. "We all love Antibes."

"You're a nice girl," Thomas said to Jean. "Now, why don't we all sit down and have our dinner?"

They could only do four knots on the one engine and Antibes harbor was silent and dark as they entered it. No horns greeted their arrival and no flowers were strewn in their wake.

IV

There was a small, insistent tapping sound in his dream and as he swam up from sleep Thomas thought, Pappy is at the door. He opened his eyes, saw that he was in his bunk with Kate sleeping beside him. He had rigged up another section to the lower bunk so that he and Kate could sleep comfortably together. The new section could be folded back during the day, to give them room to walk around the small cabin.

The tapping continued. "Who's there?" he whispered. He didn't want to wake Kate.

"It's me," came the answering whisper. "Pinky Kimball."

"In a minute," Thomas said. He didn't turn on the light, but dressed in the dark. Kate slept deeply, worn out by the day's activities.

Barefoot, in sweater and pants, Thomas cautiously opened the cabin door and went out into the gangway, where Pinky was waiting for him. There was a huge smell of drink coming from Pinky, but it was too dark in the gangway for Thomas to tell just how drunk he was. He led the way up to the pilot house, past the cabin where Dwyer and Wesley slept. He looked at his watch. Two-fifteen on the phosphorescent dial. Pinky stumbled a little going up the ladder. "What the hell is it, Pinky?" Thomas asked irritably.

"I just came from Cannes," Pinky said thickly.

"So what? Do you always wake up people when you come from Cannes?"

"You got to listen to me, mate," Pinky said. "I saw your sister-in-law in Cannes."

"You're drunk, Pinky," Thomas said disgustedly. "Go to sleep."

"In pink pants. Listen, why would I say a thing like that if I didn't glom her? I saw her all day, didn't I? I'm not that drunk. I can recognize a woman I see all day, can't I? I was surprised and went up to her and I said I thought you were on the way to Portofino and she said I am not on my way to Portofino, we had an accident and we're bloody well in Antibes harbor."

"She didn't say bloody well," Thomas said, not wishing to believe that Jean was anyplace else but on the *Clothilde*, asleep.

"A turn of phrase," Pinky said. "But I saw her."

"Where in Cannes?" He had to remember to keep his voice down, so as not to awaken the others.

"In a strip-tease joint. La Porte Rose. It's on the rue Bivouac Napoléon. At the bar with a big Yugoslav or something in a gabardine suit. I've seen him around. He's a pimp. He's done time."

"Oh, Christ. Was she drunk?"

"Looping," Pinky said. "I offered to take her back to Antibes with me but she said, This gentleman here will drive me home when we are ready."

"Wait here," Thomas said. He went down into the saloon and along the aft gangway, passing the cabins where Gretchen and Enid slept. There was no sound from either cabin. He opened the door to the master cabin in the stern. There was a light on in the gangway all night, in case Enid wanted to go to the bathroom. When Thomas opened the main cabin door, just enough to look in, he saw Rudolph sleeping in pajamas, in the big bed. Alone.

Thomas closed the door gently and went back up to Pinky. "You saw her," he said.

"What're you going to do?" Pinky asked.

"Go and get her," Thomas said.

"Do you want me to come with you? It's a rough crowd."

Thomas shook his head. Pinky sober was no help. Drunk he'd be worthless. "Thanks. You go to sleep. I'll see you in the morning." Pinky started to remonstrate, but Thomas said, "Go ahead, go ahead," and pushed him gently toward the gangplank. He watched Pinky walk unsteadily along the quay, going in and out of shadow, toward where the Vega was berthed. He felt his pockets. He had some loose change in his wallet. Then he went down to his own cabin, stepping carefully past the cabin that Dwyer and Wesley shared. He woke up Kate with a slight tap on her shoulder.

"Keep it low," he said. "I don't want to wake up the whole ship." Then he told her Pinky's news. "I've got to go get her," he said.

"Alone?"

"The fewer the better," he said. "I'll bring her back and put her in her husband's bed and tomorrow he can say his wife has a headache and is staying in bed for a day or so and nobody'll catch on to anything. I don't want Wesley or Bunny to see the lady drunk." He also didn't want Wesley or Dwyer to be around if there was going to be any trouble.

"I'll go with you," Kate said. She started to get up. He pushed her down.

"I don't want her to know that you've seen her drunk with a pimp either. We've got to live the rest of our lives as friends."

"You'll be careful, won't you?"

"Of course, I'll be careful," he said. He kissed her. "Sleep well, darling."

Any other woman would have made a fuss, he thought as he went up on deck. Not Kate. He put on the espadrilles he always left at the gangplank and went down to the quay. He was lucky. Just as he was going through the archway a taxi drove up and let off a couple in evening clothes. He got into the taxi and said, "La rue Bivouac Napoléon, Cannes."

She wasn't at the bar when he went into La Porte Rose. And there was no Yugoslav in a gabardine suit, either. There were two or three men standing at the bar, watching the show, and a couple of hookers. There were some single men at tables and three men whose looks he didn't like, sitting with one of the performers at a table near the entrance. Two elderly American couples sat at a table on the edge of the dance floor. An act was just beginning. The band was playing loudly and a red-headed girl in an evening dress was swaying around the floor in the spotlight, slowly taking off a long glove that went up nearly to her shoulder.

Thomas ordered a Scotch and soda. When the barman brought the drink and placed it in front of him, he said, in English, "I'm looking for an American lady who was in here awhile ago. Brown hair. Wearing pink pants. With a monsieur in a gabardine suit."

"Have not zee no American lady," the barman said.

Thomas put a hundred-franc note on the bar.

"Maybe I begin to remembair," the barman said.

Thomas put down another hundred-franc note. The barman looked around him quickly. The two notes disappeared. He took up a glass and began to polish it assiduously. He spoke without looking at Thomas. With all the noise from the band there was no danger of his being overheard.

"Be'ind *les toilettes*," the barman said, speaking rapidly, "is found *un escalier*, staircase, to ze cave. Ze *plongeur*, ze dishwasher, he sleep there after work. Per'aps you find what you look for in cave. The name of fellow is Danovic. *Sal* type. Be careful. He has friends."

Thomas watched while the strip-teaser took off one stocking and waved it and began to work on the garter of the other stocking. Then, still seeming to be interested in the act, he strolled slowly toward the illuminated sign in the rear that said Toilettes, Telephone. Everybody in the room seemed to be watching the girl in the spotlight and he was fairly sure that no one noticed him as he went through the archway under the sign. He passed the stink of the toilets and saw the steps going to the cellar. He went down them quickly. There was a thin, veneered wooden door at the bottom of the steps, with patched strips showing in the dim light of the small bulb that lit the stairway. Over the noise of the band, he could hear a woman's voice from behind the door, pleading hysterically, then being cut off, as though by a hand across the mouth. He tried the door, but it was locked. He backed off a little and lunged at the door. The rotten wood and the flimsy lock gave at the same time and he plunged through the doorway. Jean was there, struggling to sit up, on the dishwasher's cot. Her hair was streaming wildly about her face and her sweater was half torn from one shoulder. The man in the gabardine suit, Danovic, was standing beside her, facing the door. In the light of the one bulb strung on a wire from the ceiling, Thomas could see stacks of empty wine bottles, a work bench, some carpentry tools spread about.

"Tom!" Jean said. "Get me out of here." She had been frightened out of her drunkenness or she hadn't been as drunk as Pinky had imagined. She tried to stand up, but the man pushed her back roughly, still facing Thomas.

"What do you want?" Danovic said. He spoke English, but thickly. He was about the same size as Thomas, with heavy shoulders. He had a knife or razor scar down one side of his face.

"I came to take the lady home," Thomas said.

"I'll take the lady home when I'm good and ready," Danovic said. "*Fout-moi le camp*, Sammy." He pushed heavily at Jean's face, as she struggled again to get up.

Overhead, the noise of the band increased as another garment came off.

Thomas took a step nearer the cot. "Don't make any trouble," he said to the man quietly. "The lady's coming with me."

"If you want her, you will have to take her from me, Sammy," Danovic said. He reached back suddenly and grabbed a ball-peen hammer from the workbench and held it up in his fist.

Oh, Christ, Thomas thought, Falconettis everywhere.

"Please, please, Tom," Jean was sobbing.

"I give you five seconds to leave," Danovic said. He moved toward Thomas, the hammer ready, at the level of Thomas's face.

Somehow, Thomas knew, no matter what happened, he had to keep the hammer away from his head. If it hit him even a glancing blow, that would be the end of it. "Okay, okay," he said, retreating a little and putting up his hands placatingly. "I'm not looking for a fight." Then he dove at Davonic's legs as the hammer swung. He got his head into the crotch, butting as hard as he could. The hammer hit his shoulder and he felt the shoulder going numb. The man was reeling backward, off balance, and Thomas wrapped his arms around his knees and toppled him. His head must have hit something, because for a fraction of a second he didn't struggle. Thomas took the chance and pulled his head up. Davonic swung the hammer and hit the elbow that Thomas threw up to protect himself. He went for the hand with the hammer again, clawing at the man's eyes with his other hand. He missed the hammer and felt a stab of pain in his knee as the hammer came down again. This time he got hold of the hammer. He ignored the blows of the other hand and twisted hard. The hammer slid a little way on the cement floor and Thomas leapt for it, using his knees to keep the man away from him. They both were on their feet again, but Thomas could hardly move because of his knee and he had to switch the hammer to his left hand because his right shoulder was numb.

Over the noise of the band and his own gasping he could hear Jean screaming, but faintly, as though she were far away.

Danovic knew Thomas was hurt and tried to circle him. Thomas made himself swing around, making the leg work for him. Danovic lunged at him and Thomas hit him above the elbow. The arm dropped, but Danovic still swung the good arm. Thomas saw the opening and hit the man on the temple, not squarely, but it was enough. Danovic staggered, fell on his back. Thomas dropped on him, straddling his chest. He lifted the hammer above Danovic's head. The man was gasping, protecting his face with his arm. Thomas brought the hammer down three times on the arm, on the shoulder, the wrist and the elbow, and it was all over. Danovic's two arms lay useless alongside his body. Thomas lifted the hammer to finish him off. The man's eyes were opaque with fear as he stared up, the blood streaming down from the temple, a dark river in the delta of his face.

"Please," he cried, "please, don't kill me. *Please*." His voice rose to a shriek.

Thomas rested on Danovic's chest, getting his breath back, the hammer still raised in his left hand. If ever a man deserved to get killed, this was the man. But Falconetti had deserved to get killed, too. Let somebody else do the job. Thomas reversed the hammer and jammed the handle hard into Danovic's gaping, twitching mouth. He could feel the front teeth breaking off. He no longer was able to kill the man, but he didn't mind hurting him.

"Help me up," he said to Jean. She was sitting on the cot, holding her arms up in front of her breasts. She was panting loudly, as though she had fought, too. She stood up slowly, unsteadily, and came over and put her hands under his armpits and pulled. He rose to his feet and nearly fell as he stepped away from the shivering body beneath him. He was dizzy and the room seemed to be whirling around him, but he was thinking clearly. He saw a white-linen coat that he knew belonged to Jean thrown over the back of the room's single chair, and he said, "Put on your coat." They couldn't walk through the nightclub with Jean's sweater torn from her shoulder. Maybe he couldn't walk through the nightclub at all. He had to use his two hands to pull his bad leg up, one step after another, on the staircase. They left Danovic lying on the cement floor, the hammer sticking up from his broken mouth, bubbling blood.

As they went through the archway under the Toilettes, Telephone sign, a new strip-tease was starting. The entertainment was nonstop at La Porte Rose. Luckily, it was dark outside the glare of the spotlight on the *artiste*, who was dressed in a black, skirted riding habit, with derby and boots and whip. Leaning heavily on Jean's arm, Thomas managed not to limp too noticeably and they were almost out of the door before one of the three men sitting near the entrance with the girl spotted them. The man stood up and called, "*Allô! Vous là. Les Americains. Arrêtez. Pas si vite.*"

But they were out of the door and somehow they managed to keep walking and a taxi was passing by and Thomas hailed it. Jean struggled to push him in and then tumbled in after him and the taxi was on its way to Antibes by the time the man who had called out to them came out on the sidewalk looking for them.

In the cab, Thomas leaned back, exhausted, against the seat. Jean huddled in her white coat in a corner, away from him. He couldn't stand his own smell, mingled with the smell of Danovic and blood and the dank cellar, and he didn't blame Jean for keeping as far away from him as possible. He passed out, or fell asleep, he couldn't tell which. When he opened his eyes again they were going down the street toward the harbor of Antibes. Jean was weeping uncontrollably in her corner, but he couldn't worry any more about her tonight.

He chuckled as they came up to where the *Clothilde* was tied up.

The chuckle must have startled Jean. She stopped crying abruptly. "What're you laughing about, Tom?" she asked.

"I'm laughing about the doctor in New York," he said. "He told me to avoid any sudden movements or strenuous exertion for a long time. I'd have loved to see his face if he'd been there tonight."

He forced himself to get out of the cab unaided and paid the driver off and limped up the gangplank after Jean. He had a dizzy spell again and nearly fell sideways off the gangplank into the water.

"Should I help you to your cabin?" Jean asked, when he finally made it to the deck.

He waved her away. "You go down and tell your husband you're home," he said. "And tell him any story you want about tonight."

She leaned over and kissed him on the lips. "I swear I'll never touch another drop of liquor again as long as I live," she said.

"Well, then," he said, "we've had a successful evening, after all, haven't we?" But he patted her smooth, childish cheek, to take the sting out of his words. He watched as she went down through the saloon and to the main cabin. Then he painfully went below and opened the door to his own cabin. Kate was awake and the light was on. She made a hushed, choked sound when she saw what he looked like.

"Sssh," he said.

"What happened?" she whispered.

"Something great," he said. "I just avoided killing a man." He dropped onto the bunk. "Now get dressed and go get a doctor."

He closed his eyes, but he heard her dressing swiftly. By the time she was out of the room he was asleep.

He was up early, awakened by the sound of hissing water, as Dwyer and Wesley hosed off the deck. They had come into port too late the night before to do it then. He had a big bandage around his knee and every time he moved his right shoulder he winced with pain. But it could have been worse. The doctor said there were no broken bones, but that the knee had been badly mauled and perhaps some cartilage had been torn away. Kate was already in the galley preparing breakfast and he lay alone in the bunk, his body remembering all the other times in his life he had awakened bruised and aching. His memory bank.

He pushed himself out of the bunk with his good arm and stood in front of the little cabinet mirror on his good leg. His face was a mess. He hadn't felt it at the time, but when he had toppled Danovic his face had crashed against the rough concrete floor and his nose was swollen and his lip puffed out and there were gashes on his forehead and cheekbones. The doctor had cleaned out the cuts with alcohol and compared to the rest of him his face felt in good shape, but he hoped Enid wouldn't go screaming to her mother when she got a glimpse of him.

He was naked and there were black-and-blue welts blooming all over his chest and arms. Schultzy should see me now, he thought, as he pulled on a pair of pants. It took him five minutes to get the pants on and he couldn't manage a shirt at all. He took the shirt with him and clumped, hopping mostly, into the galley. The coffee was on and Kate was squeezing oranges. Once the doctor had assured her that nothing serious was wrong, she had become calm and businesslike. Before he had gone to sleep, after the doctor had left, he had told her the whole story.

"You want to kiss the bridegroom's beautiful face?" he said.

She kissed him gently, smiling, and helped him on with his shirt. He didn't tell her how much it hurt when he moved his shoulder.

"Does anybody know anything yet?" he asked.

"I haven't told Wesley or Bunny," she said. "And none of the others have come up yet."

"As far as anybody is concerned, I was in a fight with a drunk outside Le Cameo," Thomas said. "That will be an object lesson to anybody who goes out drinking on his wedding night."

Kate nodded. "Wesley's been down with the mask already," she said. "There's a big chunk out of the port screw and as far as he can tell the shaft is twisted, too."

"If we get out of here in a week," Thomas said, "we'll be lucky. Well, I might as well go up on deck and start lying."

He followed Kate as she went up the ladder carrying the orange juice and the coffee pot on a tray. When Wesley and Dwyer saw him, Dwyer said, "For Christ's sake what did you do to yourself?" and Wesley said, "Pa!"

"I'll tell everybody about it when we're all together," Thomas said. "I'm only going to tell the story once."

Rudolph came up with Enid and Thomas could tell from the look on his face that Jean had probably told him the true story or most of the true story. All Enid said was, "Uncle Thomas, you look funny this morning."

"I bet I do, darling," Thomas said.

Rudolph didn't say anything, except that Jean had a headache and was staying in bed and that he'd take her some orange juice after they'd all had their breakfast. They had just sat down around the table when Gretchen came up. "Good God, Tom," she said, "what in the world happened to you?"

"I was waiting for someone to ask just that question," Thomas said. Then he told the story about the fight with the drunk in front of Le Cameo. Only, he said, laughing, the drunk hadn't been as drunk as he had been.

"Oh, Tom," Gretchen said, distractedly, "I thought you'd given up fighting."

"I thought so, too," Thomas said. "Only that drunk didn't."

"Were you there, Kate?" Gretchen asked accusingly.

"I was in bed asleep," Kate said placidly. "He sneaked out. You know how men are."

"I think it's disgraceful," Gretchen said. "Big, grown men fighting."

"So do I," Thomas said. "Especially when you lose. Now let's eat breakfast."

V

Later that morning Thomas and Rudolph were up in the bow alone. Kate and Gretchen had gone to do the marketing, taking Enid along with them, and Wesley and Dwyer were down looking at the screws again with the masks.

"Jean told me the whole story," Rudolph said. "I don't know how to thank you, Tom."

"Forget it. It wasn't all that much. It probably looked a lot worse than it was to a nicely brought up girl like Jean."

"All that drinking going on all day," Rudolph said bitterly, "and then the final straw—Gretchen and me drinking here on board before dinner. She just couldn't stand it. And alcoholics can be so sly. How she could have gotten out of bed and dressed and off the ship without my waking up . . ." He shook his head. "She's behaved so well, I guess I thought there was nothing to worry about. And when she has a couple, she's not responsible. She's not the same girl at all. You don't think that when she's sober she goes around picking men up in bars in the middle of the night?"

"Of course not, Rudy."

"She told me, she told me," Rudolph said. "This polite-looking, well-spoken young man came up to her and said he had a car outside and he knew a very nice bar in Cannes that stayed open until dawn and would she like to come with him, he'd bring her back whenever she wanted . . ."

"Polite-looking, well-spoken young man," Thomas said, thinking of Danovic lying on the floor of the cellar with the handle of the ball-peen hammer sticking up from his broken teeth. He chuckled. "He's not so polite looking or well spoken this morning, I can tell you that."

"And then when they got to that bar, a strip-tease joint—God, I can't even *imagine* Jean in a place like that—he said it was too noisy for him at the bar, there was a little cosy club downstairs . . ." Rudolph shook his head despairingly. "Well, you know the rest."

"Don't think about it, Rudy, please," Thomas said.

"Why didn't you wake me up and take me along with you?" Rudolph's voice was harsh.

"You're not the sort of man for a trip like that, Rudy."

"I'm her husband, for Christ's sake."

"That was another reason for not waking you up," said Thomas.

"He could have killed you."

"For a little while there," Thomas admitted, "the chances looked pretty good."

"And you could have killed him."

"That's the one good thing about the night," Thomas said. "I found out I couldn't. Now, let's go back and see what the divers're up to." He hobbled down the deck from the bow, leaving his brother and his brother's guilts and gratitudes behind him.

VI

He was sitting alone on the deck, enjoying the calm late evening air. Kate was down below and the others had all gone on a two-day automobile trip to the hill towns and into Italy. It had been five days since the *Clothilde* had come back into the harbor and they were still waiting for the new propeller and shaft to be delivered from Holland. Rudolph had said that a little sightseeing was in order. Jean had been dangerously quiet since her night of drunkenness and Rudolph kept doing his best to distract her. He had asked Kate and Thomas to come along with them, but Thomas had said the newlyweds wanted to be alone. He had even privately told Rudolph to invite Dwyer along with the party. Dwyer had been pestering him to point out the drunk who had beaten him up outside Le Cameo and he was sure Dwyer was thinking of cooking up some crazy scheme of retaliation with Wesley. Also, Jean kept following him around without saying anything, but with a peculiar, haunted look in her eyes. Lying for five days had been something of a strain and it was a relief to have the ship to himself and Kate for a little while.

The harbor was silent, the lights out in most of the ships. He yawned, stretched, stood up. His body had gotten over feeling bruised and while he still limped, his leg had stopped feeling as though it was broken in half somewhere along the middle when he walked. He hadn't made love to his wife since the fight and he was thinking that this might be a good night to start in again, when he saw the car without lights driving swiftly along the quay. The car stopped. It was a black DS 19. The two doors on his side opened and two men got out, then two more. The last man was Danovic, one arm in a sling.

If Kate hadn't been aboard, he would have dived over the side and let them try to get him. But there was nothing for him to do but stand there. There was nobody on the boats on either side of him. Danovic remained on the quay, as the other three men came aboard.

"Well, gentlemen," Thomas said, "what can I do for you?"

Then something hit him.

He came out of the coma only once. Wesley and Kate were in the hospital room with him. "No more . . ." he said, and then slipped back into the coma again.

Rudolph had called a brain specialist in New York and the specialist was on his way to Nice when Thomas died. The skull had been fractured, the surgeon had explained to Rudolph and there had been catastrophic bleeding.

Rudolph had moved Gretchen and Jean and Enid to a hotel. Gretchen had strict orders not to leave Jean alone for a minute.

Rudolph had told the police what he knew and they had talked to Jean, who had broken down hysterically after a half hour's questioning. She had told them about La Porte Rose and they had picked up Danovic, but there had been no witnesses to the beating and Danovic had an alibi for the entire night that couldn't be shaken.

VII

The morning after the cremation Rudolph and Gretchen went by taxi to the place and got the metal box with their brother's ashes. Then they drove toward Antibes harbor, where Kate and Wesley and Dwyer were expecting them. Jean was at the hotel with Enid. It would have been too much for Kate to bear, Rudolph thought, to have to stand by Jean's side today. And if Jean got drunk, Rudolph thought, she would finally have good reason to do so.

Gretchen now knew the true story of the wedding night, as did the others.

"Tom," Gretchen said in the taxi, as they drove through the bustle of holiday traffic, "the one of us who finally made a life."

"Dead for one of us who didn't," Rudolph said.

"The only thing you did wrong," Gretchen said, "was not waking up one night."

"The only thing," Rudolph said.

After that they didn't speak until they reached the *Clothilde*. Kate and Wesley and Dwyer, dressed in their working clothes, were waiting for them on the deck. Dwyer and Wesley were red eyed from crying, but Kate, although grave faced, showed no signs of tears. Rudolph came on board carrying the box and Gretchen followed him. Rudolph put the box in the pilot house and Dwyer took the wheel and started the one engine. Wesley pulled up the gangplank and then jumped ashore to throw off the two stern lines, which Kate reeled in. Wesley leaped across open water, landed catlike on the stern, and swung himself aboard, then ran forward to help Kate with the anchor.

It was all so routine, so much like every other time they had set out from a port, that Rudolph, on the after deck, had the feeling that at any moment Tom would come rolling out of the shadow of the pilot house, smoking his pipe.

The immaculate white-and-blue little ship chugged past the harbor mouth in the morning sunlight, only the two figures standing in incongruous black on the open deck making it seem any different from any other pleasure craft sailing out for a day's sport.

Nobody spoke. They had decided what they were to do the day before. They sailed for an hour, due south, away from the mainland. Because they were only on one engine they did not go far and the coast line was clear behind them.

After exactly one hour, Dwyer turned the boat around and cut the engine. There were no other craft within sight and the sea was calm, so there wasn't even the small sound of waves. Rudolph went into the pilot house, took out the box and opened it. Kate came up from below with a large bunch of white and red gladioli. They all stood in a line on the stern, facing the open, empty sea. Wesley took the box from Rudolph's hands and, after a moment's hesitation, his eyes dry now, started to strew his father's ashes into the sea. It only took a minute. The ashes floated away, a faint sprinkling of dust on the blue glint of the Mediterranean.

The body of their father, Rudolph thought, also rolled in deep waters.

Kate threw the flowers in with a slow, housewifely gesture of her round, tanned arms.

Wesley tossed the metal box and its cover over the side, both face down. They sank immediately. Then Wesley went to the pilot house and started the engine. They were pointed toward the coast now and he held a straight course for the mouth of the harbor.

Kate went below and Dwyer went forward to stand in the prow, leaving Gretchen and Rudolph, death colored, together on the after deck.

Up in the bow, Dwyer stood in the little breeze of their passage, watching the coast line, white mansions, old walls, green pines, grow nearer in the brilliant light of the morning sun.

Rich man's weather, Dwyer remembered.